To Collin,
my buddy, my boy, my son

the winner & the simple truth

David Baldacci is an internationally acclaimed thriller writer, and all of his novels have entered the *New York Times* bestseller lists. *Absolute Power* was made into a film starring Clint Eastwood. He lives in his native state of Virginia.

DAVID BALDACCI

the winner
&
the simple truth

PAN BOOKS

The Winner first published 1997 by Warner Books/Grand Central Publishing,
a division of Hachette Book Group USA.
First published in Great Britain 1998 by Simon and Schuster UK Ltd.
First published by Pan Books 2003.
The Simple Truth first published 1998 by Warner Books/Grand Central Publishing,
a division of Hachette Book Group USA.
First published in Great Britain 1998 by Simon and Schuster UK Ltd.
First published by Pan Books 2003.

This omnibus first published 2008 by Pan Books
an imprint of Pan Macmillan Ltd
Pan Macmillan, 20 New Wharf Road, London N1 9RR
Basingstoke and Oxford
Associated companies throughout the world
www.panmacmillan.com

ISBN 978-0-330-45779-8

1 3 5 7 9 8 6 4 2

A CIP catalogue record for this book is available from
the British Library.

Printed and bound in Great Britain by
Mackays of Chatham plc, Chatham, Kent

the winner

ONE

Jackson studied the shopping mall's long corridor, noting haggard mothers piloting loaded strollers and the senior citizens group walking the mall both for exercise and conversation. Dressed in a gray pinstriped suit, the stocky Jackson stared intently at the north entrance to the shopping mall. That would no doubt be the one she would use since the bus stop was right in front. She had, Jackson knew, no other form of transportation. Her live-in boyfriend's truck was in the impoundment lot, the fourth time in as many months. It must be getting a little tedious for her, he thought. The bus stop was on the main road. She would have to walk about a mile to get there, but she often did that. What other choice did she have? The baby would be with her. She would never leave it with the boyfriend, Jackson was certain of that.

While his name always remained Jackson for all of his business endeavors, next month his appearance would change dramatically from the hefty middle-aged man he was currently. Facial features of course would again be altered; weight would probably be lost; height added or taken away, along with hair. Male or female? Aged or youthful? Often, the persona would be taken from people whom he knew, either wholly or bits of thread from different ones, sewn together until the delicate quilt of fabrication was complete. In school, biology had been a favorite subject. Specimens belonging to that rarest of all classes, the hermaphrodite, had never ceased to fascinate him. He smiled as he dwelled for a moment on this greatest of all physical duplicities.

Jackson had received a first-rate education from a prestigious Eastern school. Combining his love of acting with his natural acumen for science and chemistry, he had achieved a rare double major in drama and chemical engineering. Mornings would find him hunched over pages of complex equations or malodorous concoctions in the university's chemistry lab, while the evenings would have him energetically embroiled in the production of a Tennessee Williams or Arthur Miller classic.

Those accomplishments were serving him very well. Indeed, if his classmates could only see him now.

In keeping with today's character – a middle-aged male, overweight and out of shape from leading a sedentary lifestyle – a bead of perspiration suddenly sprouted on Jackson's forehead. His lips curled into a smile. This physical reaction pleased him immensely, aided as it was by the insulation of the padding he was wearing to provide bulky proportions and to conceal his own wiry frame. But it was something more than that too: He took pride in the fact that he became the person totally, as though different chemical reactions took place within him depending on who and what he was pretending to be.

He didn't normally inhabit shopping malls; his personal tastes were far more sophisticated. However, his clientele were most comfortable in these types of surroundings, and comfort was an important consideration in his line of work. His meetings tended to make people quite excited, sometimes in negative ways. Several interviews had become extremely animated, compelling him to think on his

2

feet. These reminiscences brought another smile to Jackson's lips. You couldn't argue with success, though. He was batting a thousand. However, it only took one to spoil his perfect record. His smile quickly faded. Killing someone was never a pleasant experience. Rarely was it justified, but when it was, one simply had to do it and move on. For several reasons he hoped the meeting today would not precipitate such an outcome.

He carefully dabbed his forehead with his pocket handkerchief and adjusted his shirt cuffs. He smoothed down a barely visible tangle in the synthetic fibers of his neatly groomed wig. His real hair was compressed under a latex skullcap.

He pulled open the door to the space he had rented in the mall and went inside. The area was clean and orderly – in fact too much so, he thought suddenly as he slowly surveyed the interior. It lacked the look of a true working space.

The receptionist seated behind the cheap metal desk in the foyer looked up at him. In accordance with his earlier instructions, she didn't attempt to speak. She had no idea who he was or why she was here. As soon as Jackson's appointment showed up, the receptionist had been instructed to leave. Very soon she would be on a bus out of town, her purse a little fatter for her minimal troubles. Jackson never looked at her; she was a simple prop in his latest stage production.

The phone beside her sat silent, the typewriter next to that, unused. Yes, absolutely, too well organized, Jackson decided with a frown. He eyed the stack of paper on the receptionist's desk. With a sudden motion he spread some of the papers around the desk's surface. He then cocked the phone around just so and put a piece of paper in the typewriter, winding it through with several quick spins of the platen knob.

3

Jackson looked around at his handiwork and sighed. You couldn't think of everything all at once.

Jackson walked past the small reception area, quickly hitting the end of the shallow space, and then turned right. He opened the door to the tiny interior office, slipped across the room, and sat down behind the scuffed wooden desk. A small TV sat in one corner of the room, its blank screen staring back at him. He pulled a cigarette from his pocket, lit it, and leaned far back in the chair, trying his best to relax despite the constant flow of adrenaline. He stroked his thin, dark mustache. It too was made of synthetic fiber ventilated on a lace foundation and attached to his skin with spirit gum. His nose had been changed considerably as well: a putty base highlighted and shadowed, to make his nose's actual delicate and straight appearance bulky and slightly crooked. The small mole resting next to the altered bridge of his nose was also fake: a concoction of gelatin and alfalfa seeds mixed in hot water. His straight teeth were covered with acrylic caps to give them an uneven and unhealthy appearance. All of these illusions would be remembered by even the most casual observer. Thus when they were removed, he, in essence, disappeared. What more could someone wholeheartedly engaged in illegal activities want?

Soon, if things went according to plan, it would all begin again. Each time was a little different, but that was the exciting part: the not knowing. He checked his watch again. Yes, very soon. He expected to have an extremely productive meeting with her; more to the point, a mutually beneficial meeting.

He only had one question to ask LuAnn Tyler, one simple question that carried the potential for very complex repercussions. Based upon his experience, he was reasonably certain of her answer, but one just

4

never knew. He dearly hoped, for her sake, that she would give the right one. For there was only one "right" answer. If she said no? Well, the baby would never have the opportunity to know its mother, because the baby would be an orphan. He smacked the desktop with the palm of his hand. She would say yes. All the others had. Jackson shook his head vigorously as he thought it through. He would make her see, convince her of the inescapable logic of joining with him. How it would change everything for her. More than she could ever imagine. More than she could ever hope for. How could she say no? It was an offer that simply no one could refuse.

If she came. Jackson rubbed his cheek with the back of his hand, took a long, slow drag on the cigarette, and stared absently at a nail pop in the wall. But, truth be known, how could she not come?

TWO

The brisk wind sailed straight down the narrow dirt road between the compression of thick woods on either side. Suddenly the road curved north and then just as abruptly dipped to the east. Over a slight rise the view yielded still more trees, some dying, bent into what seemed painful shapes by wind, disease, and weather; but the majority were ramrod straight, with thickening girths and soaring, leafy branches. On the left side of the road, the more diligent eye could discern a half circle of open space consisting of mud interspersed with patches of new spring grass. Also nestled with nature into this clearing were rusted engine blocks, piles of trash, a small mountain of bone-dry beer cans, discarded furniture, and a litany of other debris that served as visual art objects when covered with snow, and as home to snakes and other creatures when the mercury made its way north. Smack in the middle of that semicircular island rested a short, squat mobile trailer atop a crumbling cinder block foundation. Seemingly its only touch with the rest of the world were the electrical and telephone lines that ran down from the thick, leaning poles along the road and collided with one side of the trailer. The trailer was a decided eyesore in the middle of nowhere. Its occupants would have agreed with that description: The middle of nowhere was aptly applied to themselves as well.

Inside the trailer, LuAnn Tyler looked at herself in

the small mirror perched atop the leaning chest of drawers. She held her face at an unusual angle, not only because the battered piece of furniture listed to one side with a broken leg, but also because the mirror was shattered. Meandering lines grew outward on the surface of the glass like the slender branches of a sapling such that if LuAnn had looked head-on into the mirror she would have seen not one but three faces in the reflection.

LuAnn didn't smile as she studied herself; she could never really remember smiling at her appearance. Her looks were her only asset – that had been beaten into her head ever since she could remember – although she could have used some dental work. Growing up on unfluoridated well water and never stepping foot inside a dentist's office had contributed to that situation.

No smarts, of course, her father had said over and over. No smarts, or no opportunity to use them? She had never broached the subject with Benny Tyler, dead now these past five years. Her mother, Joy, who had passed away almost three years ago, had never been happier than after her husband died. That should have completely dispelled Benny Tyler's opinions of her mental ability, but little girls believed what their daddy told them, mostly unconditionally.

She looked over to the wall where the clock hung. It was the only thing she had of her mother's; a family heirloom of sorts, as it had been given to Joy Tyler by her own mother on the day she married Benny. It had no intrinsic value; you could buy one in any pawnshop for ten bucks. Yet LuAnn treasured it. As a little girl LuAnn had listened to the slow, methodical ticks of that clock far into the night. Knowing that in the middle of all the darkness it would always be there, it would always soothe her into sleep and greet her in the morning. Throughout her growing up it had been one of her few anchoring points. It had a connection, too, in that it went back to her grandmother, a woman LuAnn had adored. Having that clock around was like having her grandmother around forever. As the years had gone by, its inner workings had worn down considerably so that it produced unique sounds. It had carried LuAnn through more bad times than good, and right before Joy died she had told LuAnn to take it, to take good care of it. And now LuAnn would keep it for her daughter.

She pulled her thick auburn hair straight back, tried a bun, and then dexterously knotted a French braid. Not satisfied with either of these looks, she finally piled her thick tresses on top and secured them with a legion of bobby pins, frequently cocking her head to test the effect. At five feet ten inches tall, she also had to stoop to see herself in the mirror.

Every few seconds she looked over at the small bundle on the chair next to her. She smiled as she took in the droopy eyes, the curved mouth, the chipmunk cheeks, and doughy fists. Eight months and growing up fast. Her daughter had already started to crawl with the funny, back-and-forth gyrations of infancy. Walking would soon replace that. LuAnn stopped smiling as she looked around. It would not take Lisa long to navigate the boundaries of this place. The interior, despite LuAnn's diligent efforts to keep it clean, resembled the exterior largely due to the temperamental outbursts of the man sprawled on the bed. Duane Harvey had twitched once or twice since staggering into the house at four A.M., throwing off his clothes, and climbing into bed, but otherwise he had remained motionless. She recalled fondly that on one night early in their relationship, Duane had not come home drunk: Lisa had been the

8

result. Tears glimmered for the briefest time in LuAnn's hazel eyes. She hadn't much time or sympathy for tears, particularly her own. At twenty years of age she had already cried enough of them to last her until the end of her days, she figured.

She turned back to the mirror. While one of her hands played with Lisa's tiny fist, LuAnn used the other to pull out all the bobby pins. She swept her hair back and then let her bangs fall naturally forward over her high forehead. It was a style she had worn in school, at least through the seventh grade, when she had joined many of her friends in the rural county in dropping out and seeking work and the paycheck that came with it. They had all thought, wrongly as it turned out, that a regular paycheck beat the hell out of an education any day of the week. For LuAnn, there hadn't been much choice. Half her wages went to help her chronically unemployed parents. The other half went to pay for things her parents couldn't afford to give her, such as food and clothes.

She eyed Duane carefully as she undid her tattered robe, revealing her naked body. Seeing no sign of life from him, she swiftly pulled on her underwear. As she grew up, her blossoming figure had been a true eye-opener for the local boys, making them press for manhood even before the natural order of things would allow them official entry.

LuAnn Tyler, the movie-star-slash-supermodel-to-be. Many of the residents of Rikersville County, Georgia, had thoroughly considered the issue of LuAnn and bestowed upon her that title, weighted down as it was with the highest of expectations. She was not long for their way of life, it was plain to see, proclaimed the wrinkled, thick local women holding court on their broad, decaying porches, and no one

9

disagreed with them. The natural beauty she possessed would hold out for nothing less than the glossiest of all brass rings. She was the vicarious hope for the locals. New York or maybe Los Angeles would beckon to *their* LuAnn, it was only a matter of time. Only she was still here, still in the very same county where she had lived all her life. She was a disappointment of sorts without ever – despite being barely out of her teens – having had the opportunity to realize any of her goals. She knew the townsfolk would have been surprised to realize that her ambitions did not include lying naked in bed next to Hollywood's hunk of the month or treading the models' catwalk wearing the latest creations of the haute couture crowd. Although, as she slipped into her bra, it occurred to her that, right about now, sliding into the latest fashions in exchange for ten thousand dollars a day was not such a bad deal.

Her face. And her body. Her father had often commented on that attribute too. Voluptuous, full-figured, he had described it, as though it were an entity distinct from her. Weak mind, dazzling body. Thankfully, he had never gone beyond those verbalizations. Late at night she sometimes wondered if he had ever wanted to but simply lacked the courage or the opportunity. Sometimes the way he would look at her. On rare occasions, she would venture into the deepest parts of her subconscious and sense, like the sudden, scary prick of a needle, the disjointed pieces of memory that made her wonder if the opportunity maybe had presented itself. At that point she would always shudder and tell herself that thinking such evil of the dead was not a good thing.

She studied the contents of the small closet. Really, she owned only one dress that would be appropriate for her appointment. The short-sleeve, navy blue with white trim around the collar and hemline. She remembered the day she bought it. A whole paycheck blown. *Sixty-five entire dollars.* That was two years ago and she had never repeated that insane extravagance, in fact it was the last dress she had bought. The garment was a little frayed now, but she had done a nice touch-up job with needle and thread. A strand of small, fake pearls, a birthday gift from a former admirer, encircled her long neck. She had stayed up late methodically coloring in the nicks on her only pair of high heels. They were dark brown and didn't match the dress but they would have to do. Flip-flops or sneakers, her only other two choices, were not going to cut it today, although she would wear the sneakers on the mile-long trek to the bus stop. Today could be the start of something new, or at least different. Who knew? It could lead to somewhere, anywhere. It could carry her and Lisa away to something other than the Duanes of the world.

LuAnn took a deep breath, opened up the zippered interior pocket of her purse, and carefully unfolded the piece of paper. She had written down the address and other information from the phone call from someone who had identified herself as a Mr. Jackson, a call she had almost not answered after pulling the midnight to seven shift as a waitress at the Number One Truck Stop.

When the phone call came LuAnn's eyes had been welded shut as she sat on the kitchen floor breast-feeding Lisa. The little girl's teeth were coming in and LuAnn's nipples felt like they were on fire, but the baby formula was too damn expensive and they were out of milk. At first, LuAnn had no desire to answer the phone. Her job at the popular truck stop right off the interstate kept her running nonstop, with Lisa meanwhile tucked safely under the counter in her baby seat. Luckily, the little girl could hold a bottle and the diner's manager liked LuAnn enough that the arrangement hadn't jeopardized her position. They didn't get many calls. Mostly Duane's buddy looking for him to go drinking or strip a few cars that had broken down on the highway. Their Bud and Babe money they called it, and often right to her face. No, it was not Duane's boys calling this early. Seven A.M. would find them three hours into the deep sleep of another drinking binge.

After the third ring, for some reason, her hand had reached out and plucked up the phone. The man's voice was crisp and professional. He had sounded as though he were reading from a script and her sleep-clouded mind had pretty much reasoned that he was trying to sell her something. That was a joke! No charge cards, no checking account, just the little bit of cash hung in a plastic bag inside the hamper she used for Lisa's dirty diapers. It was the only place Duane would never search. Go ahead, mister, you just try to sell me something. Credit card number? Well let me just make one up right now. Visa? MasterCard? AmEx? Platinum. I've got 'em all, at least in my dreams. But the man had asked for her by name. And then he had mentioned the work. He wasn't selling her anything. He, essentially, was offering her employment. *How did you get my phone number?* she had asked him. The information was readily available, he had replied, so authoritatively that she instantly believed him. But she already had a job, she had told him. He asked what her salary was. She refused to answer at first and then, opening her eyes while Lisa suckled contentedly, she told him. She wasn't sure why. Later, she would think that it was a premonition of things to come.

Because that's when he had mentioned the pay.

One hundred dollars per weekday for a guaranteed two weeks. She had quickly done the arithmetic in her head. A total of one thousand dollars with the very real possibility of more work to come at those same rates. And they weren't full days. The man had said four hours tops, per day. That wouldn't affect her job at the truck stop at all. That came to twenty-five dollars per hour. No one she knew had ever earned such money. Why, at a full year that was twenty-five thousand dollars! And really, she would only be working half-time. So the rate was more like fifty thousand dollars per year! Doctors, lawyers, and movie stars earned such gigantic sums, not a high school dropout mother residing in the hopeless grip of poverty with someone called Duane. As if responding to her unspoken thoughts, Duane stirred for an instant, looking at her through brick-red eyes.

"Where the hell you going?" Duane's voice was thick with the drawl of the area. It seemed that she had heard those same words, that same tone, all her life from a variety of men. In response she picked up an empty beer can off the chest of drawers.

"How 'bout another beer, bay-bee?" She smiled coyly and arched her eyebrows wickedly. Her thick lips dangled each syllable seductively. It had the desired effect. Duane groaned at the sight of his malt and aluminum God and slumped back into the grip of his coming hangover. Despite his frequent drinking binges, he never could hold his liquor. In another minute he was asleep once more. The baby-doll smile instantly faded and LuAnn looked at the note again. The work, the man had said, involved trying new products, listening to some ads, getting her opinion on things. Sort of like a survey. Demographic analysis, he had termed it, whatever the hell that was. They did it all the time. It was connected to advertising rates, and television commercials, things like that. A hundred dollars a day for just giving her opinion, something she did for free just about every minute of her life.

Too good to be true, really. She had thought that a number of times since his phone call. She was not nearly as dumb as her father had thought. In fact, housed behind her comely face was an intellect far more powerful than the late Benny Tyler could have imagined, and it was coupled with a shrewdness that had allowed her to live by her wits for years now. However, only rarely did anyone go beyond her looks. She often dreamed of an existence where her boobs and butt weren't the first, last, and only thing anyone ever noticed about her, ever commented on.

She looked over at Lisa. The little girl was awake now, her eyes darting around the bedroom until they came to rest with much glee upon her mother's face. LuAnn's eyes crinkled back at her little girl. After all, could it be worse than her and Lisa's present reality? She normally held a job for a couple of months or, if she was really lucky, half a year, and then a layoff came with the promise of a rehire when times got better, which they never seemed to do. Without a high school diploma she was immediately categorized as stupid. By virtue of living with Duane, she had long ago decided she deserved that label. But he was Lisa's father even if he had no intention of marrying LuAnn, not that she had pushed him on that. She was not overeager to take Duane's last name or the man-child that came with it. However, having grown up in something less than the embrace of a happy, caring household, LuAnn was firmly convinced that the family unit was vitally important to a child's well-being. She had read all the magazines and watched numerous talk shows on the subject. In Rikersville, LuAnn was one step ahead of the welfare rolls most of the time; there were about twenty people for every lousy job. Lisa could and would do far better than her mother

– LuAnn had dedicated her life to making that a reality. But with a thousand dollars, perhaps LuAnn would do all right for herself. A bus ticket to somewhere else. Some money to live off until she could find a job; the little nest egg she had so desperately wanted over the years but had never been able to accumulate.

Rikersville was dying. The trailer was Duane's unofficial sepulcher. He would never have it any better and probably would have it much worse before the ground swallowed him up. It could be her crypt too, LuAnn realized, only it wouldn't be. Not after today. Not after she kept her appointment. She folded up the piece of paper and put it back in her purse. Sliding a small box out of one of the drawers, she found enough change for bus fare. She finished with her hair, buttoned her dress, swooped up Lisa, and quietly left the trailer, and Duane, behind.

THREE

There was a sharp knock on the door. The man quickly stood up from behind the desk, adjusted his tie, and opened a file folder lying in front of him. In the ashtray next to him were the remains of three cigarettes.

"Come in," he said, his voice firm and clear.

The door opened and LuAnn stepped into the room and looked around. Her left hand clutched the handle of the baby carrier where Lisa lay, her eyes looking around the room with obvious curiosity. Over LuAnn's right shoulder hung a large bag. The man observed the vein plunging down LuAnn's long, sinewy biceps until it connected with a maze of others in her muscular forearm. The woman was obvious strong, physically. What about her character? Was it as strong?

"Are you Mr. Jackson?" LuAnn asked. She looked directly at him as she spoke, waiting for his eyes to take the inevitable inventory of her face, bosom, hips, and so on. It didn't matter from what walk of life they came, in that regard men were all the same. She was thus very surprised when his gaze did not leave her face. He held out his hand and she shook it firmly.

"I am. Please sit down, Ms. Tyler. Thank you for coming. Your daughter is quite beautiful. Would you care to put her down over here?" He pointed to a corner of the room.

"She just woke up. The walk and the bus ride

makes her go to sleep every time. I'll just keep her beside me, if that's okay." As if in agreement, Lisa began to jabber and point.

He nodded his assent and then sat back down and took a moment to peruse the file.

LuAnn put Lisa and the large bag down next to her, pulled out a set of plastic keys, and handed them to her daughter to play with. LuAnn straightened back up and studied Jackson with considerable interest. He was dressed expensively. A line of perspiration was strung across his forehead like a miniature set of pearls and he appeared a little nervous. She ordinarily would put that down to her looks. Most of the men she encountered either acted like fools in attempts to impress her or shut down within themselves like wounded animals. Something told her that neither was the case with this man.

"I didn't see a sign over your office. People might not know you're even here." She looked at him curiously.

Jackson smiled tightly at her. "In our business we don't cater to foot traffic. It doesn't matter to us if people in the mall know we're here or not. All of our business is conducted via appointments, phone calls, that sort of thing."

"I must be the only appointment right now then. Y'all's waiting room is empty."

Jackson's cheek twitched as he formed a steeple with his hands. "We stagger our appointments so as not to keep people waiting. I'm the only member of the firm at this location."

"So you got other places of business?"

He nodded absently. "Would you mind filling out this information sheet for me? Take your time." He slid a piece of paper and pen over to her. LuAnn quickly filled out the form, making short, tight

17

motions with the pen. Jackson watched as she did so. He reviewed her information after she finished. He already knew everything on it.

LuAnn looked around the place. She had always been observant. Being the object of many males' desires, she typically studied the configuration of every place she was in, if only to determine the fastest exit.

When he looked up he noted her scrutinizing the office surroundings. "Something wrong?" he asked.

"It's kinda funny."

"I'm afraid I don't understand."

"You've got a funny office, is all."

"How do you mean?"

"Well, there's no clock anywhere, no trash can, no calendar, and no phone. Now, I ain't worked in any places where people wear neckties on the job, but even Red over at the truck stop keeps a calendar, and he's on the phone more than he's not. And the lady out front, she don't got a clue as to what's going on. Hell, with those three-inch nails, using that type-writer would be mighty hard anyway." LuAnn caught the stunned look on his face and quickly bit her lip. Her mouth had gotten her in trouble before, and this was one job interview she couldn't afford to blow. "I don't mean nothing by it," she said quickly. "Just talking. Guess I'm a little nervous, is all."

Jackson's lips moved for an instant and then he smiled grimly. "You're very observant."

"Got two eyes like everybody else." LuAnn smiled prettily, falling back on the old reliable.

Jackson ignored her look and rustled his papers. "You recall the terms of employment I gave to you over the phone?"

She snapped back to business. "One hundred dollars per day for two weeks, with maybe some more weeks at that same pay. I work until seven in

18

the morning right now. If it's all right I'd like to come and do this job in the early afternoon. Around about two? And is it okay if I bring my little girl? She takes her big nap around then, she won't be no trouble at all. Cross my heart." With an automatic motion LuAnn reached down and picked up the toy keys from the floor where the little girl had flung them and handed them back to Lisa. Lisa thanked her mother with a loud grunt.

Jackson stood up and put his hands in his pockets. "That's fine. It's all fine. You're an only child and your parents are dead, correct?"

LuAnn jerked at the abrupt change in subject. She hesitated and then nodded, her eyes narrowing.

"And for the better part of two years you have lived with one Duane Harvey, an unskilled laborer of sorts, currently unemployed, in a trailer in the western part of Rikersville." He looked at her as he recounted this information. He was not waiting for affirmation now. LuAnn sensed this and merely stared back at him. "Duane Harvey is the father of your daughter, Lisa, age eight months. You quit school in the seventh grade and have held numerous low-paying jobs since that time; all of them I think would be accurately summed up as dead-ends. You are uncommonly bright and possess admirable survival skills. Nothing is more important to you than your daughter's well-being. You are desperate to change the circumstances of your life and you are just as desperate to leave Mr. Harvey far behind. Right now you are wondering how to accomplish any of this when you lack the financial means to do so and likely always will. You feel trapped and well you should. You are most assuredly trapped, Ms. Tyler." He stared across the desk at her.

LuAnn's face was flushed as she stood up. "What the hell's going on here? What right do you have—"

19

He impatiently broke in. "You came here because I offered you more money than you've *ever* earned before. Isn't that right?"

"How come you know all those things "bout me?" she demanded.

He crossed his arms and studied her intently before answering. "It's in my best interests to know everything I can about someone with whom I'm about to do business."

"What does knowing about me have to do with my opinions and surveys and such?"

"Very simple, Ms. Tyler. To know how to evaluate your opinion on things I need to know intimate details about the opinion maker. Who you are, what you want, what you know. And don't know. The things you like, dislike, your prejudices, your strengths, and weaknesses. We all have them, in varying degrees. In sum, if I don't know all about you, I haven't done my job." He came around the corner of the desk and perched on the edge. "I'm sorry if I offended you. I can be rather blunt; however, I didn't want to waste your time."

Finally the anger in LuAnn's eyes passed away. "Well, I guess if you put it that way—"

"I do, Ms. Tyler. May I call you LuAnn?"

"That's my name," she said brusquely. She sat back down. "Well, I don't want to waste your time either, so what about the hours? Is the afternoon okay?"

Jackson abruptly returned to his seat and looked down at the desk, rubbing his hands slowly over its cracked surface. When he looked back up at her, his countenance was even more serious than it had been seconds before.

"Have you ever dreamed of being rich, LuAnn? I mean rich beyond all your wildest fantasies. So wealthy in fact that you and your daughter could

20

literally do anything in the world you wanted to do, when you wanted to do it? Have you ever had that dream?"

LuAnn started to laugh until she caught the look in his eyes. There was no humor, no diffidence, no sympathy in their depths, merely an intense desire to hear her answer.

"Hell, yes. Who hasn't had that dream?"

"Well, those who are already filthy rich rarely do, I can tell you that. However, you're right, most other people, at some point in their lives, have that fantasy. Yet virtually no one ever makes that fantasy a reality. The reason is simple: They can't."

LuAnn smiled disarmingly. "But a hundred bucks a day ain't bad either."

Jackson stroked his chin for several seconds, coughed to clear his throat, and then asked a question. "LuAnn, do you ever play the lottery?"

She was surprised by the inquiry but readily replied. "Now and then. Everybody around here does. It can get expensive, though. Duane plays every week, sometimes half his paycheck – that is when he pulls a paycheck, which ain't usually the case. He's all-fired certain he's going to win. Plays the same numbers every time. Says he saw them in a dream. I say he's just dumber than dirt. Why?"

"Have you ever played the national Lotto?"

"You mean the one for the whole country?"

Jackson nodded, his eyes fixed on her. "Yes," he said slowly, "that's exactly the one I mean."

"Once in a while. But the odds are so big I got a better chance of going for a stroll on the moon than I do of winning that thing."

"You're absolutely right. In fact, the odds this month are approximately one in thirty million."

"That's what I mean. I'd rather go for the dollar scratch-offs. At least then you got a chance to make

21

a quick twenty bucks. No sense throwing good money after bad. I always say, particularly when you don't get none to speak of."

Jackson licked his lips and leaned his elbows on the desk as he looked at her. "What would you say if I told you I could drastically better your chances of winning the lottery?" He kept his eyes trained resolutely on her.

"Excuse me?" Jackson said nothing. LuAnn looked around the room as if expecting to see a surveillance camera somewhere. "What's this got to do with the job? I didn't come here to play no games, mister."

"In fact," Jackson continued, ignoring her queries, "what if I could lower your odds to one in one? Would you do it?"

LuAnn exploded. "Is this some kind of big joke? If I didn't know better I'd think maybe Duane was behind this. You better tell me what the hell's going on before I really get mad."

"This is no joke, LuAnn."

LuAnn rose out of the chair. "You durn sure got something else on the burner and I don't want no parts of it. No parts! Hundred bucks a day or not," she said with deep disgust, mingled with deeper disappointment as her plans for the thousand-dollar pay-day rapidly faded away. She picked up Lisa and her bag and turned to leave.

The quiet tones of Jackson's voice rippled across her back. "I am guaranteeing that you will win the lottery, LuAnn. I am guaranteeing that you will win, *at minimum*, fifty million dollars."

She stopped. Despite her brain's telling her to run as fast as she could out of the place, she found herself slowly turning to face him.

Jackson had not moved. He still sat behind the desk, his hands clasped in front of him. "No more

Duanes, no more graveyard shifts at the truck diner, no more worrying about having food and clean clothes for your daughter. Anything you want, you can have. Anywhere you want to go, you can go. Anyone you want to become, you can." His tone remained quiet and steady.

"You mind telling me how can you do that?" *Had he said fifty million dollars? Lord Almighty!* She placed one hand against the door to steady herself.

"I need an answer to my question."

"What question?"

Jackson spread his hands. "Do you want to be rich?"

"Are you a crazy man or what? I'm strong as all get out so if you try anything I'll kick your little butt all the way down the street and leave you with half the brains you started the day with."

"Do I take that as a no?" he said.

LuAnn tossed her hair to one side and switched Lisa's carrier from her right to her left hand. The little girl was looking back and forth at them, as though absorbed in the heated conversation. "Look, there is no way in hell that you can guarantee me something like that. So I'm just gonna walk on out of here and call the nut house to come get you."

In response, Jackson looked at his watch and walked over to the TV and turned it on.

"In one minute the national daily drawing will be held. It's *only* a one million dollar payoff; however, it will serve to illustrate a point nonetheless. Understand, I do not profit from this, it's used only for demonstration purposes, to quell your quite understandable skepticism."

LuAnn turned to look at the screen. She watched as the lottery drawing began and the ball machines fired up.

Jackson glanced over at her. "The winning

23

numbers will be eight, four, seven, eleven, nine, and six, in that order." He pulled a pen and paper from his pocket and wrote the numbers down. He handed the paper to LuAnn.

She almost laughed and a loud snort did escape her mouth. It stopped just as quickly when the first number announced was eight. In rapid succession the four, seven, eleven, nine, and six balls were kicked out and announced as the winning combination. Her face pale, LuAnn stared down at the paper and then at the winning numbers on the screen.

Jackson turned off the TV. "I trust that your doubts about my abilities are now satisfied. Perhaps we can get back to my offer."

LuAnn leaned back against the wall. Her skin seemed to be humming against her bones, as though a million bees had plunged into her body. She looked at the TV. She saw no special wires or contraptions that could have aided him in predicting the outcome. No VCR. It was just plugged into the wall. She swallowed hard and looked back at him.

"How the hell did you do that?" The words came out in a hushed, fearful tone.

"You have no possible need to know that information. Just answer my question, please." His voice rose slightly.

She took a deep breath, tried to calm her twitching nerves. "You're asking me if I want to do something wrong. Then I'm telling you flat-out that I won't. I ain't got much, but I'm no criminal."

"Who says it's anything wrong?"

"Excuse me, but are you saying that guaranteeing to win the lottery ain't wrong? Sure as hell sounds like a fix to me. You think just because I work crap jobs I'm stupid?"

"I actually have a high opinion of your intelligence. That's why you're here. However, someone

24

has to win that money, LuAnn. Why not you?"

"Because it's wrong, that's why."

"And who exactly are you hurting? Besides, it's not wrong, technically, if no one ever finds out."

"I'd know."

Jackson sighed. "That's very noble. However, do you really want to spend the rest of your life with Duane?"

"He has his good points."

"Really? Would you care to enumerate them?"

"Why don't you go straight on to hell! I think my next stop's gonna be at the police station. I got a friend who's a cop. I betcha he'll be real interested to hear about all this." LuAnn turned and gripped the doorknob.

This was the moment Jackson had been waiting for. His voice continued to rise. "So Lisa grows up in a filthy trailer in the woods. Your little girl will be extraordinarily beautiful if she takes after her mother. She reaches a certain age, the young men start to get interested, she drops out of school, a baby perhaps comes along, the cycle starts anew. Like your mother?" He paused. "Like you?" Jackson added very quietly.

LuAnn turned slowly around, her eyes wide and glimmering.

Jackson eyed her sympathetically. "It's inevitable, LuAnn. I'm speaking the truth, you know I am. What future do you and Lisa have with him? And if not him, another Duane and then another and another. You'll live in poverty and you'll die in poverty and your little girl will do the same. There's no changing that. It's not fair of course, but that doesn't make it any less certain. Oh, people who have never been in your situation would say that you should just pack up and go. Take your daughter and just leave. Only they never tell you how you're supposed to do that. Where will the money for bus fare and motel rooms and food come

25

from? Who'll watch your child, first while you look for work, and then when you find it, if you ever do?" Jackson shook his head in sympathy and slid the back of one hand under his chin as he eyed her. "Of course, you can go to the police if you want. But by the time you get back, there will be no one here. And do you think they'll really believe you?" An expression of condescension played across his features. "And then what will you have accomplished? You'll have missed the opportunity of a lifetime. Your only shot at getting out. Gone." He shook his head sadly at her, as if to say, "Please don't be that stupid."

LuAnn tightened her grip on the baby carrier. An agitated Lisa was starting to struggle to get out and her mother automatically started rocking the little girl back and forth. "You talking about dreams, Mr. Jackson, I got me my own dreams. Big ones. Damn big ones." Her voice was trembling though. LuAnn Tyler had a very tough exterior built up over long, hard years of scrapping for an existence and never getting anywhere; however, Jackson's words had hurt LuAnn, or rather the truth in those words.

"I know you do. I said you were bright and you've done nothing at this meeting but reinforce that opinion. You deserve far better than what you have now. However, rarely do people get what they deserve in life. I'm offering you a way to achieve your big dreams." He abruptly snapped his fingers for effect. "Like that."

She suddenly looked wary. "How do I know you're not the police trying to set me up? I ain't going to no prison over money."

"Because it would be a clear case of entrapment, that's why. It would never hold up in court. And why in the world would the police target *you* for such an elaborate scheme?"

LuAnn leaned up against the door. Under her

dress she felt her heart beating erratically between her breasts.

Jackson stood up. "I know you don't know me, but I take my business very, very seriously. I never do anything without a very good reason. I would not be here wasting your time with some joke, and I most certainly never waste my time." Jackson's voice carried an unmistakable ring of authority and his eyes bored into LuAnn with an intensity that was impossible to ignore.

"Why me? Out of all the people in the whole friggin' world, why'd you come knocking on my door?" She was almost pleading.

"Fair question; however, it's not one I'm prepared to answer, nor is it particularly pertinent."

"How can you know I'm going to win?"

He looked at the TV. "Unless you think I was incredibly lucky with that drawing, then you shouldn't doubt the outcome."

"Huh! Right now, I doubt everything I'm hearing. So what if I play along and I still don't win?"

"Then what have you lost?"

"The two bucks it costs to play, that's what! It might not sound like much money to you, but that's bus fare for almost a whole week!"

Jackson pulled four singles from his pocket and handed them to her. "Then consider that risk eliminated and a hundred percent return on top of it."

She rubbed the money between her fingers. "I wanta know what's in it for you. I'm a little too old to believe in good fairies and wishes on a star." LuAnn's eyes were clear and focused now.

"Again, a good question, but one that only becomes applicable if and when you agree to participate. You're right, however: I'm not doing this out of the goodness of my heart." A tiny smile escaped his lips. "It's a business transaction. And in all good business

27

transactions, both sides benefit. However, I think you'll be pleased at how generous the terms will be."

LuAnn slid the money into her bag. "If you need my answer right this very minute, it's going to be a big, fat no."

"I realize that my proposition has certain complexities. Therefore, I will give you some time to think about it." He wrote a toll-free phone number down on a piece of paper and held it out to her. "But not too much time. The monthly lottery drawing takes place in four days. I have to have your answer by ten A.M. the day after tomorrow. This number will reach me anywhere."

She looked at the paper in his hand. "And if I still say no in two days, which I probably will?"

Jackson shrugged. "Then someone else will win the lottery, LuAnn. Someone else will be at least fifty million dollars richer and they certainly won't waste any time feeling guilty about it, I can assure you." He smiled pleasantly. "Believe me when I tell you that a lot of people would gladly take your place. *Gladly*." He put the paper in her hand and closed her fist around it. "Remember, one minute past ten A.M. and the offer to you is gone. Forever." Jackson of course did not mention the fact that if LuAnn said no, he would have her immediately killed. His tone was almost harsh, but then he quickly smiled again and opened the door for her, glancing at Lisa as he did so. The little girl stopped thrashing and stared wide-eyed at him. "She looks just like you. I hope she got your brains as well." As she passed through the doorway, he added, "Thank you for coming, LuAnn. And have a nice day."

"What makes me think your name ain't Jackson?" she said, giving him a piercing stare.

"I sincerely hope to hear from you soon, LuAnn. I like to see good things happen to deserving people. Don't you?" He shut the door softly behind her.

28

FOUR

On the bus ride home, LuAnn clutched both Lisa and the piece of paper bearing the phone number with equal tenacity. She had the very uncomfortable feeling that everyone on the bus was acutely aware of what had just happened to her and was judging her harshly as a result. An old woman wearing a battered coat and droopy, torn knee-high stockings gripped her plastic shopping bags and glared at LuAnn. Whether she was really privy to LuAnn's interview or simply resented her youths, looks, and beautiful baby girl, LuAnn couldn't be sure.

She sat back in her seat and let her mind race ahead to examine her life if she said yes or no to the proposal. While declining the offer seemed to carry with it certain consequences, all of them emblazoned with Duane-like features, acceptance seemed to bear its own problems. If she actually won the lottery and came into incalculable wealth, the man had said she could have anything she wanted. Anything! Go anywhere. Do anything. God! The thought of such unbridled freedom only a phone call and four days away made her want to run screaming with joy through the bus's narrow aisle. She had put aside the notion that it was all a hoax or some bizarre scheme. Jackson had asked for no money, not that she had any to give. He had also given no indication that he desired any sexual favors from her, although the full terms had not, as yet, been disclosed. However,

Jackson did not strike her as being interested in her sexually. He had not tried to touch her, had not commented on her features, at least not directly, and seemed, in every way, professional and sincere. He could be a nut, but if he was he certainly had done an admirable job of feigning sanity in front of her. Plus, it had cost money to rent the space, hire the receptionist, and so forth. If Jackson was certifiable, he definitely had his normal moments. She shook her head. And he had called every number correctly on the daily drawing, before the damn machines had even kicked them out. She couldn't deny that. So if he was telling the truth, then the only catch was that his business proposal resonated with illegality, with fraud, with more bad things than she cared to think about. That was a big catch. And what if she went along and then was caught somehow, the whole truth coming out? She could go to prison, maybe for the rest of her life. What would happen to Lisa? She suddenly felt miserable. Like most people, she had dreamt often of the pot of gold. It was a vision that had carried her through many a hopeless time when self-pity threatened to overtake her. In her dreams, though, the pot of gold had not been attached to a ball and chain. "Damn," she said under her breath. A clear choice between heaven and hell? And what were Jackson's conditions? She was sure the man would exact a very high price in exchange for transforming her from penniless to a princess.

So if she accepted and actually won, what would she do? The potential of such freedom was easy to see, taste, hear, feel. The actual implementation of it was something altogether different. Travel the world? She had never been outside Rikersville, which was best known for its annual fair and reeking slaughterhouses. She could count the times on one hand that she had ridden in an elevator. She had

30

never owned a house or a car; in fact, she had never really owned anything. No bank account had ever borne her name. She could read, write, and speak the king's English passably, but she clearly wasn't Social Register material. Jackson said she could have anything. But could she really? Could you really pluck a toad from the mud in some backwater and deposit it in a castle in France and really believe it could actually work? But she didn't need to do it all, change her life so dramatically, become something and someone that she decidedly wasn't. She shuddered.

That was the thing, though. She flipped her long hair out of her face, leaned against Lisa, and played her fingers over her daughter's forehead where the golden hairs drifted across. LuAnn took a deep breath, filling her lungs with the sweet spring air from the open bus window. The thing was, she wanted desperately to be someone else, anyone other than who she was. Most of her life she had felt, believed, and hoped that one day she would do something about it. With each passing year, however, that hope grew more and more hollow, more and more like a dream that one day would break completely free from her and drift away until finally, when she was the shrunken, wrinkled owner of a quickly fading, unremarkable life, she would no longer remember she had ever possessed such a dream. Every day her bleak future became more and more graphic, like a TV with antenna finally attached.

Now things had abruptly changed. She stared down at the phone number as the bus rolled down the bumpy street, carrying her and Lisa back to the dirt road that would lead to the dirtier trailer, where Duane Harvey lurked, awaiting their return in what she was certain would be a foul temper. He would

31

want beer money. But she brightened as she recalled she had two extra singles riding in her pocket. Mr. Jackson had already provided her with some benefit. Having Duane out of the way so she could think things through would be a start. Tonight was dollar pitcher night at the Squat and Gobble, his favorite hangout. With two bucks, Duane would happily drink himself into oblivion. She looked out the window at the world awakening from winter. Spring was here. A new beginning. Perhaps for her as well? To occur at or before ten A.M., two days from now. She and Lisa locked eyes for a long moment and then mother and daughter exchanged tender smiles. She laid her head gently down on Lisa's chest not knowing whether to laugh or cry and yet wanting very much to do both.

FIVE

The busted screen door creaked open and LuAnn passed through carrying Lisa. The trailer was dark, cool, and quiet. Duane might still be asleep. However, as she navigated through the narrow passageway, she kept her eyes and ears on high alert for movement or sound. She wasn't anything close to being afraid of Duane unless he got the drop on her. In a fair fight, she could more than hold her own. She had kicked the crap out of him on more than one occasion when he had been particularly drunk. He normally didn't try anything too outrageous when he was sober, which he would be now, or as close to it as he usually got. It was a strange relationship to have with someone who could be categorized as her significant other. However, she could name ten other women she knew who had similar arrangements, based more on pure economics, limited options, and in essence, inertia, than on anything approaching tender emotions. She had had other offers; but rarely was the grass greener elsewhere, she knew that firsthand. She picked up her pace as she heard the snores coming from the bedroom and leaned her head in the small room. She sucked in her breath as she eyed the twin figures lying under the sheets. Duane's head was visible on the right. The other person was completely covered by the sheet; however, the twin humps in the chest region suggested it was not one of Duane's male drinking buddies sleeping it off.

LuAnn quietly stepped down the hallway and placed an anxious-looking Lisa and her carrier down in the bathroom, then closed the door. LuAnn didn't want her little girl to be disturbed by what was about to happen. When she again opened the bedroom door, Duane was still snoring loudly; however, the body beside him had moved, and the dark red hair was clearly visible now. It only took a second for LuAnn to clamp a hand around the thick mane, and then she pulled with all her immense strength and the unfortunate owner of those long locks was hauled out of the bed to crash buck-naked against the far wall.

"Shit!" the woman bellowed as she landed on her butt and was immediately pulled across the rough, ragged carpet by a grim-looking LuAnn. "Dammit, LuAnn, let go."

LuAnn looked back at her for a split second. "Shirley, you slut around here again, and I swear to God I'll break your neck."

"Duane! Help me for chrissakes! She's crazy!" Shirley wailed, pulling and clawing at her hair in a futile effort to make LuAnn let go. Shirley was short and about twenty pounds overweight. Her chubby legs and full, wobbly breasts slapped back and forth against each other as the two women made their way to the bedroom door.

Duane stirred as LuAnn passed by. "What's going on here?" he said sleepily.

"Shut up," LuAnn snapped back.

As his eyes focused on the situation, Duane reached across to the nightstand and pulled out a pack of Marlboros from the drawer. He grinned at Shirley as he lit up.

"Going home so soon, Shirl?" He wiped his droopy hair out of his face as he sucked contentedly on his cigarette.

Facing to the rear as she was, Shirley glared at him, her fat cheeks a deep burgundy. "You're a piece of crap."

Duane blew her an imaginary kiss. "I love you too, Shirl. Thanks for the visit. Made my morning." He belly-laughed and slapped his thigh as he propped himself up on the pillow. Then LuAnn and Shirley disappeared through the doorway.

After depositing Shirley next to a rusted-out Ford engine block in the front yard, LuAnn turned back to the trailer.

Shirley stood up and shrieked, "You pulled half my hair out, you bitch." LuAnn kept walking, not looking back. "I want my clothes. Give me my damned clothes, LuAnn."

LuAnn turned around. "You didn't need 'em while you were here, so I can't see no reason why you'd need 'em now."

"I can't go home like this."

"Then don't go home." LuAnn went up the cinder block steps to the trailer and slammed the door behind her.

Duane met her in the hallway, dressed in his boxers, an unlit Marlboro dangling from his mouth. "Does a man good to have two alleycats fighting over him. Got my blood going, LuAnn. How 'bout you stepping up to the plate? Come on, baby, give me a kiss." He grinned at her and tried to slide an arm around her long neck. His next breath was a tortured one as her right fist smashed into his mouth, loosening a couple of his teeth. As painful as that blow was, it did not come close on the hurt scale to the knee that planted itself violently between his legs. Duane dropped heavily to the floor.

LuAnn hovered over him. "If you pull that crap again, Duane Harvey, so help me God, I'll rip it right off and flush it down the toilet."

"Crazy-ass woman," he half-sputtered, half-whimpered, clutching at his groin; blood seeped through his lips.

She reached down and clamped an iron grip across his cheeks. "No, *you're* crazy if you think for one second I'm gonna put up with that shit."

"We ain't married."

"That's right, but we live together. We got a kid together. And this place is as much mine as it is yours."

"Shirl don't mean nothing to me. What do you care?" He stared up at her, small tears gathering in the corners of his eyes as he continued to clutch his privates.

"Because that little fat piece of bacon is gonna waddle on down to the IGA and the beauty parlor and the damned Squat and Gobble and tell everybody that will listen all about it and I'm gonna look like the biggest piece of trash in the world."

"You shouldn't have left me this morning." He struggled up off the floor. "See, this here's all your fault. She came by to see you about something. What was I supposed to do?"

"I don't know, Duane, how about giving her a cup of coffee instead of your dick?"

"I don't feel so good, babe. I really don't." He leaned up against the wall.

She roughly pushed past him on her way to check on Lisa. "Best news I've heard all day."

A minute later she marched past him again and entered the bedroom, where she proceeded to rip the sheets off the bed.

Duane sulkily watched her from the doorway. "Go ahead and throw 'em away. I don't give a crap, you bought 'em."

She didn't look at him as she answered. "I'm taking 'em over to Wanda's to wash. If you're gonna sleep around with sluts, it ain't gonna cost me nothing."

As she lifted the mattress, a flash of green caught her eye. She shoved the mattress off the bed frame and then looked over at Duane. "What the hell is this?" she demanded.

Duane looked at her coldly. He sauntered into the room, scooped up the piles of cash, and stuffed them in a paper bag that had been sitting on the table beside the bed. He continued to eye her as he closed the bag. "Let's just say I won the lottery," he said arrogantly.

She perceptibly stiffened at his words as though she'd been slapped flush in the face. For a moment she felt as though she would topple right over in a dead faint. Had Duane actually been behind all of this? Were he and Jackson in this together? She could not have envisioned a more unlikely pair. It couldn't possibly be. She quickly recovered and crossed her arms. "Bull. Where'd you get it, Duane?"

"Let's just say it's a real good reason to be nice to me and to keep your mouth shut."

Angrily pushing him from the room, she locked the door. She changed into jeans, sneakers, and a sweatshirt and then quickly packed an overnight bag. When she unlocked and threw open the door, Duane hadn't budged; the bag was still clutched in his hand. She moved quickly past him, opened the door to the bathroom, and scooped up a wriggling Lisa in one arm; the dirty linen and overnight bag in her other hand, she headed for the front door.

"Where you going, LuAnn?"

"None of your damned business."

"How long you gonna be pissed about this? I didn't get mad at you for kicking me in the balls, did I? I done already forgot about it, in fact."

She whirled around for a second. "Duane, you

have got to be the dumbest person on the face of this earth."

"Is that right? Well who do you think you are? Princess Di? Why, if it weren't for me, you and Lisa wouldn't even have a damned place to stay. I took you in or you wouldn't have nothing." He lit up another cigarette but warily kept out of range of her fist. He scrunched the match out on the tattered carpet. "So maybe instead of bitching all the time, you oughta try being nice to me." He held up the paper bag stuffed with cash. "There's plenty more where this came from, too, little girl. I ain't gonna be living in this craphole much longer. You best think about it. You best think real good about that. I ain't taking crap from you or anybody else anymore. You hear me?"

She opened the front door. "Duane, I'll start being nice to you right now. You know how? I'm gonna leave before I kill you!" Lisa started to cry at her mother's angry tones as though she thought they were directed at her. LuAnn kissed the little girl and cooed in her ear to calm her down.

Duane watched LuAnn march across the muddy yard, admiring her soft behind in the tight jeans. For a moment he looked around for Shirley, but she had evidently already made a run for it, naked and all.

"I love you, babe," he yelled after LuAnn, grinning.

"Go to hell, Duane."

SIX

The mall was far busier than it had been during her visit the day before. LuAnn was grateful for the crowds as she made a wide berth around the office she had visited earlier, though she did glance in its direction as she passed by. Through the glass panes on either side of the door it seemed dark inside. She supposed if she tried the door, it would be locked. She didn't imagine that Jackson would have hung around long after she had left, and she assumed she had been his sole "client."

She had called in sick to work and spent a sleepless night at a friend's house alternating between staring at a full moon and Lisa's tiny mouth as it randomly produced smiles, grimaces, and every expression in between while the little girl slept heavily. She had finally decided not to make a decision on Jackson's proposal until she had some more information. One conclusion had come fairly rapidly: She would not go to the police. She could prove nothing, and who would believe her? There was no upside potential to such a move and at least fifty million reasons against it. For all her sense of right and wrong, she could not get past that one inescapable temptation: Incredible, sudden wealth was perhaps staring her in the face. She felt guilty that the decision wasn't more black and white. However, her latest episode with Duane had only reinforced to her that Lisa could not be allowed to grow up in such an environment. Something had to give.

The mall office was at the end of a corridor on the south side of the building. LuAnn swung open the door and went in.

"LuAnn?"

LuAnn stared at the source of this exclamation. Behind the counter, the young man was dressed neatly in a short-sleeve shirt, necktie, and black slacks. In his excitement, he repeatedly clicked a pen in his right hand. LuAnn stared at him, but no recognition was forthcoming.

The young man almost vaulted over the counter. "I didn't expect you to remember me. Johnny Jarvis. I go by John now." He extended a hand in a professional manner and then, grinning, he gave her a solid hug and spent a full minute cooing over Lisa. LuAnn pulled out a small blanket from her bag, set her daughter down on it, and gave her a stuffed animal.

"I can't believe it's you, Johnny. I haven't seen you since, what, the sixth grade?"

"You were in the seventh, I was in the ninth."

"You look good. Real good. How long you been working here?"

Jarvis grinned proudly. "After high school I went on to the community college and got my A.S. That stands for associate degree in science. Been at the mall for two years now. Started out as a data inputter but now I've moved up to sort of the assistant manager of mall operations."

"Congratulations. That's wonderful, Johnny – I mean John."

"Oh hell, you can call me Johnny. I can't believe you just walked on in that door. When I saw you, I thought I was gonna fall over and die. I never thought I'd see you again. I supposed you'd just gone on to New York City or something."

"Nope, still here," she said quickly.

40

"I'm kinda surprised I've never seen you around the mall before then."

"I don't get up here much. It's a pretty long way from where I live now."

"Have a seat and tell me what you been up to. I didn't know you had a baby. Didn't even know you were married."

"I'm not married."

"Oh." Jarvis's face reddened slightly. "Uh, you want some coffee or something? I just put on a fresh pot."

"I'm kind of in a hurry, Johnny."

"Oh, well, what can I do for you?" He suddenly looked surprised. "You aren't looking for a job, are you?"

She looked pointedly at him. "What if I was? Something wrong with that?"

"No, I mean, course not. I just meant, you know, I never expected you to hang around here, working in no mall, that's all." He smiled.

"A job's a job, ain't it? *You* work here. And while we're talking about it, exactly what am I supposed to be doing with my life?"

Jarvis's smile quickly faded and he rubbed his hands nervously down the legs of his pants. "I didn't mean nothing by it, LuAnn. I just always thought of you living in some castle somewhere wearing fancy clothes and driving fancy cars. I'm sorry."

LuAnn's anger faded as she thought back to Jackson's proposition. Castles might be within her reach now. "It's okay, Johnny, it's been a long week, you know what I mean? I'm not looking for a job. What I'm looking for is a little information about one of your renters here."

Jarvis glanced over his shoulder at the rear office area where the sounds of phones and clattering keyboards could be heard mixed with short bursts of conversation, and then he turned back to her. "Information?"

"Yeah. I came by here yesterday morning. Had an appointment."

"With who?"

"That's what I want you to tell me. It was that business on the right as you come in the mall next to the bus stop. It ain't got no sign or anything, but it's next to the ice cream place."

Jarvis looked puzzled for a second. "I thought that space was still vacant. We got a lot of that. This mall isn't exactly in the middle of a booming area."

"Well, it wasn't vacant yesterday."

Jarvis walked over to the computer on the counter and started punching buttons. "What was the appointment for?"

LuAnn's reply was immediate. "Oh, it was a sales job, you know. Pushing products door-to-door."

"Yeah, we've had some people like that come in on a temporary basis. More like an interview room than anything else. If we have the space, which we usually do, we rent it out, sometimes just for the day. Especially if it's already been built out, you know, ready-made office space."

He pulled up a screen and studied it. As voices continued to filter in from the back office he went over and shut the door. He looked a little apprehensively at LuAnn. "So what'd you want to know?"

She noted his concerned look and glanced in the direction of the door he had just shut. "You're not going to get in trouble over this, are you, Johnny?"

He waved his hand dismissively. "Hell, no. Remember, I'm the assistant manager here," he said importantly.

"Well, just tell me whatever you can. Who the people are. What the business is. An address somewhere. Stuff like that."

Jarvis looked confused. "Well, didn't they tell you that during the interview?"

"Some of it," she said slowly. "But I just want to make sure it's all legit, you know. Before I accept or not. I got to buy some nicer clothes and maybe get me a car. I don't want to do that if it's not on the up-and-up."

Jarvis snorted. "Well, you're smart to do that. I mean just because we rent space to these people, it don't mean they're shooting straight with you." He added anxiously, "They didn't ask for money from you, did they?"

"No, as a matter of fact, the money they were talking about me getting was pretty unbelievable."

"Probably too good to be true then."

"That's what I'm afraid of." She watched his fingers sail across the computer keyboard. "Where'd you learn to do that stuff?" she said with admiration.

"What, this? That's when I was at the community college. They got programs over there that teach you just about anything. Computers are cool."

"I wouldn't mind going back to school one day."

"You were always real smart in school, LuAnn. I bet you'd pick it up like nobody's business."

She gave him a pretty look. "Maybe one day. Now what'cha got for me?"

Jarvis studied the screen again. "Company's name is Associates, Inc. At least that's what they put on the rental agreement. They leased for a week, starting yesterday in fact. Paid in cash. Didn't give any other address. When they pay in cash we don't really care."

"They ain't nobody there now."

Jarvis nodded absently as he tabbed down the screen. "Guy named Jackson signed the lease agreement," he said.

"About my height with black hair, sort of fat?"

"That's right. I remember him now. He seemed very professional. Anything out of the way happen during your interview?"

"Depends on what you call out of the way. But he was real professional to me, too. Anything else you can tell me?"

Jarvis studied the screen again, hoping to find a few more kernels of information with which to entice LuAnn. Finally, strong disappointment etched across his features, he looked at her and sighed. "Not really, I guess."

LuAnn hoisted up Lisa and then eyed a stack of steno pads and a cup of pens on the counter. "Could I have one of those pads and a pen, Johnny? I could pay you something for them."

"You kidding? Good golly, take all you want."

"One of each is all I need. Thanks." She put the pad and pen in her handbag.

"No problem at all, we got tons of that stuff."

"Well, I appreciate what you told me. I really do. And it was real nice seeing you, Johnny."

"Hell, you made my whole year walking in the door like that." He took a peek at his watch. "I take my lunch break in about ten minutes. They got a nice Chinese place down at the food court. You have time? My treat. We could talk some more, catch up."

"Maybe another time. Like I said, I'm kind of in a hurry."

LuAnn observed Jarvis's disappointment and felt a little guilty. She put Lisa down and gave him a big hug. She smiled as she listened to him breathe deeply into her freshly washed hair. As he pressed his hands against the small of her back, and the warmth and softness of her chest spread over his, Jarvis's spirits were instantly rekindled. "You've done real well for yourself, Johnny," LuAnn said as she stepped back. "Always knew you'd do just fine."

Things might have been different, she thought, if she had come across Johnny a while back.

Jarvis was now treading across fine white clouds. "You did? I'm kind of surprised you even thought about me at all."

"There you go, I'm just full of surprises. Take care of yourself, maybe I'll see you around." She picked up Lisa, who was rubbing the stuffed animal against her mother's cheek and jabbering happily, and headed for the door.

"Hey, LuAnn?"

She turned back around.

"You gonna take that job?"

She considered the question for a moment. "I don't know yet. But I expect you'll probably hear about it if I do."

LuAnn's next stop was the public library, a place she had frequented when in school, but it had been years since she had last been there. The librarian was very pleasant and complimented LuAnn on her daughter. Lisa snuggled against her mother while she looked around at all the books.

"Da. Da, ooh."

"She likes books," said LuAnn. "I read to her every day."

"She's got your eyes," the woman said looking back and forth between mother and child. LuAnn's hand gently slid against Lisa's cheek.

The woman's smile faded when she saw no ring on LuAnn's finger. LuAnn noted the look. "Best thing I've ever done. I ain't got much, but this little girl's never gonna be hurting for love."

The woman smiled weakly and nodded. "My daughter is a single mother. I do what I can to help out but it's very hard. There's never enough money to go around."

"Tell me about it." LuAnn dug a bottle and a container of water out of her diaper bag, mixed some formula she had gotten from a friend together, and helped Lisa get a grip on it. "If I ever get to the end of a week with more money than I started with, I'm not going to know what to do with myself."

The woman shook her head wistfully. "I know they say that money is the root of all evil, but I often think how nice it would be not to have to worry about the bills. I can't imagine the feeling. Can you?"

"I can imagine it. I imagine it must feel pretty durn good."

The woman laughed. "Now, how can I help you?"

"You keep copies of different newspapers here on that film stuff, don't you?"

The woman nodded. "On microfilm. It's in that room." She pointed to a doorway at the far end of the library.

LuAnn hesitated.

"Do you know how to use the microfilm machine? If not, I can show you. It's not very difficult."

"That'd be real nice. Thank you."

They entered the room, which was vacant and dark. The woman turned on the overhead light, seated LuAnn at one of the terminals, and picked out a microfilm spool from one of the files. It only took a minute to insert the spool, and information appeared on the lit screen. The woman worked the controls and lines of text flashed across the screen. LuAnn watched her carefully as she removed the spool and turned the machine off. "Now, you try it," the woman said.

LuAnn expertly inserted the spool and manipulated the controls as the film advanced.

"That's very good. You learn quickly. Most people don't get the hang of it right away."

"I've always been good with my hands."

"The catalogue files are clearly marked. We carry the local paper, of course, and some of the national ones. The publication dates are printed on the outside of the file drawers."

"Thank you very much."

As soon as the woman left, LuAnn carried Lisa, who was still slurping on the bottle, and started exploring the rows of file cabinets. She set Lisa down and watched in amusement as the little girl rolled to a cabinet, put down the bottle, and tried to pull herself up. LuAnn located a major newspaper in one of the cabinets and proceeded to check the boxes housing the spools until she found the dates corresponding to the last six months. She took a minute to change and burp Lisa and then inserted the first spool into the microfilm machine. With Lisa perched on her lap and pointing excitedly and jabbering on about the sights on the screen, LuAnn's eyes scanned the front page. It didn't take long to locate the story and the accompanying two-inch headline. "Lottery Winner Nets Forty-five Million Dollars." LuAnn quickly read the story. Outside, the sound of a sudden rainstorm assailed her ears. Spring brought a lot of rain to the area, usually in the form of thunderstorms. As if in response to her thoughts, thunder boomed and the entire building seemed to shake. LuAnn glanced anxiously over at Lisa, but the little girl was oblivious to the sounds. LuAnn pulled a blanket from her bag, set it down on the floor with some toys, and put Lisa down. LuAnn turned back to the headline. She pulled the steno pad and pen out of her handbag and started scribbling notes. She flipped to the next month. The U.S. Lotto drawing was held on the fifteenth of each month. The dates she was looking at were for the sixteenth through the twentieth. Two hours later she had completed her review of the past six winners.

She unwound the last spool and replaced it in the file drawer. She sat back and looked at her notes. Her head was pounding and she wanted a cup of coffee. The rain was still coming down hard. Carrying Lisa, she went back into the library, pulled some children's books down, and showed Lisa the pictures in them and read to the little girl. Within twenty minutes, Lisa had fallen asleep and LuAnn put her in the baby carrier and set it on the table next to her. The room was quiet and warm. As LuAnn felt herself starting to doze she put one arm protectively across Lisa and gripped the little girl's leg in a gentle squeeze. The next thing she knew she was startled awake when a hand touched her shoulder. She looked up into the eyes of the librarian.

"I'm sorry to wake you, but we're closing up."

LuAnn looked around bewildered for a moment. "Good Lord, what time is it?"

"A little after six, dear."

LuAnn quickly packed up. "I'm sorry for falling asleep in here like that."

"Didn't bother me a bit. I'm just sorry I had to wake you, you looked so peaceful there with your daughter and all."

"Thanks again for all your help." LuAnn cocked her head as she listened to the rain pounding on the roof.

The woman looked at her. "I wish I could offer you a ride somewhere, but I take the bus."

"That's okay. The bus and me know each other real good."

LuAnn draped her coat over Lisa and left. She sprinted to the bus stop and waited until the bus pulled up a half hour later with a squeal of brakes and a deep sigh of its air-powered door. She was ten cents short on the fare, but the driver, a heavyset black man whom she knew by sight, waved her on

48

after dropping in the rest from his own pocket.

"We all of us need help every now and again," he said. She thanked him with a smile. Twenty minutes later, LuAnn walked into the Number One Truck Stop several hours before her shift.

"Hey, girl, what you doing here so soon?" asked Beth, LuAnn's fiftyish and very matronly coworker, as she wiped a wet cloth across the Formica counter.

A three-hundred-pound truck driver appraised LuAnn over the rim of his coffee cup and, even soaked as she was from her jaunt in the rain, he came away dutifully impressed. As always. "She come early so she wouldn't miss big old Frankie here," he said with a grin that threatened to swallow up his whole wide face. "She knew I got on the earlier shift and couldn't bear the thought of not seeing me no more."

"You're right, Frankie, it'd just break her heart if LuAnn didn't see your big old hairy mug on a regular basis," Beth rejoined, while prying between her teeth with a swizzle stick.

"Hi, Frankie, how you?" LuAnn said.

"Just fine, now," Frankie replied, the smile still cemented on his features.

"Beth, can you watch Lisa for a minute while I change into my uniform?" LuAnn asked as she wiped her face and arms down with a towel. She checked Lisa and was relieved to find her dry and hungry. "I'm going to make her up a bottle in just a minute and mix up some of that oatmeal. Then she should be ready to go down for the night even though she had a pretty big nap not too long ago."

"You bet I can take that beautiful little child into my arms. Come here, darling." Beth hoisted up Lisa and settled her against her chest, where Lisa proceeded to make all manner of noises and pull at the pen stuck behind Beth's ear. "Really, now,

LuAnn, you ain't got to be here for hours. What's up?"

"I got soaked and my uniform's the only clean thing I got. Besides, I felt bad about missing last night. Hey, is there anything left over from lunch? I sorta can't remember eating yet today."

Beth gave LuAnn a disapproving look and planted one hand on a very full hip. "If you took half as good care of yourself as you do this baby. My Lord, child, it is almost eight o'clock."

"Don't nag, Beth. I just forgot, that's all."

Beth grunted. "Right, Duane drank your money away again, didn't he?"

"You oughta drop that little sumbitch, LuAnn," Frankie grumbled. "But let me kick his ass first for you. You deserve better than that crap."

Beth raised an eyebrow that clearly signaled her agreement with Frankie.

LuAnn scowled at them. "Thank you both for your vote on *my* life, now if you'll excuse me?"

Later that evening, LuAnn sat at the far corner booth finishing a plate of food Beth had rounded up for her. She finally pushed the dinner away and sipped a cup of fresh coffee. The rain had started again and the clattering sound against the diner's tin roof was comforting. She pulled a thin sweater tighter around her shoulders and checked the clock behind the counter. She still had two hours before she went on duty. Normally, when she got to the diner early she'd try to catch a little overtime, but the manager wasn't letting her do that anymore. Hurt the bottom line, he had told LuAnn. Well, you don't want to know about my bottom line, she had told him right back, but to no avail. But that was okay, he let her bring Lisa in. Without that, there'd be no way she could work at all. And he paid her in cash. She knew he was avoiding payroll taxes that way, but she made little enough money as it was without the government taking any. She had never filed a tax return; she had lived her entire life well below the poverty line and rightly figured she didn't owe any taxes.

Lisa was in her carrier across from her. LuAnn tucked the blanket more snugly around her sleeping daughter. LuAnn had fed Lisa parts of her meal; her daughter was taking to solid food real well, but she hadn't made it through the mushed carrots before falling asleep again. LuAnn worried that her daughter wasn't getting the right kind of sleep. And she wondered, Was putting her baby under the counter of a noisy, smoky truck stop every night going to mess up Lisa's head years from now? Lower her self-esteem and do other damage LuAnn had read about in the magazines or seen on TV. That nightmarish thought had cost LuAnn more sleep than she could remember. And that wasn't all. When Lisa turned to solid food for good would there always be enough? Not having a car, always scrounging change for the bus, walking, or running through the rain. What if Lisa caught something? What if LuAnn did? What if she were laid up for a while? Who would take care of Lisa? She had no insurance. She took Lisa to the free county clinic for her shots and checkups, but LuAnn hadn't been to a doctor in over ten years. She was young, strong, and healthy, but that could change quickly. You never knew. She almost laughed when she thought of Duane trying to navigate the endless details of Lisa's daily requirements. The boy would run screaming into the woods after a few minutes. But it really wasn't a laughing matter.

While she looked at the tiny mouth opening and closing, LuAnn's heart suddenly felt as heavy as the semis parked in the diner's parking lot. Her

51

daughter depended on her for everything and the truth was LuAnn had nothing. One step from the edge every day of her life and getting closer all the time. A fall was inevitable; it was only a matter of time. She thought back to Jackson's words. A cycle. Her mother. Then LuAnn. Duane resembled Benny Tyler in more ways than she cared to think about. Next up was Lisa, her darling little girl for whom she would kill, or be killed, whatever it took to protect her. America was full of opportunity, everybody said. You just had to unlock it. Only they forgot to give out keys for LuAnn's kind. Or maybe they didn't forget at all. Maybe it was intentional. At least that's how she usually saw things when she was more than a little depressed, like now.

She shook her head clear and squeezed her hands together. That kind of thinking wasn't going to help her now. LuAnn pulled her handbag over and slid out the steno pad. What she had found at the library had greatly intrigued her.

Six lottery winners. She had started with the ones last fall and continued up to the present. She had written down their names and backgrounds. The articles had carried a photo of each winner; their smiles had seemed to stretch across the width of the page. In reverse order of winning they were: Judy Davis, age twenty-seven, a welfare mother with three young children; Herman Rudy, age fifty-eight, a former truck driver on disability with massive medical bills from an injury on the job; Wanda Tripp, sixty-six, widowed and subsisting on Social Security's "safety net" of four hundred dollars a month; Randy Stith, thirty-one, a recent widower with a young child, who had recently been laid off from his assembly line job; Bobbie Jo Reynolds, thirty-three, a waitress in New York who after winning the article said had given up her dream of starring on Broadway to take up painting in the south of France. Finally, there was Raymond Powell, forty-four, a recent bankrupt who had moved into a homeless shelter.

LuAnn slumped back in her seat. *And LuAnn, twenty years old, single mother, dirt poor, uneducated, no prospects, no future.* She would fit in perfectly with this desperate group.

She had only gone back six months. How many more of them were there? It made for great stories, she had to admit. People in dire straits hit the jackpot. Old people with newfound wealth. Young children with a suddenly bright future. All their dreams coming true. Jackson's face appeared in her thoughts. *Someone has to win. Why not you, LuAnn?* His calm, cool tones beckoned to her. In fact, those two sentences reverberated over and over in her head. She felt herself beginning to slide over the top of an imaginary dam. What was awaiting her in the deep waters below, she was not sure. The unknown both scared her and drew her, fiercely. She looked at Lisa. She could not shake the image of her little girl growing into a woman in a trailer with no way to escape while the young wolves circled.

"What'cha doing, sweetie?"

LuAnn jerked around and stared into Beth's face. The older woman expertly juggled plates full of food in both hands.

"Nothing much, just counting up all my fortune," LuAnn said.

Beth grinned and looked at the steno pad, which LuAnn quickly closed. "Well, don't forget the little people when you hit the big time, Miss LuAnn Tyler." Beth cackled and then carried the food orders to the waiting customers.

LuAnn smiled uneasily. "I won't, Beth. I swear," she said quietly.

SEVEN

It was eight o'clock in the morning on *the day*. LuAnn stepped off the bus with Lisa. This was not her usual stop, but it was close enough to the trailer that she could walk it in half an hour or so, which was nothing to her. The rain had passed and left the sky a brilliant blue and the earth a lush green. Small clusters of birds sang the praises of the changing season and the exit of another tedious winter. Everywhere LuAnn turned as she tramped along under the newly risen sun there was fresh growth. She liked this time of the day. It was calm, soothing, and she tended to feel hopeful about things.

LuAnn looked ahead to the gently rolling fields and her manner grew both somber and expectant. She walked slowly through the arched gateway and past the patinated sign proclaiming her entrance into the Heavenly Meadows Cemetery. Her long, slender feet carried her automatically to Section 14, Lot 21, Plot 6; it occupied a space on a small knoll in the shadow of a mature dogwood that would soon begin showing its unique wares. She laid Lisa's carrier down on the stone bench near her mother's grave and lifted out the little girl. Kneeling in the dewy grass, she brushed some twigs and dirt off the bronze marker. Her mother, Joy, had not lived all that long: thirty-seven years. It had seemed both brief and an eternity for Joy Tyler, that LuAnn knew. The years with Benny had not been pleasant, and had, LuAnn firmly believed now, hastened her mother's exit from the living.

"Remember? This is where your grandma is, Lisa. We haven't been for a while because the weather was so bad. But now that it's spring it's time to visit again." LuAnn held up her daughter and pointed with her finger at the recessed ground. "Right there. She's sleeping right now, but whenever we come by, she sort of wakes up. She can't really talk back to us but if you close your eyes tight as a baby bird's, and listen real, real hard, you can kinda hear her. She's letting you know what she thinks about things."

After saying this, LuAnn rose up and sat on the bench with Lisa on her lap, bundled against the chill of the early morning. Lisa was still sleepy; it usually took her a while to wake up, but once she did, the little girl wouldn't stop moving or talking for several hours. The cemetery was deserted except for a workman LuAnn could see far in the distance, cutting grass on a riding mower. The sounds of the mower's engine didn't reach her and there were few cars on the roadway. The silence was peaceful and she closed her eyes tight as a baby bird's and listened as hard as she could.

At the diner she had made up her mind to call Jackson right after she got off work. He had said anytime and she figured he would answer the phone on the first ring regardless of the time. Saying yes had seemed like the easiest thing in the world to do. And the smartest. It was her turn. After twenty years filled with grief, disappointment, and depths of despair that seemed to have endless elasticity, the gods had smiled upon her. Out of the masses of billions, LuAnn Tyler's name had turned the hat trick on the slot machine. It would never happen again, of that she was dead certain. She was also sure that the other people she had read about in the paper had made a similar phone call. She hadn't read anything about them getting in trouble. That sort of news would have been all over, certainly in as poor an area as she lived in, where everyone played the lottery in a frantic effort to throw off the bitter hopelessness of being a have-not. Somewhere between leaving the diner and stepping on the bus, however, she had felt something very deep inside of here prompting her to not pick up the phone but, instead, to seek counsel other than her own. She came here often, to talk, to lay flowers she had picked, or to spruce up her mother's final resting place. In the past, she had often thought she actually did communicate with her mother. She had never heard voices; it was more levels of feelings, of senses. Euphoria or deep sadness sometimes overtook her here, and she had finally put it down to her mother reaching out to her, letting her opinion on things having to do with LuAnn seep into her child's body, into her mind. Doctors would probably call her crazy, she knew, but that didn't take away from what she felt.

Right now she hoped for something to speak to her, to let her know what to do. Her mother had raised her right. LuAnn had never told a lie until she had started living with Duane. Then the fabrications seemed to just happen; they seemed to be an inextricable part of simply surviving. But she had never stolen anything in her life, never really done anything wrong that she knew of. She had kept her dignity and self-respect through a lot over the years and it felt good. It helped her get up and face the toil of another day when that day contained little in the way of hope that the next day and the next would be any different, any better.

But today, nothing was happening. The noisy lawn mower was drawing closer and the traffic on the road had picked up. She opened her eyes and sighed. Things were not right. Her mother apparently was not going to be available today of all days. She stood up and was preparing to leave when a feeling came over her. It was like nothing she had ever experienced before. Her eyes were automatically drawn to another section of the cemetery, to another plot that lay about five hundred yards away. Something was pulling her there, and she had no doubt what it was. Eyes wide, and her legs moving of their own accord, LuAnn made her way down the narrow, winding asphalt walkway. Something made her clutch Lisa tightly to her bosom, as though if she didn't the little girl would be snatched away by the unseen force compelling LuAnn to its epicenter. As she drew nearer to the spot, the sky seemed to turn a terrible dark. The sounds of the mowing were gone, the cars had stopped coming down the road. The only sound was the wind whistling over the flat grass and around the weathered testaments to the dead. Her hair blowing straight back, LuAnn finally stopped and looked down. The bronze marker was similar in style to her mother's, and the last name on it was identical: Benjamin Herbert Tyler. She had not been to this spot since her father had died. She had tightly clutched her mother's hand at his funeral, neither woman feeling the least bit saddened and yet having to display appropriate emotions for the many friends and family of the departed. In the strange way the world sometimes worked, Benny Tyler had been immensely popular with just about everyone except his own family because he had been generous and cordial with everyone except his own family. Seeing his formal name etched in the metal made her suck in her breath. It was as though the letters were stenciled over an office door and she would soon be ushered in to see the man himself. She started to draw back from the sunken earth, to retreat from the sharp jabs that seemed to sink in deeper with each step she had taken toward his remains. Then the intense feeling she had not realized beside her mother's grave suddenly overtook her. Of all places. She could almost see wisps of gauzy membrane swirling above the grave like a spiderweb picked up by the wind. She turned and ran. Even with Lisa, she hit an all-out sprint three steps into a run that would have made many an Olympian bristle with envy. Without missing a step and gripping Lisa to her chest, LuAnn snatched up Lisa's baby carrier and flew past the gates of the cemetery. She had not closed her eyes tight like a baby bird. She had not even been listening particularly hard. And yet the immortal speech of Benny Tyler had risen from depths so far down she could not contemplate them, and had made its way ferociously into the tender ear canals of his only child.

Take the money, little girl. Daddy says take it and damn everyone and everything else. Listen to me. Use what little brain you've got. When the body goes, you got nothing. Nothing! When did I ever lie to you, baby doll? Take it, dammit, take it, you dumb bitch! Daddy loves you. Do it for Big Daddy. You know you want to.

The man on the mower paused to watch her race away under a sky of pristine blue that begged to be photographed. The traffic on the road had picked up considerably. All the sounds of life, which had disappeared so inexplicably for LuAnn during those few moments, had once again reappeared.

The man looked over at the grave from which LuAnn had fled. Some people just got spooked in a graveyard, he figured, even in broad daylight. He went back to his mowing.

LuAnn was already out of sight.

The wind chased the pair down the long dirt road. Sweat drenched LuAnn's face as the sun bore down

58

on her from gaps in the foliage; her long legs ate up the ground with a stride that was both machine-like in its precision and wonderfully animalistic in its grace. Growing up she had been able to outrun just about everybody in the county, including most of the varsity football team. God-given world-class speed, her seventh-grade gym teacher had told her. What exactly she was supposed to do with that gift no one ever told her. For a thirteen-year-old girl with a woman's figure it had just meant if she couldn't beat up the boy who was trying to feel her up, at least she could probably outrun him.

Now her chest was burning. For a minute she wondered if she would keel over from a heart attack, as her father had. Perhaps there was some physical flaw buried deep within all the descendants of the man, just waiting for the opportunity to cleave another Tyler from the ranks. She slowed down. Lisa was bawling now and LuAnn finally stopped running and hugged her baby hard, whispering soothing words into the little girl's small pink ear while she made slow, wide circles in the dense shadows of the forest until the cries finally stopped.

LuAnn walked the rest of the way home. The words of Benny Tyler had made up her mind. She would pack what she could from the trailer and send somebody back for the rest. She would stay with Beth for a while. Beth had offered before. She had an old ramshackle house, but it had a lot of rooms and after the death of her husband her only companions were a pair of cats that Beth swore were crazier than she was. LuAnn would take Lisa into the classroom with her if need be, but she was going to get her GED and then maybe take some classes at the community college. If Johnny Jarvis could do it then she could, too. And Mr. Jackson could find somebody else to "gladly" take her place. All these answers to her life's dilemmas had come roaring in upon her so fast she could barely keep her head from exploding off her shoulders with relief. Her mother had spoken to her, in a roundabout manner perhaps, but the magic had been worked. "Never forget about the dearly departed, Lisa," she whispered to the little girl. "You just never know."

LuAnn slowed as she neared the trailer. Duane had been rolling in money the day before. She wondered how much he had left. He was quick to buy rounds at the Squat and Gobble when he had a few bucks in his pocket. Lord only knew what he had done with the wad he had under the bed. She didn't want to know where he had gotten it. She figured it was only an additional reason to get the hell out.

As she rounded the bend, a flock of blackbirds scattered from the trees overhead and scared her. She looked up at them angrily for a moment and then kept walking. As the trailer came into her line of sight, she abruptly stopped. There was a car parked out front. A convertible, big and wide, shiny black with white side-walls, and on the hood a huge chrome ornament that from a distance looked vaguely like a woman engaged in some indecent sexual act. Duane drove a battered Ford pickup truck which had been in the impoundment lot the last LuAnn had seen it. None of Duane's cronies drove anything like this crazy machine. What in the world was going on? Had Duane gone flat-out loco and bought this boat? She stole up to the vehicle and examined it, keeping one eye on the trailer. The seats were covered in a white leather with inlays of deep burgundy. The inside of the car was spotless, the dashboard clock polished enough to hurt your eye when the sunlight hit it just so. There was nothing in the front or rear seats to identify the owner. The keys hung in the ignition, a tiny Bud can attached to the ring. A phone rested in a device built specifically to hold it and attached to the hump between the front seat and the dashboard. Maybe this thing did belong to Duane. But she figured it would've taken all the cash under his mattress and then some to buy this rig.

She moved quickly up the steps and listened for sounds from within before venturing farther. When she didn't hear anything, she decided finally to brave it. She had kicked his butt the last time, she could do it again.

"Duane?" She slammed the door loudly. "Duane, what the hell did you do? Is that thing out there yours?" There was still no answer. LuAnn put an agitated Lisa down in her baby carrier and moved through the trailer. "Duane, are you here? Come on, answer me, will you, please. I don't have time to play around."

She went into the bedroom, but he wasn't there. Her eyes were riveted by her clock on the wall. It took her an instant to stuff it in her bag. She wasn't going to leave it with Duane. She exited the bedroom and moved down the hallway, passing Lisa as she did so. She stopped to calm the little girl down and placed her bag next to the baby carrier.

She finally saw Duane, lying on the raggedy couch. The TV was on, but no sound came from the battered box. A grease-stained bucket of chicken wings was on the coffee table next to what LuAnn assumed was an empty can of beer. A mess of fries and an overturned bottle of ketchup were next to the bucket of wings. Whether this was breakfast or the remnants of dinner from last night, she didn't know.

"Hey, Duane, didn't you hear me?"

She saw him turn his head, very, very slowly, toward her. She scowled. Still drunk. "Duane, ain't you never going to grow up?" She started forward. "We got to talk. And you ain't going to like it, but that's too bad becau—" She got no further as the big hand clamped over her mouth, cutting off her scream. A thick arm encircled her waist, pinning her arms to her sides. As her panicked eyes swept the room, she noted for the first time that the front of Duane's shirt was a mass of splotchy crimson. As she watched in horror, he fell off the couch with a small groan and then didn't move again.

The hand shot up to her throat and pushed her chin up so hard she thought her neck was going to snap under the pressure. She sucked in a huge breath as she saw the other hand holding the blade that descended toward her neck.

"Sorry, lady, wrong time, wrong place." LuAnn didn't recognize the voice. The breath was a mixture of cheap beer and spicy chicken wings. The foul odor pressed against her cheek as fiercely as the hand against her mouth. He had made a mistake, though. With one hand bracing her chin and the other holding the knife, he had left her arms free. Perhaps he thought she would be paralyzed with fear. She was far from it. Her foot crunched backward against his knee at the same moment her bony elbow sunk deep into his flabby gut, hitting right at the diaphragm.

The force of her blow caused his hand to jerk suddenly and the knife slashed her chin. She tasted blood. The man dropped to the floor, spitting and coughing. The hunting knife clattered to the bare carpet next to him. LuAnn hurtled toward the front door, but her attacker managed to snag a leg as she passed by and she tumbled to the floor a few feet from him. Despite being doubled over, he clamped thick fingers around her ankle and dragged her back toward him. Finally, she got a good look at him as

62

she turned over on her back, kicking at him with all her might: sunburned skin, thick, caterpillar eyebrows, sweaty, matted black hair, and full, cracked lips that were at the moment grimacing in pain. She couldn't see his eyes, which were half-closed as his body shrugged off her blows. LuAnn took in those features in an instant. What was even more evident was that he was twice her size. In the grip that tightened around her leg, she knew she had no chance against him, strength-wise. However, she wasn't about to leave Lisa to face him alone; not without a lot more fight than she had already given him.

Instead of resisting further, she threw herself toward him, screaming as loudly as she could. The scream and her sudden leap startled him. Off-balance, he let go of her leg. Now she could see his eyes; they were deep brown, the color of old pennies. In another second they were shut tightly again as she planted her index fingers in both of them. Howling again, the man fell backward against the wall but then he ricocheted off like a bounced ball and slammed blindly into her. They both pitched over the couch. LuAnn's flailing hand seized an object on the way down. She couldn't see exactly what it was, but it was solid and hard and that's all she cared about as she swung with all her might and smashed it against his head right before she hit the floor, barely missing Duane's limp body, and then she slammed headfirst into the wall.

The telephone had shattered into pieces upon impact with the man's thick skull. Seemingly unconscious, her attacker lay facedown on the floor. The dark hair was now a mass of red as the blood poured from the head wound. LuAnn lay on the floor for a moment and then sat up. Her arm tingled where she had hit the coffee table, and then it went numb on her. Her buttocks ached where she had slammed into the floor. Her head pounded where it had struck the wall. "Damn," she said as she struggled to regain her equilibrium. She had to get out of here, she told herself. Grab Lisa and keep running until her legs or lungs gave out. Her vision blurred for an instant and her eyes rolled up into her head. "Oh, Lord," she moaned as she felt it coming. Her lips parted and she sank back down to the floor, unconscious.

EIGHT

LuAnn had no idea how long she had been out. The blood that had poured out of the wound on her chin hadn't yet hardened against her skin so it couldn't have been all that long. Her shirt was ripped and bloody; one breast hung loose from her bra. She slowly sat up and rearranged herself with her good arm. She wiped her chin and touched the cut; it was jagged and painful. She slowly lifted herself up. She could not seem to catch her breath as lingering terror and physical trauma battered her from within and without.

The two men lay side by side; the big man was clearly still breathing, the expansions and contractions of his huge gut were easy to see. LuAnn wasn't sure about Duane. She dropped to her knees and felt for his pulse, but if it was there, she couldn't find it. His face looked gray, but it was hard to tell in the darkness. She jumped up and flipped on a light, but the illumination was still poor. She knelt down beside him again and touched his chest gingerly. Then she lifted his shirt. She quickly pulled it back down, nauseated at the sight of all the blood there. "Oh, Lord, Duane, what have you gone and done? Duane, can you hear me? Duane!" In the dim light she was able to see that no more blood was flowing from his wounds: a sign that his heart was probably no longer beating. She felt his arm; it was still warm to the touch, but she felt his fingers and they were already beginning to curl and grow cold. She eyed the remnants of the phone. There was no way to call the ambulance now, although it didn't look like Duane was going to need one. She should probably go fetch the police, though. Find out who the other man was, why he had cut up Duane and tried to kill her.

When LuAnn rose to leave, she noticed the small pile of bags that had been hidden behind the greasy bucket of chicken. They had fallen off the table in the scuffle. LuAnn stooped down and picked one up. It was clear plastic. Inside was a small amount of white powder. Drugs.

Then she heard the whimpering. Oh God, where was Lisa? But there was another sound. LuAnn sucked in her breath as she jerked around and looked down. The big man's hand was moving, he was starting to rise. He was coming for her! Oh sweet Lord, he was coming for her! She dropped the bag and raced to the hallway. Using her good arm to snatch up Lisa, who started screaming when she saw her mother, LuAnn bolted through the front door, slamming it back against the side of the trailer. She ran past the convertible, stopped, and turned back. The massive wall of flesh she had clocked with the phone didn't explode through the door. At least not yet. Her eyes shifted slightly to the car; the dangling keys glimmered temptingly in the sunlight. She hesitated for only an instant, then she and Lisa were in the car. LuAnn gunned the motor and fishtailed out of the muck and on to the road. She took a minute to get her nerves under control before she turned on to the main highway into town.

Now Duane's sudden wealth made a lot of sense. Selling drugs was obviously far more lucrative than stripping cars for a living. Only Duane had apparently gotten greedy and kept a little too much of the drugs or green for himself. The stupid idiot! She had to call the police. Even if Duane was alive, which she doubted, she was probably only saving him for a long spell in jail. But if he was still alive, she couldn't just leave him to die. The other fellow she didn't give a damn about. She only wished she had hit him harder. As she sped up, she looked over at Lisa. The little girl sat wide-eyed in her baby carrier, the terror still clearly observable in her quivering lips and cheeks. Lisa settled her injured arm over her daughter, biting back the pain this simple movement caused her. Her neck felt as though a car had run over it. Then her eyes alighted on the cellular phone. She pulled off the road and snatched it up.

After quickly figuring out how to work it, she started to dial 911. Then she slowly put down the phone. She looked down at her fingers. They were shaking so hard she couldn't make a fist. They were also covered with blood, and probably not just her own. It was suddenly dawning on her that she could easily be implicated in all of this. Despite his starting to move, the guy could have slumped back down, dead, for all she knew. She would have killed him in self-defense, she knew that, but would anyone else? A drug dealer. She was driving his car.

This thought made her look around suddenly to see if anyone was watching. Some cars were heading towards her. The top! She had to close the ragtop. She jumped into the backseat and gripped the stiff fabric. She pulled upward, and then the big white convertible top descended down upon them like a clam closing up. She hit the ragtop's clamps, jumped back into the driver's seat, and tore down the road.

Would the police believe that she knew nothing about Duane's selling drugs? Somehow Duane had kept the truth from her, but who would accept that as the truth? She didn't believe it herself. This reality swept over her like a fire raging through a paper house; there seemed to be no escape. But maybe there was. She almost shrieked as she thought of it. For an instant her mother's face appeared in her thoughts. It was with immense difficulty that she pushed it away. "I'm sorry, Momma. I ain't got no choices left." She had to do it: the call to Jackson.

That's when her gaze came to rest on the dashboard. For several seconds she could not even manage a breath. It was like every ounce of blood had evaporated from her body as her eyes stayed locked on the shiny clock.

It was five minutes *past* ten.

Gone. Forever, Jackson had said, and she didn't doubt for an instant he had meant it. She pulled off the road and slumped over the steering wheel in her misery. What would happen to Lisa while she was in prison? Stupid, stupid Duane. Screwed her in life, and now in death.

She slowly raised her head up and looked across the street, wiping her eyes so she could make out the image: a bank branch, squat, solid, all-brick. If she had owned a gun, she would have seriously contemplated robbing it. Even that was not an option, though; it was Sunday and the bank was closed. As her eyes drifted over the front of the bank her heart started to beat rapidly again. The change in her state of mind was so sudden as to feel almost drug-induced.

The bank clock showed four minutes *before* ten.

Bankers were supposed to be steady, reliable folk. She hoped to God their clocks were reliable as well. She snatched up the phone, at the same time digging frantically in her pocket for the slip of paper with the number on it. Her coordination seemed to have totally deserted her. She could barely force her fingers to punch in the numbers. It seemed to take forever for the line to begin ringing. Fortunately for

68

her nerves, it rang only once before being answered.

"I was beginning to wonder about you, LuAnn," Jackson said. She could envision him checking his watch, probably marveling at how close she had cut it.

She forced herself to breathe normally. "I guess the time just got away from me. I had a lot going on."

"Your cavalier attitude is refreshing, although, quite frankly, it's a bit amazing to me."

"So what now?"

"Aren't you forgetting something?"

LuAnn looked puzzled. "What?" Her brain was near serious burnout. A series of pains shot throughout her body. *If all this turned out to be a joke . . .*

"I made you an offer, LuAnn. In order to have a legally enforceable arrangement, I need an acceptance from you. A formality, perhaps, but one on which I have to insist."

"I accept."

"Wonderful. I can tell you with complete assurance that you will never regret that decision."

LuAnn looked nervously around. Two people walking on the other side of the highway were staring at the car. She put the vehicle in gear and headed down the road. "So now what?" she again asked Jackson.

"Where are you?"

Her tone was wary. "Why?" Then she added quickly, "I'm at home."

"Fine. You are to go to the nearest outlet selling lottery tickets. You will purchase one."

"What numbers do I play?"

"That doesn't matter. As you know, you have two options. Either accept a ticket with numbers automatically dispensed by the machine or pick whatever numbers you want. They're all fed into the same central computer system with up-to-the-second results and no duplicate combinations are allowed; that ensures only one winner. If you opt for a personalized combination and your first choice has already been taken, simply pick another combination."

"But I don't understand. I thought you were gonna tell me what numbers to play. The winning numbers."

"There is no need for you to understand anything, LuAnn." Jackson's voice had risen a notch higher. "You are simply to do what you're told. Once you have the combination, call me back and tell me what the numbers are. I'll take care of the rest."

"So when do I get the money?"

"There will be a press conference—"

"Press conference!" LuAnn almost flipped the car over. She fought to keep it under control with her good arm as she cradled the phone under her chin.

Now Jackson sounded truly exasperated. "Haven't you ever watched one of these things? The winner attends a press conference, usually in New York. It's televised across the country, the world. You'll have your photo taken holding a ceremonial check and then reporters will ask questions about your background, your child, your dreams, what you'll do with the money. Quite nauseating, but the Lottery Commission insists. It's terrific PR for them. That's why ticket sales have been doubling every year for the last five years. Everybody loves a deserving winner, if for no other reason than most people believe themselves to be quite deserving."

"Do I have to do it?"

"Excuse me?"

"I don't want to be on TV." ·

"Well, I'm afraid you don't have a choice. Keep in mind that you're going to be at least fifty million dollars richer, LuAnn. For that kind of money, they

70

expect you to be able to handle *one* press conference. And, frankly, they are right."

"So I have to go?"

"Absolutely."

"Do I have to use my real name?"

"Why wouldn't you want to?"

"I've got my reasons, Mr. Jackson. Would I?"

"Yes! There is a certain statute, LuAnn, not that I would expect you to be aware of it, popularly termed the 'right to know' law. To put it simply, it says that the public is entitled to know the identities, the *real* identities, of all lottery winners."

LuAnn let out a deep breath filled with disappointment. "Okay, so when do I get the money?"

Now Jackson discernibly paused. The hair on the back of LuAnn's neck started to bristle. "Listen, don't try pulling no crap on me here. What about the damn money?"

"There's no cause to get testy, LuAnn. I was merely pondering how to explain it to you in the simplest terms possible. The money will be transferred into an account of your designation."

"But I don't have any account. I've never had enough money to open a damn account."

"Calm down, LuAnn, I'll take care of all of that. You don't have to worry about it. The only thing you have to do is win." Jackson's voice tried to sound upbeat. "Go to New York with Lisa, hold that big check, smile, wave, say nice, humble things, and then spend the rest of your life on the beach."

"How do I get to New York?"

"Good question; however, one for which I have already prepared. There's no airport near where you live, but there is a bus station. You'll take a bus to the train station in Atlanta. That's on Amtrak's Crescent line. The Gainsville station is closer to you, but they don't sell tickets there. It's a long ride, about eighteen hours or so with numerous stops; however, a good part of it will be while you're sleeping. It will take you to New York and you won't have to change trains. I'd put you on a plane to New York, but that's a little more complicated. You have to show identification, and, frankly, I don't want you in New York that quickly. I'll make all the arrangements. A reserved ticket will be waiting for you at each station. You can leave for New York right after the lottery drawing takes place."

The prone figures of Duane and the man who had tried his best to kill her flashed across LuAnn's mind. "I'm not sure I want to hang around here that long."

Jackson was startled. "Why not?"

"That's my business," she said sharply, then her tone softened. "It's just that if I'm gonna win this thing, I don't want to be around here when people find out, is all. It'll be like a pack of wolves on a calf, if you know what I mean."

"That won't happen. You won't be publicly identified as the winner until the press conference occurs in New York. When you arrive in the city, someone will be waiting for you and will take you to the lottery headquarters. Your winning ticket will be confirmed and then the press conference will occur the next day. It used to take weeks to verify the winning ticket. With the technology they have today, it takes hours."

"How about if I drive to Atlanta and take the train up today?"

"You have a car? My goodness, what will Duane say?" There was considerable mirth in Jackson's tone.

"Let me worry about that," LuAnn snapped.

"You know, LuAnn, you might want to act a little more grateful, unless, of course, someone makes you rich beyond your wildest dreams on a routine basis."

LuAnn swallowed hard. She was going to be rich all right. By cheating. "I am," she said slowly. "It's just now that I made up my mind, everything's going to change. My whole life. And Lisa's, too. It's a little mind-boggling."

"Well, I understand that. But keep in mind that this particular change is definitely of the positive variety. It's not like you're going to prison or anything."

LuAnn fought back the catch in her throat and clenched her bottom lip between her teeth. "Can't I please take the train up today? Please?"

"Hold on for one minute." He clicked off. LuAnn looked up ahead. A police cruiser sat on the side of the road, a radar gun perched on the door. LuAnn automatically checked her speedometer and, although she was under the speed limit, slowed down slightly. She didn't breathe again until she was several hundred yards down the road. Jackson clicked back on, his abrupt tones startling her.

"The Crescent pulls into Atlanta at seven-fifteen this evening and arrives in New York at one-thirty tomorrow afternoon. Atlanta is only a couple hours' drive from where you are." He paused for an instant. "You're going to need money for the ticket, though, and I'm assuming you'll need additional funds, perhaps for some travel-related incidentals."

LuAnn unconsciously nodded at the phone. "Yes." She suddenly felt very dirty, like a whore pleading for some extra cash after an hour's work.

"There's a Western Union office near the train station. I'll wire you five thousand dollars there." LuAnn gulped at the amount. "Remember my initial job offer? We'll just call it your salary for a job well done. You just have to show proper identification—"

"I don't have any."

"Just a driver's license or passport. That's all they need."

LuAnn almost laughed. "Passport? You don't need a passport to go from Piggly-Wiggly to the Wal-Mart, do you? And I don't have a driver's license either."

"But you're planning to drive a car to Atlanta." Jackson's astonished tone was even more amusing to her. Here the man was, orchestrating a multi-million-dollar scam, and he could not comprehend that LuAnn would operate an automobile without a license.

"You'd be surprised how many people ain't got a license for anything and they still do it."

"Well, you can't get the money without proper identification."

"Are you anywhere nearby?"

"LuAnn, I only came to glorious Rikersville to conduct my meeting with you. Once it was done, I didn't hang around." He paused again and LuAnn could hear the displeasure in his voice when he spoke next. "Well, we have a problem then."

"Well, how much would the train ticket be?"

"About fifteen hundred."

Remembering Duane's money hoard, a sudden thought struck LuAnn. She again pulled off the road, put down the phone, and quickly searched the car's interior. The brown leather bag she pulled from underneath the front seat didn't disappoint her. There was enough cash in there probably to buy the train.

"A woman I work with, her husband left her some money when he passed on. I can ask her for the money. A loan. I know she'll give it to me," she told Jackson. "I won't need no ID for cash, will I?" she added.

74

"Money is king, LuAnn. I'm sure Amtrak will accommodate you. Just don't use your real name, of course. Use something simple, but not too phony sounding. Now go buy the lottery ticket and then call me back immediately. Do you know how to get to Atlanta?"

"It's a big place, or so I've heard. I'll find it."

"Wear something to hide your face. The last thing we need is for you to be recognized."

"I understand, Mr. Jackson."

"You're almost there, LuAnn. Congratulations."

"I don't feel much like celebrating."

"Not to worry, you have the rest of your life to do that."

LuAnn put down the phone and looked around. The car windows were tinted so she didn't think anyone had actually seen her, but that could change. She had to ditch the car as fast as possible. The only question was where. She didn't want to be seen getting out of the car. It would be pretty hard to miss a tall, blood-caked woman hauling a baby out of a car with tinted windows and a chrome figure doing nasty things on the vehicle's hood. An idea finally hit her. A little dangerous perhaps, but right now she didn't have much alternative. She did a U-turn and headed in the opposite direction. Within twenty minutes she was pulling slowly down the dirt road, and straining to see ahead as she drew nearer to her destination. The trailer finally came into view. She saw no other vehicle, no movement. As she pulled in front of the trailer cold dread poured over her as she once again felt the man's hands around her throat, as she watched the blade swooping toward her. "You see that man coming out that house," LuAnn said out loud to herself, "you're gonna run right over his butt, let his lips kiss the oil pan on this thing."

She rolled down the passenger window so she

could check for sounds coming from within but heard nothing. She pulled a diaper wipe out of Lisa's bag and methodically rubbed down all of the car's surfaces that she had touched. She had watched a few episodes of *America's Most Wanted*. If it hadn't been too dangerous she would have gone back inside the trailer and wiped down the telephone. But she had lived there for almost two years. Her fingerprints would be all over the place, anyway. She climbed out of the car, stuffing as much cash from the bag as she could under the liner of Lisa's baby seat. She pulled her torn shirt together as best she could. She noiselessly closed the car door and, holding Lisa with her good arm, she quickly made her way back down the dirt road.

From within the trailer, the pair of dark eyes watched LuAnn's hasty departure, taking in every detail. When she suddenly glanced around the man stepped back into the shadow of the trailer's interior. LuAnn didn't know him, but he wasn't taking any chances at being observed. His dark leather jacket was zipped halfway up the front, the butt of a 9-mm visible sticking out of the inside pocket. He stepped quickly over the two men lying on the floor, careful to avoid the pools of blood. He had happened along at an opportune time. He was left with the spoils of a battle he had not even had to fight. What could be better? He scooped the drug packets off both the coffee table and the floor and deposited them in a plastic bag that the man pulled from his jacket. After thinking about it for a moment, he put half the stash back where he had found it. No sense being greedy, and if the organization these boys worked for got wind that no drugs had been discovered by the police in the trailer they might start looking for who took it. If only part of the stash was missing they'd probably assume the cops had sticky fingers.

He eyed the fight scene and then noted the torn

fabric on the floor; recognition spread across his features. It was from the woman's shirt. He put it in his pocket. She owed him now. He looked at the remnants of the phone, the position of each man's body, the knife and the dents in the wall. She must have walked right into the middle of this, he deduced. Fat man got the little man, and LuAnn somehow got the fat man. His admiration for her increased as he noted the man's bulk.

As if he sensed this observation, the fat man started to stir again slowly. Not waiting for the fat man to recover further, the other man stooped down, used a cloth to snatch up the knife, and then plunged it repeatedly into the man's side. The dying man grew momentarily stiff, his fingers digging into the threadbare carpet, hanging on to the last seconds of his life, desperately unwilling to let go. After a few moments, though, his entire body shook for an instant and then slowly relaxed, his fingers uncurled and splayed out, his palms flush against the floor. His face was turned to the side; one lifeless, blood-filled eye stared up at his killer.

Next, he roughly flipped over Duane, squinting in the dim light as he tried to determine if the chest was moving up or down. Just to be safe he used several carefully aimed thrusts to make certain Duane Harvey joined the fat man in the hereafter. He tossed the knife down.

In another few seconds, he was through the front door and around the back of the trailer where he plunged into the woods. His car was parked off a little-used dirt trail that snaked through the heavy woods. It was windy and rough, but it would deliver him on to the main road in plenty of time to take up his real task: following LuAnn Tyler. When he climbed into his car, his car phone was ringing. He picked it up.

"Your duties are at an end," Jackson said. "The hunt has officially been called off. The balance of your payment will be sent to you via the usual channels. I thank you for your work and I'll keep you in mind for future employment."

Anthony Romanello gripped the phone hard. He debated whether to tell Jackson about the two bodies in the trailer and then decided not to. He might have stumbled on to something really interesting.

"I saw the little lady tearing out of here on foot. But she doesn't look like she has the resources to go very far," Romanello said.

Jackson chuckled. "I think money will be the least of her worries." Then the line went dead.

Romanello clicked off his phone and pondered the matter for a moment. Technically, he had been called off. His work was at an end and he could just return home and wait for the rest of his money. But there was something screwy going on here. Everything about the job was somehow off. Sending him down here to the sticks to kill some hick chick. And then being told not to. And there was Jackson's passing reference to money. Dollars were something that always held Romanello's interest. He made up his mind and put the car in gear. He was going to follow LuAnn Tyler.

NINE

L uAnn stopped at a gas station rest room and cleaned up as best as she could. She cleaned the wound on her jaw, pulled a Band-Aid out of Lisa's diaper bag, and covered the cut with it. While Lisa slurped contentedly on a bottle, LuAnn bought her lottery ticket and some ointment and gauze at the local 7-Eleven. As part of the ten numbers she picked, she used her own and Lisa's birthdays.

"People been coming in here like damn cattle," said the clerk, who was a friend of hers named Bobby.

"What happened there?" he asked, pointing to the large Band-Aid on her face.

"Fell and cut myself," she said quickly. "So what's the jackpot up to?" LuAnn asked.

"A cool sixty-five mil and counting." Bobby's eyes gleamed with anticipation. "I got a dozen tickets myself. I'm feeling good about this one, LuAnn. Hey, you know that movie where the cop gives the waitress half his lottery winnings? LuAnn, tell you what, darling, I win this thing, I'll give half to you, cross my heart."

"I appreciate that, Bobby, but what exactly do I have to do for the money?"

"Why, marry me, o' course." Bobby grinned as he handed her the ticket she had purchased. "So what do you say, how about half of yours if you win? We'll still get hitched."

"I think I'll just play this one all by myself.

Besides, I thought you were engaged to Mary Anne Simmons."

"I was, but that was last week." Bobby looked her up and down in obvious admiration. "Duane is dumb as dirt."

LuAnn jammed the ticket far down into her jeans. "You been seeing much of him lately?"

Bobby shook his head. "Nah, he's been keeping to himself lately. I heard he's been spending a lot of time over Gwinnett County way. Got some business over there or something."

"What kind of business?"

Bobby shrugged. "Don't know. Don't want to know. Got better things to do with my time than worry about the likes of him."

"Duane come into some money that you know of?"

"Come to think of it, he was flashing some cash around the other night. I thought maybe he won the lottery. If he did, I think I'll just go kill myself right now. Damn, she looks just like you." Bobby gave Lisa's cheek a gentle rub. "You change your mind about splitting the pot or marrying me, you just let me know, sweet cheeks. I get off at seven."

"I'll see you around, Bobby."

At a nearby pay phone, LuAnn dialed the number again and once again Jackson picked it up on the first ring. She gave him the ten digits from her ticket and she could hear him rustling paper on the other end of the line as he wrote them down.

"Read them to me once more, slowly," he said. "As you can understand, we can't have any mistakes now."

She read them again and he read them back to her.

"Good," he said. "Very good. Well, now the hard part is over. Get on the train, do your little press conference, and sail away into the sunset."

"I'm going to the train station right now."

"Someone will meet you at Penn Station and take you to your hotel."

"I thought I was going to New York."

"That's the name of the train station in New York, LuAnn," Jackson said impatiently. "The person meeting you will have a description of you and Lisa." He paused. "I'm assuming you're bringing her."

"She don't go, I don't go."

"That's not what I meant, LuAnn, of course you can bring her. However, I trust you did not include Duane in the travel plans."

LuAnn swallowed hard as she thought back to the bloodstains on Duane's shirt, how he had fallen off the couch and never moved again. "Duane won't be coming," she said.

"Excellent," Jackson said. "Enjoy your trip."

The bus dropped off LuAnn and Lisa at the train station in Atlanta. After her phone call with Jackson, she had stopped at the Wal-Mart and purchased some essentials for herself and Lisa, which were in a bag slung over her shoulder; her own torn shirt had been replaced with a new one. A cowboy hat and a pair of sunglasses hid her face. She had thoroughly cleaned and dressed the knife wound in the rest room. It felt a lot better. She went to the ticket counter to purchase her train ticket to New York. And that's when LuAnn made a big mistake.

"Name, please," the agent said.

LuAnn was fiddling with a fussing Lisa and thus answered automatically, "LuAnn Tyler." She caught her breath as soon as she said it. She looked at the clerk, who was busily typing the information into her computer. LuAnn couldn't change it now. That would obviously make the woman suspicious. She swallowed hard and hoped to God the slip would not come back to haunt her. The woman recommended the Deluxe sleeping car accommodations since LuAnn was traveling with a baby. "There's one available and it has a private shower and all," the woman said. LuAnn quickly agreed. While the ticket was being processed, the sales agent raised an eyebrow when LuAnn pulled some bills from under Lisa's baby seat to pay for the ticket, stuffing the rest in her pocket.

LuAnn observed the woman's look, thought quickly, and smiled at her. "My rainy day money. Figured I might as well use it while the weather's nice. Go up to New York and see the sights."

"Well, enjoy yourself," the woman said, "but be careful. You shouldn't be carrying a lot of cash up there. My husband and I made that mistake when we went years ago. We weren't five minutes out of the train station when we got robbed. Had to call my mother to send us some money so we could come home."

"Thanks, I'll be real careful."

The woman looked behind LuAnn. "Where's your luggage?"

"Oh, I like to travel light. Besides, we got family up there. Thanks again." LuAnn turned and walked toward the departure area.

The woman stared after her and then turned back and was startled by the person who had seemingly appeared from nowhere and was now standing in front of her window. The man in the dark leather jacket put his hands on the counter. "One-way ticket to New York City, please," Anthony Romanello said politely and then stole a sideways glance in LuAnn's direction. He had watched through the plate glass of the 7-Eleven as LuAnn had purchased her lottery ticket. Next, he had observed her make the phone

82

call from the pay phone, although he had not risked getting close enough to overhear the conversation. The fact that she was now on her way to New York had piqued his curiosity to the maximum. He had many reasons for wanting to leave the area as quickly as possible, anyway. Even though his assignment was over, finding out what LuAnn Tyler was up to and why she was going to New York was just an added inducement. It was all the more convenient because he happened to live there. It could be she was simply running from the bodies in the trailer. Or it could be more. Much more. He took the train ticket and headed toward the platform.

LuAnn stood well back from the tracks when the train came noisily into the station a bit behind schedule. With the aid of a conductor she found her compartment. The Deluxe Viewliner sleeping compartment had a lower bunk, an upper bunk, an armchair, sink, toilet, and private shower. Because of the lateness of the hour, and with LuAnn's permission, the attendant changed the compartment to its sleeping configuration. After he was finished, LuAnn closed the door to the room, sat down in the armchair, pulled out a bottle, and started feeding Lisa as the train slid smoothly out of the station half an hour later. The train gathered speed and soon LuAnn was watching the countryside sail by through the two large picture windows. She finished feeding Lisa and cradled the little girl against her chest to burp her. That accomplished, LuAnn turned Lisa around and started playing with her, doing patty cake and singing songs, which the delighted little girl joined in on in her own unique fashion. They passed an hour or so playing together until Lisa finally grew tired and LuAnn put her in the baby carrier.

LuAnn sat back and tried to relax. She had never

been on a train before, and the gliding sensation and rhythmic click of the wheels was making her drowsy as well. It was hard to remember the last time she had slept, and she started to drift off. LuAnn awoke with a start several hours later. It must be nearly midnight, she thought. She suddenly recalled that she hadn't eaten all day. It hadn't seemed important with everything that had happened. She popped her head out the compartment door, spied an attendant, and asked if there was food on the train. The man looked a little surprised and glanced at his watch. "They made the last call for dinner several hours ago, ma'am. The dining car is closed now."

"Oh," LuAnn said. It wouldn't be the first time she had gone hungry. At least Lisa had eaten.

However, when the man caught sight of Lisa and then looked at how tired LuAnn seemed, he smiled kindly and told her to wait just a bit. Twenty minutes later he came back with a tray loaded with food and even set it out for her, using the lower bunk as an impromptu table. LuAnn tipped him generously from her stash of funds. After he left, she devoured her meal. She wiped off her hands and reached carefully into her pocket and pulled out the lottery ticket. She looked over at Lisa; the little girl's hands were gently swaying in her slumber, a smile played across the small features. Must be a nice dream, LuAnn thought, smiling at the precious sight.

LuAnn's features grew softer and she leaned down and spoke quietly into Lisa's tiny ear. "Momma's gonna be able to take care of you now, baby, like I should've been doing all along. The man says we can go anywhere, do anything." She stroked Lisa's chin and nuzzled her cheek with the back of her hand. "Where you wanta go, baby doll? You name it, we'll go. How's that sound? That sound good?"

84

LuAnn locked the door and laid Lisa down on the bed, checking to make sure the straps on the baby seat were tight. LuAnn lay back on the bed and curled her body protectively around her daughter. While the train made its way to New York City, she stared out the window into the darkness, wondering mightily about what was going to come next.

TEN

The train had been delayed at several points along the route and it was nearly three-thirty in the afternoon when LuAnn and Lisa emerged into the frenzy of Penn Station. LuAnn had never seen this many people in one place in all her life. She looked around, dazed, as people and luggage flew past her like sprays of buckshot. She tightened her grip on Lisa's carrier as the train ticket agent's warning came back to her. Her arm was still throbbing painfully, but she figured she could still deck just about anybody who tried something. She looked down at Lisa. With so many interesting things going on around her, the little girl seemed ready to explode out of her seat. LuAnn moved slowly forward, not knowing how to get out of the place. She saw a sign for Madison Square Garden and vaguely recalled that several years ago she had watched a boxing match on TV that had been telecast from there. Jackson said someone would be here, but LuAnn couldn't imagine how the person would find her in the middle of all this chaos.

She jerked slightly as the man brushed against her. LuAnn looked up into dark brown eyes with a silvery mustache resting below the broad, flattened nose. For an instant LuAnn wondered if he was the man she had seen fighting at the Garden; however, she quickly realized that he was much too old, at least in his early fifties. He had the breadth of shoulders, flattened, crusty ears, and battered face, though, that marked the man as an ex-boxer.

"Miss Tyler?" His voice was low but clear. "Mr. Jackson sent me to pick you up."

LuAnn nodded and put out her hand. "Call me LuAnn. What's your name?"

The man started for an instant. "That's not really important. Please follow me, I have a car waiting." He started to walk away.

"I really like to know people's names," LuAnn said, without budging.

He came back to her, looking slightly irritated, although somewhere in his features she thought she discerned the beginnings of a smile. "Okay, you can call me Charlie. How's that?"

"That's fine, Charlie. I guess you work for Mr. Jackson. Do you use your real names with each other?"

He didn't answer as he led her toward the exit. "You want me to carry the little girl? That thing looks heavy."

"I've got it okay." She winced as another stab of pain shot through her injured arm.

"You sure?" he asked. He eyed her bandaged jaw. "You look like you've been in a fight."

She nodded. "I'm okay."

The pair exited the train station, moved past the line of people waiting in the cab stand, and Charlie opened the door of a stretch limo for LuAnn. She gawked for a minute at the luxurious vehicle before climbing in.

Charlie sat across from her. LuAnn couldn't help staring at the vehicle's interior.

"We'll be at the hotel in about twenty minutes. You want something to eat or drink in the meantime? Train food sucks," said Charlie.

"I've had a lot worse, although I am kinda hungry. But I don't want you to have to make a special stop."

He looked at her curiously. "We don't have to stop." He reached into the refrigerator and pulled out soda, beer, and some sandwiches and snack foods. He unlocked a section of the limo's interior paneling and a table materialized. As LuAnn watched in astonishment, Charlie laid the food and drink out and completed the repast with a plate, silverware, and napkin, his big hands working quickly and methodically.

"I knew you were bringing the baby, so I had the limo stocked with milk, bottles, and stuff like that. At the hotel they'll have everything you need."

LuAnn made up a bottle for Lisa, cradled her against one arm, and fed her with one hand while she devoured a sandwich with the other.

Charlie watched the tender way she handled her daughter. "She's cute, what's her name?"

"Lisa, Lisa Marie. You know, after Elvis's daughter."

"You look a little young to be a fan of the King."

"I wasn't – I mean, I don't really listen to that kind of music. But my momma did. She was a big fan. I did it for her."

"She appreciated it, I guess."

"I don't know, I hope she does. She died before Lisa was born."

"Oh, sorry." Charlie fell silent for a moment. "Well, what kind of music do you like?"

"Classical. I really don't know nothing about that kinda music. I just like the way it sounds. The way it makes me feel, sorta clean and graceful, like swimming in a lake somewhere up in the mountains, where you can see all the way to the bottom."

Charlie grinned. "I never thought about it that way. Jazz is my thing. I actually play a little horn myself. Outside of New Orleans, New York has some of the best jazz clubs around. Play until the sun

88

comes up, too. A couple of them not too far from the hotel."

"Which hotel are we going to?" she asked.

"Waldorf-Astoria. The Towers. You ever been to New York City?" Charlie took a swig of club soda and sat back against the seat, unbuttoning the front of his suit coat.

LuAnn shook her head and swallowed a bite of sandwich. "I ain't never really been anywhere."

Charlie chuckled softly. "Well then, the Big Apple is a helluva place to start."

"What's the hotel like?"

"It's real nice. First-rate, especially the Towers. Now it's not the Plaza, but then what is? Maybe you'll be staying at the Plaza one day, who knows." He laughed and wiped his mouth with a napkin. She noticed that his fingers were abnormally large and thick, the knuckles massive and knobby.

LuAnn looked at him nervously as she finished her sandwich and took a sip of Coke. "Do you know why I'm here?"

Charlie settled a keen gaze upon her. "Let's just say I know enough not to ask too many questions. Let's leave it at that." He smiled curtly.

"Have you ever met Mr. Jackson?"

Charlie's features grew grim. "Let's just leave it alone, okay?"

"Okay, just curious, is all."

"Well, you know what curiosity did to that old cat." The dark eyes glittered briefly at LuAnn as the words rolled off his tongue. "Just stay cool, do what you're told, and you and your kid have no problems, ever again. Sound good to you?"

"Sounds good to me," LuAnn said meekly, cradling Lisa closer to her hip.

Right before they climbed out of the limo, Charlie pulled out a black leather trench coat and matching wide-brimmed hat and asked LuAnn to put them on. "For obvious reasons, we don't want you to be observed right now. You can ditch the cowboy hat."

LuAnn put on the coat and hat, cinching the belt up tight.

"I'll check you in. Your suite is under the name of Linda Freeman, an American business executive with a London-based firm traveling with her daughter on a combination of business and pleasure."

"A business executive? I hope nobody asks me no questions."

"Don't worry, nobody will."

"So that's who I'm supposed to be? Linda Freeman?"

"At least until the big event. Then you can go back to being LuAnn Tyler."

Do I have to? LuAnn wondered to herself.

The suite Charlie escorted her to after he checked her in was on the thirty-second floor and was mammoth in size. It had a large sitting room and a separate bedroom. LuAnn looked around in wonderment at the elegant furnishings, and almost fell over when she saw the opulent bathroom.

"You get to wear these robes?" She fingered the soft cotton.

"You can have it if you want. For seventy-five bucks or so a pop that is," Charlie replied.

She walked over to the window and partially drew back the curtains. A goodly slice of the New York City skyline confronted her. The sky was overcast and it was already growing dark. "I ain't never seen so many buildings in all my life. How in the world do people tell 'em apart? They all look the same to me." She looked back at him.

Charlie shook his head. "You know, you're real funny. If I didn't know better, I'd think you were the biggest hick in the world."

LuAnn looked down. "I am the biggest hick in the world. At least the biggest one you'll probably ever see."

He caught her look. "Hey, I didn't mean anything by it. You grow up here, you get an attitude about things, you know what I mean?" He paused for a minute while he watched LuAnn go over and stroke Lisa's face. "Look, here's the refreshment bar," he finally said. He showed her how it worked. Next, he opened the thick closet door. "Over here is the safe." He indicated the heavy metal door inserted into the wall. He punched in a code and the cylinders whirled into place. "It's a real good idea to keep your valuables in there."

"I don't think I have anything worth putting in there."

"How about that lottery ticket?"

LuAnn gulped, dug into her pocket, and produced the lottery ticket. "So you know that much, huh?"

Charlie didn't answer her. He took the ticket, barely glancing at it, before thrusting it in the safe. "Pick a combo – nothing obvious like birthdays or stuff like that. But choose something you'll remember off the top of your head. You don't want to be writing the numbers down anywhere. Got that?" He opened the safe again.

LuAnn nodded, and input her own code and waited until the safe was in the lock mode before shutting the closet door.

Charlie headed to the door. "I'll be back tomorrow morning about nine. In the meantime, you get hungry or anything, just order up room service. Don't let the waiter get a good look at your face, though. Put your hair up in a bun or wear the shower cap, like you're about to jump in the tub. Open the door, sign the bill as Linda Freeman, and

91

then go into the bedroom. Leave some tip money on the table. Here." Charlie took a wad of bills from his pocket and handed them to her. "Generally, keep a low profile. Don't go walking around the hotel or stuff like that."

"Don't worry, I know I don't sound like no executive person." LuAnn pulled her hair out of her eyes and tried to sound flippant, although her low self-esteem was as plain as the hurt tones in Charlie's response.

"That's not it, LuAnn. I didn't mean . . ." He finally shrugged. "Look, I barely finished high school. I never went to college and I did okay for myself. So neither one of us could pass as a Harvard grad, so who the hell cares?" He touched her lightly on the shoulder. "Get a good night's sleep. When I come back tomorrow, we can go out and see some of the sights and you can talk your head off, how about that?"

She brightened. "Going out would be nice."

"It's supposed to be chilly tomorrow, so dress warmly."

LuAnn suddenly looked down at her wrinkled shirt and jeans. "Uh, these are all the clothes I have. I, uh, left home kind of quick." She looked embarrassed.

Charlie said kindly, "That's all right: No luggage, no problem." He sized her up quickly. "What, you're about five ten, right? Size eight?"

LuAnn nodded and blushed slightly. "Maybe a little bigger on top than that."

Charlie's eyes hovered over her chest area for a moment. "Right," he said. "I'll bring some clothes with me tomorrow. I'll get some things for Lisa, too. I'll need a little extra time though. I'll be here around noon."

"I can take Lisa with us, right?"

"Absolutely, the kid comes with us."

"Thanks, Charlie. I really appreciate it. I wouldn't have the nerve to go out on my own. But I'm kind of itching to, if you know what I mean. I never seen a place this big in my whole life. I betcha there's probably more people in this one hotel than in my whole hometown."

Charlie laughed. "Yeah, I guess being from here, I kind of take it for granted. But I see what you mean. I see it exactly."

After he left, LuAnn gently lifted Lisa out of her carrier and laid her in the middle of the king-size bed, stroking her hair as she did so. She quickly undressed her, gave her a bath in the oversize tub, and dressed Lisa in her pajamas. After laying the little girl back down on the bed, covering her with a blanket, and propping big pillows on either side of her so she wouldn't roll off, LuAnn debated whether to venture into the bathroom and perhaps give the tub a try as well to work the pains out of her body. That's when the phone rang. She hesitated for an instant, feeling guilty and trapped at the same time. She picked it up. "Hello?"

"Miss Freeman?"

"Sorry, you've—" LuAnn mentally kicked herself. "Yes, this is Miss Freeman," she said quickly, trying to sound as professional as possible.

"A little faster next time, LuAnn," Jackson said. "People rarely forget their own names. How are things? Are you being taken care of?"

"Sure am. Charlie's wonderful."

"Charlie? Yes, of course. You have the lottery ticket?"

"It's in the safe."

"Good idea. Do you have pen and paper?"

LuAnn looked around the room and then pulled a sheet of paper and a pen from the drawer of the antique-looking desk against the window.

Jackson continued: "Jot down what you can. Charlie will have all the details as well. You'll be happy to know that everything is in place. At six P.M. the day after tomorrow, the winning ticket will be announced nationwide. You can watch it on TV from your hotel room; all the major networks will be carrying it. I'm afraid there won't be much drama in the proceedings for you, however." LuAnn could almost envision the tight little smile on his lips as he said this. "Then the entire country will eagerly wait for the winner to come forward. You won't do it immediately. We have to give you time, in theory of course, to calm down, start thinking clearly, perhaps get some advice from financial people, lawyers, et cetera, and then you make your joyous way up to New York. Winners aren't required to come to New York, of course. The press conference can be held anywhere, even in the winner's hometown. However, many past winners have voluntarily made the trek and the Lottery Commission likes it that way. It's far easier to hold a national press conference from here. Thus, all your activities will take a day or two. Officially, you have thirty days to claim the money, so there's no problem there. By the way, in case you haven't figured it out, that's why I wanted you to wait before coming. It would not look good if people were aware you arrived in New York *before* the winning number was announced. You'll have to remain incognito until we're ready to present you as the winner." He sounded upset that his plans had been altered.

LuAnn scribbled down notes as fast as she could. "I'm sorry, but I really couldn't wait, Mr. Jackson," LuAnn said hurriedly. "I told you what it would be like back home. It's such a small place and everything. People would know I'd got the winning ticket, they just would."

94

"All right, fine, there's no sense wasting time discussing it now," he said brusquely. "The point is we have to keep you under cover until a day or so after the lottery drawing. You took the bus to Atlanta, correct?"

"Yes."

"And you took suitable precautions to disguise your appearance?"

"Big hat and glasses. I didn't see anybody I knew."

"And you of course didn't use your real name when buying your ticket?"

"Of course not," LuAnn lied.

"Good. I think your tracks have been effectively erased."

"I hope so."

"It won't matter, LuAnn. It really won't. In a few days, you'll be much farther away than New York."

"Where exactly will I be?"

"As I said before, you tell me. Europe? Asia? South America? Just name it and I'll make all the arrangements."

LuAnn thought for a moment. "Do I have to decide now?"

"Of course not. But if you want to leave immediately after the press conference, the sooner you let me know the better. I've been known to work miracles with travel arrangements, but I'm not a magician, particularly since you don't have a passport or any other identification documents." He sounded incredulous as he said this. "Those will have to be prepared as well."

"Can you get them made up? Even like a Social Security card?"

"You don't have a Social Security number? That's impossible."

"It ain't if your parents never filled out the paperwork for one," she fired back.

"I thought the hospital wouldn't let a baby leave without that paperwork having been completed."

LuAnn almost laughed. "I wasn't born in no hospital, Mr. Jackson. They say the first sight I saw was the dirty laundry stacked in my momma's bedroom because that's right where my grandma delivered me."

"Yes, I suppose I can get you a Social Security number," he said huffily.

"Then could you have them put another name on the passport, I mean with my picture on it, but with a different name? And on all the other paperwork too?"

Jackson said slowly, "Why would you want that, LuAnn?"

"Well, because of Duane. I know he looks stupid and all, but when he finds out I won all this money, he's gonna do everything he can to find me. I thought it'd be best if I disappeared. Start over again. Fresh, so to speak. New name and everything."

Jackson laughed out loud. "You honestly think Duane Harvey will be able to track you down? I seriously doubt if he could find his way out of Rikersville County if he had a police escort."

"Please, Mr. Jackson, if you could do it that way, I'd really appreciate it. Of course, if it's too hard for you, I'll understand." LuAnn held her breath desperately, hoping that Jackson's ego would take the bait.

"It's not," Jackson snapped. "It's quite simple, in fact, when you have the right connections, as I do. Well, I suppose you haven't thought of the name you want to use, have you?"

She surprised him by rattling one off immediately, as well as the place where the fictitious person was from.

"It seems you've been thinking about doing this for a while. Perhaps with or without the lottery money. True?"

"You got secrets, Mr. Jackson. Why not me, too?"

She heard him sigh. "Very well, LuAnn, your request is certainly unprecedented, but I'll take care of it. I still need to know where you want to go."

"I understand. I'll think real hard about it and let you know real soon."

"Why am I suddenly worried that I will regret having selected you for this little adventure?" There was a hint of something in his tone that caused LuAnn to shudder. "I'll be in touch after the lottery drawing, to let you know the rest of the details. That's all for now. Enjoy your visit to New York. If you need anything just tell . . ."

"Charlie."

"Charlie, right." Jackson hung up.

LuAnn went immediately to the wet bar and uncapped a bottle of beer. Lisa started to make a noise and LuAnn let her down on the floor. LuAnn watched with a big smile on her face as Lisa moved around the room. Just in the last few days, her little girl had started to really get the hang of crawling and now she was exploring the large dimensions of the suite with considerable energy. Finally, LuAnn got down on the floor and joined her. Mother and daughter made the circuit of the hotel room for about an hour until Lisa grew tired and LuAnn put her down for the night.

LuAnn went into the bathroom and started running water in the tub while she checked the cut on her jaw in the mirror. It was healing okay, but it would probably leave a scar. That didn't bother her; it could have been a lot worse. She got another beer from the refrigerator and walked back into the bathroom. She slid into the hot water and took a sip

97

of the cold beer. She figured she would need plenty of both alcohol and steamy, soothing water to get through the next couple of days.

Promptly at twelve o'clock, Charlie arrived with several bags from Bloomingdale's and Baby Gap. During the next hour, LuAnn tried on several outfits that made her tingle all over.

"You certainly do those clothes justice. More than justice," Charlie said admiringly.

"Thank you. Thanks for all this stuff. You got the size just right."

"Hell, you got the height and figure of a model. They make these clothes for people like you. You ever think about doing that for a living? Modeling, that is?"

LuAnn shrugged as she put on a cream-colored jacket over a long, pleated black skirt. "Sometimes, when I was younger."

"Younger? My God, you can't be far out of your teens."

"I'm twenty, but you feel older after having a baby."

"I guess that's true."

"No, I ain't cut out for modeling."

"Why not?"

She looked at him and said simply, "I don't like getting my picture taken, and I don't like looking at myself."

Charlie just shook his head. "You are definitely one strange young woman. Most girls your age, with your looks, you couldn't drag them away from the mirror. Narcissus personified. Oh, but you need to wear those big sunglasses and keep the hat on; Jackson said to keep you under wraps. We probably shouldn't be going out, but in a city of seven million I don't think we're going to have a problem." He

98

held up a cigarette. "You mind?"

She smiled. "Are you kidding? I work in a truck diner. They don't even let you in unless you got your smokes and plan to use 'em. Most nights the place looks like it's on fire."

"Well, no more truck diners for you."

"I guess not." She pinned a wide-brimmed, floppy hat to her hair. "How do I look?" She posed for him.

"Better than anything in *Cosmo*, that's for sure."

"You ain't seen nothing yet. You just wait till I dress my little girl," she said proudly. "Now that *is* something I dream about. A lot!"

An hour later, LuAnn put Lisa, who was decked out in the latest Baby Gap fashions, in her baby carrier and hefted it. She turned to Charlie. "You ready?"

"Not just yet." He opened the door to the suite and then looked back at her. "Why don't you close your eyes. We might as well do the whole production." LuAnn looked strangely at him. "Go on, just do it," he said, grinning.

She obeyed. A few seconds later he said, "Okay, open them up." When she did, she was staring at a brand new and very expensive baby carriage. "Oh, Charlie."

"You keep lugging that thing around much longer," he said, pointing at the baby carrier, "your hands are going to scrape the ground."

LuAnn gave him a big hug, loaded Lisa in, and they were off.

ELEVEN

Shirley Watson was madder than hell. In seeking appropriate revenge for her humiliation at the hands of LuAnn Tyler, Shirley had taxed her ingenuity, to the extent she had any, to the maximum. She parked her pickup in an out-of-the-way spot about a quarter of a mile from the trailer and got out, a metal canister held tightly in her right hand. She looked at her watch as she made her way toward the trailer, where she was pretty certain LuAnn would be deeply sleeping after working at the diner all night. Where Duane was she didn't really care. If he was there, then she might get a piece of him too for not defending her against the Amazon-like LuAnn.

With each step, the short, squat Shirley grew even angrier. She had gone to school with LuAnn, and had also dropped out before graduating. Also like LuAnn, she had lived in Rikersville all her life. Unlike LuAnn, however, she had no desire to leave it. Which made what LuAnn had done to her even more awful. People had seen her sneaking home, completely naked. She had never been more humiliated. She had gotten more crap than she knew how to deal with. She was going to have to live with that the rest of her life. Stories would be told again and again until she would be the laughingstock of her hometown. The abuse would continue until she was dead and buried; maybe even then it wouldn't stop. LuAnn Tyler was going to pay for that. So she was screwing around with Duane, so what? Everybody knew Duane had no intention of marrying LuAnn. And everyone else knew that LuAnn would probably kill herself before she would ever walk down the aisle with that man. LuAnn stayed because she had nowhere else to go, or lacked the courage to make a change, Shirley knew that – at least she believed she did – for a fact. Everyone thought LuAnn was so beautiful, so capable. Shirley fumed and grew even more flushed in the face despite the cool breeze flickering across the road. Well, she was going to love to hear what people had to say about LuAnn's looks after she got done with her.

When she drew close to the trailer, Shirley bent low and made her way from tree to tree. The big convertible was still parked in front of the trailer. Shirley could see the tire marks in the hardened mud where something had spun out. She passed the car, taking a moment to peer inside before continuing her stealthy approach. What if somebody else was there? She suddenly smiled to herself. Maybe LuAnn was getting some on the side while Duane was away. Then she could pay LuAnn back even steven. She smiled even more broadly as she envisioned a naked LuAnn running screaming from the trailer. Suddenly, everything became very quiet, very still. As if on cue, even the breeze stopped. Shirley's smile disappeared and she looked around nervously. She gripped the canister even more firmly and reached in her jacket pocket and pulled out the hunting knife. If she missed with the battery acid she was carrying in the canister, then she most assuredly wouldn't miss with the knife. She had been cleaning game and fish most of her life and could wield a blade with the best of them. LuAnn's face would get the benefit of that expertise, at least in the areas the acid missed.

"Damn," she said as she moved up to the front steps and the smell hit her right in the face. She looked around again. She hadn't experienced such an odor even when working a brief stint at the local landfill. She slipped the knife back in her pocket, unscrewed the top to the canister, and then took a moment to cover her nose with a handkerchief. She had come too far to turn back now, smell or not. She silently moved into the trailer, and made her way down to the bedroom. Edging open the door, she looked in. Empty. She closed the door softly and turned to head down the other way. Maybe LuAnn and her beau were asleep on the couch there. The hallway was dark and she felt her way along the wall. As she drew closer, Shirley steeled herself to strike. She lurched forward and, instead, stumbled over something and fell to the floor, coming face-to-face with the decaying source of the stench. Her scream could be heard almost to the main road.

"You sure didn't buy much, LuAnn." Charlie surveyed the few bags on the chaise longue in her hotel room.

LuAnn came out of the bathroom where she had changed into a pair of jeans and a white sweater, her hair done up in a French braid. "I just like looking. That was fun enough. Besides, I flat out can't believe the prices up here. Good God!"

"But I would've paid for it," Charlie protested. "I told you that a hundred times."

"I don't want you spending money on me, Charlie."

Charlie sat down in a chair and stared at her. "LuAnn, it's not *my* money. I told you that, too. I'm on an expense account. Whatever you wanted, you could have."

"Is that what Mr. Jackson said?"

"Something like that. Let's just call it an advance on your future winnings." He grinned.

LuAnn sat down on the bed and played with her hands, a deep frown on her face. Lisa was still in her baby carriage playing with some toys Charlie had bought her. Her happy sounds filled the room.

"Here." Charlie handed LuAnn a package of photos from their day in New York. "For the memory book."

LuAnn looked at the photos and her eyes crinkled. "I never thought I'd see a horse and buggy in this city. It was lots of fun riding around that big old park. Smack dab in the middle of all them buildings, too."

"Come on, you'd never heard of Central Park?"

"Sure I had. *Heard,* leastways. Only I just thought it was all made up." LuAnn handed him a double photo of herself that she picked out of the pack.

"Whoops, thanks for reminding me," said Charlie.

"That's for my passport?"

He nodded as he slipped the photo into his jacket pocket.

"Don't Lisa need one?"

He shook his head. "She's not old enough. She can travel under yours."

"Oh."

"So I understand you want to change your name."

LuAnn put the photos away and started fiddling with the packages. "I thought it'd be a good idea. A fresh start."

"That's what Jackson said you said. I guess if that's what you want."

LuAnn suddenly plopped down on the chaise longue and put her head in her hands.

Charlie looked keenly at her. "Come on, LuAnn, changing your name isn't that traumatic. What's bothering you?"

She finally looked up. "Are you sure I'm gonna win the lottery tomorrow?"

He spoke carefully. "Let's just wait until tomorrow, LuAnn, but I don't think you'll be disappointed."

"All that money, but I don't feel good about it, Charlie, not one bit."

He lit a cigarette and puffed on it as he continued to watch her. "I'm gonna order up some room service. Three courses, a bottle of wine. Some hot coffee, the works. You'll feel better after you've eaten." He opened up the hotel services book and began to peruse the menu.

"Have you done this before? I mean, looked after people that . . . Mr. Jackson has met with?"

Charlie looked up from the menu. "I've worked with him for a while, yeah. I've never met him in person. We communicate solely over the phone. He's a smart guy. A little anal for my tastes, a bit paranoid, but real sharp. He pays me well, real well. And baby-sitting people in fancy hotels and ordering room service isn't such a bad life." He added with a big smile, "I've never looked after anybody I had this much fun with, though."

She knelt down beside the baby carriage and pulled out a giftwrapped package from the storage bin underneath. She handed it to him.

Charlie's mouth gaped in surprise. "What's this?"

"I got you a present. Actually, it's from me and Lisa. I was looking for something for you and she started pointing and squealing at it."

"When did you do this?"

"Remember, while you were over looking at the men's clothing."

"LuAnn, you didn't have to—"

"I know that," she said quickly. "That's why it's called a gift, you're not supposed to have to."

Charlie gripped the box tightly in his hands, his eyes riveted on her. "Well, go ahead and open it for gosh sakes," she said.

While Charlie carefully pulled off the wrapping paper, LuAnn heard Lisa stir. She went over and picked up the little girl. They both watched Charlie as he took off the box top.

"Damn!" He gently lifted out the dark green fedora. It had an inch-wide leather band on the outside and a ribbon of cream-colored silk lining the inside.

"I saw you trying it on at the store. I thought you looked real nice in it, real sharp. But then you put it back. I could tell you didn't want to."

"LuAnn, this thing cost a lot of money."

She waved him off. "I had some saved up. I hope you like it."

"I love it, thank you." He gave her a hug and then took one of Lisa's dimpled fists in his. He gave it a gentle, formal shake. "And thank you, little lady. Excellent taste."

"Well, try it on again. Make sure you still like it."

He slid it over his head and checked himself out in the mirror.

"Slick, Charlie, real slick."

He smiled. "Not bad, not bad." He fussed with it a little until he caught the proper angle. Then he took it off and sat back down. "I've never gotten a gift from the people I've looked after. I'm usually only with them for a couple of days anyway, then Jackson takes over."

LuAnn quickly picked up on the opening. "So how'd you come to be doing this kind of work?"

"I take it you'd like to hear my life story?"

"Sure. I've been bending your ear enough."

Charlie settled back in the chair and assumed a comfortable look. He pointed to his face. "Bet you

105

didn't guess I used to ply my skills in the boxing ring." He grinned. "Mostly, I was a sparring partner – a punching bag for up-and-comers. I was smart enough to get out while I still had my brains, at least some of them. After that, I took up semipro football. Let me tell you, that isn't easier on the body, but at least you get to wear helmets and pads. I'd always been athletic, though, and to tell you the truth I liked making my living that way."

"You look like you're in real good shape?"

Charlie slapped his hard stomach. "Not bad for being almost fifty-four. Anyway, after football, I coached a little, got married, floated around here and there, never finding anything that fit, you know?"

LuAnn said, "I know that feeling real good."

"Then my career path took a big turn." He paused to crush out his cigarette and immediately lit another.

LuAnn took the opportunity to put Lisa back in the baby carriage. "What'd you do?"

"I spent some time as a guest of the U.S. government." LuAnn looked at him curiously, not getting his meaning. "I was in a federal prison, LuAnn."

She looked astonished. "You don't look the type, Charlie."

He laughed. "I don't know about that. Besides, there are lots of different types doing time, LuAnn, let me tell you."

"So what'd you do?"

"Income tax evasion. Or fraud I guess they'd call it, at least the prosecutor did. And he was right. I guess I just got tired of paying it. Never seemed like there was enough to live on, let alone giving a chunk to the government." He brushed his hair back. "That little mistake cost me three years and my marriage."

"I'm sorry, Charlie."

106

He shrugged. "Probably the best thing that ever happened to me, really. I was in a minimum security facility with a bunch of other white collar criminal types so I didn't have to worry every minute about somebody cutting my head off. I took a bunch of classes, started thinking about what I wanted to do with my life. Really only one bad thing happened to me on the inside." He held up the cigarette. "Never smoked until I got to prison. There, just about everybody did. When I got out I finally quit. For a long time. Took it back up about six months ago. What the hell. Anyway, when I got out, I went to work for my lawyer, sort of as an in-house investigator. He knew I was an honest, reliable sort, despite my little conviction. And I knew a lot of people up and down the socioeconomic scale, if you know what I mean. A lot of contacts. Plus I learned a lot while I was in the slammer. Talk about your education. I had professors in every subject from insurance scams to auto chop shops. That experience helped out a lot when I jumped to the law firm. It was a good gig, I enjoyed the work."

"So how'd you hook up with Mr. Jackson?"

Now Charlie didn't look so comfortable. "Let's just say he happened to call one day. I had gotten myself in a little bit of trouble. Nothing real serious, but I was still on parole and it could've cost me some serious time inside. He offered to help me out and I accepted that offer."

"Kind of like I did," said LuAnn, an edge to her voice. "His offers can be kind of hard to refuse."

He glanced at her, his eyes suddenly weary. "Yeah," he said curtly.

She sat down on the edge of the bed and blurted out, "I've never cheated on anything in my whole life, Charlie."

Charlie dragged on his cigarette and then put it

107

out. "I guess it all depends on how you look at it."

"What do you mean by that?"

"Well, if you think about it, people who are otherwise good, honest, and hardworking cheat every day of their lives. Some in big ways, most in small ones. People fudge on their taxes, or just don't pay 'em, like me. Or they don't give money back when somebody figures up a bill wrong. Little white lies, folks tell almost automatically on a daily basis, sometimes just to get through the day with their sanity. Then there's the big cheat: Men and women have affairs all the time. That one I know a lot about. I think my ex-wife majored in adultery."

"I got a little taste of that, too," LuAnn said quietly.

Charlie stared at her. "One dumb SOB is all I can say. Anyway, it all adds up over a lifetime."

"But not to no fifty million dollars' worth."

"Maybe not in dollar terms, no. But I might take one big cheat in a lifetime over a thousand little ones that eat away at you eventually, make you not like yourself too much."

LuAnn hugged herself and shivered.

He studied her for a moment and then looked once more at the room service menu. "I'm gonna order dinner. Fish okay with you?"

LuAnn nodded absently and stared down at her shoes while Charlie conveyed their dinner order over the phone.

That done, he flipped another cigarette out of the pack and lit up. "Hell, I don't know one single person who would turn down the offer you got. As far as I'm concerned you'd be stupid to." He paused and fiddled with his lighter. "And from the little I've seen of you, maybe you can redeem yourself, at least in your eyes. Not that you'd need much redeeming."

She stared up at him. "How can I do that?"

"Use some of the money to help other people," he said simply. "Maybe treat it like a public trust, or something like that. I'm not saying don't enjoy the money. I think you deserve that." He added, "I saw some background info on you. You haven't exactly had the easiest life."

LuAnn shrugged. "I got by."

Charlie sat down beside her. "That's exactly right, LuAnn, you're a survivor. You'll survive this, too." He looked at her intently. "You mind me asking a personal question now that I've spilled my guts to you?"

"Depends on the question."

"Fair enough." He nodded. "Well, like I said, I looked at some of your background stuff. I was just wondering how you ever hooked up with a guy like Duane Harvey. He has 'loser' stamped all over him."

LuAnn thought of Duane's slender body lying facedown on the dirty carpet, the small groan he had made before plummeting over, as though he were calling to her, pleading for help. But she hadn't answered that call. "Duane's not so bad. He had a bunch of bad breaks." She stood up and paced. "I was going through a real bad time. My momma had just died. I met Duane while I was thinking of what to do with my life. You either grow up in that county and die there or you get out just as fast as you can. Ain't nobody ever moved *into* Rikersville County, least not that I ever heard of." She took a deep breath and continued. "Duane had just moved into this trailer he had found. He had a job then. He treated me nice, we talked some about getting married. He was just different."

"You wanted to be one of the ones who was born and died there?"

She looked at him, shocked. "Hell, no. We were going to get out. I wanted to and that's what Duane

109

wanted, at least that's what he said." She stopped pacing and looked over at Charlie. "Then we had Lisa," she said simply. "That kinda changed things for Duane. I don't think having a kid was part of his plan. But we did and it's the best thing that ever happened to me. But after that, I knew things weren't going to work out between us. I knew I had to leave. I was just trying to figure out how when Mr. Jackson called."

LuAnn looked out the window at the twinkling lights etched against the darkness. "Jackson said there were some conditions with all this. With the money. I know he's not doing this because he loves me." She looked over her shoulder at Charlie.

Charlie grunted. "No, you're absolutely right about that."

"You got any idea what the conditions are?"

Charlie was shaking his head before she finished asking the question. "I do know that you'll have more money than you'll know what to do with."

"And I can use that money any way I want, right?"

"That's right. It's yours, free and clear. You can clean out Saks Fifth Avenue and Tiffany. Or build a hospital in Harlem. It's up to you."

LuAnn looked back out the window and her eyes began to shine as the thoughts plowing through her head seemed to dwarf the skyline staring back at her. Right that very instant, everything seemed to click! Even the massive number of buildings in New York City seemed far too small to hold the things she wanted to do with her life. With all that money.

TWELVE

"We should've just stayed at the hotel and watched it from there." Charlie looked around nervously. "Jackson would kill me if he knew we were here. I have strict orders never to take any of the 'clients' here." "Here" was the headquarters of the United States National Lottery Commission located in a brand new state-of-the-art, needle-thin skyscraper on Park Avenue. The huge auditorium was filled with people. Network news correspondents were scattered throughout, microphones clamped in their fists, as were representatives from magazines, newspapers, and cable TV.

Near the front of the stage, LuAnn cradled Lisa against her chest. She wore the glasses Charlie had bought for her and a baseball cap turned backward under which her long hair was balled up. Her memorable figure was hidden under the full-length trench coat.

"It's okay, Charlie, nobody's gonna remember me under all this stuff."

He shook his head. "I still don't like it."

"I had to come see. It just wouldn't be the same sitting in the hotel room watching on TV."

"Jackson's gonna probably call the hotel right after the drawing," he grumbled.

"I'll just tell him I fell asleep and didn't hear the phone."

"Right!" He lowered his voice. "You're gonna win at least fifty million bucks and you fall asleep?"

111

"Well, if I already *know* I'm gonna win, what's so exciting about it?" she shot back.

Charlie had no ready answer for that so he clamped his mouth shut and again took up a careful scrutiny of the room and its occupants.

LuAnn looked at the stage where the lottery pinball machine was set up on a table. It was about six feet long and comprised ten large tubes, each one rising above an attached bin of Ping-Pong balls. Each ball had a number painted on it. After the machine was activated, the air would circulate the balls until one made its way through the tiny hatch, popped up into the tube, and was caught and held by a special device inside the tube. Once a ball was thus captured, a bin of balls below that tube would immediately shut down and the next bin would automatically activate. Down the line it would go, the suspense building, until all ten winning numbers were finally revealed.

People were nervously looking at their lottery tickets; many held at least a dozen in their hands. One young man had an open laptop computer in front of him. The screen was filled with hundreds of lottery combinations he had purchased as he reviewed his electronic inventory. LuAnn had no need to look at her ticket; she had memorized the numbers: 0810080521, which represented her and Lisa's birthdays, and the age LuAnn would be on her next birthday. She didn't feel any more guilt as she observed the hopeful looks on the faces surrounding her. She would be able to handle their imminent disappointment. She had made up her mind, set her plan, and that decision had bolstered her spirits incredibly and it was the reason she was standing in the middle of this sea of tense people instead of hiding under the bed back at the Waldorf.

She stirred out of her musings as a man walked on

to the stage. The crowd instantly hushed. LuAnn had half-expected to see Jackson striding across the stage, but the man was younger and far better looking. LuAnn wondered for a moment if he was in on it. She and Charlie exchanged tight smiles. A blond woman in a short skirt, black nylons, and spike heels joined the man and stood next to the sophisticated-looking machine, hands clasped behind her back.

The man's announcement was brief and clear as the TV cameras focused on his handsome features. He welcomed everyone to the drawing and then he paused, stared dramatically out at the crowd, and delivered the real news of the evening: The official jackpot, based upon ticket sales up to the very last minute, was a record-setting one hundred million dollars! A collective gasp went up from the crowd at the mention of the gigantic sum. Even LuAnn's mouth dropped open. Charlie looked over at her, shook his head slightly, and a small grin escaped his lips. He playfully elbowed her, leaned close, and whispered into her ear. "Hell, you can clean out Saks and Tiffany *and* still build that hospital, just with the friggin' interest."

It was indeed the largest jackpot ever and someone, one incredibly fortunate person, was about to win it, the lottery man declared with a beaming smile and a ton of showmanship. The crowd cheered wildly. The man gestured dramatically to the woman, who hit the power switch on the side of the machine. LuAnn watched as the balls in the first bin started bouncing around. When the balls started attacking the narrow pathway into the tubes, LuAnn felt her heart race and her breathing constrict. Despite the presence of Charlie beside her, the calm, authoritative manner of Mr. Jackson, his correct predicting of the daily lottery, and all the other things she had been through in the last several days, she suddenly felt that her being here

113

was totally crazy. How could Jackson or anyone else control what those gyrating balls would do? It occurred to her that what she was witnessing resembled sperm dive-bombing an egg, something she had seen once on a TV program. What were the chances of correctly picking the one that would break through and impregnate? Her spirits plummeted as she confronted a very distinct set of options: travel back home and somehow explain the deaths of two men in a drug-filled trailer she happened to call home; or seek the hospitality of the nearest homeless shelter here in the city and contemplate what to do with the wrecked state of her life.

She clutched Lisa even more tightly and one of her hands drifted over and clasped Charlie's thick fingers. A ball squirted through the opening and was caught in the first tube. It was the number zero. It was shown on a large screen suspended over the stage. As soon as this occurred, the second bin of balls started popping. In a few seconds, it too had produced a winner: the number eight. In quick succession, six more of the balls popped through into their respective tubes and were caught. The tally now stood as follows: 0-8-1-0-0-8-0-5. LuAnn mouthed the familiar numbers silently. Sweat appeared on her forehead and she felt her legs begin to give way. "Oh my God," she whispered to herself, "it's really gonna happen." Jackson had done it; somehow, some way, the uppity anal little man had done it. She heard many moans and groans next to her as lottery tickets were torn up and thrown to the floor as the numbers stared back at the crowd from the stage. LuAnn watched, completely mesmerized, as the ninth bin of balls started bouncing. The entire process now seemed to be occurring in the slowest of slow motion. Finally, the number two ball kicked out and held in tube number nine. There were no

114

hopeful faces left in the crowd. Except for one.

The last bin fired up and the number one ball quickly fought its way right against the hatch of the last tube and appeared to be ready to shoot through to victory at any moment. LuAnn's grip on Charlie's fingers began to loosen. Then, like a pricked balloon hemorrhaging air, the number one ball suddenly slid back down to the bottom and was replaced near the hatch by a suddenly energetic and determined number four ball. With sharp, jerky motions, it grew closer and closer to the open pathway leading into the number ten and final tube, although it appeared to be repeatedly repelled from the opening. The blood slowly drained from LuAnn's face and for a moment she thought she would end up on the floor. "Oh, shit," she said out loud, although not even Charlie could hear her over the crowd noise. LuAnn squeezed Charlie's fingers so tightly he almost yelled out in pain.

Charlie's own heart was racing as if in sympathy for LuAnn. He had never known Jackson to fail, but, well, you never knew. *What the hell, it couldn't hurt*, he thought. He moved his free hand up and quietly felt under his shirt for the thick, silver crucifix he had worn for as long as he could remember. He rubbed it for good luck.

Ever so slowly, even as LuAnn's heart threatened to cease beating, the two balls, as though carefully choreographed, again swapped places with each other in the swirling spray of hot air, even ricocheting off one another at one point. After this momentary collision, the number one ball, mercifully for LuAnn, finally shot through the opening and was caught in the tenth and final tube.

It was all LuAnn could do not to scream out loud from pure relief, rather than from the excitement of having just become one hundred million dollars

115

richer. She and Charlie looked at each other, their eyes wide, both bodies shaking, faces drenched with perspiration, as though they had just finished making love. Charlie inclined his head toward her, his eyebrows arched as if to say "You won, didn't you?"

LuAnn nodded slightly, her head swaying slowly as if to the tunes of a favorite song. Lisa kicked and squirmed as though she sensed her mother's exhilaration.

"Damn," Charlie said, "I thought I was going to pee in my pants waiting for that last number to drop." He led LuAnn out of the room and in a couple of minutes they were walking slowly down the street in the direction of the hotel. It was a beautiful, brisk night; the cloudless sky housed a stretch of stars that seemingly had no end. It matched LuAnn's mood precisely. Charlie rubbed at his hand. "God, I thought you were going to snap my fingers off. What was that all about?"

"You don't wanta know," said LuAnn firmly. She smiled at him, sucked in huge amounts of the sweet, chilly air, and gave Lisa a tender kiss on the cheek. She suddenly elbowed Charlie in the side, a mischievous grin on her face. "Last one to the hotel pays for dinner." She took off like a blue streak, the trench coat billowing out like a parachute in her wake. Even as she left him in the dust, Charlie could hear her shrieks of joy flowing back to him. He grinned and then bolted after her.

Neither one would have been so happy had they seen the man who had followed them to the lottery drawing and was watching from across the street. Romanello had figured that tailing LuAnn might result in some interesting developments. But even he had to admit that his expectations had so far been exceeded.

THIRTEEN

"You're certain that's where you want to go, LuAnn?"

LuAnn spoke earnestly into the phone. "Yes sir, Mr. Jackson. I've always wanted to go to Sweden. My momma's people came from there, a long time ago. She always wanted to go there, but never had the chance. So I'd sort of be doing it for her. Is that much trouble?"

"Everything is trouble, LuAnn. It's just a matter of degrees."

"But you can get it done, can't you? I mean I'd like to go to other places, but I'd really like to start in Sweden."

Jackson said testily, "If I can arrange for someone like *you* to win one hundred million dollars, then I can certainly take care of travel plans."

"I appreciate it. I really do." LuAnn looked over at Charlie, who was holding Lisa and playing with her. She smiled at him. "You look real good doing that."

"What's that?" Jackson asked.

"I'm sorry, I was talking to Charlie."

"Put him on, we need to arrange for your visit to the lottery office so they can confirm the winning ticket. The sooner that's accomplished, the sooner we can get on with the press conference and then you can be on your way."

"The conditions you talked about—" LuAnn began.

Jackson interrupted, "I'm not ready to discuss that right now. Put Charlie on, I'm in a hurry."

LuAnn swapped the phone for Lisa. She watched closely as Charlie spoke in low tones into the phone, his back to her. She saw him nod several times and then he hung up.

"Everything okay?" Her tone was anxious as she held a rambunctious Lisa.

He looked around the room for a moment before his eyes finally met hers. "Sure, everything's A-okay. You have to go over to see the lottery people this afternoon. Enough time has passed."

"Will you go with me?"

"I'll go over in the cab with you, but I won't go in the building. I'll hang around outside until you come out."

"What all do I have to do?"

"Just present the winning ticket. They'll validate it and issue you an official receipt. There'll be witnesses there and all. You'll be confirmed every which way from Sunday. They go over the ticket with a high-tech laser to verify it's authentic. They got special fiber threads in the tickets, some of them right under the row of numbers. Kind of like U.S. currency, to prevent counterfeiting. It's impossible to duplicate, especially in a short time frame. They'll call the outlet where you bought the ticket to confirm that lottery number was indeed purchased at that site. They'll ask for background info on you. Where you're from, kids, parents, that sort of thing. It takes a few hours. You don't have to wait. They'll get in touch when the process is complete. Then they'll release a statement to the press that the winner has come forward, but they won't release your name until the press conference. You know, keep the suspense building. That stuff really sells tickets for the next drawing. You don't have to hang around for that either. The actual press conference will be the next day."

"Do we come back here?"

"Actually, 'Linda Freeman' is checking out today. We'll go to another hotel where you can check in as LuAnn Tyler, one of the richest people in the country. Fresh in town and ready to take on the world."

"You ever been to one of these press conferences before?"

He nodded. "A few. They can be a little crazy. Especially when the winners bring family with them. Money can do strange things to people. But it doesn't last too long. You get asked a bunch of questions and then off you go." He paused and then added, "That's nice what you're doing, going to Sweden for your mom like that."

LuAnn looked down as she played with Lisa's feet. "I hope so. It's sure gonna be different."

"Well, sounds like you can use a little different."

"I don't know how long I'll stay."

"Stay as long as you want. Hell, you can stay forever if you want to."

"I'm not sure I can do that. I don't think I'd fit in."

He gripped her shoulders and looked her in the face. "Listen, LuAnn, give yourself some credit. Okay, so you don't have a bunch of fancy degrees, but you're sharp, you take great care of your kid, and you got a good heart. In my book, that puts you ahead of about ninety-nine percent of the population."

"I don't know how good I'd be doing right now if you weren't here helping me out."

He shrugged. "Hey, like I said, it's part of the job." He let go of her shoulders and fished a cigarette out of his pack. "Why don't we have some quick lunch and then you go claim your prize? What do you say, you ready to be filthy rich, lady?"

119

LuAnn took a deep breath before answering. "I'm ready."

LuAnn emerged from the Lottery Commission building, walked down the street, and turned a corner, where she met Charlie at a prearranged spot. He had kept Lisa for her while she had gone in.

"She's been watching everything going by. She's a real alert kid," he said.

"Won't be long before I'm running every which way after her."

"She was doing her best to get down and crawl off, swear to God." Charlie smiled and put a very exuberant Lisa back in her carriage. "So how'd it go?"

"They were real friendly. Treated me real special. 'You want coffee, Ms. Tyler?' 'You want a phone to make calls?' One woman asked me if I wanted to hire her as my personal assistant." She laughed.

"You better get used to that. You have the receipt?"

"Yep, in my purse."

"What time's the press conference?"

"Tomorrow at six o'clock, they said." She eyed him. "What's wrong?"

As they walked, Charlie had glanced surreptitiously over his shoulder a couple of times. He looked over at her. "I don't know. When I was in prison and then doing the PI stuff I developed this kind of built-in radar that tells me when somebody's paying a little too close attention to me. My alarm's going off right now."

LuAnn started to look around, but he cut her off. "Don't do that. Just keep walking. We're fine. I checked you in at another hotel. It's another block down. Let's get you and Lisa in okay and then I'll snoop around a little. It's probably nothing."

LuAnn looked at the worry creases around his eyes and concluded his words did not match his feelings. She gripped the baby carriage tighter as they continued down the street.

Twenty yards behind and on the other side of the street, Anthony Romanello debated whether or not he had been spotted. The streets were filled with people at this hour, but something in the sudden rigidity of the people he was tracking had set off his own warning bell. He hunkered in his jacket and dropped back another ten yards, still keeping them well in sight. He kept a constant lookout for the closest taxi in case they decided to snare one. He had the advantage though, in that it would take some time to load the baby carriage and baby in. He would have plenty of opportunity to hail a cab in that time. But they continued on foot until they reached their destination. Romanello waited outside the hotel for a moment, looked up and down the street, and then went in.

"When did you get these?" LuAnn stared at the new set of luggage stacked in a corner of the hotel suite.

Charlie grinned. "You can't go on your big trip without the proper baggage. And this stuff is super-durable. Not that expensive crap that falls apart if you look at it wrong. One bag is already packed with things you'll need for the trip over. Things for Lisa and what-not. I had a lady friend of mine do it. We'll have to do some more shopping today to fill up the other bags, though."

"My God, I can't believe this, Charlie." She gave him a hug and a peck on the cheek.

He looked down in embarrassment, his face flushed. "It wasn't such a big deal. Here." He

121

handed her passport to her. She solemnly looked at the name inside, as though the fact of her reincarnation were just sinking in, which it was. She closed the small blue book. It represented a gateway to another world, a world she would soon, with a little luck, be embracing.

"Fill that sucker up, LuAnn, see the whole damned planet. You and Lisa." He turned to leave. "I'm going to check on some things. I'll be back shortly."

She fingered the passport and looked up at him, her cheeks slightly red. "Why don't you come with us, Charlie?"

He turned slowly back around and stared at her. "What?"

LuAnn looked down at her hands and spoke hurriedly. "I was thinking I got all this money now. And you been real nice to me and Lisa. And I never been anywhere before and all. And, well, I'd like you to come with us – that is, if you want to. I'll understand if you don't."

"That's a very generous offer, LuAnn," he said softly. "But you don't really know me. And that's a big commitment to make to someone you don't really know."

"I know all I need to," she said stubbornly. "I know you're a good person. I know you been taking care of us. And Lisa took to you like nobody's business. That counts for a durn lot in my book."

Charlie smiled in the little girl's direction and then looked back at LuAnn. "Why don't we both think on it, LuAnn. Then we'll talk, okay?"

She shrugged and slid several strands of hair out of her face. "I ain't proposing marriage to you, Charlie, if that's what you think."

"Good thing, since I'm almost old enough to be your grandfather." He smiled at her.

"But I really like having you with me. I ain't had that many friends, least that I can count on. I know I can count on you. You're my friend, ain't you?"

There was a catch in his throat when Charlie answered. "Yes." He coughed and assumed a more businesslike tone. "I hear what you're saying, LuAnn. We'll talk about it when I get back. Promise."

When the door closed behind him, LuAnn got Lisa ready for her nap. While the little girl drifted off to sleep, LuAnn restlessly walked the parameters of the hotel suite. She looked out the window in time to see Charlie exit the building and head down the street. She followed him with her eyes until he was out of sight. She had not seen anyone who appeared to be tracking him, but there were so many people around, she couldn't be sure. She sighed and then frowned. She was out of her element here. She just wanted to see him back safe and sound. She began to think about the press conference, but as she envisioned a bunch of strangers asking her all sorts of questions, her nerves began to jangle too much and she quit thinking about it.

The knock at the door startled her. She stared at the door, unsure what to do.

"Room service," the voice said. LuAnn went to the door and squinted through the peephole. The young man standing there was indeed dressed in a bellman's uniform.

"I didn't order anything," she said, trying hard to keep her voice from quaking.

"It's a note and package for you, ma'am."

LuAnn jerked back. "Who from?"

"I don't know, ma'am. A man in the lobby asked me to give it to you."

Charlie? LuAnn thought. "Did he ask for me by name?"

"No, he pointed you out when you were walking

to the elevator, and just said give it to you. Do you want it, ma'am?" he said patiently. "If not, I'll just put it in your box behind the registration desk."

LuAnn opened the door slightly. "No, I'll take it." She stuck out her arm and the bellman put the package in it. She immediately closed the door. The young man stood there for a moment, upset that his errand and patience had not resulted in a tip. However, the man had already rewarded him handsomely for it, so it had worked out okay.

LuAnn tore open the envelope and unfolded the letter. The message was brief and written on hotel stationery.

Dear LuAnn, how's Duane feeling lately? And the other guy, what'd you hit him with anyway? Dead as a doornail. Sure hope the police don't find out you were there. Hope you enjoy the story, a little hometown news. Let's chat. In one hour. Take a cab to the Empire State Building. It's truly a landmark worth seeing. Leave the big guy and the kid at home. XXXOOOs

LuAnn ripped off the brown packing paper and the newspaper fell out. She picked it up and looked at it: It was the *Atlanta Journal and Constitution*. It had a page marked with a yellow piece of paper. She opened to that page and sat down on the sofa.

In her agitation at seeing the headline, she jumped up. Her eyes fed voraciously on the words, occasionally darting to the accompanying photo. If possible, the trailer looked even dingier captured in grainy black and white; in fact it looked like it had actually collapsed and was merely awaiting the dump truck to cart it and its occupants away for burial. The convertible was also in the photo, its long hood and obscene ornament pointed straight at the

124

trailer like some hunting dog telling its master: There's the kill.

Two men dead, the story said. Drugs involved. As LuAnn read the name Duane Harvey, a teardrop splattered on to the page and blurred some of the text. She sat down and did her best to compose herself. The other man had not yet been identified. LuAnn read quickly, and then she stopped searching when she found her name. The police were looking for her right now; the paper didn't say she had been charged with any crime, although her disappearance had probably only increased the police's suspicions. She flinched when she read that Shirley Watson had discovered the bodies. A canister of battery acid had been found on the floor of the trailer. LuAnn's eyes narrowed. *Battery acid.* Shirley had come back to avenge herself and had brought that acid to do the job, that was clear. She doubted, though, if the police would care about a crime that had not occurred when they had their hands full with at least two that had.

While she sat staring in shock at the paper, another knock on the door almost made LuAnn jump out of her chair.

"LuAnn?"

She took a deep breath. "Charlie?"

"Who else?"

"Just a minute." LuAnn jumped up, hastily ripped the news article out of the paper and stuffed it in her pocket. She slid the letter and the rest of the newspaper under the couch.

She unlocked the door and he entered the room and shrugged off his coat. "Stupid idea, like I'm going to be able to spot somebody out on those streets." He slid a cigarette from its pack and lit up, thoughtfully staring out the window. "Still can't shake the feeling that somebody was tailing us, though."

"It could've just been somebody looking to rob us, Charlie. You got a lot of that up here, don't you?"

He shook his head. "Crooks have gotten more daring lately, but if that was the case, they would've hit us and run. Grabbed your purse and disappeared. It's not like they were going to pull a gun and stick us up in the middle of a million people. I had the sense whoever it was was tracking us for a while." He turned to stare at her. "Nothing unusual happened to you on the way up, did it?"

LuAnn shook her head, staring back at him with wide eyes, afraid to speak.

"Nobody followed you up to New York that you know of, did they?"

"I didn't see anybody, Charlie. I swear I didn't." LuAnn started to shake. "I'm scared."

He put a big arm around her. "Hey, it's okay. Probably just paranoid Charlie going off on nothing. But sometimes it pays to be paranoid. Look, how about we go do some more shopping? It'll make you feel better."

LuAnn nervously fingered the newspaper article in her pocket. Her heart seemed to be climbing up her throat, seeking a larger space in which to explode. However, when she looked up at him, her face was calm, bewitching. "You know what I really want to do?"

"What's that? Name it and it's done."

"I want to get my hair done. And maybe my nails. They both look kinda crappy. And with the press conference going on across the whole country and all, I'd like to look good."

"Damn, why didn't I think of that? Well, let's just look up the fanciest beauty parlor in the phone book—"

"There's one in the lobby," LuAnn said hurriedly. "I saw it coming in. They do hair and nails and feet, and facials, stuff like that. It looked real nice. Real nice."

"Even better then."

"Could you watch Lisa for me?"

"We can come down and hang out with you."

"Charlie, I swear. Don't you know nothing?"

"What? What'd I say?"

"Men don't come down to the beauty parlor and watch the goings-on. That's for us females to keep secret. If you knew how much trouble it takes to get us all pretty, it wouldn't be nearly as special. But you got a job to do."

"What's that?"

"You can 'ooh' and 'ahh' when I get back and tell me how beautiful I look."

Charlie grinned. "I think I can handle that one."

"I don't know how long I'll be. I might not be able to get in right away. There's a bottle ready in the refrigerator for Lisa for when she gets hungry. She's gonna want to play for a while and then you can put her down for a nap."

"Take your time, I've got nothing else on the agenda. A beer and cable TV" – he went over and lifted Lisa out of the baby carriage – "and the company of this little lady, and I'm a happy man."

LuAnn picked up her coat.

Charlie said, "What do you need that for?"

"I need to buy some personal things. There's a drug store across the street."

"You can just get them in the gift shop in the lobby."

"If they're anything like the prices at the last hotel, I'll go across the street and save myself some money, thank you very much."

"LuAnn, you're one of the richest women in the world, you could buy the whole damned hotel if you wanted."

"Charlie, I've been scraping pennies all my life. I

127

can't change overnight." She opened the door and glanced back at him, trying her best to hide the rising anxiety she was experiencing. "I'll be back as soon as I can."

Charlie moved over to the door. "I don't like it. If you go out, I'm supposed to go with you."

"Charlie, I'm a grown woman. I can take care of myself. Besides, Lisa's going to have to take a nap soon and we can't leave her here by herself, can we?"

"Well, no, but—"

LuAnn slid an arm across his shoulder. "You look after Lisa and I'll be back as soon as I can." She gave Lisa a kiss on the cheek and Charlie a gentle squeeze on the arm.

After she left, Charlie grabbed a beer from the wet bar and settled into his chair with Lisa on his lap and the TV remote in hand. He suddenly paused and looked over at the doorway, a frown appearing on his features as he did so. Then he turned back and did his best to interest Lisa in channel surfing.

FOURTEEN

When LuAnn stepped from the cab she looked up at the towering presence of the Empire State Building. She didn't have long to dwell upon the architecture, though, as she felt the arm slide around hers.

"This way, we can talk." The voice was smooth, comforting, and it made every hair on her neck stiffen.

She pulled her arm free and looked at him. Very tall and broad shouldered, his face was clean-shaven, the hair thick and dark, matching the eyebrows. The eyes were big and luminous.

"What do you want?" Now that she could actually see the man behind the note, LuAnn's fear quickly receded.

Romanello looked around. "You know, even in New York, we're bound to attract attention if we conduct this conversation out in the open. There's a deli across the street. I suggest we continue our chat there."

"Why should I?"

He crossed his arms and smiled at her. "You read my note and the news article, obviously, or you wouldn't be here."

"I read it," LuAnn said, keeping her voice level.

"Then I think it's clear we have some things to discuss."

"What the hell do you have to do with it? Were you involved in that drug dealing?"

The smile faded from the man's lips and he stepped back for a moment. "Look—"

"I didn't kill nobody," she said fiercely.

Romanello looked around nervously. "Do you want everybody here to know our business?"

LuAnn looked around at the passersby and then stalked toward the deli with Romanello right behind.

Inside they found an isolated booth far in the back. Romanello ordered coffee and then looked at LuAnn. "Anything interest you on the menu?" he asked pleasantly.

"Nothing." She glared back at him.

After the waitress departed, he looked at her. "Since I can understand your not wanting to prolong this discussion, let's get to the heart of it."

"What's your name?"

He looked startled. "Why?"

"Just make up one, that's what everybody else seems to be doing."

"What are you talking—" He stopped and considered for a moment. "All right, call me Rainbow."

"Rainbow, huh, that's a different one. You don't look like no rainbow I've ever seen."

"See, that's where you're wrong." His eyes gleamed for an instant. "Rainbows have pots of gold at the end."

"So?" LuAnn's tone was calm, but her look was wary.

"So, you're my pot of gold, LuAnn. At the end of my rainbow." He spread apart his hands. She started to get up.

"Sit down!" The words shot out of his mouth. LuAnn stopped in midrise, staring at the man. "Sit down unless you want to spend the rest of your life in prison instead of paradise." The calm returned to his manner and he politely gestured for her to resume her seat. She did so, slowly, her eyes squarely on his.

"I ain't never been real good at games, Mr. Rainbow, so why don't you say whatever the hell it is you want to say and let's be done with it."

Romanello waited for a moment as the waitress returned with his coffee. "You sure you don't want some? It's quite chilly outside."

The chill in LuAnn's eyes compelled him to move on. He waited until the waitress had set the coffee and cream down and asked if they wanted anything else. After she left, he leaned across the table, his eyes bare inches from LuAnn's. "I was at your trailer, LuAnn. I saw the bodies."

She flinched for an instant. "What were you doing there?"

He sat back. "Just happened by."

"You're full of crap and you know it."

"Maybe. The point is, I saw you drive up to the trailer in that car, the same one in the newspaper photo. I saw you pull a wad of cash out of your kid's baby seat at the train station. I saw you make a number of phone calls."

"So what? I'm not allowed to make phone calls?"

"The trailer had two dead bodies and a shitload of drugs in it, LuAnn. That was *your* trailer."

LuAnn's eyes narrowed. *Was Rainbow a policeman sent to get her to confess?* She fidgeted in her seat. "I don't know what you're talking about. I never seen no bodies. You musta seen somebody else get out of that car. And who says I can't keep my money wherever the hell I want to keep it." She dug her hand into her pocket and pulled out the newspaper article. "Here, why don't you take this back and go try scaring somebody else."

Romanello picked up the piece of paper, glanced at it, and put it in his pocket. When his hand

131

returned to view, LuAnn could barely keep from trembling as she saw the torn piece of bloody shirt.

"Recognize this, LuAnn?"

She struggled to maintain her composure. "Looks like a shirt with some stains on it. So what?"

He smiled at her. "You know, I didn't expect you to remain this calm about it. You're a dumb chick from Hooterville. I pictured you dropping to your knees pleading for mercy."

"Sorry I ain't what you imagined. And if you call me a dumb anything again, I'll knock you flat on your ass."

His face suddenly became hard and he slid down the zipper of his jacket until the butt of his 9-mm was revealed. "The last thing you want to do, LuAnn, is make me upset," he said quietly. "When I get upset, I can be very unpleasant. In fact I can be downright violent."

LuAnn barely glanced at the weapon. "What do you want from me?"

He zipped the jacket back up. "Like I said, you're my pot of gold."

"I ain't got any money," she said quietly.

He almost laughed. "Why are you in New York, LuAnn? I bet you've never been out of that god-forsaken county before. Why of all places did you take off for the Big Apple?" He cocked his head at her, waiting for an answer.

LuAnn rubbed her hands nervously across the uneven surface of the table. She didn't look at him when she finally spoke. "Okay, maybe I knew what happened in that trailer. But I didn't do nothing wrong. I had to get out, though, because I knew it might look real bad for me. New York seemed as good as anyplace." She looked up to test his reaction to her explanation. The mirth was still there.

"What are you going to do with all the money, LuAnn?"

She nearly crossed her eyes. "What are you talking about? What money? In the baby seat?"

"I would hope you weren't going to try and stuff one hundred million dollars in a baby seat." He eyed her chest. "Or, despite its obvious capacity, your bra." She just stared at him, her mouth open a notch. "Let's see," he continued, "what's the going price for blackmail these days? Ten percent? Twenty percent? Fifty percent? I mean, even at half, you're still talking millions in your bank account. That'll keep you and the kid in jeans and sneakers for life, right?" He took a sip of his coffee and sat back, idly fingering the edges of his napkin while he watched her.

LuAnn clamped a fist around the fork in front of her. For a moment she thought about attacking him, but that impulse subsided.

"You're crazy, mister, you really are."

"The press conference is tomorrow, LuAnn."

"What press conference?"

"You know, that's where you're going to hold that big old check and smile and wave to the dis-appointed masses."

"I've gotta go."

His right hand shot across and gripped her arm. "I don't think you can spend that money from a prison cell."

"I said I gotta go." She jerked her hand free and stood up.

"Don't be a fool, LuAnn. I saw you buy the lottery ticket. I was at the lottery drawing. I saw the big smile on your face, the way you ran down the street whooping and hollering. And I was inside the lottery building when you went to get your winning ticket validated. So don't try to bullshit with me. You walk out of here and the first thing I'm going to do is place a call to that Podunk county and that Podunk sheriff and tell them everything I saw. And then I'm going to send them this piece of shirt. You can't believe the high-tech stuff they've got in the lab these days. They'll start piecing it together. And when I tell them you just won the lottery and maybe they should grab you before you disappear, then you can just kiss your new life good-bye. Although I guess you can afford to put your kid up somewhere nice while you rot in jail."

"I didn't do nothing wrong."

"No, what you did was stupid, LuAnn. You ran. And when you run, the cops always figure you're guilty. It's how cops think. They'll believe you were in it up to your pretty little ass. Right now, they haven't gotten around to you. But they will. It's up to you to decide whether they start focusing on you ten minutes from now, or ten days from now. If it's ten minutes, you're dead. If it's ten days, I figure your plan is to disappear forever. Because that's what I intend to do. You only pay me once, that I'll guarantee. I couldn't spend all that money even if I tried and neither could you. We all win that way. The other way, you lose, slamdunk. So what's it gonna be?"

She stood frozen for a moment halfway out of her chair. Slowly, inch by inch, she sat back down.

"Very smart of you, LuAnn."

"I can't pay you half."

His face darkened. "Don't be greedy, lady."

"It's got nothing to do with that. I can pay you, I just don't know how much, but it'll be a lot. Enough for you to do whatever the hell you want to."

"I don't understand—" he began.

LuAnn interrupted, borrowing phraseology from Jackson. "You don't have to understand nothing. But if I do this I want you to answer one question for me and I want the truth or you can just go and call the cops, I don't care."

He eyed her cautiously. "What's the question?"

LuAnn leaned across the table, her voice low but intense. "What were you doing in that trailer? You just didn't happen on by, I know that sure as I'm sitting here."

"Look, what does it matter why I was there?" He threw his arm up in a casual motion.

LuAnn reached out as quickly as a striking rattler and grabbed his wrist. He winced as she squeezed it with a strength he had not anticipated. Big and strong as he was, it would've taken all his might to break that grip. "I said I wanted an answer, and it better be the right one."

"I earn my living" – he smiled and corrected himself – "I *used* to earn my living by taking care of little problems for people."

LuAnn continued to grip the waist. "What problems? Did this have to do with the drugs Duane was dealing?"

Romanello was already shaking his head. "I didn't know anything about the drugs. Duane was already dead. Maybe he was holding out on his supplier or maybe skimming off the top and the other guy cut him up. Who knows? Who cares?"

"What happened to the other guy?"

"You were the one who hit him, weren't you? Like I said in the note, dead as a doornail." LuAnn didn't answer. He paused and took a breath. "You can let go of my wrist any time now."

"You haven't answered my question. And unless you answer it, you can just go call the sheriff, because you ain't getting one red cent from me."

Romanello hesitated, but then his greed won out over his better judgment. "I went there to kill you," he said simply.

135

She slowly let go of his wrist after giving it one more intense ratchet. He took a minute to rub the circulation back in.

"Why?" LuAnn demanded fiercely.

"I don't ask questions. I just do what I'm paid to do."

"Who told you to kill me?"

He shrugged. "I don't know." She reached for his wrist again, but this time he was ready for her and jerked it out of danger. "I'm telling you I don't know. My clients don't just drop by and have coffee and chat about who they want me to take out. I got a call, I got half the money up front. Half when the job was done. All through the mail."

"I'm still alive."

"That's right. But only because I got called off."

"By who?"

"By whoever hired me."

"When did you get the call?"

"I was in your trailer. I saw you get out of the car and take off. I went to my car and got the call then. Around ten-fifteen."

LuAnn sat back as the truth dawned on her: Jackson. So that's how he took care of those who refused to go along.

When she didn't say anything, Romanello leaned forward. "So now that I've answered all your questions, why don't we discuss the arrangements for our little deal?"

LuAnn stared at him for a full minute before speaking. "If I find out you're lying to me, you won't like it one bit."

"You know, somebody who kills for a living usually strikes a little more fear into people than what you're showing," he said, his dark eyes flickering at her. He partially unzipped his jacket again so that the butt of the 9-mm was once more visible. "Don't push it!" His tone was menacing.

LuAnn glanced at the pistol with contempt before settling her eyes back on his. "I growed up surrounded by crazy people, *Mr. Rainbow*. Rednecks getting drunk and pointing twelve-gauge shotguns in people's faces and then pulling the trigger just for fun, or cutting somebody up so bad their momma wouldn't have knowed them and then betting on how long they'd take to bleed to death. Then there was the black boy who ended up in a lake with his throat slashed and his private parts gone, 'cause somebody thought he was too uppity hanging around a white girl. I'm pretty sure my daddy had something to do with that, not that the police down there gave a damn. So your little gun and your big man bullshit don't mean crap to me. Let's just get this over with and then you can get the hell out of my life."

The danger in the depths of Romanello's eyes rapidly dissipated. "All right," he said quietly, zipping his jacket back up.

FIFTEEN

A half hour later Romanello and LuAnn exited the deli. LuAnn climbed into a cab and headed back to her hotel where, to follow through on her cover story to Charlie, she would spend the next several hours at the beauty salon. Romanello walked down the street in the opposite direction, silently whispering to himself. Today had been a very good day. The arrangements he had made with LuAnn weren't a hundred percent foolproof, but his gut told him she would honor the deal she had made. If the first installment of the money wasn't in his account by close of business two days from now, then he would be on the phone to the police in Rikersville. She would pay, Romanello was sure of that. Why bring all that grief on yourself?

Since he was in a festive mood, he decided to stop and buy a bottle of Chianti on the way to his apartment. His thoughts were already focused on the mansion he would buy in some faraway land to replace it. He had earned good money over the years exterminating human beings, but he had to be careful in how he spent it or where he kept it. The last thing he wanted was the IRS knocking on his door asking to see his W-2s. Now that problem was behind him. Instant, massive wealth allowed one to soar beyond the reach of the Revenue boys, and everyone else. Yes, it had been a great day, Romanello concluded.

Not finding a cab handy, he opted for the subway. It was very crowded and he could barely find standing room in one of the train cars. He rode the subway for a number of stops before pushing through the masses and once again hitting the street. He turned the key in his door, closed and locked it, and walked into the kitchen to drop off the bottle. He was about to take off his jacket and pour himself a glass of Chianti when someone knocked at the door. He squinted through the peephole. The brown uniform of the UPS man filled his line if vision.

"What's up?" he asked through the door.

"Got a delivery for an Anthony Romanello, this address." The UPS man was busily scanning the package, an eight-by-eleven-inch container that bulged out at the center.

Romanello opened the door.

"You Anthony Romanello?"

He nodded.

"Just sign right here, please." He handed Romanello a pen attached to what looked to be an electronic clipboard.

"You're not trying to serve me with legal papers, are you?" Romanello grinned as he signed for the package.

"They couldn't pay me enough to do that," the UPS man replied. "My brother-in-law used to be a process server up in Detroit. After he was shot the second time, he went to work driving a bakery truck. Here you go. Have a good one."

Romanello closed the door and felt the contents of the package through the thin cardboard. A smile broke across his lips. The second installment of his LuAnn Tyler hit. He had been told of the possibility of being called off. But his employer had assured him that the rest of the money would be forthcoming regardless. The smile froze on his face as it suddenly struck him that the payment should have been mailed to his post office box. Nobody was supposed to know where he lived. Or his real name.

He whirled around at the sound behind him.

Jackson emerged from the shadows of the living room. Dressed as immaculately as when he had interviewed LuAnn, Jackson leaned against the doorway to the kitchen and looked Romanello up and down behind a pair of dark glasses. Jackson's hair was streaked with gray and a neatly trimmed beard covered his chin. His cheeks were large and puffy, the ears red and flattened-looking, both the result of carefully designed latex molds.

"Who the hell are you and how did you get in here?"

In response, Jackson pointed one gloved hand at the package. "Open it."

"What?" Romanello growled back.

"Count the money and make certain it's all there. Don't worry, you won't hurt my feelings by doing so."

"Look—"

Jackson slipped off the glasses and his eyes bored into Romanello. "Open it." The voice was barely above a whisper and spoken in an entirely non-threatening manner that made Romanello wonder why he was shivering inside. After all, he had murdered six people in premeditated fashion over the span of the last three years. Nobody intimidated him.

He quickly ripped open the package and the contents spilled out. Romanello watched as the cut-up newspaper drifted to the floor.

"Is this supposed to be funny? If it is, I'm not laughing." He glowered at Jackson.

Jackson shook his head sadly. "As soon as I hung up with you I knew my little slip over the phone

140

would prove to be serious. I made mention of LuAnn Tyler and money, and money, as you well know, makes people do strange things."

"What exactly are you talking about?"

"Mr. Romanello, you were hired to perform a job for me. Once that task was called off, your participation in my affairs was at an end. Or let me rephrase that: Your participation in my affairs was *supposed* to be at an end."

"They were at an end. I didn't kill the lady and all I get from you is cut-up newspaper. I'm the one who should be pissed."

Jackson ticked the points off with his fingers. "You followed the woman back to New York. You, in fact, have been following her all over the city. You sent her a note. You met with her, and while I wasn't privy to the conversation itself, from the looks of things the subject matter wasn't pleasant."

"How the hell do you know all that?"

"There isn't much I don't know, Mr. Romanello. There really isn't." Jackson put the glasses back on.

"Well, you can't prove anything."

Jackson laughed, a laugh that sent every hair on Romanello's neck skyward and made him reach for his gun, a gun that was no longer there.

Jackson looked at the man's amazed face and shook his head sadly. "Subways are so crowded this time of night. Pickpockets, I understand, can stalk honest people with impunity. There's no telling what else you might find missing."

"Well, like I said, you can't prove it. And it's not like you can just go to the cops. You hired me to kill someone. That doesn't do a whole lot for your credibility."

"I have no interest in going to the authorities. You disobeyed my instructions and in doing so jeopardized my plans. I came here to inform you that I was

141

aware of this, to plainly show you that the rest of your money has been forfeited because of your improper actions, and that I have decided upon the appropriate punishment. A punishment that I fully intend to mete out now."

Romanello drew himself up to his full six feet three inch height, towering over Jackson, and laughed heartily. "Well, if you came here to punish me, I hope you brought somebody else with you to do the punishing."

"I prefer to handle these matters myself."

"Well, then this is going to be your last job." In a flash, Romanello's hand went down to his ankle and he was erect again in a second, the jagged-edge blade in his right hand. He started forward and then stopped as he eyed the device in Jackson's hand.

"The touted advantages of strength and superior size are so often overrated, wouldn't you agree?" said Jackson. The twin darts shot out from the taser gun and hit Romanello dead center in the chest. Jackson continued to squeeze the trigger, sending 120,000 volts of electricity along the thin metal cords that were attached to the darts. Romanello went down as though poleaxed, and he lay there staring up as Jackson stood over him.

"I've held the trigger down for a full minute now, which will incapacitate you for at least fifteen minutes, more than ample for my purposes."

Romanello watched helplessly as Jackson knelt down beside him and gingerly pulled the two darts free and packed the apparatus back in his pocket. He carefully opened Romanello's shirt. "Quite hairy, Mr. Romanello. A medical examiner will never pick up on the extremely small holes in your chest." The next item Jackson withdrew from his coat would have left Romanello numb if he hadn't already been. With his tongue feeling as big as a knobby tree root,

Romanello thought he had suffered a stroke. His limbs were useless to him: there was no physical sensation at all. He could still see clearly, however, and suddenly wished he had been blinded as well. He watched in horror as Jackson methodically checked the hypodermic needle he held in his hand.

"It's mostly an innocuous saline solution, you know," Jackson said as though he were addressing a science class. "I say mostly, because what's lurking in here can be quite deadly under certain conditions." He smiled down at Romanello and paused for a moment as he considered the import of his own words and then continued. "This solution contains prostaglandin, a substance produced naturally in the body. Normal levels are measured in micrograms. I'm about to give you a dose several thousand times that, measured in milligrams in fact. When this dose hits your heart it will cause the coronary arteries to severely constrict, triggering what doctors would technically term a myocardial infarction or coronary occlusion, also known as a heart attack of the most devastating kind. To tell you the truth, I've never combined the effects of electrification caused by the stun gun with this method of inflicting death. It might be interesting to observe the process." Jackson was betraying no more emotion than if he were about to dissect a frog in biology class. "Since prostaglandin occurs naturally in the body, as I mentioned, it's also naturally metabolized by the body, meaning there will be no suspiciously high traces left for a medical examiner to detect. I'm currently working on a poison to which I will attach an enzyme, encapsulated by a special coating. The protective cover is quickly broken down by the components in the bloodstream; however, the poison will have ample time to do its work before that occurs. Once the protective

143

coating is gone the enzymes will instantly react with the poison compound and break it down, in effect destroying it. They use a similar process to clean up oil slicks. It's absolutely untraceable. I was planning to use it on you tonight; however, the process is not yet perfected and I hate to rush things of that nature. Chemistry, after all, requires patience and precision. Hence, the fallback to the old reliable: prostaglandin."

Jackson held the needle very close to Romanello's neck, seeking the perfect entry site. "They will find you here, a young, strapping man felled in his prime by natural causes. Another statistic in the ongoing health debate."

Romanello's eyes almost exploded out of his head as he struggled with every ounce of will to break the grip of inertia the stun gun had caused. The veins stood out on his neck with the effort he was exerting and Jackson quietly thanked him for providing such a convenient place, right before the needle plunged into the jugular vein and its contents poured into his body. Jackson smiled and gently patted Romanello on the head as his pupils shot back and forth like a metronome.

From his bag, Jackson extracted a razor blade. "Now, a sharp-eyed medical examiner might pick up on the hypodermic's entry site, so we will have to address that." Using the razor, Jackson nicked Romanello's skin at the precise place the needle had gone in. A drop of blood floated to the surface of the skin. Jackson replaced the razor in the bag and pulled out a Band-Aid. He pressed it across the fresh cut and sat back to study his handiwork, smiling as he did so.

"I'm sorry that it's come to this, as your services might have been useful to me in the future." Jackson picked up one of Romanello's limp hands and made

144

the sign of the cross over the stricken man's chest. "I know that you were raised Roman Catholic, Mr. Romanello," he said earnestly, "although you obviously have strayed from the teachings of the Church, but I'm afraid a priest to administer last rites is out of the question. I hardly think it matters where you're going anyway, do you? Purgatory is such a silly notion after all." He picked up Romanello's knife and placed it back in the sheath strapped to his ankle.

Jackson was about to stand up when he noted the edge of the newspaper sticking out from the inside of Romanello's jacket pocket. He nimbly plucked it out. As he read the article detailing the story of the two murders, drugs, LuAnn's disappearance, and the police's search for her, his features became grim. That explained a lot. Romanello was blackmailing her. Or attempting to. Had he discovered this piece of information a day earlier, Jackson's solution would have been simple. He would've executed LuAnn Tyler on the spot. Now he could not do that and he hated that he had lost partial control of the situation. She had already been confirmed as the winning ticket holder. She was scheduled to appear to the world in less than twenty-four hours as the lottery's newest winner. Yes, now her requests made more sense. He folded up the piece of paper and put it in his pocket. Like it or not, he was wedded to LuAnn Tyler, warts and all. It was a challenge, and, if nothing else, he loved a challenge. However, he would take control back. He would tell her exactly what she had to do, and if she didn't follow his instructions precisely, then he would kill her after she won the lottery.

Jackson gathered up the shredded newspaper and remnants of the UPS package. The dark suit he was wearing came off with a tug on certain discreet parts of the garment, and together with the now revealed body moldings that had given Jackson his girth, all of these items were packed in a pizza carrier bag that Jackson pulled from a corner of the living room. Underneath, a much slimmer Jackson was wearing the blue and white shirt proclaiming him to be a Domino's Pizza delivery person. From one of his pockets, he pulled out a piece of thread and, edging it carefully under the putty on his nose, lifted the piece cleanly off and stuck it in the pizza box. The mole, beard, and ear pieces he similarly discarded. He swabbed his face down with alcohol from a bottle pulled from his pocket, removing the shadows and highlights that had aged his face. His hands worked quickly and methodically from years of long practice. Last, he combed a gel through his hair that effectively removed the sprayed-on streaks of gray. He checked his altered appearance in a small mirror hanging on the wall. Then this chameleon landscape was swiftly altered by a small bristly mustache applied with spirit gum, and a hair extender hung in a long ponytail out from under the Yankee baseball cap he was now putting on. Dark glasses covered his eyes; dress shoes were replaced with tennis shoes. He once again checked his appearance: completely different. He had to smile. It was quite a talent. When Jackson quietly left the building a few seconds later, Romanello's features were relaxed, peaceful. They would forever remain so.

SIXTEEN

"Everything will be all right, LuAnn." Roger Davis, the young, handsome man who had announced the lottery drawing, said these words as he patted her on the hand. "I know you have to be nervous but I'll be right there with you. We'll make it as painless as possible for you, I give you my word," he said gallantly.

They were in a plush room inside the lottery building, just down the corridor from the large auditorium where a mass of press and regular folk awaited the latest lottery winner's arrival. LuAnn wore a pale blue knee-length dress with matching shoes, her hair and makeup impeccable thanks to the in-house staff at the Lottery Commission. The cut on her jaw had healed enough that she had opted for makeup instead of the bandage.

"You look beautiful, LuAnn," said Davis. "I can't remember a winner looking so ravishing, I mean that." He sat down right next to her, his leg touching hers.

LuAnn flashed him a quick smile, slid a couple of inches away and turned her attention to Lisa. "I don't want Lisa to have to go out there. All them lights and people would just scare her to death."

"That's fine. She can stay in here. We'll have someone watching her of course, every minute. Security is very tight here as you can imagine." He paused while he once again took in LuAnn's shapely form. "We'll announce that you have a daughter,

147

though. That's why your story is so great. Young mother and daughter, all this wealth. You must be so happy." He patted her on the knee and then let his hand linger for a moment before pulling it away. She wondered again whether he was in on all of it. Whether he knew she had won an enormous fortune by cheating. He looked the type, she concluded. The kind who would do anything for money. She imagined he would be very well paid for helping to pull off something this big.

"How long until we go out there?" she asked.

"About ten minutes." He smiled at her again and then said as casually as possible, "Uh, you weren't exactly clear on your marital status. Will your husband—"

"I'm not married," LuAnn said quickly.

"Oh, well, will the father of the child be attending?" He added quickly, "We just have to know for scheduling purposes."

LuAnn looked dead at him. "No, he won't."

Davis smiled confidently and inched closer. "I see. Hmmm." He made a steeple with his hands and rested them against his lips for a moment and then he laid one arm casually across the back of her seat. "Well, I don't know what your plans are, but if you need anyone to show you around town I am absolutely here for you, LuAnn, twenty-four hours a day. I know after living all your life in a small town, that the big city" – Davis lifted his other arm dramatically toward the ceiling – "must be very overwhelming. But I know it like the back of my hand. The best restaurants, theaters, shopping. We could have a great time." He edged still closer, his eyes hugging the contours of her body as his fingers drifted toward her shoulder.

"Oh, I'm sorry, Mr. Davis, I think maybe you got the wrong idea. Lisa's father ain't coming for the press conference, but he's coming up after. He had to get leave first."

"Leave?"

"He's in the Navy. He's with the SEALs." She shook her head and stared off as if digging up some shocking memories. "Let me tell you, it downright scares me some of the stuff he's told me about. But if there's anybody that can take care of himself it's Frank. Why, he beat six guys unconscious in a bar one time 'cause they were coming on to me. He probably would've killed them if the police hadn't pulled him off, and it took five of them to do it, big, strong cops, too."

Davis's mouth dropped open and he scooted away from LuAnn. "Good Lord!"

"Oh, but don't say nothing about that at the press conference, Mr. Davis. What Frank does is all top-secret-like and he'd get real pissed at you if you said anything. Real pissed!" She stared intently at him, watching the waves of fear pour over his pretty-boy features.

Davis stood up abruptly. "No, of course not, not one word. I swear." Davis licked his lips and put a shaky hand through his heavily moussed hair. "I'd better go check on things, LuAnn." He managed a weak smile and gave her a shaky thumbs-up.

She returned the gesture. "Thanks so much for understanding, Mr. Davis." After he had gone, LuAnn turned back to Lisa. "You ain't never gonna have to do that, baby doll. And pretty soon, your momma ain't gonna have to do it no more either." She cradled Lisa against her chest and stared across at the clock on the wall, watching the time tick down.

Charlie glanced around the crowded auditorium while he methodically pushed his way toward the front of the stage. He stopped at a spot where he could see clearly and waited. He would've liked to be up on the stage with LuAnn, giving her what he knew would be much needed moral support. However, that was out of the question. He had to remain in the background; raising suspicion was not part of his job description. He would see LuAnn after the press conference was completed. He also would have to tell her his decision about whether he would accompany her or not. The problem was he hadn't made up his mind yet. He stuffed his hand in his pocket for a cigarette and then remembered smoking wasn't permitted in the building. He really was craving the soothing influences of the tobacco and for a brief instant he contemplated sneaking outside for a quick one, but there wasn't enough time.

He sighed and his broad shoulders collapsed. He had spent the better part of his life roaming from point to point with nothing in the way of a comprehensive plan, nothing resembling long-term goals. He loved kids and would never have any of his own. He was paid well, but while money went a long way toward improving his physical sur-roundings it didn't really contribute to his genuine overall happiness. At his age, he figured this was as good as it was going to get. The avenues he had taken as a young man had pretty much dictated what the remaining years of his life would be like. Until now. LuAnn Tyler had offered him a way out of that. He held no delusions that she was interested in him sexually, and in the cold face of reality, away from her unpretentious and yet incredibly seductive presence, Charlie had concluded that he did not want that either. What he wanted was her sincere friendship, her goodness – two elements that had been appallingly lacking in his life. And that brought him back to the choice. Should he go or not? If he went, he had little doubt that he would enjoy the hell out of LuAnn and Lisa, with an added plus of being a father figure for the little girl. For a few years anyway. But he had sat up most of the night thinking about what would happen after those first few years.

It was inevitable that beautiful LuAnn, with her new wealth, and the refinement that would come from those riches, would be the target of dozens of the world's most eligible men. She was very young, had one child, and would want more. She would marry one of these men. That man would assume the responsibility of fathering Lisa, and properly so. He would be the man in LuAnn's life. And where would that leave Charlie? He edged forward, squeezing between two CNN cameramen as he thought about this again. At some point, Charlie figured, he would be compelled to leave them. It would be too awkward. It wasn't like he was family or anything. And when that time came it would be painful, more painful than allowing his body to be used for a punching bag during his youth. After spending only a few days with them, he felt a bond with LuAnn and Lisa that he had not managed to form in over ten years of marriage with his ex-wife. What would it be like after three or four years together? Could he calmly walk away from Lisa and her mother without suffering an irreparably broken heart, a screwed-up psyche? He shook his head. What a tough guy he had turned out to be. He barely knew these simple people from the South and he was now engulfed in a life-churning decision the consequences of which he was extrapolating out years into the future.

A part of him said simply go for the ride and enjoy the hell out of yourself. You could be dead from a heart attack next year, what the hell did it matter? The other part of him, though, he was afraid, was

151

winning the day. He knew that he could be LuAnn's friend for the rest of his life, but he didn't know if he could do it close-up, every day, with the knowledge that it might end abruptly. "Shit," he muttered. It came down to pure envy, he decided. If he were only twenty – he shrugged – okay, thirty years younger. Envy of the guy who would eventually win her. Win her love, a love that he was sure would last forever, at least on her side. And heaven help the poor man who betrayed her. She was a hellcat, that was easy to see. A firecracker with a heart of gold, but that was a big part of the attraction: Polar opposites like that in the same fragile shell of skin and bones and raw nerve endings was a rare find.

Charlie abruptly stopped his musings and looked up at the stage. The entire crowd seemed to tense all at once, like a biceps flexing and forming a ridge of muscle. Then the cameras started clicking away as LuAnn, tall, queenly, and calm, walked gracefully into their field of vision and stood before them all. Charlie shook his head in silent wonderment. "Damn," he said under his breath. She had just made his decision that much harder.

Sheriff Roy Waymer nearly spit his mouthful of beer clear across the room as he watched LuAnn Tyler waving back at him from the TV. "Jesus, Joseph, Mary!" He looked over at his wife, Doris, whose eyes were boring into the twenty-seven-inch screen.

"You been looking for her all over the county and there she is right there in New York City," Doris exclaimed. "The gall of that girl. And she just won all that money." Doris said this bitterly as she wrung her hands together; twenty-four torn-up lottery tickets resided in the trash can in her back yard.

Waymer wrestled his considerable girth out of his

152

La-Z-Boy and headed toward the telephone. "I phoned up to the train stations around here and at the airport in Atlanta, but I hadn't heard nothing back yet. I didn't take her to be heading up to no New York, though. I didn't put no APB out on LuAnn because I didn't think she'd be able to get out of the county, much less the state. I mean, the girl ain't even got a car. And she had the baby and all. I thought for sure she'd just hightailed it over to some friend's house."

"Well, it sure looks like she slipped right out on you." Doris pointed at LuAnn on the TV. "Right or wrong there ain't many people that look like that, that's for sure."

"Well, Mother," he said to his wife, "we don't exactly have the manpower of the FBI down here. With Freddie out with his back I only got two uniformed officers on duty. And the state police are up to their eyeballs in work; they couldn't spare nobody." He picked up the phone.

Doris looked at him anxiously. "You think LuAnn killed Duane and that other boy?"

Waymer held the phone up to his ear and shrugged. "LuAnn could kick the crap out of most men I know. She sure as hell could Duane. But that other guy was a hoss, almost three hundred pounds." He started punching in numbers on the phone. "But she coulda snuck up behind him and smashed that phone over his head. She'd been in a fight. More than one person saw her with a bandage on her chin that day."

"Drugs was behind it, that's for sure," Doris said. "That poor little baby in that trailer with all them drugs."

Waymer was nodding his head. "I know that."

"I bet'cha LuAnn was the brains behind it all. She's sharp, all right, we all know that. And she was

153

always too good for us. She tried to hide it, but we could all see through that. She didn't belong here, she wanted to get out, but she didn't have no way. Drug money, that was her way, you mark my words, Roy."

"I hear you, Mother. Except she don't need drug money no more." He nodded toward the TV.

"You best hurry up then, before she gets away."

"I'll contact the police up in New York to go pick her up."

"Think they'll do that?"

"Mother, she's a possible suspect in a double murder investigation," he said importantly. "Even if she ain't done nothing wrong, she's probably gonna be what they call a material witness."

"Yeah, but you think those Yankee police up in New York gonna care about that? Huh!"

"Police is police, Doris, North or South. The law's the law."

Unconvinced of the virtues of her Northern compatriots, Doris snorted and then suddenly looked hopeful. "Well, if she's convicted wouldn't she have to give back the money she won?" Doris looked back at the TV, at LuAnn's smiling face, wondering whether to go out to the trash and try to reconstruct all those lottery tickets. "She sure as heck wouldn't need all that money in prison, would she?"

Sheriff Waymer didn't answer. He was now trying to get through to the NYPD.

LuAnn held the big check, waved, and smiled at the crowds and answered a barrage of questions thrown at her from all sides of the vast room. Her picture was transported across the United States and then across the world.

Had she definitive plans for the money? If so, what were they?

154

"You'll know," LuAnn answered. "You'll see, but you'll just have to wait."

There were a series of predictably stupid questions such as "Do you feel lucky?"

"Incredibly," she responded. "More than you'll ever know."

"Will you spend it all in one place?"

"Not likely unless it's a really, really big place."

"Will you help your family?"

"I'll help all the people I care about."

Three times her hand was sought in matrimony. She answered each suitor differently and with polite humor but the bottom line was always "No." Charlie silently fumed at these exchanges; and then, checking his watch, he made his way out of the room.

After more questions, more photos, and more laughter and smiles, the press conference was finally over and LuAnn was escorted off the stage. She returned to the holding room, quickly changed into slacks and a blouse, erased all the makeup from her face, piled her long hair under a cowboy hat, and picked up Lisa. She checked her watch. Barely twenty minutes had passed since she had been introduced to the world as the new lottery winner. She expected that the local sheriff would be contacting the New York police by now. Everyone from LuAnn's hometown watched the lottery drawing religiously including Sheriff Roy Waymer. The timing would be very tight.

Davis leaned his head in the door. "Uh, Ms. Tyler, there's a car waiting for you at the rear entrance to the building. I'll have someone escort you down if you're ready."

"Ready as I'll ever be." When he turned to leave, LuAnn called after him. "If anybody shows up asking for me, I'll be at my hotel."

Davis looked at her coldly. "Are you expecting anyone?"

"Lisa's father, Frank."

Davis's face tightened. "And you're staying at?"

"The Plaza."

"Of course."

"But please don't tell anybody else where I am. I haven't seen Frank in a while. He's been on maneuvers for almost three months. So we don't want to be disturbed." She arched her eyebrows wickedly and smiled. "You know what I mean?"

Davis managed a very insincere smile and made a mock bow. "You can trust me implicitly, Ms. Tyler. Your chariot awaits."

Inwardly, LuAnn smiled. Now she was certain that when the police came for her, they would be directed as fast as possible to the Plaza Hotel. That would gain her the precious moments she would need to escape this town, and this country. Her new life was about to begin.

SEVENTEEN

The rear exit was very private and thus very quiet. A black stretch limo confronted LuAnn as she left the building. The chauffeur tipped his hat to her and held open the door. She got in and settled Lisa in the seat next to her.

"Good work, LuAnn. Your performance was flawless," Jackson said.

LuAnn nearly screamed out as she jerked around and stared into the dark recesses of the limo's far corner. All the interior lights in the rear of the limo were off except for a solitary one directly over her head that suddenly came on, illuminating her. She felt as though she were back on the stage at the lottery building. She could barely make out his shape as he hunkered back into his seat.

His voice drifted out to her. "Really very poised and dignified, a touch of humor when it was called for, the reporters eat that up, you know. And of course the looks to top it all off. *Tres* marriage proposals during one press conference is certainly a record as far as I'm aware."

LuAnn composed herself and settled back into her seat as the limo proceeded down the street. "Thank you."

"Quite frankly I was concerned that you would make a complete fool of yourself. Nothing against you of course. As I said before, you are an intelligent young woman; however, anyone, no matter their sophistication, thrust into a strange situation, is more apt to fail than not, wouldn't you agree?"

"I've had a lot of practice."

"Excuse me?" Jackson leaned forward slightly but still remained hidden from her view. "Practice with what?"

LuAnn stared toward the darkened corner, her vision blocked by the shining light. "Strange situations."

"You know, LuAnn, you really do amaze me sometimes, you really do. In some limited instances your perspicacity rivals my own and I don't say that lightly." He stared at her for several more seconds and then opened a briefcase lying on the seat next to him and pulled out several pieces of paper. As he sat back against the soft leather, a smile played across his features and a sigh of contentment escaped his lips.

"And now, LuAnn, it's time to discuss the conditions."

LuAnn fumbled with her blouse before crossing her legs. "We need to talk about something first."

Jackson cocked his head. "Really? And what might that be?"

LuAnn let out a deep breath. She had stayed awake all night deciding how best to tell him about the man calling himself Rainbow. She had first wondered whether Jackson needed to know at all. Then she decided that since it was about the money, then he would probably find out at some point. Better it be from her.

"A man came and talked to me yesterday."

"A man, you say. What about?"

"He wanted money from me."

Jackson laughed. "LuAnn, my dear, everybody will want money from you."

"No, it's not like that. He wanted half of my winnings."

"Excuse me? That's absurd."

"No it ain't. He . . . he had some information about me, things that had happened to me, that he said he would tell, if I didn't pay him."

"My goodness, what sorts of things?"

LuAnn paused and looked out the window. "Can I have something to drink?"

"Help yourself." A gloved finger came out of the darkness and pointed to the door built into one side of the limo. LuAnn did not look in his direction as she opened the refrigerator door and pulled out a Coke.

She took a long drink, wiped her lips, and continued. "Something happened to me right before I called to tell you I was going to take your offer."

"Would that possibly be the two dead bodies in your trailer? The drugs there? The fact that the police are looking for you? Or perhaps something else you tried to hide from me?" She didn't answer at first, nervously cradling the soda in her lap, the astonishment clear on her face.

"I didn't have nothing to do with those drugs. And that man was trying to kill me. I was just protecting myself."

"I should have realized when you wanted to leave town so quickly, change your name, all that, that there was something up." He shook his head sadly. "My poor, poor LuAnn. I guess I would've left town quickly too, confronted with those circumstances. And who would have thought it of our little Duane. Drugs! How terrible. But I tell you what, out of the goodness of my heart, I won't hold it against you. What's past is past. However" – here Jackson's tone became starkly forceful – "don't ever try to hide anything from me again, LuAnn. Please don't do that to yourself."

"But this man—"

Jackson spoke impatiently. "That's taken care of. You certainly won't be giving any money to him."

She stared into the darkness, amazement spreading across her face. "But how could you have done that?"

"People are always saying that about me: How could I have done that?" Jackson looked amused and said in a slightly hushed voice, "I can do anything, LuAnn, don't you know that by now? Anything. Does that frighten you? If it doesn't, it should. It even frightens me sometimes."

"The man said he was sent to kill me."

"Indeed."

"But then he got called off."

"How terribly peculiar."

"Timewise, I figure he got called off right after I called you and said I'd do it."

"Life is chock full of coincidences, isn't it?" Jackson's tone had become mocking.

Now LuAnn's features took on their own glint of ferocity. "I get bit, I bite back, real hard. Just so we understand each other, Mr. Jackson."

"I think we understand each other perfectly, LuAnn." In the darkness, she heard papers rustling. "However, this certainly complicates matters. When you wanted your name changed, I thought we could still do everything aboveboard."

"What do you mean?"

"Taxes, LuAnn. We do have the issue of taxes."

"But I thought all that money was mine to keep. The government couldn't touch it. That's what all the ads say."

"That's not exactly true. In fact the advertising is very misleading. Funny how the government can do that. The principal is not tax-free, it's *tax-deferred*. But only for the first year."

"What the hell does that mean?"

"It means that for the first year the winner pays no federal or state taxes, but the amount of that tax is simply deferred until the next year. The underlying tax is still owed, it's just the timing that's affected. No penalties or interest will accrue of course, so long as payment is made on a timely basis during the next tax year. The law states that the tax must be paid over ten years in equal installments. On one hundred million dollars, for example, you will owe roughly fifty million dollars in state and federal income tax, or one half the total amount. You're obviously in the highest tax bracket now. Divided by ten years the tax payment comes to five million dollars per year. In addition to that, generally speaking, any money you earn from the principal amount is taxable without any type of tax-deferred status.

"And I must tell you, LuAnn, I have plans for that principal, rather grand plans. You will make a great deal more money in the coming years; however, it will almost all be taxable income, dividends, capital gains, interest from taxable bonds, that sort of thing. That ordinarily would not present a problem, since law-abiding citizens who are not on the run from the police under an assumed name can file their tax returns, pay their fair share of tax, and live quite nicely. You can no longer do that. If my people filed your tax return under the name LuAnn Tyler with your current address and other personal inform-ation, don't you think the police might come knocking on your door?"

"Well, can't I pay tax under my new name?"

"Ah, potentially a brilliant solution; however, the IRS tends to get quite curious when the very first tax return filed by someone barely out of her teens has so many zeros on it. They might wonder what you were doing before and why all of a sudden you're richer than a Rockefeller. Again, the result would probably be the police, or even more likely the FBI, knocking on your door. No, that won't really do."

"So what do we do?"

When Jackson next spoke, the tone that reached LuAnn's ears made her tighten her grip on Lisa.

"You will do exactly as I tell you, LuAnn. You are ticketed on a flight that will take you out of the country. You will never return to the United States. This little mess in Georgia has bestowed upon you a life on the move. Forever, I'm afraid."

"But—"

"There's no *but* to it, LuAnn, that is the way it will be. Do you understand?"

LuAnn sat back against the leather seat and said stubbornly, "I got enough money now to where I can handle myself okay. And I don't like people telling me what to do."

"Is that right?" Jackson's hand closed around the pistol he had lifted from his briefcase. In the darkness he could have swung it up in an instant: mother and child obliterated. "Well, then why don't you take your chances on getting out of the country by yourself. Would you like to do that?"

"I can take care of myself."

"That's not the point. You made a deal with me, LuAnn. A deal I expect you to honor. Unless you're a fool you will work with me and not against me. You will see that in the long run your and my interests are the same. Otherwise, I can stop the limo right here, toss you and the child out, and I'll phone the police to come and pick you up. It's your choice. Decide. Now!"

Confronted with that option, LuAnn looked desperately around the interior of the limo. Her eyes finally settled on Lisa. Her daughter looked up at her with big, soft eyes; there was complete faith there.

LuAnn let out a deep breath. What choice did she really have?

"All right."

Jackson again rustled the papers he held. "Now, we have just enough time to go over these documents. There are a number of them for you to sign, but let me discuss the principal terms first. I will try to be as simple in my explanation as possible.

"You have just won one hundred million dollars and change. As we speak, that money has been placed in a special escrow account set up by the Lottery Commission under your name. By the way, I have obtained a Social Security number for you, under your *new* name. It makes life so much easier when you have one of those. Once you execute these papers my people will be able to transfer the funds out of that account and into one over which I will have complete and total control."

"But how do *I* get to the money?" LuAnn protested.

"Patience, LuAnn, all will be explained. The money will be invested as I see fit and for my own account. However, from those investment funds you will be guaranteed a minimum return of twenty-five percent per annum, which comes to approximately twenty-five million dollars per year. Those funds will be available to you all during the course of the year. I have accountants and financial advisors who will handle all of that for you, don't worry." He held up a cautionary finger. "Understand that that is income from principal. The one hundred million is never touched. I will control that principal amount for a period of ten years and invest it however I choose. It will take several months or more to fully implement my plans for the money, so the ten-year period will commence approximately in the late fall of this year. I will provide you with the exact date later. Ten years from that date, you will receive the full one hundred million dollars back. Any of the yearly income you've earned over the ten years is of course yours to keep. We will invest that for you as well, free of charge. I'm sure you're ignorant of this, but at that rate, your money, compounded, less even an exorbitant personal allowance, will double approximately every three years, particularly when you don't pay any taxes. Under practically any reasonable projection, you will be worth hundreds of millions of dollars at the end of the ten-year period, risk-free." Jackson's eyes sparkled as he rattled off the figures. "It's positively intoxicating, isn't it, LuAnn? It just beats the hell out of a hundred dollars a day, doesn't it? You've come a long way in less than a week, you truly have." He laughed heartily. "To start you off, I will advance you the sum of five million dollars, interest-free. That should be sufficient to keep you until the investment earnings come rolling in."

LuAnn swallowed hard at the mention of the gigantic sums. "I don't know nothing about investing, but how can you guarantee me so much money each year?"

Jackson looked disappointed. "The same way I could *guarantee* that you would win the lottery. If I can perform that magic, I think I can handle Wall Street."

"What if something should happen to me?"

"The contract you will be signing binds your heirs and assigns." He nodded at Lisa. "Your daughter. However, that income would go to her and at the end of the ten-year period so would the principal amount. There's also a power of attorney form. I took the liberty of already having filled in the notary panel. I'm a man of many talents." He chuckled lightly. From out of the darkness, Jackson extended the packet of documents and a pen to her. "They're clearly marked where your signature is required. I trust that you are satisfied with the terms. I told you from the start that they would be generous, didn't I?"

LuAnn hesitated for an instant.

"Is there a problem, LuAnn?" Jackson asked sharply.

She shook her head, quickly signed the documents, and handed them back. Jackson took the documents and slid open a compartment in the console of the limo.

LuAnn heard Jackson make some tapping sounds and a loud screech ensued and then stopped.

Jackson said, "Faxes are wonderful things especially when time is of the essence. Within ten minutes the funds will be wired into my account." He picked the papers up as they slid out of the machine and placed them back into his briefcase.

"Your bags are in the trunk. I have your plane tickets and hotel reservations with me. I have planned your itinerary out for the first twelve months. It will be a great deal of travel; however, I think the scenery will be pleasant enough. I have honored your request to travel to Sweden, the land of your maternal ancestors. Think of it all as an extremely long vacation. I may have you end up in Monaco. They have no personal income tax. However, out of an abundance of caution I'm putting together and thoroughly documenting an intricate cover story for you. In sum, you left the States as a very young girl. You met and married a wealthy foreign national. The money will be kept only in foreign banks and offshore accounts. U.S. banks have stringent reporting requirements to the IRS. None of your money will ever, ever be kept in the United States. However, keep in mind that you will be traveling under a United States passport as a

United States citizen. Some accounts of your wealth may well trickle back here. We have to be prepared for that. However, if the money is all your husband's, who is not an American citizen, who does not reside at any time in this country, who earns no income directly in America, or from investments or business endeavors connected to this country, then, generally speaking, the IRS cannot touch you. I won't bore you with the complex tax rules having to do with U.S. source income such as interest on bonds issued by U.S. concerns, dividends paid by U.S. corporations, other transactions and sales of property having some tangible connection to the United States that could trip up the unwary. My people will take care of all that. Believe me when I say it won't be a problem."

LuAnn reached out for the tickets.

"Not quite yet, LuAnn, we have some steps to take. The police," he said pointedly.

"I took care of that."

"Oh, did you now?" His tone was one of amusement. "Well, I would be very surprised if New York's Finest weren't stationing themselves at every airport, bus, and train station right this very minute. Since you're a felon fleeing across state lines, they've probably called the FBI in as well. They're sharp. It's not like they'll be waiting patiently at your hotel for you to show up." He looked out the window of the limo. "We have some preparations to take care of. It'll give the police additional time to set up their net; however, it's a trade-off we have to make."

As Jackson was talking, LuAnn felt the limo slow down and then stop. Then she heard a long, slow clanking sound, as though a door were being raised. When it stopped, the limo pulled through and then stopped again.

The limo phone rang and Jackson quickly

answered it. He listened for a few moments and then hung up. "Confirmation that the hundred million dollars has been received; though it's after regular banking hours, I'd had special arrangements in place. Omniscience is such a rewarding gift."

He patted the seat. "Now I need you to sit next to me. First, close your eyes and then give me your hand so I can guide you," Jackson said, reaching for it out of the darkness.

"Why do I have to close my eyes?"

"Indulge me, LuAnn. I can't resist a little drama in life, particularly since it's so rare. I can assure you that what I'm about to do will be absolutely essential to your safely evading the police and starting your new life."

LuAnn started to question him again but then thought better of it. She took his hand and closed her eyes.

He settled her down beside him. She could feel a light shine down on her features. She jerked as she felt the scissors cut into her hair. Jackson's breath was right next to her ear. "I would advise you not to do that again. It's hard enough to do this in such a small space with limited time and equipment. I wouldn't want to do you serious damage." Jackson continued cutting until her hair stopped just above her ears. He periodically stuffed the cut hair into a large trash bag. A wet substance was continually run through the remaining strands and then it quickly hardened almost like concrete. Jackson used a styling brush to manipulate the remaining strands into place.

Jackson next clamped a portable mirror surrounded by non-heating light bulbs to the edge of the limo's console. Ordinarily, with the nose job he was going to perform, he would employ two mirrors to test profile constantly; however, he didn't have that

167

luxury sitting in a limo in a Manhattan underground parking garage. He opened up his kit, a ten-tray case filled with makeup supplies and a myriad of tools with which to apply them and then set to work. She felt his nimble fingers flying over her face. He blocked out her eyebrows with Kryolan's eyebrow plastic, covered them with a sealer, dressed the area with a creme stick, and then powdered it. Then he created totally new ones using a small brush. He thoroughly cleansed the lower part of her face with rubbing alcohol. He applied spirit gum to her nose, and let it dry. While it did so, he applied K-Y lubricating jelly to his fingers so the putty he was going to use wouldn't stick to them. He let the putty heat up in his hand, and then commenced applying the malleable substance to her nose, methodically kneading and pressing until a satisfactory shape was created. "Your nose is long and straight, LuAnn, classic, really. However, a little putty, a little shadowing and highlighting and, *voilà*, we have a thick, crooked piece of cartilage that isn't nearly as becoming. However, it's only temporary. Everyone, after all, is only temporary." He chuckled lightly at this philosophical statement as he went through the process of stippling the putty with a black stipple sponge, powdering the surface, stippling in a foundation color, and adding rouge to the nares to give a natural appearance. Using subtle shadowing and highlights, he made LuAnn's eyes seem closer together, and made her chin and jawline seem less prominent with the aid of powders and creams. Rouge was placed skillfully on the cheekbones to lessen their impact on her overall appearance.

She felt him gently examining the wound on her jaw. "Nasty cut. Souvenir from your trailer experience?" When LuAnn didn't answer, he said, "You know this will require some stitching. Even with that, it's deep enough that it probably will scar. Don't worry, after I'm done, it will be invisible. But eventually, you may want to consider plastic surgery." He chuckled again and added, "In my professional opinion."

Next, Jackson carefully painted her lips. "A little thinner, I'm afraid, than the classical model, LuAnn. You may want to consider collagen at some point."

It was all LuAnn could do not to jump up and run screaming from him. She had no idea what she was going to look like; it was as though he were some mad scientist bringing her back from the dead.

"I'm stippling in freckles now, along the forehead, around the nose and cheeks. If I had time, I'd do your hands as well, but I don't. No one would notice anyway, most people are so unobservant." He spread open the collar of her shirt and applied foundation and stippling around her neck. Then he buttoned her shirt up, repacked his equipment, and guided her back to her seat.

"There's a small mirror in the compartment next to you," Jackson informed her.

LuAnn slowly pulled out the mirror and held it up in front of her face. She gasped. Looking back at her was a redheaded woman with short, spiky hair, a very light, almost albino complexion, and an abundance of freckles. Her eyes were smaller and closer together, her chin and jawline less prominent, the cheeks flat and oval. Her lips were a deep red and made her mouth look huge. Her nose was much broader and bore a distinctive curve to the right. Her dark eyebrows were now tinted a much lighter color. She was completely unrecognizable to herself.

Jackson tossed something on her lap. She looked down. It was a passport. She opened it. The photo staring back at her was the same woman whom she had looked at in the mirror.

"Wonderful work, wouldn't you say?" Jackson said.

As LuAnn looked up, Jackson hit a switch and a light illuminated him. Or her, rather, as LuAnn received a second jolt. Sitting across from her was her double, or the double of the woman she had just become. The same short red hair, facial complexion, crooked nose, everything – it was as though she had suddenly discovered a twin. The only difference was she was wearing jeans and her twin was wearing a dress.

LuAnn was too amazed to speak.

Jackson quietly clapped his hands together. "I've impersonated women before, but I believe this is the first time I've impersonated an impersonation. That photo of me, by the way. Taken this morning. I think I hit it rather well, although I don't think I did your bust justice. Well, even 'twins' needn't be identical in every respect." He smiled at her shocked look. "No need to applaud, however I do think that considering the working conditions, it does deserve some degree of acclaim."

The limo started moving again. They exited the garage and a little more than half an hour later, they arrived at JFK.

Before the driver opened the door, Jackson looked sharply at LuAnn. "Don't put on your hat or your glasses, as that suggests attempting to hide one's features and you could conceivably mess up the makeup. Remember, rule number one: When trying to hide, make yourself as obvious as possible, put yourself right out in the open. Seeing adult twins together is fairly rare, however, but while people – the police included – will notice us, perhaps even gawk, there will be no levels of suspicion. In addition, the police will be looking for one woman. When they see two together, and twins at that, even

170

with a child, they'll discount us entirely, even as they stare at us. It's just human nature. They have a lot of ground to cover and not much time."

Jackson reached across for Lisa. LuAnn automatically blocked his hand, looking at him suspiciously.

"LuAnn, I am trying my best to get you and this little girl safely out of the country. We will shortly be walking through a squadron of police and FBI agents who will be doing their best to apprehend you. Believe me, I have no interest in keeping your daughter, but I do need her for a very specific reason."

Finally, LuAnn let go. They climbed out of the limo. In high heels Jackson was a little taller than LuAnn. She noted that he had a long, lean build that, she had to admit, looked good in the stylish clothing. He put a black coat on over his dark dress.

"Come on," he said to LuAnn. She stiffened at the new tone of his voice. Now he also *sounded* exactly like her.

"Where's Charlie?" LuAnn asked as they entered the terminal a few minutes later, a chubby skycap with the bags in tow.

"Why?" Jackson said quietly. He expertly maneuvered in the high heels.

LuAnn shrugged. "Just wondering. He'd been taking me around before. I thought I'd see him today."

"I'm afraid Charlie's duties with you are at an end."

"Oh."

"Don't worry, LuAnn, you're in much better hands." They entered the terminal and Jackson glanced up ahead. "Please act natural; we're twin sisters, if anyone asks, which they won't. However, I have identification to support that cover just in case they do. Let me do the talking."

LuAnn looked up ahead and swallowed quickly as she eyed the quartet of police officers carefully scrutinizing each of the patrons at the crowded airport.

They passed by the officers, who did indeed stare at them. One even took a moment to check out Jackson's long legs as the coat he was wearing flapped open. Jackson seemed pleased at the attention. Then, just as Jackson had predicted, the police quickly lost interest in them and focused on other persons coming into the terminal.

Jackson and LuAnn stopped near the international flight check-in for British Airways. "I'll check in at the ticket counter for you while you wait over near that snack bar." Jackson pointed across the broad aisle of the terminal.

"Why can't I check in myself?"

"How many times have you flown overseas?"

"I ain't never flown."

"Precisely. I can get through the process a lot faster than you. If you messed up something, said something you weren't supposed to, then we might attract some attention that we don't really need right now. Airline personnel aren't the most security conscious people I've ever run across but they're not idiots either and you'd be surprised what they pick up on."

"All right. I don't want to mess nothing up."

"Good, now give me your passport, the one I just gave you." LuAnn did so and watched as Jackson, the skycap behind him, swung Lisa's baby carrier in one hand as he sauntered over to the ticket counter. Jackson had even picked up that mannerism of hers. LuAnn shook her head in awe and moved over to the spot designated by Jackson.

Jackson was in the very short first-class line and it

172

moved very quickly. He rejoined LuAnn in a few minutes. "So far, so good. Now, I wouldn't recommend changing your appearance for several months. You can wash the red dye out of course, although, frankly, I think the color works well on you." His eyes twinkled. "Once things die down, and your hair grows out, you can use the passport I originally made up for you." He handed a second U.S. passport to her, which she quickly put in her bag.

From the corner of his eye, Jackson watched as two men and a woman all dressed in suits moved down the aisle, their eyes sweeping the area. Jackson cleared his throat and LuAnn glanced in their direction and then away again. LuAnn had spied, in one of their hands, a piece of paper. On it was a picture of her, no doubt taken at the press conference. She froze until she felt Jackson's hand inside hers. He gave it a reassuring squeeze. "Those are FBI agents. But just remember that you don't look anything like that photo now. It's as if you're invisible." His confident tones assuaged her fears. Jackson moved forward. "Your flight leaves in twenty minutes. Follow me." They went through security and down to the departure gate and sat down in the waiting area.

"Here." Jackson handed her the passport, along with a small packet. "There's cash, credit cards, and an international driver's license in there, all in your new name. And your new appearance with respect to the driver's license." He took a moment to toy with her hair in a completely clinical fashion. He scrutinized her altered features and came away duly impressed with himself again. Jackson took a moment to grip her by the hand and even patted her shoulder. "Good luck. If you find yourself in difficulty at any time, here is a phone number that will reach me anywhere in the world day or night. I will tell you, though, that unless there is a problem you and I will

173

never meet or speak to each other again." He handed her the card with the number on it.

"Isn't there something you want to say to me, LuAnn?" Jackson was smiling pleasantly.

She looked at him curiously and shook her head. "Like what?"

"Perhaps, thank you?" he said, no longer smiling.

"Thank you," she said very slowly. It was difficult pulling her gaze away from him.

"You're welcome," he said very slowly back, his eyes riveted to hers.

Finally, LuAnn nervously looked down at the card. She hoped she would never have to use it. If she never looked upon Jackson's face again, it would be all right with her. The way she felt around the man was too close to the feeling she had experienced at the cemetery when her father's grave had threatened to swallow her up. When she looked up again, Jackson had disappeared into the crowd.

She sighed. She was already tired of running and now she was about to start a lifetime of just that.

LuAnn took out her passport and looked at its blank pages. That would soon change. Then she turned back to the first page and stared at the strange photo and the stranger name underneath it. A name that would not be so unusual after a while: Catherine Savage from Charlottesville, Virginia. Her mother had been born in Charlottesville before moving as a young girl into the deep South. Her mother had spoken to LuAnn often of the good times she had as a child in the beautiful, rolling countryside of Virginia. Moving to Georgia and marrying Benny Tyler had abruptly ended those good times. LuAnn thought it appropriate that her new identity should call that city her hometown as well. Her new name had been well thought out too. A savage she was and a savage she would remain despite an enormous fortune at her command. She looked at the photo again and her skin tingled as she remembered that it was Jackson staring back at her. She quickly closed the passport and put it away.

She touched her new face gingerly and then looked away after she eyed another policeman making his way toward her. She couldn't tell if he was one of the ones who might have seen Jackson check in for her. If so, what if he watched her get on the plane instead of Jackson? Her mouth went dry and she silently wished that Jackson hadn't left. Her flight was called. As the policeman approached, LuAnn willed herself to stand. As she picked up Lisa her packet of documents tumbled to the floor. Her heart trembling, she bent down to retrieve them with one hand, at the same time awkwardly balancing Lisa in her car seat with her other. She suddenly found herself staring at a pair of black shoes. The cop bent down and looked her over. In one hand he held a photo of her. LuAnn froze for an instant as his dark eyes bored into hers.

A kindly smile emerged on his face. "Let me help you, ma'am. I've got kids of my own. Traveling with them is never easy."

He scooped up the papers, replaced them in the packet, and handed it to her. LuAnn thanked him and he tipped his cap to her before moving off.

LuAnn was sure that if someone had cut her at that instant no blood would have come out. It was all frozen inside her.

Since first-class passengers could board at their leisure, LuAnn took some time to look around; however, her hopes were fading. It was clear that Charlie wasn't coming. She walked down the jet-walk and the flight attendant greeted her warmly while LuAnn marveled at the interior size of the Boeing 747.

"Right this way, Ms. Savage. Beautiful little girl." LuAnn was led up a spiral staircase and escorted to

175

her seat. With Lisa in the seat next to her, LuAnn accepted a glass of wine from the cabin attendant. She again looked around the lavish space in awe and noted the built-in TV and phone at each seat. She had never been on a plane before. This was quite a princely way to experience it for the first time.

The darkness was rapidly gathering as she looked out the window. For now Lisa was content to look around the cabin and LuAnn used the time to think while she sipped on her wine. She took a series of deep breaths and then studied the other passengers as they entered the first-class compartment. Some were elderly and expensively dressed. Others were in business suits. One young man wore jeans and a sweatshirt. LuAnn thought she recognized him as a member of a big-time rock band. She settled back in her seat and then jumped a bit as the plane pushed back from its moorings. The flight attendants went through their pre-flight safety drill and within ten minutes the giant plane was lumbering down the runway. LuAnn held on to the sides of her seat and gritted her teeth as the plane rocked and swayed while it gathered speed. She didn't dare look outside the window. Oh Lord, what had she done? One of her arms flew protectively over Lisa, who appeared far calmer than her mother. Then with a graceful motion, the plane lifted into the air and the lurching and swaying stopped. LuAnn felt as though she were floating into the sky on an enormous bubble. A princess on a magic carpet; the image swept into her mind and stayed there. Her grip relaxed, her lips parted. She looked out the window and down at the twinkling lights of the city, the country she was leaving behind. Forever, according to Jackson. She gave a symbolic wave out the window and then leaned back against the seat.

Twenty minutes later she had put on her headphones and was gently swaying her head to some classical music. She jerked upright when the hand fell upon her shoulder and Charlie's voice filtered down to her. He wore the hat she had bought him. His smile was big and genuine, but there was a nervousness evident in his body language, the twitching of his eyes. LuAnn took off the headphones.

"Good gosh," he whispered. "If I hadn't recognized Lisa I would've passed right by you. What the hell happened?"

"A long story." She gripped his wrist tightly and let out a barely audible sigh. "Does this mean you're finally gonna tell me your real name, Charlie?"

A light rain had started to fall on the city shortly after the 747 had lifted off. Walking slowly down the street in midtown Manhattan with the aid of a cane, the man in the black trench coat and waterproof hat seemed not to notice the inclement weather. Jackson's appearance had changed drastically since his last encounter with LuAnn. He had aged at least forty years. Heavy pouches hung under his eyes, a fringe of brittle white hair circled the back of his bald head, which was mottled all over with age spots. The nose was long and saggy, the chin and neck equally so. His gait, slow and measured, matched the feebleness of his character. He often aged himself at night, as though when darkness came he felt compelled to shrink down, to draw nearer to old age, to death. He looked up into the cloudy sky. The plane would be over Nova Scotia about now as it traveled along its convex path to Europe.

And she had not gone alone; Charlie had gone off with her. Jackson had stayed behind after dropping off LuAnn and watched Charlie board the aircraft, not knowing his employer was only a few feet away. That arrangement might work out all right after all, Jackson

177

thought. He had doubts about LuAnn, serious doubts. She had withheld information from him, usually an unpardonable sin. He had managed to avoid a serious problem by eliminating Romanello, and he had to concede that the difficulty had been partially his in the making. He had, after all, hired Romanello to kill his chosen one if she had failed to accept his offer. However, he had never before had a winner on the run from the police. He would do what he always did when confronted with a possible disaster: He would sit back and observe. If things continued to run smoothly he would do nothing. At the slightest sign of trouble, however, he would take immediate and forceful action. So having capable Charlie along with her might prove to be a good thing. LuAnn was different from the others, that was certain.

Jackson pulled his collar up and slowly ambled down a side street. New York City in the darkness and rain held no terror for him. He was heavily armed and expertly skilled in innumerable ways of killing anything that breathed. Anyone targeting the "old man" as easy pickings would painfully realize the mistake. Jackson had no desire to kill. It was sometimes necessary, but he took no pleasure in it. Only the attainment of money, power, or ideally both, would suffice as justification in his mind. He had far better things to do with his time.

Jackson turned his face once again to the sky. The light rain fell on the latex folds of his "face." He licked at them; they were cool to the touch, felt good against his real skin. Godspeed to you both, he said under his breath and then smiled.

And God help you if you ever betray me.

He continued down the street, thinking intently and whistling while he did so. It was now time to plan for next month's winner.

PART TWO

Ten Years Later

EIGHTEEN

The small private jet landed at the airstrip at Charlottesville-Albemarle Airport and taxied to a halt. It was nearly ten o'clock at night and the airport had pretty much shut down for the day. The Gulfstream V was the day's last incoming flight in fact. The limousine was waiting on the tarmac. Three people quickly exited the plane and climbed into the limo, which immediately drove off and a few minutes later was heading south on Route 29.

Inside the limo, the woman took off her glasses and laid her arm across the young girl's shoulder. Then LuAnn Tyler slumped back against the seat and took a deep breath. Home. Finally, they were back in the United States. All the years of planning had finally been executed. She had thought about little else for some time now. She glanced over at the man who sat in the rear-facing seat. His eyes stared straight ahead, his thick fingers drummed a somber rhythm across the car's window. Charlie looked concerned, and he was concerned, but he still managed a smile, a reassuring grin. If nothing else he had always been reassuring for her over the last ten years.

He put his hands in his lap and cocked his head at her. "You scared?" he asked.

LuAnn nodded and then looked down at ten-year-old Lisa, who had immediately slumped over her mother's lap and fallen into an exhausted sleep. The trip had been a long and tedious one.

"How about you?" she asked back.

He shrugged his thick shoulders. "We prepared as well as we could, we understand the risks. Now we just live with it." He smiled again, this time more broadly. "We'll be okay."

She smiled back at him, her eyes deep and heavy. They had been through a lot over the last decade. If she never climbed aboard another airplane, never passed through another Customs post, never again wondered what country she was in, what language she should be trying to muddle through, it would be perfectly fine with her. The longest trip she wanted to take for the rest of her life was strolling down to the mailbox to pick up her mail, or driving down to the mall to go shopping. God, if it could only be that easy. She winced slightly and rubbed in a distracted fashion at her temples.

Charlie quickly picked up on this. Over the years he had acquired a heightened sensitivity to the subtle tracks of her emotions. He scrutinized Lisa for a long moment to make sure she was indeed sleeping. Satisfied, he undid his seat belt, sat down next to LuAnn, and spoke in soft tones.

"He doesn't know we've come back. Jackson doesn't know."

She whispered back to him. "We don't know that, Charlie. We can't be sure. My God, I don't know what's scaring me the most: the police or him. No, that's a lie. I know, it's him. I'd take the police over him any day. He told me never to come back here. Never. Now I am back. We all are."

Charlie laid his hand on top of hers and spoke as calmly as he could. "If he knew, do you think he'd have let us get this far? We took about as circuitous a route as anybody could take. Five plane changes, a train trip, four countries, we zigzagged halfway across the world to get here. He doesn't know. And

182

you know what, even if he does he's not going to care. It's been ten years. The deal's expired. Why should he care now?"

"Why should he do any of the things he's done? You tell me. He does them because he wants to."

Charlie sighed, undid his jacket button, and lay back against the seat.

LuAnn turned to him and gently rubbed his shoulder. "We're back. You're right, we made the decision and now we're going to live with it. It's not like I'm going to announce to the whole world that I'm around again. We're going to live a nice, quiet life."

"In considerable luxury. You saw the photos of the house."

LuAnn nodded. "It looks beautiful."

"An old estate. About ten thousand square feet. Been on the market for a long time, but with an asking price of six million bucks, can't say I'm surprised. Let me tell you, we got a deal at three point five mil. But then I drive a hard bargain. Although, of course, we dumped another million into renovation. About fourteen months' worth, but we had the time, right?"

"And secluded?"

"Very. Almost three hundred acres, plus or minus as they say. About a hundred of those acres are open, 'gently rolling land.' That description was in the brochure. Growing up in New York, I never saw so much green grass. Beautiful Piedmont, Virginia, or so the realtor kept telling me on all those trips I took over here to scout for homes. And it was the prettiest home I saw. True it took a lot of work to get it in shape, but I got some good people, architects and what-not representing our interests. It's got a truckload of outbuildings, caretaker's house, three-stall horse barn, a couple of cottages, all vacant by

183

the way; I don't see us taking in renters. Anyway, all those big estates have that stuff. It's got a pool. Lisa will love that. Plenty of room for a tennis court. The works. But then there's dense forest all around. Look at it as a hardwood moat. And I've already started shopping around for a firm to construct a security fence and gate around the property line fronting the road. Probably should have already gotten that done."

"Like you didn't have enough to do. You do too much as it is."

"I don't mind. I kind of like it."

"And my name's not on the ownership papers?"

"Catherine Savage appears nowhere. We used a straw man for the contract and closing. Deed was transferred in the name of the corporation I had set up. That's untraceable back to you."

"I wish I could have changed my name again, just in case he's on the lookout for it."

"That would've been nice except the cover story he built for you, the same one we used to appease the IRS, has you as Catherine Savage. It's complicated enough without adding another layer to it. Geez, the death certificate we had made up for your 'late' husband was hell to get."

"I know." She sighed heavily.

He glanced over at her. "Charlottesville, Virginia, home to lot of rich and famous, I hear. Is that why you picked it? Private, you can live like a hermit, and nobody'll care?"

"That was one of two reasons."

"And the other?"

"My mother was born here," LuAnn said, her voice dropping a notch as she delicately traced the hem of her skirt. "She was happy here, at least she told me she was. And she wasn't rich either." She fell silent, her eyes staring off. She jolted back and

184

looked at Charlie, her face reddening slightly. "Maybe some of that happiness will rub off on us, what do you think?"

"I think so long as I'm with you and this little one," he said, gently stroking Lisa's cheek, "I'm a happy man."

"She's all enrolled in the private school?"

Charlie nodded. "St. Anne's-Belfield. Pretty exclusive, low student-to-teacher ratio. But, hell, Lisa's educational qualifications are outstanding. She speaks multiple languages, been all over the world. Already done things most adults will never do their whole life."

"I don't know, maybe I should have hired a private tutor."

"Come on, LuAnn, she's been doing that ever since she could walk. She needs to be around other kids. It'll be good for her. It'll be good for you too. You know what they say about time away."

She suddenly smiled at him slyly. "Are you feeling claustrophobic with us, Charlie?"

"You bet I am. I'm gonna start staying out late. Might even take up some hobbies like golf or something." He grinned at LuAnn to show her he was only joking.

"It's been a good ten years, hasn't it?" Her voice was touched with anxiety.

"Wouldn't trade 'em for anything," he said.

Let's hope the next ten are just as good, LuAnn said to herself. She laid her head against his shoulder. When she had stared out at the New York skyline all those years ago, she had been brimming with excitement, with the potential of all the good she could do with the money. She had promised herself that she would and she had fulfilled that promise. Personally, however, those wonderful dreams had not been met. The last ten years had only been good to her if you

185

defined good as constantly on the move, fearful of discovery, having pangs of guilt every time she bought something because of how she had come by the money. She had always heard that the incredibly rich were never really happy, for a variety of reasons. Growing up in poverty LuAnn had never believed that, she simply took it to be a ruse of the wealthy. Now, she knew it to be true, at least in her own case.

As the limo drove on, she closed her eyes and tried to rest. She would need it. Her "second" new life was about to commence.

NINETEEN

Thomas Donovan sat staring at his computer screen in the frenetic news room of the *Washington Tribune*. Journalistic awards from a number of distinguished organizations dotted the walls and shelves of his cluttered cubicle, including a Pulitzer he had won before he was thirty. Donovan was now in his early fifties but still possessed the drive and fervor of his youth. Like most investigative journalists, he could dish out a strong dose of cynicism about the workings of the real world, if only because he had seen the worst of it. What he was working on now was a story the substance of which disgusted him.

He was glancing at some of his notes when a shadow fell across his desk.

"Mr. Donovan?"

Donovan looked up into the face of a young kid from the mail room.

"Yeah?"

"This just came in for you. I think it's some research you had requested."

Donovan thanked him and took the packet. He dug into it with obvious zeal.

The lottery story he was working on had so much potential. He had already done a great deal of research. The national lottery took in billions of dollars each year in profits and the amount was growing at more than twenty percent a year. The government paid out about half its revenue in prize money, about ten percent to vendors and other operating costs, and kept forty percent as profit, a margin most companies would kill for. Surveys and scholars had argued for years about whether the lottery amounted to a regressive tax with the poor the chief loser. The government maintained that, demographically, the poor didn't spend a disproportionate share of their income on the game. Such arguments didn't sit well with Donovan. He knew for a fact that millions of the people who played the game were borderline poverty-level, squandering Social Security money, food stamps, and anything else they could get their hands on to purchase the chance at the easy life, even though the odds were so astronomically high as to be farcical. And the government advertisements were highly misleading when it came to detailing precisely what those odds were. But that wasn't all. Donovan had turned up an astonishing seventy-five percent bankruptcy rate per year for the winners. Nine out of every twelve winners each year subsequently had declared bankruptcy. His angle had to do with financial management companies and other scheming, sophisticated types getting hold of these poor people and basically ripping them off. Charities calling up and hounding them relentlessly. Purveyors of every type of sybaritic gratification selling them just about anything they didn't need, calling their wares "must-have" status items for the nouveaux riches and charging a thousand percent markup for their trouble. It didn't stop there. The sudden wealth had destroyed families and life-time friendships as greed supplanted all rational emotions.

And the government was just as much to blame, Donovan felt, for these financial crashes. About twelve years ago they had bestowed the initial prize in one lump sum and given it tax-deferred status for one year to attract more and more players. The advertisements had played up this fact dramatically, touting the winnings as "tax-free" in the large print and counting on the "fine print" to inform the public that the amounts were actually tax-deferred and only for one year. Previously, the winnings had been paid out over time and taxes taken out automatically. Now the winners were on their own as far as structuring the payment of taxes went. Some, Donovan had learned, thought they owed no tax at all and went out and spent the money freely. All the earnings on that principal were subject to numerous taxes as well, and hefty ones. The Feds just hung the winners out there with a pat on the back and a big check. And when the winners weren't astute enough to set up sophisticated accounting and financial systems, the tax boys would come after them and take every last dime they had, under the guise of penalties and interest and what-not, and leave them poorer than when they started out.

It was a game designed for the ultimate destruction of the winner and it was done under the veil of the government's doing good for its people. It was the devil's game and our own government was doing it to us, Donovan was firmly convinced. And the government did it for one reason and one reason only: money. Just like everybody else. He had watched other papers give the problem lip service. And whenever a real attack or exposé was formed in the news media, government lottery officials quickly squelched it with oceans of statistics showing how much good the lottery monies were doing. The public thought the money was earmarked for education, highway maintenance, and the like, but a large part of it went into the general purpose funds and ended up in some very interesting places, far away from buying school books and filling potholes.

Lottery officials received fat paychecks and fatter bonuses. Politicians who supported the lottery saw large funds flow to their states. All of it stunk and Donovan felt it was high time the truth came out. His pen would defend the less fortunate, just as it had over his entire career. If he did nothing else, Donovan would at least shame the government into reconsidering the morals of this gargantuan revenue source. It might not change anything, but he was going to give it his best.

He refocused on the packet of documents. He had tested his theory on the bankruptcy rate going back five years. The documents he was holding took those results back another seven years. As he paged through year after year of lottery winners, the results were almost identical, the ratio staying at virtually nine out of twelve a year declaring personal bankruptcy. Absolutely astonishing. He happily thumbed through the pages. His instincts had been dead-on. It was no fluke.

Then he abruptly stopped and stared at one page, his smile disappearing. The page represented the list of twelve consecutive lottery winners from exactly ten years ago. It couldn't be possible. There must be some mistake. Donovan picked up the phone and made a call to the research service he had engaged to do the study. No, there was no mistake, he was told. Bankruptcy filings were matters of public record.

Donovan slowly hung up the phone and stared again at the page. Herman Rudy, Bobbie Jo Reynolds, LuAnn Tyler, the list went on and on, twelve winners in a row. Not one of them had declared personal bankruptcy. Not one. Every twelve-month period for the lottery except this one had resulted in nine bankruptcies.

Most reporters of Thomas Donovan's caliber lived or died by two intangibles: perseverance and instincts. Donovan's instinct was that the story he might be on to right now would make his other angle seem about as exciting as an article on pruning.

He had some sources to check and he wanted to do them in more privacy than the crowded newsroom allowed. He threw the file in his battered briefcase and quickly left the office. In non-rush hour traffic he reached his small apartment in Virginia in twenty minutes. Twice divorced with no children, Donovan led a life focused solely on his work. He had a relationship slowly percolating with Alicia Crane, a well-known Washington socialite from a wealthy family, which had once been politically well connected. He had never been fully comfortable moving in these circles; however, Alicia was supportive and devoted to him, and truth be known, flitting around the edges of her luxurious existence wasn't so bad.

He settled into his home office and picked up the phone. There was a definite way to obtain information on people, particularly rich people, no matter how guarded their lives. He dialed the number of a longtime source at the Internal Revenue Service. Donovan gave that person the names of the twelve consecutive lottery winners who had not declared bankruptcy. Two hours later he got a call back. As he listened, Donovan checked off the names on his lists. He asked a few more questions, thanked his friend, hung up, and looked down at his list. All the names were crossed off except for one. Eleven of the lottery winners had duly filed their tax returns each year, his source had reported. That was as far as his source would go, however. He would tell Donovan no specifics except to add that the income reported on all of the eleven tax returns was enormous. While the question still intrigued Donovan as to how all of them had avoided bankruptcy and apparently done very well over the last ten years, another more puzzling question had emerged.

He stared down at the name of the sole lottery winner that wasn't crossed off. According to his source, this person had not filed any tax returns, at least under her own name. In fact this person had outright disappeared. Donovan had a vague recollection of the reason why. Two murders, her boyfriend in rural Georgia and another man. Drugs had been involved. The story had not interested him all that much ten years ago. He would not have recalled it at all except that the woman had disappeared just after winning a hundred million dollars and the money had disappeared with her. Now his curiosity was much greater as he eyed that particular name on his list: "LuAnn Tyler." She must have switched identities on her run from the murder charge. With her lottery winnings she could easily have invented a new life for herself.

Donovan smiled for an instant as it suddenly occurred to him that he might have a way of discovering LuAnn Tyler's new identity. And maybe a lot more. At least he could try.

The next day Donovan telephoned the sheriff in Rikersville, Georgia, LuAnn's hometown. Roy Waymer had died five years ago. Ironically, the current sheriff was Billy Harvey, Duane's uncle. Harvey was very talkative with Donovan when the subject of LuAnn came up.

"She got Duane killed," he said angrily. "She got him involved in those drugs sure as I'm talking to you. The Harvey family ain't got much, but we got our pride."

"Have you heard from her in any way over the last ten years?" Donovan asked.

Billy Harvey paused for a lengthy moment. "Well, she sent down some money."

"Money?"

"To Duane's folks. They didn't ask for it, I can tell you that."

"Did they keep it?"

"Well, they're on in years and poorer'n dirt. You don't just turn your back on that kind of money."

"How much are we talking about?"

"Two hundred thousand dollars. If that doesn't show LuAnn's guilty conscience, I don't know what would."

Donovan whistled under his breath. "Did you try to trace the money?"

"I wasn't sheriff then, but Roy Waymer did. He even had some local FBI boys over to help, but they never turned up a durn thing. She's helped some other people round here too, but we could never get a handle on her whereabouts from them either. Like she was a damned ghost or something."

"Anything else?"

"Yeah, you ever talk to her, you tell her that the Harvey family ain't forgot, not even after all these years. That murder warrant is still outstanding. We get her back to Georgia, she'll be spending some nice quality time with us. I'm talking twenty to life. No statute of limitations on murder. Am I right?"

"I'll let her know, Sheriff, thanks. Oh, I'm wondering if you could send me a copy of the file on the case. The autopsy reports, investigative notes, forensics, the works?"

"You really think you can find her after all this time?"

"I've been doing this kind of stuff for thirty years and I'm pretty good at it. I'm sure going to try."

"Well, then I'll send it up to you, Mr. Donovan."

Donovan gave Harvey the *Trib*'s FedEx number

and address, hung up, and wrote down some notes. Tyler had a new name, that was for certain. In order even to begin to track her down, he had to find out what that name was.

He spent the next week exploring every crevice of LuAnn's life. He got copies of her parents' death notices from the *Rikersville Gazette*. Obituaries were full of interesting items: birthplaces, relatives, and other items that could conceivably lead him to some valuable information. Her mother had been born in Charlottesville, Virginia. Donovan talked to the relatives listed in the obituary, at least the few who were alive, but received few useful facts. LuAnn had never tried to contact them.

Next, Donovan dug up as many facts as he could on LuAnn's last day in the country. Donovan had conversations with personnel from the NYPD and the FBI field office in New York. Sheriff Waymer had seen her on TV and immediately notified the police in New York that LuAnn was wanted in Georgia in connection with a double murder and drug trafficking. They, in turn, had put a blanket over the bus and train stations, and the airports. In a city of seven million, that was the best they could do; they couldn't exactly put up roadblocks. However, there hadn't been one sign of the woman. That had greatly puzzled the FBI. According to the agent Donovan talked to who was somewhat familiar with the file, the Bureau wanted to know how a twenty-year-old woman with a seventh-grade education from rural Georgia, carrying a baby no less, had waltzed right through their net. An elaborate disguise and cover documents were out of the question, or so they thought. The police had thrown out their net barely a half hour after she had appeared on national television. No one was that fast. And all the money had disappeared as well. At the time, some at the FBI had wondered whether she had had help. But that lead had never been followed up as other crises of more national importance had swallowed up the Bureau's time and manpower. They had officially concluded that LuAnn Tyler had not left the country, but had simply driven out of New York or taken the subway to a suburb and then lost herself somewhere in the country or perhaps Canada. The NYPD had reported its failure to Sheriff Waymer and that had been the end of it. Until now. Now, Donovan was greatly intrigued. His gut told him that LuAnn Tyler had left the country. Somehow she had gotten past the law. If she had gotten on a plane, then he had something to work with.

He could narrow the list down in any event. He had a certain day to work with, even a block of hours on that day. Donovan would begin with the premise that LuAnn Tyler had fled the country. He would focus on international flights departing from JFK during that time frame, ten years ago. If the records at JFK turned up nothing, he would focus on LaGuardia and then Newark International Airport. At least it was a start. There were far fewer international flights than domestic. If he had to start checking domestic flights, he concluded he would have to try another angle. There were simply too many. As he was about to start this process a package arrived from Sheriff Harvey.

Donovan munched on a sandwich at his cubicle while he looked through the files. The autopsy photos were understandably gruesome; however, they didn't faze the veteran reporter. He had seen far worse in his career. After an hour of reading he laid the file aside and made some notes. From the looks of it, he believed LuAnn Tyler to be innocent of the charges for which Harvey wanted to arrest her. He had done some independent digging of his own into

Rikersville, Georgia. By virtually all accounts, Duane Harvey was a lazy good-for-nothing with no greater ambition than to spend his life drinking beer, chasing women, and adding nothing whatsoever of value to mankind. LuAnn Tyler, on the other hand, had been described to him by several persons who had known her as hardworking, honest, and a loving, caring mother to her little girl. Orphaned as a teenager, she seemed to have done as well as she could under the circumstances. Donovan had seen photos of her, had even managed to dig up a videotape of the press conference announcing her as the lottery winner ten years ago. She was a looker all right, but there was something behind that beauty. She hadn't scraped by all those years on her physical assets alone.

Donovan finished his sandwich and took a sip of his coffee. Duane Harvey had been cut up badly. The other man, Otis Burns, had also died from knife wounds to his upper torso. There had been serious but nonfatal head trauma also present, and the clear signs of a struggle. LuAnn's fingerprints had been found on the broken phone receiver and also all over the trailer. No surprise since she happened to live there. There had been one witness account of seeing her in Otis Burns's car that morning. Despite Sheriff Harvey's protests to the contrary, Donovan's research led him to believe that Duane was the drug dealer in the family and had been caught skimming. Burns was probably his supplier. The man had a lengthy rap sheet in neighboring Gwinnett County, all drug related. Burns had probably come to settle the score. Whether LuAnn Tyler knew of Duane's drug dealing was anybody's guess. She had worked at the truck stop up until the time she had bought her lottery ticket and disappeared only to resurface, however briefly, in New York City. So if she had known of Duane's sideline, she hadn't reaped any discernible benefits from it. Whether she had been in the trailer that morning and had had anything to do with either man's death was also unclear. Donovan really didn't care one way or another. He had no reason to sympathize with Duane Harvey or Otis Burns. At this point he didn't know what he felt about LuAnn Tyler. He did know that he wanted to find her. He wanted that very much.

TWENTY

Jackson sat in a chair in the darkened living room of a luxurious apartment in a prewar building overlooking Central Park. His eyes were closed, his hands neatly folded in his lap. Approaching forty years of age he was still lean and wiry in build. His actual facial features were androgynous, although the years had etched fine lines around his eyes and mouth. His short hair was cut stylishly, his clothing was quietly expensive. His eyes, however, were clearly his most distinctive feature, which he had to disguise very carefully when he was working. He rose and moved slowly through the amply proportioned apartment. The furnishings were eclectic: English, French, and Spanish antiques mixed liberally with Oriental art and sculpture.

He entered an area of his apartment reminiscent of a Broadway star's dressing room. It was his makeup room and workshop. Special recessed lighting covered the ceiling. Multiple mirrors with their own special nonheating bulbs ringed the room. Two padded reclining leather chairs sat in front of two of the largest mirrors. The chairs had casters which allowed them to be rolled about the room. Innumerable photos were neatly pinned to cork bulletin boards on the walls. Jackson was an avid photographer, and many of his subjects were the basis for most of the identities he had created over the years. Both full wigs and hairpieces, neatly separated into toupees and falls, lined one wall, each hanging on special cotton-covered wire. Customized wall cabinets housed dozens of latex caps and other body pieces along with acrylic teeth, caps, and molds, and other synthetic materials and putties. One massive storage unit contained absorbent cotton, acetone, spirit gum, powders, body makeup; large, medium, and small brushes with bristles of varying rigidity; cake makeup, modeling clay, collodion to make scars and pock marks; crepe hair to make beards, mustaches, and even eyebrows; Derma wax to alter the face, creme makeup, gelatin, makeup palettes; . netting, toupee tape, sponges, ventilating needles to knot hair into net or gauze for beards and wigs; and hundreds of other devices, materials, and substances designed solely to reshape one's appearance. There were three racks of clothing of all descriptions and several full-length mirrors to test the effect of any disguise. In a specially built case with multiple drawers were over fifty complete sets of identification documents that would allow Jackson to travel the world as a man or a woman.

Jackson smiled as he noted various articles in the room. This was where he was most comfortable. Creating his numerous roles was the one constant pleasure in his life. Acting out the part, however, ran a close second as his favorite endeavor. He sat down at the table and ran his hand along its top. He stared into a mirror. Unlike anyone else looking into a mirror, Jackson didn't see his reflection staring back at him. Instead, he saw a blank countenance, one to be manipulated, carved, painted, covered, and massaged into someone else. Although he was perfectly content with his intellect and personality, why be limited to one physical identity one's whole life, he thought, when there was so much more out there to experience? Go anywhere, do anything. He had told that to all twelve of his lottery winners. His baby ducklings all in a row. And they had all bought it, completely and absolutely, for he had been dead right.

Over the last ten years he had earned hundreds of millions of dollars for each of his winners, and billions of dollars for himself. Ironically, Jackson had grown up in very affluent circumstances. "Old money" his family had been. His parents were long dead. The old man had been, in Jackson's eyes, a typical example of those members of the upper class whose money and position had been inherited rather than earned. Jackson's father had been both arrogant and insecure. A politician and insider in Washington for many years, the old man had taken his family connections as far as he could until his decided lack of merit and marketable skills had done him in and the escalator had stopped moving upward. And then he had spent the family money in a futile attempt to regain that upward momentum. And then the money was gone. Jackson, the eldest, had often taken the brunt of the old man's wrath over the years. Upon turning eighteen, Jackson discovered that the large trust fund his grandfather had set up for him had been raided illegally so many times by his father that there wasn't anything left. The continuing rage and physical abuse the old man had wielded after Jackson had confronted him with this discovery had left a profound impression on the son.

The physical bruises eventually had healed. The psychological damage was still with Jackson and his own inner rage seemed to grow exponentially with each year, as though he were trying to outdo his elder in that regard.

It might seem trite to others, Jackson understood that. Lost your fortune? So what? Who gives a damn? But Jackson gave a damn. Year after year he had counted on that money to free him from his father's tyrannical persecution. When that long-held hope was abruptly torn away, the absolute shock had carved a definite change in him. What was rightfully his had been stolen from him, and by the one man who shouldn't have done it, by a man who should have loved his son and wanted the best for him, respected him, wanted to protect him. Instead Jackson had gotten an empty bank account and the hate-filled blows of a madman. And Jackson had taken it. Up to a point. But then he hadn't taken it anymore.

Jackson's father had died unexpectedly. Parents killed their small children every day, never with good reason. By comparison, children killed their parents only rarely, usually with excellent purpose. Jackson smiled lightly as he thought of this. An early chemical experiment, administered through his father's beloved scotch, the rupturing of a brain aneurysm the result. As with any occupation, one had to start somewhere.

When those of average or below-average intelligence committed crimes such as murder, they usually did so clumsily, with no long-range planning or preparation. The result was typically swift arrest and conviction. Among the highly intelligent, serious crimes evolved from careful planning, long-term approaches, many sessions of mental gymnastics. As a result, arrests were rare, convictions even rarer. Jackson was definitely in the latter category.

The eldest son had been compelled to go out and earn the family fortune back. A college merit scholarship to a prestigious university and graduation at the top of his class had been followed by his careful nurturing of old family contacts, for those embers could not be allowed to die out if Jackson's long-range plan was to succeed. Over the years he had devoted himself to mastering a variety of skills, both corporeal and cerebral, that would allow him to pursue his dream of wealth and the power that came with it. His body was as fit and strong as his mind, the one in precise balance with the other. However, ever mindful of not following in his father's footsteps, Jackson had set a far more ambitious goal for himself: He would do all of it while remaining completely invisible from scrutiny. Despite his love of acting, he did not crave the spotlight as his politician father had. He was perfectly content with his audience of one.

And so he had built his invisible empire albeit in a profoundly illegal manner. The results were the same regardless of where the dollars had originated. Go anywhere, do anything. It didn't only apply to his ducklings.

He smiled at this thought as he continued to move through the apartment.

Jackson had a younger brother and sister. His brother had inherited their father's bad habits and consequently expected the world to offer up its best for nothing of comparable value in return. Jackson had given him enough money to live a comfortable but hardly luxurious existence. If he ran through that money there would be no more. For him, that well was dry. His sister was another matter. Jackson cared deeply for her, although she had adored the old man with the blind faith a daughter often shows to her father. Jackson had set her up in grand style but never visited her. The demands on his time were too immense. One night might find him in Hong Kong, the next in London. Moreover, visits with his sister would necessitate conversation and he had no desire to lie to her about what he had done and continued to do for a living. She would never be a

202

part of that world of his. She could live out her days in idle luxury and complete ignorance looking for someone to replace the father she believed had been so kind, so noble.

Still, Jackson had done right by his family. He had no shame, no guilt there. He was not his father. He had allowed himself one constant reminder of the old man, the name he used in all his dealings: Jackson. His father's name was Jack. And no matter what he did, he would always be Jack's son.

As he continued to drift around his apartment he stopped at a window and looked out at a spectacular evening in New York. The apartment he was living in was the very same one he had grown up in, although he had completely gutted it after purchasing it; the ostensible reason had been to modernize and make it suitable for his particular needs. The more subtle motivation had been to obliterate, to the extent he could, the past. That compulsion did not only apply to his physical surroundings. Every time he put on a disguise, he was, in effect, layering over his real self, hiding the person his father had never felt deserved his respect or love. None of the pain would ever be fully wiped away, though, so long as Jackson lived, as long as he could remember. The truth was, every corner of the apartment held the capability of flinging painful memories at him at any moment. But that wasn't so bad, he had long since concluded. Pain was a wonderful motivational tool.

Jackson entered and exited his penthouse by private elevator. No one was ever allowed in his apartment under any circumstances. All mail and other deliveries were left at the front desk; but there was very little of that. Most of his business was conducted by means of phone, computer modem, and fax. He did his own cleaning, but with his traveling schedule and spartan habits, these were not overly time-consuming chores, and were certainly a small price to pay for absolute privacy.

Jackson had created a disguise for his real identity and used it whenever he left his apartment. It was a worst-case scenario plan, in the event the police ever came calling at his door. Horace Parker, the elderly doorman who greeted Jackson each time he left his apartment, was the same one who had tipped his cap to the shy, bookish boy clutching his mother's hand all those years ago. Jackson's family had left New York when he was a teenager, because his father had fallen on bad times, so the aged Parker had accepted Jackson's altered appearance as simply maturation. Now with the "fake" image firmly in people's minds, Jackson was confident that no one could ever identify him.

For Jackson, hearing his given name from Horace Parker was comforting and troubling at the same time. Juggling so many identities was not easy, and Jackson occasionally found himself not responding when he heard his real name uttered. It was actually nice being himself at times, however, since it was an escape of sorts where he could relax, and explore the never-ending intricacies of the city. But no matter which identity he assumed, he always took care of business. Nothing came before that. Opportunities were everywhere and he had exploited them all.

With such limitless capital, he had made the world his playpen for the last decade, and the effects of his manipulations could be felt in financial markets and political paradigms all across the globe. His funds had propelled enterprises as diverse as his identities, from guerrilla activities in Third World countries to the cornering of precious metal markets in the industrialized world. When one-could mold world events in that way, one could profit enormously in the financial markets. Why gamble on futures markets, when one could manipulate the underlying product itself, and thereby know precisely which way the winds would be blowing? It was predictable and logical; risk was controlled. These sorts of climates he loved.

He had exhibited a distinctly benevolent side as well, and large sums of money had been funneled to deserving causes across the globe. But even with those situations he demanded and received ultimate control however invisible it was, figuring that he could exercise far better judgment than anyone else. With so much money at stake, who would deny him? He would never appear on any power list or hold any political office; no financial magazine would ever interview him. He floated from one passion to another with the utmost ease. He could not envision a more perfect existence, although he had to admit that even his global meanderings were becoming a little tedious lately. Redundancy was beginning to usurp originality in his numerous lines of business and he had begun searching around for a new pursuit that would satisfy an ever-growing appetite for the unusual, for the extremely risky, if only to test and retest his skills of control, of domination, and ultimately, of survival.

He entered a smaller room which was filled floor to ceiling with computer equipment. This represented the nerve center of his operation. The flat screens told him in real time how his many world-wide interests were doing. Everything from stock exchanges to futures markets to late-breaking news stories was captured, catalogued, and eventually analyzed here by him.

He craved information, absorbed it like a three-year-old learning a foreign language. He only needed to hear it once and he never forgot it. His eyes scanned each of the screens, and from long habit he was able to separate the important from the mundane, the interesting from the obvious in a matter of minutes. Investments of his colored in soft blue on the screens meant he was doing very well; those mired in harsh red meant he was doing less well. He sighed in satisfaction as a sea of blue blinked back at him.

He went into another, larger room that housed his collection of mementos from past projects. He pulled out a scrapbook and opened it. Inside were photographs of and background information on his twelve precious pieces of gold – the dozen individuals upon whom he had bestowed great wealth and new lives; and who, in turn, had allowed him to recoup his family's fortune. He flipped idly through the pages, occasionally smiling as various pleasant memories flickered through his mind.

He had handpicked his winners carefully, culling them from welfare rolls and bankruptcy filings; logging hundreds of hours tramping through poor, desolate areas of the country, both urban and rural, searching for desperate people who would do anything to change their fortunes – normal law-abiding citizens who would commit what was technically a financial crime of immense proportion without blinking an eye. It was wonderful what the human mind could rationalize given the appropriate inducement.

The lottery had been remarkably easy to fix. It was often that way. People just assumed institutions like that were absolutely above corruption or reproach. They must have forgotten that government lotteries had been banned on a wholesale basis in the last century because of widespread corruption. History did tend to repeat itself, if in a more sophisticated and focused manner. If Jackson had learned one thing over the years it was that nothing, absolutely nothing, was above corruption so long as human beings were involved, because, in truth, most people were not above the lure of the dollar or other material enticements, particularly when they worked around vast sums of money all day. They tended to believe that part of it was rightfully theirs anyway.

And an army of people wasn't required to carry out his plans. Indeed, to Jackson, the notion of a "widespread conspiracy" was an oxymoron anyway.

He had a large group of associates working for him around the globe. However, none of them knew who he really was, where he lived, how he had come by his fortune. None of them were privy to the grand plans he had laid, the worldwide machinations he had orchestrated. They simply performed their small slice of the pie and were very well compensated for doing so. When he wanted something, a bit of information not readily available to him, he would contact one of them and within the hour he would have it. It was the perfect setting for contemplation, planning, and then action – swift, precise, and final.

He completely trusted no one. And with his ability to create flawlessly more than fifty separate identities, why should he? With state-of-the-art computer and communications technology at his fingertips, he could actually be in several different places at the same time. As different people. His smile broadened. Could the world be any more his personal stage?

As he perused one page of the scrapbook his smile faded and was replaced with something more understated; it was a mixture of discernible interest and an emotion that Jackson almost never experienced: uncertainty. And something else. He would never have characterized it as fear; that particular demon never bothered him. Rather he could adequately describe it as a feeling of destiny, of the unmistakable conviction that two trains were on a collision course and no matter what one or the other did, their ominous meeting would take place in a very memorable manner.

Jackson stared at the truly remarkable countenance of LuAnn Tyler. Of the twelve lottery winners, she had been by far the most memorable. There was danger in that woman, danger and a definite volatility that drew Jackson like the most powerful magnet in the world. He had spent several weeks in Rikersville, Georgia, a locale he had picked for one simple reason: its irreversible cycle of poverty, of hopelessness. There were many such places in America, so well documented by the government under such categories as "lowest per capita income levels," "below standard health and education resources," "negative economic growth." Stark fiscal terms that did little or nothing to enlighten anyone as to the people behind the statistics; to shed light on a large segment of the population's free fall into misery. Ever the capitalist, Jackson surprisingly did not mind the added element of his actually doing some good here. He never picked rich people to win, although he had no doubt most of them would have been far easier to persuade than the poor he solicited.

He had discovered LuAnn Tyler as she rode the bus to work. Jackson had sat across from her, in disguise, of course, blending into the background in his torn jeans, stained shirt, and Georgia Bulldogs cap, a scruffy beard covering the lower part of his face, his piercing eyes hidden behind thick glasses. Her appearance had struck him immediately. She seemed out of place down here; everyone else looked so unhealthy, so hopeless, as though the youngest among them were already counting the days until burial. He had watched her play with her daughter; listened to her greet the people around her, and watched their dismal spirits noticeably lifted by her thoughtful comments. He had proceeded to investigate every element of LuAnn's life, from her impoverished background to her life in a trailer home with Duane Harvey. He had visited that trailer several times while LuAnn and her "boyfriend" had not been there. He had seen the small touches LuAnn had employed to keep the place neat and clean despite Duane Harvey's slovenly lifestyle. Everything having to do with Lisa was kept separate and immaculate by LuAnn. Jackson had seen that clearly. Her daughter was her life.

Disguised as a truck driver, he had spent many a night in the roadside diner where LuAnn worked. He had watched her carefully, seen the terms of her life grow more and more desperate, observed her stare woefully into her infant daughter's eyes, dreaming of a better life. And then, after all this observation, he had chosen her as one of the fortunate few. A decade ago.

And then he had not seen or spoken to her in ten years; however, a rare week went by that he did not at least think of her. At first he had kept quite a watchful eye on her movements, but as the years went by and she continued to move from country to country in accordance with his wishes, his diligence had lessened considerably. Now, she was pretty much off his radar screen entirely. The last he had heard she was in New Zealand. Next year could find her in Monaco, Scandinavia, China, he well knew. She would float from one locale to the next until she died. She would never return to the United States, of that he was certain.

Jackson had been born to great wealth, to every material advantage, and then it had all been taken away. He had had to earn it back through his skill, his sweat, his nerve. LuAnn Tyler had been born to nothing, had worked like a dog for pennies, no way out, and look at her now. He had given LuAnn Tyler the world, allowing her to become who she had always wanted to be: someone other than LuAnn Tyler. Jackson smiled. With his complete love of deception, how could he not appreciate that irony? He had spent most of his adult life pretending to be other people. LuAnn had spent the last ten years of hers living another life, filling in the dimensions of another identity. He stared into the lively hazel eyes, studied the high cheekbones, the long hair; he traced with his index finger the slender yet strong neck and began to wonder once more about those trains, and the truly wonderful collision they might one day create. His eyes began to shine with the thought.

TWENTY-ONE

Donovan entered his apartment and sat down at the dining room table, spreading the pages he had taken out of his briefcase in front of him. His manner was one of subdued excitement. It had taken several weeks, dozens of phone calls, and a massive amount of leg work to accumulate the information he was now sifting through.

Initially, the task seemed more than daunting; indeed it had seemed destined for failure through sheer numbers. During the year LuAnn Tyler had disappeared, there had been over seventy thousand scheduled international passenger-aircraft movements at JFK. On the day she presumably fled there had been two hundred flights, or ten per hour, because there had been no flights between one and six A.M. Donovan had whittled down the parameters of his search at JFK to include women between the ages of twenty and thirty traveling on an international flight on the date of the press conference ten years ago, between the hours of seven P.M. and one A.M.. The press conference had lasted until six-thirty and Donovan doubted she could have made a seven o'clock flight, but the flight could have been delayed, and he wasn't taking any chances. That meant checking sixty flights and about fifteen thousand passengers. Donovan had learned during his investigation that most airlines kept active records of passengers going back five years. After that the information was archived. His task promised to be easier because most airline records had been computerized in the mid-seventies. However, Donovan had met a stone wall in seeking passenger records from ten years ago. The FBI could get such records, he had been told, but usually only through a subpoena.

Through a contact at the Bureau who owed him a favor, Donovan had been able to pursue his request. Without going into particulars and naming names with his FBI contact, Donovan had been able to convey the precise parameters of his search, including the fact that the person he was seeking had probably been traveling under a newly issued passport and traveling with a baby. That had narrowed things down considerably. Only three people satisfied those very narrow criteria and he was now looking at a list of them together with their last known addresses.

Next, Donovan pulled out his address book. The number he was calling was a firm called Best Data, a well-known national credit check agency. Over the years the company had amassed a large database of names, addresses, and, most important, Social Security numbers. They serviced numerous firms requiring that information, including collection agencies and banks checking up on the credit of potential borrowers. Donovan gave the three names and last known addresses of the people on his list to the person at Best Data, and then provided his credit card number to pay for Best Data's fee. Within five minutes he was given the Social Security numbers for all three people, their last known addresses, and five "nearbys," or neighbors' addresses. He checked those against the records from the airlines. Two of the women had moved, which wasn't surprising given their ages ten years ago; in the interim they had probably moved on to careers and marriages.

One woman, however, had not changed her address. Catherine Savage was still listed as living in Virginia. Donovan called directory assistance in Virginia, but no number came up for that name and address. Undeterred, he next called the Virginia Department of Motor Vehicles, or DMV, and gave the woman's name, last known address, and Social Security number, which in Virginia was also the driver's license number. The person at DMV would only tell Donovan that the woman had a current, valid Virginia driver's license but would not reveal when it had been issued or the woman's current address. Unfortunate, but Donovan had chased lots of leads into brick walls in the past. At least he knew she was now living in Virginia or at least had a driver's license in the commonwealth. The question now was Where in the commonwealth might she be? He had ways of finding that out, but decided in the meantime to dig up some more information on the woman's history.

He returned to the office where he had an on-line account through the newspaper and accessed the Social Security Administration's PEBES, or Personal Earnings and Benefit Estimate Statement database on the World Wide Web. Donovan was from the old school when it came to research methods, but even he occasionally lumbered out to do some Net surfing. All one needed to find out information on a person was their Social Security number, mother's maiden name, and the birthplace of the person. Donovan had all of these facts in hand. LuAnn Tyler had been born in Georgia, that he knew for certain. However, the first three digits of the Social Security number he had been given identified Catherine Savage as having been born in Virginia. If LuAnn Tyler and Catherine Savage were one and the same, then Tyler had obtained a phony SSN. It wasn't all that difficult to do, but he doubted whether the woman would've had the connections to do it. The PEBES listed a person's earnings going back to the early fifties, their contributions to the Social Security fund, and their expected benefits upon retirement based upon those contributions. That was normally what was shown. However, Donovan was looking at a blank screen. Catherine Savage had no history of wage earnings of any kind. LuAnn Tyler had worked, Donovan knew that. Her last job had been at a truck diner. If she had received a paycheck, her employers should have withheld payroll taxes, including amounts for Social Security. Either they hadn't or LuAnn Tyler didn't have a Social Security number to begin with. Or both. He called up Best Data again and went through the same process. The answer this time, however, was different. As far as the Social Security Administration was concerned, LuAnn Tyler didn't exist. She simply did not have a Social Security number. There was no more to be learned here. It was time for Donovan to take some more serious steps.

That evening Donovan returned home, opened a file, and took out IRS form 2848. The form was entitled "Power of Attorney and Declaration of Representative." A relatively simple form as Internal Revenue documents went, but one that carried extraordinary power. With it Donovan could obtain all sorts of confidential tax documents on the person he was investigating. True, he would have to stretch the truth a little in filling out the form, and a little falsification of signature was involved, but his motives were pure, and, thus, his conscience was clear. Besides, Donovan knew that the IRS received tens of millions of requests a year from taxpayers for information about their tax returns. The fact that somebody would take the time to match signatures

214

was beyond the realm of probability. Donovan smiled. The odds of it would be greater even than the odds of winning the lottery. He filled out the form, listing the woman's name and last known address, put in her Social Security number, listed himself as the woman's representative for tax purposes, and requested the woman's federal income tax returns for the last three years, and mailed it off.

It took two months and numerous prodding phone calls, but the wait was worth it. Donovan had devoured the contents of the package from the IRS when it finally came. Catherine Savage was an awfully wealthy woman and her tax return from the prior year, at a full forty pages in length, reflected that wealth and the financial complexities that level of income bore. He had requested her last three years' worth of returns, but the IRS had only sent one for the simple reason that she had only filed one return. The mystery behind that had been cleared up quickly, because Donovan, as Catherine Savage's tax representative, had been able to contact the IRS and ask virtually every question that he wanted about the taxpayer. Donovan had learned that Catherine Savage's tax situation had sparked a great deal of initial interest with the IRS. A U.S. citizen with such an extraordinary level of income filling a tax return for the first time at age thirty was enough to jump-start even the most drone-like of Revenue agents into action. There were over a million Americans living abroad who simply never filed returns, costing the government billions in unpaid taxes, and consequently this was an area that always received the IRS's attention. However, the initial interest had been quickly dissipated as every question the agency had asked had been answered and every

215

question had been supported by substantial documentation, Donovan had been told.

Donovan looked at his notes from the conversation with the IRS agent. Catherine Savage had been born in the United States, in Charlottesville, Virginia, in fact, and then left the country as a young girl when her father's business had taken him overseas. As a young woman living in France, she had met and married a wealthy German businessman who was a resident of Monaco at the time. The man had died a little over two years ago and his fortune had duly passed to his young widow. Now, as a U.S. citizen with control of her own money, all of which was passive, unearned income, she had begun paying her income taxes to her homeland. The documents in the file were numerous and legitimate, the IRS agent had assured Donovan. Everything was aboveboard. As far as the IRS was concerned, Catherine Savage was a responsible citizen who was lawfully paying her taxes although residing outside the United States.

Donovan leaned back in his chair and studied the ceiling, his hands clasped behind his head. The agent had also provided Donovan with another piece of interesting news. The IRS had very recently received a change of address form for Catherine Savage. She was now in the United States. In fact, she had returned, at least according to her records, to the town of her birth: Charlottesville, Virginia. The same town where LuAnn Tyler's mother had been born. That was far too much of a coincidence for Donovan.

And with all that information in hand, Donovan was fairly certain of one thing: LuAnn Tyler had finally come home. And now that he was so intimately familiar with virtually every facet of her life, Donovan felt it was time that they actually meet. How and where was what he started to think about.

TWENTY-TWO

Sitting in his pickup truck parked on the side of a sharp bend in the road, Matt Riggs surveyed the area through a pair of lightweight field binoculars. The tree-filled, steeply graded land was, to his experienced eye, impenetrable. The half mile of winding asphalt private road running to his right formed a T-intersection with the road he was on; beyond that, he knew, sat a grand country estate with beautiful vistas of the nearby mountains. However, the estate, surrounded by thick woods, couldn't be seen from anywhere except overhead. Which made him wonder again why the owner would want to pay for an expensive perimeter security fence in the first place. The estate already had the very best of nature's own handiwork for protection.

Riggs shrugged and bent down to slip on a pair of Overland boots, then pulled on his coat. The chilly wind buffeted him as he stepped from his truck. He sucked the fresh air in and put a hand through his unkempt dark brown hair, working a couple of kinks out of his muscular frame before donning a pair of leather gloves. It would take him about an hour to walk the front location of the fence. The plans called for the fence to be seven feet high, made of solid steel painted glossy black, with each post set in two feet of concrete. The fence would have electronic sensors spaced randomly across its frame, and would be topped by dangerously sharp spike finials. The front gates, set on six-foot-high, four-foot-square concrete monuments with a brick veneer, would be of similar style and construction. The job also called for a video camera, intercom system, and a locking mechanism on the huge gates that would ensure that nothing less than the head-on impact of an Abrams tank could ever open it without the permission of the owner. From what he could tell, Riggs didn't expect such permission to be granted very often.

Bordered by Nelson County on the southwest, Greene County to the north, and Fluvanna and Louisa counties on the east, Albemarle County, Virginia, was home to many wealthy people, some famous and some not. However, they all had one thing in common: They all craved privacy and were more than willing to pay for it. Thus, Riggs was not entirely surprised at the precautions being undertaken here. All the negotiations had been handled through a duly authorized intermediary. He reasoned that someone who could afford a fence such as this, and the cost was well into the hundreds of thousands of dollars, probably had better things to do with his time than sit down and chat with a lowly general contractor.

Binoculars dangling around his neck, he dutifully trudged down the road until he found a narrow pathway into the woods. The two most difficult parts of the job were clear to him: getting the heavy equipment up here and having his men work in such cramped surroundings. Mixing concrete, punching postholes, laying out the frames, clearing land, and angling sections of a very heavy fence, all of that took space, ample space that they would not have here. He was very glad to have added a healthy premium to the job, plus a provision for a cost overrun for exactly those reasons. The owner, apparently, had not set a limit as to the price, because the representative had promptly agreed to the huge dollar amount Riggs had worked up. Not that he was complaining. This single job would guarantee his best year ever in business. And although he had only been on his own for three years, his operation had been growing steadily ever since the first day. He got to work.

The BMW pulled slowly out from the garage and headed down the drive. The road going down was lined on either side with four-board oak fencing painted a pristine white. Most of the cleared land was surrounded by the same style of fencing, the white lines making a stunning contrast to the green landscape. It was not quite seven in the morning and the stillness of the day remained unbroken. These early morning drives had become a soothing ritual for LuAnn. She glanced back at the house in her rearview mirror. Constructed of beautiful Pennsylvania stone and weathered brick with a row of new white columns bracketing a deep front porch, a slate roof, aged-looking copper gutters, and numerous French doors, the house was elegantly refined despite its imposing size.

As the car passed down the drive and out of sight of the house, LuAnn turned her eyes back to the road and suddenly took her foot off the gas and hit the brake. The man was waving at her, his arms crisscrossing themselves as he flagged her down. She inched forward and then stopped the car. He came up to the driver's side window and motioned for her to open it. Out of the corner of her eye she saw the black Honda parked on a grass strip bordering the road.

She eyed him with deep suspicion but hit the button and the window descended slightly. She kept one foot on the accelerator ready to mash it down if the situation called for it. His appearance was innocent enough: middle-aged and slight of build, with a beard laced around the edges with gray.

"Can I help you?" she asked, her eyes attempting to duck his gaze at the same time she tried her best to note any sudden movements on his part.

"I think I'm lost. Is this the old Brillstein Estate?" He pointed up the road toward where the house was.

LuAnn shook her head. "We just recently moved in, but that wasn't the name of the owners before us. It's called Wicken's Hunt."

"Huh, I could've sworn this was the right place."

"Who were you looking for?"

The man leaned forward so that his face filled her window. "Maybe you know her. The name is LuAnn Tyler, from Georgia."

LuAnn sucked in a mouthful of air so quickly she almost gagged. There was no hiding the astonishment on her face.

Thomas Donovan, his face full of satisfaction, leaned even closer, his lips right at her eye level. "LuAnn, I'd like to talk to you. It's important and—"

She hit the accelerator and Donovan had to jump back to avoid having his feet crushed by the car tires.

"Hey!" he screamed after her. The car was almost out of sight. Donovan, his face ashen, ran to his car, started it up, and roared off down the road. "Christ!" he said to himself.

Donovan had tried directory assistance in Charlottesville, but they had no listing for Catherine Savage. He would have been shocked if they had. Someone on the run all these years didn't ordinarily give out her phone number. He had decided, after much thought, that the direct approach would be, if not the best, at least the most productive. He had

220

watched the house for the last week, noted her pattern of early morning drives, and chosen today to make contact. Despite being almost run over, he had the satisfaction of knowing that he had been right. Throwing the question at her out of the blue like that, he knew, was the only sure way to get the truth. And now he had it. Catherine Savage was LuAnn Tyler. Her looks had changed considerably from the video and photos he had seen from ten years ago. The changes were subtle, no one single alteration really dramatic, yet the cumulative effect had been marked. Except for the look on her face and her abrupt departure, Donovan wouldn't have known it was her.

He now focused on the road ahead. He had just glimpsed the gray BMW. It was still far ahead, but on the curvy mountain road his smaller and more agile Honda was gaining. He didn't like playing the daredevil role; he had disdained it in his younger days when covering dangerous events halfway around the world, and he disliked it even more now. However, he had to make her understand what he was trying to do. He had to make her listen. And he had to get his story. He hadn't worked twenty-hour days the last several months tracking her down simply to watch her disappear again.

Matt Riggs stopped for a moment and again studied the terrain. The air was so clean and pure up here, the sky so blue, the peace and quiet so ethereal, he again marveled at why he had waited so long to chuck the big city, and come to calmer, if less exciting, parts. After years of being in the very center of millions of tense, increasingly aggressive people, he now found being able to feel like you were all alone in the world, for even a few minutes, was more soothing than he could have imagined. He was about to pull the property survey out of his jacket to study in more detail the dimensions of the property line when all thoughts of work amid the peaceful countryside abruptly disappeared from his mind.

He jerked his head around and whipped the binoculars up to his eyes to focus on what had suddenly destroyed the morning's calm. He quickly located the origin of the explosion of sound. Through the trees he spied two cars hurtling down from the road where the country estate was situated, their respective engines at full throttle. The car in front was a big BMW sedan. The car behind it was a smaller vehicle. What the smaller car lacked in muscle power to the big Bimmer, it more than made up for in agility around the winding road. At the speeds the two were doing, Riggs thought it most likely they would both end up either wrapped around a tree or upside down in one of the steep ditches that bordered either side of the road.

The next two visuals he made through his binoculars made him turn and run as fast as he could back to his truck.

The look of raw fear on the woman's face in the Bimmer, the way she looked behind to check her pursuer's progress, and the grim countenance of the man apparently chasing her were all he needed to kick-start every instinct he had ever gained from his former life.

He gunned the engine, unsure exactly what his plan of action would be, not that he had much time to come up with one. He pulled on to the road, strapping his seat belt across him as he did so. He normally carried a shotgun in the truck to ward off snakes, but he had forgotten it this morning. He had some shovels and a crowbar in the truck bed, although he hoped it wasn't going to come to that.

As he flew down the road, the two cars appeared in front of him on the main road. The Bimmer took

222

the turn almost on two wheels before stabilizing, the other car right behind it. However, now on the straightaway, the three hundred plus horses of the BMW could be fully used, and the woman quickly opened a two-hundred-yard gap between herself and her pursuer, a gap that grew with every second. That wouldn't last, Riggs knew, because a curve that would qualify for deadman's status was fast approaching. He hoped to God the woman knew it; if she didn't he would be watching the BMW turn into a fireball as it sailed off the road and crashed into an army of unyielding hardwoods. With that prospect nearly upon them, his plan finally came together. He punched the gas, the truck flew forward, and he gained on what he now saw was a black Honda. The man apparently had all of his attention focused on the BMW, because when Riggs passed him on the left, the man didn't even look over. However, he took abrupt and angry notice when Riggs cut in front of him and immediately slowed down to twenty miles an hour. Up ahead, Riggs saw the woman glance back in her rearview mirror, her eyes riveted on Riggs and his fortuitous appearance on the scene as the truck and Honda fought a pitched battle for supremacy of the road. Riggs tried to motion to her to slow down, to make her understand what he was trying to do. Whether she got the message or not, he couldn't tell. Like the coils of a sidewinder, the truck and the Honda swayed back and forth across the narrow roadway, coming dangerously close to the sheer drop on the right side. Once, the truck's wheel partially skidded in the gravel shoulder and Riggs braced himself for the plunge over, before he barely managed to regain control. The driver of the Honda tried mightily to pass, leaning on his horn the whole time. But in his past career Riggs had done his share of dangerous, high-speed driving and he expertly matched the other man maneuver for maneuver. A minute later they rounded the almost V-shaped curve, a wall of sheer jutting rock on his left and an almost vertical drop to the right. Riggs anxiously looked down that steep slope for any sight of the Bimmer's wreckage. He breathed a sigh of relief as he saw none. He looked up the once again straight road. He saw the glint of a bumper far up ahead and then the big sedan was completely out of sight. Admiration was his first thought. The woman hadn't slowed down much, if any, coming around that curve. Even at twenty miles an hour Riggs hadn't felt all that safe. Damn

Riggs reached across to his glove box and pulled out his portable phone. He was just about to punch in 911 when the Honda now took the very aggressive tack of ramming his truck from behind. The phone flew out of his hand and smashed into several pieces against the dashboard. Riggs cursed, shook off the impact, clenched the wheel hard, shifted into low gear, and slowed down even more as the Honda repeatedly smashed into him. What he was hoping would happen eventually did, as the Honda's front bumper and the truck's heavy-duty rear one locked together. He could hear the gears grinding in the Honda as the driver tried to extricate his vehicle without success. Riggs peered into the rearview mirror and he saw the man's hand slide over to his glove compartment. Riggs wasn't going to wait around to see whether a weapon emerged from it or not. He jerked the truck to a stop, slammed the gear in reverse, and the two vehicles roared backward down the road. He watched with satisfaction as the man in the Honda jerked back upright and gripped the steering wheel in a panic. Riggs slowed as he came to the curve, cleared it and then shot forward again. As he came to a straightaway, he cut the wheel sharply to the left and slammed the Honda into the rocky side of the road. The force of that collision uncoupled the two vehicles. The driver appeared unhurt. Riggs slammed the truck into drive and quickly disappeared down the road in pursuit of the BMW. He continually looked back for several minutes but there was no sign of the Honda. Either it had been disabled upon impact, or the driver had decided not to pursue his reckless actions further.

The adrenaline continued to course through Riggs's body for several minutes until it finally dissipated. Five years removed from the dangers of his former profession, Riggs was aware that this morning's five-minute episode had reminded him vividly of how many close calls he had survived. He had neither expected nor ever wanted to rekindle that anxious feeling in the sleepy morning mists of central Virginia.

His damaged bumper clanking loudly, Riggs finally slowed down, as further pursuit of the BMW was hopeless. There were innumerable roads off the main track and the woman could have taken any one of them and be long gone by now. Riggs pulled off the road and stopped, plucked a pen from his shirt pocket and wrote the license plate numbers of the Honda and BMW down on the pad of paper he kept affixed to his dashboard. He ripped the paper off the pad and tucked it in his pocket. He had a pretty good idea who was in the Bimmer. Someone who lived in the big house. The same big house he had been hired to surround with a state-of-the-art security fence. Now the owner's request started to make a whole lot more sense to Riggs. And the question he was most interested in now was why? He drove off, deep in thought, the morning's peacefulness irretrievably shattered by the look of sheer terror on a woman's face.

TWENTY-THREE

The BMW had indeed pulled off on a side road
several miles away from where Riggs and the
Honda had tangled. The driver's side door was
open, the motor running. Arms clutched tightly
around her sides, LuAnn walked in tight, frenetic
circles in the middle of the road, shooting frosty
breaths skyward in her agitation. Anger, confusion,
and frustration raced across her features. All traces
of fear were gone, however. The present emotions
were actually far more damaging to her. Fear almost
always passed; these other mental battering rams
did not retreat so easily. She had learned this over
the years, and had even managed to cope with it as
best as she could.

Now thirty years old, LuAnn Tyler still carried the
impulsive energy and sleek animal movements of
her youth. The years had grafted on to her a more
complete, mature beauty. However, the basic
elements of that beauty had been discernibly altered.
Her body was leaner, the waist even tighter. The
effect was to make her appear even taller than she
already was. Her hair had grown out and now was
far more blond than auburn, and cut in a sophisticated manner that highlighted her more defined
facial features, including the minor nose job done for
disguise rather than aesthetics. Her teeth were now
perfect, having benefitted from years of expensive
dentistry. There was, however, one imperfection.
She had not followed Jackson's advice regarding

226

the knife wound to her jaw. She had had it stitched, but let the scar remain. It wasn't all that noticeable, but every time she looked in the mirror, it was a stark reminder of where she had come from, how she had gotten here. It was her most visible tie to the past, and not a pleasant one. That was the reason she would not cover it over with surgery. She wanted to be reminded of the unpleasantness, of the pain.

People she had grown up with would probably have recognized her; however, she never planned to see anyone like that here. She had resigned herself to wearing a big hat and sunglasses whenever she ventured out into public, which wasn't very often. A lifetime of hiding from the world: that had come with her deal.

She went and sat back down on the front seat of the BMW, rubbing her hands back and forth across the padded steering wheel. She continually looked back down the road for any sign of her pursuer; however, the only sounds were her car's engine and her own uneven breathing. Huddled in her leather jacket, she hitched up her jeans, swung her long legs inside the car, and closed the door and locked it.

She took off and for a few moments as she drove her thoughts centered on the man in the truck. He had obviously helped her. Was he just a good Samaritan who had happened along at the right time? Or was he something else, something more complex than that? She had lived with this paranoia for so long now that it was like an exterior coating of paint. All observations had to pass through its screening first, all conclusions were based in some way upon how she perceived the motivation of anyone colliding unexpectedly with her universe. It all came down to one grim fact: fear of discovery. She took one long, deep breath and wondered for the hundredth time if she had made a grievous mistake by returning to the United States.

Riggs drove his battered truck up the private road. He had kept a close eye out for the Honda on his return down the road, but the car and driver had not reappeared. Going up to the house, he figured, was the quickest way to find a telephone, and perhaps also seek an explanation of sorts for this morning's events. Not that he deserved one, but his intervention had helped the woman and he felt that was worth something. In any event, he couldn't exactly let it rest now. He was surprised that no one stopped him on the drive up. There was no private security, apparently. He had met with the owner's representative in town; this was his first visit to the estate, which had been christened Wicken's Hunt long ago. The home was one of the most beautiful in the area. It had been constructed in the early 1920s with craftsmanship that was simply nonexistent today. The Wall Street magnate who had had it built as a summer retreat had jumped off a New York skyscraper during the stock market crash of '29. The home had passed through several hands, and had been on the market six years before being sold to the current owner. The place had required substantial renovation. Riggs had talked to some of the subcontractors employed to do that work. They had spoken with awe of the craftsmanship and beauty of the place.

Whatever moving trucks had hauled the owner's possessions up the mountain road had apparently done so in the middle of the night, because Riggs could find no one who had seen them. No one had seen the owner, either. He had checked at the courthouse land records. The home was owned by a corporation that Riggs had never heard of. The usual channels of gossip had not yielded an answer to the mystery, although St. Anne's-Belfield School had admitted a ten-year-old girl named Lisa Savage who had given Wicken Hunt as her home address. Riggs had heard that a tall young woman would occasionally drop off and pick up the child; although she had always worn sunglasses and a large hat. Most often picking up the little girl would be an elderly man who had been described to Riggs as built like a linebacker. A strange household. Riggs had several friends who worked at the school but none of them would talk about the young woman. If they knew her name, they wouldn't say what it was.

When Riggs rounded a curve, the mansion suddenly appeared directly in front of him. His truck resembled a plain, squat tug bearing down on the *QEII.* The mansion stood three stories tall, with a double doorway spanning at least twenty feet.

He parked his truck in the wraparound drive that encircled a magnificent stone fountain that, on this cold morning, was not operating. The landscaping was as lush and as carefully planned as the house; and where annuals and even late-blooming perennials had died out, evergreens and other hardy foliage of all descriptions filled in the spaces.

He slid out of his seat, making sure he had the piece of paper with the license plate numbers still in his pocket. As he walked up to the front door, he wondered if a place like this would condescend to have a doorbell; or would a butler automatically open the door at his approach? Actually, neither happened, but as he cleared the top step, a voice did speak to him from a brand new-looking intercom built into the side of the wall next to the door.

"Can I help you?" It was a man's voice, big, solid, and, Riggs thought, slightly threatening.

"Matthew Riggs. My company was hired to build the privacy fence on the property's perimeter."

"Okay."

The door didn't budge, and the tone of the voice made clear that unless Riggs had more information to impart, this status was not going to change. He looked around, suddenly conscious that he was being observed. Sure enough, above his head, recessed within the back of one of the columns, was a video camera. That looked new as well. He waved.

"Can I help you?" the voice said again.

"I'd like to use a telephone."

"I'm sorry, that's not possible."

"Well, I'd say it should be possible since I just crashed my truck into a car that was chasing a big charcoal gray BMW that I'm pretty sure came from this house. I just wanted to make sure that the woman driving the car was okay. She looked pretty scared the last time I saw her."

The next sound Riggs heard was the front door being unbolted and thrown open. The elderly man facing him matched the six foot one Riggs in height, but was far broader across the shoulders and chest. However, Riggs noted that the man moved with a slight limp as though the legs and, perhaps, the knees in particular were beginning to go. The possessor of a very strong, athletic body himself, Riggs decided he would not want to have to take this guy on. Despite his advancing age and obvious infirmities, the man looked strong enough to break Riggs's back with ease. This was obviously the guy seen at the school picking up Lisa Savage. The doting linebacker.

"What the hell are you talking about?"

Riggs pointed toward the road. "About ten minutes ago, I was out doing a preliminary survey of the property line in advance of ordering up men and equipment when this BMW come bolting down the road, a woman driving, blond from what I could see,

230

and scared to death. Another car, a black Honda Accord, probably a 1992 or '93 model, right on her butt. A guy was driving that one and he looked determined as hell."

"The woman, is she all right?" The elderly man edged forward perceptibly. Riggs backed up a notch, unwilling to let the guy get too close until he had a better understanding of the situation. For all he knew, this guy could be in cahoots with the man in the Honda. Riggs's internal radar was all over the place on this one.

"As far as I know. I got in between them and took the Honda out, banged the crap out of my truck in the process." Riggs briefly rubbed his neck as the recollection of his collision brought several distinct painful twinges to that location. He would have to soak in the tub tonight.

"We'll take care of the truck. Where's the woman?"

"I didn't come up here to complain about the truck, mister—"

"Charlie, call me Charlie." The man extended his hand, which Riggs shook. He had not under-estimated the strength the old guy possessed. As he took his hand back Riggs observed the indentations in his fingers caused by the other man's vise-like grip. Whether he was merely anxious about the safety of the woman, or he mangled visitors' fingers on a routine basis, Riggs didn't know.

"I go by Matt. Like I said, she got away, and as far as I know, she's fine. But I still wanted to call it in."

"Call it in?"

"The police. The guy in the Honda was breaking at least several laws that I know of, including a couple of felonies. Too bad I didn't get to read him his rights."

"You sound like a cop."

231

Had Charlie's face darkened, or was that his imagination, Riggs wondered.

"Something like that. A long while back. I got the license plate number of both cars." He looked at Charlie, studying the battered and grizzled face, trying to get beyond the solid stare he was getting in return. "I'm assuming the BMW belongs to this house, and the woman."

Charlie hesitated for a moment and then nodded. "She's the owner."

"And the Honda?"

"Never seen it before."

Riggs turned and looked back down the road. "The guy could've been waiting partially down the entry road. There's nothing stopping him from doing that." Riggs turned and looked back at Charlie.

"That's why we contracted with you to build the fence and gate." A glint of anger rose in Charlie's eyes.

"Now I can see why that might be a good idea, but I only got the signed contract yesterday. I work fast, but not that fast."

Charlie relaxed at the obvious logic of Riggs's words and looked down for a moment.

"What about using that phone, Charlie?" Riggs took a step forward. "Look, I know a kidnap attempt when I see one." He looked up at the facade of the house. "It's not hard to see why either, is it?"

Charlie took a deep breath, his loyalties sharply divided. He was sick with worry about LuAnn – *Catherine*, he corrected himself mentally; despite the passage of ten years, he had never been comfortable with her new name. He was finding it close to impossible to allow the police to be called in.

"I take it you're her friend or family—"

"Both actually," Charlie said with renewed vigor as he stared over Riggs's shoulder, a smile

232

breaking across his face.

The reason for that change in attitude reached Riggs's ears a second later. He turned and watched the BMW pull up behind his truck.

LuAnn got out of the car, glanced at the truck for a moment, until her eyes riveted on the damaged bumper; then she strode up the steps, passing over Riggs to focus on Charlie.

"This guy said you ran into some trouble," said Charlie, pointing at Riggs.

"Matt Riggs." Riggs extended his hand. In her boots, the woman wasn't much shorter than he. The impression of exceptional beauty he had gotten through his binoculars was considerably magnified up close. The hair was long and full, with golden highlights that seem to catch every streak of the sun's rays as it slowly rose over them. The face and complexion were flawless to the point of seeming impossible to achieve naturally, yet the woman was young so the cut of the plastic surgeon's knife could not have beckoned to her yet. Riggs reasoned the beauty must be all her own. Then he spotted the scar that ran along her jawline. That surprised him, it seemed so out of place with the rest of her. The scar also intrigued Riggs because, to his experienced eye, the wound seemed to have been made by a knife with a serrated edge. Most women, he figured, especially those who had the kind of money she obviously did, would have paid any amount to cover up that blemish.

The pair of calm, hazel eyes that stared into Riggs made him conclude that this woman was different. The person he was looking at was one of those rare creations: a very lovely woman who cared little about her looks. As his eyes continued to sweep over her, he noted the lean, elegant, body; but from the smallish hips and waist there grew a breadth of shoulders that suggested exceptional physical strength. When her hand closed around his, he almost gasped. The grip was almost indistinguishable from Charlie's.

"I hope you're okay," said Riggs. "I got the plate number of the Honda. I was going to call it in to the cops, but my cell phone got broken when the guy hit me. The car's probably stolen anyway. I got a good look at the guy. This is a pretty isolated place. We should be able to nail him, if we act fast enough."

LuAnn looked at him, confusion on her face. "What are you talking about?"

Riggs blinked and stepped back. "The car that was chasing you."

LuAnn looked over at Charlie. Riggs watched closely but he saw no discernible signals passing between them. Then LuAnn pointed over at Riggs's truck. "I saw that truck and another car driving erratically, but I didn't stop to ask any questions. It was none of my business."

Riggs gaped for a moment before he responded. "The reason I was doing the two-step with the Honda was because he was trying his best to run you off the road. In fact, I almost took your place as the wreck of the week."

"Again, I'm sorry, but I don't know what you're talking about. Don't you think I would know if someone were trying to run me off the road?"

"So you're saying that you always drive eighty miles an hour around curvy, mountainous roads just for the fun of it?" Riggs asked heatedly.

"I don't think my driving methods are any of your concern," she snapped back. "However, since you happen to be on my property, I think it is my concern to know why you're here."

Charlie piped in. "He's the guy who's building the security fence."

234

LuAnn eyed Riggs steadily. "Then I would strongly suggest you concentrate on that task rather than come up here with some outrageous account of my being chased."

Riggs's face flushed and he started to say something, but then decided against it. "Have a good day, ma'am." He turned and headed back to his truck.

LuAnn didn't look back. She passed by Charlie without a glance and walked quickly into the house. Charlie stared after Riggs for a moment before shutting the door.

As Riggs climbed back in his truck another car pulled up the drive. An older woman was driving. The back seat of the car was stacked with groceries. The woman was Sally Beecham, LuAnn's live-in housekeeper, just back from early-morning grocery shopping. She glanced over at Riggs in a cursory fashion. Though his features were laced with anger, he curtly nodded at her and she returned the gesture. As was her custom, she pulled around to the side-load garage and hit the garage door opener clipped to the car's visor. The door in from the garage led directly to the kitchen, and Beecham was an efficient person who detested wasted effort.

As Riggs pulled off he glanced back up at the massive house. With so many windows staring back at him he didn't catch the one framing LuAnn Tyler, arms folded across her chest, looking resolutely at him, a mixture of worry and guilt on her face.

TWENTY-FOUR

The Honda slowed down, turned off the back road, then made its way over a rustic wooden bridge spanning a small creek, and then disappeared into the thickness of the surrounding forest. The antenna clipped some of the overhanging branches, sending a shower of dewdrops on to the windshield. Up ahead, under an umbrella of oak trees, a small, ramshackle cottage was visible. The Honda pulled into the tiny backyard and then into a small shed located behind the cottage. The man closed the doors of the shed and walked up to the house.

Donovan rubbed his lower back and then worked his neck around some in an attempt to overcome the aftereffects of his early morning escapade. He was still visibly shaking. Donovan stamped into the house, threw off his coat, and proceeded to make coffee in the small kitchen. Nervously smoking a cigarette while the coffee percolated, he looked outside the window with a slight feeling of apprehension, although he was fairly certain no one had followed him. He rubbed his brow. The cottage was isolated and the landlord didn't know his real name or the reason he had decided to take up temporary residence here.

The guy in the truck, who the hell had he been? Friend of the woman or some guy who had happened by? Since he had been seen, Donovan would have to shave off his beard and do something with his hair. He would also have to rent another car. The Honda was damaged and the guy in the truck could've gotten the license plate number. But the Honda was a rental, and Donovan had not used his real name in leasing it. He wasn't worried about the woman doing anything about it, but the guy might put a crimp in his plans. He wouldn't risk driving the Honda back into town to exchange it for another rental. He didn't want to be spotted driving it, and he didn't want to have to explain the damage to the bumper right now. Tonight, he'd walk to the main road and catch a bus into town, where he would pick up another rental car.

He poured a cup of coffee and walked into the dining room that had been set up as an office. A computer terminal, printer, and fax and phone were set up on one table. File boxes were stacked neatly in one corner. On two walls hung several large bulletin boards. They were filled with newspaper clippings.

The car chase had been stupid, Donovan muttered to himself. It was a miracle both of them weren't dead in some ravine right now. Tyler's reaction had absolutely astonished him. Although, thinking about it now, it probably shouldn't have. She was scared, and she had ample reason to be. Donovan's next problem was apparent. What if she disappeared again? Finding her the first time had been part hard work and part luck. There was no guarantee he would be as fortunate the next time. However, there was nothing he could do about that now. He could only wait and watch.

He had established a contact at the regional airport who would advise Donovan if any person matching LuAnn Tyler's description or traveling under the name Catherine Savage was headed out of the area via plane. Unless she had another identity already set up, it would be difficult for Tyler to travel any time soon except under the name Catherine Savage, and that would leave him a trail. If she left the area by means other than airplane, well, he could watch the house, but he couldn't do it twenty-four hours a day. He briefly contemplated calling in reinforcements from the *Trib*, but there were many factors that cautioned him against doing that. He had worked alone for almost thirty years, and bringing in a partner now was not very appealing, even if the newspaper would consent to do it. No, he would do what he could to dog her movements, and he would work very hard to set up another face-to-face. He was convinced that he could make the woman trust him, work with him. He didn't believe that she had killed anybody. But he was fairly certain that she and perhaps some of the other winners were hiding something about the lottery. He wanted that story, wherever it led him.

A fire blazed in the hearth of the spacious two-story library, which had floor-to-ceiling maple bookcases on three walls and inviting, overstuffed furniture arranged in intimate conversation patterns. LuAnn sat on a leather sofa, her legs drawn up under her, bare feet protruding, an embroidered cotton shawl covering her shoulders. A cup of tea and a plate of uneaten breakfast sat on the table next to her. Sally Beecham, dressed in a gray uniform with a sparkling white apron, was just leaving, carrying the serving tray. Charlie closed the arched double doors behind her and sat down next to LuAnn.

"Listen, are you gonna tell me what really happened or not?" When LuAnn didn't answer, Charlie gripped one of her hands. "Your hands are like ice. Drink the tea." He rose and stoked the fire until the flames made his face redden. He looked at her expectantly. "I can't help you if you don't tell me what's wrong, LuAnn."

Over the last ten years a lasting bond had been built between the two that had seen them through many crises, both minor and major, in their travels. From the time Charlie had touched her shoulder as the 747 climbed into the skies, until they had arrived back in America, they had been inseparable. Even though his given name was Robert, he had taken "Charlie" as his accepted name. It wasn't too far from the truth, as his middle name was Charles. What was in a name anyway? However, he referred to her as LuAnn only in private, as now. He was her closest friend and confidant, really her only one, since there were things she could not even tell her daughter.

As he sat back down, Charlie winced in pain. He was acutely aware that he was slowing down, a process that was exacerbated by the rough treatment of his body in his youth. The difference in years between the two was now more pronounced than ever, as nature took its toll on him. Even with all that, he would do anything for her, would face any danger, confront any enemy she had with every ounce of strength and ingenuity he had left.

It was the look in Charlie's eyes as LuAnn read these very thoughts that made her finally start talking.

"I had just left the house. He was standing in the middle of the driveway waving for me to stop."

"And you did?" Charlie's tone was incredulous.

"I didn't get out of the car. I couldn't exactly run over the man. If he tried anything, or pulled a gun, you can bet I would've done just that."

Charlie hitched one leg up over the other, an action that was accompanied by another painful wince. "Go on. Eat while you're talking, and drink your tea! Your face is white as a sheet."

LuAnn did as he said, managing to get some bites of egg and toast down and a few sips of the hot tea. Putting the cup back down, she wiped her mouth with a napkin. "He motioned for me to roll the window down. I cracked it a bit and asked him what he wanted."

"Wait a minute, what'd he look like?"

"Medium height, full beard, a little gray at the edges. Wire-rimmed glasses. Olive complexion, maybe a hundred sixty pounds. Probably late forties or early fifties." Over the last ten years, memorizing minute details of people's appearances had become second nature to LuAnn.

Charlie mentally filed away her description of the man. "Go on."

"He said he was looking for the Brillstein Estate." She hesitated and took another sip of tea. "I told him that this wasn't the place."

Charlie leaned forward. "What'd he say then?"

Now LuAnn was perceptibly shaking. "He said he was looking for somebody."

"Who? Who?" Charlie asked again as LuAnn's blank stare dropped to the floor.

She finally looked up at him. "LuAnn Tyler from Georgia."

Charlie sat back. After a decade, they had pretty much put the fear of exposure on the back burner, though it was still there and always would be. Now that flame had just been rekindled.

"Did he say anything else?"

LuAnn rubbed the napkin across her dry lips and then sat back up. "He said something about wanting to talk to me. Then . . . I . . . I just went blank, slammed the accelerator, and almost ran over him." She let all the air drain out of her after speaking. She looked over at Charlie.

"And he chased you?"

She nodded. "I've got strong nerves, Charlie, you know that, but they have their limits. When you're going out for a relaxing early morning drive and you get hit with something like that instead?" She cocked her head at him. "God, I was just starting to feel comfortable here. Jackson hasn't shown up, Lisa loves school, this place is so beautiful." She fell silent.

"What about the other guy, Riggs? Is his story true?"

Suddenly agitated, LuAnn stood up and paced the room. She stopped and ran her hand fondly along a row of finely bound novels resting on the shelves. Over the years, she had read just about every book in the room. Ten years of intensive education with some of the finest private tutors had produced an articulate, polished, cosmopolitan woman far removed from the one who had run from that trailer, from those bodies. Now those bloody images would not budge from her mind.

"Yes. He just jumped right into the middle of it. I probably would've lost the guy, anyway." She added quietly, "But he did help me. And I would've liked to have thanked him. But I couldn't exactly do that, could I?" She threw up her hands in frustration and sat back down.

Charlie rubbed his chin as he pondered the situation.

"You know, legally, the lottery scam amounts to a bunch of felonies, but the statute of limitations has expired on all of them. The guy can't really hurt you there."

"What about the murder charge? There's no statute of limitations on that. I did kill the man, Charlie. I did it in self-defense, but who the hell would believe me now?"

"True, but the police haven't pursued the case in years."

"Okay, do you want me to go turn myself in?"

"I'm not saying that. I just think you might be blowing this out of proportion."

LuAnn trembled. Going to jail over the money or the killing was not her biggest concern. She put her hands together and looked over at Charlie.

"My daddy probably never said one word to me that was true. He did his best to make me feel like the most worthless piece of trash in the world and any time I built up some confidence he'd come along and tear it down. The only thing I was good for according to him was making babies and looking pretty for my man."

"I know you had it rough, LuAnn—"

"I swore to myself that I would never, ever do that to any child of mine. I swore that to God on a stack of Bibles, said it on my mother's grave, and whispered it to Lisa while I was carrying her and every night for six months after she was born." LuAnn swallowed hard and stood up. "And you know what? Everything I've told her, everything she knows about herself, you, me, every damned molecule of her existence is a lie. It's all made up, Charlie. Okay, maybe the statute of limitations is expired, maybe I won't go to jail because the police don't care that I killed a drug dealer. But if this man has found out my past and he brings it all out into the open, then Lisa will know. She'll know that her mother told her more lies than my daddy probably ever thought of in his entire life. I'll be a hundred times worse than Benny Tyler, and I'll lose my little girl as certain as the sun comes up. I'll lose Lisa." After this outburst, LuAnn shuddered and closed her eyes.

"I'm sorry, LuAnn, I hadn't thought about it like that." Charlie looked down at his hands.

LuAnn's eyes opened and they held a distinctly fatalistic look. "And if that happens, if she finds out,

242

then it's over for me. Jail will seem like a day in the park, because if I lose my little girl, then I won't have any reason to be anymore. Despite all this." She swept her arms around the room. "No reason at all."

LuAnn sat back down and rubbed at her forehead.

Charlie finally broke the silence. "Riggs got the license plate number. On both cars." He fiddled with his shirt and added, "Riggs is an ex-cop, LuAnn."

Her head in her hands, LuAnn looked at him. "Oh God! And I didn't think it could get any worse."

"Don't worry, he runs your plate, he gets nothing except Catherine Savage with this address, legit Social Security number, the works. Your identity has no holes in it. Not after all this time."

"I think we have a very big hole, Charlie. The guy in the Honda?"

Charlie conceded the point with a quick nod of his head. "Right, right, but I'm talking about Riggs. Your end with him is okay."

"But if he tracks the other guy down, maybe talks to him?"

"Then maybe we got a big problem." Charlie finished the thought for her.

"You think Riggs might do that?"

"I don't know. I do know that he didn't buy your story about not knowing you were being chased. Under the circumstances, I don't blame you for not acknowledging it, but an ex-cop? Hell, he's got to be suspicious. I don't think we can count on him letting it lie."

LuAnn rubbed the hair out of her eyes. "So what do we do?"

Charlie gently took one of her hands. "*You* do nothing. You let old Charlie see what he can find us. We've been in tight places before. Right?"

She slowly nodded and then licked her lips nervously. "But this might be the tightest one of them all."

＊＊

Matt Riggs walked quickly up the steps of the old Victorian with a wraparound porch that he had meticulously restored over the last year. He had had a few years of carpentry and woodworking experience before coming to Charlottesville. They had been pursuits he had taken up to alleviate the stress that had come with what he used to do for a living. He wasn't thinking about the graceful lines of his home right now, however.

He went inside and down the hall to his office, for his home also housed his business. He shut the door, grabbed the phone, and placed a call to an old friend in Washington, D.C. The Honda had D.C. tags. Riggs was pretty sure what running the license plate would reveal: either a rental or stolen. The BMW would be another matter. At least he would find out the woman's name, since it had suddenly occurred to him on the drive home that neither the man calling himself Charlie nor the woman had ever mentioned it. He was assuming the last name would be Savage and that the woman in the BMW was either Lisa Savage's mother or perhaps, from her youthful looks, an older sister.

A half hour later he had his answers. The Honda was indeed a rental out of the nation's capital. Tom Jones was the name of the lessee and he had rented the vehicle two weeks ago. Tom Jones! That was real clever, Riggs thought. The address he had for the man would be as phoney as the name, he was certain. A total deadend; he had expected nothing less.

Then he stared down at the woman's name he had written on a piece of paper. Catherine Savage. Born in Charlottesville, Virginia. Age: thirty. Social Security number had checked out, current address was correct: Wicken's Hunt. Unmarried. Excellent credit, no priors. No red flags at all in her background. He had a good slice of her past right there in his hand in less than half an hour. Computers were wonderful. And yet . . .

He looked at her age again. Thirty years old. He thought back to the house and substantial grounds, three hundred acres of prime Virginia real estate. He knew the asking price for Wicken's Hunt had been six million dollars. If she had struck a wonderful deal, Ms. Savage could conceivably have gotten it for between four and five million, but from what he heard the renovation work had easily run to seven figures. Where the hell does a woman that young get that kind of money? She wasn't a movie star or rock star; the name Catherine Savage meant nothing to him, and he wasn't that far out of the loop on popular culture.

Or was it Charlie who had the bucks? They weren't husband and wife, that was clear. He had said he was family, but something was off there too. He leaned back in his chair, slid open a drawer of his desk, and popped a couple of aspirin, as his neck threatened to stiffen up again. It could be she had inherited serious family money or been the extraordinarily rich widow of some old duffer. Recalling her face, he could easily see that. A lot of men would shower her with everything they had.

So what now? He looked out the window of his office at the beauty of the surrounding trees with their vibrant fall colors. Things were going well for him: An unhappy past behind him; a thriving business in a place he loved. A low-key lifestyle that he figured would add lots of quality years to his life. And now this. He held the piece of paper with her name on it up to eye level. Despite having no material incentive to care at all about her, Riggs's curiosity was at a high pitch.

"Who the hell are you, Catherine Savage?"

TWENTY-FIVE

"You about ready, honey?" LuAnn peeked in the door and cast her gaze fondly on the back of the young girl who was finishing dressing.

Lisa looked around at her mother. "Almost."

With a face and athletic build that mirrored LuAnn's, Lisa Savage was the one immovable landmark in her mother's life.

LuAnn stepped into the room, closed the door, and settled on the bed. "Miss Sally says you didn't eat much breakfast, are you feeling all right?"

"I have a test today. I guess I'm just a little nervous." One result of having lived all over the world was that her speech carried myriad traces of the different cultures, dialects, and accents. The mesh was a pleasing one, although several months in Virginia had already started to graft upon Lisa the beginnings of a mild Southern inflection.

LuAnn smiled. "I would've thought that by now, after so many straight A's, you wouldn't get so nervous." She touched her daughter's shoulder. During the time spent traveling, LuAnn had thrown every ounce of energy and a great deal of money into reshaping herself to be who she had always wanted to be, which was as far from Southern white trash named LuAnn Tyler as she could get. Well-educated, able to speak two foreign languages, she noted with pride that Lisa could speak four, as much at home in China as in London. She had covered several lifetimes in the last ten years. With this morning's developments, maybe that was a good thing. Had she run out of time?

Lisa finished dressing and sat down with her back to her mother. LuAnn picked up a brush and started doing her daughter's hair, a daily ritual between the two that allowed them to talk and catch up with each other.

"I can't help it, I still do get nervous. It's not always easy."

"Most things worthwhile in life aren't easy. But, you work hard and that's the important thing. You do your best, that's all I'll ever ask, regardless of what your grades are." She combed Lisa's hair into a thick ponytail and then clipped on a bow. "Just don't bring home any B's." They both laughed.

As they walked downstairs together, Lisa looked over at her mother. "I saw you talking to a man outside this morning. You and Uncle Charlie."

LuAnn tried to hide her apprehensiveness. "You were up? It was pretty early."

"Like I said, I was nervous about the test."

"Right."

"Who was he?"

"He's putting up the security fence and gate around the property. He had some questions about the plans."

"Why do we need a security fence?"

LuAnn took her hand. "We've talked about this before, Lisa. We're, well, we're very well-off financially. You know that. There are some bad people in the world. They might try to do things, to get money from us."

"Like robbing us?"

"Yes, or maybe something else."

"Like what?"

LuAnn stopped and sat down on the steps,

beckoning Lisa to join her. "Remember how I'm always telling you to be careful, watch out for people?" Lisa nodded. "Well, that's because some bad people might try to take you away from me."

Lisa looked frightened. "I'm not telling you that to scare you, baby, but in a way I guess I do want you to be concerned, to be aware of what's going on. If you use your head and keep your eyes open, everything will be fine. Me and Uncle Charlie won't let anything happen to you. Mommy promises. Okay?"

Lisa nodded and they went down the stairs hand in hand.

Charlie met them in the hallway. "My, don't we look extra pretty this morning."

"I've got a test."

"You think I don't know that? I was up last night until ten-thirty with you going over the stuff. You're gonna ace it, sure as anything. Go get your coat, I'll be out front in the car."

"Isn't Mommy taking me today?"

Charlie glanced over at LuAnn. "I'm gonna give your mom a break this morning. Besides, it'll give us one more time to go over the test stuff, right?"

Lisa beamed. "Right."

After Lisa had gone, Charlie turned a very serious face to LuAnn. "I'm gonna check some things out in town after I drop Lisa off."

"You think you can find this guy?"

Charlie shrugged as he buttoned up his overcoat. "Maybe, maybe not. It's not a big town, but it's got lots of hiding places. One reason *we* picked it, right?"

LuAnn nodded. "What about Riggs?"

"I'll save him for later. I go knock on his door now, he might get more suspicious than he already is. I'll call from the car if I find out anything."

LuAnn watched the two climb into Charlie's Range Rover and drive off. Deep in thought, she pulled on a heavy coat, walked through the house and out the back. She passed the Olympic-size pool with surrounding flagstone patio and three-foot-high brick wall. At this time of year, the pool was drained and protected by a metal cover. The tennis court would probably go in next year. LuAnn cared little for either activity. Her underprivileged childhood had yielded no opportunities to idly hit a yellow ball around or lounge in chlorinated water. But Lisa was an avid swimmer and tennis player, and upon arriving at Wicken's Hunt, she had pressed eagerly for a tennis court. Actually, it was nice to know she was going to be around in one spot long enough actually to plan something like the construction of a tennis court down the road.

The one activity LuAnn had picked up in her travels was what she was heading to do right now. The horse barn was about five hundred yards behind the main house and surrounded on three sides by a thick grove of trees. Her long strides took her there quickly. She employed several people full-time to care for the grounds and horse barn, but they were not yet at work. She pulled the gear from the tack room and expertly saddled her horse, Joy, named for her mother. She snagged a wide-brimmed Stetson hat and leather gloves off the wall, and swung herself up on to her ride. She had had Joy for several years now; the horse had traveled with them to several countries, not an easy task, but one that was quite manageable when your pocketbook was bottomless. LuAnn and company had arrived in the United States via plane. Joy had made the crossing by boat.

One reason she and Charlie had decided upon the property was its myriad of riding trails, some probably dating from Thomas Jefferson's days.

She started off at a good pace and soon left the

house behind. Twin clouds of breath escorted the pair as they made their way down a gradual decline and then around a curve, the trees hugging either side of the trail. The morning's briskness helped to clear LuAnn's head, let her think about things.

She had not recognized the man, not that she had expected to. Counterintuitively, she had always expected discovery to come from unknown quarters. He had known her real name. Whether that was a recent discovery on his part or he had found out long ago, she had no way of knowing.

Many times she had thought about going back to Georgia and telling the truth, just making a clean breast of it and attempting to put all of it behind her. But these thoughts had never managed to work themselves into cohesive actions and the reasons were clear. Although she had killed the man in self-defense, the words of the person calling himself Mr. Rainbow had continually come back to her. She had run. Thus, the police would assume the worst. On top of that, she was vastly rich, and who would have any sympathy or compassion for her now? Especially people from her hometown. The Shirley Watsons of the world were not so rare. Added to that was the fact that she had done something that was absolutely wrong. The horse she was riding, the clothes she was wearing, the home she was living in, the education and worldliness she had obtained over the years for herself and Lisa, all had been bought and paid for with what amounted to stolen dollars. In stark fiscal terms, she was one of the biggest crooks in history. If need be, she could endure prosecution for all that, but then Lisa's face sprung up in her thoughts. Almost simultaneously, the imagined words of Benny Tyler that day at the graveyard came filtering back to her.

Do it for Big Daddy. When did I ever lie to you,

baby doll? Daddy loves you.

She pulled Joy to a halt and sunk her head in her hands as a painful vision entered her head.

Lisa, sweetheart, your whole life is a lie. You were born in a trailer in the woods because I couldn't afford to have you anywhere else. Your father was a no-account loser who got murdered over drugs. I used to stick you under the counter at the Number One Truck Stop in Rikersville, Georgia, while I waited tables. I've killed a man and run from the police over it. Mommy stole all this money, more money than you could dream of. Everything you and I have came from that stolen money.

When did Mommy ever lie to you, baby doll? Mommy loves you.

LuAnn slowly dismounted and collapsed on a large stone that jutted at an angle from the ground. Only after several minutes did she slowly come around, her head swaying in long, slow movements, as though she were drunk.

She finally rose and took a handful of pebbles from the ground. She idly skipped the stones across the smooth surface of a small pond, sending each one farther and farther with quick, graceful flicks of her wrist. She could never go back now. There was nothing to go back to. She had given herself a new life, but it had come with a terrifyingly high cost. Her past was total fabrication, thus her future was uncertain. Her day-to-day existence vacillated between fear of total collapse of the flimsy veneer shrouding her true identity and immense guilt for what she had done. But if she lived for anything, it was to ensure that Lisa's life would not be harmed in any way by her mother's past – or future – actions. Whatever else happened, her little girl would not suffer because of her.

LuAnn remounted Joy, cantering along until she slowed the mare down to a walk as they passed

251

through some overhanging tree branches. She guided Joy to the edge of the trail and watched the swift, powerful thrust of the swollen creek that cut a jagged path across her property. There had been recent heavy rains, and early snow in the mountains had turned the usually docile water into a dangerous torrent. She backed Joy away from the edge and continued on.

Ten years ago, just after she, Charlie, and Lisa had landed in London, they had immediately boarded a plane for Sweden. Jackson had given them detailed marching orders for the first twelve months and they had not dared to deviate from them. The next six months had been a whirlwind zigzag through western Europe and then several years in Holland and then back to Scandinavia where a tall, light-haired woman would not seem so out of place. They had also spent time in Monaco and surrounding countries. The last two years had them in New Zealand, where they had all enjoyed the quiet, civilized, and even somewhat old-fashioned lifestyle. While Lisa knew multiple languages, English had been her primary one; LuAnn had been firm on that. LuAnn was an American despite spending so much time away.

It had indeed been fortunate that Charlie was a seasoned traveler. It had been largely through his efforts that potential disaster had been avoided at several different times. They had not heard from Jackson, but both assumed that he knew Charlie was with her. Thank God he was. If he hadn't gotten on that plane, LuAnn didn't know what she would've done. As it stood now, she couldn't function without him. And he wasn't getting any younger. She shook at the thought of life without the man. To be robbed of the one person in her life who shared her secret, who loved her and Lisa. There was nothing Charlie

252

wouldn't do for them, and when his life ended and that void erupted . . . She drew in a deep breath.

Their new identities had been cemented over the years as LuAnn had taken great pains to establish the history Jackson had concocted for her and her daughter. The toughest part by far had been Lisa. Lisa believed her father to have been an extremely wealthy European financier who had died when Lisa was very young and who had left behind no family other than them. Charlie's role, while never fully explained, was clearly one of family and the "uncle" label had seemed a natural one. There were no photographs of Mr. Savage. LuAnn had explained to Lisa that her father was very reclusive and a touch eccentric and had allowed none to be taken. LuAnn and Charlie had long debated whether actually to create a man, photos and all, but had decided that it would be too dangerous. A wall with holes punched through it would eventually fall. Thus, Lisa believed her mother to be the very young widow of an extremely wealthy man, whose wealth, in turn, had made her mother one of the wealthiest women in the world. And one of the most generous.

LuAnn had sent Beth, her former coworker, enough money to start her own chain of restaurants. Johnny Jarvis from the mall had received enough to pay for several advanced degrees at the country's most prestigious universities. Duane's parents had received enough money to keep them secure in their retirement. LuAnn had even sent money to Shirley Watson, a guilty reaction to having lashed the woman with a negative reputation in the only place where Shirley would ever have the ambition or courage to live. Finally, LuAnn's mother's gravesite was now marked with a far more elaborate monument. The police, she was sure, had done all they could to track her down through this largesse, but without success. Jackson had hidden the money well and there had been absolutely no trace for the authorities to follow.

In addition, half her yearly income had been donated anonymously to a number of charities and other good works that she and Charlie had identified over the years. They were ever on the lookout for more deserving homes for the lottery money. LuAnn was determined to do as much good as she could with the money to atone, at least in part, for the manner in which she had acquired it. Even with all that, the money came in far faster than they could dispose of it. Jackson's investments had paid off more handsomely than even he had envisioned and the anticipated twenty-five million dollars in earnings each year had actually exceeded forty million per annum. All money unspent by LuAnn had also been reinvested by Jackson and the surplus had kept compounding until the assets LuAnn now held in her own name were almost half a billion dollars. She shook her head at the thought of the staggering sum. And the original lottery prize money, one hundred million dollars, was to be returned to her very shortly, the ten-year period having expired, as her contract with Jackson had stated. That mattered little to LuAnn. Jackson could keep it; it wasn't as though she needed it. But he would return it. The man, she had to admit, had been utterly faithful to his promise.

Over all these years, every quarter the detailed financial statements had arrived, no matter where they happened to be in the world. But since only the papers and never the man showed up, LuAnn's anxiety finally had passed. The letter accompanying all the financial packets was from an investment company with a Swiss address. She had no idea of Jackson's ties to this firm, nor did she care to explore

254

that area further. She had seen enough of him to be respectful of his volatility; and more disturbingly, of the extreme consequences which he was capable of causing. She also remembered how he had been prepared to kill her if she had rejected his offer. There was something not quite natural about him. The powers he seemed to possess could hardly be of this world.

She stopped at a large oak. From one of its branches a long knotted rope dangled. LuAnn gripped the rope and lifted herself off the saddle, while Joy, already quite familiar with this ritual, waited patiently. Her arms moving like wonderfully calibrated pistons, LuAnn swiftly climbed to the other end of the rope, which was tied around a thick branch almost thirty feet off the ground, and then made her way back down. She repeated the process twice more. She had a fully equipped gymnasium in her home where she worked out diligently. It wasn't vanity; she had little interest in how it made her look. She was naturally strong, and that physical strength had carried her through many a crisis. It was one of the few constant things in her life and she was loath to let it disappear.

Growing up in Georgia, she had climbed many trees, run through miles of countryside, and jumped many ravines. She had just been having fun; the concept of exercise hadn't come into the equation. And so, in addition to pumping the iron, she had built a more natural exercise course across her extensive grounds. She pulled herself up the rope one more time, the muscle cords in her arms and back tight as rebar.

Breathing hard, she settled lightly back into the saddle and made her way back to the horse barn, her heart lightened and her spirits raised by the invigorating ride through the countryside and the strenuous rope climb.

In the large storage building next to the horse barn, one of the groundspeople, a beefy man in his early thirties, had just started splitting logs with a sledgehammer and wedge. LuAnn glanced at him through the open doorway as she rode by. She quickly unsaddled Joy and returned the horse to its stall. She walked over to the doorway of the outbuilding. The man briefly nodded to her and then continued his work. He knew she lived in the mansion. Other than that, he knew nothing about her. She watched the man for a minute and then took off her coat, lifted a second sledgehammer off the wall, squeezed a spare wedge between her fingers, testing its weight, set a log up on the block, tapped the wedge into its rough surface, stepped back, and swung cleanly. The wedge bit deep, but didn't cleave the log in two. She hit it again, dead center, and then again. The log broke clean. The man glanced at her in surprise, then shrugged and kept splitting. They both pounded away, barely ten feet from each other. The man could split a log with one swing of the hammer, while it continued to take LuAnn two and sometimes three blows. He smiled over at her, the sweat showing on his brow. She kept pounding away, though, her arms and shoulders working in precise unity, and within five minutes she was cracking a log with one blow, and before he knew it she was doing it faster than he.

The man picked up his pace, the sweat falling faster across his brow, his grin gone as his breaths became more painful. After twenty minutes, he was taking two and three strikes to crack a log as his big arms and shoulders started to tire rapidly, his chest heaving and his legs rubbery. He watched in growing amazement as LuAnn continued, her pace steady, the strength of her blows against the wood totally undiminished. In fact, she seemed to be hitting the wedge harder and harder. The sound of metal on metal rang out louder and louder. Finally, the man dropped the sledgehammer and leaned back against the wall, his gut heaving, his arms dead, his shirt drenched in perspiration despite the chilly weather. LuAnn finished her pile of logs and, barely missing a stroke, finished off his stack as well. Her work complete, she wiped her forehead and replaced the sledgehammer on the wall hook before glancing over at the puffing man as she shook out her arms.

"You're very strong," she said, looking at the substantial pile of wood he had split as she put her coat back on.

He looked at her in surprise and then started laughing. "I was thinking that too before you came along. Now I've half a mind to go work in the kitchen."

She smiled and patted him on the shoulder. She had chopped wood virtually every day of her life from the time she had started school until she was sixteen. She hadn't done it for exercise, like now; back then she had done it to keep warm. "Don't feel bad, I've had a lot of practice."

As she walked back up to the house she took a moment to admire the rear facade of the mansion. The purchase and renovation of this house had been, by far, her greatest extravagance. And she had done it for two reasons. First, because she was tired of traveling and wanted to settle down, although she would've been happy in something far less magnificent than what she was staring at. Second, and most important, she had done it for the same reason she had done most things over the years: for Lisa. To give her a real home with a sense of permanence where she could grow up, marry, and have children of her own. Home the last ten years

257

had been hotels, rented villas, and chalets, not that LuAnn was complaining about existing in such luxury, but none of them were home. The tiny trailer in the middle of the woods all those years ago had had far deeper roots for her than the most extravagant residence in Europe. Now they had this. LuAnn smiled at the sight: big, beautiful, and safe. At the thought of the last word, LuAnn suddenly huddled in her coat as a wind broke through the stand of trees.

Safe? When they had gone to bed last night they had been safe and secure, or as much as one could be living the kind of existence they all did. The face of the man in the Honda sprang up before her and she closed her eyes tightly until it finally went away. In its place came another image. The man's face stared at her with many emotions passing across it. Matthew Riggs had risked his life for her and the best she could do was accuse him of lying. And with that response she had only served to make him more suspicious. She pondered a moment, and then sprinted toward the house.

Charlie's office was straight out of a men's club in London, with a magnificent wet bar of polished walnut occupying one corner. The custom-built mahogany desk had neatly sorted piles of correspondence, bills, and other household matters. LuAnn quickly flipped through his card file until she found the one she wanted and plucked it out. She then took out a key Charlie kept high up on a shelf and used it to open a drawer in his desk. She took out the .38 revolver, loaded it, and carried it upstairs with her. The weight of the compact weapon restored some of her confidence. She showered, changed into a black skirt and sweater, threw on a full-length coat, and went down to the garage. As she drove down the private road, one hand tight around the pistol in her coat pocket, LuAnn anxiously looked around, for the Honda could be lurking. She breathed a sigh of relief when she hit the main road and was still all alone. She glanced at the address and phone number on the business card and wondered whether she should call first. Her hand hesitated over the car phone and then she decided just to chance it. If he wasn't there, then maybe it was best. She didn't know whether what she was planning would help or hurt matters. Ever one to choose action over passivity, she couldn't change her ways now. Besides, it was her problem, not anyone else's. She would have to deal with it eventually.

Eventually, she would have to deal with it all.

TWENTY-SIX

Jackson had just arrived back from a cross-country trip and was in his makeup room divesting himself of his most recent disguise when the phone rang. It was not his residential phone. It was his business line, an untraceable communications linkage, and it almost never rang. Jackson called out on the line often during the business day to convey precise instructions to his associates across the globe. Almost no one ever called him, however; and that was the way he wanted it. He had a myriad of other ways to ascertain whether his instructions were being carried out. He snatched up the phone.

"Yes?"

"I think we might have a problem here, or it may be nothing," the voice said.

"I'm listening." Jackson sat down and used a long piece of string to lift the putty off his nose. Then he removed the latex pieces adhering to his face by tugging gently on their edges.

"As you know, two days ago we wired income from the last quarter to Catherine Savage's account in the Caymans. To Banque Internacional. Just like always."

"So? Is she complaining about the rate of return?" Jackson said sarcastically. He tugged firmly on the back edges of his snow white wig and then pulled up and then forward. He next removed the latex skullcap and his own hair sprang free.

"No, but I got a call from the wire department at

Banque and they wanted to confirm something."

"What was that?" Jackson cleansed his face while he was listening, his eyes scanning the mirror as layer after layer of concealment was removed.

"That they had wired all the monies from Savage's accounts to Citibank in New York."

New York! As he absorbed this stunning news, Jackson opened his mouth wide and removed the acrylic caps. Instantly, dark, misshapen teeth became white and straight. His dark eyes glittered menacingly and he stopped removing his disguise. "First, why would they call you if it was her account?"

"They shouldn't have. I mean they never have before. I think the guy at the wire desk down there is new. He must have seen my name and phone number on some of the paperwork and figured I was a principal on the receiving account instead of being on the other end of the transaction, the sending account."

"What did you tell him? I hope you didn't excite any suspicion."

"No, not at all," the voice said nervously. "I simply thanked him and said that was correct. I hope I did the right thing, but of course I wanted to report it to you right away. It seemed unusual."

"Thank you."

"Anything you want me to do on follow-up?"

"I'll handle it." Jackson hung up the phone. He sat back and fiddled absently with the wig. None of LuAnn's money was ever, ever supposed to end up in the United States. Money in the United States was traceable. Banks filed 1099s with the IRS, and other documents detailing income and account balances. Social Security numbers were communicated and kept as part of the official record; filings with the IRS on behalf of the taxpayer were required. None of that was ever supposed to happen in LuAnn's case.

LuAnn Tyler was a fugitive. Fugitives did not return to their homeland and start paying their taxes, even under assumed names.

He picked up his phone and dialed a number.

"Yes, sir?" the voice asked.

Jackson said, "The taxpayer's name is Catherine Savage." Jackson provided her Social Security number and other pertinent information. "You will find out immediately whether she has filed a U.S. tax return or any other type of documents with the IRS. Use all the sources at your disposal, but I need this information within the hour."

He hung up again. For the next forty-five minutes, he walked around his apartment, wearing the portable phone and headset, a requirement when you liked to pace and your apartment was as large as Jackson's was.

Then the phone rang again.

The voice was crisp. "Catherine Savage filed an income tax return last year. I couldn't get full particulars in such a short time frame; however, according to my source, the income reported was substantial. She also recently filed a change of address form with the IRS."

"Give it to me." Jackson wrote the Charlottesville, Virginia, address down on a piece of paper and put it in his pocket.

"One more thing," the voice said. "My source pulled up a very recent filing in connection with Savage's tax account."

"By her?"

"No. It was a Form 2848. It gives a third party a power of attorney to represent the taxpayer with respect to just about anything having to do with their tax matters."

"Who was the requesting party?"

"A fellow named Thomas Jones. According to the

file, he's already received information on her account, including her change of address and last year's income tax return. I was able to get a facsimile of the 2848 form he filed. I can send it to you right now."

"Do so."

Jackson hung up and a minute later had the fax in his hands. He looked at Catherine Savage's signature on the form. He pulled out the originals of the documents LuAnn had signed ten years earlier in connection with their agreement for the lottery winnings. The signatures weren't even close, not that the IRS, cumbersome institution that it was, would ever have taken the time to compare signatures. A forgery. Whoever the man was, he had filed this document without the woman's knowledge. Jackson studied the address and phone number that Tom Jones had given for himself. The address was a P.O. box. Jackson was certain that would also be another dead end. The man was privy to Catherine Savage's tax situation and her new address and his background was a complete sham.

That startling fact was not what annoyed Jackson the most, troubling as it was. He sat down in a chair and studied the wall as his mind moved in ever expanding circles of thought. LuAnn had come back to the United States, despite his explicit instructions to the contrary. She had disobeyed him. That was bad enough. The problem was compounded by the fact that someone else was now interested in her. For what reason? Where was this person now? Probably the same place Jackson was just about to head to: Charlottesville, Virginia.

The lights of the two trains were becoming clearer. The possibility of that collision with LuAnn Tyler crept closer and closer to reality. Jackson went back to his makeup room. It was time for another creation.

TWENTY-SEVEN

After dropping Lisa off at St. Anne's, taking care to walk her directly into the classroom, as was his and LuAnn's practice, Charlie had wheeled the Range Rover out of the parking lot and headed into town. Over the last few months while LuAnn had remained reclusive inside their mountainside fortress, Charlie had been the point man, meeting with prominent townsfolk, making the rounds of businesses and charities and university officials. He and LuAnn had decided that they could not keep secret her wealth and presence in this small, albeit cosmopolitan town and any attempt to do so would invite more suspicion rather than less. Thus, Charlie's task was to lay the groundwork with the town's leaders for the eventual emergence of LuAnn into their society. However, it would only be a very limited emergence. Everyone could understand the need for privacy of the extremely wealthy. And there were many organizations very eager to receive donations from LuAnn, so that maximum cooperation and understanding would likely be forthcoming. That pipeline had already been opened, as LuAnn had donated over a hundred thousand dollars to several local causes. As he headed down the road Charlie shook his head wearily. All these plans, strategies, and what-not. Being phenomenally wealthy was a big pain in the ass. Sometimes he yearned for the old days. A few bucks in his pocket, a beer nearby, and a pack of smokes when he wanted it; a fight on the tube. He smiled wryly. LuAnn had finally gotten him to stop smoking about eight years ago and he knew that had prolonged his life considerably. But he was allowed an occasional cigar. She wasn't about to mother him to death.

Charlie's earlier forays into Charlottesville society had produced one contact in an extremely useful position, a contact that he now intended to pump for information that would allow him and LuAnn to check out her pursuer and, if possible, forestall any real problem. If the man wanted money, that was one thing. Money was not an issue. LuAnn's pocketbook was more than sufficient to satisfy even the most outrageous blackmailer. But what if the issue wasn't simply money? The problem was, Charlie was unsure exactly what the man knew or didn't know. He had mentioned LuAnn's real name. Did he also know about Duane Harvey's murder and LuAnn's relationship to the dead man? The warrant that had been issued for LuAnn's arrest ten years ago? And how had he tracked LuAnn down after all these years? The next issue was even more critical: Did the man know about the lottery fix? LuAnn had told Charlie all about the man calling himself Rainbow. Rainbow might have figured it out. He had followed her, watched her buy a lottery ticket, leave immediately for New York, and win a fortune. Had the man known it was rigged? And had he told anyone? LuAnn had not been sure.

And what had happened to Rainbow? Charlie licked his lips nervously. He had never really known Jackson, never even seen him. But while he had worked for him, he had talked to the man often. The tones of Jackson's voice had been unremarkable: even, calm, direct, supremely confident. Charlie had known people just like that. These men weren't the

265

blusterers, the ones who always said a hell of a lot more than they ever had the courage or ability to back up in reality. They were the ones who looked you dead in the eye, said precisely what they intended to do with little fanfare or hyperbole, and then simply did it. These types would efficiently disembowel you and not lose any sleep over it. Jackson, Charlie had long ago decided, was one of those. Despite his own toughness and strength, Charlie shivered slightly. Wherever Rainbow was, it wasn't among the living, that was for damn sure. Charlie drove on, lost in thought.

TWENTY-EIGHT

uAnn pulled her car into the driveway and stopped in front of the house. She didn't see the pickup truck anywhere. He probably was off at another job. She was about to leave, but the simple beauty of Matt Riggs's home made her stop, get out of the BMW, and go up the plank steps. The graceful lines of the old structure, the obvious care and skill which had gone into rehabbing it, made her eager to explore the place, even if its owner was absent.

She moved around the broad porch, running her hand along its intricate wooden scrollwork. She opened the screen door and knocked at the front door, but there was no answer. She hesitated and then tried the doorknob. It turned easily in her hand. People had not locked their doors where she had grown up either. As security conscious as she was now, it was good to know there were still places like that left in the world. She hesitated again. Entering the man's home without his knowledge might only compound matters. However, if he never found out? She might be able to obtain some useful information about him, something she could use to help extricate herself from this potential disaster.

She pushed open the front door and then closed it softly behind her. The living room had random-width oak flooring splotched and mottled with age. The furnishings were simple but carefully arranged and each was of excellent quality. LuAnn wondered whether Matt Riggs bought the pieces in broken condition and then worked on them. She moved through the rooms, stopping to admire the man's handiwork here and there. The slight smell of varnish hovered over various pieces of furniture. The place was neat and clean. There were no pictures of family: no wife, no kids. She didn't know why but this struck her as odd. She reached his office and peered inside. Quietly moving over to his desk, she stopped for a moment as she thought she heard a sound come from somewhere within the house. Her heart started to race and she briefly contemplated fleeing. The sound wasn't repeated, however, and she calmed down and seated herself behind the desk. The first thing that caught her eye was the paper on which Riggs had jotted down the notes. Her name and other information about her. Then she glanced at the information on the Honda. She looked at her watch. Riggs was clearly not a man who believed in idleness. And he was able to get information from sources that were obviously more than a little sophisticated. That was troubling. LuAnn jerked her head up as she looked out the broad window into the backyard. There was a barn-like structure there. The door was open slightly. LuAnn had thought she had noted movement there. As she got up to go outside, her hand dipped into her jacket pocket and closed around the .38.

When she exited the house she started to head back to her car. Then her curiosity got the better of her and she crept over to the barn door and peered inside. An overhead light illuminated the area well. It was set up as a workshop and storage facility. In front of two entire walls were sturdy work benches and tables and more tools than LuAnn had ever before seen in one place. The two other walls had shelving where wood supplies and other materials

268

were stacked in precise configurations. As LuAnn moved inside she eyed the staircase at the rear of the structure. In former times she was certain it would have led to a hayloft. Riggs, however, had no animals in need of hay, at least that she could see. She wondered what it housed now.

She took the steps slowly. When she reached the top, she stared in amazement. The place was set up as a small study and observation area. Two book-cases, a beat-up leather chair and ottoman, and an ancient potbellied stove stared back at her. In one corner, an old-fashioned telescope was set up to look out a huge window in the rear of the barn. As LuAnn climbed up and looked through the window, her heart started to pound. Riggs's truck was parked behind the barn.

As she turned to run down the stairs, she found herself staring down the barrel of a twelve-gauge shotgun.

When Riggs saw who it was he slowly lowered the weapon. "What the hell are you doing here?" She tried to move past him, but Riggs grabbed her arm. She just as quickly pulled it free.

"You scared me to death," she said.

"Sorry. Now what the hell are you doing here?"

"Is this how you usually welcome company into your home?"

"Company usually comes in through the front door, and only after I've opened it." He looked around. "This sure as hell isn't my front door, and I don't remember inviting you in."

LuAnn moved away from him as she looked around the space and then returned her gaze to his angry features.

"This is a nice place to come and think. How would you like to build me something like this at my house?"

Riggs leaned up against the wall. He still held the shotgun in the down position but he could swing it up into a firing position in the matter of a second. "I would think you'd want to see my work on the fence before you hired me for something else, Ms. Savage."

She feigned surprise at the sound of her name but apparently not enough to satisfy Riggs.

"So, did you find anything else of interest in my office besides my homework on you?"

She looked at him with even more respect. "I'm a little paranoid about my privacy."

"So I noticed. Is that why you carry a pistol?"

LuAnn looked down at her pocket. A sliver of the .38 was visible.

"You have good eyes."

"A thirty-eight doesn't have such great stopping power. If you're serious about your privacy, and your security, you might want to step up to a nine millimeter. A semiautomatic over a revolver is a no-brainer." The hand holding the shotgun twitched for an instant. "I tell you what, you take the revolver out, muzzle first, and I'll stop fussing with my shotgun here."

"I'm not going to shoot you."

"That's absolutely right, you're not," he said evenly. "Please do as I say, Ms. Savage. And do it very slowly."

LuAnn took the pistol out, holding it by the barrel.

"Now unload it and put the bullets in one pocket and the pistol in the other. And I can count to six so don't try to be cute."

LuAnn did as she was told, looking at him angrily. "I'm not used to being treated like a criminal."

"You break into my house carrying a weapon, that's exactly how I'm going to treat you. Count yourself lucky that I didn't shoot first and ask questions later. Buckshot can be very irritating to the skin."

270

"I didn't break in. The door was open."

"Don't try that one in a court of law," he fired back.

When Riggs had confirmed that she had emptied the revolver, he broke open the shotgun and laid it down on the bookcase. He crossed his arms and studied her.

Slightly unnerved, LuAnn went back to her original train of thought. "My circle of friends is very small. When somebody intrudes on that circle I tend to get curious."

"That's funny. You call it intrusion, but what I did this morning ordinarily would be called coming to the rescue."

LuAnn brushed a strand of hair out of her face and looked away for a moment. "Look, Mr. Riggs—"

"My friends call me Matt. We're not friends, but I'll allow you the privilege," he said coolly.

"I'd rather call you Matthew. I don't want to break any of your rules."

Riggs looked startled for a moment before settling back down. "Whatever."

"Charlie said you were a cop."

"I never said so."

She looked at him, surprise now clear on her features. "Well, were you?"

"What I was really isn't any of your business. And you still haven't told me what you're doing here."

She rubbed her hand across the old leather chair. She didn't answer right away and Riggs was content to let the silence endure until she broke it. "What happened this morning is a little more complicated than it appeared. It's something that I'm taking care of." She paused and looked up at him, her eyes searching his. "I appreciate what you did. You helped me and you didn't have to. I came here to thank you."

271

Riggs relaxed a little bit. "Okay, although I didn't expect any thanks. You needed some help and I was around to give it. One human being to another. The world would be a hell of a lot better place if we all lived by that rule."

"I also came to ask a favor."

Riggs inclined his head toward her, waiting.

"The situation this morning, I would appreciate it if you'd just forget about it. Like I said, Charlie and I are taking care of it. If you got involved, it might make things more difficult for me."

Riggs took this in for a few moments.

"Do you know the guy?"

"I really don't want to get into it."

Riggs rubbed his chin. "You know, the guy banged me up. So I already feel like I'm involved."

LuAnn moved closer to him. "I know you don't know me, but it would mean a lot if you would just drop it. It really would." Her eyes seemed to widen with each word spoken.

Riggs felt himself drawing closer to her although he hadn't physically budged an inch. Her gaze seemed to be pasted on to his face, all the sunlight streaming through the window seemed to be blocked out as though an eclipse were occurring.

"I'll tell you what: Unless the guy gives me any more trouble, I'll forget it ever happened.

LuAnn's tensed shoulders slumped in relief. "Thank you."

She moved past him toward the stair. The scent of her perfume drifted through his nostrils. His skin started to tingle. It had been a long time since that had happened.

"Your home is beautiful," she said.

"It certainly doesn't compare to yours."

"Did you do it all yourself?"

"Most of it. I'm pretty handy."

272

"Why don't you come by tomorrow and we can talk about you doing some more work for me."

"Ms. Savage—"

"Call me Catherine."

"Catherine, you don't have to buy my silence."

"Around noon? I can have some lunch ready."

Riggs gave her a searching look and then shrugged. "I can make that."

As she started down the stairs, he called after her. "That guy in the Honda. Don't assume he's going to give up."

She glanced back at the shotgun for one significant moment before settling her gaze on him.

"I never assume anything anymore, Matthew."

"Well, it's a good cause, John, and she likes to help good causes." Charlie leaned back in his chair and sipped the hot coffee. He was sitting at a window table in the dining room of the Boar's Head Inn, off Ivy Road a little west of the University of Virginia. Two plates held the remnants of breakfast. The man across from him beamed.

"Well, I can't tell you how much it means to the community. Having her here – both of you – is just wonderful." Wearing a costly double-breasted suit, with a colorful handkerchief dangling from the outer pocket and matching his polka-dot tie, the wavy-haired John Pemberton was one of the area's most successful and well-connected real estate agents. He also sat on the boards of numerous charities and local committees. The man knew virtually everything that happened in the area, which was precisely the reason Charlie had asked him to breakfast. Further, the commission on the sale of LuAnn's home had landed six figures in Pemberton's pocket and he was, thus, an eternal friend.

Now he looked down at his lap and a sheepish grin appeared on his handsome features when he looked back up at Charlie. "We are hoping to actually *meet* Ms. Savage at some point."

"Absolutely, John, absolutely. She's looking forward to meeting you too. It'll just take some time. She's a very private person, you understand."

"Of course, of course, this place is full of people like that. Movie stars, writers, people with more money than they know what to do with."

An involuntary smile played across Pemberton's lips. Charlie assumed the man was daydreaming about future dollars of commission when these wealthy folk moved in or out of the area.

"You'll just have to live with my company for a little while longer." A grin creased Charlie's features.

"And very enjoyable company it is too," Pemberton replied automatically.

Charlie put down his coffee cup and pushed his breakfast plate away. If he still smoked cigarettes he would've stopped to light one up. "We have Matt Riggs doing some work for us."

"Putting in the security fence. Yes, I know. Undoubtedly his biggest job to date."

Upon noting Charlie's surprised look, Pemberton smiled in an embarrassed fashion. "Despite its cosmopolitan appearance, Charlottesville really is a small town. There is very little that happens that isn't known by most people soon thereafter."

At those words, Charlie's spirits plummeted. *Had Riggs already told someone? Had they made a mistake coming here? Should they have planted themselves amid the seven million residents of New York City instead?*

With an effort, he shook off these numbing thoughts and plunged ahead. "Right. Well, the guy had some terrific references."

"He does very good work, dependable and

274

professional. He hasn't been here all that long by the standards of most locals, about five years, but I've never heard a bad word said about him."

"Where'd he come from?"

"Washington. D.C., not the state of." Pemberton fingered his teacup.

"So he was a builder up there then?"

Pemberton shook his head. "No, he got his general contractor's license after he got here."

"Still, he could've apprenticed up there."

"I think he had some natural talent for the trade. He's a first-rate carpenter, but he apprenticed with Ralph Steed, one of our best local builders for two years. Ralph passed away about that time and that's when Riggs went out on his own. He's done very well. He's a hard worker. And landing that fence job doesn't hurt any."

"True. Still, the guy just shows up in town one day and plunges into something new. That takes some balls. I mean I've met him, and it wasn't like he would've been fresh out of college when he came here."

"No, he wasn't." Pemberton looked around the small dining area. When he spoke next it was with a lowered voice. "You're not the first person who has been curious about Riggs's origins."

Charlie leaned forward, adding to the conspiratorial image of the pair. "Is that right? What do we have here, a little local intrigue?" Charlie tried to make his tone appear light and unconcerned.

"Of course rumors come and go, and you know the questionable veracity of most of them. Still, I have heard from various sources that Riggs held some important position in Washington." Pemberton paused for effect. "In the intelligence community."

Behind the stone mask Charlie fought the urge to abruptly give back his breakfast. Although LuAnn had had the good luck to be one of the recipients of Jackson's control of the lottery, she might have just matched that luck with a dose of incredibly bad fortune. "In intelligence, you say? Like a spy?"

Pemberton threw up his hands. "Who knows. Secrets are a way of life with people like that. Torture them and they won't say a thing. Probably bite on their cyanide pill or whatever and go peacefully into the night." Pemberton obviously enjoyed a touch of the dramatic mixed in with elements of danger and intrigue, particularly at a safe distance.

Charlie rubbed at his left knee. "I had heard he was a cop."

"Who told you that?"

"I don't recall. Just heard it in passing."

"Well, if he was a policeman that's something that can be checked. If he was a spy, there'd be no record of it, would there?"

"So he never talked to anyone here about his past?"

"Only in vague terms. That's probably why you heard he was a policeman. People hear bits and pieces, they start to fill in the holes themselves."

"Well, son of a gun." Charlie sat back, trying hard to appear calm.

"Still, he's an exceptional builder. He'll do good work for you." Pemberton laughed. "Just so long as he doesn't start snooping around. You know if he was a spy, those habits probably die hard. I've led a pretty squeaky clean life, but everybody has skeletons in their closet, don't you think?"

Charlie cleared his throat before answering. "Some more than others."

Charlie leaned forward again, his hands clasped in front of him on the table; he was quite eager to change the subject and had the vehicle to do so.

"John," Charlie's voice dipped low, "John, I've got a small favor to ask of you."

Pemberton's smile broadened. "Just ask it, Charlie. And consider it done."

"A man came by the house the other day asking for a donation to a charitable foundation he said he headed."

Pemberton looked startled. "What was his name?"

"He wasn't local," Charlie said quickly. "He gave me a name but I'm not sure it was his real one. It all seemed suspicious, you understand what I'm saying."

"Absolutely."

"Someone in Ms. Savage's position has to be careful. There are a lot of scams out there."

"Don't I know it. How upsetting."

"Right. Well, anyway, the guy said he was staying in the area for a while. Asked for a follow-up meeting with Ms. Savage."

"I hope you're not going to agree to that."

"I haven't yet. The guy left a phone number, but it's not a local one. I called it. It was an answering service."

"What was the name of the foundation?"

"I don't remember exactly, but it had something to do with medical research of some kind."

"That's so easy to concoct," Pemberton said knowingly. "Of course I have no personal experience with frauds like that," he added huffily, "but I understand that there is a proliferation of them."

"That was exactly my read. Well, to make a long story short, since the guy said he was going to be around awhile, I thought it probable that he was renting someplace hereabouts, instead of sacking out at a hotel. That gets to be expensive after a while, especially if you're living scam to scam."

"And you want to know if I can find out where he might be staying?"

"Exactly. I wouldn't ask it if it weren't real important. With things like this I'm never too careful. I want to know who I'm dealing with in case he shows up again."

"Of course, of course." Pemberton let out a shallow breath and sipped at his tea. "I'll certainly look into it for you. My sympathies lie with you and Ms. Savage."

"And we will be very grateful for any assistance you can give us. I've mentioned several of the other charities you head up to Ms. Savage and she spoke very positively about all of them and your work with them."

Pemberton was glowing now. "Why don't you give me a description of the man? I have the morning free and I can start my own little investigation. If he's within fifty miles of here, with my connections, I'm certain I can find him."

Charlie described the man, laid some cash on the table for the meal, and stood up. "We really appreciate it, John."

TWENTY-NINE

Thomas Donovan scanned the city streets for a parking spot. Georgetown was not known for its abundance of places to leave one's vehicle. He was driving a new rental car, a late model Chrysler. He turned right from M Street on to Wisconsin Avenue, and finally managed to snag a spot on a side street not too far from where he was heading. A light rain began to fall as he walked down the street. The quiet area he soon found himself in harbored an elite neighborhood of towering brick and clapboard residences which were home to high-ranking businessmen and political types. He eyed some of the homes as he walked along. In the lights visible through intricately designed windows Donovan could make out well-dressed owners settling down in front of warm fires, coddling drinks and exchanging light kisses as they went through their rituals of relaxation after another day of perhaps changing the world, or merely adding to their already hefty investment portfolios.

So much wealth and power rested in this area that an energy seemed to wash up from the brick sidewalks and hurtle Donovan along at a furious clip. Money and power had never been overriding ambitions of his. Despite that, his occupation often placed him in close proximity to those who held the attainment of one or both of these prizes above all else. It was a wonderful position from which to play the altruistic cynic and Donovan often played that role to the fullest for the simple reason that he genuinely believed in what he did for a living. The irony of this was not lost on him. For without the rich and powerful and their evil ways, at whom would he throw his sharp-edged stones?

Donovan finally stopped at one formidable residence: a one-hundred-year-old three-story brick townhouse sitting behind a waist-high brick wall topped by black wrought-iron fencing of a style found throughout the area. He inserted a key into the gate's lock and went up the sidewalk. Another key allowed him entry through the massive wooden front door and he shook off his coat.

The housekeeper appeared immediately and took the wet coat from him. She wore a traditional maid's uniform and spoke with a practiced degree of deference.

"I'll tell the missus you're here, Mr. Donovan."

He nodded quickly and moved past her into the drawing room where he took a moment to warm himself before the blazing fire and then looked around with contentment. His upbringing had been decidedly blue collar but he did not attempt to hide his pleasure at occasionally dabbling in luxury. It was an incongruity in his nature that had bothered him greatly in his youth, but much less so now. Some things did become better as one aged, he mused, including layers of personal guilt that one ended up shedding like peeling an onion.

By the time he had mixed himself a drink from the stock housed behind a cabinet in one corner of the drawing room, the woman had appeared.

She moved quickly to him and gave him a deep kiss. He took her hand and caressed it lightly.

"I missed you," she said.

He led her over to the large sofa against one wall. Their knees touched as they sat close together.

Alicia Crane was petite, in her mid-thirties, with long hair that was looking more ash than blond with each passing day. Her dress was costly and the jewelry clinging to her wrists and ears easily matched the richness of the garment; however, the image was one of quiet wealth and sophistication. Her features were delicate, the nose so small as to be barely noticeable between the deep luster of the dark brown eyes. While she was not a traditional beauty, her obvious wealth and refinement had inspired a certain look that was pleasant enough. On her best days she would be described as very well put together.

Her cheek trembled slightly as he stroked it.

"I missed you too, Alicia. A lot."

"I don't like it when you have to be away." Her voice was cultured and dignified, its cadence slow and exact. It was a voice seemingly too formal for a relatively young woman.

"Well, it's part of the job." He smiled at her. "But you're making that job a lot more difficult to do." He *was* attracted to Alicia Crane. While not the brightest star in the universe, she was a good person, without the pretenses and airs that her level of wealth usually stamped on its possessors.

With a start, she stared. "Why in the world did you shave off your beard?"

Donovan rubbed his hand across the smooth skin. "Change of pace," he said quickly. "You know men go through their own form of menopause. I think it took about ten years off the mug. What do you think?"

"I think you're just as handsome without it as you were with it. In fact, you remind me a little of Father. When he was a younger man, of course."

"Thanks for lying to an *old* man." He smiled. "But being compared to him, well that's high praise."

"I can have Maggie put on some supper. You must be starved." She gripped his hand with both of hers.

"Thank you, Alicia. And maybe a hot bath after that."

"Of course, the rain is so chilling at this time of year." She hesitated for a moment. "Will you have to leave again soon? I was thinking we could go down to the islands. It's so beautiful this time of year."

"That sounds wonderful, but I'm afraid it'll have to keep. I have to leave tomorrow."

Her disappointment shone through on her face before her gaze dropped. "Oh, I see."

He tucked one hand under her chin and stared into her eyes. "Alicia, I had a breakthrough today. A breakthrough that I wasn't sure would happen. It was a risk on my part, but sometimes you have to take risks if you want the payoff." He remembered from that morning, the haunted look in LuAnn Tyler's eyes. "All that sniffing around, never sure if anything's going to turn up. But that's all part of the game."

"That's wonderful, Thomas, I'm so happy for you. But I hope you didn't place yourself in personal danger. I don't know what I would do if anything happened to you."

He sat back as he contemplated his daredevil morning. "I can take care of myself. But I don't take unnecessary risks. I leave that for the kiddies coming up." His voice was calming.

He glanced over at her; the look on her face was that of a child listening to her favorite hero recount a past adventure. Donovan finished his drink. A hero. He liked the feeling. Who wouldn't? Who didn't need that kind of unadulterated admiration every now and then? He smiled deeply and gripped Alicia's small hand in his.

"I promise you something. After I break this story,

282

we're going to take a long vacation. Just you and me. Someplace warm, with plenty to drink, and I can dust off my talents as a sailor. I haven't done that in a long time and I can't think of anyone I'd rather do it with. How's that sound?"

She laid her head against his shoulder and squeezed his hand tightly. "Wonderful."

THIRTY

"You invited him for lunch?" Charlie stared at LuAnn with a mixture of anger and frustration on his grizzled face. "Would you mind telling me why you did that? And would you mind telling me why the hell you went there in the first place?"

They were in Charlie's office. LuAnn stood next to the bulky desk while Charlie sat in front of it. He had unwrapped a thick cigar and was about to light it when LuAnn had delivered the news of her excursion that morning.

Defiance was all over LuAnn's features as she scowled back at him. "I couldn't just sit around and do nothing."

"I told you I was going to handle it. What, you don't trust my judgment anymore?"

"Of course I do, Charlie, it's not that." LuAnn dropped her defiant stance, perched on the edge of his chair and ran her fingers through his thinning hair. "I figured if I could get to Riggs before he had a chance to do anything, apologize and then get him to drop it, we'd be free and clear."

Charlie shook his head, wincing as a small pain worked at his left temple. He took a deep breath and put an arm around her waist. "LuAnn, I had a very informative conversation with John Pemberton this morning."

"Who?"

"Real estate agent. Guy who sold us the house.

That's not important. What is relevant is the fact that Pemberton knows everybody and everything that goes on in this town. He's trying to track down the guy in the Honda for us right now."

LuAnn jerked back. "You didn't tell him—"

"I concocted a cover story and fed it to him. He slurped it up like it was the sweetest ice cream in the world. We both have gotten real good with making up stuff over the years, haven't we?"

"Sometime too good," LuAnn said gloomily. "It's getting harder and harder to remember what's true and what's not."

"I also talked to Pemberton about Riggs. Trying to get some of the guy's history out, to try and get a feel for the guy."

"He's not a cop. I asked him and he said he wasn't. You said he was."

"I know, a screw-up on my part, but Riggs led me to believe he was."

"So what the heck was he? And why all the secrecy?"

"A funny question coming from you." LuAnn jabbed an elbow playfully into Charlie's side. Her smile disappeared with Charlie's next words. "Pemberton thinks Riggs was a government spy."

"A spy? Like the CIA?"

"Who the hell knows. It's not like the guy's gonna advertise what outfit he was with. Nobody really knows for sure. His background is kind of a blur as far as Pemberton can tell."

LuAnn shuddered, remembering the info Riggs had gathered on her so quickly. Now it perhaps made sense. But she was still unconvinced. "And now he builds fences in rural Virginia. I didn't think they ever let spies retire."

"You've been watching too many mob movies. Even spies change jobs or retire, especially with the

285

Cold War ending. And there are a lot of specialities in intelligence gathering. Not all of them involve trench coats, pistols up the sleeve, and assassination plots working against foreign dictators. He could've been just some schlep working in an office looking at aerial photos of Moscow."

LuAnn recalled her meeting with Riggs at his home. The way he had handled the shotgun, his observation skills and his knowledge of firearms. And finally his confident and cool demeanor. She shook her head firmly. "He doesn't strike me as the office type."

Charlie sighed deeply. "Me either. So how did it go?"

LuAnn stood back up and leaned against the doorjamb, her fingers hooked through the belt loops on the jeans she had changed into. "He had already dug up some info on me and the Honda. The cover stuff came up on me, so we're okay there."

"Anything on the Honda?"

LuAnn shook her head. "Rental up in D.C. Name looked phony. Probably a dead-end."

"Riggs moves fast. How'd you find that out?"

"I did a little snooping around his office. When he caught me he was holding a shotgun."

"Good gosh, LuAnn, if the guy was a spy you're lucky he didn't blow your head off."

"It didn't seem so risky while I was doing it. It turned out all right anyway."

"You and your risk-taking. Like going to the drawing that night in New York. I should really start putting my foot down around here. What else?"

"I admitted to him that the car chase was something we were concerned about and that we were handling it."

"And he accepted that? No questions?" Charlie's tone was skeptical.

"I was telling the truth, Charlie," she said heatedly. "I get kind of tingling all over when the rare occasion happens along that I can do that."

"Okay, okay. I didn't mean to put a stick in your spokes. God, we sound like an old married couple here."

LuAnn smiled. "We *are* an old married couple. We just have a few more secrets to share than most."

Charlie flashed her a quick grin and took a moment to light his cigar. "So you really think Riggs is okay? He won't keep nosing around?"

"I think he's very curious, and he should be. But he told me he wasn't going to pursue it and I believe him. I'm not exactly sure why, but I do. There doesn't appear to be much B.S. in the man."

"And him coming over for lunch tomorrow? I take it you want to get to know him a little better."

LuAnn studied Charlie's face for a moment. Was there a touch of jealousy there? She shrugged her shoulders. "Well, it's a way to keep an eye on him, and maybe learn a little more about him. Maybe he's got some secrets, too. It certainly sounds like it, anyway."

Charlie puffed on his cigar. "So if things are cool with Riggs then we got only the guy in the Honda to worry about."

"Isn't that enough?"

"It's better than two headaches at one time. If Pemberton can trace him maybe we have clear sailing."

LuAnn looked nervously at him. "If he finds him, what are you going to do?"

"I've been thinking about that. I think I've decided to play straight with the man, call his hand and see what the hell he wants. If it's money, maybe we see what we can work out."

"And if it's not just money he wants?" She had

287

difficulty getting the next part out. "What if he knows about the lottery?"

Charlie took the cigar from his mouth and stared at her.

"I can't see how he could. But in the billion to one chance he does, there are a lot of other places in the world we can live, LuAnn. We could be gone tomorrow if need be."

"On the run again," she said, her tone bone-tired.

"Consider the alternative. It's not pleasant."

She reached out and plucked the cigar from between his fingers. Clenching it between her teeth, she drew the smoke in and then let it slowly out. She handed it back to him.

"When is Pemberton supposed to get back to you?"

"No set time. Could be tonight, could be next week."

"Let me know when you hear from him."

"You'll be the first to know, milady."

She turned to leave.

"Oh, am I invited to this lunch tomorrow?" he asked.

She glanced back. "I was kind of counting on it, Charlie." She smiled prettily and left. He stood up and watched her glide gracefully down the hallway. Then he closed the door to his study and sat down at his desk puffing thoughtfully on his stogie.

Riggs had put on a pair of chino pants, and the collar of his button-down shirt peeked out from under his patterned sweater. He had driven over in a Jeep Cherokee he had borrowed while his pickup truck was in the shop having its bumper repaired. The Jeep seemed more fitting to the affluent surroundings than his battered truck anyway. He smoothed down his freshly washed hair before climbing out of the Cherokee and walking up the steps of the mansion. These days he didn't usually dress up, except for the occasional social event he attended in town. He had finally decided a jacket and dress slacks was too pretentious. It was only lunch after all. And who knew? The lady of the house might ask him to do some on-site work.

The door was answered by the maid who escorted Riggs to the library. Riggs wondered if he had been watched as he had pulled up in the circle. Maybe there were video cameras trained on that area as well, with Catherine Savage and her sidekick Charlie sitting in some observation room crammed floor to ceiling with TV monitors.

He looked around the spacious area and noted with due respect the numerous volumes lining the walls. He wondered if they were for show only. He had been in places where that was the case. Somehow he didn't think that was true here. His attention fell upon the photos lining the fireplace mantel. There were ones there of Charlie and a little girl who strongly resembled Catherine Savage, but none of Catherine Savage. That seemed odd, but the woman was odd, so there was some semblance of consistency there.

He turned when the double doors to the library opened. His first real encounter with the woman, in his reconfigured hayloft, had not prepared him for his second.

The golden hair tumbled down the stylishly flared shoulders of a black one-piece dress that ended at her bare calves and didn't miss any contour of her long, curvy body along the way. It struck him that on her the garment would have seemed equally appropriate at a state fair or a White House dinner. She wore matching black low heel shoes. The image of a sleek, muscular panther gliding toward him held fast in his mind. After giving it some thought, Riggs had decided that the woman's beauty was undeniable, but wasn't perfect. After all, whose was? And another remarkable detail now emerged: While there were fine lines beginning to carve themselves around her eyes, Riggs noticed the almost complete absence of lines around her mouth, as though she had never smiled.

Curiously, the small scar on her jaw considerably heightened her attraction, he felt. Perhaps by silently forging a layer of danger, of adventure into her past?

"I'm glad you could make it," she said, moving briskly forward and extending a hand, which Riggs shook. He was again amazed at the strength he felt in that grip; her long fingers seemed to swallow his big, callused hand. "I know contractors have numerous emergencies during the day. Your time is never your own."

Riggs eyed the walls and ceilings of the library. "I heard about some of the renovations you had done here. I don't care how good the G.C. is, something this complex, things get out of whack every now and then."

"Charlie handled all of that. But I think things went fairly smoothly. I'm certainly pleased with the end product."

"I could see that."

"Lunch will be ready in a few minutes. Sally is setting it up in the rear verandah. The dining room seats about fifty and I thought it might be a little overwhelming for three. Would you like something to drink beforehand?"

"I'm okay." He pointed at the photos. "Is that your daughter? Or younger sister?"

She blushed and then followed his gesture, but settled herself on the couch before answering. "My daughter, Lisa. She's ten years old. I can't believe that, the years go by so quickly.

Riggs looked her over in an unassuming manner. "You must have had her very young then."

"Younger than I probably should have, but I wouldn't give her back for anything in the world. Do you have children?"

Riggs shook his head quickly and looked down at his hands. "Never been that lucky."

LuAnn had noted the absence of a wedding ring, although some men never wore them. She assumed a man who worked with his hands all day might not wear it simply for safety reasons.

"Your wife—"

"I'm divorced," he interjected. "Almost four years now." He put his hands in his pockets and again ran his eyes around the room. He could sense her following the path of his observations. "You?" he asked, settling his eyes back upon her.

"Widowed."

"I'm sorry."

She shrugged. "It was a long time ago," she said simply. There was a ring in her voice that told Riggs the years had not managed to diminish the impact of the loss.

"Ms. Savage—"

"Please, call me Catherine." She smiled impishly. "All my close friends do."

He smiled back and sat down next to her. "So where's Charlie?"

"He's out running some errands. He'll be joining us for lunch though."

"So he's your uncle?"

LuAnn nodded. "His wife passed on years ago. Both my parents are dead. We're really all the family left."

"I take it your late husband did very well for himself. Or maybe you did. I don't want to sound politically incorrect." Riggs grinned suddenly. "Either that, or one of you won the lottery."

LuAnn's hand tightened perceptibly on the edge of the couch. "My husband was a brilliant business-man who obviously left me very well-off." She managed to say this with a casual air.

"He sure did," Riggs agreed.

"And you? Have you lived here all your life?"

"Gee, after my visit here yesterday I thought you would have checked out my background thor-oughly."

"I'm afraid I don't have quite the level of sources you obviously do. I didn't think builders had such an information network." Her eyes remained fixed on his.

"I moved here about five years ago. Apprenticed with a local builder who taught me the trade. He died about three years ago and that's when I set up my own shop."

"Five years. So your wife lived here with you for a year."

Riggs shook his head. "The divorce was *final* four years ago, but we had been separated for about fourteen months. She's still up in D.C. Probably always will be."

"Is she in politics?"

"Attorney. Big partner, at a big firm. She has some politically connected clients. She's very successful."

"She must be good then. That's still very much a man's world. Like a lot of other ones."

Riggs shrugged. "She's smart, a great business-getter. I think that's why we broke up. The marriage thing got in the way."

"I see."

"Not what you'd call an original story, but it's the only one I have. I moved down here and never looked back."

292

"I take it you like what you do."

"It can be a hassle sometimes, just like any job. But I like putting things together. It's therapeutic. And peaceful. I've been lucky, got some good word of mouth and the business has been steady. As you probably know, there's a lot of money in this area. Even before you came."

"So I understand. I'm glad your career change has worked out."

He sat back while he digested her words, his lips pursed, his hands balled up into fists, but not in a threatening way.

He chuckled. "Let me guess, you heard that I was either a CIA operative or an international assassin who abruptly decided to chuck all that and take up hammering and sawing in more placid surroundings."

"Actually, I hadn't heard the assassin angle."

They exchanged brief smiles.

"You know if you just told people the truth, they'd stop speculating." She couldn't believe she had just made that statement, but there it was. She looked at him with what she hoped was an air of complete innocence.

"You're assuming that I care if people speculate about me. I don't."

"That's beneath you, I take it."

"If I've learned anything in life, it's that you don't worry about what other people think or say. You worry about yourself and that's good enough. Otherwise you're setting yourself up to be a basket case. People can be cruel. Especially people who supposedly cared about you. Believe me, I speak from experience."

"I take it the divorce wasn't exactly amicable?"

He didn't look at her when he spoke. "I'm not taking anything away from you, but sometimes losing a spouse isn't as traumatic or painful as going through a divorce. They each have their own degrees of hurt, I guess."

He looked down at his hands. There was a definite ring of sincerity in his words and LuAnn felt instant guilt that she in fact had not been widowed, at least not by the falsehood of losing a wealthy husband. It was as though he were baring his wounds in return for LuAnn baring hers. As usual, it was all lies on her part. Could she even speak the truth anymore? In fact how could she? Speaking the truth would destroy her, all the lies would immediately fall to earth like those old buildings demolished by explosives that caused them to implode.

"I can understand that," she said.

Riggs didn't appear inclined to continue.

LuAnn finally looked at her watch. "Lunch should be just about ready. I thought after we eat you could look at a site at the rear grounds where I'm thinking of having you build a small studio." She stood up and Riggs did too. He appeared immeasurably relieved that this particular conversation was over.

"That sounds good, Catherine. In my business, work is always welcome."

As they walked to the rear of the house, Charlie joined them. The two men shook hands. "Glad to see you again, Matt. I hope you're hungry. Sally usually puts out a good spread."

Lunch was devoted to enjoying the food and drink and discussing innocuous subjects of local interest. However, there was an energy between Charlie and Catherine Savage that was unmistakable to Riggs. A strong bond, he concluded. Unbreakable, in fact. They were family, after all.

"So what're we looking at timewise on the fence, Matt?" Charlie asked. He and Riggs were on the rear terrace overlooking the grounds. Lunch was over and LuAnn had gone to pick up Lisa. School had ended early because of a scheduled teacher workshop. She had asked Riggs to remain until she returned so they could talk about the studio construction. Riggs wondered if her going to get Lisa had been a deliberate maneuver to leave Charlie behind to pump him for information. Whatever the reason, he remained on guard.

Before Riggs had a chance to answer him about the fence, Charlie extended a cigar. "You smoke these things?"

Riggs took it. "After a meal like that, and a gorgeous day like this, even if I didn't, I'd be tempted." He snipped off the end with a cutter Charlie handed him and they took a moment to get their respective smokes going.

"I figure a week to dig all the postholes. Two weeks clearing land, and assembling and installing the fencing. That includes pouring the cement for the posts. Another week to install the gate and security systems. One month total. That's about what I estimated in the contract."

Charlie looked him over. "I know, but sometimes what you put on paper doesn't work exactly that way in reality."

"That pretty much sums up the construction business," Riggs agreed. He puffed on his cigar. "But we'll get in before the frost, and the lay of the land isn't as bad as I originally thought." He paused and eyed Charlie. "After yesterday, I wish I could have that sucker in today. I'm sure you do too."

It was an open invitation for discussion and Charlie didn't disappoint Riggs. "Have a seat, Matt." Charlie indicated a pair of white wrought-iron chairs next to the balustrade. Charlie sat down gingerly. "God these suckers are uncomfortable as hell, and for what they cost you'd think they were made out of gold. I'm thinking the interior designer we used must've gotten some kind of kickback on them." He smoked his cigar while he looked over the landscape. "Damn, it's beautiful here."

Riggs followed his gaze. "It's one reason I came here. A big reason."

"What were the other reasons?" Charlie grinned at him. "I'm just kidding. That's *your* business." The emphasis on the word was not lost on Riggs. Charlie wriggled in the seat until he managed to find a semicomfortable position. "Catherine told me about your little discussion yesterday."

"I assumed she would. She shouldn't go sneaking around people's houses, though. That's not always a healthy thing to do."

"That's exactly what I told her. I know it might be hard to see, but she's rather headstrong."

The two men exchanged knowing chuckles.

"I do appreciate your agreeing not to pursue it," Charlie said.

"I told her so long as the guy didn't bother me, I wouldn't bother him."

"Fair enough. I'm sure you can see that with all of Catherine's wealth, she's a target for a variety of scams, hustles, or downright threats. We have Lisa to worry about too. We keep a real close eye on her."

"You sound like you speak from experience."

"I do. This isn't the first time. And it won't be the last. But you can't let it get to you. I mean Catherine could buy a deserted island somewhere and make it impossible for anyone to reach her, but what kind of life would that be? For her or Lisa?"

"And you. It's not like you're tapping on the grave, Charlie. You look like you could suit up for the Redskins on Sunday."

Charlie beamed at the compliment. "I actually

played some semipro ball way back when. And I take care of myself. And Catherine nags me about my diet. I think she lets me smoke these things out of pity." He held up the cigar. "Although lately I'm feeling old beyond my years. But yeah, I don't want to live on a deserted island."

"So any luck finding the guy in the Honda?" Riggs asked.

"I'm working on it. Got some inquiries going."

"Don't take offense at this, but if you find him, what do you plan on doing about it?"

Charlie looked over at him. "What would you do?"

"Depends on his intentions."

"Exactly. So until I find him and determine what his intentions are, I don't know what I'm going to do." There was a slight trace of hostility in Charlie's tone that Riggs chose to ignore. He looked back over the countryside.

"Catherine says she wants to put up an outdoor studio. Do you know where?"

Charlie shook his head. "I really haven't discussed it with her. I think it was a recent impulse on her part."

Riggs again looked over at him. Had that been a conscious slip on his part? It was as though Charlie were telling him pointblank that the potential new piece of business was the payoff for Riggs keeping his mouth shut. Or was there another reason?

"What would she be using it for, the studio?"

Charlie glanced at him. "Does it matter?"

"Actually it does. If it's an art studio, I'd make sure there was sufficient lighting, maybe put in some skylights, and a ventilation system to carry the paint fumes out. If she just wants to use it to get away, read or sleep, I'd configure it differently."

Charlie nodded thoughtfully. "I see. Well, I don't

297

know what she plans to use it for. But she doesn't paint, that I know."

The men fell silent until that silence was interrupted by the sounds of LuAnn and Lisa approaching. The door to the terrace opened and the pair came out.

In person, Lisa Savage resembled her mother even more than in the photo. They both walked the same way, easy glides, no wasted energy.

"This is Mr. Riggs, Lisa."

Riggs had not been around many children in his life, but he did what came naturally. He put out his hand. "Call me Matt, Lisa. Pleased to meet you."

She smiled and squeezed his hand in return. "Pleased to meet you, Matt."

"That's quite a grip." He glanced up at LuAnn and then Charlie. "That particular attribute must run in the family. If I keep coming over here I might have to start wearing a steel glove."

Lisa smiled.

"Matthew is going to build a studio for me, Lisa. Out there somewhere." She pointed toward the rear grounds.

Lisa looked up at the house in undisguised wonderment. "Isn't our house big enough?"

All the adults burst into laughter at that one and finally Lisa joined in too.

"What's the studio for?" Lisa asked.

"Well, maybe it'll be kind of a surprise. In fact, I might let you use it too, sometimes."

Lisa grinned broadly at the news.

"But only if you keep your grades up," said Charlie. "By the way, how'd your test go?" Charlie's tone was gruff, but it clearly was all a facade. It was obvious to Riggs that the old guy loved Lisa as much as he did her mother, if not more.

Lisa's mouth dropped into a pout. "I didn't get an A."

298

"That's okay, sweetie," Charlie said kindly. "Probably my fault. I'm not all that good with math."

Lisa suddenly broke into a big smile. "I got an A plus."

Charlie playfully cuffed her head. "You got your mother's sense of humor, that's for sure."

LuAnn said, "Miss Sally has some lunch ready for you. I know you didn't get a chance to eat at school. Run along and I'll see you after I finish up with Matthew."

LuAnn and Riggs walked through the rear grounds. Charlie had begged off. He had some things to do, he had said.

After Riggs had walked the property he pointed to a clearing that was level, had an unobstructed view of the distant mountains, but still had shade trees on two sides. "That looks like a nice spot. Actually, with this much land, you probably have a number of potential locations. By the way, if I knew what you were going to use the place for I could make a more informed choice for the site." He looked around. "And you have a number of outbuildings already. Another option would be to convert one of those into a studio."

"I'm sorry, I thought I was clear on that. I want it done from scratch. None of the other buildings would really do. I want it set up like yours. Two stories. The first floor could be set up as a workshop for some of my hobbies, that is, when I get around to having some hobbies. Lisa is into drawing and she's getting pretty good. Maybe I could take up sculpting. That seems like a very relaxing pastime. On the second level I want a woodstove, a telescope, comfortable furniture, built-in bookcases, maybe a small kitchen, bay windows."

Riggs nodded and looked around. "I saw the pool area. Are you planning on a poolhouse and maybe tennis courts?"

299

"Next spring. Why?"

"I was just thinking that we might want to tie those and the studio into an overall plan. You know, use the same materials or some combo thereof with the poolhouse and the studio."

LuAnn shook her head. "No, I want it separate. We'll put in a large gazebo for outdoor entertaining and all that. It'll be mostly Lisa using the pool and tennis courts. I want those facilities closer to the main house. The pool is already close. The studio I want farther away. Sort of hidden."

"That's fine. You certainly have the land." He checked out the slope of the property. "So do you swim or play tennis?"

"I can swim like a fish, but I've never played tennis and I really don't have any desire to start."

"I thought all rich people played tennis. That and golf."

"Maybe if you're born with money. I haven't always been wealthy."

"Georgia."

LuAnn looked sharply at him. "What?"

"I've been trying to place your accent. Lisa's is all over the place. Yours is very faint, but it's still there. I'd guess you spent a lot of years in Europe, but you know what they say, you can take the girl out of Georgia but you can't take Georgia out of the girl."

LuAnn hesitated for a moment before replying. "I've never been to Georgia."

"I'm surprised. I'm usually pretty good at gauging that."

"Nobody's perfect." She flicked her hair out of her eyes. "So what do you think?" She looked at the clearing.

Riggs stared at her curiously for a moment before answering. "We'll have to draw up plans. They'll help you get it exactly the way you want, although it

300

sounds like you have a pretty good idea already. Depending on the size and complexity, it could take anywhere from two to six months."

"When could you start?"

"Not any time this year, Catherine."

"You're that busy?"

"It's got nothing to do with that. No sane builder would start on a project like that now. We need architectural plans and we also need to get building permits. The ground will be freezing soon and I don't like to pour footers after that. And we wouldn't be able to get it framed and under roof before winter set in. Weather can get real nasty up here. This is definitely a next spring project."

"Oh." LuAnn sounded deeply disappointed. She stared off at the site as though she were seeing her hideaway fully completed.

Trying to make her feel better Riggs said, "Spring will be here before you know it, Catherine. And the winter will allow us to work up a really good set of plans. I know a first-rate architect. I can set up a meeting."

LuAnn was hardly listening. Would they even be here next spring? Riggs's news about the construction schedule had dissipated much of her enthusiasm for the project.

"I'll see. Thanks."

As they walked back to the house Riggs touched her shoulder. "I take it you're not into delayed gratification. If I could put it up for you right now, I would. Some sleazy builders might take on the job and charge you a healthy premium and then proceed to turn out a piece of crap that'll fall down in a year or two. But I take pride in my work and I want to deliver a quality job for you."

She smiled at him. "Charlie said you had excellent references. I guess I can see why."

301

They were passing by the horse barn. LuAnn pointed at it and said, "I guess that counts as a hobby. You ride?"

"I'm no expert, but I won't fall off either."

"We should go for a ride sometime. There are some beautiful trails around here."

"I know," was Riggs's surprising reply. "I used to walk them before this property was sold. You made an excellent choice in real estate, by the way."

"Charlie found it."

"He's a good person to have around."

"He makes my life a lot easier. I don't know what I'd do without him."

"Nice to have somebody like that in your life."

She cast a furtive glance at him as they continued back to the house.

THIRTY-ONE

Charlie met them at the rear entrance. There was a suppressed excitement in his manner, and the darting glances he gave LuAnn told her the reason: Pemberton had found where the man in the Honda was staying.

While not showing it, Riggs picked up on the subtle undercurrents.

"Thanks for the lunch," he said. "I'm sure you've got things to do and I've got some appointments to take care of this afternoon." He looked over at LuAnn. "Catherine, let me know about the studio."

"I will. Call me about going for a ride."

"I'll do that."

After he left, Charlie and LuAnn went into Charlie's study and closed the door.

"Where is the guy?" she asked.

"He's our neighbor."

"What?"

"A little rental cottage. Pretty isolated. It's not more than four miles from here up Highway Twenty-two. I looked at some land up near there when we were thinking of building. Used to be a big estate up there but now there's just the caretaker's cottage. Remember, we took a drive up there a while back?"

"I remember exactly. You could walk or ride it through the back trails. I've done it. The guy could have been spying on us for a while."

"I know. That's what worries me. Pemberton gave

me exact directions to the place." Charlie laid the paper with the directions down on his desk while he pulled on his coat.

LuAnn took the opportunity to scan surreptitiously the directions and commit them to memory.

Charlie unlocked a drawer of his desk. LuAnn's eyes widened as she watched him pull out the .38. He proceeded to load it.

"What are you going to do?" she said fiercely.

He didn't look at her as he checked the safety and put the gun in his pocket. "Like we planned, I'm going to go check it out."

"I'm going with you."

He looked at her angrily. "The hell you are."

"Charlie, I am."

"What if there's trouble?"

"You're saying that to me?"

"You know what I mean. Let me check it out first, see what the guy's up to. I'm not going to do anything dangerous."

"So why the gun?"

"I said *I'm* not going to do anything dangerous. I don't know about him."

"I don't like it, Charlie."

"You think I do? I'm telling you, it's the only way. Something happens, the last thing I want is you in the middle of it."

"I've never expected you to fight my battles for me."

He touched her cheek gently. "You're not exactly twisting my arm here. I want you and Lisa to be safe and sound. In case you hadn't noticed, I've kind of made that my life's work. By choice." He smiled.

She watched him open the door and start to head out. "Charlie, please be careful."

He looked back, noting the worry in her features.

"LuAnn, you know I'm always careful."

304

As soon as he left, LuAnn went to her room, changed into jeans and a warm shirt, and pulled on sturdy boots.

In case you hadn't noticed, Charlie, my *life's work is to make sure* you and Lisa *are safe and sound.*

She grabbed a leather jacket from her closet and raced out of the house in the direction of the horse barn. She saddled Joy and then galloped off toward the maze of trails behind the mansion.

As soon as Charlie hit the main road, Riggs started to follow from a safe distance in the Cherokee. Riggs had thought it a fifty-fifty possibility that something was going to happen as soon as he left. A friend of Riggs had mentioned seeing Pemberton and Charlie having breakfast the day before. That was smart on Charlie's part, and indeed, was probably the path Riggs would have taken to track down the man in the Honda. That and Charlie's excited manner had been enough to convince Riggs that something was up. If he had been wrong, he wouldn't have wasted much time. He kept the Range Rover just in sight as it turned north on to Highway 22. It wasn't easy being invisible on the rural road, but Riggs was confident he could manage it. On the seat next to him was his shotgun. This time he would be prepared.

Charlie glanced to the right and left as he pulled the Range Rover underneath the cover of trees and then stopped. He could see the cottage up ahead. He might have wondered who would have built the place in the middle of nowhere, but Pemberton had informed him that the house had been a caretaker's cottage for a vast estate that was no longer in existence. Ironic that the tiny structure had outlived the main house. He gripped the pistol in his pocket and got out. Threading his way through the thick trees behind the cottage, he made his first stop the shed. Rubbing away the dirt and grime on the window he was able barely to make out the black Honda inside. For this, he and LuAnn owed Pemberton a nice little donation to a charity of his choice.

Charlie waited about another ten minutes, his gaze glued to the small cottage, looking for any movement, any shadows falling across the windows. The place appeared unoccupied but the car in the shed belied that appearance. Charlie moved forward cautiously.

He glanced around but did not notice Riggs crouched behind a stand of thick holly bushes to the left of the house.

Riggs lowered his binoculars and surveyed the area. Like Charlie, he had detected no movement or sound coming from the cottage but that didn't mean anything. The guy could be in there just waiting for Charlie to put in an appearance. Shoot first and ask questions later. Riggs gripped his shotgun and waited.

The front door was locked. Charlie could have smashed a glass pane next to the door and unlocked the door from the inside, or simply kicked the door until it tore loose from the doorjamb – it didn't look all that sturdy. However, if the house was indeed occupied, knocking down the door might prompt a deadly response. And, if it wasn't occupied, he didn't want to leave any evidence that he had been to the cottage. Charlie knocked on the door, his pistol half out of his pocket. He waited and knocked again. There was no answer. He slid the gun back in his pocket and looked at the lock, a common pin tumbler, to his expert eye. He pulled out two items from his inner coat pocket: a straight pick and a tension tool. Fortunately, arthritis had not yet set into his fingers or he would not have had the dexterity needed to pick the lock. He first slid the pick into the keyhole and then eased the tension tool underneath the pick. Using the pick, Charlie raised the tumbler pins to their open position, and the constant pressure from the tension tool kept the tumbler pins open. Charlie manipulated the pick, sensing the subtle vibrations of the pins until he was rewarded with a click. He turned the doorknob and the door swung open. He replaced his tools in his coat. His State Pen degree had once again worked its magic. All the while he listened intently. He was well aware that a trap could be awaiting him. His hand closed around the .38. If the guy gave Charlie the opportunity to use it he would. The ramifications of such an act were too numerous to analyze; however, at least a few of them would be better than outright exposure.

The cottage's interior was of a simple configuration. The hallway ran from front to back, splitting the space into roughly equivalent halves. The kitchen was in the back on the left; the small dining room fronted that. On his right was an equally modest living room. Tacked on to the rear of that was a combination mud room/laundry room. Plain wooden stairs on the right made their way to the bedrooms on the second floor. Charlie observed little of this, because his attention was riveted on the dining room. He stared in amazement at the computer, printer, fax, and stacks of file boxes. He moved closer as his eyes swept to the bulletin board with all the news clippings and photos affixed to it.

He mouthed the headlines. LuAnn's face was prominent among the various photos. The whole story was there: the murders, LuAnn winning the lottery, her disappearance. Well, that had confirmed his suspicions. Now it remained to discover who the man was and, more important, what he wanted from them.

He made his way around the room, carefully lifting papers here and there, studying the clippings, examining the file boxes. His eyes diligently search-ed for anything that would identify the man; however, there was nothing. Whoever was pursuing them knew what he was doing.

Charlie moved to the desk and carefully slid open a drawer. The papers in there yielded nothing new. He tried the other drawers with similar results. For a moment he thought about turning on the computer but his skills with that technology were about nil. He was about to begin a search of the rest of the house when a solitary box in the far corner caught his eye. He might as well hit that too, he figured.

Lifting off the top, Charlie's eyes immediately started to twitch uncontrollably. The word "shit" passed almost silently from between his lips and his legs made a serious threat of giving out on him.

A single piece of paper stared back at him. The names were listed neatly on it. LuAnn's name was there. Most of the remaining names represented people Charlie was also familiar with: Herman Rudy, Wanda Tripp, Randy Stith, Bobbie Jo Reynolds among others. All past lottery winners. Most of them Charlie had personally escorted, like LuAnn. All of them, he knew, had won their fortunes with Jackson's help.

Charlie steadied himself by placing a shaking hand on top of the windowsill. He had been pre-pared to find evidence of the man knowing all about the murders and LuAnn's involvement. He had not been at all prepared to learn that the lottery scam had been uncovered. The hairs on his forearms felt like they had suddenly been electrified.

How? How could the guy have found out? Who the hell was he? He quickly put the boxtop back, turned, and headed out the door. He made sure it was locked before shutting it. He swiftly retraced his steps to the Range Rover, climbed in, and drove off.

Donovan headed down Route 29. He had been on the road the better part of two hours on his return trip from Washington and he was anxious to get back on the hunt. He sped up as he neared his final destination. On the drive down, he had thought of the next steps he would employ against LuAnn Tyler. Steps designed to make her cave in and do so quickly. If one approach failed, he would find another. The saving grace in all of this – a look of deep satisfaction came to his features as he thought of it – was that he had LuAnn Tyler over a barrel. The oft-quoted phrase was quite true: A chain was only as strong as its weakest link. And LuAnn, you are that rusty link, he said to himself. And you're not going to get away. He checked his watch. He would be at the cottage shortly. On the seat next to him was a small-caliber pistol. He didn't like guns, but he wasn't stupid either.

THIRTY-TWO

As Riggs watched Charlie drive off he caught only a glimpse of the man's face. However, it was enough to tell him that something was up. And that what was up was all bad. After the Range Rover disappeared from his line of sight, Riggs turned around and stared at the cottage. Should he make an attempt as well to search the place? It might answer a lot of questions. He had almost decided to flip a coin when another development caused him to crouch down behind the holly tree again and return to his role of observer.

LuAnn had tethered Joy to a tree in the woods about a hundred yards from the clearing in which the cottage stood. She emerged from outside the tree line with the same graceful movements Riggs had observed in her before. She squatted down on her haunches and waited, surveying the area with quick, darting movements of her head. Despite the impenetrable bulk of the holly tree, Riggs almost felt naked before her intense gaze.

LuAnn studied the road at the same time Riggs studied her. Was she aware that Charlie had already come and gone? Probably not. However, her features gave away nothing.

LuAnn silently watched the cottage for a time before moving over to the shed. Glancing through the same window Charlie had, she looked over the Honda. Then she lifted some dirt and grime from the windowsill and covered over the small opening

Charlie had made in the filth. Riggs watched this procedure with growing respect. Even he might not have thought to do that. Charlie certainly hadn't.

LuAnn turned her attention to the house. Both hands were in the pockets of her coat. She knew Charlie had been here but had already left. The smeared window had told her that. She also deduced he hadn't stayed very long because she had ridden Joy hard on the way over, and her route had been far more direct than the one Charlie had had to drive, although he had had a head start. His short stay meant he had found either nothing, or something highly incriminating. Her instincts told her that it was almost undoubtedly the latter. Should she leave and return home and let him fill her in? While that would have been the most prudent thing to do, LuAnn quickly made her way to the front porch and her hand closed around the doorknob. It didn't budge despite the immense pressure she was exerting. She had no special tools to jimmy it as Charlie had; thus she moved on, looking for another way in and finding it at the rear of the cottage. The window finally opened under her persistent tuggings and she quickly climbed inside.

She silently descended from the windowsill to the floor and immediately crouched down. From her line of sight she could make out the kitchen. She had very acute hearing, and if someone had been in the small house she was certain she would have heard his breathing no matter how shallow. She edged forward until she reached what should have been the dining room but had been set up as an office. LuAnn's eyes widened as she saw the news clippings on the bulletin board. As LuAnn's gaze swept around the room, she sensed there was something more at work here than a blackmail scheme.

* * *

"Oh, hell." Riggs ducked down after saying the words and watched in dismay as the Chrysler passed by him on the way to the cottage. The man was hunched over the steering wheel, but Riggs had no trouble recognizing him despite the beard's having been shaved off. Thinking quickly, Riggs gripped his shotgun and hurried to his Cherokee.

LuAnn flew to the back of the cottage as soon as she heard the car drive up. She raised her head a few inches above the windowsill; her heart sank. "Dammit!" She watched Donovan pull around to the rear of the cottage and climb out of the Chrysler. Her eyes were riveted on the pistol he held in his right hand. He headed straight for the rear door. LuAnn backed away, her eyes darting every which way, looking desperately for an exit. The problem was there wasn't any, at least none that would be unobserved. The front door was locked and if she attempted to open it, he would hear her. There was no time to wriggle through a window. The cottage was so small that he couldn't possibly fail to see her if she remained on the first floor.

Donovan inserted the key in the door lock. If he had glanced through the paned door window, he would have spotted LuAnn immediately. The door began to open.

LuAnn edged back into the dining room and was about to head upstairs and try for an escape from the second floor when she heard it.

The car horn was loud and shrill and the sound pattern kept repeating itself, like a car alarm that had been activated. She crept back to the window and watched as Donovan jerked to a halt, slammed the door closed, and then ran around to the front of the cottage.

LuAnn lost no time. She launched herself through

the same window she had used to enter, did a roll, and came up running. She made it to the shed and crouched down. The horn was still beeping. She ran to the far side of the shed, peered around the edge, and watched as Donovan advanced down the road, away from her, toward the sound, his pistol making wide sweeps as he did so.

The hand that suddenly gripped LuAnn's shoulder almost made her scream.

"Where's your horse?" Riggs's voice was even and calm.

She looked at him, the whiplash of fear receding as quickly as it had appeared. "About a hundred yards that way." She jerked her head in the direction of the thick woods. "Is that your car alarm?"

Riggs nodded and gripped his car keys tightly. One eye on Donovan and the other on their avenue of escape, Riggs rose to his feet and pulled LuAnn up with him. "Ready, go." Bursting out from their cover they raced across the open ground. Keeping his eyes on Donovan's back, Riggs unfortunately caught his foot on a root and he went down, his finger gripping the key ring, accidentally pressing the alarm's shut-off button. Donovan whipped around and stared at them. LuAnn had Riggs up again in a moment and they raced off into the woods. Donovan lurched toward them, his pistol making broad sweeps. "Hey," he screamed. "Dammit, hold it right there." Donovan waved the gun around, but he wasn't going to shoot; he wasn't a killer.

LuAnn ran like the wind and Riggs found it impossible to keep up with her. He had slightly twisted his ankle, he told himself, but truth be known, even at full speed he probably could not have caught her. They reached Joy, who stood patiently awaiting her owner's arrival. LuAnn quickly released the tether and jumped into the saddle without even bothering to use the stirrup. She flicked out a hand and hauled Riggs up behind her. The next moment they were racing up the trail astride the fleet mare. Riggs looked back for an instant, but Donovan was nowhere in sight. They had moved so fast he wasn't surprised. Riggs gripped LuAnn's waist with both hands and hung on for dear life as she whipped Joy at a breakneck pace through the swerving trails.

They had returned Joy to the horse barn and were walking back to the main house before Riggs broke the silence. "I take it that's how you handle those kind of situations. Break into the place. See what you can find. I don't know why I should be surprised. That's what you did with me." He looked at LuAnn with angry eyes.

She matched the look. "I didn't break into your place. And I don't remember asking you to follow me."

"I followed Charlie, not you," he corrected her. "But it's a damn good thing I was there, wasn't it? Two times in two days. At this rate you'll wear out your nine lives in a week." She kept walking, her arms crossed in front of her, her eyes staring resolutely ahead. Riggs stopped.

She stopped too and looked down for an instant. When she looked up there was a far softer countenance confronting him. "Thank you. Again. But the more distance you put between the three of us and yourself, the better off you'll be, I guarantee it. Forget the fence. I don't think we'll be staying on here. Don't worry, I'll pay you for it anyway." She stared at him for a moment longer, trying to push away feelings that had been strangers to her for so long that they now simply frightened her. "Have a good life, Matthew." She turned and headed for the house.

314

"Catherine?" She kept walking. "Catherine," he said again.

She finally stopped.

"Would you please tell me what's going on? I might be able to help you."

"I don't think so."

"You never know."

"Believe me, I know."

She started toward the house again.

Riggs stood there staring after her. "Hey, in case you forgot, I don't have a car to get home in."

When she turned around, the key ring was already sailing through the air. Riggs caught it in the palm of his hand.

"Take my car. It's parked out front. Keep it as long as you like. I've got another one."

On that she spun back around and disappeared into the house.

Riggs slowly pocketed the keys, shaking his head in absolute frustration.

THIRTY-THREE

"Where the hell have you been?" Charlie came out of his study and leaned up against the doorjamb. His face was still pale, a detail LuAnn picked up on immediately.

"Same place you were," she said.

"What? LuAnn, I told you—"

"You weren't alone. Riggs followed you. In fact he managed to save me again. If he happens to do it once more, I might have to consider marrying the man."

Charlie went a shade paler. "Did he go inside the house?"

"No, but I did."

"How much did you see?" Charlie asked nervously.

LuAnn swept past him and into the office. "I don't want Lisa to hear."

Charlie closed the door behind them. He went straight over to the liquor stand and poured himself a drink. LuAnn watched his movements in silence for a moment before speaking.

"Apparently, you saw more than I did."

He turned to her and downed the drink in one motion. "The news clippings on the lottery? The murders?"

LuAnn nodded. "I saw them. After my first encounter with the man, I wasn't very surprised to see that."

"I wasn't either."

"Apparently there was more, though." She looked

at him pointedly at the same time she sat down on the sofa, folding her hands in her lap and collecting her nerves as best she could.

There was a haunted look in Charlie's features, as though he had awoken from a nightmare and attempted to laugh it off, only to find out he wasn't dreaming. "I saw some names. A list of them in fact. Yours was on there." He paused and put the glass down. His hands were shaking. LuAnn braced herself. "Herman Rudy. Wanda Tripp. Randy Stith. They were on there too. I escorted them all in New York."

LuAnn slowly rested her head in her hands.

Charlie sat down beside her, put one beefy hand on her back, and slowly rubbed it.

She sat back and slumped against him; a painful weariness laced her words. "We have to go, Charlie. We have to pack up and go. Tonight."

He considered the request before running a hand across his forehead. "I've been thinking about that. We can run, like we've done before. But there's a difference now."

LuAnn's response was immediate. "He knows about the lottery fix *and* he knows LuAnn Tyler and Catherine Savage are one and the same. Our cover isn't going to work anymore."

Charlie nodded glumly. "We've never been confronted with both of those before. It makes disappearing a little trickier."

She suddenly stood up and started her ritualistic pacing, moving in fluid circles around the room. "What does he want, Charlie?"

"I've been thinking about that too." He went over to the liquor stand with his empty glass, hesitated, and decided against a second round. "You saw the guy's setup. What did it look like to you?" he asked.

LuAnn stopped pacing and leaned up against the

fireplace mantel. In her mind, she went through every detail of the place.

"His car was a rental, under an assumed name. So he doesn't want us to be able to trace his real identity. I didn't recognize the man, but there must be another reason he's going incognito."

"Right." Charlie studied her. Over the years, he had learned that LuAnn missed almost nothing and her instincts were first-rate.

"He tried to spook me, which he did. I take that as a warning, a message that he's a player and he wants us to be aware of that for the next time he calls."

"Go on," he encouraged.

"The place, the little I saw of it, was set up like an office. Very neat, very orderly. Computer, fax, printer, files. It was like he had made all of this some special research project."

"Well, he would've had to do a ton of research to figure out the lottery scam. Jackson is no dummy."

"How do you think he did it, Charlie?"

He rubbed his chin and sat down in front of his desk. "Well, we don't know for absolute certain that he has figured it all out. I just saw the list. That's all."

"With the names of all those lottery winners? Come on. How long did Jackson run the scam anyway?"

Charlie shook his head. "I don't know. I mean, I was there for nine of them, including you. Started in August. You were Miss April, my last gig."

LuAnn shook her head stubbornly. "He knows, Charlie; we have to assume that to be true. However he did it, he did it."

"Okay. So it seems pretty clear the guy wants money."

She shook her head. "We don't know that. I mean, why would he set up shop here and bring all that stuff with him? He didn't need to do that. He could just send me a letter from parts unknown with the

318

same info, and a demand for money to be wire-transferred to his bank account."

Charlie sat back, his face carrying extreme confusion. He had not looked at the matter in that light. "That's true."

"And I don't think the guy's hurting for money. He was wearing really nice clothes. Two leased cars, the rent on that cottage isn't cheap, I'm thinking, and all that equipment he had. He's not digging his dinner out of garbage cans."

"Right, but unless he's already a millionaire, going after you would significantly enrich his bank account," said Charlie.

"But he hasn't done that. He hasn't asked for anything. I wish I knew why." She was lost deep in thought for a moment and then looked up. "How long did Pemberton say the cottage had been rented?"

"About a month."

"That makes it even more unlikely he was going to blackmail us. Why wait? Why come right out and warn me that he knows everything? How does he know I won't just disappear in the middle of the night? If I do that, he's not going to be filling up his bank account with my funds."

Charlie sighed deeply. "So what do we do now?"

"Wait," was finally the answer from LuAnn's lips. "But make arrangements for us to leave the country on a moment's notice. By private jet. And since he knows about Catherine Savage, we're going to need another set of identification papers. Can you get them?"

"I'll have to look up some old contacts, but I can do it. It'll take a few days."

LuAnn stood up.

"What about Riggs?" Charlie asked. "The man's not going to let it go now."

"There's nothing we can do about that. He doesn't trust us and I don't blame him."

319

"Well, I doubt if he'll do anything that'll end up hurting you."

She looked sharply at him. "How do you know that?"

"Look, LuAnn, it doesn't take a rocket scientist to see Riggs has a thing for you." A hint of resentment tinged his response. His tone softened, however, with his next words. "Seems like a nice guy. Under different circumstances, who knows. You shouldn't spend your life alone, LuAnn."

A flush swept over her face. "I'm not alone. I've got Lisa and I've got you. I don't need anybody else. I can't handle anybody else." She looked away. How could she invite anyone into her life? It was impossible. Half truths competing with complete falsehoods. She was no longer a real person. She was a thirty-year-old shell, period. Everything else had been bartered away. Jackson had taken the rest of it. He and his offer. If she hadn't made that call way back when. If she hadn't panicked? She wouldn't have spent ten years turning herself into the woman she always wanted to be. She wouldn't be living in a million-dollar mansion. But as ironic as it sounded, she would probably have had far more of a life than she had now. Whether it was to be spent in another wrecked mobile trailer or slinging fried foods at the truck stop, LuAnn Tyler, the pauper, would probably have been happier than Catherine Savage, the princess, ever dreamt of being. But if she hadn't accepted the offer, Jackson would have had her killed. There was no way out. She turned back to Charlie and spread her arms wide.

"That's the trade-off, Charlie. For this. For all this. You, me, and Lisa."

"The Three Musketeers." Charlie attempted a smile.

"Let's pray for a happy ending." LuAnn opened the door and disappeared down the hallway in search of her daughter.

320

THIRTY-FOUR

"Thank you for meeting with me on such short notice, Mr. Pemberton."

"John, please call me John, Mr. Conklin." Pemberton shook the other man's hand and they sat down at the small conference table in Pemberton's real estate office.

"I go by Harry," the other man said.

"Now you mentioned over the phone that you were interested in a house, but you really didn't say what area or price range."

Without seeming to do so, Pemberton looked Harry Conklin over. Probably in his sixties, expensive clothing, air of assurance, undoubtedly liked the good things in life. Pemberton swiftly calculated his potential commission.

"I got your name on good reference. I understand that you specialize in the upper-end market around here," Conklin said.

"That's correct. Born and raised here. Know everybody and every property worth knowing about. So would that be a price range you're interested in? The upper end?"

Conklin assumed a comfortable look. "Let me tell you a little about myself. I make my living on Wall Street and it's a damn good living if I do say so myself. But it's also a young man's game and I'm not a young man anymore. I've made my fortune and it's substantial. I've got a penthouse in Manhattan, a place in Rio, a home on Fisher Island in Florida, and a country estate outside London. But I'm looking to get out of New York and radically simplify my life. And this place is about as beautiful as they come."

"Absolutely right," Pemberton chimed in.

"Now, I do a lot of entertaining, so it would have to be a substantial place. But I want privacy as well. Something old, and elegant, but restored. I like old things, but not old plumbing, you understand me?"

"Perfectly."

"Now, I'm assuming that there are probably a number of properties around here that fit the bill."

"There are. Most assuredly," Pemberton said excitedly.

"But see, I've got one in mind. One I heard about from my father, in fact. He was in the stock market too. Back in the twenties. Made a bundle and was fortunate to get out before the crash. He used to come here and stay with a good friend of his who was in the market too. My father, God rest his soul, loved it there, and I thought it would be appropriate for his son to buy it and live in it."

"What a truly inspiring idea. Certainly makes my job easier. Do you know the name of the place?" Pemberton's smile was broadening.

"Wicken's Hunt."

Pemberton's smile quickly faded.

"Oh." He licked his lips, made a clicking sound with his tongue against his teeth. "Wicken's Hunt," he repeated, looking depressed.

"What's the matter? Did it burn down or something?"

"No, no. It's a beautiful place, wonderfully restored." Pemberton sighed deeply. "Unfortunately it's no longer on the market."

"You sure?" Conklin sounded skeptical.

"I'm certain. I was the selling agent."

"Damn, how long ago?"

"About two years, although the people have only been in it for several months. There was a lot of renovation work to do."

Conklin looked at him slyly, eyebrows cocked. "Think they might want to sell?"

Pemberton's mind raced through the possibilities. Flipping a property like that within the relatively short span of two years? What a wonderful impact on his wallet.

"Anything's possible. I've actually gotten to know them – well, one of them anyway – fairly well. Just had breakfast with him, in fact."

"So it's a couple then, old like me, I guess. Wicken's Hunt isn't exactly a starter home from what my father told me."

"Actually, they're not a couple. And he's older, but the property doesn't belong to him. It belongs to her."

Conklin leaned forward. "To her?"

Pemberton looked around for a moment, got up and fully shut the door to his conference room, and then sat back down.

"You understand that I'm telling you this in confidence."

"Absolutely. I didn't survive all those years on Wall Street without understanding confidences."

"While the land records show a corporation as the title holder, the real owner of Wicken's Hunt is a young woman. Catherine Savage. Obviously incredibly wealthy. Quite frankly, I'm not certain what the source of that wealth is, nor is it my business to ask. She lived abroad for years. Has a little girl about ten. Charlie Thomas – the older man – he and I have had some nice little discussions. They've been very generous with several local charities. She doesn't come out in public very much, but that's understandable."

323

"Sure is. If I moved here, you might not see me for weeks on end."

"Exactly. They seem to be real good people, though. They seem very happy here. Very happy."

Conklin sat back and it was his turn to sigh. "Well, I guess they won't be looking to move any time soon. Damn shame too." He eyed Pemberton intently. "Real damn shame, since I make it my practice to pay a finder's fee on top of any real estate commission you might collect from the seller."

Pemberton perked up noticeably. "Is that right?"

"Now, there aren't any ethical considerations that would prevent you from accepting such an inducement, are there?"

"None that I can think of," Pemberton said quickly. "So, how much would that inducement come to?"

"Twenty percent of the purchase price." Harry Conklin drummed his fingers on the tabletop and watched Pemberton's face turn different colors.

If Pemberton hadn't been sitting down, he would've toppled to the floor. "That's very generous," he finally managed to say.

"If I want something done, I find the best way to accomplish my goal is to provide decent incentives to those in a position to help me achieve that goal. But from the looks of things here, I don't think it's likely. Maybe I'll try North Carolina, I hear good things about it." Conklin started to get up.

"Wait a minute. Please wait just a minute."

Conklin hesitated and then slowly resumed his seat.

"Actually, your timing may be perfect."

"Why's that?"

Pemberton leaned even closer to him. "There have been recent developments, very recent developments, that might give us an opening to approach them about selling."

"If they just moved in, seem happy here, what kind of developments are we talking about? The place isn't haunted, is it?"

"No, nothing like that. As I said, I had a breakfast meeting with Charlie. He was concerned about a person who had come to visit them. Asking for money."

"So? That happens to me all the time. You think that'll make them pack up and leave?"

"Well, I wouldn't have thought so at first either, but the more I thought about it, the more unusual it sounded. I mean, you're right, the rich get approached all the time, so why should this man upset them so? But he obviously did."

"How do you know that?"

Pemberton smiled. "In many ways, in fact, in more ways than people around here care to admit, Charlottesville is a small town. Now I know for a fact that very recently Matt Riggs was up surveying Ms. Savage's property line when he became engaged in a reckless chase with another car that almost got him killed."

Conklin shook his head in confusion. "Who's Matt Riggs?"

"A local contractor hired by Ms. Savage to install a security fence around her property."

"So he was chasing another car? How does that tie in with Catherine Savage?"

"A friend of mine was heading to work that morning. He lives up in that same area and works in town. He was about to turn on to the main road heading into town when a charcoal gray BMW flew by. He said it must've been doing eighty. If he had pulled out a second sooner that BMW would've torn his car in half. He was so shaken, he couldn't budge for a full minute. Good thing too, because while he's sitting there trying to keep his breakfast down, Matt

325

Riggs's pickup comes barreling by and another car is locked on his bumper. They were obviously going at it."

"Do you know who was in the BMW?"

"Now, I've never met her but I know people who have seen her. Catherine Savage is a tall, blond woman. Real good-looking. My friend only got a glimpse of the driver, but he said she was blond and pretty. And I saw a charcoal gray BMW parked up at Wicken's Hunt when I went up to do a preclosing walk-through with Charlie."

"So you think somebody was chasing her?"

"And I think Matt Riggs must've run smack into it. I know that his truck's in the shop with a busted bumper. I also know that Sally Beecham – she's the maid up at Wicken's – saw Riggs walking off in a huff from the house later that same morning."

Conklin stroked his chin. "Very interesting. Guess there's no way to find out who was chasing her?"

"Yes there is. I mean I did. At least his location. You see, it gets even more interesting. As I said, Charlie invited me to breakfast. That's when he told me about this man who had come by the house wanting money. Charlie wanted my help in finding out if the man was staying in the area. Of course, I agreed to do what I could. At that point I didn't know about the car chase. I found that out later."

"You said you were able to find the man? But how could you? Lots of places to hide around here, I would think." Conklin asked this in a nonchalant manner.

Pemberton smiled triumphantly. "Not much escapes my notice, Harry. Like I said, I was born and raised here. Charlie gave me a description of the man and the car. I used my contacts and in less than twenty-four hours I had located him."

"Probably holed up pretty far away, I'll bet."

Pemberton shook his head. "Not at all. He was right under their noses. A small cottage. It's barely ten minutes from Wicken's Hunt by car. But very isolated."

"Help me out here. I don't have my bearings here yet. Is it near Monticello?"

"Well, in the general vicinity, but the area I'm talking about is north of that, north of Interstate Sixty-four, in fact. The cottage isn't too far from the Airslie Estate, off Highway Twenty-two, the Keswick Hunt area it's called. The man had leased the cottage about a month ago."

"Good gosh, did you get a name?"

"Tom Jones." Pemberton smiled knowingly. "Obviously false."

"Well, I guess they appreciated your help. So what happened?"

"I don't know. My business keeps me hopping. I really haven't talked to them about it any more."

"Well, this Riggs fellow, I bet he's sure sorry he got involved."

"Well, he can take care of himself."

"Maybe so, but getting banged around in a car in a high-speed chase? Most general contractors don't do that."

"Well, Riggs wasn't always a G.C."

"Really?" Conklin said, his features inscrutable. "You really do have the Peyton Place here. So what's his story?"

Pemberton shrugged his shoulders. "Your guess is as good as mine. He never talks about his past. He just appeared one day about five years ago, started learning the building trade and he's been here ever since. Pretty mysterious. Charlie thought he was a policeman. Frankly, I think he was with the government in some secret capacity and they put him out to pasture. Call it my gut."

"That's real interesting. Old guy then."

"No. Mid- to late thirties. Tall, strong, and very capable. Excellent reputation."

"Good for him."

"Now about our arrangement. If this man really is dogging them, I can talk to Charlie, see what he has to say. Maybe they will agree to move. It's certainly worth asking."

"I tell you what, you let me think about it for a few days."

"I can get the process started anyway."

Conklin put up one hand. "No, I don't want you doing that. When I'm ready to move, we'll move fast, don't you worry about that."

"I just thought—"

Conklin abruptly got up. "You'll hear from me very soon, John. I appreciate the insight, I really do."

"And if they won't move, there are at least a dozen other estates I can show you. They would serve your purposes equally well, I'm sure."

"This fellow in the cottage intrigues me. You wouldn't happen to have an exact address and directions, would you?"

Pemberton was startled by the question. "You certainly don't want to talk to him, do you? He might be dangerous."

"I can take care of myself. And I've learned in my business that you never know where you might find an ally." Conklin looked at him keenly until understanding spread across Pemberton's face. He wrote the information down on a piece of paper and handed it to the other man.

Conklin took an envelope out of his pocket and handed it to Pemberton, motioning for him to open it.

"Oh my God." Pemberton sat there gaping at the wad of cash that spilled out. "What's this for? I haven't done anything yet."

Conklin eyed Pemberton steadily. "You've given me information, John. Information is always worth a great deal to me. I'll be in touch." The men shook hands and Conklin took his leave.

Back at the country inn where he was staying, Harry Conklin walked into the bathroom, closed the door, and turned on the water. Fifteen minutes later the door opened and Jackson emerged, the remnants of Harry Conklin bundled in a plastic bag which Jackson deposited in a side pouch of his luggage. His conversation with Pemberton had been very enlightening. His encounter with the man had not been by chance. Upon arriving in Charlottesville, Jackson had made discreet inquiries around town that had quickly identified Pemberton as the selling agent for Wicken's Hunt. He sat on the bed and opened a large, detailed map of the Charlottesville area, noting and committing to memory the places he and Pemberton had discussed and the written directions to the cottage. Before talking to Pemberton he had educated himself on some of the history of Wicken's Hunt, which had been nicely detailed in a book on local area estates and their original owners at the county library. It had given him enough background information to form his cover story and draw out Pemberton on the subject.

Jackson closed his eyes, deep in thought. Right now he was planning how best to begin his campaign against LuAnn Tyler and the man who was pursuing her.

THIRTY-FIVE

Riggs had given it a day before he had attempted to retrieve his Jeep. Just in case the guy was still around, he went armed and he went at night. The Cherokee looked undamaged. Riggs made a quick check of it before heading toward the cottage. The Chrysler was nowhere to be seen. He shone his flashlight in the window of the shed. The Honda was still there. Riggs went up to the front door and wondered for the hundredth time if he should just leave this business alone. Dangerous things seemed to happen around Catherine Savage. He had had his fill of such events and he had come to Charlottesville in search of other things. Still, he could not stop his hand from carefully turning the doorknob. The door swung open.

The flashlight in one hand, his pistol in the other, Riggs moved forward slowly. He was reasonably certain that the place was empty, but assumptions like that could earn you an unwanted trip to the morgue with a tag around your big toe. He could see most of the first floor from where he was standing. He shone his flashlight slowly around the room. There was a light switch on the wall, but he wasn't about to use it. In what had been the dining room, he discerned dust patterns on the floor that showed certain objects had been removed. He ran his fingers over these areas and then moved on. He moved into the kitchen where he lifted the phone. There was no

330

dial tone. He moved back into the dining room.

As Riggs's eyes swept the room, they passed right over the figure dressed all in black standing just inside the half-opened closet door next to the stairs.

Jackson closed his eyes the second before the light moved across his hiding place so that his pupils would not reflect off it. When the arc of illumination had passed, Jackson reopened his eyes and gripped the handle of the knife tightly. He had heard Riggs before he had ever set foot on the porch. It was not the man who had leased the cottage. He was long gone; Jackson had already searched the place thoroughly. This man had come to reconnoiter the place as well. Riggs, it must be, Jackson concluded. In fact, Jackson found Riggs almost as interesting as the man he had come to kill tonight. Ten years ago Jackson had predicted that LuAnn would be a problem, and now that prediction was coming true. He had done some preliminary checking on Riggs's background after his discussion with Pemberton. The fact that there was little to find out had intrigued him greatly.

When Riggs passed within a few feet of him, Jackson contemplated killing him. It would take just a flick of the razor-sharp blade against his throat. But as quickly as the homicidal impulse flared through his system, it passed. Killing Riggs would further no purpose, at least not at present. Jackson's hand gripping the knife relaxed. Riggs would live another day. If there was a next time, Jackson decided, the outcome might be far different. He didn't like people meddling in his business. If nothing else, he would now check into Riggs's background with far greater intensity.

Riggs left the cottage and headed toward his Cherokee. He glanced back at the cottage. A sensation had just come over him, as though he had just survived a close call. He shrugged it off. He had once lived by his instincts; however, he assumed they had rusted somewhat since his occupation had changed. It was an empty house and nothing more.

Watching from the window, Jackson picked up on Riggs's slight hesitation, and with it his curiosity grew even more. Riggs would possibly make an interesting project, but he would have to wait. Jackson had something more pressing to take care of. From the floor of the closet Jackson picked up what looked like a doctor's bag. He moved to the dining room, crouched down, and unpacked the contents of a first-rate fingerprint kit. Jackson then moved over to the light switch and hit it from various angles with a handheld laser carried in his jacket pocket. Several latent prints sprang to life under the beam. Jackson dusted the area with a fiberglass brush dipped in black powder and gently brushed around the area of the light switch, outlining the latent prints. The kitchen counter, telephone, and doorknobs were subjected to the same process. The telephone, especially, evidenced very clear fingerprints. Jackson smiled. Riggs's real identity would not be a mystery much longer. Using pressure-wound tape, he then lifted the prints from each of the areas and transferred them to separate index cards. Humming quietly to himself, Jackson marked the cards with special identification hieroglyphics and placed them in separate plastic-lined containers. He then carefully removed all evidence of the fingerprint powder from each of the surfaces. He loved the methodology of it all. Precise steps that reached a precise conclusion. It took him only a few minutes to repack his kit and then he left the cottage. He took a side trail to his waiting car and drove off. It was not often that one captured two birds with one stone. Tonight's work was beginning to look like precisely that.

THIRTY-SIX

"I like Mr. Riggs, Mom."

"Well, you don't really know him, do you?"

LuAnn sat on the edge of her daughter's bed and fingered the bed covers absentmindedly.

"I have good instincts about these things."

Mother and daughter exchanged smiles. "Really? Well, maybe you can share some of your insights with me."

"Seriously, is he going to come back soon?"

LuAnn took a deep breath. "Lisa, we may have to go away soon."

Lisa's hopeful smile faded away at this abrupt change of subjects. "Go away? Where?"

"I'm not sure just yet. And it's not for certain. Uncle Charlie and I haven't finished talking about it yet."

"Were you going to include me in those discussions?"

The unfamiliar tone in her daughter's voice startled LuAnn. "What are you talking about?"

"How many times have we moved in the last six years? Eight? And that's just as far back as I can remember. God knows how many times we did when I was really little. It's not fair." Lisa's face colored and her voice shook.

LuAnn swept an arm around her shoulders. "Sweetie, I didn't say it was for certain. I just said maybe."

"That's not the point. Okay, so it's maybe now. Or maybe next month. But then one day it'll be 'we're moving' and there's nothing I can do about it."

LuAnn put her face in Lisa's long hair. "I know it's hard on you, baby."

"I'm not a baby, Mom, not anymore. And I'd really like to know what we're running from."

LuAnn stiffened and raised her head back up, her eyes searching out Lisa's.

"We're not running from anything. What would we possibly be running from?"

"I was hoping you would tell me. I like it here, I don't want to leave, and unless you can give me a really good explanation why we have to, I'm not going."

"Lisa, you're ten years old and even though you're a very intelligent and mature ten-year-old, you're still only a child. So where I go, you go."

Lisa turned her face away. "Do I have a big trust fund?"

"Yes, why?"

"Because when I turn eighteen I'm going to have my own home and I'm going to stay there until I die. And I don't want you to ever visit me."

LuAnn's cheeks reddened. "Lisa!"

"I mean it. And then maybe I'll have friends and can do the things I want to do."

"Lisa Marie Savage, you've been all over the world. You've done things most people will never get a chance to do their entire lives."

"Well, you know what?"

"What?" LuAnn shot back.

"Right now, I'd trade with them in a heartbeat."

Lisa lay down in the bed and put the covers up almost over her head. "And right now, I'd like to be alone."

LuAnn started to say something and then thought

334

better of it. Biting her lip hard, she raced down the hallway to her room, where she collapsed on the bed.

It was unraveling. She could feel it, like a big ball of twine someone had tossed down a long set of stairs. She rose, went into the bathroom, and started the shower. She pulled off her clothes and stepped under the steaming water. Leaning up against the wall she closed her eyes and tried to tell herself that it would be okay, that in the morning Lisa would be all right, that her love for her mother remained undiminished. This was not the first serious argument mother and daughter had had over the years. Lisa did not just share her mother's physical attributes; LuAnn's independence and stubborn streak had been replicated in her daughter. After a few minutes LuAnn finally calmed down and let the soothing water envelop her.

When she opened her eyes another image invaded her thoughts. Matthew Riggs must believe her to be insane by now. Insane and dishonest as hell. Quite a combination if you were trying to make an impression. But she wasn't. If anything, she felt sorry for him, having risked his life twice and gotten kicked in the gut both times for his trouble. He was a very attractive man, but she wasn't looking for a relationship. How could she? How could she even contemplate partnering with someone? She'd be afraid to speak for fear of letting a secret scurry free. With all that, the image of Matt Riggs remained fixed in her head. A very handsome man. Strong, honest, courageous. And there was secrecy in his background too. And hurt. She suddenly cursed out loud that her life wasn't normal. That she couldn't attempt even a friendship with him.

She moved her hands fiercely along her limbs as she soaped up and released her frustrations at the same time. The harsh movements against her skin rekindled a disturbing revelation. The last man she had slept with was Duane Harvey over ten years ago. As her fingers moved over her breasts, Riggs's face appeared again in her thoughts. She shook her head angrily, closed her eyes again, and laid her face against the wall of the shower. The costly imported tile was wet and warm. She remained in that position despite danger signs flashing in her mind. So wet. So warm. So safe. Almost unconsciously her hands dipped to her waist and then over her buttocks and all the while Matthew Riggs resided in her thoughts. She kept her eyes scrunched tight. The fingers of her right hand slithered around to her navel. Her breaths became heavier. Under the sounds of the water, a low moan passed over her lips. A large tear made its way down her face before it was washed away. Ten years. Ten damned years. The fingers of her two hands were touching now, intermeshed in a way, like the gears of a clock. Slow, methodical, reliable. Back and forth . . . She jerked straight up so quickly she almost smashed her skull against the showerhead.

"Good Lord, LuAnn!" She exclaimed this to herself. She cut off the water and stepped out of the shower. She sat down on the lid of the toilet and hung her head between her knees; the lightheadedness was already passing. Her wet hair sprawled across her long, bare legs. The floor became sopping wet as the water poured off her body. She glanced over at the shower, a guilty look on her face. The muscles in her back bunched together, the veins in her arms swelled large. It wasn't easy. It just wasn't easy at all.

She rose on unsteady legs, toweled off, and went into the bedroom.

Among the costly furnishings of her bedroom was

a very familiar object. The clock her mother had given her ticked away, and as LuAnn listened, her nerves began to reassemble themselves. Thank God she had stuffed it in her bag right before almost being killed in that trailer so many years ago. Even now she would lie awake at night listening to its clunkiness. It skipped every third beat and at around five o'clock in the afternoon it would make a noise like someone had lightly smacked a cymbal. The gears and wires, the guts of the contraption, were tired; but it was like listening to an old friend strum on a weathered guitar, the notes not what they should be, ideally, but holding comfort for her, some peace.

She pulled on a pair of panties and then went back into the bathroom to dry her hair. Looking in the mirror she saw a woman on the brink of something: disaster probably. Should she start seeing a shrink? Didn't you have to be truthful in therapy in order to make any progress? She mouthed this question to her reflection in the mirror. No, psychotherapy wasn't going to be an option. As usual, she would just go it alone.

She traced the scar on her face, letting her finger feel each contour of the ridged, damaged skin, in essence reliving the painful events of her past. *Never forget*, she told herself. *It's all a sham. All a lie.*

She finished drying her hair, and was about to go back into the bedroom and collapse on to the bed when Lisa's words came back to her. She just couldn't let that resentment and anger fester all night. She had to talk to her daughter again. Or at least try to.

She went back into the bedroom to put on her robe before heading for Lisa's room.

"Hello, LuAnn."

So stunned was LuAnn that she had to reach out

337

and grip the doorjamb or she would've sagged to the floor. As LuAnn stared at him, she found that the muscles in her face had ceased to function. She couldn't even form a response, as though she had just suffered a stroke.

"It's been a long time." Jackson stepped away from the window and sat down on the edge of the bed.

His casual movements finally broke LuAnn free from her inertia. "How the hell did you get in here?"

"Not relevant." The words and tone were instantly familiar to her. All those years ago came rushing back with such speed that the effect was nearly incapacitating.

"What do you want?" She forced the words to come out.

"Ah, very relevant. However, we have much to discuss, and I would suggest you do so in the comfort of some clothing." He stared pointedly at her body.

LuAnn found it extremely difficult to take her eyes off him. Being half naked in front of the man was far less disturbing than having to turn her back on him. Finally, she threw open her closet door, pulled out a knee-length robe, and quickly put it on. She cinched the robe tightly around her waist and turned back around. Jackson wasn't even looking at her. His eyes roamed the spectacular parameters of her boudoir; his gazed rested on the clock on the wall briefly and then moved on. Apparently, the brief view of her body – a sight many men would have paid hard cash for – had inspired in him nothing more than extreme diffidence.

"You've done well for yourself. If I remember correctly, your previous decorating tastes were limited to dirty linoleum and Goodwill castoffs."

"I don't appreciate this intrusion."

He swiveled his head around and his eyes flashed into hers. "And I don't appreciate having to take time away from a very busy schedule to rescue you yet again, LuAnn. By the way, do you prefer LuAnn or Catherine?"

"I'll let you choose," she said sharply. "And I don't need to be rescued by anyone, certainly not by you."

He rose from the bed and scrutinized her altered appearance closely. "Very good. Not quite as good as I could have done, but I won't nit-pick," he finally said. "Still, the look is very chic, very sophisticated. Congratulations."

LuAnn responded by remarking, "The last time I saw you, you were wearing a dress. Other than that, you haven't changed much."

Jackson still had on the dark clothing he had worn at the cottage. His features were the same as for their first meeting, although he had not covered his lean frame with padding. He thrust his head forward; the smile seemed to engulf his entire face. "Didn't you know?" he said. "Aside from my other remarkable abilities, I also never age." His smile receded as quickly as it had appeared. "Now, let's talk." He once again perched on the edge of the bed and motioned for LuAnn to sit at a small antique writing desk situated against one wall. She did so.

"What about?"

"I understand you had a visitor. A man who chased you in a car?"

"How the hell do you know that?" LuAnn said angrily.

"You just won't accept the fact that you can't conceal information from me. Like the fact that you have reentered the United States against my most explicit instructions."

"The ten years are up."

"Funny, I don't remember setting an expiration date on those instructions."

"You can't expect me to run for the rest of my life."

"On the contrary, that is exactly what I expect. That is exactly what I *demand*."

"You cannot run my life."

Jackson looked around the room again and then stood up. "First things first. Tell me about the man."

"I can handle this situation by myself."

"Is that right? From what I can tell, you've committed one blunder after another."

"I want you to leave right now. I want you to get the hell out of my house."

Jackson calmly shook his head. "The years have done nothing to ameliorate your temper. An unlimited supply of money can't purchase good breeding or tact, can it?"

"Go to hell."

In response Jackson reached one hand inside his jacket.

In an instant LuAnn had snatched up a letter opener from her writing desk. She cocked her arm back in preparation to hurl it. "I can kill you with this from twenty feet. Money *can* buy a lot of things."

Jackson shook his head sadly. "Ten years ago I found you, a young girl with a good head on her shoulders in very difficult circumstances. But you were still white trash, LuAnn. And, I'm afraid to say, some things just don't change." His hand slowly came out of his jacket. In it he held a slip of paper. "You can put your little toy away. You won't need it." He looked at her with a calmness that managed, under the circumstances, to paralyze her. "At least not tonight." He unfolded the paper. "Now, I understand that two men have recently entered your life: Matthew Riggs is one; the other is as yet unidentified."

LuAnn slowly dropped her arm, but she still clutched the letter opener in her hand.

Jackson looked up from the paper. "I have a vested interest in ensuring that your secret never be found out. I have a number of ongoing business activities, and above all I value anonymity. You're one in a line of dominoes. And when they start to fall, they tend to keep falling until they reach the end. I am that end. Do you understand?"

LuAnn sat back down in the chair and crossed her legs. "Yes," she answered curtly.

"You have unnecessarily complicated my life by coming back to the United States. The man who is following you discovered your identity, in part, through your tax records. That is why I never wanted you to come back."

"I probably shouldn't have," LuAnn conceded. "But you try moving just about every six months, a new country, a new language. And try doing it with a little girl."

"I appreciate your difficulties; however, I assumed that being one of the richest women on earth would more than make up the difference."

"Like you said, money can't buy everything."

"You never met the man before? In your extensive travels? You're absolutely certain?"

"I would've remembered. I've remembered everything the last ten years." She said this softly.

Jackson studied her closely. "I believe you. Do you have any reason to think that he knows about the lottery?"

LuAnn hesitated a second. "No."

"You're lying. Tell me the truth immediately or I'll kill everyone in this house starting with you." This abrupt threat, delivered calmly and precisely, made her suck in her breath.

She swallowed with difficulty. "He had a list. A

341

list with twelve names on it. Mine, Herman Rudy, Bobbie Jo Reynolds, and some others."

Jackson assimilated this information rapidly and then looked down at the paper. "And the man Riggs?"

"What about him?"

"There's some confusion as to his background."

"Everyone has secrets."

Jackson smiled. "Touché. Under other circumstances that would not bother me. However, in this instance it does."

"I'm not following you."

"Riggs has a mysterious past and he just happens to be around when you need assistance. I take it he did help you."

LuAnn looked at him quizzically. "Yes, but he's been here for five years, long before I got here."

"That's not the point. I'm not suggesting the man is a plant. I am suggesting that he could well be something entirely different than what he claims. Now he coincidentally collides with your world. That's what worries me."

"I don't think it was anything other than a coincidence. He was hired to do a job for me. It was perfectly natural that he would be nearby when the other man started chasing me."

Jackson shook his head. "I don't like it. I saw him tonight." LuAnn stiffened perceptibly. "At the cottage. I was this close to him." He spread his hands about two feet apart. "I contemplated killing him on the spot. It would have been extremely easy."

LuAnn's face turned white and she licked dry lips. "There's no reason to do that."

"You have no way of knowing that. I'm going to check him out and if I find anything in his background to suggest trouble for me, then I will eliminate him. It's that simple."

342

"Let me get that information for you."

"What?" Jackson looked startled.

"Riggs likes me. He's already helped me, probably saved my life. It would be natural for me to show my gratitude. Get to know him better."

"No, I don't like it."

"Riggs is a nobody. A local builder. Why trouble yourself with him? Like you said, you're busy."

Jackson studied her intensely for a moment. "All right, LuAnn, you do that. However, any information you obtain better be reported to me in a timely fashion or, with respect to Mr. Riggs, I will take matters into my own very capable hands. Clear?"

LuAnn let out a deep breath. "Clear."

"The other man, of course, I must find. It shouldn't be too terribly difficult."

"Don't do that."

"Excuse me?"

"You don't have to do that. Find him."

"I am very much certain that I do."

The memory of Mr. Rainbow came flooding back to her. She did not want another death on her conscience. She wasn't worth it. "If he shows up again, we're just going to leave the country."

Jackson refolded the paper and replaced it in his pocket. He made a precise steeple with his hands. "You obviously do not fully understand the situation. Were you the only one he was on to, then perhaps your simplistic solution might resolve the matter, at least temporarily. However, the man has a list with the names of eleven other people with whom I worked. I would submit that a resolution involving all of them fleeing the country almost simultaneously would be essentially unworkable."

LuAnn drew in a sharp breath. "I could pay the man. How much money can he want? That would take care of it."

Jackson smiled tightly. "Blackmailers are a bad lot. They never seem to go away." He added sharply, "Unless they receive extreme persuasion to do so."

"Mr. Jackson, please don't do it," she said again.

"Don't do what, LuAnn? Ensure your survival?" He glanced around. "And with it all of this?" He rested his gaze back upon her. "How is Lisa, by the way? As beautiful as her mother?"

LuAnn felt her throat constrict. "She's fine."

"Excellent. Let's keep it that way, shall we?"

"Can't you just let it go? Let me handle it."

"LuAnn, many years ago we were confronted with a situation regarding another would-be blackmailer. I took care of that incident and I will take care of this one. In matters like this I almost never opt for delegation. Count your blessings that I'm allowing Riggs to live. For now."

"But that man can't prove anything. How can he? And even if he could, they'll never be able to trace anything to you. Maybe I'll go to jail, but you won't. Hell, I don't even know who you really are."

Jackson stood up, his lips pursed. He took a moment to rub his left hand delicately along the edge of the bedspread.

"Beautiful needlework here," Jackson commented. "Indian isn't it?"

Distracted for an instant by his query, LuAnn was suddenly staring down the barrel of a 9-mm, a suppressor attached to its muzzle.

"One potential solution could involve my killing all twelve of you. That would certainly qualify as a startling dead-end for our inquisitive friend. Remember that the ten-year period is up. The lottery's principal amount has already been returned to a Swiss account that I have set up in your name. I would strongly advise against transferring that money into the United States." He pulled

344

another slip of paper from his pocket and put it down on her bed. "Here are the authorization codes and other account information that will enable you to access it. The funds are untraceable. There you have it. As agreed." Jackson's fingers curled around the trigger of his weapon. "However, now I really don't have any incentive to keep you around, do I?" He advanced toward her. LuAnn's fingers tightened around the letter opener.

"Put it down, LuAnn. Granted, you're remarkably athletic, but you're not faster than a bullet. Put it down. *Now!*"

She dropped the letter opener and backed up against the wall.

Jackson stopped a few inches from her. While he lined up the pistol with her left cheekbone, he ran a gloved hand along her right cheek. There was no sexual content to the motion. Even through the glove, LuAnn could sense the purely clinical chill of his touch.

"You should have thrown it the first time, LuAnn. You really should have." His eyes were mocking.

"I'm not going to kill someone in cold blood," said LuAnn.

"I know. You see, that is your greatest shortcoming, because that's precisely when you should strike."

He removed his hand and looked at her.

"Ten years ago I felt you were the weak link in the chain. During the intervening years, I thought perhaps I was wrong. Everything was going so smoothly. But now I find my initial intuition was correct. Even if I were in no personal danger of discovery, were I to let this man blackmail you or perhaps even expose the manipulations of the lottery, then that would be a failure on my part. I do not fail. Ever. And I do not let other people have any control whatsoever over plans of mine, for that, in itself, would be a form of failure. Besides, I couldn't bear to let such a grand performance be ruined.

"Just think about the wonderful life I've given you, LuAnn. Remember what I told you all those years ago: 'Go anywhere, do anything.' I gave that to you. The impossible. All yours. Look at you now. Flawless beauty." His hand went to the front of her robe. With slow movements he undid the strap and the robe fell open, fully exposing her quivering breasts and flat belly. He slid the robe over her shoulders and it fell to the floor.

"The most prudent action on my part, of course, would be to kill you. Right here and right now. In fact, what the hell." He pointed the gun directly at her head and pulled on the trigger. LuAnn jerked back, her eyes slamming shut.

When she reopened them, Jackson was studying her reaction. She was shaking terribly; her heart was thumping around inside her, she couldn't catch her breath.

Jackson shook his head. "Your nerves don't seem to be as strong, LuAnn, as when we were last together. And nerves, or a lack thereof, really are the whole ball of wax." He looked at the pistol for a moment, slipped off the safety, and continued speaking calmly. "As I was saying, the most prudent thing, when one is confronted with a weak link, is to snip it out." He paused and then continued, "I'm not going to do that with you, at least not yet. Not even after you've disobeyed me, jeopardized everything. Would you like to know why?"

LuAnn remained planted against the wall, afraid to move, her eyes fixed on his.

He took her silence for assent. "Because I feel you have a greater destiny to fulfill. A dramatic statement, but I'm a dramatic person; I think I'll allow

346

myself that. It's really as simple as that. And in very large measure, you are a creation of mine. Would you be living in this house, speaking and thinking as an educated person, traveling the world on a whim, without me? Of course not. In killing you, I would, in effect, be killing part of myself. That, as I'm sure you can appreciate, I am loath to do. Nevertheless, please keep in mind that a wild animal, when trapped, will ultimately sacrifice a limb in order to escape and survive. Don't think for one moment that I am not capable of that sacrifice. If you do, you're a fool. I sincerely hope that we are able to extricate you from this little problem." He shook his head sympathetically, much as he had ten years earlier during their very first meeting. "I really do, LuAnn. However, if we can't, we can't. Problems come up in business all the time, and I'm counting on you to do your part, to do all you can to ensure that we successfully navigate this one." Jackson's tone once again became businesslike as he ticked off items with his fingers. "You will not leave the country. You obviously went to a great deal of trouble to get back in, so stay and enjoy it for a while. You will immediately report to me any further contact with our mysterious stranger. The number I gave you ten years ago will still reach me. I will be in touch on a regular basis. Whatever additional instructions I give you, you will follow precisely. Understood?"

She quickly nodded.

"I'm quite serious, LuAnn. If you disobey me again, I will kill you. And it will be slow and unbelievably painful." He studied her reaction to these words for a moment. "Now go into the bathroom and compose yourself."

She started to turn away.

"Oh, LuAnn?"

She looked back.

347

"Keep in mind that if we do fail to contain this problem and I have to eliminate that weak link, there will be no reason that I can see to stop there." He glanced ominously in the direction of the doorway leading to the hallway, where barely twenty feet away Lisa lay sleeping. He turned back to her. "I like to give my business associates as much incentive as possible to achieve success. I find that they're much more likely not to disappoint."

LuAnn ran into the bathroom, locking the door after her. She gripped the cold marble of the vanity, every limb shaking uncontrollably, as though she had left her skeleton back there with him. Wrapping a thick, full-length towel around her, she sank down to the floor. Her natural courage was tempered with a strong dose of common sense and she understood quite clearly the serious personal jeopardy she was in. But that was far from her greatest fear. The fact that Jackson might set his murderous sights on Lisa made her nearly delirious with terror.

Curiously enough it was with this thought that LuAnn's features grew deadly still in their own right. Her eyes stared across at the doorway, on the other side of which stood a person to whom she was probably more similar than dissimilar. They both had secrets; they both were incredibly rich from ill-gotten gains. They both had mental and physical abilities above and beyond the norm. And perhaps most telling, they both had killed someone. Her act had been spontaneous, survival the only motive. Jackson's had been premeditated, but survival of sorts had also been his motivation. Perhaps not as wide a chasm as it looked on the surface. The results, after all, had been the deaths of two human beings.

She slowly rose from the floor. If Jackson ever came after Lisa, then either he would die or LuAnn would; there would be no other possibilities. She let

348

the towel fall to the floor. She unlocked the door. There seemed to exist an ethereal connection between Jackson and LuAnn Tyler that defied a logical explanation. It was as though, even after all this time apart, that their synapses had become fused together at a certain, almost psychic level. For she was absolutely certain what she would find when she returned to the bedroom. She threw open the door.

Nothing. Jackson was gone.

LuAnn pulled on some clothes and hurried down the hallway to check on Lisa. The little girl's steady breathing told her mother that she was asleep. For a while, LuAnn simply hovered over Lisa, afraid to leave her. She didn't want to wake her. She wouldn't be able to hide the terror she was feeling from her daughter. Finally, LuAnn made certain the windows were locked and left the room.

Next she made her way to Charlie's bedroom and gently roused him from sleep.

"I just had a visitor."

"What? Who?"

"We should've known he'd find out," she said wearily.

When the meaning behind her words worked through his grogginess, Charlie sat straight up in bed, almost knocking over the lamp on the nightstand. "Good God, he was here? Jackson was here?"

"When I finished my shower I found him waiting for me in my bedroom. I don't think I've ever been that scared in my life."

"Oh, God, LuAnn, baby." Charlie hugged her tightly for several moments. "How the hell – how the hell did he find us?"

"I don't know, but he knows everything. The man who chased me. About Riggs. I, I told him about the list of lottery winners. I tried to lie, but he knew I

349

was. He threatened everyone in the house if I didn't tell him the truth."

"What's he going to do?"

"He's going to find the guy and then he's going to kill him."

Charlie leaned up against the headboard and LuAnn sat down next to him. Charlie put a big hand across his face and shook his head. He looked over at her. "What else did he say?"

"That we weren't to do anything. Be careful around Riggs and to let him know if the other guy showed up again."

"Riggs? Why'd he mention him?"

She looked over at him. "Jackson seemed very suspicious of him. Like maybe he has an ulterior motive for being involved."

"Son of a bitch," Charlie moaned and abruptly rolled out of bed. He stood up and started getting dressed.

"What are you doing?"

"I don't know, but I feel like I've got to do something. Warn Riggs. If Jackson's after him—"

She reached up and gripped his arm. "If you tell Riggs about Jackson, then all you're doing is guaranteeing his death. Somehow, some way, Jackson will find out. He always does. I've got Riggs safe, at least for now."

"How'd you do that?"

"Jackson and I worked out a little arrangement. At least I think he bought it. Who can tell with him?"

Charlie stopped pulling on his pants and looked over at her.

LuAnn continued, "For now anyway, Jackson's going to focus on the other man. He'll find him, and it's not like we can warn him, because we don't even know who he is."

Charlie sat back down on the bed. "So what do we do?"

LuAnn took his hand in hers. "I want you to take Lisa away. I want both of you to go away."

"There's no way I'm leaving you alone with that guy in the neighborhood. No way in hell."

"Yes you will, Charlie, because you know I'm right. By myself, I'm okay. But if he were to get hold of Lisa . . ." She didn't need to finish the thought.

"Why don't you go with her and let me stay here and handle it?"

LuAnn shook her head. "That won't work. If I leave Jackson will come looking. Looking hard. So long as I'm around, he's not going to stray too far. In the meantime, you two can get away."

"I don't like it. I don't want to abandon you, LuAnn. Not now."

She put her arms around his burly shoulders. "My God, you're not abandoning me. You're going to be taking care of the most precious thing I have—" She broke off here, as Jackson's face planted itself squarely in her thoughts.

Finally Charlie took her hand. "Okay. When do you want us to leave?"

"Right now. I'll go get Lisa ready while you pack. Jackson just left, so I doubt if he's going to be watching the place. He probably figures I'm too frozen with fear to do anything. Actually, he wouldn't be too far from the truth."

"Where do we go?"

"You pick the place. I don't want to know. That way nobody can get the information out of me. Call when you get there and then we'll make arrangements to safely communicate after that."

Charlie shrugged. "I never thought it would come to this."

She kissed him lightly on the forehead. "We'll be

351

okay. We just need to be really careful."

"And what about you? What are you going to do?"

LuAnn took a deep breath. "Whatever it takes to make sure we all survive this."

"And Riggs?"

She looked squarely at him. "Especially Riggs."

"I hate this, Mom. I hate it." Lisa stomped around the room in her pajamas as LuAnn hurriedly packed her daughter's bags.

"I'm sorry, Lisa, but you're just going to have to trust me on this."

"Trust, ha, that's a funny one coming from you." Lisa glared at her from across the room.

"I don't need that kind of talk right now, young lady."

"And I don't need this." Lisa sat down on the bed and stubbornly crossed her arms.

"Uncle Charlie is ready, you need to get a move on."

"But we're having a party at school tomorrow. Can't it at least wait until after that?"

LuAnn slammed the suitcase shut. "No, Lisa, I'm afraid it really can't."

"When is this going to stop? When are you going to stop dragging me all over the place?"

LuAnn ran a shaky hand through her hair and sat down next to her daughter, putting an arm around Lisa's quaking form. She sensed the pain coursing through the small body. Could the truth hurt her daughter any worse than this? LuAnn clenched her fist and pushed it against her right eye as she tried to stop her nerves from pouring right out of her body.

She turned to her daughter. "Lisa?" The little girl refused to look at her mother.

"Lisa, please look at me."

Finally, Lisa looked at her mother, her small face a blend of anger and disappointment, a combination that was crushing to LuAnn.

LuAnn spoke slowly. The words she was uttering would have been unthinkable an hour ago. But then Jackson had shown up and his appearance had changed a lot of things. "I promise that one day, very soon, I will tell you everything you want to know. In fact, more than you will ever want to know about me, about you, about everything. All right?"

"But why—"

LuAnn put her hand gently across her daughter's mouth, silencing her. "But I'm telling you right now that when I do it will shock you, it will hurt you and you might never understand or appreciate why I did what I did. You may hate me for it, you may be sorry I'm your mother" – she paused, biting hard into her lip – "but however you feel, I want you to know that I did what I thought was best at the time. I did what I thought was best for you. I was very young and I really didn't have anyone to help me make my decision."

She cupped Lisa's chin with her hand and tilted her daughter's face up to hers. Lisa's eyes were now filled with tears. "I know I'm hurting you now. I don't want you to go away, but I will die before I'd let anything happen to you. So would Uncle Charlie."

"Mom, you're scaring me."

LuAnn gripped Lisa with both hands. "I love you, Lisa. More than I've ever loved anything in my whole life."

"I don't want anything to happen to you." Lisa touched her mother's face. "Mom, will you be okay?"

LuAnn managed a reassuring smile. "A cat always lands on its feet, sweetie. Mommy'll be just fine."

THIRTY-SEVEN

The next morning LuAnn rose early after a mostly sleepless night. Saying good-bye to her daughter had been the most wrenching thing she had ever done; however, she knew that task would seem easy compared to the day she would tell Lisa the truth about her life, about her mother's life. LuAnn hoped she would have the opportunity to do that. And yet a huge wave of relief had swept over her when she had watched the lights of the Range Rover disappear down the road the night before.

Now her biggest concern was devising a way to reapproach Riggs without making him even more suspicious. But she didn't have much time. If she didn't report back to Jackson with some information soon, then he would turn his attention fully on Riggs. She was not going to let that happen.

She was thinking this through as she drew back her bedroom curtains and peered out on to the rear lawn. Her bedroom was on the third floor and provided an inspiring view of the surrounding countryside. A balcony opened off the bedroom through a pair of French doors. LuAnn wondered if that was how Jackson had gained access to the room last night. Normally she activated the burglar alarm right before she went to bed. She might start doing it earlier, although she had little hope that any security system would pose much of a challenge for the man. He seemed to be able to walk right up and then through walls.

She brewed a pot of coffee in the small kitchenette next to her dressing room. Then she put on a silk robe and, holding a cup of steaming coffee in one hand, she stepped out on to the balcony. A table and two chairs were set up there; however, she chose to perch on the marble railing and look out over her property. The sun was on its way up and the rays of pink and gold formed a backdrop to a sea of equally colorful foliage. The view was almost enough to raise her sagging spirits. What she saw next almost caused her to fall off the balcony.

Matthew Riggs was kneeling in the grass near the spot where she had wanted her studio to be built. From her vantage point LuAnn watched in amazement as Riggs unrolled a thick set of blueprints and eyed the lay of the land. LuAnn clambered up on top of the railing and, one hand clinging to the brick wall of the house for support, she stood on tip-toe for a better look. Now she could make out stakes planted in the ground at various points. While she watched, Riggs unraveled some twine and, tying one end to a stake, he started laying out what looked to be the footprint of a building.

She tried calling to him, but her voice couldn't carry far enough.

LuAnn jumped down from the railing, raced through her bedroom, not even pausing to put on shoes. She took the stairs two at a time and unlocked the back door. Sprinting across the dewy grass in her bare feet, the silk robe clung to her form, showing a good deal of her long legs in the process.

Breathing hard, she reached the spot where Riggs had been and looked around. Her breaths were visible in the early morning chill and she pulled the sheer robe tight around her.

Where the hell had he gone? She hadn't imagined it. The stakes were there, the string affixed to them.

She stared at them as if they would eventually reveal the secret of the man's whereabouts.

"Morning."

LuAnn whirled around and stared at him as he emerged from the stand of trees, a large rock in his hand. He set it down ceremoniously in the middle of the staked-out area.

"Your stone chimney," he proclaimed, grinning.

"What are you doing?" LuAnn asked in an amazed tone.

"You always run around outside in that? You're going to catch pneumonia." He stared at her and then discreetly looked away as the emerging sun's rays cleared the tops of the trees and made the thin robe virtually transparent; she wasn't wearing anything underneath. "Not to mention what it's doing to me," he muttered to himself.

"I don't usually see someone on my property at the crack of dawn putting stakes into the ground."

"Just following orders."

"What?"

"You wanted a studio, I'm building you a studio."

"You said there wasn't enough time before winter set in. And you needed plans and permits."

"Well, you admired mine so much, I had the brilliant idea of using those diagrams for this one. That'll save a lot of time. And I've got contacts at the inspector's office so we can expedite the approval process." He paused and looked at her as she stood there shivering. "Now don't rush to thank me," he said.

She crossed her arms. "It's not that, I—" She shuddered again as a brisk wind sailed down the tree line. Riggs took off his heavy coat and draped it around her shoulders.

"You know you really shouldn't be outside in your bare feet."

"You don't have to do this, Matthew. I think I've

356

intruded on your time and patience enough."

He shrugged and looked down at the ground, tapping one of the stakes lightly with his foot. "I don't really mind, Catherine." He coughed in an embarrassed fashion and looked up at the tree line. "There are a lot worse things than hanging out with a woman like you." He shot her a quick glance and then looked away.

LuAnn blushed, biting nervously at her bottom lip while Riggs shoved his hands in his pockets and stared off at nothing. The pair unconsciously emulated two teens nervously feeling each other out for that vital first date.

She looked over at the staked-out area. "So, it'll be just like yours?"

Riggs nodded. "I had the time since you fired me on the fence job."

"I told you I'd pay you and I meant it."

"I'm sure you meant it, but I have a policy of not accepting payment for a job I didn't do. I'm kind of funny that way. Don't worry, I'll charge you plenty for this one."

Riggs once again looked at the surrounding country. "It doesn't get much prettier than this, I can tell you that. Once I build this thing, you probably won't want to leave it."

"That sounds very nice, but hardly realistic."

He glanced over at her. "I guess you travel a lot. A person in your position."

"It's not that. But I do travel a lot." She added wearily, "Too much."

Riggs looked around again. "It's good to see the world. But it's nice to come home too."

"You sound like you speak from experience." She looked at him curiously.

He grinned sheepishly. "Me? I haven't really been anywhere."

357

"But you still like to come home. For some peace?" she said quietly, her big eyes locked on his.

His grin disappeared and he looked at her with renewed respect. "Yes," he finally said.

"How about some breakfast?"

"I already ate, but thanks."

"Coffee?" She was balancing on one bare foot and then the other as the cold ate at her skin.

Riggs watched her movements and then said, "I'll take you up on that one." Riggs tugged off his work gloves and stuffed them in his pants pocket. He turned around and bent down. "Climb on."

"Excuse me?"

"Climb on." He patted his back. "I know I'm not as bulky as your horse but just pretend."

LuAnn didn't budge. "I don't think so."

Riggs turned and looked at her. "Will you come on? I'm not kidding about the pneumonia. Besides, I do this with billionaires all the time, I'm telling you."

LuAnn laughed, pulled his coat on all the way, and hoisted herself up piggyback style, wrapping her arms around his neck. He locked his arms around her bare thighs. "Are you sure you're up to it? It's a pretty long way and I'm not exactly petite."

"I think I can manage, just don't shoot me if I collapse." They started off.

Halfway there she jabbed him playfully in the sides with her knees.

"What the hell was that for?"

"I'm pretending, just like you said. So giddy-up."

"Don't push it," he groused back and then smiled.

In the woods near the horse barn, Jackson repacked his sound wand and made his way through the woods to his car parked on a side road. He had watched in some amusement as Riggs carried LuAnn back to the house. He had also noted the rough

358

footprint for the structure Riggs was apparently building for her. Considering how she was dressed, Jackson thought it likely that LuAnn and the handsome Riggs would probably be enjoying an intimate moment very shortly. That was good, since it would give her an opportunity to pump him for information. Using the sound wand, he had also recorded Riggs's voice, an asset that might prove valuable later. He reached his car and drove off.

Riggs sipped on a cup of coffee in the kitchen while LuAnn munched on a piece of buttered toast. She rose and fixed herself another cup of coffee and freshened his.

Riggs couldn't help but stare when her back was turned. She hadn't changed her clothes and the clingy robe was making him think about things he probably shouldn't be. He finally looked away, his face hot.

"If I get another horse, I think I'll name it after you," LuAnn said.

"Thanks bunches." He looked around. "Everybody else still sleeping?"

She put the coffeepot back down and took a moment to sponge up a bit of spillage on the counter. "Sally has the day off. Charlie and Lisa went on a little vacation."

"Without you?"

She sat back down, her eyes roaming the room before she looked back at him and spoke casually. "I had some things to take care of. I might have to leave for Europe soon. If I do, I'll meet up with them and then we'll all go together. Italy is beautiful this time of year. Have you ever been?"

"The only Rome I've been to is in New York."

"In your past life?" She looked at him over the top of her coffee cup.

"There we go with that past life thing again. It's really not all that exciting."

"So why not tell me about it then?"

"So what's the quid pro quo?"

"Ah, I assume you learned that phrase from your attorney ex-wife."

"Assumptions are dangerous things. I like facts a lot better."

"So do I. So shower me with them."

"Why are you so interested in what I did before I came to Charlottesville?"

Because I'm doing my best to keep you alive, and it sickens me every time I think how close you came to being dead because of me. LuAnn struggled to keep her tone at an even level despite that painful reality. "I'm just a naturally curious person."

"Well, so am I. And I have a hunch your secrets are a lot more interesting than mine."

She tried her best to look surprised. "I don't have any secrets."

He put down his coffee cup. "I can't believe you can actually say that with a straight face."

"I have a lot of money. Some people would like to take it away from me any way they can. That doesn't exactly qualify for shocker status."

"So, you've concluded the guy in the Honda was a potential kidnapper."

"Maybe."

"Funny kidnapper."

"What do you mean?"

"I've been thinking a lot about it. The guy looked like a college professor. He rented a place in the area and furnished it. When he attempted to 'kidnap' you he wasn't even wearing a mask. And when I showed up on the scene, instead of hightailing it off, he tried to drive right through me even though he had no chance of catching you. And in my experience most

360

kidnappers don't work solo. Logistically, it's difficult to go it alone."

"In your experience?"

"See, I'm showering you with secrets."

"Maybe he was trying to frighten me before he actually made the kidnap attempt."

"Don't think so. Why put you on your guard? Kidnappers kind of like the element of surprise."

"If he's not a kidnapper, what then?"

"I was hoping you could tell me. Charlie went into the cottage and so did you. What did you find?"

"Nothing."

"That's bullshit and you know it."

LuAnn stood up and glared at him. "I don't appreciate being called a liar."

"Then stop lying."

Her lips trembled and she abruptly turned away from him.

"Catherine, I'm trying to help you here. Okay, in my past life I did deal with the criminal class quite a bit. I've got some insights and some skills that might prove useful if you'd just tell me the truth."

He rose and put a hand on her shoulder. He turned her around to face him. "I know you're scared. And I also know you've got stronger nerves and more spirit than just about anybody I've ever run across, so I'm assuming whatever you're facing is pretty bad. And I want to help you. I *will* help you, if you'll just let me." He cupped her chin with his hand. "I'm playing straight with you, Catherine. I really am."

She winced slightly as he said her name again. Her *fake* name. She finally reached up and lightly caressed his fingers with her own. "I know you are, Matthew, I know." She looked up at him and her lips parted slightly. Their eyes did not budge from each other as their fingers exchanged touches that were

361

suddenly electrifying both their bodies. The spontaneity of the sensation absolutely immobilized them. But not for long.

Riggs swallowed hard, dropped his hands to her bottom, and abruptly pulled LuAnn against him. The warmth and softness of her breasts burned invisible holes through his thick flannel shirt. Their mouths erupted against each other as he yanked the robe free and it fell to the floor. LuAnn moaned and closed her eyes, her head swaying drunkenly from side to side as Riggs attacked her neck. She pulled at his hair and then wrapped her arms around his head as he hoisted her up in the air, his face buried in her chest. She wrapped her legs around his torso.

Following her frantic, whispered directions, Riggs lunged blindly along the hallway to the small first-floor guest bedroom. Riggs pushed open the door. LuAnn jerked away from him and sprawled flat on her back on the bed, the muscles in her long legs tensing in anticipation. She reached up and pulled at him.

"Dammit, Matthew, hurry!" At his subconscious level Riggs noticed the abrupt return of the Georgia drawl but he was far too intoxicated with the passion of the moment to do anything about it.

Riggs's heavy work boots hit the hardwood floor with a loud thump and his pants followed immediately. She jerked his shirt off, popping several buttons in the process, then slid his boxers down. They didn't bother with the bed covers although Riggs did manage to back-kick the door closed before he plunged on top of her.

362

THIRTY-EIGHT

J ackson sat at the table and studied the laptop's small screen. His suite was large and airy and furnished with eighteenth-century reproductions. The aged hardwood floors were partially covered with area rugs stitched with early American colonial themes. A large wooden carving of a duck in flight hung on one wall. A set of framed prints, each depicting a Virginia native who had gone on to become president of his country long ago, was on another wall. The inn was located in close proximity to his area of focus, was quiet, and allowed Jackson the greatest freedom of unobserved movement. The night before, he had checked out as Harry Conklin and checked back in under another name. He liked to do that. He became uncomfortable staying in one character too long. Besides, he had met with Pemberton in the Conklin role and he didn't want to run into the man again. Now a baseball cap covered his head. Heavy latex eye pouches bracketed the fake nose. The hair was blondish-gray and tied in a ponytail that sprouted out the back of the cap. His neck was long and wrinkled and his build was stocky. He looked like an aging hippie. His luggage was stacked neatly in one corner. He had a practice of not unpacking when he traveled; his line of work sometimes necessitated rapid exits.

Two hours earlier he had scanned one set of fingerprints lifted from the cottage into his hard drive and transmitted them via modem to one of his information contacts. He had already called this person and told him what was coming. This particular contact had access to a database that housed oceans of the most interesting facts, the sole reason that Jackson had enlisted his services many years ago. It wasn't certain that the man who was pursuing LuAnn would have his fingerprints on file anywhere, but Jackson had nothing to lose by checking. If the man did, Jackson's task of tracking him down would become far easier.

Jackson smiled as his computer screen started filling up with data. A digitized photo of the man had even accompanied the personal details.

Thomas J. Donovan. The photo was three years old, but Jackson reckoned that at this time of life, Donovan wouldn't have changed all that much. He studied the nondescript features of the man carefully and then checked the contents of his portable makeup kit and various hairpieces he had brought with him. Yes, if it came down to it, he could impersonate the man. Donovan's name was actually familiar to Jackson. Donovan was an award-winning journalist at the *Washington Tribune*. In fact, about a year ago he had done an in-depth piece on Jackson's father's career as a United States senator.

Jackson had read the story and quickly condemned it as a fluff piece that came nowhere near to addressing the personal side of his father and his monstrous behavior. The history books would smile upon the man; his son knew better.

Jackson's hunch had proven correct. He had figured the man trailing LuAnn wasn't your typical blackmailer. It had taken a lot to track her down and an investigative journalist or perhaps ex-law enforcement person would have the skills, knowledge, and more important, the informational resources to have successfully done so.

Jackson sat back and mused for a moment. Actually, a true blackmailer would have posed less of a difficulty for him. Donovan was undoubtedly on to a story, an enormous story, and he would not stop until he achieved his goal. Or until someone stopped him. It was an interesting challenge. Simply killing the man wouldn't do any good, however. That might make people suspicious. Also, Donovan might have told others of his investigations, although most journalists of Donovan's capabilities, Jackson was aware, kept their cards close to the vest until they broke the story, for a variety of reasons not the least of which was the fear of being scooped.

He had to determine how much Donovan knew and whether he had told anyone else. He picked up the phone, got the number for the *Trib*, and dialed it. He asked for Thomas Donovan. He was told that Donovan had taken a leave of absence. He slowly hung up the phone. He wouldn't have talked to the man if he had come on the phone. He did want to hear his voice, though, in case that knowledge should become useful later. Jackson was also an accomplished mimic and impersonating someone's voice was a wonderful way to manipulate others.

According to Pemberton, Donovan had been in the Charlottesville area for at least a month. Jackson focused briefly on one obvious question: Of all the lottery winners why had the man targeted LuAnn? Jackson almost immediately answered his own query. Because she was the only one running from a murder charge. The only one who had disappeared for ten years and then resurfaced. But how could Donovan possibly have picked up her trail? The cover had been deep and it had been buried even deeper with the passage of ten years, even though LuAnn had committed a tremendous blunder by coming back to the States.

He had a sudden thought. Donovan apparently knew the names of all or some of the lottery winners for the year Jackson had fixed the game. What if he attempted to contact some of the others? If he didn't get what he wanted from LuAnn, and Jackson felt reasonably sure he wouldn't, the next logical step would be to seek out the others. Jackson took out his electronic Rolodex and started making phone calls. After half an hour he had finished contacting the other eleven. Compared to LuAnn, they were sheep to be led around. What he told them to do, they did. He was their savior, the man who had led them to the Promised Land of wealth and leisure. Now, if Donovan bit, the trap would spring.

Jackson began to pace the room. He paused and opened his briefcase. He pulled out the photos. They had been taken on his first day in Charlottesville, even before meeting with Pemberton. The quality of the photos was good considering he had been using a long-range lens and the early morning light had not been the best. The faces stared back at him. Sally Beecham looked tired and bothered. In her forties, tall and slender, she was LuAnn's live-in house-keeper. Her suite was on the first floor on the north side of the mansion. He studied the next two photos. The two young Hispanic women constituted the cleaning staff. They came at nine and left at six. Finally came the photos of the groundspeople. Jackson studied each of their faces. When taking the photographs, he had watched the people intently; how they moved, how they gestured. His handheld sound wand had picked up their voices perfectly. He had listened to their voices over and over as he had just listened to Riggs's. Yes, it was coming together nicely. Like pieces in a strategic battle plan, he was positioning his soldiers to optimal advantage. Possibly, none of the information he had painstakingly gathered about Catherine Savage's daily world would ever come into play. But, on the chance that it might, he would be more than ready. He put the photos away and closed the briefcase.

From a hidden compartment in his suitcase he drew out a short-handled throwing knife. Hand-crafted in China, the blade was so sharp it couldn't even be touched by a bare hand without drawing blood; it was thrown by means of the perfectly balanced teak handle. Jackson strolled around the room, as his mind was sidetracked for a moment. LuAnn was uncommonly fast, lithe, agile, words that would equally be applied to himself. Yes, she had certainly upgraded herself. What else had she learned? What other skills had she acquired? He wondered whether she had experienced the same premonition he had: that their paths would cross again one day like two trains colliding. And had she done her utmost to prepare for that eventuality? Twenty feet. Using the letter opener, she could have killed him from that distance. Fast as he was, the blade would have been imbedded in his heart before he had a chance to react.

On this last thought Jackson wheeled around and let the knife fly. It sailed across the room, splitting the duck's head completely in half upon impact and burrowing several inches into the wall. Jackson eyed the distance between himself and his target: At least *thirty* feet, he estimated. He smiled. LuAnn would have been far wiser to have killed him. She had, no doubt, been constrained by her conscience. That was her greatest weakness and Jackson's greatest advantage, for he had no such parallel compunction.

Ultimately, if it came down to it, he knew that would be the difference.

THIRTY-NINE

LuAnn watched Riggs, who lay dozing next to her. She let out a small breath and stretched her neck. She had felt like a virgin while they made love. An incredibly energetic display of sex, she was surprised the bed hadn't caved in; they'd probably be sore tomorrow. A grin spread over her face. She stroked his shoulder and huddled next to him, putting one of her bare legs across both of his. With this movement he finally stirred and looked over at her.

A boyish smile cracked his face.

"What?" she asked, her eyes impish.

"I'm just trying to remember how many times I said 'oh, baby.'"

She rubbed her hand across his chest, letting the nails bite in just enough to make him playfully grab her hand. LuAnn said, "I think it was more often than I screamed 'yes, yes,' but that was only because I couldn't catch my breath."

He sat up and put a hand through her hair. "You make me feel young and old all at the same time."

They kissed again and Riggs lay back while LuAnn nestled on his chest. She noticed a scar on his side.

"Let me guess, old war wound?"

He looked up surprised and then followed her gaze to the scar. "Oh, yeah, real exciting, appendicitis."

"Really? I didn't think people came with two appendixes."

"What?"

She pointed to another scar on his other side.

"Hey, can we just enjoy the moment here and stop with the observations and questions?" His tone was playful, but she noted the serious intent just below the surface.

"Well, you know, if you come over every day to work on the studio, we might make this a regular thing, sort of like breakfast." LuAnn smiled and then almost immediately caught herself. *What was the chance of that happening?* The impact of this thought was crushing.

She quickly moved away from him and started to get up.

Riggs could hardly miss this dramatic transformation.

"Was it something I didn't say?"

She turned to find him looking at her. As if suddenly self-conscious about her nakedness, she pulled the bedspread off the bed and draped it around her. "I've got a lot to do today."

Riggs sat up and grabbed at the bedspread. "Well, excuse the hell out of me. I didn't mean to get in the way of your schedule. I guess I had the six A.M. to seven A.M. slot. Who's up next? The Kiwanis Club?"

She jerked the bedspread free. "Hey, I don't deserve that."

Riggs rubbed his neck and started to pull on his clothes. "Okay. It's just that I'm having trouble switching gears as fast as you. Going nonstop from the most intensive passion I can ever remember to discussing the day's workload sort of rubbed me the wrong way. I'm sorry as hell if I offended you."

LuAnn looked down and then moved over and sat next to him. "That's how it was for me too, Matthew," she said quietly. "I'm embarrassed to tell you how long it's been." She paused and then said almost to herself, "Years."

369

He looked at her incredulously. "You've gotta be kidding." She didn't answer and he was reluctant to break the silence. The ringing phone did.

Hesitating for a moment, LuAnn picked it up. She hoped to God it was Charlie and not Jackson. "Hello?"

It turned out to be neither. "We're going to talk, Ms. Tyler, and we're going to do it today," Thomas Donovan said.

"Who is this?" LuAnn demanded.

Riggs quickly looked over at her.

"We had a brief meeting the other day when you were out driving. The next time I saw you was when you were sneaking out of my place with your boyfriend."

"How did you get this number? It's unlisted."

Donovan silently laughed. "Ms. Tyler, no information is safe, if you know where to look. I'm assuming by now that you realize I know where to look."

"What do you want?"

"Like I said, I want to talk."

"I don't have anything to say to you."

Riggs went over to the phone and held the receiver with her. At first LuAnn tried to push him off but Riggs held firm.

"Sure you do. And I have a lot to say to you. I can understand your reaction the other day. Maybe I should have approached you differently, but that's past. I know beyond a doubt that you're sitting on a story of immense importance, and I want to know what it is."

"I have nothing to say to you."

Donovan considered this for a moment. He ordinarily didn't like to take this tack, but right now he couldn't think of an alternative strategy. He made up his mind. "I'll give you this as an inducement. If you talk to me, I'll give you forty-eight hours to leave the country before I go public. If you don't talk to me then I go public with everything I have as soon as I get off the phone." He struggled internally for a moment and then added quietly, "Murder doesn't have a statute of limitations, LuAnn."

Riggs stared over at LuAnn, wide-eyed. She looked away from him.

"Where?" she asked.

Riggs was shaking his head fiercely but LuAnn ignored him.

"Let's make it a very public place," Donovan said. "Michie's Tavern. I'm sure you know where that is. One o'clock. And don't bring anyone with you. I'm way too old for guns and speeding cars. I catch a whiff of your boyfriend or anyone else, the deal is off and I call the sheriff in Georgia. Do you understand?"

LuAnn ripped the phone free from Riggs and slammed it down.

Riggs faced her. "Would you like to fill me in on what's going on? Who are you supposed to have murdered? Someone in Georgia?"

LuAnn stood up and pushed past him, her face crimson from the abrupt revealing of this secret. Riggs grabbed her arm and pulled her back roughly. "Dammit, you're going to tell me what's going on."

She snapped around and, quick as a ferret, connected her right fist flush with his chin, causing his head to snap back and hit hard against the wall.

When he came to Riggs was lying on the bed. LuAnn sat next to him holding a cold compress to his bruised chin and then pressed it against the growing knot on his head.

"Damn!" he said as the cold went through his system.

"I'm sorry, Matthew. I didn't mean to do that. I just—"

371

He rubbed his head in disbelief. "I can't believe you knocked me out. I'm not a chauvinist, but I can't believe a woman just flattened my butt with one punch."

She managed a feeble smile. "I had a lot of practice growing up, and I'm pretty strong." She added kindly, "But I think your head hitting the wall had a lot to do with it."

Riggs rubbed his jaw and sat up. "Next time we're having an argument and you're thinking about popping me, just let me know and I'll surrender on the spot. Deal?"

She touched his face gently and kissed him on the forehead. "I'm not going to hit you anymore."

Riggs looked over at the phone. "Are you going to meet him?"

"I don't have a choice – that I can see."

"I'm going with you."

LuAnn shook her head. "You heard him."

Riggs sighed. "I don't believe you murdered anyone."

LuAnn took a deep breath and decided to tell him. "I didn't murder him. It was self-defense. The man I was living with ten years ago was involved in drugs. I guess he was skimming off the top and I walked right into the middle of it."

"So you killed your boyfriend?"

"No, the man who killed my boyfriend."

"And the police—"

"I didn't stay around long enough to find out what they were going to do."

Riggs looked around the room. "The drugs. Is that where all this came from?"

LuAnn almost laughed. "No, he was a small-timer. Drug money didn't have anything to do with this."

Riggs wanted desperately to ask what did, but

372

refrained from doing so. He sensed that she had divulged enough of her past life for now. Instead he watched in silent frustration as LuAnn slowly got up and started to leave the room, the bedspread dragging behind her, the well-defined muscles in her bare back tensing with each stride.

"LuAnn? That's your real name?"

She turned to look at him and nodded faintly. "LuAnn Tyler. You were right about Georgia. Ten years ago I was a lot different. A lot."

"I believe it, although I bet you've always had that right cross." He attempted a smile, but neither of them was buying it.

She watched Riggs as he dug into his pants pocket. He tossed something to her. She caught the keys in the palm of her hand. "Thanks for letting me use your BMW; you might need the horsepower in case he starts chasing you again."

She frowned, looked down, and then walked out of the room.

FORTY

Wearing a long black leather coat and a matching hat, her eyes hidden behind a pair of Ray-Bans, LuAnn stood outside the "Ordinary," an aged wooden building that was part of Michie's Tavern, a historic structure originally built in the late 1700s and later moved to its current location down the road from Monticello in the late 1920s. It was lunchtime and the place was starting to fill up with tourists either lining their stomachs with the fried chicken buffet offered there after touring Jefferson's home and its neighbor Ash Lawn, or fueling up before setting out on the tour. Inside, a fire blazed in the hearth and LuAnn, who had arrived early to check things out, had soaked in the warmth from the flames before deciding to wait for him outside. She looked up when the man walked toward her. Even without his beard she recognized him.

"Let's go," Donovan said.

LuAnn looked at him. "Go where?"

"You follow me in your car. I'll be checking my rearview mirror. If I see anyone who remotely looks like they're following us, then I pick up my cell phone and you go to prison."

"I'm not following you anywhere."

He leaned into her face and said quietly, "I think you might want to reconsider."

"I don't know who you are or what you want. You said you wanted to meet. Well, I'm here."

Donovan looked around at the line of people making their way into the tavern. "I had in mind a little more privacy than this."

"You picked the place."

"That I did." Donovan jammed his hands in his pocket and stared at her in obvious discomfort.

LuAnn broke the silence. "I'll tell you what, we'll go for a drive in my car." She stared at him ominously and spoke in low tones. "But don't try anything because if you do, I *will* hurt you."

Donovan snorted for a moment and then just as quickly stopped as he stared into her eyes. An involuntary shiver swept over him. He followed her long strides to her car.

LuAnn got on Interstate 64 and put the big sedan on cruise control.

Donovan turned to her. "You know, you threatened me back there with bodily injury. Maybe you did kill that guy in the trailer."

"I didn't *murder* anyone. I didn't do anything wrong in that trailer."

Donovan studied her features and then looked away. When he spoke next, his tone was softer, calmer. "I didn't spend the last several months tracking you down, LuAnn, in order to destroy your life."

She glanced over at him. "Then what did you track me down for?"

"Tell me what did happen in that trailer."

LuAnn shook her head in frustration and remained silent.

"I've dug through a lot of dirt over the years, and I can read between the lines with the best of them. I don't believe you murdered anyone," Donovan said. "Come on, I'm not a cop. You can check me for a wire if you want. I've read all the newspaper accounts. I'd like to hear your version."

LuAnn let out a deep sigh and looked over at him. "Duane was dealing drugs. I didn't know anything about it. I just wanted to get out of that life. I went to the trailer to tell him so. Duane was cut up very badly. A man grabbed me, tried to cut my throat. We fought. I hit him with the telephone and he died."

Donovan looked puzzled. "You just hit him with the telephone?"

"Really hard. I guess I cracked his skull."

Donovan rubbed his chin thoughtfully. "The man didn't die from that. He was stabbed to death."

The BMW almost ran off the road before LuAnn regained control. LuAnn stared over at him, her eyes wide. "What?" she gasped.

"I've seen the autopsy reports. He did have a wound to the head, but it wasn't fatal. He died from multiple stab wounds to his chest. No doubt about it."

It didn't take LuAnn long to realize the truth. *Rainbow*. Rainbow had killed him. And then lied to her. She shook her head. Why should that be such a big surprise, she thought. "All these years, I believed that I had killed him."

"That's a horrible thing to carry around inside. I'm glad I could clear your conscience on it."

"The police can't still be interested in all this. It's been ten years," LuAnn said.

"That's where you've run into some incredibly bad luck. Duane Harvey's uncle is the sheriff in Rikersville now."

"Billy Harvey is sheriff?" LuAnn said in astonishment. "He's one of the biggest crooks down there. He had an auto chop shop. He ran gambling in the back rooms of the bars; he was into everything you could earn a buck from illegally. Duane kept trying to get in on it, but Billy knew Duane was too stupid and unreliable. That's probably why he ended up selling drugs over in Gwinnett."

"I don't doubt it. But the fact is he's sheriff. Probably figured the best way to avoid trouble with the police was to become the police."

"So you talked to him?"

Donovan nodded. "According to him, the whole family has never gotten over poor Duane and his hasty exit from the living. He said the drug dealing sort of besmirched the whole family. And the money you sent? Instead of salving over those wounds, they took it as pouring salt on them, like you were trying to buy them off somehow. I mean they spent it and all, but they still didn't like it, at least according to the illustrious Billy Harvey. Bottom line is, he told me that the investigation is still active and he's not going to rest until LuAnn Tyler is brought in for trial. From what I can tell his theory is that you're the one who was involved in the drug dealing because you wanted to escape Duane and the boring life. Duane died trying to protect you and then you murdered the other guy, who allegedly was your partner."

"That's a bunch of lies."

Donovan shrugged. "You know it is, I know it is. But the people deciding that will be a jury of your peers down in Rikersville, Georgia." He took a moment to appraise her expensive clothing. "Or a jury of whom your peers *used* to be. I wouldn't recommend that you wear that outfit to the trial. It might rub people the wrong way. Duane being flower food and all these last ten years while you were living the high life and doing a pretty good impersonation of Jackie O, it just wouldn't sit well with the good folks down there."

"Tell me something I don't know." She paused for a moment. "So is that your deal? If I don't talk, you're going to throw me to Billy Harvey?"

Donovan patted the dashboard. "It may surprise

you to know that I don't give a damn about all that stuff. If you hit that man, you did it in self-defense. That I believe."

LuAnn lifted her sunglasses and stared across at him. "Then what do you care about?"

He leaned toward her. "The lottery." His eyebrows arched.

LuAnn spoke evenly. "What about it?"

"You won it ten years ago. One hundred million dollars."

"So?"

"So, how'd you do it?"

"I bought a ticket that turned out to be the winning number, how else do you do it?"

"I don't mean that. Let me fill you in on something. Without getting too technical, I went back through years' worth of lottery winners. There's a constant rate of bankruptcy declared by all those winners. Nine out of twelve every year. Bang, bang, you can set your clock by it. Then I run across twelve consecutive winners who somehow managed to avoid the big 'B' and you were smack in the middle of that unique group. Now how is that possible?"

She glanced over at him. "How should I know? I've got good money managers. Maybe they do too."

"You haven't paid taxes on your income nine out of the last ten years; I guess that helps."

"How do you know that?"

"Again, all sorts of information is available. You just have to know where to look. I know where to look."

"You'd have to talk to my financial people about that. I was in other parts of the world during that time, maybe the income wasn't taxable in the U.S."

"I doubt that. I've written enough financial stories to know that there's almost nothing Uncle Sam won't tax, if he can find it, that is."

"So call up the IRS and report me."

"That's not the story I'm looking for."

"Story?"

"That's right. I forgot to fill you in on the reason I came to visit you. My name's Thomas Donovan. You probably haven't heard of me, but I'm a journalist for the *Washington Trib* going on thirty years now and a damned good one even if I am blowing my own horn. A while back I decided to do a story on the national lottery. Personally, I think the whole thing is a travesty. Our own government doing that to the poorest among us. Dangling carrots like that, all the catchy ads, enticing people to cash in their Social Security checks to play something with odds at millions to one. Excuse the soapbox, but I only write about things I feel passionate about. Anyway, my original angle was the rich sucking it back out of the poor after they hit the jackpot. You know, investment shysters, people peddling one scheme after another, and the government just letting them go right ahead and do it, and then when the winners' finances are so screwed up, they haven't paid enough tax or what-not, the IRS comes in and takes every last dime, leaving them poorer than before they won. A good story, and one I feel needs to be told. Well, while I'm researching the story, I find out this interesting coincidence about all the lottery winners from your year: They didn't lose a dime of their money. In fact, using their tax returns as a gauge, they're all richer now. A lot richer. So I track you down and here I am. What I want is simple: the truth."

"And if I don't tell you, I end up in a Georgia prison, is that it? That's what you implied over the phone."

Donovan stared across at her angrily. "I won two Pulitzers before I was thirty-five. I've covered Vietnam, Korea, China, Bosnia, South Africa. Gotten my ass shot up twice. I've spent my life chasing

379

every hot spot in the world. I'm as legit as they come. I'm not going to blackmail you, because I don't operate that way. I told you that over the phone just to get you to meet with me. If Sheriff Billy catches up to you it's not going to be with my help. Personally, I hope he never does."

"Thank you."

"But if you don't tell me the truth, I'll find it out someplace else. And then I'm going to write that story. And if you don't tell me your side of things, I can't guarantee how flatteringly I can portray you. I report the facts, guilt will fall where it may. If you're willing to talk to me, I can guarantee only one thing: that your side of the story will be heard. But if you've broken the law somehow, there's nothing I can do about that. I'm not a cop, and I'm not a judge." He paused and looked at her. "So what's it going to be?"

She didn't speak for several minutes, her eyes staring down the road. He could see the conflict going on inside her.

Finally she looked over at him. "I want to tell you the truth. God, I want to tell somebody the truth." She took a deep breath that almost turned into a shudder. "But I can't."

"Why not?"

"You're already in a great deal of danger. If I were to talk to you, that danger would turn to an absolute certainty that you're going to die."

"Come on, LuAnn, I've been in dangerous spots before. It comes with the territory. What is it, and who's behind it?"

"I want you to leave the country."

"Excuse me?"

"I'll pay. You pick a place, I'll make all the arrangements. I'll set up an account for you."

"Is that your way of dealing with problems? Send them off to Europe? Sorry, but I've got a life right here."

"That's just it. If you stay you're not going to have a life."

"You're really going to have to do better than that. If you'd work with me, we could really accomplish something here. Just talk to me. Trust me. I didn't come down here to shake you down. But I also didn't come down here to be thrown a bunch of bullshit."

"I'm telling you the truth. You are in serious danger!"

Donovan wasn't listening now. He rubbed his chin as he thought out loud. "Similar backgrounds. All poor, desperate. It made for great stories, really picked up the numbers of players." He looked at her, clutched her arm. "Come on, LuAnn, you had help leaving the country ten years ago. You've gotten a whole lot richer. I can smell the story here, if you'd just give me the right angle. This could rank right up there with the Lindbergh baby and who shot JFK. I've got to know the truth. Is the government behind this, whatever this is? They're making billions off this thing every month, sucking it out of the rest of us. Taxation without representation." Donovan rubbed eager hands together. "Are we talking all the way to the White House? Please tell me we are."

"I'm not telling you anything. And I'm doing it to keep you as safe as I can."

"If you work with me, we both win."

"I don't consider being murdered winning. Do you?"

"Last chance."

"Will you please believe me?"

"Believe what? You haven't told me anything," he bellowed.

"If I tell you what I know, it's like I'm putting a pistol against your head and pulling the trigger myself."

Donovan sighed. "Then why don't you take me

back to my car. I don't know, LuAnn, I guess I expected more from you. You grew up dirt-poor, raised a kid by yourself, and then got this incredible break. I thought you might give a crap."

LuAnn put the car in gear and they started off again. She glanced once or twice at him and then started speaking in a very low voice, as though she were afraid of being overheard. "Mr. Donovan, the person who is looking for you right this very minute is not someone you want to mess around with. He told me he's going to kill you because you might know too much. And he will. Unless you leave right now, he'll find you for sure and when he does it won't be pretty. This person can do anything. Anything."

Donovan snorted and then his face froze. He slowly turned and looked at her as the answer finally hit him. "Including making a poor woman from Georgia rich?"

Donovan saw LuAnn jerk slightly as he said the words. His eyes widened. "Jesus, that's it, isn't it? You said this man can do anything. He made you the lottery winner, didn't he? A woman barely out of her teens running from the police after believing she committed a murder—"

"Mr. Donovan, please."

"She stops to buy a lottery ticket and then just happens to travel to New York where the lottery drawing is being held. And what do you know, she wins a hundred million bucks." Donovan slapped the dashboard with the palm of his hand. "Good God, the national lottery was fixed."

"Mr. Donovan, you have got to let it drop."

Donovan's face flushed crimson. "No way, LuAnn. No way am I letting this drop. Like I said, you couldn't have eluded the NYPD and the FBI all by yourself. You had help, a lot of help. This elaborate cover story you had in Europe. Your 'perfect' money managers.

This guy set all of it up. All of it, didn't he? Didn't he?" LuAnn didn't answer. "God, I can't believe I didn't see it all before. Sitting here talking to you, it just all fell into place. I've been drifting in circles for months and now—" He turned sideways in his seat. "You're not the only one either, are you? The other eleven non-bankrupts? Maybe more. Am I right?"

LuAnn was shaking her head hard. "Please stop."

"He didn't do it for free. He must've gotten some of your winnings. But, Christ, how did he fix it? Why? What's he doing with all that money? It can't be just one guy." Donovan fired questions left and right. "Who, what, when, why, how?" He gripped her shoulder. "Okay, I'll accept your statement that whoever is behind this is one very dangerous individual. But don't discount the power of the press, LuAnn. It's toppled crooks bigger than this guy. We can do it, if we work together." When LuAnn didn't respond, Donovan let go of her shoulder. "All I'm asking is that you think about it, LuAnn. But we don't have a lot of time."

When they returned to his car Donovan got out and then poked his head back in the door. "This number will reach me." He handed across a card. LuAnn didn't take it.

"I don't want to know how to reach you. You'll be safer that way." LuAnn suddenly reached across and grabbed his hand. Donovan winced from the pressure of her fingers.

"Will you please take this?" She reached in her purse and took out an envelope. "There's ten thousand dollars in here. Pack your bags, go to an airport, get on a plane, and get the hell out of here. Call me when you get to wherever you're going and I'll send enough money to keep you in hotels and restaurants for as long as you want."

"I don't want money, LuAnn. I want the truth."

383

LuAnn pushed back the urge to scream. "Dammit I'm trying my best to save your life."

He dropped the card on to her front seat. "You warned me and I appreciate that. But if you won't help me, I'll get it from somewhere else. One way or another, this story is being told." He looked at her ominously. "If this person is half as dangerous as you say he is, you might want to think about getting the hell out of here. My butt may be in the crosshairs now, but it's only my butt. You've got a kid." He paused again and right before he turned to leave he said, "I hope we both make it through this, LuAnn. I mean that."

He walked across the parking lot to his car, got in, and drove off. LuAnn watched him go. She took a deep breath, trying to calm her shaken nerves. Jackson was going to kill the man unless she did something. But what could she do? For one thing, she wasn't going to tell Jackson about her meeting with Donovan. She looked around the parking lot for any sign of him. But what was the use? He could be anyone. Her heart took another jolt. He could've tapped her phone lines. If so he would know about Donovan's phone call, that they had planned to meet. If he knew that, it was highly likely that he had followed her. Then Jackson would already be tracking Donovan. She looked down the road. Donovan's car was already out of sight. She slammed her fists into the steering wheel.

Although LuAnn didn't know it, Jackson had not tapped her phone line. However, as she drove off, she also had no inkling that directly beneath her seat a small transmitter had been affixed to the floorboard. Her entire conversation with Donovan had just been heard by someone else.

FORTY-ONE

Riggs turned off the receiving unit and the sounds of LuAnn's BMW coming through his earphones vanished. He slowly took off the headphones, sat back in his desk chair, and let out a long breath. He had anticipated obtaining some information about LuAnn Tyler and her discussions with the man he now knew to be Thomas Donovan, a newspaper reporter. The name was familiar to Riggs; he had seen the guy's byline in past years. However, Riggs hadn't anticipated stumbling across something that had all the earmarks of a major conspiracy.

"Damn." Riggs stood up and looked out the window of his home office. The trees were stunning, the sky a pale blue that was both dazzling and soothing. To the right a squirrel scampered up a tree, a chestnut secured between its jaws. Farther back, through the thickness of the trees, Riggs could make out a slender procession of deer headed by a six-point buck as they made their way cautiously toward the small spring-fed pond situated on Riggs's property. So peaceful, so serene, all that he had hoped for. He looked back at the receiving device he had used to listen in on LuAnn and Donovan's conversation. "LuAnn Tyler," Riggs said out loud. Not Catherine Savage, not even close, she had said. New identity, new life, far, far away. That was something Riggs could certainly relate to. He eyed the phone, hesitated, then picked it up. The number he was calling had been given to him five years ago, for emergencies, just as, unknown to Riggs, Jackson had provided one to LuAnn ten years ago. Just for emergencies. Well, Riggs decided as he punched in the numbers, he supposed this qualified as such.

An automated voice came on the line. Riggs left a series of numbers and then his name. He spoke slowly in order to let the computer verify the authenticity of his voice patterns. He put down the phone. One minute later it rang. He picked it up.

"That was fast," Riggs said, sitting back down.

"That number gets our attention. What's the situation? You in trouble?"

"Not directly. But I've come across something I need to check up on."

"Person, place, or thing?"

"Person."

"I'm ready, who is it?"

Riggs took a silent breath and hoped to God he was doing the right thing. He would at least hedge his bets until he understood matters a little better. "I need to find out about someone named LuAnn Tyler."

LuAnn's car phone buzzed as she was driving back home.

"Hello?"

The voice on the other end of the line made her breathe easier.

"Don't tell me where you are, Charlie, we can't be sure this line is safe." She checked where she was on the road. "Give me twenty minutes and then call me at the prearranged spot." She hung up. When they had come to the area, they had identified a pay phone at a McDonald's that would receive incoming calls. That was their safe phone.

Twenty minutes later she was standing at the pay phone, snatching it up on the first ring.

"How's Lisa?"

386

Charlie's tone was low. "Fine, we're both okay. She's still bumming, but who can blame the kid."

"I know. Did she talk to you at all?"

"A little. Although, I think we're both the enemy as far as she's concerned right now. That little girl's playing it close to the vest. Chip off the old block, right?"

"Where is she?"

"Crashed on the bed. We drove all night, and she didn't sleep much, just stared out the car window."

"Where are you?"

"Right now we're at a motel on the outskirts of Gettysburg, Pennsylvania, just across the Maryland state line. We had to stop, I was falling asleep at the wheel."

"You didn't use a credit card, did you? Jackson can trace that."

"You think I'm a novice at being on the run? All cash."

"Any sign that you've been followed?"

"I've varied my route, gone the interstate, back roads, lots of stops in very public places. I've checked every car that even looks remotely familiar. No one's on to us. How's it on your end? You hook up with Riggs?"

LuAnn blushed at the question. "You could say that." She paused and cleared her throat. "I met up with Donovan."

"Who?"

"The guy from the cottage. His name is Donovan. He's a reporter."

"Aw, crap!"

"He knows about the twelve lottery winners."

"How?"

"It gets complicated, but basically because none of us declared bankruptcy. In fact we all became a lot richer through shrewd investment advice. I guess that's pretty unusual with lottery winners."

"Damn, I guess Jackson isn't infallible."

"That's a comforting thought. I've got to go. Give me the number there." Charlie did so.

"I brought the portable cell phone too, LuAnn. You've got the number, right?"

"Memorized."

"I don't like it that you're all alone in this. I really don't."

"I'm holding my own. I've just got to think things through a little. When Jackson shows up again, I want to be ready."

"I'm not sure that's possible. The guy's not human."

LuAnn hung up the phone and walked back to her car. As unobtrusively as she could, she scanned the parking lot for anyone looking remotely suspicious. But that was the problem: Jackson never looked suspicious.

Charlie hung up the phone, checked on Lisa, and then went to the window of the ground-floor motel room. The building was constructed in the shape of a horseshoe so that Charlie was looking out not only at the parking lot but also at the motel units on the other side of the parking lot. He had a habit of checking the parking lots every thirty minutes to see who had pulled in after them. He had selected fairly isolated places that would make it easier to flush out someone who was following them. Despite his sharp scrutiny he could not have seen the pair of binoculars focused on him from the dark recesses of the motel room directly across from his. This person's car was not in the parking lot because he was not a paying guest of the motel. He had broken into the room when Charlie and Lisa had gone out to eat. The man put down the binoculars and jotted some words down in a notebook before taking up his sentry once again.

FORTY-TWO

The BMW pulled into the front drive. LuAnn sat in the car and stared up at the house. She had not gone home. After driving around for a while, she had decided to come here. The Jeep was there, so he must be as well. She got out of the sedan and walked up the wide steps of the Victorian.

Riggs heard her coming. He was just finishing up his phone call, the paper in front of him covered with notes, more information than he had ever wanted to know. His gut was cramping up just thinking about it all.

He opened the door to her knock and she passed through the doorway without looking at him.

"How'd it go?" he asked.

LuAnn drifted around the room before settling down on the couch and looking up at him with a shrug. "Not all that well, really." Her voice was listless. Riggs rubbed his eyes and sat down in the chair opposite her.

"Tell me about it."

"Why? Why in the hell would I want to get you involved in all this?"

He paused and briefly considered what he was about to say. He could walk away from this. She was obviously giving him the opportunity to do so. He could just say you're right and escort her to the door and out of his life. As he looked at her, so tired, so alone, he spoke quietly and intensely.

"I want to help you."

"That's nice, but I really wouldn't know where to begin."

"How about ten years ago, Georgia, and you're running from the cops for a murder you didn't commit."

She stared at him, biting her lip. She wanted desperately to trust the man; it was an almost physiologically compelling need. And yet, as she stared down the hallway to where his study was, where she had previously seen the information he had obtained on her so easily, so quickly, the doubts came flooding back to her. Jackson was suspicious of the man. Who was he? Where had he come from? What had he done in his past life?

When she looked back over at him, he was watching her closely. He read the uncertainty, the suspicions there.

"LuAnn, I know you really don't know me. Yet. But you *can* trust me."

"I want to, Matthew. I really do. It's just—" She stood up and started her ritualistic pacing. "It's just that I've made a habit the last ten years of never trusting anyone. Anyone other than Charlie."

"Well, Charlie's not here, and from the looks of things, you're not going to be able to handle this alone."

She stiffened at the words. "You'd be surprised at what I can handle."

"I don't doubt that. Not at all," he said in a sincere, if disarming, manner.

"And getting you involved means, ultimately, placing you in danger. That's not something I want on my conscience."

"You'd be surprised at how accustomed I am to dangerous things. And people."

She stared at him, a glimmer of a smile on her lips. Her deep hazel eyes were intoxicating to him, calling

390

up the fresh memory of their lovemaking.

"I still don't want you to get hurt."

"Then why are you here? In spite of how terrific this morning was, I doubt if you're here for a nooner. You've got other things on your mind, I can tell."

She sat back down and clasped her hands together. After thinking the matter over a minute she started speaking earnestly. "The man's name was Thomas Donovan. He's a reporter of some kind. He started investigating me."

"Why? Why you? The murder?"

LuAnn hesitated before answering. "That was part of it."

"What was the other part?"

LuAnn didn't answer now; she looked at the floor. Imparting personal information to anyone other than Charlie went against every instinct she possessed.

Riggs decided to take a shot. "Did it have to do with the lottery?"

She slowly looked up, the astonishment starkly on her face.

"I knew your real name; something clicked. You won a hundred million dollars ten years ago, a lot of stories about you back then. Then you disappeared."

She studied him warily, alarm bells ringing. His face, though, was one of complete sincerity, and finally that look subdued her suspicions, at least temporarily.

"Yes, I won that money."

"So what did Donovan want? Your story on the killing?"

"Partly."

"What was the other part?" he asked persistently.

Now the alarm bells started ringing again, and this time Riggs's honest features did not silence them. LuAnn rose. "I've got to be going."

"Come on, LuAnn. Talk to me."

"I think I've said more than I should have."

Riggs knew far more than she had already told him, but he had wanted to hear it from her. His source for the information on LuAnn had naturally desired to know why he wanted it. He had lied, or gotten close to it. He wasn't going to give LuAnn Tyler away, at least not yet. He had no reason to trust her, and many reasons not to. But he did trust her. He did believe in her.

As her hand closed over the doorknob he called to her.

"LuAnn, if you change your mind, I'll be here."

She didn't look at him, fearful of what might happen if she did. She wanted to tell him everything. She wanted his help, she wanted to make love to him again. After all these years of fabrication, of lies, deceit, and constant fear of exposure, she just wanted to be held; to be loved for herself, not for the enormous wealth she possessed.

Riggs watched the BMW pull out of his driveway. When it had disappeared from view he turned and went back to his study. Because of his inquiries into LuAnn Tyler, Riggs knew the Feds would undoubtedly get around to dispatching some agents to Charlottesville to talk to him or at least get the local FBI office involved. But because of his special status, they would have to jump through some bureaucratic hoops before that could be accomplished. He had some time, but not much. And once the Bureau boys showed up, it was over for LuAnn Tyler. All of her diligent work over the last ten years to remain hidden Riggs could blow up in the next few days. A very strong emotion told Riggs he could not allow that to happen, despite what he knew about the woman. In the course of his past career, deception had become a way of a life. So also had reading people, telling the good ones from the bad, to the

392

extent you could. LuAnn was a good person, Riggs had long ago concluded. Even if she didn't want his help, she was going to get it. But she was obviously involved with some very dangerous people. And now, Riggs thought to himself, so was he.

FORTY-THREE

When LuAnn arrived home it was late; the household staff had gone, and Sally Beecham would not return until tomorrow. She went in the house through the garage, punched in the alarm code, and threw her coat and purse down on the kitchen island. She went upstairs to shower and change. She had a lot of things to think through right now.

In the shrubs bordering the edge of the expensive lawn by the garage side of the house, Jackson knelt in the mulch and smiled to himself. He lowered the small piece of equipment he was holding in his hand. On its digital face were the six numbers constituting LuAnn's pass code for the home's alarm system. The scanner had picked up the electrical impulses thrown off when LuAnn inputted her pass code and then it had unscrambled them. With the pass code Jackson could come and go freely.

When he got back to his rental car, his cell phone buzzed. He spoke for a few minutes and then hung up. Charlie and Lisa were at a motel outside of Gettysburg. They would probably be on the move again soon. LuAnn had tried to get them away from him, or rather Lisa away from him. Charlie could take care of himself, Jackson well knew. If it came to it, Lisa was the Achilles' heel of her mother.

LuAnn had watched out the window as the figure

made its way down the tree line toward the main road. The steps had been animal-like in their stealth and precision, much as hers would have been. She didn't know what had drawn her to the window at that precise instant. She felt no fear or even apprehension as she watched Jackson move down the hillside. She had expected him to be there. For what specific reason or for how long Jackson had been watching the house, she wasn't sure; but it was completely logical that he should be. She was now his main focus, she knew. And to be the main focus of the man was akin to treading on the very edge of the grave. She drew the curtains shut and sat on her bed. The enormous house felt cold and threatening, as though she were all alone in a mausoleum of immense proportion, just waiting for something unspeakably horrible to happen to her.

Was Lisa truly safe, beyond the reach of the man? The answer to that question was so obvious that it hit her like a hard slap in the face.

I can do anything, LuAnn.

The mocking words came back to her after all these years and sent a shiver through her. Riggs was right, she couldn't get through this alone. He had offered help, and this time she needed it. Whether she was making the right decision or not, she didn't care. Right now, she just needed to do something. She jumped up, grabbed her car keys, unlocked a box in her closet, and placed the loaded nickel-plated .44 Magnum in her purse. She ran down the stairs and into the garage. A minute later the BMW was flying down the road.

Riggs was in the room over his barn when he heard the car drive up and park next to the garage. He watched out the window as LuAnn came into view. She started toward the house but then, as if sensing his presence, she turned to stare at him.

Their eyes stayed locked for a long time as each silently probed the other. A minute later she was sitting across from him, warming her hands from the heat of the stove.

This time Riggs felt no compunction to mince words.

"The lottery was fixed, wasn't it? You knew you were going to win, didn't you?"

LuAnn jolted upright for an instant, but then let out an almost simultaneous breath of relief.

"Yes." With that one word she felt as though the last ten years of her life had suddenly evaporated. It was a cleansing feeling. "How'd you figure it out?"

"I had some help."

LuAnn tensed and slowly rose. Had she just made the biggest mistake of her life?

Riggs sensed her sudden change and put up a hand. As calmly as he could, he said, "Nobody else knows right now. I pulled some pieces of information from different sources and then took a wild stab." He hesitated and then added, "I also bugged your car. I heard your entire conversation with Donovan."

"Who the hell are you?" LuAnn hissed, her hand feeling for her purse catch and the gun inside even as she stared at him.

Riggs just sat there and stared back at her. "I'm someone very much like you," was his surprising reply. Those words stopped her cold. Riggs stood and put his hands in his pockets, leaned up against the bookcase, and eyed the gently swaying trees through the window. "My past is a secret, my present is all made up." He looked over at her. "A lie. But for a good reason." He raised his eyebrows. "Like you."

LuAnn trembled for an instant. Her legs felt weak and she abruptly sat down on the floor. Riggs swiftly knelt beside her, taking her hand in his. "We don't have a lot of time so I'm not going to sugarcoat things. I made some inquiries about you. I did it discreetly, but it's going to have ripple effects nonetheless." He looked at her intently. "Are you ready to hear this?"

LuAnn swallowed hard and nodded; the fear passed from her eyes and was replaced with an inexplicable calmness.

"The FBI has been interested in you ever since you fled the country. The case has been dormant for a while, but that's not going to last. They know something is up with you, and maybe with how you won the money, but they don't know what, and they haven't been able to prove anything."

"If you bugged the car, you know how Donovan got on to it."

Riggs nodded and helped her up. They both sat on the couch. "Bankruptcy. Pretty clever. I know the Feds haven't latched on to that angle yet. Do you know how it was rigged?"

LuAnn shook her head.

"Is it a group, an organization behind it? Donovan thought it was the government. Please don't tell me it is. That gets way too complicated."

"It's not." LuAnn was speaking clearly now, although traces of fear, the effect of the sudden exposure of long-held secrets, flitted over her features. "It's one person, as far as I know."

Riggs sat back with an amazed look. "One person. That isn't possible."

"He had some people working for him, at least two that I know of, but I'm pretty sure he was the boss." That was an understatement. LuAnn could not imagine Jackson taking orders from anyone.

"Was Charlie one of those people?"

LuAnn started again. "What makes you say that?"

397

Riggs shrugged. "The uncle story was a little lame. And you two seemed to be sharing a secret. There wasn't any mention in all my research about you of any uncle, so I assumed he came into the picture after the lottery scam."

"I'm not going to answer that." The last thing she was going to do was incriminate Charlie.

"Fair enough. What about this person behind it? What can you tell me about him?"

"He calls himself Jackson." LuAnn stopped suddenly, astonished that she was telling anyone this. As the name passed over her lips, she closed her eyes and imagined for an instant what Jackson would do to her, to all of them, if he had any idea what she was revealing. She instinctively looked over her shoulder.

Riggs gripped her arm. "LuAnn, you're not alone anymore. He can't hurt you now."

She almost laughed out loud. "Matthew, if we're the luckiest people in the world, he'll kill us quick instead of making us suffer."

Riggs felt her arm shaking. As strong and resourceful as he knew her to be, she was clearly afraid.

"If it makes you feel any better," he said, "I've dealt with some pretty bad people in my time, and I'm still here. Everyone has weaknesses."

"Sure, right." LuAnn's voice was hushed, her words lifeless.

Riggs's tone was harsh. "Well, if you want to roll over for him and play dead, go ahead. I don't see how that's going to help Lisa, though. If this guy's as scary as you say, you think he's going to let her walk?"

"I haven't told her about any of this."

"Jackson's not going to assume that. He's going to assume that she knows everything, and that she's going to have to be eliminated if things turn against him."

"I know," she finally said. She rubbed her face and glanced wearily at him. "I don't understand. Why do you want to help me? You don't even know me. And I just told you I did something illegal."

"Like I said, I checked you out. I know your background. Jackson took advantage of you. Hell, if it had been me in your same position, I would've jumped at the chance to be rich too."

"That's just it, I didn't. I had decided not to go along, but then I walked into Duane's drug deal, and the next thing I know two men are dead and I'm running as fast as I can with a baby in my arms. I . . . I didn't think I had any choice left. I just wanted to get away."

"I can understand that, LuAnn. I really can."

"I've been running ever since, scared of my shadow, afraid somebody would find everything out. It's been ten years, but it's felt like a hundred." She shook her head and gripped her hands together.

"So I take it Jackson's in the area."

"He was in my garden about forty-five minutes ago."

"What?"

"I'm not sure what he was up to, but I'm assuming he's laying the groundwork for whatever plan he's about to implement."

"What sort of plan?"

"He's going to kill Donovan for starters."

"So I heard you tell Donovan."

"And then Jackson will probably come after us." LuAnn put her face in her hands.

"Well, you won't be seeing him again."

"You're wrong there, Matthew. I have to meet with him. And very soon."

He looked at her in absolute shock. "Are you crazy?"

"Jackson suddenly appeared in my bedroom last night. We had quite a lengthy discussion. I told him I was going to get to know you better. I don't think he had sex in mind, it just worked out that way."

"LuAnn, you don't—"

"He was going to kill you. In the cottage last night. I guess you went back for your truck. He said he was two feet from you. You're lucky to be alive. Very lucky."

Riggs sat back. His instincts had been right. That was a little heartening, despite the close call he had unwittingly experienced.

"He was going to check you out. He was concerned about your background, it was fuzzy. He was going to look into your background, and if he found anything worrisome, he was going to kill you."

"But?"

"But I told him I'd check you out instead."

"You took a risk there."

"Not as many as you've taken for me. I owed you. And I didn't want anything to happen to you. Not because of me."

Riggs spread his hands wide. "So why? Why the lottery fix? Did you give him some of your winnings?"

"All of it." Riggs looked blankly at her. LuAnn said, "He had control of the money for ten years; that period just ended. He invested the money and paid me some of the income from those investments."

"He had a hundred million to invest. How much did you earn each year?"

"Around forty million on the initial principal. He also invested any amounts I didn't spend. I earned tens of millions more on that each year."

Riggs gaped at her. "That's a forty percent return on your lottery money alone."

"I know. And Jackson made a lot more than that, I'm certain. He wasn't in this out of the goodness of

400

his heart. It was a business transaction, plain and simple."

"So if you made forty percent, he probably made at least that and maybe more. That's a minimum of eighty percent return on your money. He could only have done that through illegal channels."

"I don't know about that."

"And at the end of ten years?"

"I got the hundred million back."

Riggs rubbed at his brow. "And if there were twelve of you at, say, an average of seventy million dollars each, this guy had almost one billion dollars to invest."

"He's got a lot more than that now, I'm sure." She looked at him, saw the worry lines. "What, what are you thinking?"

He looked at her steadily. "Another thing that's had the FBI's dander up." She looked puzzled. Riggs started to explain. "I know for a fact that for years now the FBI, Interpol, and a few other foreign law enforcement agencies have been aware of something: Tremendous amounts of money have been funneled into lots of activities across the globe, some legit, others not. At first the Feds thought it was drug cartel money, either from South America or Asia, partly to launder it. That didn't turn out to be the case. They picked up threads here and there, but the leads always fizzled. Someone with that much money can cover himself really well. Maybe that someone is Jackson." Riggs fell silent.

"You're sure the Feds don't know about the lottery?"

Riggs looked uneasy. "I can tell you, if they do, they didn't learn it from me. But they do know of my inquiries about you. There was no getting around that."

"And if they've figured it out for themselves?

401

Then we have Jackson *and* the federal government coming for us. Right?"

Riggs looked away for a moment and then stared her directly in the eye. "Right."

"And to tell you the truth, I'm not sure which one frightens me more."

They looked at each other, similar thoughts running through their minds. Two people against all of this.

"I need to go now," LuAnn said.

"Go where?"

"I'm pretty certain that Jackson's been following my movements closely. He'll know we've seen each other several times. He may know I've met with Donovan. If I don't report back to him right away" – here she took a painful swallow – "well, it won't be pretty."

Riggs gripped her shoulders tightly. "LuAnn, this guy is a psycho, but he must be brilliant as well. That makes him even more dangerous. You walk in there, the guy gets the least bit suspicious . . ."

She gently rubbed his arms with her hands. "Well, I just have to make sure he doesn't get suspicious."

"How in the hell are you going to do that? He already must be. I say we bring in the troops, set the guy up and take him."

"And me, what about me?"

Riggs stared at her. "I'm sure you could probably work a deal with the authorities," he said lamely.

"And the folks down in Georgia? You heard Donovan, they want to lynch me."

"The Feds could talk to them, they . . ." Riggs broke off as he realized absolutely none of what he was saying could be guaranteed.

"And maybe I work a deal with all of them. I give back the money. It might surprise you, but I really don't care about that. And then maybe I get a sympathetic judge, or judges, and they give me a break. Cumulatively what could I be looking at? Twenty years?"

402

"Maybe not that much."

"How much then?"

"I can't tell you that. I don't know."

"I'd make a real sympathetic defendant, wouldn't I? I can see the headlines now: Drug dealer-turned-murderess-turned-dream-stealer-turned-fugitive LuAnn Tyler living like a queen while people blow their Social Security checks on the lottery. Maybe they'd give me a prize instead of throwing away the key. What do you think?"

Riggs didn't answer and he couldn't manage to look at her either.

"And let's say we set Jackson up? What if we miss and he gets away? Or what if we nail him? Do you think with all his money, all his power, he might beat the rap? Or maybe he just might pay someone to carry out his revenge for him. Given that, what do you think my life is worth? And my daughter's life?"

Riggs did answer this time. "Nothing. Okay, I hear where you're coming from. But listen, why can't you report back to the guy over the phone? You don't need to see him in person."

LuAnn considered this for a minute. "I'll try," was all she could promise.

LuAnn stood up to her full height and gazed down at him. She looked twenty again, strong, rangy, confident. "Despite having zillions of dollars and traveling all over the world, I'm not the FBI. I'm still just a dumb girl from Georgia, but you might be a little surprised at what I can do when I set my mind to it." Lisa's face was conjured up in her thoughts. "And I've got a lot to lose. Too much." Her eyes seemed to look right through his, seeing something far, far down the road. When she spoke, her voice carried the full measure of her deep Southern roots. "So I'm not going to lose."

FORTY-FOUR

George Masters stared down at the file intently.
He was sitting in his office at the Hoover
Building in Washington. Masters had been
with the FBI for over twenty-five years. Ten of those
years had been spent in the FBI's New York office.
And now Masters was staring down at a name that
he had become intimately familiar with ten years
ago: LuAnn Tyler. Masters had been part of the
federal investigation of Tyler's flight from the
United States, and although the investigation had
been officially closed years ago due to basic inertia,
Masters had never lost interest mainly because none
of it made sense. Things that didn't make sense
bothered the veteran FBI agent greatly. Even after
transferring to Washington, he had kept the case in
the back of his mind. Now there were recent events
that had ignited that spark of interest into a full
flame. Matthew Riggs had made inquiries about
LuAnn Tyler. Riggs, Masters knew, was in
Charlottesville, Virginia. Masters knew Riggs, or
who Riggs used to be, very well. If someone like
Riggs was interested in Tyler, so was Masters.

After failing to prevent LuAnn Tyler's escape
from New York, Masters and his team had spent
considerable time trying to reconstruct the last
several days leading up to her disappearance. He
had figured that she would have either driven up
from Georgia to New York or taken the train. She
didn't have a driver's license or a car. The big

convertible she had been spotted in had been found in front of the trailer, so she hadn't used that vehicle. Masters had then focused on the trains. At the station in Atlanta, Masters had hit the jackpot. LuAnn Tyler had taken the Amtrak Crescent to New York City on the day the authorities believed the murders were committed. But that wasn't all she had done. LuAnn had made a phone call from Otis Burns's car phone. Burns was the other dead man in the trailer. The FBI had traced the phone call. The number was an eight hundred number, but it had already been disconnected. Investigations into who had leased the phone number had run into a complete dead-end. That had gotten Masters's curiosity up even more.

Now that he was once again focused on LuAnn Tyler, Masters had instructed his men to go over NYPD records looking for any unusual events occurring around the time of LuAnn's disappearance. One item his men had just discovered had interested Masters greatly. A man named Anthony Romanello had been found dead in his New York apartment the night before the press conference announcing LuAnn as the lottery winner. The discovery of a dead body in New York City was hardly news; however, the police had been suspicious of Romanello's death because he had a long arrest record and was suspected of hiring himself out as an assassin. The police had probed into the details of what he had done on his last day among the living. Romanello and a woman had been seen at a restaurant shortly before Romanello had died; they had been observed having a serious argument. Barely two hours later, Romanello was dead. The official cause of death had been ruled cardiac arrest; however, the autopsy had revealed no sign of heart trouble in the youthful and strongly built man. None of these details had gotten Masters excited. What had gotten his adrenaline going was the description of the woman: It matched LuAnn Tyler precisely.

Masters shifted uncomfortably in his chair and lit up a cigarette. And then came the kicker: Found on Romanello's person was a receipt for a train ticket. Romanello had been in Georgia and returned to New York on the very same train with LuAnn, although they had been seated in separate compartments. Was there a connection? Drawing on information that had been long buried in his mind, the veteran FBI agent was beginning to piece things together from a clearer perspective. Maybe being away from the case all these years had been a good thing.

He had finished poring over the files he had accumulated on LuAnn Tyler, including records from the lottery. The winning ticket had been purchased at a 7-Eleven in Rikersville, Georgia, on the day of the trailer murders, presumably by LuAnn Tyler. Pretty nervy for her to stop and buy a ticket after a double homicide, Masters thought. The winning ticket had been announced on the following Wednesday at the drawing in New York. The woman fitting LuAnn's description had been seen with Romanello on Friday evening. And the press conference announcing LuAnn as the winner had been held on Saturday. But the thing was, according to Amtrak records and the ticket found on Romanello, both Tyler and Romanello had taken the Crescent train on the *previous* Sunday getting them into New York on Monday. If so, that meant LuAnn had left for New York City *before* she had known she had even won the lottery. Was she just running from a possible murder charge and coincidentally chose New York in which to hide, and then just happened to win a hundred million bucks? If so, she must be

406

the luckiest person in the world. George Masters did not believe that anyone could be that lucky. He ticked off the points on his hand. Murders. Telephone call. Purchase of lottery ticket. Train to New York before winning ticket announced. LuAnn Tyler wins the lottery. Romanello and Tyler argue. Romanello dies. LuAnn Tyler, a twenty-year-old with a seventh-grade education and a baby, walks right through a massive police net and successfully disappears. She could not, Masters decided, have done that alone. All of this had been planned well in advance. And that meant one thing. Masters suddenly gripped the arms of his chair tightly as the conclusion hit him.

LuAnn Tyler knew that she was going to win the lottery.

The implications of that last thought sent a deep shudder through the grim-faced agent. He couldn't believe he hadn't seen that possibility ten years ago, but he had to admit it had never even occurred to him. He was looking for a potential murderer and nothing else. He drew solace from the fact that ten years ago he didn't have the Romanello angle to chew on.

Masters obviously wasn't old enough to remember all the lottery corruption from the last century, but he certainly remembered the game show scandals in the 1950s. Those would seem laughable by comparison to what the country might be now facing.

Ten years ago someone may have corrupted the United States Lottery. At least once, possibly more. The ramifications were truly terrifying to think about. The federal government depended on the revenue from that lottery to fund a myriad of programs, programs that were now so entrenched politically that it would be impossible to repeal them. But if the source of those funds was contaminated? If the American People ever discovered that fact?

Masters's mouth went dry with the thought. He swallowed some water from a carafe on his desk and downed a couple of aspirin to combat the beginnings of what would still become a torturous headache. He composed himself and picked up his phone. "Get me the director," he instructed. While he waited for the call to go through, Masters sat back in his chair. He knew this eventually would have to go up to the White House. But he'd let the director talk to the attorney general and the A.G. could talk to the president. If his conclusions were right, so much shit would hit the fan that everyone would eventually be covered in it.

FORTY-FIVE

J ackson was again in his suite and was again staring at his laptop. LuAnn had met with Riggs several times now. Jackson would give her another few hours to call. He was disappointed in her nonetheless. He had not tapped LuAnn's phone line, an oversight that he had decided was not worth remedying at this point. She had caught him a little off-guard by sending Lisa away so quickly. The associate he had retained to track LuAnn's movements had been compelled to follow Charlie and Lisa, thereby depriving Jackson of a valuable pair of eyes. Thus, he did not know that LuAnn and Donovan had already met.

He had contemplated sending for more people so that all bases would be covered, but too many strangers lurking around town would probably raise suspicion. He wanted to avoid that if possible. Particularly because there was a wild card out there he was unsure of: Matt Riggs. He had transmitted Riggs's fingerprints to the same information source and was awaiting a reply.

Jackson's mouth sagged as the information spread over the screen. The name that appeared as the owner of the fingerprints was not Matthew Riggs. For a moment Jackson wondered if he could have lifted someone else's prints in the cottage by mistake. But that was impossible; he had seen the exact area the man calling himself Matt Riggs had touched. There could have been no mistake there. He quickly decided to check the other source of a possible mistake. He dialed the number and spoke at length to the person on the other end.

"This one was tricky," the voice said. "We went through normal channels initially to avoid any suspicions. We believe the request was kicked to senior level and we received back a 'no-fingerprint-found' reply."

"But a person was identified," Jackson said.

"Right, but only after we went back through other channels." Jackson knew that meant hacking into a database. "That's when we pulled up the information we transmitted to you."

"But it's a different name than the one he's using now and it lists him as being deceased."

"Right, but the thing is, when a criminal dies, the standard procedure is to fingerprint the corpse and transmit the prints to the FBI for verification. When that's completed, the pointer – the linkage used to retrieve the print from the database – is deleted. The result is that there are, technically, no prints of deceased criminals on the database."

"So how do you explain what you just sent me? Why would they want to have this person listed as deceased but under another name?"

"Well, that tells me that the name listed on the database is his real one and the one he's using now is phony. The fact that he's listed as dead tells me that the Feds want people to believe he's dead, including anyone who might try to get access to their database to check. I've seen the Feds do that before."

"Why?"

The answer the man gave him caused Jackson to slowly hang up the phone. Now it all made sense. He stared at the screen.

Daniel Buckman: Deceased.

It was less than three minutes after LuAnn left that

Riggs received a telephone call. The message was terse, but still managed to chill Riggs to the bone.

"Someone just made an unauthorized access of your fingerprint file through the Automated Fingerprint Identification System. And it was somebody who knew what he was doing because we didn't realize it happened until after the fact. Exercise extreme care, we're checking it out right now."

Riggs slammed down the phone and grabbed his receiving unit. He took a moment to unlock a drawer of his desk. He pulled out two pistols, two ammo clips, and an ankle holster. The larger pistol he put in his pocket and the smaller one he inserted in the holster he belted around his ankle. Then he ran for his Jeep. He hoped to God LuAnn hadn't found and removed the transmitter from her car.

FORTY-SIX

From the car phone LuAnn called the number Jackson had given her. He buzzed her back less than a minute later.

"I'm on the move too," he said. "We need to talk."

"I'm reporting back to you, like you said."

"I'm sure you are. I trust you have a good deal to tell me."

"I don't think we have a serious problem on our hands."

"Oh, really, I'm so very glad to hear it."

LuAnn responded testily. "Do you want to hear it or not?"

"Yes, but in person."

"Why?"

"Why not?" he fired back. "And I have some information that might be of interest to you."

"About what?"

"No, about whom. Matt Riggs. Like his real name, his real background, and why you should take every caution in dealing with him."

"You can tell me all that over the phone."

"LuAnn, perhaps you didn't hear me. I said you're going to meet me in person."

"Why should I?"

"I'll give you a wonderful reason. If you don't I'll find Riggs and kill him in the next half hour. I'll cut off his head and mail it to you. If you call to warn him, then I'll go to your home and kill everyone there from the maids to the gardeners and then I'll

412

burn it to the ground. Then I'll go to your precious daughter's exclusive school and slaughter everyone there. You can keep calling, trying to warn the whole town, and I'll just start killing people at random. Is that a good enough reason, LuAnn, or do you want to hear more?"

LuAnn, pale and trembling at this verbal onslaught, had to force her next breath out. She knew that he meant every insane word. "Where and when?"

"Just like old times. Speaking of old times, why don't you ask Charlie to join us. This applies to him as well."

LuAnn held the phone away from her, staring at it as though she wanted to melt it down along with the man on the other end. "He's not around right now."

"My, my. And I thought he never left your side, the faithful sidekick."

Something in his tone touched a chord in LuAnn's memory. She couldn't think of what it was. "We're not exactly joined at the hip. He's got a life to live."

For now, Jackson thought. *For now, just like you. I'm having my doubts, though, I really am.*

"Let's meet at the cottage where our inquisitive friend was nesting. Thirty minutes, can you manage it?"

"I'll be at the cottage in thirty minutes."

Jackson hung up the car phone and with an automatic motion felt for the knife hidden in his jacket.

Ten miles away LuAnn almost mirrored that movement, slipping off the safety on her .44.

Dusk was gathering as LuAnn drove down the tree-lined, leaf-strewn dirt road. The area was very dark. It had rained heavily the night before and a spray of water kicked up on her windshield as she drove through a deep puddle; she was momentarily startled. The cottage was up ahead. She slowed down and swept the terrain with her eyes. She saw no car, no person. She knew that meant nothing. Jackson seemed to appear and disappear whenever he damn well pleased with less rippling than a pebble flung across the ocean. She pulled the BMW to a stop in front of the ramshackle structure and climbed out. She knelt down for a moment and eyed the dirt. There were no other tire tracks and the mud would have shown any very clearly.

LuAnn studied the exterior of the cottage. He was already there, she was certain. It was as though the man carried a scent that was detectable only to her. It smelled like the grave, moldy and dank. She took one last breath and started toward the door.

Upon entering the cottage, LuAnn surveyed the small area.

"You're early." Jackson stepped from the shadows. His face was the same one from each of their face-to-face encounters. He liked to be consistent. He wore a leather jacket and jeans. A black ski cap covered the top of his head. Dark hiking boots were on his feet. "But at least you came alone," he added.

"I hope the same can be said of you." LuAnn shifted slightly so that her back was against a wall rather than the door.

Jackson interpreted her movements and smiled slightly. He folded his arms and leaned against the wall, his lips pursed. "You can start delivering your report," he ordered.

LuAnn kept her hands in her jacket, one fist closed around her pistol; she managed to point the muzzle at Jackson through the pocket.

Her movements were slight but Jackson cocked his head and smiled. "Now I distinctly remember you saying you wouldn't kill in cold blood."

"There are exceptions to everything."

"Fascinating, but we don't have time for games. The report?"

LuAnn started speaking in short bursts. "I met with Donovan. He's the man who was following me, Thomas Donovan." LuAnn assumed that Jackson had already run down Donovan's identity. She had decided on the drive over that the best approach was to tell Jackson mostly the truth and to only lie at critical junctures. Half truths were a wonderful way to inspire credibility, and right now she needed all she could muster. "He's a reporter with the *Washington Tribune*."

Jackson squatted on his haunches, his hands pressed together in front of him. His eyes remained keenly on her. "Go on."

"He was doing a story on the lottery. Twelve of the winners from ten years ago." She nodded toward Jackson. "You know the ones; they've all flourished financially."

"So?"

"So, Donovan wanted to know how, since so many of the other winners have gone belly-up. A very consistent percentage, he said. So your twelve sort of stuck out."

Jackson hid his chagrin well. He didn't like having loose ends, and this one had been glaring. LuAnn studied him closely. She read the smallest of self-doubts in his features. That was enormously comforting to her, but this was not the time to dwell on it.

"What did you tell him?"

"I told him I had been referred to an excellent investment firm by someone from the lottery. I gave him the name of the investment firm you used. I'm assuming they're legitimate."

"Very," Jackson replied. "At least on the surface. And the others?"

415

"I told Donovan I didn't know about them, but that they could have been referred to the same firm for all I knew."

"And he bought that?"

"Let's just say that he was disappointed. He wanted to write a story about the wealthy screwing the poor – you know, they win the lottery and then parasitic investment firms churn their accounts, earn their pieces of the pie, and leave the winner with nothing but attorney fees for filing bankruptcy. I told him that I certainly didn't support that conclusion. I had done just fine."

"And he knew about your situation in Georgia?"

"That's what drew him to me initially, I would imagine." LuAnn drew in a small breath of relief as she saw Jackson nod slightly at this remark. He apparently had arrived at the same conclusion. "He thought I would confess to some big conspiracy, I guess."

Jackson's eyes glittered darkly. "Did he mention any other theories, like the lottery being fixed?"

To hesitate now would be disastrous, LuAnn knew, so she plunged ahead. "No. Although he thought he had a big story. I told him to talk directly to the investment firm, that I had nothing to hide. That seemed to take the wind out of his sails. I told him if he wanted to contact the Georgia police he could go ahead. Maybe it was time to get things out in the open."

"You weren't being serious."

"I wanted him to believe I was. I figured if I made a big deal out of resisting or wanting to hide anything, he'd get even more suspicious. As it was, everything sort of fizzled for him."

"How did you leave it?"

"He thanked me for meeting with him, even apologized for troubling me. He said he might

416

contact me later, but kind of doubted it." Once again LuAnn saw Jackson incline his head slightly. This was working out better than she could have expected. "He got out of my car and into his. That's the last I saw of him."

Jackson was silent for several moments and then he slowly rose, silently clapping his hands together. "I love a good performance and I think you handled the situation very well, LuAnn."

"I had a good teacher."

"What?"

"Ten years ago. The airport, where you impersonated an impersonation. You told me the best way to hide is to stick out, because it runs counterintuitive to human nature. I used the same principle. Be overly open, cooperative, and honest, and even suspicious people tend to rethink things."

"I am honored that you remembered all that."

A little ego-stroking went a long way with most men, LuAnn knew, and Jackson, exceptional though he was in many ways, was no exception in that regard. In an understatement of mammoth proportions, LuAnn said, "You're a little hard to forget. So you don't have to do anything with Donovan, he's harmless. Now tell me about Riggs."

A smile formed on the man's lips. "I witnessed your impromptu meeting with Riggs on the rear grounds this morning. It was rather picturesque. From your state of undress, I imagine he had quite a pleasant morning."

LuAnn hid her anger at this barb. Right now she needed information. She replied, "All the more reason why I should know all about him."

"Well, let's start with his real name: Daniel Buckman."

"Buckman? Why would he have a different name?"

"Funny question coming from you. Why do people change their names, LuAnn?"

Perspiration sprouted on her forehead. "Because they have something to hide."

"Precisely."

"Was he a spy?"

Jackson laughed. "Not quite. Actually, he's not anything."

"What do you mean by that?"

"I mean that dead men, technically, can't be anything other than dead, correct?"

"Dead?" LuAnn's entire body froze. *Had Jackson killed Matthew? It couldn't be.* She fought with all her might not to plunge to the floor. Luckily, Jackson continued.

"I obtained his fingerprints, had them run through a database and the computer told me that he's dead."

"The computer's wrong."

"The computer only relays what it's been told. Someone wanted it to appear that Riggs was dead in case anyone came looking."

"Came looking? Like who?"

"His enemies." When LuAnn didn't respond, Jackson said, "Have you ever heard of the Witness Protection and Relocation Program?"

"No. Should I?"

"You've lived abroad for so long, I suppose not. It's run by the federal government, more particularly by the United States Marshal's Service. It's to protect persons testifying against dangerous criminals or organizations. They get new identities, new lives. Officially, Riggs is dead. Shows up in a small town, starts a new life under a new identity. Maybe his features have been altered somewhat. I don't know for certain, but it's an educated guess on my part that Riggs is a member of that select group."

418

"Riggs – Buckman – was a witness? To what?"

Jackson shrugged. "Who knows? Who cares? What I'm telling you is that Riggs is a criminal. Or was a criminal. Probably drugs or something like that. Maybe Mafia informant. Witness Protection isn't used for purse snatchers."

LuAnn settled back against the wall to keep herself from falling. *Riggs was a criminal.*

"I hope you haven't confided anything to him. There's no telling what his agenda might be."

"I haven't," LuAnn managed to say.

"So what can you tell me about the man?"

"Not as much as you just told me. He doesn't know any more than he did before. He's not pushing the issue. He thinks Donovan was a potential kidnapper. From what you just said, I'm sure he doesn't want to draw any attention to himself."

"True, that's very good for us. And I'm sure your little rendezvous this morning didn't hurt at all."

"That's really none of your business," she retorted hotly. With their exchange of information at an end, she wasn't going to let that remark pass.

"Ah, your first mistake this session. You just can't make it through without committing some blunder, can you?" He pointed a slender finger at her. "Everything about you is my business. I made you. And in a real sense I feel responsible for your well-being. I don't take that responsibility lightly."

LuAnn blurted out, "Look, the ten years is up. You've made your money. I've made mine. I say we call it a day, forever. In thirty-six hours I'll be on the other side of the world. You go your way, I'll go mine, because I'm more than real tired of this."

"You disobeyed me."

"Right, well I spent ten damn years in twenty different countries, constantly looking over my shoulder, obeying *your* instructions. And I guess

419

now I'll spend the rest of my life doing the same thing. So let me get to it." The two engaged in a stare-down of prolonged duration.

"You'll leave right away?"

"Just give me time to pack my bags. We'll be gone by tomorrow morning."

Jackson rubbed his chin as he considered this proposal. "Tell me something, LuAnn, tell me why I shouldn't kill you right now."

She had been prepared for that question. "Because Donovan might find it a little peculiar that right after he talks to me I end up a corpse. He's not suspicious now. I think I can guarantee you that would get his radar going. You really want that kind of trouble?"

Jackson pursed his lips for a moment and then motioned to the door. "Go pack."

LuAnn looked at him and motioned to the door. "You first."

"Let's leave together, LuAnn. That way, we'll each have a reasonable chance at reciprocating in kind in the event one of us tries something violent."

They went to the door together, their gazes glued to each other.

Right when Jackson put his hand on the door-knob, the door burst open, almost knocking him down.

Riggs stood there, his gun leveled on Jackson. Before he could fire, Jackson pulled LuAnn in front of him, his hand edging downward.

"Matthew, don't," LuAnn cried out.

Riggs shot her a glance. "LuAnn—"

LuAnn sensed rather than saw Jackson cock his arm. He was using an underhand throwing method to hurl the knife, but it wouldn't be any less deadly that way.

Her hand shot out, partially colliding with Jackson's forearm. The next instant Riggs was grunting in

420

pain, the knife sticking out of his arm. He dropped to the floor, clutching at the blade's handle. LuAnn pulled her gun out of her pocket and whipped around, trying to draw a bead on Jackson. At the very same time, Jackson pulled her backward against him.

Their combined momentum sent Jackson and LuAnn crashing through the glass window. LuAnn landed on top of him as they hit the porch, hard. LuAnn's pistol squirted free from her hand and slid across the porch. Each felt the subtle but undeniable strength of the other as they wrestled amid the thick, slippery shards of glass, trying to gain some footage. He clutched at her neck, she kicked at his groin, one of her elbows levered against his chin. Locked tightly together, they both rose slowly, each seeking an advantage. She noted the blood pouring from the grisly wound on Jackson's hand; he must have cut it going through the window. His grip couldn't be a hundred percent, she thought. With a sudden burst of strength that seemed to astonish even Jackson, LuAnn tore free from him, seized him by his belt and shirt front, and threw him face first against the side of the cottage where he slumped down, momentarily stunned from the impact. Without wasting an instant or any unnecessary motion, LuAnn propelled herself forward, straddled his back, gripped his chin with both hands, and pulled it backward, trying her best to crack his spine. Jackson screamed in pain as she pulled harder and harder. Another inch and he was a dead man. Her hands, however, suddenly slipped and she fell backward, landing in the glass. She exploded up and then froze as she looked down. In her hands was Jackson's face.

Jackson staggered up. For one terrible instant their eyes locked on each other. And for the first time, LuAnn was staring at Jackson's real face.

421

Jackson looked down at her hands. He touched his face, felt his own skin, his own hair, his breath coming in great gasps. Now she could identify him. Now she had to die.

The same thought occurred to LuAnn. She dove for the gun at the same time Jackson pounced on her; they slid together along the porch, both straining for the gun.

"Get off her, you bastard!" Riggs screamed. LuAnn turned to see the man, deathly pale, standing at the window, his shirt entirely red, the gun in his shaky hands. With an enviable bit of speed Jackson leapt over the porch railing. Riggs fired an instant too late, the bullets striking the porch instead of flesh.

"Shit!" Riggs groaned and dropped to his knees, disappearing from LuAnn's line of sight.

"Matthew!" LuAnn sprung to the window. Meanwhile, Jackson had disappeared into the woods.

LuAnn raced through the door, pulling off her jacket as she did so. She was next to Riggs in an instant. "Wait, don't pull it out, Matthew." Using her teeth, she tore her jacket sleeve apart and into strips. Next, she ripped open his shirtsleeve and exposed the wound. At first she tried to staunch the bleeding with the cloths, but she couldn't. She searched under Riggs's armpit and applied pressure with her finger at a certain spot. The flow of blood finally stopped. As gently as she could LuAnn pulled the knife free while Riggs's fingers dug into her arm, his teeth almost biting through his lip. She tossed the blade down.

"Matthew, hold your finger right here, don't push too hard, you need to allow a little blood to flow through." She guided his finger to the pressure point under his arm that she had been pressing against.

"I've got a first-aid kit in my car. I'll dress it as best

422

as I can. Then we need to get you to a doctor."

LuAnn retrieved her gun from the porch and they hustled out to the BMW, where LuAnn cleaned and dressed the wound using the first-aid kit from her glove compartment. As she cut the last piece of tape off with her teeth and wound it around the gauze, Riggs looked at her. "Where did you learn to do this stuff?"

LuAnn grunted. "Hell, the first time I ever saw a doctor was when Lisa was born. And even then it was only for about twenty minutes. You live in the boonies with no money, you have to learn how to do this just to survive."

When they got to an urgent care center off Route 29, LuAnn started to get out of the car to help Riggs in. He stopped her.

"Look, I think it'll be better if I go in alone. I've been to this place before, they know me. General contractors get hurt a lot. I'll tell 'em I slipped and stuck a hunting knife in my arm."

"You're sure?"

"Yeah, I think I made a big enough mess for you already."

He struggled out of the car.

"I'll be here when you get out, I promise," she said.

He smiled weakly, and holding his injured arm, he went inside.

LuAnn pulled the BMW around and backed into the parking space so she could see anyone coming in. She locked the doors and then swore under her breath. Riggs had come to her rescue, for that she could hardly fault him. But right before that she had Jackson convinced that everything was okay. Another minute and they would've been home free. God, the timing. She slumped against the seat. It was possible that she could explain Riggs's sudden and

423

armed presence away. Riggs had been concerned for her safety, followed her, thinking maybe that the man she was meeting was Donovan. But Riggs had done something else, something that she couldn't explain away. She let out a loud groan as she watched the traffic pass by on Route 29.

In front of Jackson, Riggs had called her LuAnn. That one word had destroyed everything. There was no way he would've missed that. Now, Jackson knew she had lied to him about what Riggs knew. She had no doubt what the punishment for that would be. Her spirits had been so high barely thirty minutes ago. Now all bets were off.

She glanced down at the seat and saw the white piece of paper there. She picked up Donovan's card and looked at the phone number. She thought for a moment and then picked up the phone. She silently cursed when she only got the answering machine. She left a lengthy message telling Donovan what had happened. She implored him once again to go underground, that she would pay for everything. He was a good man looking for the truth. She didn't want him to die. She didn't want anyone else to die because of her. She hoped to God he would live to get the message.

Jackson pressed the cloth against his palm. He had indeed badly cut his hand going through the glass. Damn the woman. Riggs would've been dead if she hadn't hit Jackson's arm a millisecond before he released the knife.

He gingerly touched his real skin. A small lump had appeared thanks to one of her blows. He had finally felt her raw strength and he had to admit, it exceeded his own. Who would have thought it? The big muscle-bound types never possessed genuine God-given strength like that; the kind you couldn't

424

manufacture in a health spa. It was a combination of both inner and outer phenomena, working in precise, albeit spontaneous, bursts when called upon. One couldn't measure it or quantify it, because it came and went upon demand by its owner and varied in its intensity depending on the situation, rising to the occasion and mustering just enough reserve so that failure was never a possibility. Either you had that type of power or you didn't. LuAnn Tyler clearly did. He would not forget that. He would not seek to conquer her that way, but, as always, he would adapt around it. And the stakes were as high as they were ever likely to climb, for one specific reason.

The irony was he had believed her. He had been prepared to let her walk away. LuAnn had confided in Riggs, that was clear. Riggs knew her real name. There were few actions that angered Jackson more than prevarication by his own people. Disloyalty could not and would not be tolerated. If she had lied about Riggs, it was more than probable that she had lied about Donovan. Jackson had to assume that the *Trib* reporter was closing in on the truth. Thus, he had to be stopped as well.

As these thoughts were going around in Jackson's mind, his portable phone rang. He picked it up. He listened, asked a few questions, conveyed some clear instructions, and when he hung up, a deep look of satisfaction graced his true features. The timing couldn't have been better: His trap had just been sprung.

FORTY-SEVEN

The Bell Ranger helicopter landed in a grassy field where three black sedans bearing government license plates were waiting. George Masters alighted from the chopper, another agent, Lou Berman, right at his elbow. They climbed in one of the cars and started off. Riggs had seriously underestimated the quickness of the response time from Washington.

Twenty minutes later the procession made its way down the gravel road and stopped in front of Riggs's home. Car doors swung open and serious-looking men, weapons out and ready, swarmed the front and back of the house and barn.

Masters strode up to the front door. When his knocks were not answered, he motioned to one of the men. The burly agent planted one foot directly against the lock and the door flew open, crashing against the interior wall. After they searched the house thoroughly, they finally converged in Riggs's office.

Masters sat down at the desk and quickly rustled through the papers, his eyes alighting on one set of notes. Masters leaned back in the chair and intently studied Riggs's scribbles on LuAnn Tyler and someone named Catherine Savage. He looked up at Berman. "Tyler disappears and Catherine Savage reappears. That's the cover."

"We can check the airports, see if Catherine Savage flew out ten years ago," Berman said.

Masters shook his head. "We don't need to do that. They're one and the same. Tyler is here. Find out Savage's address pronto. Call up some of the high-end real estate agents around here. I don't think her highness will be living in another trailer."

Berman nodded, pulled out a portable phone, and went to confer with the local FBI agents who had accompanied them here.

Masters ran his eyes around Riggs's office. He was wondering how Riggs fit into all this. He had it nice here, new life, new career, peaceful, lot of good years left to live. But now? Masters had been at the White House meeting with the president, the attorney general, and the director of the FBI. As Masters had outlined his theory, he had watched each of their faces go sickly pale. A scandal of horrific proportions. The government lottery, fixed. The American people would believe that their own government had done it to them. How could they not? The president had publicly announced his support for the lottery, even appeared in a TV commercial touting it. So long as the billions flowed in, and a few lucky people were elevated to millionaire status, who cared?

The concept of the lottery had received attacks claiming that what it spent on furthering the public welfare was largely negated by what it cost in others: breakup of families, gambling addiction, making poor people even poorer, causing people to eschew hard work and industriousness for the unrealistic dream of winning the lottery. One critic had said it was much like inner city kids striving for the NBA instead of an MBA. However, the lottery had remained bulletproof from those attacks.

If it came out, however, that the game was fixed, then the bullets would rapidly shatter that bubble. There would be a tremendous blood-letting and

427

everyone from the president on down was going to take a major hit. As Masters had sat in the Oval Office he saw that clearly in all their features: the FBI director, the nation's top lawman; the attorney general, the nation's top lawyer; the president, the number one of all. The responsibility would fall there and it would fall heavily. So Masters had been given explicit instructions: Bring in LuAnn Tyler, at any cost and by any means possible. And he intended to do just that.

"How's it feel?"

Riggs climbed slowly into the car. His right arm was in a sling. "Well, they gave me enough pain-killers to where I'm not sure I can feel anything."

LuAnn put the car in gear and they sped out on to the highway.

"Where are we going?" he asked.

"McDonald's. I'm starving and I can't remember the last time I had a Big Mac and fries. Sound good?"

"Sounds good."

She pulled into the drive-through of a McDonald's, ordering some burgers, fries, and two coffees.

They ate as they drove. Riggs put down his coffee, wiped his mouth, and nervously fingered the dash-board with his good arm. "So tell me, how badly did I screw things up for you?"

"Matthew, I'm not blaming you."

"I know," he said sheepishly. He slapped the seat. "I thought you were walking into a trap."

She stared over at him. "And why's that?"

Riggs looked out the window for a long moment before answering. "Right after you left I got a call."

"Is that right? Who from, and what did it have to do with me?"

He sighed deeply. "Well, for starters, my name's not Matthew Riggs. I mean it's been my name for the last five years, but it's not my real name."

"Well, at least we're even on that score."

He said with a forced grin, "Daniel Buckman." He held out his hand. "My friends call me Dan."

LuAnn didn't take it. "You're Matthew to me. Do your friends also know that technically you're dead and that you're in the Witness Protection Program?"

Riggs slowly withdrew his hand.

She flipped him an impatient look. "I told you that Jackson can do anything. I wish you'd start believing me."

"I was betting he was the one who tapped into my file. That's why I followed you. If he knew about me, I didn't know how he'd react. I thought he might kill you."

"That's always a possibility with the man."

"I got a good look at him."

LuAnn was exasperated. "That wasn't his real face. Dammit, it's never his real face." She thought of the rubbery flesh she had held. She had seen his real face. *His real face.* She knew what that meant. Jackson would now do everything in his power to kill her.

She slid her hands nervously over the steering wheel. "Jackson said you were a criminal. So what'd you do?"

"Are you telling me you believe everything that guy says to you? Just in case you didn't notice, he's a psycho. I haven't seen eyes like that since they executed Ted Bundy."

"Are you saying you're not in Witness Protection?"

"No. But the program isn't just for the bad guys."

She looked at him, puzzled. "What does that mean?"

"Do you think criminals can pick up the phone and get the sort of info I got on you?"

"I don't know, why can't they?"

"Pull over."

429

"What?"

"Just pull the damn car over!"

LuAnn turned into a parking lot and stopped the car.

Riggs leaned over and pulled out the listening device from under LuAnn's seat. "I told you I had bugged your car." He held up the sophisticated device. "Let me tell you, they almost never give out equipment like this to felons."

LuAnn looked at him, her eyes wide.

Riggs took a deep breath. "Up until five years ago, I was a special agent with the FBI. I'd like to think a *very* special agent. I worked undercover infiltrating gangs operating both in Mexico and along the Texas border. These guys were into everything from extortion to drugs to murder for hire; you name it, they were doing it. I lived and breathed with that scum for a year. When we busted the case open, I was the lead witness for the prosecution. We knocked out the entire operation, sent a bunch of them to prison for life. But the big bosses in Colombia didn't take all that kindly to my depriving them of about four hundred million a year in disposable income from the drug operation component. I knew how badly they'd want me. So I did the brave, honorable thing. I asked to disappear."

"And?"

"And the Bureau turned me down. They said I was too valuable in the field. Too experienced. They did have the courtesy to set me up in another town, in another gig. A desk job for a while."

"So there was no wife. That was all made up."

Riggs rubbed his injured arm again. "No, I was married. After I relocated. Her name was Julie."

LuAnn said very quietly, "Was?"

Riggs shook his head slowly and took a weary sip

430

on his coffee. The steam from the liquid fogged the window and he traced his real initials in it, forming the D and the B for Dan Buckman with great care as though doing it for the very first time. "Ambush on the Pacific Coast Highway. Car went over the cliff with about a hundred bullet holes in it. Julie was killed by the gunfire. I took two slugs; somehow neither of them hit any vitals. I was thrown clear of the car, landed on a ledge. Those were the scars you saw."

"Oh, God. I'm so sorry, Matthew."

"Guys like me, we probably shouldn't get married. It wasn't something I was looking for. It just happened. You know, you meet, you fall in love, you want to get married. You expect everything to sort of click after that. Things that you know might come up to ruin it, you sort of will them away. If I had resisted that impulse, Julie would still be alive and teaching first grade." He looked down at his hands as he spoke. "Anyway, that was when the brilliant higher-ups at the Bureau decided I just might want to retire and change my identity. Officially, I died in the ambush. Julie's six feet under in Pasadena and I'm a general contractor in safe, pastoral Charlottesville." He finished his coffee. "Or at least it used to be safe."

LuAnn slid her hand across the front seat and took his in a firm grip.

He squeezed back and said, "It's tough wiping out so many years of your life. Trying not to think about it, forgetting people and places, things that were so important to you for so long. Always afraid you're going to slip up." He stared at her. "It's damn tough," he said wearily.

She raised her hand up and stroked his face. "I never realized how much we had in common," she said.

431

"Well, here's another one." He paused for a second as their eyes locked. "I hadn't been with a woman since Julie."

They kissed tenderly and slowly.

"I want you to know," Riggs said, "that that wasn't the reason this morning happened. I've had other opportunities over the years. I just never felt like doing anything about them." He added quietly, "Until you."

She traced his jaw line with her index finger and then her finger curled up to his lips. "I've had other chances too," she said. They kissed again and then their bodies instinctively embraced and held tightly like two pieces from a mold, joined at last. They sat and rocked together for several minutes.

When they finally pulled away, Riggs checked the parking lot, refocusing on the present situation.

"Let's get to your house, pack some clothes, and whatever else you need. Then we'll go to my house and I'll do the same. I left the notes I made from my phone calls about you on my desk. I don't want to leave a trail for anyone."

"There's a motel off twenty-nine about four miles north of here."

"That's a start."

"So, what do you think Jackson's going to do now?"

"He knows I lied about you. He has to assume I lied about Donovan. Since I have every reason not to reveal the truth and Donovan is trying his best to do that, Jackson will go after him first and me second. I called Donovan and left a message warning him."

"Boy, that's real encouraging, being number two on Master Psycho's hit list," Riggs said, tapping his hand against the gun in his pocket.

A few minutes later they pulled up the private drive to Wicken's Hunt. The house was dark. LuAnn parked in front and she and Riggs got out. LuAnn

432

punched in the home's security code and they went inside.

Riggs sat alertly on the bed while LuAnn stuffed some things in a small travel bag.

"You're sure Lisa and Charlie are okay?"

"As sure as I can be. They're far away from here. And him. That can only be a good thing."

Riggs went over to the window that overlooked the front drive. What he saw coming up the driveway made his knees buckle for an instant. Then he snatched LuAnn by the hand and they were racing down the stairs and out the rear entrance.

The black sedans stopped in front of the house and the men quickly scrambled out. George Masters laid a hand on the BMW's hood and immediately scanned the area. "It's warm. She's here somewhere. Find her." The men fanned out and surrounded the house.

LuAnn and Riggs were racing past the horse barn and were headed into the deep woods when LuAnn pulled up.

Riggs stopped too, clutching at his arm, sucking in air. They were both trembling.

"What are you doing?" he gasped.

She motioned toward the horse barn. "You can't run with that arm. And we can't just go floundering around in the woods."

They entered the horse barn. Joy immediately started to make some noise and LuAnn quickly darted over and soothed the animal. While LuAnn readied their mount, Riggs pulled a pair of binoculars off the wall and went outside. Setting up in some thick bushes that hid the horse barn from the house, Riggs focused the binoculars. He automatically jerked back as he saw, under the flood lights that fully illuminated the entire rear law, the man moving across the back of the house, rifle in hand and the letters "FBI" emblazoned across his jacket. The next sight made Riggs mutter under his breath. It was five years since he had seen the man. George Masters hadn't changed much. The next instant the men disappeared from view as they entered the house.

Riggs hustled back to the horse barn where LuAnn was checking the cinches on the saddle. She patted Joy's neck, whispering calming words to the horse as she slid on the bridle.

"You ready?" she asked Riggs.

"Better be. As soon as they find the house empty, they're going to check the grounds. They know we're around somewhere – the car's engine would've still been warm."

LuAnn planted a wooden crate next to Joy, swung up, and reached out a hand for Riggs. "Step on that crate and hold on tight to me."

Riggs managed to struggle up in this fashion, clutching his arm as he did so. He planted his good arm around LuAnn's waist.

"I'll go as slow as I can, but it's going to jostle you a lot regardless. Horseback riding does that."

"Don't worry about me. I'll take a little pain to having to try and explain everything to the FBI."

As they started off on the trail LuAnn said, "So that's who it was? Your old friends?" Riggs nodded.

"At least one old friend in fact. Used to be a friend anyway. George Masters. He's the one at the Bureau who said I was too valuable in the field, who wouldn't let me enter Witness Protection until my wife was dead."

"Matthew, it's not worth it. There's no reason you should be running from them, you haven't done anything wrong."

"Look, LuAnn, it's not like I owe those guys anything."

434

"But if I'm caught and you're with me?"

"Well, we just won't get caught." He grinned.

"What's so funny?"

"I was just thinking how bored I'd been the last few years. I guess I'm not really happy unless I'm doing something where I have a reasonable shot at getting my head blown off. I might as well own up to it."

"Well, you picked the right person to hang with then." She looked up ahead. "The motel's probably out of the question."

"Yep, they'll cover every place like that. Besides, riding up on a horse might make the motel manager suspicious."

"I've got another car back at the house, fat lot of good that'll do us."

"Wait a minute. We do have a car."

"Where?"

"We've got to get to the cottage, pronto."

When they arrived at the cottage, Riggs said, "Keep a sharp eye out in case you know who decided to come back." He opened up the doors to the rear shed and went inside. In the darkness, LuAnn couldn't see what he was doing. Then she heard a motor turn over and then die. Then it kicked over again and this time it kept running. A moment later, Donovan's black Honda, torn-up front bumper and all, appeared in the doorway. Riggs pulled it to a stop outside the shed doors and climbed out.

"What do you want to do with the horse?"

LuAnn looked around. "I could send her back up the trail. She'd probably go back to the horse barn on her own, but in the dark like this, she might miss the trail or wander off and fall in a hole or maybe the creek."

"How about we put her in the shed and then you can call somebody to come get her?" he offered.

"Good idea." She swung down and led Joy inside the shed.

She looked around and noted the watering trough, tack wall, and two small bales of hay stored in the back of the shed.

"It's perfect. The tenant before Donovan must have kept a horse and used this as a stable."

Lifting off the saddle and slipping off the horse's bridle, LuAnn tethered Joy to a hook on the wall with a piece of rope she found. LuAnn scrounged up a bucket and, using water from the outside tap, she filled up the watering trough, and laid out the hay in front of Joy. The horse immediately dipped her head to the trough and then started to munch the hay. LuAnn shut the doors and climbed in the driver's seat of the Honda while Riggs eased in the other side.

There was no key in the ignition. LuAnn glanced under the steering column and saw a bundle of exposed wires hanging down. "They teach hot wiring at the FBI?"

"You learn a lot of things going through life."

She put the car in gear. "Tell me about it."

They were silent and still for a moment and then Riggs stirred. "We may only have one shot at getting out of this relatively intact."

"And what's that?"

"The FBI can be accommodating to people who cooperate."

"But, Matthew—"

He broke in, "But they can be absolutely forgiving to people who give them what they really want."

"Are you suggesting what I think you are?"

"All we need to do is deliver Jackson to them."

"That's good to hear. For a minute there I thought it might be something difficult."

They drove off in the Honda.

436

FORTY-EIGHT

It was ten o'clock in the morning. Donovan stared through a pair of binoculars at the large Southern colonial home set amid mature trees. He was in McLean, Virginia, one of the most affluent locales in the United States. Million-dollar properties were the norm here and that was typically only on one acre of land or less. The home he was staring at rested on five secluded acres. You have to have substantial wealth for a place like this. As he looked at the columned portico, Donovan knew without a doubt that the current owner had more than enough.

As he watched, a brand new Mercedes drove down the street from the opposite direction and approached the massive gates to the property. As the Mercedes nosed toward the entrance, the gates parted and the car entered the private drive. Through the binoculars, Donovan eyed the woman driving. In her forties now, she still matched her lottery photo from ten years ago pretty well. Lots of money could slow down the aging process, Donovan figured.

He checked his watch. He had gotten here early just to scope things out. He had checked his answering machine and had listened to LuAnn Tyler's warning. He wasn't going to run yet, but he had taken her advice quite seriously. He would've been a fool to think there weren't some serious forces behind all this. He took out the gun from his pocket and checked to make sure it was fully loaded. He scanned the area intently once more. He waited a few more minutes to give her time to get settled, then tossed his cigarette out the window, rolled it up, and drove toward the house.

He pulled up to the gates and spoke into an intercom. The voice answering him sounded nervous, agitated. The gates opened and a minute later he was standing inside the foyer that rose a full three stories above his head.

"Ms. Reynolds?"

Bobbie Jo Reynolds was trying her best not to meet his eye. She didn't speak, but simply nodded. She was dressed in a way Donovan would describe as very put together. You wouldn't have suspected that barely ten years ago she had been a starving actress wannabe hustling tables. She had been back in the country for almost five years now after a lengthy sojourn in France. During his investigation into the lottery winners, Donovan had checked her out thoroughly. She was now a very respected member of the Washington social community. He suddenly wondered if Alicia Crane and she knew each other.

After failing to get anywhere with LuAnn, Donovan had contacted the eleven other lottery winners. They had been far easier to track down than LuAnn; none of them were fugitives from the law. Yet.

Reynolds was the only one who had agreed to speak with him. Five of the winners had hung up on him. Herman Rudy had threatened bodily harm and used language Donovan hadn't heard since his Navy days. The others hadn't called back after he had left messages.

Reynolds escorted him into what Donovan figured was the living room – large, airy, and filled, presumably under an interior designer's tasteful eye, with contemporary furnishings, sprinkled here and there with costly antiques.

Reynolds sat down in a wingback chair and motioned Donovan to the settee across from her. "Would you like some tea or coffee?" She still didn't look at him, her hands nervously clasping and unclasping.

"I'm fine." He hunched forward, took out his notebook, and slipped a tape recorder from his pocket. "You mind if I record this conversation?"

"Why is that necessary?" Reynolds was suddenly showing a little backbone now, he thought. Donovan quickly decided to squelch that tendency before it gained any further strength.

"Ms. Reynolds, I assumed when you called me back that you were prepared to talk about things. I'm a reporter. I don't want to put words in your mouth, I want to get the facts exactly straight, can you understand that?"

"Yes," she said nervously, "I suppose I can. That's why I called you back. I don't want my name besmirched. I want you to know that I've been a very respectable member of this community for years. I've given generously to numerous charities, I sit on several local boards—"

"Ms. Reynolds," Donovan interrupted, "do you mind if I call you Bobbie Jo?"

There was a perceptible wince on Reynolds's face. "I go by Roberta," she said primly.

Reynolds reminded Donovan so much of Alicia he was tempted to ask if they knew each other. He decided to pass on that impulse.

"All right, Roberta, I know you've done a ton of good for the community. A real pillar. But I'm not interested in the present. I want to talk about the past, specifically ten years ago."

"You mentioned that on the phone. The lottery." She swept a shaky hand through her hair.

"That's right. The source of all this." He looked around at the opulence.

"I won the lottery ten years ago, that's hardly news now, Mr. Donovan."

439

"Call me Tom."

"I would prefer not."

"Fine. Roberta, do you know someone named LuAnn Tyler?"

Reynolds thought a moment and then shook her head. "It doesn't seem familiar. Should I know her?"

"Probably not. She won the lottery too, in fact two months after you did."

"Good for her."

"She was a lot like you. Poor, not a lot to look forward to. No way out, really."

She laughed nervously. "You make it sound like I was destitute. I was hardly that."

"But you weren't exactly rolling in dough, were you? I mean that's why you played the lottery, right?"

"I suppose. It's not like I expected to win."

"Didn't you, Roberta?"

She looked startled. "What are you talking about?"

"Who manages your investments?"

"That's none of your business."

"Well, my guess is it's the same person who manages the money of eleven other lottery winners, including LuAnn Tyler."

"So?"

"Come on, Roberta, talk to me. Something's up. You know all about it and I want to find out all about it. In fact, you knew you were going to win the lottery."

"You're crazy." Her voice was trembling badly.

"Am I? I don't think so. I've interviewed lots of liars, Roberta, some very accomplished. You're not one of them."

Reynolds stood up. "I don't have to listen to this."

Donovan persisted. "The story's going to come out, Roberta. I'm close to breaking through on a variety of fronts. It's only a matter of time. The question is: Do you want to cooperate and maybe get out of this whole thing relatively unscathed or do you want to go down with everybody?"

"I . . . I . . ."

Donovan continued in a steady voice. "I'm not looking to wipe out your life, Roberta. But if you participated in a conspiracy to fix the lottery, in whatever manner, you're going to take some lumps. But I'll offer you the same deal I offered Tyler. Tell me all you know, I go and write my story and you do whatever you want to do until the story hits. Like disappear. Consider the alternative. It's not nearly as pretty."

Reynolds sat back down and looked around her home for a moment. She took a deep breath. "What do you want to know?"

Donovan turned on the recorder. "Was the lottery fixed?" She nodded. "I need an audible response, Roberta." He nodded toward the recorder.

"Yes."

"How?" Donovan was almost shaking as he waited for the answer.

"Would you mind pouring me a glass of water from that carafe over there?"

Donovan jumped up, poured the water, and set the glass down in front of her. He sat back down.

"How?" he repeated.

"It had to do with chemicals."

Donovan cocked his head. "Chemicals?"

Reynolds pulled a handkerchief from her pocket and wiped at a sudden cluster of tears in her eyes.

As Donovan watched her, he figured she was near the breaking point. Ironic that the one to call him back would be the nervous Nellie type.

"I'm no scientist, Roberta, give it to me as simply as you can."

Reynolds gripped the handkerchief tightly. "All but one ball, the one with the winning number, was sprayed with some chemical. And the passageway through which the ball traveled was sprayed with something. I can't explain it exactly, but it made certain that only the ball that wasn't sprayed with anything went through. It was the same for all the other ball bins."

"Damn!" Donovan stared at her in amazement. "Okay, Roberta, I got a million questions. Do the other winners know about this? How it was done? And by whom?" He thought back to LuAnn Tyler. She knew, that was for damned sure.

"No. None of the winners knew how it was done. Only the people who did it knew." She pointed to his tape recorder. "Your recorder's stopped." She added bitterly, "I'm sure you don't want to miss one word of this."

Donovan picked up the recorder and studied it as he reflected on her words. "But that's not exactly right, because you knew how the lottery was fixed, Roberta, you just told me. Come on, give me the whole truth."

The crunching blow to his upper torso sent Donovan over the top of the settee. He landed hard on the oak floor, his breath painfully gone. He could feel shattered ribs floating inside him.

Reynolds hovered over him. "No, the truth is only the *person* who came up with the whole scheme knew how it was done." The feminine hair and face came off and Jackson stared down at the injured man.

Donovan tried desperately to get up. "Christ."

Jackson's foot slammed into his chest, knocking him back against the wall. Jackson stood erect. "Kick-boxing is a particularly deadly art form. You can literally kill someone without using your

442

however, the result isn't bad for a half hour's work."

"I need to get to a doctor." Donovan managed to get the words out through blood-caked lips.

"I'm afraid that's not going to happen. But I will take a couple of minutes to explain some things to you. For what it's worth, I believe that I owe you that. You were quite ingenious in figuring out the bankruptcy angle. That, I admit, had never occurred to me. My main concern was to ensure that none of my winners would want for money. Any shortage of funds might give them motivation to tell all. Fat and happy people rarely double-cross their benefactor. You found the hole in that plan."

Donovan coughed and, with a sudden motion, managed to sit up straight. "How'd you pick up my trail?"

"I knew LuAnn would tell you basically nothing. What would you do next? Ferret out another source. I phoned all my other winners and alerted them that you might call. Ten of them I instructed to blow you off. I told Bobbie Jo – excuse me, Roberta – to meet with you."

"Why her?"

"Simple enough. Geographically, she was the closest one to me. As it is, I had to drive through the night to get here and set everything up. That was me in the Mercedes, by the way. I had a description of you. I thought that was you in the car watching the house."

"Where's Bobbie Jo?"

"Not relevant." Jackson smiled both in his eagerness to explain and in his triumph and total control over the veteran reporter. "Now, to continue. The substance applied to nine of the ten balls was a clear light acrylic. If you care for precise details, it was a diluted solution of polydimethyl siloxane that I made a few modifications to, a turbocharged version if you will. It builds up a powerful static charge and also increases the size of the ball by approximately one thousandth of an inch without, however, a measurable change in weight or appearance or even smell. They do weigh the balls, you know, to ensure that all are of equal weight. In each bin the ball with the winning number on it had no chemicals applied to it. Each passageway through which the winning ball must travel was given a small trace of the modified polydimethyl siloxane solution as well. Under those precisely controlled conditions, the nine balls with the static charge could not enter a passageway coated with the same substance; indeed, they repelled each other, much like a force field. Thus they could not be part of the winning combination. Only the uncoated ball would be able to do so."

The awe was clear on Donovan's face, but then his features clouded. "Wait a minute: If the nine balls were coated with the same charge, why wouldn't they be repelling each other in the bin? Wouldn't that make people suspicious?"

"Wonderful question. I thrive on the details. I further modified the chemical so that it would be instantly activated by the heat given off by the air flow into the machines to make the balls gyrate. Until then, the balls would remain motionless."

Jackson paused, his eyes shining. "Inferior minds seek convoluted scenarios; it takes a brilliant one to achieve simplicity. And I'm sure your background research revealed that all of my winners were poor, desperate, searching for a little hope, a little help. And I gave it to them. To all of you. The lottery loved it. The government looked like saints helping the impoverished like that. You people in the media got to write your teary-eyed stories. Everybody won. Including me." Donovan half expected the man to

446

take a bow.

"And you did this all by your lonesome?" Donovan sneered.

Jackson's retort was sharp. "I didn't need anyone else, other than my winners. Human beings are infinitely fallible, completely unreliable. Science is not. Science is absolute. Under strict principles, if you do A and B, then C will occur. That rarely happens if you inject the inefficiencies of humanity into the process."

"How'd you get the access?" Donovan was starting to slur his words as his injuries took their toll.

Jackson's smile broadened. "I was able to gain employment as a technician at the company that provided and maintained the ball machines. I was drastically overqualified for the position, which was one reason I got it. No one really cared about the geeky little techie, it was like I wasn't even there. But I had complete and unrestricted access to the machines. I even bought one of the ball machines so that I could experiment in private as to the right combinations of chemicals. So there I am, mister technician, spraying the balls with what everyone thought was a cleansing solution to get rid of dust and other grime that might have gotten into the bins. And all I had to do was hold the winning ball in my hand while I did so. The solution dries almost immediately. I surreptitiously drop the winning ball back into the bin and I'm all set."

Jackson laughed. "People really should respect the technicians of the world more, Mr. Donovan. They control everything because they control the machines that control the flow of information. In fact, I use many of them in my work. I didn't need to buy off the leaders. They're useless because they're incompetent showpieces. Give me the worker bees

447

any day."

Jackson stood up and put on a pair of thick gloves. "I think that covers everything," he said. "No, after I finish with you, I'm going to visit LuAnn."

Damn me for a fool for not listening to you, LuAnn, Donovan thought to himself.

Through the glove Jackson rubbed his injured hand where the glass had cut him. He had many paybacks planned for LuAnn.

"Piece of advice, A-hole," Donovan sputtered, "tangle with that woman and she'll cut your balls off."

"Thank you for your point of view." Jackson gripped Donovan tightly by the shoulders.

"Why're you keeping me alive, you son of a bitch?" Donovan tried to pull back from him, but was far too weak.

"Actually, I'm not." Jackson suddenly placed both hands around the sides of Donovan's head and gave it an abrupt twist. The sound of bone cracking was slight but unmistakable. Jackson lifted the dead man up and over his shoulder. Carrying him down to the garage, Jackson opened the front door of the Mercedes and pressed Donovan's fingers against the steering wheel, dash, cock, and several other surfaces that would leave good prints. Finally, Jackson clinched the dead man's hand around the gun he had used to kill Bobbie Jo Reynolds. Wrapping the body in a blanket, Jackson loaded it in the trunk of the Mercedes. He raced back into the house, retrieved his bag and Donovan's recorder, then returned to the garage and climbed behind the wheel of the Mercedes. In a few minutes the car had left the very quiet neighborhood behind. Jackson stopped by the side of the road, rolled down the window, and hurled the gun into the woods before pulling off again. Jackson would wait until nightfall

448

and then a certain local incinerator he had found on an earlier reconnaissance would prove to be Thomas Donovan's final resting place.

As he dróve on, Jackson thought briefly of how he would deal with LuAnn Tyler and her new ally, Riggs. Her disloyalty was now firmly established and there would be no more reprieves. He would focus his undivided attention on that matter shortly. But first he had something else to take care of.

Jackson entered Donovan's apartment, closed the door, and took a moment to survey the premises. He was still wearing the dead man's face. Thus, even if he had been spotted, it was of no concern to him. Donovan's body had been incinerated, but Jackson had a limited amount of time to complete his search of the late reporter's apartment. A journalist kept records, and those records were what Jackson had come for. Very soon the housekeeper would discover Bobbie Jo Reynolds's body and would call the police. Their search would very quickly, largely through Jackson's efforts, lead to Thomas Donovan.

He searched the apartment rapidly but methodically and soon found what he was looking for. He stacked the record boxes in the middle of the small foyer. They were the same ones Donovan had kept in the cottage in Charlottesville, filled with the results of his investigation into the lottery. Next he logged on to Donovan's computer and did a search of the hard drive. Thankfully, Donovan had not bothered to employ any passwords. The hard drive was clear. He probably kept everything on disk for portability. He looked at the back of the computer and then behind the desk. No phone modem. Just to be sure, Jackson again checked the icon screen. No computer services like America Online were present. Thus there was no e-mail to search. How old-fashioned of Donovan, he thought. Next he checked a stack of floppies in the desk drawer and piled them all in one of the boxes. He would look at them later.

He was preparing to leave when he noted the phone answering machine in the living room. The red light was blinking. He went over to the phone and hit the playback button. The first three messages were innocuous. The voice on the fourth message made Jackson jerk around and bend his head low to catch every single word.

Alicia Crane sounded nervous and scared. Where were you, Thomas, she implored. You haven't called. What you were working on was too dangerous. Please, please call me, the message said.

Jackson rewound the tape and listened to Alicia's voice again. He hit another button on the machine. Finally, he picked up the boxes and left the apartment.

FORTY-NINE

LuAnn looked at the Lincoln Memorial as she drove the Honda over the Memorial Bridge. The water of the Potomac River was dark and choppy. Flecks of white foam appeared but then quickly dissipated. It was the morning rush hour and the traffic over the bridge was heavy. They had spent one night in a motel near Fredericksburg while they decided what to do. Then they had driven to the outskirts of Washington, D.C., and spent the night at a motel near Arlington. Riggs had made some phone calls and visited a couple of retail establishments preparing for the events that would take place the next day. Then they had sat in the motel room eating while Riggs had gone over the plan, the details of which LuAnn quickly memorized. With that completed they had turned out the lights. One slept while the other kept watch. That was the plan at least. However, neither one got much rest. Finally, they both sat up, one curled around the other. Under any other circumstances they would have probably made love. As it was they spent the night looking out the window on to the dark street, listening for any sound that might herald another wave of danger.

"I can't believe I'm doing this," LuAnn said as they drove along.

"Hey, you said you trusted me."

"I do. I do trust you."

"LuAnn, I know what I'm doing. There are two

451

things I know: how to build things, and how the Bureau works. This is the way to do it. The only way that makes sense. You run, they'll eventually find you."

"I got away before," she said confidently.

"You had some help and a better head start. You'd never get out of the country now. So if you can't run, you do the reverse, you go right at them, take the offensive."

LuAnn focused on the traffic at the same time she was thinking intently about what they were about to do. What she was about to do. The only man she had ever absolutely trusted was Charlie. And that complete trust had not come quickly, it had been built and then cemented over a ten-year period. She had only known Riggs for a very short time. And yet he had earned her trust, even in a matter of days. His actions reached her far more deeply than any words he could try to tempt her with.

"Aren't you nervous?" she asked. "I mean you don't really know what you're going to be walking into."

He grinned at her. "That's the really great part, isn't it?"

"You're a crazy man, Matthew Riggs, you really are. All I want in my life is a little predictability, a semblance of tranquillity, of normalcy even, and you're salivating over walking along the edge of the cliff."

"It's all in how you look at it." He looked out the window. "Here we are." He pointed to an open spot on the curb and she pulled over and parked. Riggs got out and then poked his head back in. "You remember the plan?"

LuAnn nodded. "Going over everything last night helped. I can find it with no trouble."

"Good, see you soon."

As Riggs walked down the street to the pay phone,

LuAnn looked up at the large, ugly building. The J. EDGAR HOOVER BUILDING was stenciled on its facade. Home of the Federal Bureau of Investigation. These people were looking for her everywhere and here she was parked ten feet from their damned headquarters. She shivered and put on her sunglasses. Putting the car in gear, she tried to keep her nerves in check. She hoped to hell the man really knew what he was doing.

Riggs made the phone call. The man on the other end was understandably excited. Within a few minutes Riggs was inside the Hoover Building and being escorted by an armed guard to his destination.

The conference room he was deposited in was large but sparsely furnished. He passed by the chairs gathered around the small table, and remained standing waiting for them to arrive. He took a deep breath and almost cracked a smile. He had come home, in a manner of speaking. He scanned the room for any hidden cameras, and saw nothing obvious, which meant the room was probably under both audio and video surveillance.

He swung around when the door opened and two men dressed in white shirts and similar ties entered.

George Masters extended his hand. He was large, nearly bald, but his figure was trim. Lou Berman sported a severe crew cut and a grim demeanor.

"It's been a long time, Dan."

Riggs shook his hand. "It's Matt now. Dan's dead, remember, George?"

George Masters cleared his throat, looked nervously around, and motioned Riggs to sit down at the nicked-up table. After they were all seated, George Masters inclined his head toward the other man. "Lou Berman, he's heading up the investigation we discussed over the phone." Berman nodded curtly at Riggs.

Masters looked at Berman. "Dan" – Masters

paused, correcting himself – "Matt was one of the best damned undercover agents we ever had."

"Sacrificed a lot in the name of justice, didn't I, George?" Riggs eyed him evenly.

"Gave it up, too dangerous." He looked over at Berman. "George here will tell you I stayed in the ball game one inning too many. Right, George? Sort of against my will, though."

"That was all a long time ago."

"Funny, it still seems like yesterday to me."

"Goes with the territory, Matt."

"That's easy to say when you haven't watched your wife get her brains blown out because of what her husband did for a living. How's your wife by the way, George? Three kids too, right? Having kids and a wife must be nice."

"All right, Matt. I get your point. I'm sorry."

Riggs swallowed hard. He was feeling far more emotion than he had expected, but it did feel like yesterday and he had waited half a decade to say this. "It would've meant a lot more if you had said it five years ago, George."

Riggs's stare was so intense that Masters finally had to look away.

"Let's get down to it," Riggs finally said, breaking out of the past.

Masters put his elbows up on the table and glanced over at him. "FYI, I was in Charlottesville two nights ago."

"Beautiful little college town."

"Visited a couple of places. Thought I might see you."

"I'm a working man. Gotta keep busy."

Masters eyed the sling. "Accident?"

"The construction business can be very hazardous. I'm here to strike a deal, George. A mutually satisfactory deal."

454

"Do you know where LuAnn Tyler is?" Berman leaned forward, his eyes darting all over Riggs's face.

Riggs cocked his head at the other man. "I've got her down in the car, Lou, you want to go check? Here." Riggs reached in his pocket, pulled out a set of keys, and dangled them in front of the FBI agent. They were the keys to his house, but Riggs figured Berman wouldn't take him up on the offer.

"I'm not here to play games," Berman snarled.

Riggs put the keys away and leaned forward. "Neither am I. Like I said, I'm here to make a deal. You want to hear it?"

"Why should we deal? How do we know you're not working with Tyler?"

"What do you care if I am?"

Berman's face turned red. "She's a criminal."

"I worked with criminals most of my career, Lou. And who says she's a criminal?"

"The state of Georgia."

"Have you really looked at the case? I mean really looked at it. My sources say it's bullshit."

"Your sources?" Berman almost laughed.

Masters intervened. "I've looked at it, Matt. It probably *is* bullshit." He glowered over at Berman. "And even if it isn't, it's Georgia's problem, not ours."

"Right, and your interests should lie elsewhere."

Berman refused to give it up. "She's also a tax evader. She won a hundred million bucks and then disappeared for ten years and hasn't paid Uncle Sam a dime."

"I thought you were an FBI agent, not an accountant," Riggs shot back.

"Let's settle down, guys," Masters said.

Riggs leaned forward. "I thought you'd be a lot more interested in the person behind LuAnn Tyler, the person behind a lot of people. The invisible guy with billions of dollars running around the planet playing games, causing havoc, making your lives miserable. Now, do you want to get to him, or do you want to talk to LuAnn Tyler about her itemized deductions?"

"What are you suggesting?"

Riggs sat back. "Just like old times, George. We reel in the big fish and let the little one go."

"I don't like it," Berman grumbled.

Riggs's eyes played over the man's features. "Based upon my experience at the Bureau, catching the big fish gets you promoted and, more important, gets you pay raises; delivering the small fry doesn't."

"Don't lecture me on the FBI, Riggs, I've been around the block a few times."

"Good, Lou, then I shouldn't have to waste time on this crap. We deliver you the man and LuAnn Tyler walks. And I mean from everything – federal, taxes, and the state of Georgia."

"We can't guarantee that, Matt. The boys at the IRS go their own way."

"Well, maybe she pays some money."

"Maybe she pays a lot of money."

"But no jail. Unless we agree on that, it's a no go. You have to make the murder charge go away."

"How about we arrest you right now and hold you until you tell us where she is?" Berman was inching forward, crowding Riggs.

"Then how about you never break the biggest case of your career. Because LuAnn Tyler will disappear again and you'll be stuck at point A again. And on what charge would you be holding me by the way?"

"Accessory," Berman fired back.

"Accessory to what?"

Berman thought for a moment. "Aiding and abetting a fugitive."

"What proof do you have of that? What actual proof do you have that I even know where she is, or have ever even met her?"

"You've been investigating her. We saw the notes in your house."

"Oh, so you came by my house on your visit to Charlottesville? You should've called ahead. I would've fixed up something nice for dinner."

"And we found lots of interesting stuff," Berman snapped.

"Good for you. Can I see the search warrant you used to enter my premises without permission?"

Berman started to say something and then clamped his mouth shut.

A thin smile broke across Riggs's face. "Great. No search warrant. All inadmissible. And since when is it a crime to make a phone call and get some *public* information on someone? Considering that I got that information from the Feds."

"Your WPP handler, not us," Berman said threateningly.

"I guess I treat all you guys as one big, happy family."

Masters started speaking slowly. "Supposing we do go along, you haven't given us the connection between Tyler and this other person."

Riggs had been expecting this question and was surprised it hadn't come up before. "He had to get the money from somewhere."

Masters considered this statement for a moment, and then his eyes flickered. "Listen, Matt, this is a little bigger than you probably know." He looked over at Berman briefly before continuing. "We know – or rather we think – the lottery was . . ." Masters paused, searching for the right words. "We believe

457

the lottery may have been compromised. Was it?"

Riggs sat back in his chair and tapped his fingers on the table. "Maybe."

Masters again chose his words carefully. "Let me make this real clear to you. The president, the A.G., the director of the FBI, they've all been apprised of this possibility. I can tell you that their collective reaction was one of absolute shock."

"Bully for them."

Masters ignored Riggs's sarcastic tone. "If the lottery was fixed, then this situation has to be handled very delicately."

Riggs chuckled. "Translation: If it ever gets out to the public, half the guys in Washington, including the president, the A.G., the director, and you two guys, will probably be looking through the want ads. So what you're suggesting is a major cover-up."

"Hey, this all probably happened ten years ago. It didn't occur on our watch," Berman said.

"Gee, Lou, that'll go over real big with John Q. Public. All of your butts are on the line here and you know it."

Masters banged his fist down on the table. "Do you realize what would happen if it becomes public that the lottery was fixed?" Masters said hotly. "Can you imagine the lawsuits, the investigations, the scandals, the blow it would give the old U.S. of A. right in the gut? It would almost be like the country defaulting on its debt. It cannot be allowed to happen. It *will not* be allowed to happen."

"So what's your suggestion, George?"

Masters rapidly calmed down and ticked off the points with his fingers. "You bring in Tyler. We question her, we get her cooperation. With that information in hand we bring in the people—"

"*Person*, George," Riggs interrupted. "There's just one of him, but let me tell you, he's a very special one."

458

"Okay, so with Tyler's help we nail him."

"And what happens to LuAnn Tyler?"

Masters spread his hand helplessly. "Come on, Matt, she's got a state murder warrant out. She hasn't paid taxes for almost a decade. I have to assume she was in on the lottery scam. That all adds up to a few lifetimes in prison, but I'll settle for just one, maybe half of one if she's real cooperative, but I can't guarantee it."

Riggs stood up. "Well, guys, it was nice talking to you."

Berman was up in an instant and he slid over to the door, blocking Riggs's exit.

"Lou, I've still got one good arm, and the fist attached to it is just itching like hell to plant one right across your face." Riggs started to advance menacingly toward the door.

"Wait a minute, just hold it. Both of you sit down," Masters bellowed.

Riggs and Berman engaged in a suitably lengthy stare-down and then slowly returned to their seats.

Riggs stared over at Masters. "If you think the woman's going to waltz in here so she can risk her life in order to bring this guy down and then be rewarded by spending the rest of her life in prison, then you've hung around the Bureau too long, George. Your brains are gone."

Riggs pointed a finger at him. "Let me fill you in on something. It's the game of life and it's called 'who's got the leverage.' You call up the state of Georgia and tell them that LuAnn Tyler is no longer wanted for murder there, or for anything else. If she's got a friggin' parking ticket outstanding, then it's wiped out. You understand me? Squeaky clean. Then you call up the IRS and you tell them that she'll pay what she owes, but they can forget jail time. As far as being involved in any lottery scam, if the

459

statute of limitations hasn't already expired, then that goes away too. The tiniest infraction that could possibly put her in jail for even a second gets blotted out. Gone. She's a free person."

"Are you nuts?" Berman said.

"Or?" Masters said quietly, his eyes fixed on Riggs.

"Or, we go public with everything, George. What does she have to lose? If she's going to go to prison for life, then she's going to have to have some hobbies to fill up her days. I'm thinking appearances on *Sixty Minutes*, *Dateline*, *Prime Time Live*, maybe even *Oprah*. A book deal would probably be in the cards too. She can just talk her little heart out about the lottery being fixed, how the president and the A.G. and the FBI director wanted to cover it all up to save their jobs and how they were stupid enough to let a master criminal who's been wreaking world-wide havoc for years walk away so they could put a young woman who grew up dirt-poor in prison for doing something all of us would've done in an instant!"

Riggs sat back and looked at both men. "That, gentlemen, is what I mean by leverage."

While Masters considered this, Berman snorted. "One guy? I don't believe that. We're looking at a big organization. No way could one person do all the stuff I've been seeing on my radar screen. We haven't been able to prove anything, but we know there are multiple players."

Riggs thought back to the cottage, right before the knife sliced into his arm. He had stared right into the most deadly pair of eyes he had ever seen. Over the years working undercover in some very dangerous situations, he had been scared before; he was only human after all. But he had never before felt the nervous terror those eyes had aroused in him. If he had had a crucifix handy, he would have pulled it out to ward the guy off.

He looked at Berman. "You know, Lou, you'd be surprised. This guy is a master of disguise. He can probably play enough roles to fill a Broadway musical. And by going it alone, he never has to worry about anyone turning snitch on him or trying to cut him out."

Masters started speaking in low tones as he tried a different tack. "Remember, Matt, not so long ago, you were one of us. You might want to think about that. You've obviously gained Tyler's confidence. You bring her in, well, let's just say your government would be very grateful. No more sawing and hammering to make a living."

"Let me think about that for a second, George." Riggs closed his eyes, reopened them almost instantaneously, and said, "Go to hell."

He and Masters locked eyes. "What do you say, George? Is it a deal? Or do I go and phone Oprah?"

Slowly, almost imperceptibly, Masters nodded.

"I'd really love to hear you *say* it, George."

Berman started to cut in, but Masters stared him into silence.

"Yes, it's a deal," Masters said, "no jail."

"Georgia too?"

"Georgia too."

"You sure you can do that? I know your authority is limited there." Riggs's tone was taunting.

"Mine is, but I don't think the president of the United States has that same problem. My instructions are to avoid public exposure at all costs. I guarantee that either he or the A.G. will make that phone call."

"Good, now get the director and the attorney general in here, because I want to hear the same things from them. By the way, is the president busy today?"

461

"There's no way in hell the president is meeting with you."

"Then get the director and the A.G. in here, George. Right now."

"You don't trust my word?"

"Let's just say your track record hasn't inspired my confidence all that much. And I take comfort in numbers." He nodded at the phone. "Make the call."

Masters and Riggs stared across at each other for at least a minute. Then Masters slowly picked up the phone and spoke into it at length. It took some schedule-juggling, but within thirty minutes the director of the FBI and the attorney general of the United States were sitting across from Riggs. Riggs presented the same deal to them he had presented to Masters, and he extracted the same promises.

Riggs rose. "Thank you for your cooperation."

Berman got up too. "All right, if we're working together now, bring Tyler in, we can wire her, get a team together, and go get this 'one man crime wave.'"

"Uh-uh, Lou. The deal was *I'd* bring him in, not the FBI."

Berman looked ready to explode. "Listen you—"

"Shut up, Lou!" The FBI director's eyes bored into him and then he turned to look at Riggs. "You really think you can pull this off?"

Riggs smiled. "Have I ever let you guys down before?" He glanced over at Masters.

Masters didn't return the smile, but just continued to study Riggs's face. "If you don't, all bets are off. For Tyler." He paused and then added ominously, "And you. Your cover's blown. And I'm not sure how much incentive we'd have to reestablish it. And your enemies are still plenty active."

Riggs walked across the room to the door, but then turned back. "Well, George, I never really expected anything less from you guys. Oh, and don't try to have me followed. That'll just piss me off and waste a lot of time. Okay?"

Masters nodded quickly. "Sure, don't sweat it."

The big-voiced attorney general asked a final question. "Was the lottery fixed, Mr. Riggs?"

Riggs looked back at her. "You bet it was. And you want to know the kicker? It looks like the United States Lottery was used to finance the plans of one of the most dangerous psychopaths I've personally ever seen. I truly hope this never makes it on to the six o'clock news." His eyes swept the room taking in the steadily rising panic in each of their faces. "Have a good day." Riggs closed the door behind him.

The rest of the group looked around at each other. "Holy shit," was all the director could say, his head swaying from side to side.

Masters picked up the phone and spoke into it. "He's leaving the building now. He'll know he's being followed. Make it a short leash, but give him some room. He's an expert at this stuff, so he'll take you for a waltz around the city and then try to lose you. Be alert! When he hooks up with Tyler, communicate with me immediately. Keep them under surveillance, but don't approach them." He looked over at the A.G., who nodded her assent. Masters hung up the phone and took a deep breath.

"Do you believe Riggs's story that it's only one man behind all this?" the director asked, looking nervously at Masters.

"It sounds incredible, but I hope to God it's true," said Masters. "I'd rather be dealing with one guy than some worldwide crime syndicate." The A.G. and director both nodded in agreement.

Berman looked around with questioning eyes. "So what's the plan here?"

The director cleared his throat heavily and said,

"We can't ever let this come out, you all know that. No matter what happens. No matter who gets hurt. Even if Riggs is successful and we are able to apprehend this person and any others involved in the scheme, then we still face a major problem."

The A.G. folded her arms across her chest and picked up this line of thought. "Even if we can build a case against him on all the other activities this person will know he has 'leverage,' to use Riggs's terms. And he'll use the same threat Riggs used. Deal with him or he goes public. I can just see his defense lawyer salivating over that one." She involuntarily shuddered.

"So what you're saying is this thing can never go to trial," Berman said. "What then?"

The A.G. ignored the question and instead asked Masters, "You think Riggs is playing straight with us?"

Masters shrugged. "He was one of the best at undercover operations. To do that you have to lie on a regular basis and appear not to be. Truth takes a backseat. Sometimes reality becomes blurred. And old habits die hard."

"Meaning we can't completely trust him," the A.G. said.

Masters looked thoughtful for a moment. "No more than he can trust us."

"Well," the director said, "there's the strong possibility that we won't bring this guy in alive." He looked around the room. "Right?"

They all nodded. Masters ventured, "If he's half as dangerous as Riggs says he is, I'd shoot first and ask no questions later. Then maybe our problem goes away."

"And what about Riggs and Tyler?" the A.G. asked.

Berman answered, "Well, if we're going to go that

464

route, you never know who might get caught in the crossfire. I mean none of us wants that to happen, of course," he quickly added, "but like Riggs's wife, you know, innocent people sometimes die."

"Tyler is hardly innocent!" the director said angrily.

"That's right," Masters said. "And if Riggs is tying his allegiances to her instead of us, well then he has to accept the consequences. Whatever they may be."

All of them looked at each other uneasily. Under normal circumstances, none of them would have been remotely contemplating any of this. They had dedicated their lives to apprehending criminals and then seeing them receive a fair trial before a court of law for their offenses. Their now silently praying that justice wouldn't happen this time, that instead several human beings would die before a judge or jury ever heard their case, was not sitting well with any of them. However, in this present case, they were all confronted with something much larger than merely hunting down a criminal. Here the truth was far more dangerous.

"Whatever the consequences may be," the director quietly repeated.

FIFTY

Walking down the street, Riggs looked at his watch. The clock housing was actually a sophisticated recording device; the tiny perforations in the leather strap were the speaker component. The day before, he had spent some time in a well-known "spy shop" four blocks from the FBI building. The technology had certainly gotten better over the years. At least his deal with the government was recorded somewhere other than in his memory. With operations like this, he shouldn't put too much faith in anyone, no matter which side he was on.

Riggs knew that the government could never allow the truth to come out. In this case capturing the criminal alive was just as bad as not capturing him, maybe worse. And anyone who knew the truth was in serious jeopardy, and not just from Jackson. Riggs knew that the FBI would never intentionally gun down an innocent person. But he knew the FBI hardly regarded LuAnn as innocent. And since Riggs had thrown his support her way, he was automatically lumped with her as the enemy. If it got dicey toward the end, which Riggs knew it would, and if LuAnn were anywhere near Jackson, well, the FBI might not be real careful about who they were firing at. Riggs didn't expect Jackson to go down quietly. He would take out as many agents as he could. Riggs had seen that in his eyes at the cottage. The man had no respect for human life. To him a person was merely a factor to be manipulated and eliminated if circumstances called for it. As an undercover agent, Riggs had dealt with people like that for years. People almost as dangerous as Jackson. Given those elements, the FBI would err on the side of killing the man rather than taking him alive; they wouldn't risk the life of an agent in order to ensure that the man would stand trial. Riggs was well aware that the government had no incentive to bring Jackson to trial and every incentive not to. So Riggs's job was to flush out Jackson and then the Feds could do what they wanted. If that was pumping the man full of lead, Riggs would be glad to help them do so. But he was going to keep LuAnn as far away from the man as humanly possible. She was not going to be caught in the crossfire. He had been through that once. History was not going to repeat itself.

Riggs didn't bother to look behind him. He knew he was already under surveillance. Despite Masters's assurances to the contrary, he would have immediately ordered a tail. Riggs would've done the same thing in his position. Now he had to beat the trail before meeting up with LuAnn. He smiled. Just like old times.

While Riggs had been dealing with the FBI, LuAnn had driven to another pay phone and dialed a certain phone number. It rang several times and LuAnn thought she would probably get the standard automated message. Then a voice answered. She could barely recognize it, the connection was so bad.

"Charlie?"

"LuAnn?"

"Where are you?"

"On the road. I can barely hear you. Hold on, I'm passing some power lines."

467

In a moment, the connection was much clearer.

"That's better," LuAnn said.

"Hang on, there's someone who wants to talk to you."

"Mom?"

"Hello, baby."

"Are you okay?"

"I'm fine, sweetie, I told you Mommy would be fine."

"Uncle Charlie said you and Mr. Riggs saw each other."

"That's right. He's helping me. With things."

"I'm glad you're not alone. I miss you."

"I miss you too, Lisa, I can't tell you how much."

"Can we come home soon?"

Home? Where was home now? "I think so, baby. Mommy's working really hard on that right now."

"I love you."

"Oh, sweetie, I love you too."

"Here's Uncle Charlie."

"Lisa?"

"Yes?"

"I mean to keep my promise to you. I'm going to tell you everything. The truth. Okay?"

The voice was small, a little scared. "All right, Mom."

When Charlie came back on the phone, LuAnn told him to just listen. She filled him in on the latest events including Riggs's plan and his real background.

Charlie could barely contain himself. "I'm pulling over at a rest stop in two minutes. Call me back."

When LuAnn did so, Charlie's tone was heated. "Are you crazy?"

"Where's Lisa?"

"In the rest room."

"Is it safe?"

468

"I'm right outside the door and the place is packed with families. Now answer my question."

"No, I don't think I'm crazy."

"You let Riggs, an ex-FBI agent, walk into the Hoover Building and cut a deal for you. How in hell do you know he's not selling you down the river right now?"

"I trust him."

"Trust him?" Charlie's face turned crimson. "You barely know him. LuAnn, this is a big mistake, darling. A damned big one."

"I don't think so. Riggs is playing straight. I know he is. I've learned some things about him in the last few days."

"Like he's an experienced undercover agent who's an expert at lying."

LuAnn blinked for a second as these words sunk in. A small seed of doubt suddenly grew, invading her confidence in Matthew Riggs.

"LuAnn, are you there?"

She gripped the phone hard. "Yes. Well, if he did sell me down the river, it won't be long before I find out."

"You've got to get out of there. You said you've got the car. Get the hell out of there."

"Charlie, he saved my life. Jackson almost killed him while he was trying to help me."

Charlie was silent for a moment. He was having an internal conflict and was highly uncomfortable with it. From everything LuAnn had just told him, Riggs probably was going to bat for her. Charlie thought he knew why: The man was in love with her. Was LuAnn in love with him? Why shouldn't she be? And where did that leave him? The fact was, Charlie wanted Riggs to be lying. He wanted the man out of their lives. That thought was skewing his whole mental process. But Charlie did love LuAnn.

And he loved Lisa too. He had always put his own interests behind theirs. And with that thought his inner conflict disappeared. "LuAnn, I'll go with your instincts. Riggs is probably okay, now that I think about it. Just keep your eyes open, will you?"

"I will, Charlie. Where are you?"

"We headed through West Virginia, then into Kentucky, skirted the edge of Tennessee, and now we're floating back toward Virginia."

"I've gotta go now. I'll call later today and fill you in."

"I hope the rest of today isn't as exciting as the last two were."

"You and me both. Thanks, Charlie."

"For what? I haven't done anything."

"Now who's lying?"

"Take care of yourself."

LuAnn hung up the phone. She would be meeting Riggs soon if everything went according to plan. As she walked back to the car, Charlie's initial reaction came back to her. Could she trust Riggs? She slid into the front seat of the Honda. She had left it running because she had no keys and didn't share Riggs's skills at hot-wiring automobiles. She was about to put the car in gear when her hand stopped. This was no time for doubts, and yet she was suddenly overwhelmed with them. Her hand refused to move.

FIFTY-ONE

Riggs walked slowly down Ninth Street, looking casually around, as if he had all the time in the world. A gust of freezing air hit him. He stopped, gingerly slipped off the sling, and put his injured arm in the sleeve of his overcoat, buttoning it all the way up. As the bitter wind continued to blow down the street, Riggs pulled up the collar of his overcoat, took a knit cap emblazoned with the Washington Redskins logo from his pocket, and pulled it tightly over his head so that only the lower part of his reddening face was visible. He entered a corner convenience store.

The two teams of agents that were following him, one on foot, the other in a gray Ford, swiftly moved into position. One team covered the front of the store, the other the rear. They knew Riggs was an experienced undercover agent and they weren't taking any chances.

Riggs appeared carrying a newspaper under his arm, walked down the street, and hailed a taxi. The agents quickly climbed into the sedan, and it followed the taxi.

Moments after the sedan disappeared, the real Matt Riggs, wearing a dark felt cap, emerged from the store and walked quickly in the opposite direction. The key had been the brightly colored knit cap. His pursuers would have focused on the burgundy and gold colors like a ship's beacon to pinpoint their man and would not notice the subtle differences in the overcoats, pants, and shoes. He had called in a favor last night from an old friend who had thought Riggs long dead. The FBI was now tailing that old friend to his job at a law firm near the White House. The man lived near the FBI building, so his being in the vicinity would not be difficult to explain. And a lot of Washingtonians wore Redskins knit caps this time of year. Finally, the FBI couldn't possibly know of the long ago connection between the two men. The agents would question him briefly, realize their mistake, report back to Masters and the director, and get their heads handed to them for their morning troubles.

Riggs climbed in a cab and gave an address. The car sped off. He ran a hand through his hair. He was glad to get that one under his belt. He and LuAnn were a long way from being home free, but it felt good to know he still had it, at least in small doses. As the cab stopped at a red light, Riggs opened the newspaper he had purchased at the store.

Staring back at him from the front page were two photos. One person he knew, the other was a stranger to him. He quickly read the story and then looked at the pictures again. With a press badge dangling around his neck and a small notepad and pen peeking out from his shirt pocket, a sleepy-eyed Thomas Donovan looked like he had just climbed off a plane from covering some major news event on the other side of the world.

The woman in the photo next to him could not have struck a greater contrast to the reporter's disheveled image. The dress was elegant, the hair and makeup obviously professionally done and thus impeccable, the background almost surreal in its abundant luxury: a charity event where the rich and famous caucused to raise money for the less fortunate. Roberta Reynolds had been a longtime participant in such events and the story said her brutal murder had robbed the Washington area's charitable community of a great benefactor. Only one line of the story recounted the source of Reynolds's wealth: a sixty-five-million-dollar lottery win ten years earlier. She was apparently worth far more than that now. Or, at least, now her estate was.

She had been murdered – allegedly, the story reported, by one Thomas Donovan. he had been seen around the woman's home. A message from Donovan requesting an interview was on the dead woman's answering machine. Donovan's prints had been found on a carafe of water and a glass in Reynolds's home, which indicated the two had indeed met. And, finally, the pistol apparently used to slaughter Roberta Reynolds had been found in a wooded area about a mile from her home, along with her Mercedes, with Donovan's prints all over both of them. The murdered woman had been discovered lying on her bed. Evidence indicated she had been bound and held for some period of time, so that the crime was obviously premeditated, the paper said. There was an APB out on Donovan and the police were confident they would soon apprehend him.

Riggs finished reading the story and slowly folded up the newspaper. He knew the police were completely wrong. Donovan hadn't killed Reynolds. And it was highly likely that Donovan was dead as well. Riggs took a deep breath and thought about how he would break the news to LuAnn.

FIFTY-TWO

The burly man looked around at the other pricey homes in the Georgetown neighborhood. Fiftyish with pale skin and a neatly trimmed mustache, the man hitched up his pants, tucked his shirt in, and rang the bell to the front door.

Alicia Crane opened the door, looking anxious and tired.

"Yes?"

"Alicia Crane?"

"Yes."

The man flashed his identification. "Hank Rollins, homicide detective, Fairfax County, Virginia."

Alicia stared at the man's photo and the badge affixed to it. "I'm not sure—"

"Are you an acquaintance of Thomas Donovan?"

Alicia closed her eyes and bit her lip on the inside. When she reopened her eyes she said, "Yes."

Rollins rubbed his hands together. "Ma'am, I've got some questions to ask you. We can either do it down at the station or you can ask me in before I freeze to death, it's your call."

Alicia immediately opened the door. "Of course, I'm sorry." She led him down the hallway to the living room. After settling him down on the sofa she asked him if he wanted coffee.

"That'd be great, yes, ma'am."

As soon as she left the room, Rollins lurched to his feet and looked around the room. One item commanded his immediate attention. The photo of Donovan, his arm around Alicia Crane. It looked to be of recent vintage. They both looked extremely happy.

Rollins was holding the photo in his hands when Alicia walked back in carrying a tray with two cups of coffee and some creamer and two blue packets of Equal.

She lowered the tray to the coffee table. "I couldn't find the sugar. The housekeeper ran an errand. She'll be back in about an hour and I don't usually—" Her eyes caught the photo.

"May I have that?" she asked. She set down the tray and held out her hand.

Rollins quickly passed the photo over and returned to his seat. "I'll get to the point, Ms. Crane. You've read the newspaper, I assume?"

"You mean that pack of lies." Her eyes flashed for an instant.

"Well, I'll agree that it's all largely speculation at this time; however, there's a lot of things pointing toward Thomas Donovan having killed Roberta Reynolds."

"His fingerprints and his gun?"

"It's an active homicide investigation, Ms. Crane, so I can't really go into it with you, but, yes, things like that."

"Thomas wouldn't hurt anyone."

Rollins shifted his bulk around, picked up a cup of coffee, and stirred some cream into it. He tasted the result and then poured the contents of an Equal pack into the cup before he resumed speaking. "But he did go visit Roberta Reynolds."

Alicia crossed her arms and glared at him. "Did he?"

"He never mentioned it to you, that he was going to meet with her?"

"He told me nothing."

Rollins pondered this for a moment. "Ma'am, we got your name off Donovan's answering machine at his apartment. You sounded upset, said what he was working on was dangerous." Alicia didn't take the bait. "Also his place had been ransacked, all his records, files, everything gone."

Alicia started to shake, finally steadying herself by grasping the arm of the chair she was sitting in.

"Ms. Crane, you might want to have some of that coffee. You don't look too good."

"I'm all right." However, she did raise the cup and take several nervous sips.

"Well, if, as you say, someone went through Thomas's apartment, then there must be someone else involved. You should focus your efforts on apprehending that person."

"I'm not arguing with you on that point, but I have to have something to go on. I guess I don't have to tell you that Ms. Reynolds was a very prominent member of the community and we're getting a lot of heat to find her killer, pronto. Now I've already talked to someone at the *Trib*. He told me Donovan was working on a story having to do with lottery winners. And Roberta Reynolds was one of those winners. Now, I'm not a reporter, but when you're talking that kind of money, maybe somebody would have a motive for murder."

Alicia smiled for an instant.

"Something you want to tell me?"

Alicia returned to her prim manner and shook her head.

"Ms. Crane, I've been working homicide since my youngest was born and now he's got his own kids. Don't take this the wrong way, but you're holding out on me and I'd like to know why. Murder isn't something you want to screw around with." He looked at the elegant room. "Murderers and those

476

who *assist* murderers don't end up in places nearly as nice as this one.''

Alicia's eyes bulged at him. "What are you implying?"

"I'm not implying a damn thing. I came here looking for facts. I listened to your voice on Donovan's answering machine. That voice told me two things: First, you were scared for him; second, you knew exactly why you were scared for him."

Alicia kneaded and kneaded her lap with her fisted hands. She closed and opened her eyes several times. Rollins waited patiently while she went through her decision-making process.

When she started speaking it was in quick bursts. Rollins whipped out his notebook and scribbled.

"Thomas had initially started investigating the lottery because he was convinced that several top money management firms were taking the winners' money and either losing it or charging such huge commissions, churning, he called it, that the winners were left with nothing. He also hated the government for, in essence, leaving these poor people exposed to all of that. And then so many of them not understanding how to handle their taxes, and then the IRS coming in and taking everything back. And more. Leaving them with nothing.''

"How did he arrive at that conclusion?"

"Bankruptcies," she said simply. "All these people were winning all this money and then they were declaring bankruptcy."

Rollins scratched his head. "Well, I've read about that from time to time. I always chalked it up to the winners' not being money savvy. You know, spend everything they get, forget to pay taxes, that kind of stuff, like you said. Pretty soon, you can work your way right through all those winnings. Hell, I'd probably do the same thing, just go nuts."

"Well, Thomas didn't think that was all there was to it. But then he discovered something else." She took another sip of coffee, her face coloring prettily as she recalled Thomas Donovan's cleverness.

"Which was?" Rollins prodded.

"Which was the fact that twelve lottery winners in a row didn't declare bankruptcy." ·

"So?"

"So Thomas's research went back many years. In all that time the ratio of winners to bankrupt was completely consistent. Then, right in the middle of this consistency were twelve who didn't. Not only didn't they declare bankruptcy but they grew far wealthier."

Rollins rubbed his chin, unconvinced. "I'm still not seeing a story here."

"Thomas wasn't clear in his mind about that yet. But he was getting closer. He called me regularly from the road to let me know how things were going, what he had found out. That's why I was so worried when I hadn't heard from him."

Rollins looked at his notebook. "Right. You mentioned danger in your phone message."

"Thomas tracked down one of the twelve lottery winners." Alicia paused and struggled to remember the name. "LuAnn somebody. Tyler, that's right, LuAnn Tyler. He said she was charged with murdering somebody right before she won the lottery and then she disappeared. He tracked her down, partly through her tax records. He went to visit her."

"Now, where was this?" Rollins was again scribbling in his notebook.

"Charlottesville. Lovely country, some of the most beautiful estates. Have you ever been?"

"On my salary, I'm not really into estate shopping. What next?"

"He confronted the woman."

478

"And?"

"And she cracked. Or almost did. Thomas said you can always tell by the eyes."

"Uh-huh." Rollins rolled his own eyes. "So what was Donovan's angle?"

"Excuse me?"

"His angle. What story was he going to write that you thought put him in danger?"

"Oh, well, the woman was a murderer. She had killed once, she could kill again."

Rollins smiled lightly. "I see."

"I don't think you're taking this seriously."

"I take my work very seriously. I just don't see the connection. Are you suggesting that this LuAnn person killed Roberta Reynolds? Why would she do that? We don't even know if they knew each other. Are you suggesting that she may have threatened Donovan?"

"I'm not suggesting that LuAnn Tyler threatened or murdered anyone. I mean I have no proof of that."

"Then what?" Rollins was struggling to maintain his patience.

Alicia looked away. "I . . . I don't know. I mean I'm not sure."

Rollins stood up, closing his notebook. "Well, if I need any more information I'll be in touch."

Alicia just sat there, her face pale, her eyes shut. Rollins was almost at the door when she spoke. "The lottery was fixed."

Rollins slowly turned and walked back into the living room. "Fixed?"

"He called two days ago and told me that. Thomas made me promise not to breathe a word to anyone." She clutched at the hem of her skirt in anxiety. "That LuAnn Tyler person practically admitted that the lottery was fixed. Thomas sounded, well, he sounded a little frightened. And now, I'm just so worried about him. He was supposed to call again, but never did."

Rollins parked his bulk on the sofa once more. "What else did he tell you?"

"That he had contacted the other eleven winners, but that only one had called him back." Her lips trembled. "Roberta Reynolds."

"So Donovan did meet with her." His tone was accusatory.

Alicia rubbed a tear from her eye. She didn't speak but merely shook her head. Finally she said, "He had been working on this story for a long time, but he only recently confided in me. He was scared. I could tell in his voice." She cleared her throat. "He had at least arranged to meet with Roberta Reynolds. The meeting was to take place yesterday morning. I haven't heard from him since that time, and he'd promised to call me right after it was over. Oh, God, I know something terrible has happened."

"Did he tell you who fixed the lottery?"

"No, but LuAnn Tyler told him to watch out for somebody. A man. That this person would kill him, that he was on Thomas's trail and would find him. That he was very dangerous. I'm sure this person had something to do with that woman's death."

Rollins sat back and stared sadly at her and took a big gulp of the hot coffee.

Alicia didn't look up. "I told Thomas to go to the police with what he knew."

Rollins sat forward. "Did he?"

She shook her head fiercely. "Dammit no!" A huge breath escaped her lungs. "I pleaded with him to. If someone had fixed the lottery, all that money. I mean people would kill for that. You're a policeman, aren't I right about that?"

"I know people who'd cut your heart out for a couple of singles," was Rollins's chilling reply. He looked down at his empty coffee cup. "Got any more?"

Alicia started. "What? Oh, yes, I just made a fresh pot."

Rollins took out his notepad again. "Okay, when you get back, we'll have to go over every detail and then I'm calling in some reinforcements. I'm not afraid to admit that this one is looking like it's way over my head. You up for a trip to police headquarters?"

Alicia nodded without much enthusiasm and left the room. She came back a couple of minutes later balancing the wooden tray, her eyes focused on the filled coffee cups, trying not to spill them. When she looked up her eyes widened in utter disbelief and she dropped the entire tray on the floor.

"Peter?"

The remnants of Detective Rollins – wig, mustache, facial mask, and malleable rubber padding – were neatly positioned on the wingback chair. Jackson, or Peter Crane, Alicia Crane's elder brother, was looking back at her, his features infinitely troubled as his right cheek rested on his right palm.

Donovan's observation that Bobbie Jo Reynolds had looked a lot like Alicia Crane was right on the mark. However, it had been Peter Crane's alias, Jackson, disguised as Bobbie Jo Reynolds, who looked a lot like Alicia Crane. The family resemblance was remarkable.

"Hello, Alicia."

She stared at the discarded disguise. "What are you doing? What is all this?"

"I think you should sit down. Would you like me to clean up that mess?"

"Don't touch it." She put one hand against the doorjamb to steady herself.

"I didn't mean to upset you so," said Jackson with

481

sudden sincere remorse. "I . . . I guess when faced with confrontation, I'm just more comfortable not being myself." He smiled weakly.

"I don't appreciate this at all. I almost had a heart attack."

He rose quickly, encircled her waist with one of his arms, and guided her over to the sofa. He patted her hand kindly. "I'm sorry, Alicia, I really am."

Alicia again stared over at the remains of the beefy homicide detective. "What is this all about, Peter? Why were you asking me all those questions?"

"Well, I needed to know how much you knew about everything. I needed to know what Donovan had told you."

She jerked her hand from under his. "Thomas? How do you know about Thomas? I haven't seen or spoken to you in three years."

"Has it been that long?" he said evasively. "You don't need anything, do you? You just had to ask."

"Your checks come like clockwork," she said, a bit bitterly. "I don't need any more money. It would have been nice to have seen you once in a while. I know you're very busy, but we are family."

"I know." He looked down for a moment. "I always said I would take care of you. And I always will. Family is family."

"Speaking of, I spoke with Roger the other day."

"And how is our decadent, undeserving younger brother?"

"He needed money, like always."

"I hope you didn't send him any. I gave him enough to last a lifetime, even invested it for him. All he had to do was stay within a reasonable budget."

"There's nothing reasonable about Roger, you know that." She looked at him a little nervously. "I sent him some money." Jackson started to say something, but she hurried on. "I know what you

482

said all those years ago, but I just couldn't let him be thrown out on the street."

"Why not? It might be the best thing that ever happened to him. He shouldn't live in New York. It's too expensive."

"He wouldn't survive. He's not strong, not like Father."

Jackson held his tongue at the mention of their father. The years had not cleared up his sister's blindness in that regard. "Forget it, I'm not going to waste my time discussing Roger."

"I want you to tell me what's going on, Peter."

"When did you meet Donovan?"

"Why?"

"Please just answer the question."

"Almost a year ago. He did a lengthy piece on Father and his distinguished career in the senate. It was a wonderful, compelling testimonial."

Jackson shook his head in disbelief. She would have viewed it that way: the exact opposite of the truth.

"So I called Thomas up to thank him. We had lunch and then dinner and, well, it's been wonderful. Extraordinarily wonderful. Thomas is a noble man with a noble purpose in life."

"Like Father?" Jackson's mouth curled into a smirk.

"Very much like him," she said indignantly.

"It's truly a small world." He shook his head at the irony.

"Why do you say that?"

Jackson stood up and spread his arms to show the entire sweep of the room. "Alicia, where exactly do you think all of this came from?"

"Why, from the family money, of course."

"The family money? That was gone. All of it. Has been for years."

"What are you talking about? I know that Father

ran into some financial difficulties along the way, but he recovered. He always did."

Jackson looked at her with contempt. "He recovered shit, Alicia. He didn't earn a dime of it. It was all made long before he was around. All he did was blow it. My inheritance, your inheritance. He pissed it away on himself and his lousy dreams of greatness. He was a fake and a loser."

She jumped up and slapped his face. "How dare you! Everything you have is because of him."

Jackson slowly rubbed his skin where she had hit him. His real skin was pale, smooth as though he had lived his life in a temple like a Buddhist monk, which in one sense he had.

"Ten years ago, *I* fixed the national lottery," he said quietly, his dark eyes glittery as he stared at her small, stunned face. "All that money, everything you have came from that money. From me. Not dear old Dad."

"What do you mean? How could you—"

Jackson pushed her down on the sofa as he interrupted.

"I collected almost one billion dollars from twelve lottery winners, the very same ones Donovan was investigating. I took their winnings and I invested the money. You remember Grandfather's network of Wall Street elite? He actually *earned* his money. I maintained those contacts over the years for a very specific purpose. With the fortune I amassed from the lottery winners, which Wall Street assumed came from the 'family money,' I was one of their preferred customers. I negotiated the best deals, was given first choice of all the initial public offerings, the sure-fire winners. That's a well-kept secret of the rich, Alicia. They get first dibs on everything: A stock that I get at ten dollars a share right before it hits the market goes to seventy dollars a share in the twenty-four hours after it hits the market. I sell it to the ordinary folks, collect my six hundred percent return, and move on to the next windfall. It was like printing money; it's all in who you know and what you bring to the table. When you bring a billion dollars, believe me, everybody sits up and takes notice. The rich get richer and the poor never will."

Alicia's lips had begun trembling halfway through her brother's explanation, as his speech and mannerisms grew more and more intense, more and more feverish. "Where is Thomas?" Her question was barely audible.

Jackson looked away and licked his dry lips. "He was no good for you, Alicia. No good at all. An opportunist. And I'm sure he loved all of this. All that you had. All that I had given you."

"*Was? Was* no good?" Alicia stood up, her hands clamped so tightly together the skin looked boiled.

"Where is he? What have you done to him?"

Jackson stared at her, searching her features for something. It suddenly occurred to him that he was looking for some redeeming quality. From afar he had long held idyllic visions of his only sister, putting her perhaps on a pedestal. Face-to-face with her he found that image was unsustainable. The tone of his response was casual, his words far from casual, as he finally made up his mind.

"I killed him, Alicia."

She stood there frozen for an instant and then started toppling to the floor. He grabbed her and laid her on the couch, this time not so gently. "Now don't be this way. There will be other men. I can assure you of that. You can walk the earth searching for Father. Donovan wasn't him, but I'm sure you'll keep trying." He didn't try to hide the sarcasm.

She wasn't listening to him, however. The tears stained her cheeks.

He continued despite her tears, pacing in front of her, the professor in front of his class of one. "You'll have to leave the country, Alicia. I erased your phone message to Donovan, so the police won't have that to go on. However, since your relationship has endured for a year, it must be well known to others. The police will come calling at some point. I'll make all the arrangements. As I recall, you've always loved New Zealand. Or perhaps Austria. We had several lovely times there as children."

"Stop it! Stop it, you animal."

He turned to find her on her feet.

"Alicia—"

"I'm not going anywhere."

"Let me be quite clear. You know too much. The police will ask questions. You have no experience in these matters. They will get the truth from you quite easily."

"You're right about that. I intend to call them right now and tell them everything."

She started for the phone, but he blocked her way. "Alicia, be reasonable."

She hit him with her fists as violently as she could. They did no physical damage to him; however, the blows conjured up the memory of another violent confrontation with another family member. His father, back then, had been physically stronger than he, was able to dominate him in ways that Jackson had never let himself be dominated since.

"I loved him, damn you! I loved Thomas," Alicia shrieked in his face.

Jackson focused a pair of watery eyes upon her. "I loved someone too," he said. "Someone who should have loved me back, respected me, but who didn't." Despite the years of pain, of guilt and embarrassment, Jack's son still held long-buried feelings for the old man. Feelings that he had never dwelt

486

upon or vocalized until now. The resurgence of this emotional maelstrom had a violent impact on him.

He grabbed her by the shoulders and threw her roughly on the sofa.

"Peter—"

"Shut up, Alicia." He sat down next to her. "You're leaving the country. You are not going to call the police. Do you understand?"

"You're crazy, you're insane. Oh, God, I don't believe this is happening."

"Actually, right now, I'm absolutely certain I'm the most rational member in the family." He stared into her eyes and repeated the words very slowly. "You're not talking to anyone, Alicia, do you understand?"

She looked at his eyes and suddenly shivered to the depths of her soul. For the first time during this confrontation, terror had suddenly replaced her anger. It had been a long time since she had seen her brother. The boy she had happily romped with, and whose maturity and intelligence she had been fascinated by, was now unrecognizable to her. The man across from her was not her brother. This manifestation was something else altogether.

She hastily changed course and spoke as calmly as she could. "Yes, Peter, I understand. I . . . I'll pack tonight."

Jackson's face took on a level of despair that it had not carried for many years. He had read her thoughts, her fears; they were so plainly written on the thin parchment of her soft features. His fingers clutched the large throw pillow on the sofa between them.

"Where would you like to go, Alicia?"

"Anywhere, Peter, anywhere you say. New Zealand, you mentioned New Zealand. That would be fine."

"It is a beautiful country. Or Austria, as I said, we had good times there, didn't we?" He tightened his grip on the pillow. "Didn't we?" he asked again.

"Yes we did." Her eyes dipped to follow his movements and she tried to swallow but her throat was too dry. "Perhaps I could travel there first and then on to New Zealand."

"And not a word to the police? You promise?" He lifted up the pillow.

Her chin trembled uncontrollably as she watched the pillow come toward her. "Peter. Please. Please don't."

His words were stated very precisely. "My name is Jackson, Alicia. Peter Crane doesn't live here anymore."

With a sudden pounce, he pushed her flat against the couch, the pillow completely covering her face. She fought hard, kicking, scratching, gyrating her body, but she was so small, so weak; he barely felt her fighting for her life. He had spent so many years making his body hard as rock; she had spent that time waiting for a precise replica of her father to stride gallantly into her life, her muscles and her mind growing soft in the process.

Soon, it was over. As he watched, the violent movements diminished quickly and then stopped altogether. Her pale right arm slid down to her side and then dangled off the couch. He removed the pillow and forced himself to look down at her. She at least deserved that. The mouth was partially open, the eyes wide and staring. He quickly closed them and sat there with her, patting her hand gently. He did not try to hold back his own tears. That would've done no good. He struggled to remember the last time he had cried but couldn't. How healthy was it when you couldn't even recall?

He placed her arms across her chest but then

decided to have them clasped at her waist instead. He carefully lifted her legs up on the sofa and put the pillow he had used to kill her under her head, arranging her pretty hair so that it swept out evenly over the pillow. He thought she was very lovely in death despite the utter stillness. There was a peace there, a serenity that was at least heartening to him, as though what he had just done wasn't all that terrible.

He hesitated for a moment and then went ahead: He checked her pulse and laid her hand back down. If she'd still been alive, then he would've left the room, fled the country, and left it at that. He wouldn't have touched her like that again. She was family after all. But she was dead. He rose and looked down at her one last time.

It needn't have ended this way. Now all the family he had left was the useless Roger. He should go kill his brother right now. It should have been him lying there, not his cherished Alicia. However, Roger wasn't worth the effort. He froze for an instant as an idea occurred to him. Perhaps his brother could play a supporting role in this production. He would call Roger and make him an offer. An offer he knew his younger brother would be unable to resist as it would be all cash; the most potent drug in existence.

He gathered up the elements of his disguise, and methodically reapplied them, all the time making little darting glances at his dead sister. He had coated his hands with a lacquer-like substance, so he wasn't concerned about leaving fingerprints. He left by the back door. They would find her soon enough. Alicia had said her housekeeper had gone out to run an errand. It was a better than even chance that the police would think Thomas Donovan had continued his homicidal rampage by murdering his lady friend, Alicia Morgan Crane. Her obituary would be extensive, her family had been very important; there would be much to write about. And at some point, Jackson would have to come back, as himself once more, to bury her. Roger could hardly be trusted to do that. *I am sorry, Alicia. It shouldn't have come to this.* This unexpected turn of events had come closer than anything he could remember to completely immobilizing him. Above all else he cherished complete control and it suddenly had been stripped from him. He looked down at his hands, the instruments of his sister's death. His sister. Even now his legs felt rubbery, his body not in sync with his mind.

As he walked down the street, still reeling from what he had just done, Jackson's mental energies finally were able to focus on the one person he clearly saw as responsible for all of it.

LuAnn Tyler would experience the brunt of everything he was now feeling. The pain that slashed so viciously through him would be multiplied a hundredfold upon her until she would beg him to just finish her, make her stop breathing because every breath would be a hell, would be beyond what any person could endure. Even her.

And the grand part of it all was that he would not have to go looking for her. She would come to him. She would run to him with all the speed and strength her extraordinary physical specimen of a body could inspire. For he would have something that LuAnn would go anywhere, do anything for. He would hold something that LuAnn Tyler would die for. *And so you will LuAnn Tyler slash Catherine Savage.* As he disappeared down the street he swore this, over the mental image of a still-warm body whose dear face strongly resembled his own.

FIFTY-THREE

For the tenth time Riggs looked around the Mall and then checked his watch. In cutting his deal with the FBI, he had just shimmied out on to the most fragile limb in the world and LuAnn was three hours late. If she never showed up, where did that leave him? Jackson was still out there, and Riggs doubted if the knife would miss its mark a second time. If he didn't produce Jackson, fulfill his deal with his former employer, and have his cover reestablished, the cartel members who had sworn to kill him five years ago would soon learn that he was alive and they would surely try again. He couldn't return to his house. His business was probably already going to hell, and to top it off, he had five bucks in his pocket and no car. If he could have screwed up his life to any greater degree he was at a loss as to how.

He slumped on a bench and stared up at the Washington Monument while the cold wind whipped up and down the flat, open space that stretched from the Lincoln Memorial to the United States Capitol. The sky was overcast; it would be raining again soon. You could smell it in the air. Just wonderful. *And you're right between a rock and a hard place, Mr. Riggs,* he said to himself. His emotional barometer had dropped to its lowest point since finding out his wife had perished in the gang attack five years ago. Had it really been less than one week ago that he had been leading a relatively normal life?

Building things for wealthy people, reading books by his woodstove, attending a few night classes at the university, thinking seriously about taking a real vacation for a change?

He blew on his cold fingers and stuffed them in his pockets. His injured shoulder ached. He was just about to leave when the hand touched his neck.

"I'm sorry."

As he turned his head, his spirits soared with such swiftness that he felt dizzy. But he couldn't help smiling. He needed desperately to smile.

"Sorry for what?"

He watched as LuAnn settled in beside him, slipping her arm through his. She didn't answer right away. After staring off for a minute and then taking a heavy breath, she turned to him, stroked his hand with hers.

"I had some misgivings."

"About me?"

"I shouldn't have. After all you've done, I shouldn't have any doubts left."

He looked at her kindly. "Sure you should. Everybody has doubts. After the last ten years, you should have more than most." He patted her hand, looked into her eyes, noted their moist edges, and then said, "But you're here now. You came. So it must be okay, right? I passed the test?"

She simply nodded her head, unable to speak.

"I vote for finding a warm place where I can fill you in on developments and we can discuss our plan of attack. Sound good?"

"I'm all yours." Her grip tightened on his hand as though she would never let go. And right now, that was just fine with him.

They ditched the Honda, which was acting up, and rented a sedan. Riggs was getting tired of hot-wiring the car anyway.

492

They drove to the outskirts of western Fairfax County and stopped for lunch at a nearly empty restaurant. On the drive out Riggs filled her in on the meeting at the Hoover Building. They walked past the bar area and sat at a table in the corner. LuAnn absently watched the bartender tinker with the TV to better the reception of a daytime soap he was watching. He slouched against the bar and pried between his teeth with a swizzle stick as he watched the small screen. It would be wonderful, she thought, to be that relaxed, that laid back.

They ordered food and then Riggs pulled out the newspaper. He didn't say a word until LuAnn had read the entire story.

"Good Lord."

"Donovan should have listened to you."

"You think Jackson killed him?"

Riggs nodded grimly. "Probably set him up. Had Reynolds call him, say she was gonna spill her guts. Jackson is there and pops them both with the result that Donovan gets blamed for it all."

LuAnn let her head rest in her hands.

Riggs gently touched her head. "Hey, LuAnn, you tried to warn the guy. There was nothing else you could do."

"I could have said no to Jackson ten years ago. Then none of this would've happened."

"Yeah, but I bet if you had, he would've done you right then and there."

LuAnn wiped her eyes with her sleeve. "So now I've got this great deal with the FBI you negotiated for me, and in order to finalize it all we need to do is drop a net over Lucifer." She sipped on her coffee. "Would you care to tell me how we're going to do that?"

Riggs put away the paper. "I've been giving it a lot of thought as you might have guessed. The problem

493

is we can't be too simplistic or too complicated. Either way, he'll smell a trap."

"I don't think he'll take another meeting with me."

"No, I wasn't going to suggest that. He wouldn't show, but he'd send somebody to kill you. That's way too dangerous."

"Didn't you know, I like danger, Matthew. If I wasn't constantly smothered in the stuff, I wouldn't know what to do with myself. Okay, no meeting, what else?"

"Like I said before, if we can find out who he really is, track him down, then we might be in business." Riggs paused as their food came. After the waitress left he picked up his sandwich and started talking in between bites. "You don't remember anything about the guy? I mean anything that could start us in the right direction to finding out who he really is?"

"He was always disguised."

"The financial documents he sent you?"

"They were from a firm in Switzerland. I've got some back at the house, which I guess I can't get to. Even with our deal?" She raised an eyebrow.

"I wouldn't advise that, LuAnn. The Feds run across you now, they might forget all about our little deal."

"I've got some other documents at my bank in New York."

"Still too risky."

"I could write the firm in Switzerland, but I don't think they're going to know anything. And if they do, I don't think they're going to talk. I mean, that's why people bank in Switzerland, right?"

"Okay, okay. Anything else? There's gotta be something you remember about the guy. The way he dressed, smelled, talked, walked. Any particular interests? How about Charlie? Would he have any ideas?"

LuAnn hesitated. "We could ask him," she said, wiping her hands on her napkin, "but I wouldn't bet on it. Charlie told me he'd never even met Jackson face-to-face. It was always over the phone."

Riggs slumped back and touched his injured arm. "I just don't see any way to get to him, Matthew."

"There is a way, LuAnn. In fact I had already concluded it was the only way. I was just going through the motions with all those questions."

"How?"

"You have a phone number where you can reach him?"

"Yes. So?"

"We set up a meeting."

"But you just said—"

"The meeting will be with me, not you."

LuAnn half stood up in her anger. "No way, Matthew, there is no way in hell I'm going to let you near that guy. Look what he did to you." She pointed at his arm. "The next time will be worse. A lot worse."

"It would've been a lot worse if you hadn't messed up his aim." He smiled tenderly at her. "Look, I'll call him. I tell him that you're leaving the country and all these problems behind. You know Donovan is dead, so Jackson doesn't have that issue anymore. Everybody's home free." LuAnn was vigorously shaking her head as she sat back down.

"Then I'll tell him," Riggs continued, "that I'm not such a happy camper. I've got it all figured out: I'm a little tired of construction work, and I want my payoff."

"No, Matthew, no!"

"Jackson figures I'm a criminal anyway. Trying to extort him wouldn't seem out of line at all. I'll tell him I bugged your bedroom, that I've got a recording of a conversation he had with you, that night at your house, where you both talked a lot about things."

"Are you nuts?"

"I want money. Lots of it. Then he gets the tape."

"He will kill you."

Now Riggs's face darkened. "He'll do that anyway. I don't like sitting around waiting for the other shoe to drop. I'd rather go on the offensive. Make him sweat for a change. And I may not be the killing machine he is, but I'm no slouch either. I'm a veteran FBI agent. I've killed before, in the line of duty, and if you think I'd hesitate one second before blowing his brains out, then you really don't know me."

Riggs looked down for a moment, trying to make himself calm down. His plan was risky, but what plan wouldn't be? When he looked back up at LuAnn, he was about to say something else but the look on her face froze the words in his mouth.

"LuAnn?"

"Oh, no!" Her voice was filled with panic.

"What is it? What's the matter?" Riggs grabbed her shoulder, which was quivering. She didn't answer him. She was looking at something over his shoulder. He whirled around, expecting to see Jackson coming for them, foot-long knives in either hand. He scanned the nearly empty restaurant and then his eyes settled on the TV where a special news report was being broadcast.

A woman's face spread across the screen. Two hours ago, Alicia Crane, prominent Washingtonian, had been found dead in her home by her house-keeper. The evidence collected so far suggested that she had been murdered. Riggs's eyes widened as he listened to the broadcaster mention that Thomas Donovan, prime suspect in the Roberta Reynolds murder, apparently had been dating Alicia Crane.

496

LuAnn could not pull her eyes away from that face. She had seen those features, those eyes staring at her from the front porch of the cottage. Jackson's eyes bored into her.

His real face.

She had shuddered when she had actually seen it, or realized what she was seeing. She had hoped to never lay eyes on those features again. Now she was staring at them. They were planted on the TV.

When Riggs looked back at her, she raised a shaky finger toward the screen. "That's Jackson," she said, her voice breaking. "Dressed up like a woman."

Riggs looked back at the screen. That couldn't be Jackson, he thought. He turned back to LuAnn. "How do you know? You said he was always in disguise."

LuAnn could barely take her eyes away from the face on the screen. "At the cottage, when he and I went through the window. We fought and his face, plastic, rubber, whatever, came off. I saw his real face. That face." She pointed to the screen.

Riggs's first thought was the correct one. *Family?* God, could it be? The connection to Donovan couldn't be a coincidence, could it? He raced to the phone.

"Sorry I lost your boys, George. Hope that didn't cost you any brownie points with the top brass."

"Where the hell are you?" Masters demanded.

"Just listen." Riggs recounted the news story he had just heard.

"You think he's related to Alicia Crane?" Masters asked, the excitement echoing in his voice, his anger at Riggs completely gone, for now.

"Could be. Ages are about right. Older or younger brother maybe, I don't know."

"Thank God for strong genes."

"What's your game plan?"

"We check her family. Shouldn't be too hard to do. Her father was a U.S. senator for years. Very prominent lineage. If she has brothers, cousins, whatever, we hit 'em fast. Bring them in for questioning. Hell, it can't hurt."

"I don't think he's going to be waiting for you to knock on the front door."

"They never do, do they?"

"If he is around, be careful, George."

"Yeah. If you're right about all this—"

Riggs finished for him: "The guy just killed his own sister. I'd hate to see what he'd do to a non-family member."

Riggs hung up. For the very first time he actually felt hopeful. He was under no delusions that Jackson would be around for the FBI to take into custody. He would be flushed out, cut off from his home base. He'd be pissed, full of revenge. Well, let him be. He'd have to cut Riggs's heart out before he'd get to LuAnn. And they wouldn't be sitting targets. Now was the time to keep on the move.

Ten minutes later they were in the car heading for points unknown.

FIFTY-FOUR

Jackson boarded the Delta shuttle for New York. He needed additional supplies and he was going to pick up Roger. He couldn't count on him to travel by himself and get to where he was supposed to be. Then they would head back south. During the short flight Jackson checked in with the man following Charlie and Lisa. They had made a rest stop. Charlie had talked on the phone. No doubt checking in with LuAnn. They had gone on and were now close to reentering Virginia on the southern side. It was all working out very well. An hour later, Jackson was in a cab threading its way through Manhattan toward his apartment.

Horace Parker looked around with intense curiosity. A doorman for over fifty years at a building where average apartments covered four thousand square feet and went for five million, and the penthouse that covered triple that space and went for twenty mil, he had never seen anything like this before. He watched as the small army of men in FBI windbreakers swept through the lobby and into the private elevator that went only to the penthouse. They looked deadly serious and had the weaponry to prove it.

He went back outside and looked up and down the street. A cab pulled up and out stepped Jackson. Parker immediately went over to him. The doorman had known him for most of his life. Years ago he had skipped pennies in the lobby's massive fountain with Jackson and his younger brother, Roger. To earn extra money he had baby-sat them and taken them to Central Park on the weekends; he had bought them their first beers when they were barely into puberty. Finally, he had watched them grow up and then leave the nest. The Cranes, he had heard, had fallen on hard times, and they had left New York. Peter Crane, though, had come back and bought the Penthouse. Apparently, he had done awfully well for himself.

"Good evening, Horace," Jackson said cordially.

"Evening, Mr. Crane," Parker said and tipped his cap.

Jackson started past him.

"Mr. Crane, sir?"

Jackson turned to him. "What is it? I'm in a bit of a hurry, Horace."

Parker looked upward. "There's some men come to the building, Mr. Crane. They went right up to your apartment. A bunch of them. FBI. Guns and everything, never seen nothing like it. They're up there right now. I think they're waiting for you to get home, sir."

Jackson's reply was calm and immediate. "Thank you for the information, Horace. Simply a misunderstanding."

Jackson put out his hand, which Parker took. Jackson immediately turned and walked away from the apartment building. When Parker opened his hand, there was a wad of hundred-dollar bills there. He looked around discreetly before stuffing the cash in his pocket and taking up his position by the door once more.

From the shadows of an alley across the street, Jackson turned and looked up at his apartment building. His eyes kept going up and up until they came to rest upon the windows of the penthouse. His penthouse. He could see the silhouettes move slowly across the windows, and his lips started to tremble at this outrageous invasion of his home. The possibility that they could have traced him to his personal residence had not occurred to him. How in the hell? He couldn't worry about it now, though. He went down the cross street and made a phone call. Twenty minutes later a limousine picked him up. He called his brother and told him to leave his apartment immediately – not even bothering to pack a bag – and meet Jackson in front of the St. James Theater. Jackson wasn't sure how the police had found out his identity, but he couldn't be sure they wouldn't wind up at Roger Crane's apartment at any minute. Then he made a quick stop to gather together some necessary supplies from another smaller apartment he kept under a phony name. Under the ownership of one of his myriad corporate shells he maintained a private jet and full-time crew at La Guardia. He called ahead so that the pilot on duty would be able to file his flight plan as quickly as possible. Jackson did not intend to spend time twiddling his thumbs in the waiting area. The limo would take them right to the plane. That accomplished, he collected his brother from in front of the theater.

Roger was two years younger and slimly built but wiry like his older brother. He also shared the same shock of dark hair and delicate facial features. He was certainly curious about his brother's abrupt return to his life. "I couldn't believe you called like that out of the blue. What's up, Peter?"

"Shut up, I need to think." He suddenly turned to his younger brother. "Have you seen the news?"

He shook his head. "I don't usually watch TV. Why?"

501

He obviously didn't know of Alicia's death. That was good. Jackson didn't answer his brother; he settled back in the seat, his mind racing through a seemingly infinite number of scenarios.

In a half hour they were at La Guardia Airport. Soon they had left the Manhattan skyline behind on their way south.

The FBI did converge on Roger Crane's small apartment building, but a little too late. Yet they were far more intrigued by what they had discovered at Peter Crane's penthouse.

Masters and Berman, walking around the massive penthouse, came across Jackson's makeup and archives rooms and his computerized control center.

"Holy shit," Berman said, his hands in his pockets as he stared at the masks, makeup bins, and racks of clothing.

Masters held the scrapbook gingerly in his gloved hands. FBI technicians roamed everywhere collecting evidence.

"Looks like Riggs was right. One guy. Maybe we *can* survive all this," Masters said.

"So what's our next move?"

Masters answered immediately. "We focus on Peter Crane. Put a blanket on the airports and train and bus stations. I want road blocks posted on all the major arteries leading out of town. You're to instruct all the men that he's extremely dangerous and a master of disguise. Send out photos of the guy everywhere, fat lot of good that'll do us. We've cut off his home base, but he's obviously got enormous financial resources. If we do manage to track him down, I want no unnecessary chances. Tell the men that if there's the slightest threat, to shoot him down."

"How about Riggs and Tyler?" Berman asked.

"So long as they don't get in the way, they'll be okay. If they get mixed up with Crane along the way, well, there's no guarantee. I'm not going to jeopardize my men to make sure they don't get hurt. As far as I'm concerned LuAnn Tyler belongs in jail. But that's why we've got some ammo with her. We can send her to jail or threaten to. I think she'll keep her mouth shut. Why don't you go oversee the rest of the evidence collection."

While Berman did so, Masters sat down and read the background information on LuAnn that accompanied her photo.

He was finishing up when Berman returned.

"You think Crane's going to go after Tyler now?" Berman asked.

Masters didn't answer. Instead he looked down at the picture of LuAnn Tyler staring back at him from the photo album. He now understood why she had been picked as a lottery winner. Why they had all been picked. He now had a much clearer idea of who LuAnn Tyler was and why she had done what she had. She had been destitute, stuck in a cycle of poverty, with an infant daughter. No hope. All of the chosen winners had shared this common denominator: no hope. They were ripe for this man's scheme. Masters's features betrayed the emotions he was feeling. Right at that very moment, and for a number of reasons, George Masters was starting to feel immense guilt.

It was nearing midnight when Riggs and LuAnn stopped at a motel. After checking in, Riggs phoned George Masters. The FBI agent had just returned from New York and he detailed to Riggs what had happened since they had last spoken. After receiving this briefing Riggs hung up the phone and looked over at a very anxious LuAnn.

"What happened? What did they say?"

Riggs shook his head. "As expected. Jackson wasn't there, but they found enough evidence to keep him in prison for the rest of his life and then some. Including a scrapbook on all the lottery winners."

"So he *was* related to Alicia Crane."

Riggs nodded grimly. "Her older brother, Peter. Peter Crane is Jackson. Or at least everything points that way."

LuAnn was wide-eyed. "Then he murdered his own sister."

"Looks that way."

"Because she knew too much? Because of Donovan?"

"Right. Jackson couldn't take a chance on that. Maybe he shows up disguised or maybe as his true self. He gets what he wants out of her, maybe he tells her he killed Donovan. Who knows. She apparently was dating the guy. She might have gone nuts, threatened to go to the police. At some point he murdered her, I feel sure of that."

LuAnn shuddered. "Where do you think he is?"

Riggs shrugged. "The Feds got to his house, but from the looks of the place the man has money to burn, a million different places he could go, a dozen faces and identities he could go there under. It's not going to be easy to catch him."

"To finish our deal?" LuAnn's tone was slightly sarcastic.

"We handed the Feds his friggin' identity. They're at his 'world' headquarters right now. When I said we'd deliver him, I didn't necessarily mean in a box with a ribbon on it, laid on the doorstep of the Hoover Building. As far as I'm concerned we've lived up to our end of the bargain."

LuAnn let out a deep breath. "So does that mean

everything's square? With the FBI? And Georgia?"

"We'll have some details to work out, but yeah, I think so. Unknown to them, I recorded the entire meeting at the Hoover Building. I've got Masters, the director of the FBI, and the attorney general of the United States herself, acting upon the authority of the president of the United States no less, all on tape agreeing to the deal I proposed. They've got to play straight with us now. But I've gotta be straight with you too. The IRS is going to put a big dent in your bank account. In fact after so many years of compounded penalties and interest, I'm not sure how much money you're going to have left, if any."

"I don't care about that. I want to pay my taxes, even if it takes everything I've got. The truth is, I stole the money to begin with. I just want to know if I have to keep looking over my shoulder for the rest of my life."

"You're not going to prison, if that's what you mean." He touched her cheek with his hand. "You don't look too happy."

She blushed and smiled at him. "I am." Her smile quickly faded though.

"I know what you're thinking."

She blurted out, "Until they catch Jackson, my life's not worth spit. Or yours. Or Charlie's." Her lips trembled. "Or Lisa's." She suddenly jumped up and grabbed the phone.

"What are you doing?" Riggs asked.

"I need to see my daughter. I need to know that she's safe."

"Wait a minute, what are you going to tell them?"

"That we can meet up somewhere. I want her near me. Nothing's going to happen to her without it happening to me first."

"LuAnn, look—"

"This subject isn't open for discussion." Her tone was ferocious.

505

"All right, all right, I hear you. But where are we going to meet them?"

LuAnn passed a hand over her forehead. "I don't know. Does it matter?"

Riggs said, "Where are they now?"

"The last I heard, they were heading back into southern Virginia."

He rubbed his chin. "What's Charlie driving?"

"The Range Rover."

"Terrific. It'll hold all of us. We'll meet them wherever they are right now. We'll leave the rental and head out. Go somewhere and wait for the FBI to do its thing. So call them and I'll run up to that all-night burger place we saw on the way in and get us some food."

"Good enough."

When Riggs got back with two bags of food, LuAnn was no longer on the phone.

"You reach them?"

"They're at a motel on the outskirts of Danville, Virginia. But I need to call them back and let them know when we're going to be there." She looked around. "Where the hell are we?"

"We're in Edgewood, Maryland, north of Baltimore. Danville is a little over a hundred miles south of Charlottesville, which means we're about five or six hours from Danville."

"Okay, if we start right now—"

"LuAnn, it's after midnight. They're probably in bed, right?"

"So?"

"So, we can catch some sleep, which we both really need, get up early, and meet them tomorrow around noon."

"I don't want to wait. I want Lisa safe with me."

"LuAnn, driving when you're exhausted isn't real safe. Even if we start right now, we won't make it

506

until five or six in the morning. Nothing's going to happen between now and then. Come on, I think we've had enough excitement for one day. And if Lisa knows you're coming tonight, she won't get a wink of sleep."

"I don't care. I'd rather she be sleepy and safe."

Riggs shook his head slowly. "LuAnn, there's another reason we might not want to hook up with them right now, and it has to do with keeping Lisa safe."

"What are you talking about?"

Riggs put his hands in his pockets and leaned up against the wall. "Jackson is somewhere out there, that we know. Now, the last time we saw him he was running off into the woods. He could have easily come back and followed us."

"But what about Donovan and Bobbie Jo Reynolds and Alicia Crane? He killed them."

"We believe he killed them, or had someone kill them. Or he could've killed all of them personally and hired someone to follow us. That man has a deep pocketbook; there isn't much he can't buy."

LuAnn reflected briefly on Anthony Romanello. Jackson had hired him to kill her. "So Jackson could know about your meeting with the FBI? He could know where we are right now?"

"And if we go running off to see Lisa, then we lead him right to her as well."

LuAnn slumped down on the bed. "We can't do that, Matthew," she said wearily.

He rubbed her shoulders. "I know."

"But I want to see my little girl. Can't I do that?"

Riggs thought for a few minutes and then sat on the bed beside her and held her hands with his. "Okay, we'll stay here for the night. It would be a lot easier for someone to follow us at night and remain unseen. Tomorrow, we'll get an early start and head

507

down to Danville. I'll keep an eagle eye out for anyone remotely suspicious. As an undercover agent, I got pretty good at that. We'll take secondary roads, make frequent stops, and occasionally take the interstate. It'll be impossible for anyone to trail us. We'll meet Charlie and Lisa at the motel and then we'll have Charlie take her directly to the local FBI office in Charlottesville. We'll follow in our car but we won't go in. I don't want them getting hold of you just yet. But since we struck a deal with the Feds, we might as well avail ourselves of some of their protection resources. How's that sound?"

She smiled. "So I'll see Lisa tomorrow?"

He cupped her chin in his hand. "Tomorrow."

LuAnn called Charlie back, setting the meeting time at one o'clock the following day at the motel in Danville. With Charlie, Riggs, and herself around her little girl, Jackson could just come on and try something, because she liked their odds of survival under those circumstances.

They slid into bed and Riggs wrapped his good arm around her slim waist and snuggled against her. His 9-mm was under his pillow, a chair wedged tightly under the door lock. He had unscrewed a light bulb, broken it, and sprinkled the remains in front of the door. Although he didn't expect anything to happen, he wanted as much advance warning as he could get if it did.

As he lay next to her he was both confident and uneasy. She apparently sensed this and turned to face him, her hand gently stroking his face.

"Got something on your mind?"

"Anticipation, I guess. When I was with the FBI I had to work hard to keep my patience. I seem to have a natural aversion to delayed gratification."

"That all?" Riggs slowly nodded. "You sure you're not sorry you got involved in all this?"

508

He pulled her closer to him. "Why in the world would I be?"

"Well, let me list some things for you. You've been stabbed, and came within an inch of dying. A madman is probably going to try his best to kill us. You stuck your neck out with the FBI for me and your cover is blown, with the result that the people who tried to kill you before may try again. You're running around the country with me trying to stay one step ahead of everybody and your business is going to hell and it doesn't look like I'll have two dimes to rub together to even begin to repay you for everything you've done. That cover it?"

Riggs stroked her hair and figured he might as well say it now. Who knew how things were going to go. He might not get another chance.

"You left out the part about me falling in love with you."

Her breath caught as her eyes drifted over him, taking in every subtle quiver, trying to give them all simultaneous meaning. All the while his words echoed in her head. She tried to say something but couldn't.

He filled in the silence. "I know it's probably the world's worst timing, but I just wanted you to know."

"Oh, Matthew," she finally managed to say. Her voice was trembling, everything about her was.

"I'm sure you've heard those words before. Lots of times, from guys probably a lot better suited—"

She covered his mouth with her hand but she didn't say anything for a long minute. He gently kissed her fingers.

Her voice was husky as though she were reaching down deep in order to utter the words. "Other men have said them. But this is the first time I've really been listening."

She stroked his hair and then her lips searched out and found his in the darkness and sunk in, slowly and deeply. They blindly undressed each other, their fingers probing and gently caressing. LuAnn began to softly cry as the unlikely twins of nervous fear and intense happiness fought for dominance. Finally, she just stopped thinking and gave herself over to what she had been looking for for so many years, across so many countries; from precious dreams that rudely dissolved into nightmares, which viciously framed realities that never came close to inspiring in her any more than an extreme ambivalence about her life. She clutched Matthew Riggs hard, as if realizing that this might be her last chance. Their bodies gripped each other for a long time before relaxing. They fell into an exhausted sleep safely in each other's arms.

FIFTY-FIVE

Charlie rubbed the sleep from his eyes and stared over at the phone. It had been a couple of hours since LuAnn had filled him in on all the recent developments and he still couldn't get to sleep. So Jackson was really Peter Crane. That information personally did him no good, but Charlie figured it would help immeasurably the authorities' efforts to track the man down. On the downside, if Jackson knew his identity had been discovered, Charlie figured he would be one pissed-off person. And Charlie wouldn't want anyone he cared for to be in the vicinity of the gentleman if that was the case.

He pulled himself up from the couch. His knees were aching more than usual. All the driving was getting to him. He was very much looking forward to seeing LuAnn. And Riggs too, he supposed. Sounded like the guy had really come through for LuAnn. If he could pull all this off, well, it would be a miracle.

He went into the adjoining room and checked on Lisa. She was still sleeping soundly. He looked at her delicate features, seeing so much of her mother in them. She was going to be tall too. The last ten years had gone by so fast. Where would they all be next week? Where would he be? Maybe with Riggs in the equation, his run was coming to an end. He had no doubt that LuAnn would take care of him financially, but it would never be the same. But what the hell, the whirlwind that represented the last ten years with her and Lisa had been far more than he deserved anyway.

The ringing phone startled him. He checked his watch. Almost two A.M. He snatched up the receiver.

"Charlie?"

Charlie didn't recognize the voice at first. "Who's this?"

"Matt Riggs."

"Riggs? Where's LuAnn? Is she okay?"

"She's more than okay. They caught him. They caught Jackson." His tone was one of unbridled joy.

"Christ Almighty. Hallelujah! Where?"

"In Charlottesville. The FBI had put a team of agents together at the airport and he and his brother walked right into it. I guess he was coming to pay LuAnn back."

"His brother?"

"Roger. The FBI doesn't know if he's involved in all this, but I don't think they care. They've got Peter Crane. They want LuAnn to come to Washington in the morning to give a deposition."

"Tomorrow? What about meeting us down here?"

"That's why I called. I want you and Lisa to get packed up right now and meet us in Washington. At the Hoover Building. Ninth Street and Pennsylvania Avenue. They'll be expecting you. I set it all up. If you leave now, you can meet us for breakfast. I personally want to celebrate."

"And the FBI? The murder charge?"

"All taken care of, Charlie. LuAnn's home free."

"That's great, Riggs. That's the most wonderful news I've heard in I can't remember how long. Where's LuAnn?"

"She's on the other phone talking to the FBI. Tell Lisa that her mother loves her and can't wait to see her."

512

"You got it." He hung up and immediately started to pack. He would've loved to have seen Jackson's face when the FBI busted him. The prick. He figured he'd pack the car before waking Lisa. Might as well let her sleep as long as possible. When she heard the news about her mother Charlie was sure further sleep would not be possible for the little girl. It looked like Riggs had come through after all.

His heart lighter than it had been in years, Charlie, a bag under each arm, opened the front door.

He immediately froze. The man was standing in the doorway, his face covered by a black ski mask, a pistol in his hand. With a scream of rage, Charlie threw the bag at him, knocking the gun free. Next, Charlie grabbed the man by the mask and hurled him into the room, where he slammed against a wall and went down. Before the man could get up, Charlie was on top of him, hammering him with lefts and rights, his old boxing skills coming back as though he had never left the ring.

The piston-like battering took its toll as the man slumped down, groaning from the furious beating, and lay still. Charlie turned his head as he felt the second presence in the room.

"Hello, Charlie." Jackson closed the door behind him.

As soon as he recognized the voice, Charlie leapt for him, surprising Jackson with his quickness. The twin darts from the stun gun hit Charlie in the chest, but not before his massive fist collided with Jackson's chin, knocking him back against the door. However, Jackson continued to squeeze the trigger, sending the massive electrical current into Charlie's body.

Charlie was on his knees using all of his strength to try to rise, to kick the shit out of the man, to beat him into oblivion where he could hurt no one else.

513

He tried to propel himself forward, every mental impulse in his brain craving nothing less than the man's complete destruction. But his body refused to follow his orders. As he slowly sank to the floor, he stared at a terrified Lisa standing in the doorway leading into the bedroom.

He tried to say something, tried to scream to her to run, to run like hell, but all that came out was something that would hardly qualify as a whisper.

He watched in horror as Jackson staggered up, flew over to Lisa, and pressed something against her mouth. The girl struggled valiantly but it was no use. As her nostrils sucked in the chloroform she was soon on the floor next to Charlie.

Jackson wiped the blood from his face and roughly pulled his associate up. "Take her to the car and don't let anyone see you."

The man nodded dully, his entire body one large hurt from Charlie's fists.

Charlie watched helplessly as the man carried the unconscious Lisa out. Then his eyes slid over to Jackson, who knelt down next to him, rubbing his chin gingerly.

Then, speaking in a voice that exactly impersonated Riggs, he said, "They caught Jackson. They caught him. I feel like celebrating." Then Jackson laughed out loud.

Charlie didn't say anything. He just lay there, watching, waiting.

In his own voice, Jackson said, "I knew my phone call would make you drop your guard just enough. Opening the door without checking first, no gun ready. How lax. You were really very diligent about not being followed, though. I knew you would be. That's why on the very first night I was in Charlottesville, I entered the garage at Wicken's Hunt and placed a transmitter inside the wheel well

514

of each vehicle there, including your Range Rover. This particular transmitter was originally designed for military use and employs satellite-tracking technology. I could have followed you around the globe. It was very expensive, but obviously was well worth it.

"I knew after I met with LuAnn that she would send Lisa off with you and I needed to know exactly where you were just in case I needed little Lisa for the final showdown. I love strategic thinking, don't you? It's so rare when someone does it correctly. As it turns out, I do need her. That's why I'm here."

Charlie winced slightly when Jackson pulled the knife from his coat and he flinched again when Jackson pulled up the sleeve of Charlie's shirt.

"I really love this device," Jackson said, looking at the stun gun. "It's one of the few instruments I'm aware of that allows one to have full control over another without seriously injuring them and still leaving them fully conscious."

Jackson packed the stun gun away in his coat. He left the darts in Charlie. He wasn't worried about leaving any evidence behind this time.

"You sided with the wrong person." As Jackson said this he ripped open the shirtsleeve up to Charlie's shoulder to give himself a clear space in which to work. "You were loyal to LuAnn and look where it got you." Jackson shook his head sadly, but the smile on his face betrayed his true feelings of glee.

As slowly as he could, Charlie tried to flex his legs. He grimaced a little, but he could feel something down there. It hurt, but at least he could feel it. What Jackson didn't know was that one of the darts had hit Charlie's thick Crucifix, imbedding completely in it. The other dart had partially hit the medallion before entering his chest, with the result that the

515

voltage that had rocked his body was far less than Jackson had counted on it to be.

"Now, the stun charge will last approximately fifteen minutes," Jackson lectured him. "Unfortunately, the cut I'm about to inflict upon you will only take about ten minutes to cause you to bleed to death. However, you won't feel anything, physically. Mentally, well, it might be rather unnerving watching yourself bleed to death and being absolutely powerless to do anything about it. I could kill you quick, but this way seems far more gratifying to me personally."

As he spoke, Jackson made a precise and deep gash in Charlie's upper arm. Charlie bit the inside of his jaw as he felt the sharp blade slice through his skin. As Charlie's blood started to pour out in a steady flow, Jackson rose.

"Good-bye, Charlie, I'll tell LuAnn you said hello. Right before I kill her." Jackson snapped this last sentence out, his face a twisted mass of hatred. Then he smiled and closed the door.

Inch by agonizing inch, Charlie managed to roll over on to his back. Then, after an equally hard struggle, he brought his massive hands up, up until they closed around the darts. He was already dizzy from the blood loss. The sweat pouring off his brow, he pulled with all his strength and, little by little, the darts came loose and he tossed them aside. That didn't lessen the numbness of his body, but it felt good nonetheless. With what little control he had over his limbs, he slid over to the wall backward and inched his torso up to a sitting position by levering himself against this solid surface. His legs were on fire, the equivalent of a million burning needles stuck in them, and his body was covered in blood, but he managed to thrust himself upward as though he were squatting weights and his legs held, his knees locked

516

in place. Ironically, the stun gun's impact had made his knees feel better than they had in years. Keeping himself pressed against the wall for support, he made it to the closet, which he managed to throw open. He pushed himself into the closet and gripped a wooden suit hanger with his teeth. All his limbs were on fire now, which was exhilarating because the slow return of his motor functions was becoming evident all over his body. He managed to grip the suit hanger in one hand and rip off the slender stem that normally kept trousers neatly in place. Dropping the rest of the hanger, he pushed off from the wall, propelling himself to the bed. Using his teeth and one of his hands, he shredded the bed sheet into strips. He worked more quickly now as his limbs returned to a semblance of normalcy. He was starting to feel nauseated; the blood loss was taking its toll. He was running out of time. As quickly as he could he wound a long strip directly above the cut and then used the thin piece of wood to torque down on it. The rude tourniquet worked its life-saving magic and the flow of blood finally halted. Charlie knocked the phone receiver off and punched in 911. After giving his location he sat back on the bed, sweat pouring off him, his entire body crimson from his own blood. He was still uncertain whether he was going to live or not, and yet all he could think about was the fact that Jackson had Lisa. He knew exactly what Jackson was going to do with her. The girl was bait. Bait to lure the mother. And when LuAnn went for that bait, Charlie knew exactly what would happen: Jackson would slaughter them both.

This terrifying thought was his last before he lost consciousness.

As the van moved down the highway, Jackson looked over at the unconscious Lisa, finally shining a penlight on her features so he could see them more clearly. "The spitting image of her mother," he said to himself. "She has her fighting spirit too," he added.

Jackson reached over and touched the young girl's face. "You were just an infant when I last saw you." He paused for a moment and looked out into the darkness before returning his gaze to her. "I'm very sorry it had to come to this."

He rubbed her cheek lightly, before slowly withdrawing his hand. Roberta, Donovan, his sister, Alicia, and now the little girl. How many more people was he going to have to kill? After this was all over, he told himself, he would go to the most remote location he possibly could find and do nothing for the next five years. When he had cleansed his mind of the events of this past week, he would go on with his life. But first he had to take care of LuAnn. That was one death he was not going to lose much sleep over.

"I'm coming, LuAnn," he said to the darkness.

LuAnn sat bolt upright in bed feeling as if every nerve were on fire. Her breath came in big chunks, her heart pounding out of control.

"Sweetie, what is it?" Riggs sat up and wrapped an arm around her quivering shoulders.

"Oh, God, Matthew."

"What? What is it?"

"Something's happened to Lisa."

"What? LuAnn, you were dreaming. You had a bad dream, that's all."

"He's got her. He's got my baby. Oh, God, he was touching her. I saw it."

Riggs pulled her around to face him. Her eyes were careening all over the room. "LuAnn, there's nothing wrong with Lisa. You had a nightmare.

518

Perfectly natural under the circumstances." He tried to sound as calm as possible, although being wakened out of a dead sleep by this hysterical outburst had certainly unnerved him.

She pushed him off, jumped up, and started tossing things off the table next to the bed.

"Where's the phone?"

"What?"

"Where's the damned phone?" she screamed. As soon as she said it, she uncovered the phone.

"Who are you calling?"

She didn't answer. Her fingers flew across the face of the receiver as she punched in the cell phone number. She was almost vibrating off the ground as she waited for an answer. "They're not answering."

"So? Charlie probably turned off the phone. Do you know what time it is?"

"He wouldn't turn off the phone. He *never* turns off the damned phone." She redialed, with the same result.

"Well, if that's the case, maybe the battery's dead. If he didn't plug it in when he got to the motel."

LuAnn was shaking her head. "Something's happened. Something's wrong."

Riggs got up and went over to her. "LuAnn, listen to me." He shook her to the extent his wound would allow him. "Will you listen for a minute?"

She finally calmed down a bit and managed to look at him.

"Lisa is fine. Charlie is fine. You had a nightmare and that's all." He put his arm around her, squeezed her tightly to him. "We're going to see them tomorrow. And everything is going to be fine, okay? If we go tonight and we are being followed, we'll never know it. Don't let a nightmare make you do something that could end up *really* putting Lisa in danger."

She stared at him, terror still in her eyes.

He continued to murmur in her ear and his soothing tones finally reached her. She let him draw her back over to the bed and they climbed in. As he settled back to sleep, however, LuAnn stared at the ceiling, silently praying that it really had only been a nightmare. Something deep within her kept telling her it wasn't. In the darkness she could see what looked to be a hand reaching out for her. Whether in a friendly gesture or not she couldn't tell, because it never fully formed and then it was gone. She put an arm around the sleeping Riggs, holding him protectively. She would have given anything to be doing the same for her daughter.

FIFTY-SIX

The two FBI agents sipped hot coffee and enjoyed the late morning calm and beauty of the area. The winds were whipping up, however, as a storm system approached with the promise of even higher winds and a lot of rain, that night and into the next day. Stationed at the road leading up to LuAnn's home, the veteran agents had seen little activity, but they kept alert despite the tedium.

At eleven o'clock a car approached their checkpoint and stopped. The window came down on the driver's side.

Sally Beecham, LuAnn's housekeeper, looked expectantly at one of the agents and he quickly waved her through. She had gone out two hours before to run some errands. When she had passed the checkpoint earlier she had been very nervous. The FBI hadn't explained much to her, but they had made it clear that she wasn't in trouble. They wanted her to go about her normal duties, keep everything the same. They had given her a number to call in case she noticed anything suspicious.

As she passed through the checkpoint this time, she looked more comfortable, perhaps even a touch self-important with all of this official attention.

One of the agents commented to the other, "I don't think Tyler's going to be coming back to eat any of that food." His colleague smirked knowingly.

The next vehicle that came down the road and

stopped at the checkpoint drew some special attention. The older man driving the van explained that he was the groundskeeper. The younger man in the passenger seat was his assistant. They produced ID, which the agents checked thoroughly, then made some phone calls to verify. The agents opened the back of the van and it was indeed filled with tools, boxes, and old rolled-up tarps. Just to make sure, one of the agents followed the van up the road.

Sally Beecham's car was parked in front; a shrill beep emanated from the house. The front door was open and the agent could see her just inside the door deactivating the alarm system, he presumed. He was proven correct when the beep stopped. The agent watched the men get out of the van, pull some tools from the back of the vehicle, stack them in a wheelbarrow, and head around to the back of the house. Then the agent got in his car and drove back to the checkpoint.

LuAnn and Riggs were standing in the parking lot of the motel outside Danville, Virginia. Riggs had talked to the motel manager. The police had been summoned the night before. The man in Room 112 had been attacked and badly injured. Because of the severity of the wound, a medevac helicopter had been called to airlift out the man. The name the man had given was not Charlie's; however, that meant nothing. And the manager was not aware of a young girl being with the man.

"You're sure they were in room one twelve?"

LuAnn whirled around. "Of course I'm sure."

She closed her eyes, stopped pacing, and rocked on her heels. She knew! She knew what had happened. The thought of Jackson touching Lisa, hurting her, all because of what LuAnn had done or hadn't done. It was numbing, absolutely and totally incapacitating.

"Look, how was I supposed to know you have some kind of psychic connection with this guy?" Riggs replied.

"Not him dammit. Her! My daughter."

This statement stopped Riggs dead in his tracks. He looked down and then watched her resume her pacing.

"We need some information, Matthew. Right now."

Riggs agreed, but he didn't want to go to the police. That would entail wasting a lot of time in explanations and the end result might very well be the local cops taking LuAnn into custody.

Finally, Riggs said, "Come on."

They went into the motel office and Riggs walked over to a pay phone. Riggs phoned Masters. The FBI still had no leads on Jackson and Roger Crane still had not surfaced, Riggs was told.

Riggs briefly explained the situation at the motel the night before to Masters.

"Hold on," Masters said.

While Riggs did so he looked over at LuAnn staring at him. She was silently waiting for the worst news she could possibly receive, of that he was certain. He tried to smile reassuringly at her, but then stopped. The last thing he could be right now was reassuring, particularly since he had nothing to base it upon. Why set her up even further for the long fall.

When Masters came back on, his tone was low and nervous. Riggs turned away from LuAnn while he listened.

Masters said, "I just checked with the local police in Danville. Your information is correct, a man was stabbed at that motel on the outskirts of town. The ID found on him gave his name as Robert Charles Thomas."

Charlie? Riggs licked his lips, gripped the phone. "His ID? He couldn't tell the police?"

"He was unconscious. Lost a lot of blood. Damn miracle he's even alive, they tell me. The wound was professionally administered, designed to slow-bleed the person. They found darts from a stun gun in the room. Guess that was how he was incapacitated. As of early this morning, they weren't sure if he was going to make it."

"What's he look like?" Riggs heard some paper rustling over the line. He was almost certain it was Charlie, but he needed to be absolutely sure.

Masters started speaking again. "Over six feet, in his sixties, strongly built, must be strong as an ox to have survived to this point."

Riggs breathed deeply. No doubt now. It was Charlie. "Where is he now?"

"The medevac took him to the UVA trauma center in Charlottesville."

Riggs felt the presence next to him. He turned to find Lisa staring at him; the look in her eyes was scary.

"George, was there any mention of a ten-year-old girl being with him?"

"I asked. The report said that the man came to for a few seconds and started shouting a name."

"Lisa?"

Riggs heard Masters clear his throat. "Yes." Riggs remained silent. "It was her daughter, wasn't it? This guy's got her, doesn't he?" Masters asked.

"Looks like it," Riggs managed to get out.

"Where are you?"

"Look, George, I don't think I'm ready to give you that information yet."

Masters started speaking more forcefully. "He's got the little girl. You two could be next, Matt. Think about it. We can protect you both. You have got to come in."

"I don't know."

"Look, you can go back to her house. I've got the entrance under twenty-four-hour guard. If she agrees to go there, I'll fill the place up with agents."

"Hold on, George." Riggs held the phone against his chest and looked at LuAnn. His eyes told her all she needed to know.

"Charlie?"

"Unconscious. They don't know if he's going to make it. The good news is that a medevac helicopter flew him to the trauma center at UVA hospital."

"He's in Charlottesville?" she asked.

Riggs nodded. "It's only a short hop from Danville by air, and the trauma unit there is top-notch. He'll get the best care."

She continued to stare at him, waiting. And he knew exactly what for.

"Jackson probably has Lisa." He moved on quickly. "LuAnn, the FBI wants us to come in. So they can protect us. We can go to Wicken's Hunt if you want. Agents are already guarding the entrance. They think—"

She snatched the phone out of his hand.

She screamed into it. "I don't want protection. I don't need your damned protection. He's got my daughter. And the only thing I'm going to do is find her. I'm going to get her back. You hear me?"

"Ms. Tyler, I'm assuming this is LuAnn Tyler—" Masters started to say.

"You just stay out of the way. He'll kill her sure as hell if he even *thinks* you're around."

Masters tried to remain calm even as he said the awful words. "Ms. Tyler, you can't be sure he hasn't already done something to her."

Her reply was surprising, both for its content and its intensity. "I know he hasn't hurt her. Not yet."

"The man's a psycho. You can't be sure—"

"The hell I can't. I know exactly what he wants. And it's not Lisa. You just stay out of the way, FBI man. If my daughter dies because you got in the way, there won't be any place on this earth that I won't find you."

Sitting at his desk in the heavily guarded Hoover Building, with twenty-five years of high-level criminal detection work behind him, during which he'd confronted more than his share of evil, now surrounded by a thousand superbly trained, hardened FBI special agents, George Masters actually shivered as he listened to those words.

The next sound he heard was the phone slamming down.

Riggs raced after LuAnn as she stormed to the car.

"LuAnn, will you wait a damned minute?" She whirled around, waiting for him to speak. "Look, what George said makes a lot of sense."

LuAnn threw up her hands and started to get in the car.

"LuAnn, you go in to the FBI. Let them protect you from this guy. Let me stay on the outside. Let me track him down."

"Lisa is my daughter. I'm the reason she's in this danger and I'm the one who's going to get her out. Just me. Nobody else. Charlie's almost dead. You were almost killed. Three other people have been slaughtered. I'm not involving anybody else in my screwed up, miserable, sonofabitchin' excuse for a life." She screamed the words at him; when she stopped, both their chests were heaving.

"LuAnn, I'm not letting you go after him alone. If you don't want to go to the FBI, fine. I won't go either. But you're not, repeat not, going after him alone. That way you both die."

"Matthew, did you hear me? Just get out of this.

Go to your buddies at the FBI and let them get you a new life somewhere the hell away from all of this. The hell away from me. Do you want to die? Because if you hang around me, you're going to, sure as I'm looking at you." The polished facade had fallen away, shed like a snake's skin in autumn. She was one long, raw muscle standing alone.

"He'll come after me, regardless, LuAnn," Riggs said quietly. "He'll find me and he'll kill me whether I go to the FBI or not." She didn't respond so he continued. "And to tell you the truth, I'm too old, too tired of running and hiding to start it up again. I'd rather go down the cobra's hole and meet him head-on. I'll take my chances with you next to me. I'd rather have you than every agent at the Bureau, than every cop in the country. We're probably only going to have one shot at this, and I'll take that shot with you." He paused for a moment as she stared at him, her eyes wild, her long hair billowing in the wind, her strong hands balling up into fists and then uncurling. Then he said, "If you'll take that shot with me."

The wind was really picking up now. They each stood barely two feet apart from the other. The gap would either swell or diminish with LuAnn's answer. Despite the chill, cold sweat clung to each of their faces. She finally broke the silence.

"Get in."

The room was completely dark. Outside the rain was pouring down and had been for most of the day. Sitting in the very center of the space, her body bound tightly to a chair, Lisa was trying, without much success, to use her nose to inch up the mask that covered her eyes. The intense darkness – being totally and completely blind – was unnerving to her. She had the impression that perilous things were lurking very near her. In that regard she was completely right.

"Are you hungry?" The voice was right at her elbow and her heart nearly stopped.

"Who is it? Who are you?" Her voice quavered.

"I'm an old friend of your mother's." Jackson knelt beside her. "These bindings aren't too tight, are they?"

"Where's Uncle Charlie? What did you do to him?" Lisa's courage suddenly resurfaced.

Jackson quietly chuckled. "Uncle, is it?" He stood back up. "That's good, very good."

"Where is he?"

"Not relevant," Jackson snapped. "If you're hungry, tell me so."

"I'm not."

"Something to drink then?"

Lisa hesitated. "Maybe some water."

She heard some tinkling of glass in the background and then she felt a coldness against her lips and jerked back.

"It's only water. I'm not going to poison you." Jackson said this in such a commanding fashion that Lisa quickly opened her mouth and drank deeply. Jackson patiently held the cup until she was finished.

"If you need anything else, to use the bathroom for instance, then just say so. I'll be right here."

"Where are we?" When Jackson didn't answer, she asked, "Why are you doing this?"

Standing there in the darkness, Jackson considered the question carefully before answering. "Your mother and I have some unfinished business. It has to do with things that occurred a long time ago, although there have been repercussions of a very recent vintage that are motivating me."

"I bet my mom didn't do anything to you."

"On the contrary, while she owes her entire life to me, she has done everything in her power to hurt me."

"I don't believe that," Lisa said hotly.

"I don't expect you to," Jackson said. "You're loyal to your mother, as you should be. Family ties are very important." He crossed his arms and thought for a moment on the status of his own family, of Alicia's sweet, peaceful face. *Sweet and peaceful in death.* With an effort he shrugged the vision off.

"My mom will come and get me."

"I certainly expect her to."

Lisa blinked rapidly as his meaning suddenly dawned upon her. "You're going to hurt her, aren't you? You're going to try and hurt my mom when she comes to get me." Her voice had risen.

"Call if you need anything. I don't intend to make you suffer unduly."

"Don't hurt my mom, please." The tears materialized behind the mask.

Jackson did his best to ignore the pleas. Finally, the crying turned to bawling and then dissolved into exhausted whimpering. He had first seen Lisa as an eight-month-old infant. She had certainly grown up into a lovely child. Had LuAnn not accepted his offer, the orphaned Lisa would probably be in a foster home somewhere. He looked over at her, suffering terribly inside, her head slumped on to her chest in her private agony. A lot for a ten-year-old to handle. Maybe she would have been better off in that foster home, without ever really having known her mother. The woman Jackson was going to now eliminate from her life. He had no desire to cause pain to the daughter, but such was life. It wasn't fair. He had told LuAnn that the very first day they had met: Life was not fair. If you wanted something you had to take it. Before someone else took from you.

Neatly dissected down to its essence, life was one long series of lily pad hoppings. The quick and the resourceful were able to adapt and survive; all others were simply crushed as a more nimble creature landed on the lily pad they had occupied for too long.

He stood completely motionless as though conserving all his energies for what lay ahead. He stared off into the darkness. Very soon it would all begin. And very soon it would all end.

FIFTY-SEVEN

The medical facility at the University of Virginia was a teaching component of the medical school as well as a highly regarded public hospital with a level-one trauma center. LuAnn raced down the corridor. Riggs was parking the car and then would follow her in. She reflected briefly on the fact that she had never before been in a hospital. She quickly concluded that she didn't care for either the smell or atmosphere. A lot of that was probably due to the reason she was here: to see Charlie.

He was in a private room. A member of the Charlottesville police force stood guard outside his door. LuAnn shot right past him and started to enter the room,.

"Whoa, there, ma'am. No visitors," said the police officer, a solidly built man in his early thirties, holding out a beefy arm for emphasis.

LuAnn had whirled around ready for a fight when Riggs hustled up.

"Hey, Billy."

The officer turned around. "Hey, Matt, how you doing?"

"Not so good. Won't be playing basketball at the Y with you for a while."

Billy looked at his sling. "How'd you do that?"

"Long story. The guy in there is her uncle." He nodded at LuAnn.

Billy looked embarrassed. "I'm sorry, ma'am, I

didn't know. They told me no visitors, but I know they didn't mean family. You go on in."

"Thanks, Billy," Riggs said.

LuAnn pushed open the door and went in. Riggs was right behind her.

LuAnn stared across at Charlie lying in the bed. As if he sensed her presence, he looked over and a smile spread across his face. He looked pale but his eyes were quick and active.

"Damn, now that's a real pleasant sight," he said.

LuAnn was next to him in an instant, taking his big hand in hers. "Thank God, you're okay."

Charlie was about to say something when the door opened and a middle-aged man in a white coat popped his head in. "Just making rounds, folks." He opened the door all the way and came in. He carried a clipboard.

"Dr. Reese," he said, introducing himself.

"Matt Riggs. This is Charlie's niece, Catherine." Riggs pointed at LuAnn, who shook the doctor's hand.

Dr. Reese checked Charlie's vital signs while he spoke. "Well, it's very lucky Charlie was so good with a tourniquet. Stopped the blood loss before things got really nasty."

"So he's going to be okay?" LuAnn asked anxiously.

Reese peered at her over his glasses. "Oh, yes. He's in no danger. We replaced the blood he lost, the wound is all stitched up. All he needs is some rest, get his strength back." Reese noted his findings on Charlie's record log.

Charlie half-sat up. "I feel fine. When can I check out?"

"I think we'll give you a couple of more days to get back on your feet."

Charlie was clearly not pleased with that answer.

"I'll be back in the morning," Reese said. "Don't stay too long, folks, let him get some rest."

As soon as Reese was gone, Charlie sat all the way up. "Any word on Lisa?"

LuAnn closed her eyes and looked down. Thick tears slid out from under her eyelids. Charlie looked over at Riggs for the first time.

"We think he has her, Charlie," said Riggs

"I *know* he has her. I told the cops everything I knew as soon as I came to."

"I'm sure they're working on it," Riggs said lamely.

Charlie banged his fist against the metal sides of the bed. "Dammit, they're not going to catch him. He's long gone. We've got to do something. He hasn't tried to contact you?"

"I'm going to contact him," LuAnn said, opening her eyes. "But I had to come see you first. They said – they said you might not make it." Her voice shook and her hand gripped his tighter.

"It'd take a lot more than one cut to send yours truly into oblivion." He paused, struggling with what he was about to say. "I'm sorry, LuAnn. That bastard's got her and it's my fault. He called in the middle of the night, impersonated Riggs's voice. Said that the FBI had Jackson. That I was to come up to Washington and rendezvous with you at the FBI building. I dropped my guard. I walked right into his trap." Charlie shook his head. "God, I should've suspected something, but he sounded just like Riggs."

LuAnn leaned over and hugged him. "Damn you, Charlie, you almost got yourself killed for her. And for me."

Charlie wrapped his big arms around her while Riggs watched in respectful silence as the two shook and swayed together.

"Lisa will be okay, Charlie." She sounded a lot more confident than she actually felt. However, it would do Lisa no good if LuAnn allowed herself to become hysterical and thus useless.

"LuAnn, you know that guy. He could do anything to her."

"He wants me, Charlie. His whole world is falling apart. The Feds are on to him, he killed Donovan and Bobbie Jo Reynolds and probably his own sister as well. And I know he thinks I'm the cause of all of it."

"That's nuts."

"It's not nuts if he believes it."

"Well, you can't just walk in there and give yourself to him."

Riggs piped in, "My sentiments exactly. You can't just call the guy up and say 'Don't worry, I'll be right over so you can kill me.'"

LuAnn didn't answer him.

"He's right, LuAnn," Charlie said. He started to get up.

"What the hell are you doing?" she said sharply.

"Getting dressed."

"Excuse me, didn't you hear the doctor?"

"I'm old, my hearing's going. And so am I. Going, that is."

"Charlie—"

"Look," he said angrily as he stumbled trying to get his pants on. LuAnn gripped his good arm, while Riggs steadied him on the other side. "I'm not going to lie here in this bed while that son of a bitch has Lisa. If you don't understand that, I really don't care."

LuAnn nodded in understanding and helped him get his pants on. "You're a big old ornery bear, you know that?"

"I've got one good arm, and just let me get it around that guy's neck."

534

Riggs held up his own injured arm. "Well, between us we have two good arms. I owe the guy too."

LuAnn put her hands on her hips and looked around. "There's a cop outside."

"I can take care of him," Riggs said.

LuAnn picked up the rest of Charlie's belongings, including the portable cell phone, and put them in a plastic hospital bag.

When Charlie was finished dressing, Riggs stepped out the door and spoke to Billy.

"Billy, you mind going down to the cafeteria and getting a couple of coffees and maybe some stuff to munch on? I'd go but I can't carry anything with this bum arm." He jerked his head toward the room. "And she's pretty hysterical right now. I don't want to leave her."

"I'm really not supposed to leave my post, Matt."

"I'll hang out here, Billy, it'll be okay." Riggs held up some money. "Here, get yourself something too. Last time we played hoops I remember you eating a whole pizza by yourself afterward." He eyed Billy's healthy dimensions. "I don't want you to wilt away to nothing."

Billy took the money and laughed. "You sure know the way to a fella's heart."

As soon as Billy got into the elevator and the doors closed, Charlie, LuAnn, and Riggs left the room and made their way out by the back stairs. With LuAnn and Riggs supporting Charlie, they quickly walked through the pouring rain to the car. With the thick clouds, it was already dark and the visibility was getting worse every minute.

Shortly, the three of them were in the car heading down Route 29. Charlie used the opportunity to tell them everything that had happened at the motel, including the fact that Jackson had had another man

535

with him. After he finished, Charlie leaned forward from the back seat. "So what's the plan?" He winced as the car bounced over a pothole and jostled his arm.

LuAnn pulled into a gas station. She pulled out a slip of paper from her pocket. "I'm going to call him."

"And then what?" Riggs asked.

"I'll let him tell me," she replied.

"You know what the hell he's going to say," Charlie rejoined. "He's going to set up a meeting, just you and him. And if you go, he's going to kill you."

"And if I don't go, he's going to kill Lisa."

"He'll kill her anyway," Riggs said hotly.

LuAnn looked over at him. "Not if I get him first." She thought back to her last encounter with Jackson, at the cottage. She was stronger than he was. Not by much, but she had the clear advantage there. However, he knew that too. She had seen that in his eyes. That meant he would not go toe-to-toe with her again, at least not physically. She would have to remember that. If he could adapt, so could she.

"LuAnn, I have a lot of confidence in you," Riggs said, "but this guy is something else again."

"He's right, LuAnn," Charlie added.

"Thanks for the vote of confidence, guys." She didn't wait for them to answer. She pulled the portable phone out of the bag and punched in the number. Before it started ringing, she looked at both of them. "But remember, I've got *two* good arms."

Riggs slid his hand down into his coat until it touched the reassuring metal of his pistol. His aim would have to be a lot better this time around. He hoped not to have the painful distraction of a knife sticking out of his arm.

He and Charlie watched as LuAnn spoke into the

receiver, leaving the number of the cell phone. She hung up and waited, still not looking at them. Barely three minutes had passed before the phone rang.

Before LuAnn could say anything, Jackson said, "Please know that I have a device attached to my phone that will indicate whether this call is being traced, just in case you happen to be sitting at police headquarters. It will tell me in about five seconds if that is occurring. If you are, I will immediately hang up and slit your daughter's throat."

"I'm not at the police and I'm not tracing your call."

He didn't say anything for five seconds. She could envision him eyeing his device, perhaps hoping she was lying to him. "I applaud you for avoiding the obvious," he finally said quite pleasantly.

"When and where?" LuAnn said.

"No greeting? No small talk? Where are your manners? Has the expensively constructed princess deteriorated that suddenly? Like a flower without water? Without sunshine?"

"I want to talk to Lisa. Right now."

"Sorry about Uncle Charlie," Jackson said. He was sitting on the floor almost in total darkness. He held the phone close to his mouth, speaking slowly and in as casual a tone as he could muster. He wanted her panic level to rise steadily, he wanted her to feel his absolute control of the situation. When the time came he wanted her to come obediently forward to receive her punishment. He wanted her to come meekly to confront her executioner.

She wasn't about to tell Jackson that Charlie was sitting right behind her wanting nothing more than to wring the life out of him. "I want to talk to Lisa!"

"How can you be sure I haven't killed her already?"

"What?" she gasped.

537

"You can talk to her, but how will you know it's not me mimicking her voice? 'Mommy, Mommy,' I could say. 'Come help me.' I could say all those things. So if you want to talk to her, you can, but it will prove nothing."

"You son of a bitch!"

"Would you still like to talk to her?"

"Yes," LuAnn said pleadingly.

"Manners now. Yes, what?"

She hesitated for an instant, taking a deep breath, trying to keep her wits and her nerves together. "Yes, please," she said.

"Just a minute. Now where have I put that child?"

Riggs was doing his best to listen in. Exasperated, LuAnn finally opened the door and got out of the car.

She strained to hear any sound in the background.

"Mom, Mom, is that you?"

"Honey, baby, it's Mom. Oh, God, sweetie, I'm so sorry."

"Oh, excuse me, LuAnn, that's still me," Jackson said. "Oh, Mom, Mommy, are you there?" he said again, mimicking Lisa's voice precisely.

LuAnn was too stunned to say anything.

The next voice she heard was Jackson's real one. His tone almost bit into her ear it was said with such forcefulness. "I'll let you talk to her, really talk to her. You can have your mother–daughter emotional exchange. But when you're done I will tell you exactly what you will do. If you deviate in any way from my instructions . . ."

He didn't finish. He didn't have to. They both sat there on the phone, not saying anything, simply listening to each other's breathing, two trains careening out of control, about to slam into each other across the wireless void. LuAnn tried with all her might to hold back the thick gush of air that was

538

ramming against her throat. She knew what he was doing. What he was doing to her mind. But she was equally aware that she could do nothing about it. At least not right now.

"Do you understand?"

"Yes." As soon as she said the word, she heard it. She heard the sound in the background that made her both smile and grimace simultaneously. She looked at her watch. Five o'clock. The smile increased at the same time her eyes took on a gleam. A gleam of hope.

The next minute she was talking to Lisa, quickly asking her questions that only her little girl would know the answer to. They both desperately wanted to reach through the darkness that separated them.

And then Jackson came back on the line and gave her the instructions, the where and the when. None of it surprised her as she focused again on the sounds occurring in the background on his end. He ended the call by saying, with daunting finality, "See you soon."

She clicked off the phone and got back in the car. She spoke with a calmness that astonished the two men, particularly under the circumstances.

"I'm to call him tomorrow ten A.M. He'll give me the meeting place then. He'll let Lisa go if I come alone. If he even thinks anyone else is around, he'll kill her."

"So it's you for Lisa," Riggs said.

She looked at both of them. "That's the way it's going to be."

"LuAnn—"

"That's the way it's going to be," she said more forcefully.

"How do you know he'll let her go? You can't trust him," Charlie implored.

"On this I can. He just wants me."

"There's got to be another way," Riggs exclaimed.

"There's only one way, Matthew, and you know it." She looked at him sadly before putting the car in gear and driving off.

She had one more card to play. But Charlie and Riggs weren't going to be invited to the game. They had already sacrificed too much for her. Jackson had nearly killed both men, and she wasn't about to give the man another try on either. If Jackson were given an extra shot, she knew what the outcome would be. It was now up to her. It was up to her to save her daughter, and that, she felt, was the way it should be. She had been self-reliant for most of her life, and truth be known, that was the way she liked it. That knowledge was reassuring. And she knew something else.

She knew where Jackson and Lisa were.

FIFTY-EIGHT

The rain had finally slackened off but the spring showers were far from over. LuAnn had tacked up a blanket over the shattered window of the cottage. Riggs had turned the heat fully on and it was comfortable enough. The remnants of a meal rested on the kitchen sink. Riggs eyed the stains on the dining room floor. His blood. Charlie and Riggs had pulled mattresses down from the upstairs bedroom and laid them out on the floor. They had decided the cottage was the best place to spent the night. Charlie and Riggs had argued with LuAnn for hours trying to change her mind. Finally, she said she would call the FBI in the morning before she called Jackson. It was possible the FBI could trace the call. That had appeased the men enough that they agreed to let LuAnn keep the first watch. Riggs would relieve her in two hours.

Exhausted, both men soon began snoring deeply. LuAnn stood with her back to the window and silently observed them. She looked at her watch; it was after midnight. She made sure her gun was loaded, then she knelt next to Charlie and gave him a light kiss on the cheek. He barely moved.

She moved over to Riggs and watched the even rise and fall of his chest. Brushing the hair out of his eyes, she watched him a while longer. She knew the odds were not good that she would ever see either man again. She kissed him gently on the lips and then rose. For one long moment she leaned back against the wall, taking deep breaths as everything she was confronted with threatened to simply overwhelm her.

Then she was on the move again, climbing through the window to avoid the squeaky front door. She put up her hood against the fine rain falling. Ignoring the car and the unavoidable noise it would make, she went to the shed and opened the door. Joy was still there. LuAnn had forgotten to call anyone to come get the horse; however, the shed was dry and warm and there was still water and hay left. She quickly saddled the animal and swung on to Joy's back. Easing her out of the shed, they made it to the woods with scarcely any noise.

When she reached the edge of her property, she dismounted and led Joy back to the horse barn. She hesitated for a moment and then she took the binoculars off the wall, edged through the thick brush, and set up surveillance in a narrow break in the tree line, exactly where Riggs had earlier. She scanned the rear of the house. She jerked back as a car's headlights glinted off the binoculars. The car pulled around to the garage side, but the garage doors didn't budge. As LuAnn watched, a man got out of the car and walked around the rear of the house as if on patrol. Under the rear floods, LuAnn could see the FBI insignia emblazoned on his windbreaker. Then the man got back in the car and it pulled off.

LuAnn broke from the trees and raced across the open ground. She made it to the side of the house in time to see the car head back down the private drive toward the main road, the one where she had fled from Donovan, the encounter that had started this whole nightmare. The FBI was guarding the entrance to her home. She suddenly remembered that Riggs had mentioned that to her during his

542

conversation with Masters. She would have dearly loved to have enlisted the agents' very able assistance, but they no doubt would have arrested her on the spot. Yet fear of arrest wasn't the chief factor. She simply refused to involve anyone else in her problems. No one else was going to be stabbed or killed because of her. Jackson wanted her and only her. She knew he expected her to walk meekly to him, to receive her punishment in exchange for her daughter's release. Well, in this case, he was going to get more than he wanted. A lot more. She and Lisa were going to survive this. He wasn't.

As she started to head back to the rear of the house, she noticed something else. Sally Beecham's car out front. That puzzled her. She shrugged and went around to the rear door.

The sound she had heard in the background during Jackson's call to her was what had brought her here. The absolutely unique sounds of the old clock, the family heirloom, passed down to her from her mother, the very same one LuAnn had diligently refused ever to part with. It had proved to be the most valuable possession she had because she had heard it in the background during her phone conversation with Jackson.

Jackson had been in her house, had called from her house. And LuAnn was absolutely convinced that Lisa was there now. Jackson was here too, she knew. LuAnn had to admire the man's nerve, to come here, with the FBI waiting just down the road. In a very few minutes, she would come face-to-face with her worst nightmare.

She pressed herself flat against the brick wall and peered in the side door, squinting hard through the pane of glass to see if the alarm light that was visible from this point was red or green. She breathed a quiet sigh of relief when she saw the friendly green.

She knew the code to disarm it of course, but disarming it would produce one shrill beep that might jeopardize everything.

LuAnn inserted her key in the lock and slowly opened the door. She paused for a minute; the gun she held made quick, darting movements all around. She heard nothing. It was well past midnight now so that wasn't so surprising. Something was bothering her, however.

Being back in her own house should have brought some comfort to her, but it didn't. If anything it was close to unnerving. Letting her guard down now, letting herself be lulled by the familiarity of the surroundings, could easily result in her and Lisa's not being around to see the sun come up.

She continued down the hallway and then froze. She heard voices clearly. Several people; she recognized none of them. She slowly let out her breath as the music from a commercial came on. Someone was watching TV. A glint of light came from a doorway at the end of the hallway. LuAnn quietly moved forward, stopping right before her shadow would pass across the small opening between door and wall. She listened for a few seconds more. Then she edged open the door with her left hand as she pointed her gun through the opening with her right. The door swung silently inward and LuAnn leaned in. The room was dark, the only light coming from the TV. What she saw next made her freeze once again. The dark hair, cut short around the neck and built high up in the form of a modified beehive, was directly in front of her. Sally Beecham was in her bedroom watching TV. Or was she? She was sitting so still that LuAnn couldn't tell if she was alive or not.

For an instant: the image of LuAnn threading her way through that trailer ten years ago, spotting

Duane on the couch. Going toward him, walking right up to him. And seeing him turn, turn so slowly toward her, the blood all over his chest, his face as gray as a Navy ship. And watching him fall off that couch, dying. And then the hand clamping over her mouth from behind. From behind!

She whirled but there was no one there; however, her abrupt movements had made some noise. When she looked back Sally Beecham was staring at her with horror in her eyes. When she recognized LuAnn she seemed to catch her breath. A hand fluttered up to her chest, which was heaving.

She started to say something, but LuAnn put a finger up to her lips and whispered, "Shh."

"There's someone here," LuAnn said. Sally looked confused. "Have you seen anyone here?" Sally shook her head and pointed to herself, the worry lines sprouting all over her ghastly pale face.

And that's when it hit LuAnn, and her own face went pale.

Sally Beecham never parked in front of the house. She always parked in the garage which led directly into the kitchen. LuAnn's hand tightened on the gun. She looked at the face again. It was hard to tell in the dark light, but she wasn't taking any chances. "I'll tell you what, Sally. I want you to get in the kitchen pantry and I'm going to lock you in. Just to be safe."

LuAnn watched as the eyes darted over her face. Then one of the hands started to move behind the woman's back.

LuAnn thrust the gun forward. "And we're going to do it right now or I'll shoot you right here. And pull out the gun, butt-first."

When the pistol emerged, LuAnn motioned to the floor. The gun clunked when it hit the hardwood.

When the person moved in front of LuAnn,

LuAnn quickly reached out and jerked the wig off, revealing the man. He had short, dark hair. He jerked around for an instant, but LuAnn shoved the gun in his ear.

"Move, Mr. Jackson! Or should I say, Mr. Crane?" She had no false hopes as to the fate of Sally Beecham, but with everything else confronting her, LuAnn did not have the opportunity to dwell on it. She hoped she would have the chance to grieve for the woman.

When they reached the kitchen, LuAnn shoved him inside the pantry and locked the door from the outside. The door was an original from the house, solid oak, three inches thick with a deadbolt. It would hold him. At least for a while. She didn't need long.

She raced to the end of the hallway and flew up the carpeted stairs. LuAnn made her way from door to door. She was fairly certain that Lisa was in her mother's bedroom but she couldn't take any chances. Her eyes had adjusted well to the darkness and she quickly surveyed room after room. All empty. She went on. There was only one more bedroom left: hers. LuAnn willed her hearing to the highest possible acuity. All she wanted to hear was Lisa sighing, mumbling, breathing, anything to let her mother know she was okay. She couldn't call out, that was too dangerous. She recalled that Jackson now had someone with him. Where was that person?

She reached the door, slid her hand around the doorknob, took a deep breath, and turned it.

A long bolt of lightning cut across the sky, followed by a deafening clap of thunder. At the same instant, the blanket was blown off the window and rain started coming in. The combination of these events finally woke Riggs. He sat up, disoriented for a moment, and then looked around. He saw the open window, the wind and rain coming through. He glanced over at Charlie, who was still sleeping. Then it hit him.

He staggered up. "LuAnn? LuAnn?" His cries roused Charlie.

"What the hell?" he said.

In a minute they had searched the small cottage.

"She's not here," he screamed to Charlie.

They both raced outside. The car was still there. Riggs looked around bewildered.

"LuAnn," Charlie screamed over the sounds of the storm.

Riggs looked over at the shed. The doors were open. It hit him. He raced over and looked in the empty shed. He looked down at the mud in front of the shed. Even in the darkness, he could make out the hoof prints. He followed the tracks to the edge of the woods. Charlie ran up beside him.

"Joy was in the shed," he told Charlie. "It looks like she's gone back to the house."

"Why would she do that?"

Riggs thought hard for a minute. "Were you surprised she agreed to finally calling the FBI tomorrow?"

"Yes," Charlie said, "but I was too damn tired and too relieved to think much about it."

"Why would she go to the house?" Riggs repeated Charlie's question. "The FBI is guarding the place. What would be there that she'd take that sort of risk?"

Charlie went pale and he staggered slightly.

"What is it, Charlie?"

"LuAnn once told me something Jackson had told her. A rule he lived by."

"What was it?" Riggs demanded.

"If you want to hide something, put it out in plain sight because no one would see it."

Now it was Riggs's turn to go pale as the truth hit him. "Lisa's at the house."

"And so is Jackson."

They raced to the car.

As the sedan flew down the road Riggs picked up the portable phone. He dialed the police and then the local FBI. He was shocked to hear Masters's voice come on the line.

"He's here, George. Crane's at Wicken's Hunt. Bring everything you got." Riggs heard the phone drop to the desk and footsteps running off. Then he clicked off the phone and floored the car.

As the door swung open, LuAnn darted into the room. Smack in the center was a chair and in that chair was Lisa, slumped over, exhausted. The next sound LuAnn heard was the labored ticking of that clock, that wonderful, beautiful clock. She closed the door behind her and ran to her daughter, hugged her. Her face dissolved into a big smile when her daughter's eyes met her mother's.

And then a loop of thick cord was around LuAnn's neck, was pulled tight, and LuAnn's breath was suddenly gone; her gun fell to the floor.

Lisa screamed and screamed in agonizing silence, the tape still tightly across her mouth. She kicked at her chair, trying to topple it over, trying to reach her mother, help her in some way before this man killed her.

Jackson was fully behind LuAnn now. He had watched from the darkness next to the dresser as LuAnn had sailed toward Lisa, oblivious to his presence in the room. Then he had struck. The cord had a piece of wood attached to it and Jackson was winding it tighter and tighter. LuAnn's face was turning blue, her senses were slipping away as the cord dug deeply into the skin of her neck. She tried to punch him but it was too awkward, her fists flailed helplessly, sapping away what remaining strength she had. She kicked at him, but he was too quick and dodged those blows as well. She dug at the rope with her strong fingers but it was so imbedded in her skin that there was no space left to get a grip.

He whispered into her ear. "Tick-tock, LuAnn. Tick-tock of the little clock. Like a magnet, it led you right to me. I held the phone right next to it so you couldn't help but hear it. I told you I find out everything about someone I do business with. I visited your trailer in good old Rikersville. I listened to the rather unique sounds of that timepiece several times. And then seeing it on the wall of the bedroom the night I visited you. Your little, cheap family heirloom." He laughed. "I would have loved to have seen your face when you thought you had outsmarted me. Was it a happy face, LuAnn? Was it?"

Jackson's smile deepened as he felt her giving way, her vaunted strength almost gone. "Now don't forget your daughter. There she is." He hit a light switch and swung her around violently so that she could see Lisa reaching for her. "She'll watch you die, LuAnn. And then it will be her turn. You cost me a family member. Someone I loved. How does it feel to be responsible for her death?" He yanked on the cord harder and harder. "Die, LuAnn. Just give in to it. Close your eyes and just stop breathing. Just do it. It's so easy. Just do it. Do it for me. You know you want to," he hissed.

LuAnn's eyes were close to erupting out of their sockets now, her lungs almost dead. She felt like she was deep under water; she would give anything to take one breath, just one long drink of air. As LuAnn listened to those taunting words she was swept back to a graveyard, to a plot of dirt, to a small brass marker in the ground many years ago. Exactly where she was heading. *Do it for Big Daddy, LuAnn. It's so easy. Come and see Big Daddy. You know you want to.*

From the corner of her blood-filled right eye she could barely see Lisa silently screaming for her mother, reaching for her across a chasm that was barely seconds from becoming eternal. At that very moment and from a place so deep that LuAnn never even knew she possessed it, there came a rush of strength so unbelievably powerful that it almost knocked her over. With a shriek, LuAnn jerked upright and then bent forward, lifting an astonished Jackson completely off the floor in the process. She clamped her arms around his legs so that she was carrying him piggyback style. Then she exploded backward, her legs pumping like a long jumper about to erupt into flight until she slammed Jackson violently into the heavy dresser against the wall. The sharp wooden edge caught him dead on the spine.

He screamed in pain but hung on to the cord. LuAnn reached up and dug her fingernails right into the recent wound on his hand – the one from the fight at the cottage – tearing the cut wide open. Jackson screamed again and this time he let go of the cord. Feeling the rope go lax, LuAnn whipped her torso forward and Jackson went flying over her shoulders and crashing into a mirror hanging on the wall.

LuAnn staggered drunkenly around in the middle of the room sucking in huge amounts of air. She reached up to her throat and pulled off the cord. Then her eyes settled dead center on the man.

Jackson grabbed at his injured back and struggled

to stand up. It was too little too late, as with a guttural scream LuAnn pounced. She flattened him to the floor and pinned him there. Her legs clamped against his, immobilizing them. Her hands encircled his throat and now *his* face started to turn blue. The grip he felt against his throat was ten times as strong as the one he had battled on the cottage porch. He looked into her blood-filled eyes, red with burst capillaries from her near strangling, and he knew there was no way he could ever break her choke hold. His hands groped the floor as she continued to squeeze the life out of him. A series of visions proceeded across his mind, but there was no rush of strength to accompany it. His body started to go limp. His eyes rolled in their sockets, his neck constricted to the breaking point under the ever increasing pressure. His fingers finally closed around a bit of glass from the shattered mirror and held. He swung it upward, catching her in the arm and cutting through her clothing and into her skin. She didn't release her grip. He cut her again and then again but to no avail. She was beyond pain; she would simply not let go.

Finally, with the last bit of strength he had left, his fingers felt under her arm and he pressed as hard as he could. Suddenly, LuAnn's arms went dead as Jackson found the pressure point and her grip was abruptly broken. In an instant he had pushed her off and sprinted across the room, gasping for breath.

LuAnn watched in horror as he grabbed Lisa's chair and dragged it across the room to the window. She got to her feet, flying toward them. She knew exactly what he was going to do, but damn if she was going to let him do it. He was lifting the chair and Lisa with it, and LuAnn dove for it, her hand closing around her daughter's leg as the chair smashed against the window that overlooked the brick patio almost thirty feet below. LuAnn and Lisa crashed to the floor amid the shattered glass.

Jackson tried to snatch up her gun but LuAnn was one step ahead of him. LuAnn's leg flew up and caught Jackson, who had strayed a little too close, directly in the crotch. He bent down, groaning. She jumped up and landed a powerful right hand squarely against Jackson's chin. He went down to the floor.

In the distance they all heard the police sirens coming. Jackson swore under his breath, picked himself up, and, clutching his privates, raced through the doorway and then slammed and locked the door.

LuAnn let him go. Screaming and crying in relief, she gently pulled off the tape and undid the ropes holding Lisa. Mother and daughter held each other tightly. LuAnn clutched at Lisa's body, she pushed her face in Lisa's hair, her nose drank in every wonderful smell of her little girl. Then LuAnn stood and picked up her gun and fired two shots out the window.

Riggs and Charlie and the FBI agents were engaged in an animated discussion at the entrance to the private road when they heard the shots. Riggs threw the car into gear and roared up the road. The FBI agents ran to their car.

Jackson bolted down the hallway, suddenly stopped, and looked in Sally Beecham's bedroom. Empty. He spied the gun on the floor and snatched it up. Then he heard the pounding. He raced to the kitchen and unlocked and threw open the pantry door. Roger Crane, squinting and quivering, stumbled out.

"Thank God, Peter. She had a gun. She put me in here. I . . . I did exactly as you told me."

552

"Thank you, Roger." He lifted up the pistol. "Tell Alicia I said hello." Then he fired point blank into his brother's face. The next instant he was out the door and racing across the lawn for the woods.

As they jumped out of their car Riggs saw Jackson first and sprinted after him. Charlie, despite his weakened state, was right behind. When the lawmen pulled up seconds later, they ran to the house.

LuAnn met them on the stairs. "Where are Matthew and Charlie?"

The men looked at each other. "I saw somebody running into the woods," one of them answered.

They all ran out on to the front lawn. That's when they heard it, the drone of the helicopter as the blades cut through the rain and wind. It landed on the front lawn. They all saw the FBI insignia on the side. The group raced over; LuAnn and Lisa reached it first.

Several police cars pulled up next to the fountain and a small army of officers poured out.

George Masters climbed out of the helicopter followed by a team of FBI agents. He looked at her. "LuAnn Tyler?" She nodded. Masters looked at Lisa. "Your daughter?"

"Yes," LuAnn said.

"Thank God." He let out a deep sigh of relief and held out his hand. "George Masters, FBI. I came into town to interview Charlie Thomas. When I got to the hospital he was gone."

"We've got to go after Jackson, I mean Peter Crane. He went into the woods," LuAnn said. "Matthew and Charlie went after him. But I want Lisa safe. I can't leave her without knowing she'll be completely safe."

Masters looked between mother and daughter, spitting images of each other. Then he looked at the helicopter.

553

"We'll transport her to the FBI office here in Charlottesville in this helicopter. I'll put her smack in the center of a room with a half dozen heavily armed FBI agents. That good enough?" He smiled weakly.

A grateful look crossed her face. "Yes. Thanks for understanding."

"I've got children too, LuAnn."

While Masters gave instructions to the pilot, LuAnn gave Lisa one more hug and kiss and then turned and raced for the woods, a swarm of FBI agents and police officers right behind her. As fleet of foot as she was, and knowing the terrain as well as she did, she soon left them far behind.

Riggs could hear the feet flying in front of him. Charlie had dropped back a bit, but Riggs could hear his heavy breathing not far behind. The woods were wreathed in almost complete darkness and the rain continued to pour down. Riggs blinked his eyes rapidly to gain some degree of night vision. He pulled his gun, slipped the safety off with a quick punch of his finger. Then he halted abruptly as the sounds ahead of him stopped. He crouched and swept the area with his eyes, his gun making wide arcs. He heard the sound behind him an instant too late as the foot slammed into his back, sending him lunging forward and then down. He hit the wet ground hard, his face sliding painfully across the grass and dirt, and he ended up slamming against a tree, his gun smacking hard against the trunk. The impact caused his wounded arm to start bleeding again. When he flipped over on his back, he saw the man flying at him, the foot poised to deliver another crunching blow. Then Charlie blindsided Jackson and the two men went sprawling.

An incensed Charlie pounded Jackson with his fists and then cocked his arm back to deliver a knock-out punch. Quick as an eel, Jackson made a direct hit on Charlie's wound, a blow that made him scream and double over. Then, with the same motion employed in striking a cymbal, Jackson smashed both palms against Charlie's ears, forcing a sudden, painful rush of air into his ear canals and rupturing an eardrum. Nauseated and dizzy from the combined blows, Charlie fell off Jackson and lay on the ground groaning.

"I should've slit your throat at the motel," Jackson spat down at him. Jackson was about to deliver a crushing kick to Charlie's head when he heard Riggs scream at him.

"Get the hell away from him before I blow your damn head off."

When Jackson looked over, Riggs's gun was pointed directly at him. Jackson stepped away from Charlie.

"Finally, we meet. Riggs the criminal. How about discussing a financial arrangement that will make you very rich?" Jackson said. His voice was hoarse and weak from his near strangling by LuAnn. He clutched at his torn hand; his face was bleeding from Charlie's blows.

"I'm not a criminal, asshole. I was an FBI agent who testified against a cartel. That's why I was in Witness Protection."

Jackson circled closer to Riggs. "Ex-FBI? Well, then at least I'm certain you won't shoot me down in cold blood." He pointed a warning finger at Riggs. "Understand though, if I go down, so does LuAnn. I'll tell your former employers that she was in on everything, even helped me plan it. I'll paint a picture so dark that she'll be grateful for a life sentence. My attorneys will see to that. But don't worry, I understand you can have yearly conjugal visits in some prisons now."

555

"You're going to rot in jail."

"I hardly think that. I can only imagine what sort of deal I can cut with the Feds. I would think they'd do anything to avoid public disclosure of all this. When this is all over, I'm sure I'll be seeing you again. In fact, I look forward to it."

Jackson's mocking tones burned through every fiber of Riggs's body. What was even more maddening was the fact that everything Jackson had predicted could very well happen. But it wouldn't, Riggs swore to himself. "That's where you're wrong," Riggs said.

"About what?"

"About killing you in cold blood." Riggs pulled the trigger. The sound that *didn't* occur seemed to drive all the blood from Riggs's body. The gun didn't fire; the impact with the tree had jammed it. He pulled the trigger again with the same sickening result.

Jackson instantly drew his own gun and pointed it at Riggs.

Riggs dropped the useless pistol and backed up as Jackson advanced. He finally stopped retreating when his foot felt nothing but air. He looked behind him: a sheer drop. Down below, the fast-moving water. He looked back at Jackson, who smiled and then fired.

The bullet hit right in front of Riggs's feet and he stepped back a half inch, teetering on the edge.

"Let's see how well you swim with no arms." The next shot hit Riggs's good arm. He grunted in pain and doubled over, clutching it, trying to maintain his balance. Then he looked up at the sneering face of Jackson.

"Take the bullet or the jump, it's your choice. But do it quick, I don't have much time."

Riggs had only an instant. As he crouched over,

556

the arm that had just been hit slid up the length of his sling – a very natural movement under the circumstances. Jackson had underestimated his resourcefulness. Jackson wasn't the only one who had lived by his wits, who had gotten himself out of tight spots by acting nimbly. What Riggs was about to do had saved his life while working undercover during a drug deal that had gone sour. It would not save his life this time. But it would save several others, including one that he cared more about than his own: LuAnn's.

He locked eyes with Jackson. His anger was so intense that it blocked out the pain in both arms. His hand closed around the butt of the compact gun taped inside his sling, the one he had originally had in his ankle holster. Its muzzle was pointed right at Jackson. Wounded arm and all, his aim was as sharp as ever. And Jackson was only a few feet away. But Riggs had to make the first shot count.

"Riggs!" Charlie screamed.

Jackson didn't take his eyes off Riggs. "You're next, *Uncle Charlie*."

Matt Riggs would never forget the look on Jackson's face as the first shot Riggs fired erupted through the sling and hit the man flush in the face, tearing first through the powder, putty, and spirit gum, and then slamming a microsecond later into real flesh and bone. The gun fell from an astonished Jackson's hand.

Riggs kept pulling the trigger, sending bullet after bullet slamming into Jackson. Head, torso, leg, arm – there wasn't a piece of him Riggs missed until the firing pin banged empty twelve shots later. And all the time Jackson's countenance held a look of supreme disbelief as blood mixed with fake hair and skin; creams and powders mutated into a dull crimson. The total effect was eerie, as though the

557

man were dissolving. Then Jackson dropped to his knees, blood pouring from a dozen wounds, and then he fell face forward to the ground and did not move again. His last performance.

That's when Riggs went fully over the edge. The multiple kicks from the pistol were enough to completely unsettle his balance, and his feet were unable to counter the slippery red clay. But as he went over, a look of grim satisfaction came over his face even as he stared down at the abyss he was plummeting toward. Two useless arms, both bleeding him to death, deep, fast, icy water, nothing to grab. It was over.

He heard Charlie scream his name one more time, and then he heard nothing else. He felt no pain now, only peace. He hit the water awkwardly and went under.

Charlie scrambled over and was just about to plunge in when a body hurtled by him and went over the edge.

LuAnn broke the surface of the water cleanly and almost instantly reappeared. She scanned the surface of the rapidly moving water that was already pulling her downstream.

From the bank, Charlie stumbled along through the thick trees and heavy underbrush, trying to keep up. The shouts of the FBI agents and police officers were getting louder, but it didn't look as though their help would arrive in time.

"Matthew!" LuAnn screamed. Nothing. She dove under, methodically pushing off from bank to bank searching for him. Twenty seconds later she re-surfaced, sucking in air.

"LuAnn!" Charlie yelled at her.

She ignored his cries. As the cold rain pelted her, she sucked in another lungful of air and went under again. Charlie stopped, his eyes darting everywhere, trying to pinpoint where she would come up. He wasn't about to lose both of them.

When LuAnn broke the surface again she wasn't alone. She gripped Riggs tightly around the chest as the current swept them along. He gagged and spit up water as his lungs struggled to function again. She tried to swim cross-current but was making little progress. She was freezing. In another minute hypothermia could well incapacitate her. Riggs was sheer dead weight, and she felt his strength fading. She scissored her legs around his upper torso, angling just enough that his face was above the water's surface. She kept putting pressure on his stomach, making his diaphragm kick up and down, helping him clear his lungs.

She looked desperately behind her, searching for some way out. Her eyes fell upon a fallen tree, and, more important, the thick branch that was suspended partially out over the water. It would be close. She readied herself, gauging the distance and height. She tensed her legs around Riggs and then made her lunge. Her hands closed around the branch and held. She raised herself up. She and Riggs were now partially out of the water. She tried to pull herself up more, but couldn't; Riggs was too heavy. She looked down and saw him staring at her, his breath coming in short gasps. Then she watched horrified as he started to unwrap her legs from around him.

"Matthew, don't! Please!"

Through blue lips that moved in a painfully slow manner he said, "We're not going to both die, LuAnn." He pushed her legs again and she was now fighting him and the current and the weary ache in her limbs as the numbing cold settled deeply within her. Her lips were trembling with both rage and helplessness. She looked down at him again as he

559

tried desperately to free himself, to rid her of the burden. She could simply let go, fall with him, but what about Lisa? She had seconds to make a choice, but then she didn't have to. For the first time in her life, her strength failed, and her grip was broken. She started to plummet downward.

The thick arm that clamped around her body ended her fall and the next thing she felt was herself and Riggs being lifted completely out of the water.

She cocked her head back and her eyes fell upon his face.

Straddling the tree trunk, Charlie, bad arm and all, grunted and grimaced and finally pulled them safely to a narrow dirt bank where they all three collapsed, the water inches from them. LuAnn's legs were still locked in a death grip around Riggs She lay back, her head on Charlie's chest, which was heaving mightily from his efforts. LuAnn slid her right hand down to Riggs, who took it, laying it against his cheek. Her left hand went up and gripped Charlie's shoulder. He covered her hand with his. None of them said a word.

FIFTY-NINE

"Well, it's all done," Riggs said, gingerly hanging up the phone. They were in his home office, LuAnn, Charlie, and Lisa. A gentle snow was falling outside. Christmas was rapidly closing in.

"So what's the bottom line?" LuAnn asked.

LuAnn and Charlie were healed. Riggs was out of his sling, and the cast he had had to wear to mend the bone Jackson's bullet had broken had recently been removed as well. He still moved slowly, though.

"Not great. The IRS finished its calculations of the back taxes you owed, penalties and interest all compounded for the last eight or so years."

"And?"

"And it came to all the cash you had, all the investments you had, and all the property you had, including Wicken's Hunt." He managed a grin, trying to ease the impact of the depressing news. "You were actually short sixty-five cents so I threw it in for you, no charge."

Charlie snorted. "What a Christmas present. And the other lottery winners get to keep all their money. That's not fair."

"They paid their taxes, Charlie," Riggs replied.

"She's paid taxes."

"Only since coming back to this country and only under the name Catherine Savage."

"Well, she couldn't before. Not without probably going to prison for a crime she didn't commit."

561

"Well, gee, that's a real winning argument."

"Yeah, but they all won by cheating too," Charlie retorted.

"Well, the government isn't about to announce that to the world. They make billions off the lottery. Telling the truth might just mess that up, don't you think?"

"How about all the millions she gave to charity, doesn't that count for something?" Charlie said angrily.

"The IRS applauded LuAnn's generosity but said they really couldn't help on that because she had never filed a return. I'm telling you it's not a bad deal. She could have gone to prison for a long time over this. Except for that fact, she probably could have kept some of the money. But that was a very real threat over her head. Sheriff Harvey didn't go away very easily."

"I can't believe this crap. After all she's been through. She broke up Crane's worldwide criminal syndicate, the FBI looks like heroes, they confiscated all his property, billions of bucks into the Treasury, and she winds up with nothing. Not even a pat on the back. It's not fair!"

LuAnn put a hand on a seething Charlie's shoulder. "It's okay, Charlie. I didn't deserve any of that money. And I wanted to pay what I owed. I just want to be LuAnn Tyler again. I told Matthew that. But I didn't murder anyone. All the charges against me are gone, right?" She looked at Riggs for confirmation.

"That's right. Federal, state, everything. Free as a bird."

"Yeah, and poor as a church mouse," Charlie added angrily.

"Is that it, Matthew? They can't come back on me later? The IRS, I mean? For more money?"

"All the papers are signed. They dropped everything. It's over. They confiscated all your accounts, they foreclosed on the house. Anyway, even if they came after you, which they can't, you don't have any more money."

Lisa looked at him. "Maybe we can move in here, Mom." She added quickly, "I mean for a little while." She looked between LuAnn and Riggs nervously. LuAnn smiled at Lisa. Telling her daughter the entire truth had been the hardest thing she had ever had to do. But the second she had finished, she had never felt greater relief. Lisa had taken the news admirably. Now at least their relationship could take on a semblance of normalcy.

Riggs looked at LuAnn, a little nervous himself. "I was thinking along those lines myself." He swallowed hard. "Can you excuse us for a minute?" he asked Charlie and Lisa.

He took LuAnn by the arm and they left the room. Charlie and Lisa watched them go and then exchanged smiles.

Riggs sat LuAnn down by the fireplace and stood in front of her. "I'd love for all of you to move in here. There's plenty of room. But—" He looked down.

"But what?" she asked.

"I was thinking about a more permanent arrangement."

"I see."

"I mean, I earn a good living and, well, now that you don't have all that money." She cocked her head at him as he blew out a deep breath. "I just never wanted you to think I was after you because of your wealth. It would've driven me crazy. It was like this big roadblock I couldn't get around. I don't want you to think that I'm happy you're not rich anymore.

If there had been some way for you to keep the money, that would've been great. But, now that you don't have it, I just want you to know . . ." Here he stumbled again, unable to continue, suddenly terrified at the deep waters he had ventured into.

"I love you, Matthew," LuAnn said simply.

Riggs's features fully relaxed. He didn't look terrified anymore. In fact, he couldn't remember ever being this happy before. "I love you too, LuAnn Tyler."

"Have you ever been to Switzerland?" she asked.

He looked surprised. "No. Why?"

"I always thought about honeymooning there. It's so romantic, so beautiful. Especially at Christmas time."

Riggs looked troubled. "Well, sweetie, I work hard, but small-town, one-man-shop general contractors don't make enough money to do those sorts of things. I'm sorry." He licked his lips nervously. "I'll understand if you can't accept that, after all these years of being so rich."

In response, LuAnn opened her purse and took out a slip of paper. On it was an account number at a bank in Switzerland. The account had been opened with one hundred million dollars: Jackson's return of her principal. It was all there, just waiting. It cranked out six million a year in interest alone. She would retain her lottery prize after all. And she wasn't feeling any guilt about it this time around. Right now in fact, it seemed like she had earned it. She had spent the last ten years trying to be someone she wasn't. It had been a life of great wealth and great misery. Now she was going to spend the rest of her life being who she really was and enjoying it. She had a beautiful, healthy daughter and *two* men who loved her. No more running, no more hiding for LuAnn Tyler. She was truly blessed.

She smiled at him, stroked his face.

"You know what, Matthew?"

"What?"

Right before she kissed him she said, "I think we'll be just fine."

ACKNOWLEDGMENTS

To Michelle, for keeping everything going while I'm off in my dream world.

To Jennifer Steinberg, for superb research, as always.

To Catherine Broome, M.D., for taking the time from a very busy schedule to talk poisons with me over lunch.

To Steve Jennings, for his always sharp editorial eye.

To Carl Patton, my favourite accountant, and Tom DePont of NationsBank, for much needed help on complex tax issues.

To Larry Kirshbaum, Maureen Egen, and the rest of the Warner crew, for being so supportive and just plain, good people.

To Aaron Priest, for being my sage, my mentor, and, most important, my friend.

To Frances Jalet-Miller, for once again making the story immeasurably better.

To the rest of my family and friends, for their continued love and support.

the sin

To Michelle:
The simple truth is,
my life doesn't work without you

This book is also lovingly dedicated
to the memory of Brenda Gayle Jennings,
a special child

The Truth is rarely pure and never simple.
—Oscar Wilde

ACKNOWLEDGMENTS

To Jennifer Steinberg, once more for superb research.

To Lou Saccoccio, for his able assistance on military legal matters.

To Lee Calligaro, whose stories about his tenure as a JAG attorney during the Vietnam War fascinated me, and who is also the finest trial lawyer I have ever met.

To Steve Jennings, for his astute editorial comments.

To the Warner Books family—Larry, Maureen, Mel, Emi, Tina, Heather, Jackie J. and Jackie M. and all the rest of an incredibly fine and dedicated group of people who make my life so much more enriched.

To my mother, for the finer points of southwest Virginia, an area she knows awfully well.

To Karen Spiegel, who has been with me for a long time on this story.

To attorney Ed Vaughn, for educating me on some of the finer points of Virginia law and practice.

To those other sources, for their help in enlightening me on that fascinating place, the United States Supreme Court.

To my friend and agent, Aaron Priest, who provided me, as always, with a lot of good counsel as I worked my way through this novel.

To Frances Jalet-Miller, for putting so much time, effort and spirit into helping me realize the full potential of this work. I couldn't have done it without you.

CHAPTER ONE

At this prison the doors are inches thick, steel; once factory smooth, they now carry multiple dents. Imprints of human faces, knees, elbows, teeth, residue of blood are harvested large on their gray surface. Prison hieroglyphics: pain, fear, death, all permanently recorded here, at least until a new slab of metal arrives. The doors have a square opening at eye level. The guards stare through it, use the small space to throw bright lights at the human cattle on their watch. Without warning, batons smack against the metal with the pop of gun reports. The oldies bear it well, looking down at the floor, studying nothing—meaning their lives—in a subtle act of defiance, not that anyone notices or cares. The rookies still tense when the pop or light comes; some dribble pee down their cotton pants, watch it flow over their black low-quarter shoes. They soon get over it, smack the damn door back, fight down the push of schoolboy tears and belly bile. If they want to survive.

At night, the prison cells hold the darkness of a cave but for odd shapes here and there. On this night a thunderstorm grips the area. When a lightning bolt dips from the sky, it splashes illumination into the cells through the small Plexiglas windows. The honeycomb pattern of the chicken wire stretched tight across the glass is reproduced on the opposite wall with each burst.

During the passage of such light, the man's face emerges from the dark, as though having suddenly parted the surface of water. Unlike those in the other cells, he sits alone, thinks alone, sees no one in here. The other prisoners fear him; the guards too, even armed as they are, for he is a man of intimidating proportions. When he passes by the other cons, hardened, violent men in their own right, they quickly look away.

His name is Rufus Harms and his reputation at Fort Jackson Military Prison is that of a destroyer: He will crush you if you come at him. He never takes the first step, but he will the last. Twenty-five years of incarceration have taken a considerable toll on the man. Like the age rings of a tree, the ruts of scars on Harms's skin, the poorly healed fractures of bone on his skeleton are a chronicle of his time here. However, far worse damage lies within the soft tissue of his brain, within the centers of his humanity: memory, thought, love, hate, fear, all tainted, all turned against him. But mostly memory, a humbling tumor of iron against the tip of his spine.

There is substantial strength left in the massive frame, though; it is evident in the long, knotty arms, the density of Harms's shoulders. Even the wide girth of his middle carries the promise of exceptional power. But Harms is still a listing oak, topped out on growth, some limbs dead or dying, beyond the cure of pruning, the roots ripped out on one side. He is a living oxymoron: a gentle man, respectful of others, faithful to his God, irreversibly cast in the image of a heartless killer. Because of this the guards and the other prisoners leave him be. And he is content with that. Until this day. What his brother has brought him. A package of gold, a surge of hope. A way out of this place.

Another burst of light shows his eyes brimming with deep red, as though bloodied, until one sees the tears that stain his dark, heavy face. As the light recedes, he smooths out the piece of paper, taking care not to make any sound, an invitation to the guards to come sniffing. Lights have been extinguished for several hours now, and he is unable to reverse that. As it has been for a quarter century, his darkness will end only with the dawn. The absence of light matters little, though. Harms has already read the letter, absorbed every word. Each syllable cuts him like the quick bite of a shiv. The insignia of the United States Army appears bold at the top of the paper. He knows the symbol well. The Army has been his employer, his warden for almost thirty years.

The Army was requesting information from Rufus Harms, a failed and forgotten private from the era of Vietnam. Detailed information. Information Harms had no way of giving. His finger navigating true even without light, Harms touched the place in the letter that had first aroused fragments of memory drifting within him all these years. These particles had generated the incapacitation of endless nightmare, but the nucleus had seemed forever beyond him. Upon first reading the letter, Harms had dipped his head low to the paper, as though trying to reveal to himself the hidden meanings in the typewritten squiggles, to solve the greatest mystery of his mortal life. Tonight, those twisted fragments had suddenly coalesced into firm recollection, into the truth. Finally.

Until he read the letter from the Army, Harms had only two distinct memories of that night twenty-five years ago: the little girl; and the rain. It had been a punishing storm, much like tonight. The girl's features were delicate; the

nose only a bud of cartilage; the face as yet unlined by sun,
age or worry; her staring eyes blue and innocent, the
ambitions of a long life ahead still forming within their
simple depths. Her skin was the white of sugar, and
unblemished except for the red marks crushed upon a neck
as fragile as a flower stem. The marks had been caused by
the hands of Private Rufus Harms, the same hands that
now clutched the letter as his mind careened dangerously
close to that image once more.

Whenever he thought of the dead girl he wept, had to,
couldn't help it, but he did so silently, with good reason.
The guards and cons were buzzards, sharks, they sniffed
blood, weakness, an opening, from a million miles away;
they saw it in the twitch of your eyes, the widened pores
of your skin, even in the stink of your sweat. Here, every
sense was heightened. Here, strong, fast, tough, nimble
equaled life. Or not.

He was kneeling beside her when the MPs found
them. Her thin dress clung to her diminutive frame,
which had receded into the saturated earth, as though
she had been dropped from a great height to form the
shallowest of graves. Harms had looked up at the MPs
once, but his mind had registered nothing more than a
confusion of darkened silhouettes. He had never felt
such fury in his life, even as the nausea seized him, his
eyes losing their focus, his pulse rate, respiration, blood
pressure all bottoming out. He had gripped his head as
if to prevent his bursting brain from cleaving through
the bone of his skull, through tissue and hair, and
exploding into the soaked air.

When he had looked down once more at the dead girl,
and then at the pair of twitching hands that had ended
her life, the anger had drained from him, as though
someone had jerked free a plug embedded within. The
functions of his body oddly abandoning him, Harms
could only remain kneeling, wet and shivering, his

knees sunk deeply into the mud. A black high chieftain in green fatigues presiding over a small pale-skinned sacrifice, was how one stunned witness would later describe it.

The next day he would come to learn the little girl's name: Ruth Ann Mosley, ten years old, from Columbia, South Carolina. She and her family had been visiting her brother, who was stationed at the base. On that night Harms had only known Ruth Ann Mosley as a corpse, small—tiny, in fact—compared to the stunning breadth of his six-foot-five-inch, three-hundred-pound body. The blurred image of the rifle butt that one of the MPs smashed against his skull represented the last mental sliver Harms carried from that night. The blow had dropped him to the ground right next to her. The girl's lifeless face pointed upward, collecting droplets of rain in every still crevice. His face sunken into the mud, Rufus Harms saw nothing more. Remembered nothing more.

Until tonight. He swelled his lungs with rain-drenched air and stared out the half-open window. He was suddenly that still rare beast: an innocent man in prison.

He had convinced himself over the years that such evil had been lurking, cancerlike, within him. He had even thought of suicide, to make penance for stealing the life of another, more pitiably a child's. But he was deeply religious, and not a fleeting jailhouse convert to the Lord. He thus could not commit the sin of prematurely forcing his last breath. He also knew the girl's killing had condemned him to an afterlife a thousand times worse than the one he was now enduring. He was unwilling to rush to its embrace. Better this place, this man-made prison, for now.

Now he understood that his decision to live had been right. God had known, had kept him alive for this moment. With stunning clarity he recalled the men who had come for him that night at the stockade. His mind once more clearly held every contorted face, the stripes on the uniforms some of them wore—his comrades in arms. He recalled the way they circled him, wolves to prey, emboldened only by their numbers; the telling hatred of their words. What they had done that night had caused Ruth Ann Mosley to die. And in a very real sense, Harms had died as well.

To these men Harms was an able-bodied soldier who had never fought in defense of his country. Whatever he got, he deserved, they no doubt believed. Now he was a middle-aged man slowly dying in a cage as punishment for a crime of long-ago origin. He had no power to see that any semblance of justice was done on his behalf. And yet with all that, Rufus Harms stared into the familiar darkness of his crypt, a single passion empowering him: After twenty-five years of terrible, wrenching guilt that had relentlessly taunted him until he was just barely in possession of a ruined life, he knew that it was now their turn to suffer. He gripped the worn Bible his mother had given him, and he promised this to the God who had chosen never to abandon him.

CHAPTER TWO

The steps leading up to the United States Supreme Court building were wide and seemingly endless. Trudging up them was akin to laboring toward Mount Olympus to request an audience of Zeus, which in a real sense you were. Engraved in the facade above the main doorway were the words EQUAL JUSTICE UNDER LAW. The phrase came from no significant document or court ruling but from Cass Gilbert, the architect who had designed and built the courthouse. It was a matter of spacing: The words fit perfectly into the area designated by Gilbert for a memorable legal phrase.

The majestic building rose four stories above ground level. Ironically, Congress had appropriated the funds to construct it in 1929, the same year the stock market crashed and helped bring on the Great Depression. Almost a third of the building's $9 million cost had gone to the purchase of marble. Pure Vermont was on the exterior, hauled down by an army of freight cars; crystal-lined

Georgia rock padded the four interior courts; and milky Alabama stone lay over most of the floors and walls of the interior, except in the Great Hall. Underfoot there was a darker Italian marble, with African stone in other places. The columns in the hall had been cast from blocks of Italian marble quarried from the Montarrenti site and shipped to Knoxville, Tennessee. There ordinary men struggled to cast the blocks into thirty-foot shapes to help support the building that had been the professional home to nine men since 1935 and, since 1981, to at least one woman, all of extraordinary achievement. Its supporters deemed the building a fine example of the Corinthian style of Greek architecture. Its detractors decried it as a palace for the insane pleasures of kings, rather than a place for the rational dispensation of justice.

And yet since John Marshall's time, the Court had been the defender and interpreter of the Constitution. It could declare an act of Congress unconstitutional. These nine people could force a sitting president to turn over tapes and documents that would ultimately lead to his resignation and disgrace. Crafted alongside the legislative authority of the Congress and the executive power of the presidency by the Founding Fathers, the American judiciary, headed by the Supreme Court, was an equal branch of government. And govern it did, as the Supreme Court bent and shaped the will of the American people by virtue of its decisions on any number of significant issues.

The elderly man walking down the Great Hall carried on this honored tradition. He was tall and bony, with soft brown eyes in no need of glasses, his eyesight still excellent even after decades of reading small print. His hair was nearly gone; his shoulders had narrowed and curved over the years, and he walked with a slight limp. Still, Chief Justice Harold Ramsey had a nervous energy about him and a peerless intellect that more than compensated for any physical slide. Even his footfalls seemed to carry special purpose.

He was the highest-ranking jurist in the land, and this was his Court, his building. The "Ramsey Court," the media had long deemed it, like the Warren Court and its other predecessors—his legacy for all time. Ramsey ran his court tight and true, cobbling together a consistent majority that was now going on ten years running. He loved the wheeling and dealing that went on behind the scenes at the Court. A carefully placed word or paragraph here or there, give a little on one point with the favor to be repaid later. Waiting patiently for just the right case to come along as a vehicle for change, sometimes in ways unexpected by his colleagues. Culling together the five votes necessary for a majority was an absolute obsession with Ramsey.

He had come to the Court as an associate justice and then been elevated to the top rank a decade ago. Merely first among equals in theory, but something more than that in reality. Ramsey was a man of intense beliefs and personal philosophies. Fortunately for him, he had been nominated to the Court when the selection process had nothing of the political sophistication of today. There were no bothersome questions about a candidate's positions on specific legal issues like abortion, capital punishment and affirmative action, queries that now littered the highly politicized process of becoming a Supreme Court justice. Back then, if the president nominated you, if you possessed the requisite legal pedigree, and if there were no particularly bad skeletons lying in wait, you were in.

The Senate had confirmed Ramsey unanimously. It really had no choice. His educational and legal backgrounds were of the first order. Multiple degrees, all from Ivy League schools, and top of his class in every one of them. Next had come an award-winning stint as a law professor with original, sweeping theories on the direction the law and, by extension, humanity should take. Then he had been nominated to the federal appellate bench, quickly becoming chief judge of his circuit. During his tenure on the appellate bench, the Supreme Court had never reversed one of his majority opinions. Over the years he had built the right network of contacts, done all the necessary things in his pursuit of the position he now held as tightly as he could.

He had earned the position. Nothing had ever been given to him. That was another of his firm beliefs. If you worked hard, you would succeed in America. No one was entitled to any handouts, not the poor, not the rich, not the middle class. The United States was the land of opportunity, but you had to work for it, sweat for it, sacrifice for its bounty. Ramsey had no patience for people's excuses for not getting ahead. He had been born to abysmal poverty and an abusive, hard-drinking father. Ramsey had found no refuge with his mother; his father had crushed any maternal instincts she might have had. Not a promising start in life, and look where he now stood. If he could survive and flourish under those circumstances, then others could too. And if they didn't it was their fault, and he would not hear otherwise.

He let out a contented sigh. Another Court term had just begun. Things were going smoothly. But there was one hitch. A chain was only as strong as its weakest leak. And he had one of those. His potential Waterloo. Things might be going well now, but what about five years down the road? Those problems were better dealt with early on, before they surged out of control.

He knew he was close to meeting his match with Elizabeth Knight. She was as smart as he, and just as tough, perhaps. He had known this the day her nomination had been approved. A young-blood female on a court of old men. He had been working on her from day one. He would assign her opinions when he thought she was on the fence, with the hope that the responsibility of penning a draft that would bring together a majority would put her firmly in his camp. He had tried to place her under his wing, to guide her through the intricacies of the Court process. Still, she had shown a very stubborn independent streak. He had watched other chief justices grow complacent, let their guard down, with the result that their leadership had been usurped by others more diligent. Ramsey was determined never to join that group.

"Murphy's concerned about the *Chance* case," Michael Fiske said to Sara Evans. They were in her office on the second floor of the Court building. Michael was six-two and handsome, with the graceful proportions of the athlete he once was. Most clerks did a one-year stint at the Supreme Court before moving on to prestigious positions in private practice, public service or academia. Michael was beginning an almost unprecedented third year here as senior clerk to Justice Thomas Murphy, the Court's legendary liberal.

Michael was the possessor of a truly wondrous mind. His brain was like a money-sorting machine: Data poured into his head and was swiftly sorted and sent to its proper location. He could mentally juggle dozens of complex factual scenarios, testing each to see how it would impact on the others. At the Court he happily labored over cases of national importance, surrounded with mental sabers equal to his own. And Michael had found that, even in the context of rigorous intellectual discourse, there was time and opportunity for something deeper than what the stark words of a law proclaimed. He really didn't want to leave the Supreme Court. The outside world held no appeal for him.

Sara looked concerned. Last term, Murphy had voted to hear the *Chance* case. Oral argument was set, and the bench memo was being prepared. Sara was in her mid-twenties, about five-five, slender, but her body possessed subtle curves. Her face was nicely shaped, the eyes wide and blue. Her hair was thick and light brown—it still turned blondish in the summer—and seemed always to carry a fresh, pleasing scent. She was the senior clerk for Justice Elizabeth Knight. "I don't understand. I thought he was behind us on this. It's right up his alley. Little person against a big bureaucracy."

"He's also a firm believer in upholding precedent."

"Even if it's wrong?"

"You're preaching to the choir, Sara, but I thought I'd pass it along. Knight's not going to get five votes without him, you know that. Even with him she might fall short."

"Well, what does he want?"

This was how it went most of the time. The famed clerk network. They hustled and debated and scrounged for votes on behalf of their justices like the most shameless political hucksters. It was beneath the justices to openly lobby for votes, for a particular phrasing in an opinion, or for a specific angle, addition or deletion, but it wasn't below the clerks. In fact, most of them took great pride in the process. It was akin to an enormous, never-ending gossip column with national interests at stake. In the hands of twenty-five-year-olds at their first real job, no less.

"He doesn't necessarily disagree with Knight's position. But if she gets five votes at conference, the opinion will have to be very narrowly drawn. He's not going to give away the farm. He was in the military in World War II. He holds it in the highest regard. He believes it deserves special consideration. You need to know that when you're putting together the draft opinion."

She nodded her head in appreciation. The backgrounds of the justices played more of a role in their decision making than most people would suspect. "Thanks. But first Knight has to get the opinion to write."

"Of course she will. Ramsey is not voting to overturn *Feres* and *Stanley*, you know that. Murphy will probably vote in favor of Chance at the conference. He's the senior associate, so he gets to assign the opinion. If she gets her five votes at conference, he'll give Knight her shot. If she delivers the goods—meaning no broad, sweeping language—we're all okay."

United States v. Chance was one of the most important cases on the docket for this term. Barbara Chance had been a private in the Army. She had been bullied, harassed and frightened into repeatedly having sexual intercourse with several of her male superiors. The case had gone through the internal channels of the Army with the result that one of the men had been court-martialed and imprisoned. Barbara Chance, however, had not been content with that. After leaving the military, she had sued the Army for damages, claiming that it had allowed this hostile environment to exist for her and other female recruits.

The case had slowly worked its way through the proper legal channels, Chance losing at each stop. The matter presented enough gray areas in the law that it had eventually been plopped like a big tuna on the doorstep of this place.

The current law said that Chance had, ironically, no chance of winning. The military was virtually immune from suit by its personnel for any damages, regardless of the cause or the element of fault. But the justices could change what the law said. And Knight and Sara Evans were working hard behind the scenes to do just that. The support of Thomas Murphy was critical to that plan. Murphy might not support overturning completely the military's immunity right, but the Chance case could at least punch a hole in the Army's wall of invincibility.

It seemed premature to be discussing resolution of a case that had not yet been heard, but in many cases and for many justices, oral argument was anticlimactic. By the time it rolled around, most had already made up their minds. The argument phase of the process was more an opportunity for the justices to showcase their positions and concerns to their colleagues, often by use of extreme hypotheticals. They were akin to mental scare tactics, as if to say, "See what could happen, Brother Justice, if you vote that way?"

Michael stood and looked down at her. It was at his urging that Sara had signed up for another term at the Court. Raised on a small farm in North Carolina and educated at Stanford, Sara had, like all the clerks here, a wonderful professional future waiting once she left the Court. Having a clerkship at the Supreme Court on one's résumé was a gold key to entry at just about any place an attorney would care to put down his briefcase. That had affected some clerks in a negative way, giving them inflated egos that their actual accomplishments did not quite back up. Michael and Sara, though, had remained the same people they had always been. Which was one reason, aside from her intelligence, good looks and refreshingly balanced personality, that Michael had asked her a very important question a week ago. A question he hoped to receive an answer to soon. Perhaps now. He had never been a particularly patient man.

Sara looked up at him expectantly.

"Have you given my question any thought?"

She had known it was coming. She had avoided it long enough. "That's all I've been thinking about."

"They say when it takes that long, it's a bad sign." He said this jokingly, but the humor was obviously forced.

"Michael, I like you a lot."

"*Like?* Oh boy, another bad sign." His face suddenly grew warm.

She shook her head. "I'm sorry."

He shrugged. "Probably not half as sorry as I am. I've never asked anyone to marry me before."

"You're actually my first too. And I can't tell you how flattered I am. You've got it all."

"Except for one thing." Michael looked down at his hands as they quivered a bit. His skin suddenly seemed too tight for his body. "I respect your decision. I'm not one of those who thinks you can learn to love someone over time. It's either there or not."

"You'll find someone, Michael. And that woman will be very lucky." Sara felt so awkward. "I hope this doesn't mean I'm losing my best friend on the Court."

"Probably." He held up a hand as she started to protest. "I'm just kidding." He sighed. "I don't mean this to sound egotistical, but this is the first time anybody's really turned me down for anything."

"I wish my life had been so easy." Sara smiled.

"No, you don't. It makes rejection a lot harder to accept." Michael went over to the doorway. "We're still friends, Sara. You're too much fun to be around. I'm too smart to let that go. And you'll find someone too, and he'll be very lucky." He didn't look at her when he added, "Have you found him yet, by the way?"

She started slightly. "Why do you ask that?"

"Call it a sixth sense. Losing is a little easier to accept if you know who you lost out to."

"There's no one else," she said quickly.

Michael didn't look convinced. "Talk to you later."

Sara stared after him, very troubled.

"I remember my first years on the Court." Ramsey was staring out the window, a smile working across his face.

He was seated across from Elizabeth Knight, the Court's most junior associate. Elizabeth Knight was in her mid-forties, average height, with a slender body, and long black hair tied back in a harsh, unflattering bun. Her face possessed sharply edged features, and her skin was unlined, as though she never spent any time outdoors.

Knight had quickly established a reputation as one of the most vocal questioners at oral argument and as one of the most hardworking of all the justices.

"I'm sure they're still vivid." Knight leaned back in her desk chair as she mentally checked off her work schedule for the rest of the day.

"It was quite a *learning* process."

She stared at him. He was now looking directly at her, his large hands clasped behind his head.

"It took me five years just to figure out things, really," Ramsey continued.

Knight managed not to smile. "Harold, you're being much too modest. I'm sure you had it all figured out before you walked in the door."

"Seriously, it does take time. And I had many fine examples with whom to work. Felix Abernathy, old Tom Parks. Respecting the experience of others is nothing to be ashamed of. It's an indoctrination process we all go through. Though you certainly have progressed faster than most," he quickly added. "Still, here, patience is a very cherished virtue indeed. You've been here only three years. I've called this place home for over twenty. I hope you understand my point."

Knight hid a smile. "I understand you are a little perturbed that I led the way for *U.S. v. Chance* to be put on the docket at the end of the last term."

Ramsey sat up straight. "Don't believe everything you hear around here."

"On the contrary, I've found the clerk grapevine to be extraordinarily accurate."

Ramsey sat back once more. "Well, I have to admit that I was a little surprised about it. The case presents no unsettled question of law that requires our intervention. Need I say more?" He threw up his hands.

"In your opinion?"

A tinge of red eased across Ramsey's face. "In the

published opinions of this Court over the last fifty years. All I ask is that you accord the Court's precedents the respect they deserve."

"You'll find no one who holds this institution in higher regard than I do."

"Very happy to hear that."

"And I'll be delighted to entertain your thoughts further on the *Chance* case after we hear oral argument."

Ramsey looked at her dully. "It will be a very short discussion, considering that it doesn't take long to say yes or no. Bluntly speaking, at the end of the day, I'll have at least five votes and you won't."

"Well, I convinced three other justices to vote to hear the case."

Ramsey looked as though he might laugh. "You'll quickly learn that the difference between votes to hear a case and votes to decide it is enormous. Rest assured, I will have the majority."

Knight smiled pleasantly. "Your confidence is inspiring. That I *can* learn from."

Ramsey rose to leave. "Then consider this other lesson: Small mistakes tend to lead to large ones. Ours is a lifetime appointment, and all you have is your reputation. Once it's gone, it doesn't come back." Ramsey went to the door. "I wish you a productive day, Beth," he said before leaving her.

CHAPTER THREE

"Rufus?" Samuel Rider cautiously pressed the phone to his ear. "How did you track me down?"

"Ain't many lawyers up these parts, Samuel," Rufus Harms said.

"I'm not in the JAG anymore."

"Being on the outside pays good, I guess."

"Some days I miss the uniform," Rider lied. He had been a terrified draftee, fortunately with a law degree in hand, and had chosen a safe role in the Judge Advocate General's Office—or JAG—over toting a gun through the jungles of Vietnam as a pudgy, fear-soaked GI, a sure beacon for enemy fire.

"I need to see you. Don't want to say why over the phone."

"Everything okay up at Fort Jackson? I heard you were transferred there."

"Sure. Prison's just fine."

"I didn't mean that, Rufus. I was just wondering why you looked me up after all this time."

"You're still my lawyer, ain't you? Only time I ever needed one."

"My schedule's kind of tight, and I don't usually travel over that way." Rider's hand tightened on the phone with Harms's next words.

"I really need to see you tomorrow, Samuel. You think you owe me that?"

"I did all I could for you back then."

"You took the deal. Quick and easy."

"No," Rider countered, "we did the pretrial agreement with the convening authority, and the trial counsel signed off on it, and that was the smart thing to do."

"You didn't really try to beat it none on the sentencing. Most try to do that."

"Who told you that?"

"Learn a lot in prison."

"Well, you can't waive the sentencing phase. We put on our case to the members, you know that."

"But you didn't call no witnesses, didn't really do much that I could see."

Rider now got very defensive. "I did the best I could. Remember something, Rufus, they could've executed you. A little white girl and all. They would've gone for first degree, they told me that. At least you got to live."

"Tomorrow, Samuel. I put you on my visitors' list. Around about nine A.M. Thank you. Thank you kindly. Oh, bring a little radio with you." Before Rider could ask him why he should bring such a device, or why he should even come to see him, Harms had hung up the phone.

Rider eased back in his very comfortable chair and looked around his spacious, wood-paneled office. He practiced law in a small rural town some distance from Blacksburg, Virginia. He made a fine living: nice house, new Buick every three years, vacations twice annually. He had put the past behind him, particularly the most horrible case he had ever handled in his brief career as a military lawyer. The kind of case that had the same effect on your stomach as curdled milk, only no amount of Pepto-Bismol could right the discomfort.

Rider touched a hand to his face as his thoughts now drifted back to the early seventies, a time of chaos in the military, the country, the world. Everybody blaming everybody else for everything that had ever gone wrong in the history of the universe. Rufus Harms had sounded bitter over the phone, but he *had* killed that little girl. Brutally. Right in front of her family. Crushed her neck in a few seconds, before anyone could even attempt to stop him.

On Harms's behalf, Rider had negotiated a pretrial agreement, but then, under the rules of military law, he had the right to attempt to beat that deal in the sentencing phase. The defendant would either receive the punishment in the pretrial agreement, or the one meted out by the judge or by the members—the military counterpart of a jury—whichever involved less prison time. Harms's words gnawed at the lawyer, though, for Rider had been persuaded at the time not to put on much of a case at the sentencing phase. He had agreed with the prosecutor not to bring in any witnesses from outside the area who could attest to Harms's character and so forth. He had also agreed to rely on stipulations from the official record instead of attempting to find fresh evidence and witnesses.

That was not exactly playing by the rules, because a defendant's right to beat the deal was not supposed to be waived or bargained away in any substantive manner. But without Rider working behind the scenes like that, the prosecutor would have gone for the death penalty, and with those facts, he probably would have gotten it. It mattered little that the murder had happened so quickly that proving premeditation would have been very difficult. The cold body of a child could derail the most logical of legal analyses.

The bald truth was nobody cared about Rufus Harms. He was a black man who had spent most of his Army career locked in the stockade. His senseless murder of a child certainly had not improved his standing in the eyes of the military. Such a man was not entitled to justice, many had felt, unless it was swift, painful, and lethal. And maybe Rider was one of those who felt that way. So he hadn't exactly practiced the scorched-earth policy in his defense of the man, but Rider had gotten Rufus Harms life. That was the best any lawyer could have done.

So what could Rufus want to see him about? he wondered.

CHAPTER FOUR

As John Fiske rose from the counsel's table he glanced over at his opponent, Paul Williams. The young assistant commonwealth attorney, or ACA, had just finished confidently stating the particulars of his motion. Fiske whispered, "Your ass is grass, Paulie. You messed up."

When Fiske turned to face Judge Walters, his manner was one of subdued excitement. Fiske was broad-shouldered, though at six feet he was a couple of inches shorter than his younger brother. And unlike Michael Fiske, his features were far from classically handsome. He had chubby cheeks, a too-sharp chin and a twice-broken nose, one time from high school wrestling, the other time a carryover from his cop days. However, Fiske's black hair was swept over his forehead in an unkempt manner that somehow managed to be attractive and intimate, and his brown eyes housed an intense core.

"Your Honor, in the interest of not wasting the court's time, I would like to make an offer in open court to the

Commonwealth Attorney's Office regarding its motion. If they agree to withdraw with prejudice and contribute one thousand dollars to the public defender's fund, I will withdraw my response, not file for sanctions and we can all go home."

Paul Williams leaped to his feet so quickly his eyeglasses fell off and hit the table. "Your Honor, this is outrageous!"

Judge Walters looked over his crowded courtroom, silently contemplated his equally bulging docket and flicked a weary hand at both men. "Approach."

At the sidebar, Fiske said, "Judge, I'm only trying to do the commonwealth a favor."

"The commonwealth doesn't need favors from Mr. Fiske," Williams said with disgust.

"Come on, Paulie, a thousand bucks, and you can get a beer before you go back and explain to your boss how you messed up. I'll even buy you the beer."

"Not in ten thousand years will you get a dime from us," Williams said disdainfully.

"Well, Mr. Williams, this motion is a little unusual," Judge Walters said. In the Richmond criminal courts, motions were heard before or during trial. And there weren't lengthy briefs attached to them. The sad truth was, most issues of criminal law were well settled. Only in the unusual case in which the judge was unsure of a ruling after he had heard the lawyers' oral arguments would he ask for written briefs to review before making his decision. Thus, Judge Walters was a little bewildered by the unsolicited and lengthy brief filed by the commonwealth.

"I know, Your Honor," said Williams. "However, as I stated, this is an unusual situation."

"Unusual?" Fiske said. "Try nuts, Paulie."

Judge Walters impatiently broke in. "Mr. Fiske, I have admonished you before regarding your unorthodox behavior in my courtroom, and I will not hesitate to find you in contempt if your future actions warrant it. Get on with your response."

Williams returned to his seat and Fiske stepped to the lectern. "Your Honor, in spite of the fact that the commonwealth's 'emergency' motion was faxed to my office in the middle of the night and I haven't had time to prepare a truly proper response, I believe that if you would refer to each of the second paragraphs on pages four, six and nine of the commonwealth's memorandum, you will conclude that the facts relied upon therein, particularly with regard to the defendant's prior criminal record, the statements of the arresting officers and the two eyewitness accounts at the location of the crime allegedly committed by my client, are unsustainable with the established record in this case. Further, the principal precedent cited by the commonwealth on page ten was very recently overturned by a decision of the Virginia Supreme Court. I've attached the pertinent materials to my response and highlighted the discrepancies for your ease of review."

As Judge Walters examined the file in front of him, Fiske leaned over to Williams and said, "See what happens when you draft this shit in the middle of the night?" Fiske dropped his reply brief in front of Williams. "Since I only had about five minutes to read your brief, I thought I'd return the favor. You can read along with the judge."

Walters finished reviewing the file and gave Williams a stare that chilled even the most casual observer in the courtroom.

"I hope the commonwealth has an appropriate response to this, Mr. Williams, although I'm at a loss as to what it could possibly be."

Williams rose from his chair. As he tried to speak, he suddenly discovered that his voice, along with his hubris, had deserted him.

"Well?" Judge Walters said expectantly. "Please say

something or I've a mind to grant Mr. Fiske's motion for sanctions before I've even heard it."

When Fiske glanced over at Williams, his expression softened somewhat. You never knew when you might need a favor. "Your Honor, I'm certain the factual and legal errors in the commonwealth's motion are due to the overworked lawyers there rather than anything intentional. I'll even cut my settlement offer to five hundred dollars, but I'd like a personal apology from the commonwealth on the record. I really could've used some sleep last night." That last comment brought laughter from around the courtroom.

Suddenly a voice boomed out from the back of the courtroom. "Judge Walters, if I may intercede, the commonwealth will accept that offer."

Everyone looked at the source of the announcement, a short, almost bald, thick-bodied man dressed in a seersucker suit, his hairy neck pinched by his starchy collar. "We'll take the offer," the man said again in a gravelly voice laced with both the pleasing drawl of a lifelong Virginian and the rasp of a lifelong smoker. "And we do apologize to the *court* for taking up its valuable time."

"I'm glad you happened by when you did, Mr. Graham," Judge Walters said.

Bobby Graham, commonwealth attorney for the city of Richmond, nodded curtly before leaving through the double glass doors. He had offered no apology to Fiske; however, the defense lawyer chose not to push it. In a court of law, you rarely got everything you asked for.

Judge Walters said, "Commonwealth's motion is dismissed with prejudice." He looked at Williams. "Mr. Williams, I think you should go have that beer with Mr. Fiske, only I think you should be the one doing the buying, son."

As the next motion was called, Fiske snapped shut his

briefcase and walked out of the courtroom, Williams right next to him.

"Should've taken my first offer, Paulie."

"I won't forget this, Fiske," Williams said angrily.

"Don't."

"We're still going to put Jerome Hicks away," Williams sneered. "Don't think we're not."

For Paulie Williams and most of the other assistant commonwealth attorneys Fiske faced, Fiske knew his clients were like their personal, lifelong enemies, undeserving of anything other than the harshest of punishments. In some cases, Fiske knew, they were right. But not in all.

"You know what I'm thinking?" Fiske asked Williams. "I'm thinking how fast ten thousand years can go by."

As Fiske left the third-floor courtroom, he passed police officers he had worked with when he was a Richmond cop. One of them smiled, nodded a hello, but the others refused to look at him. To them he was a traitor to the ranks, suit and briefcase traded for badge and gun. Mouthpiece for the other side. Rot in hell, Brother Fiske.

Fiske looked at one group of young black men, crewcuts so severe they looked bald, pants pushed down to the crotch, boxers showing, puffy gang jackets, bulky tennies with no laces. Their open defiance of the criminal justice system was clear; they were imperiously sulky in their sameness.

These young men crowded around their attorney, a white guy, office-chunky, sweaty, expensive pinstripe soiled at the cuffs, slick-skinned loafers on his feet, horn-rim glasses twisting a little as he hammered home a point to his scout troop. He banged his fist into his meaty palm as the young black men, abdominals racked under their silk drug-trove shirts, listened intently, the only time they figured they would need this man, would bother to even look at him other than with contempt, or through a gun sight. Until the next time they needed him. And they would. In this building, he was magic. Here Michael Jordan could not touch this white man. They were Lewis and Clark. He was their Sacajewea. Shout the mystical words, Sac. Don't let them do us.

Fiske knew what the suit was saying, knew it as if he could read the man's lips. The man specialized in defending gang members on any crime they cared to commit. The best strategy: stone silence. Seen nothing, heard nothing, remembered nothing. Gunshots? Car backfire, most likely. Remember this, boys: Thou Shalt not kill; but if thou Shalt kill, thou Shalt not rat on each other about it. He smacked his palm against his briefcase for added emphasis. The huddle broke and the game commenced.

Along another part of the hallway, sitting on the boxy gray-carpeted seating built into the wall, were three hookers, working teens of the night. A variety pack: one black, one Asian, one white, they waited their turn before justice. The Asian looked nervous, probably needing a calming smoke or the sting of a needle. The others were vets, Fiske knew. They strolled, sat, showed some thigh, the jiggle of breast occasionally when some good old boys or young turks prowled by. Why miss some business over a little court thing? This was America, after all.

Fiske took the elevator down and was just passing by the metal detector and X-ray machine, standard equipment in virtually every courthouse these days, when Bobby Graham approached him, an unlit cigarette in his hand. Fiske liked the man neither personally nor professionally. Graham selected cases for prosecution based on the size of the headlines they would garner for him. And he never took on a case he would have to work real hard to win. The public doesn't like prosecutors who lose.

"Just a little pretrial motion in a dime-a-dozen case. The big man has better things to do with his time, don't you, Bobby?" said Fiske.

"Maybe I had an inkling that you were going to chew up and spit out one of my baby lawyers. It wouldn't have been so easy if you'd been up against a real attorney."

"Who, like you?"

With a wry smile, Graham put the unlit cigarette in his mouth. "Here we are, living in arguably the damned tobacco capital of the world, the biggest cigarette manufacturing facility on the planet just a spit on down the road, and one can't even smoke in the halls of justice." He chewed on the end of his unfiltered Pall Mall, noisily sucking in the nicotine. Actually there were still designated smoking areas in the Richmond court building, only not where Graham happened to be standing.

The prosecutor let slip a triumphant grin. "Oh, by the way, Jerome Hicks was picked up this morning on suspicion of murdering a guy over on Southside. Black on black, drugs involved. Wow, what a surprise. Apparently he wanted to increase his inventory of coke and didn't want to go through the normal acquisition channels. Only your guy didn't know we had his target staked out."

Fiske wearily leaned up against the wall. Court victories were often empty, particularly when your client couldn't keep a lid on his felonious impulses. "Really? That's the first I've heard about it."

"I was coming down here anyway for a pretrial conference, thought I'd fill you in. Professional courtesy."

"Right," Fiske said dryly. "If that's the case, why did you let Paulie's motion go forward?" When Graham didn't respond, Fiske answered his own question. "Just making me jump through the hoops?"

"A man's got to have some fun with his work."

Fiske balled up a fist, and then just as quickly he uncurled it. Graham wasn't worth it. "Well, as a professional courtesy, were there any eyewitnesses?"

"Oh, about a half dozen, murder weapon found in Jerome's car, along with Jerome. He almost ran down two policemen trying to get away. We've got blood, the drugs, the whole candy store, really. Guy shouldn't have been granted bail in the first place. Anyway, I've a mind to drop this rinky-dink distribution charge you're representing him on and just focus on this new development. Got to maximize my scarce resources. Hicks is a bad one, John. I think we're gonna have to seek a capital murder indictment on this one."

"Capital case? Come on, Bobby."

"The willful, deliberate and premeditated killing of any person in the commission of a robbery equals capital murder equals death penalty. At least that's what my Virginia statute book says."

"I don't give a shit what the law says, he's only eighteen years old."

Graham's face tensed. "Funny talk coming from a lawyer, an officer of the court."

"The law's a sieve I have to slip my facts through, because my facts always suck."

"They're scum. Come out of the womb looking to hurt people. We oughta start building baby prisons before the sonsofbitches can really hurt anybody."

"Jerome Hicks's entire life can be summed up—"

"Right, blame it on his piss-poor childhood," Graham interrupted. "Same old story."

"That's right, *same* old story."

Graham smiled and shook his head. "Look, I didn't grow up with a silver spoon in my mouth, okay? Wanta know my secret? I worked my ass off. If I can do it, they damn well can too. Case closed."

Fiske started to walk off and then looked back. "Let me take a look at the arrest report and I'll call you."

"We got nothing to talk about."

"Killing him won't get you the AG slot, Bobby, you know that. Aim higher." Fiske turned and walked away.

Graham twisted the cigarette between his fingers. "Try getting a real job, Fiske."

A half hour later, John Fiske was at a suburban county jail meeting with one of his clients. His practice often took him outside of Richmond, to the counties of Henrico, Chesterfield, Hanover, even Goochland. His ever-expanding pool of work was not something he was particularly pleased about, but it was like the sun rising. It would continue until the day it stopped for good.

"I've got a plea to talk to you about, Derek."

Derek Brown—or DB1, as he was known on the street—was a light-skinned black, with tattoos of hate, obscenity and poetry running down his arms. He spent enough time in jail to be buffed; wormy veins split his biceps. Fiske had once seen Derek playing basketball in the jail's recreation yard; shirt off, well muscled, more tattoos on his back and shoulders. It looked like a damn musical score from a distance. Rising from the air like a jet on takeoff, gliding smooth, held up by something Fiske couldn't see, the guards and other cons turning to look in admiration, the young man slammed the ball home, finishing with high-fives all around. Never good enough, though, to play college ball, much less NBA. So here they were looking at each other in the county lockup.

"ACA's offered malicious wounding, Class Three felony."

"Why not Class Six?"

Fiske stared at him. These guys were in and out of the criminal system so often they knew the criminal code better than most lawyers.

"Class Six is heat of the moment. Your heat came the next day."

"He had a gun. I ain't going up against Pack when he got his shooter and I ain't got mine. What, you stupid?"

Fiske wanted to reach across and wipe the man's attitude

right off his face. "Sorry, the Commonwealth isn't budging from Class Three."

"How much time?" Derek said stonily. His ears were pierced, by Fiske's count twelve times.

"Five, with time already served."

"Bullshit. Five years for cutting somebody a little with a damn pocketknife?"

"Stiletto, six-inch blade. And you stabbed him ten damn times. In front of witnesses."

"Shit, he was feeling up my bitch. Ain't that a defense?"

"You're lucky you're not looking at murder in the first, Derek. The docs said it was a miracle the guy didn't bleed to death right there on the street. And if Pack weren't such a dangerous slimeball you wouldn't just be looking at malicious wounding either. You could've been looking at aggravated malicious wounding. That's twenty to life. You know that."

"Messing with my bitch." Derek leaned forward and popped his bony knuckles to emphasize the absolute logic of both his legal and moral positions.

Derek had a good-paying job, Fiske knew, albeit an illegal one. He was a first lieutenant for the number two drug distribution ring in Richmond, hence his street name of DB1. Turbo was the boss, all of twenty-four years old. His empire was well organized, discipline enforced, and included the facade of legality with dry-cleaning operations, a café, a pawnshop, and a stable of accountants and lawyers to deal with the drug funds after they had been laundered. Turbo was a very smart young man, good head for numbers and business. Fiske had always wanted to ask him why he didn't try running a Fortune 500 company. The pay was almost as good, and the mortality rate was considerably lower.

Normally, Turbo would have one of his three-hundred-dollar-an-hour Main or Franklin Street lawyers take care of Derek. But Derek's offense was unrelated to Turbo's business, so that accommodation had not been made. Sloughing him off to someone like Fiske was a form of punishment for Derek doing something as stupid as losing his head over a female. Turbo had no reason to fear Derek's turning snitch. The prosecutor hadn't even made any noises along those lines, knowing it was futile. You talk, you die—in or out of prison, it made no difference.

Derek had grown up in a nice middle-class neighborhood, with nice middle-class parents, before he decided to drop out of high school and take the easy route of drug dealing over actually working for a living. He had every advantage, could have done anything with his life. There were just enough Derek Browns around to make the world largely apathetic to the horrific lives of the kids who turned to the sugar-elixir provided by people like Turbo. Which made Fiske want to take Derek out to an alley late at night with a baseball bat in hand and teach the young man some good old-fashioned values.

"The ACA doesn't give a damn about what he was doing to your girlfriend that night."

"I can't believe this shit. Buddy of mine cut up somebody last year and he got two years, half that suspended. Out in three months with time served. And I'm looking at five damn years? What kinda shitty lawyer are you?"

"Did your buddy have a prior felony conviction?" Was your good old buddy one of the top men for one of Richmond's worst diseases? Fiske wanted to ask, and he would have but it would be wasted breath. "I tell you what—I'll go back with three and time served."

Now Derek looked interested. "You think you can get that?"

Fiske stood up. "Don't know. I'm just a shitty lawyer."

On the way out, Fiske looked out the barred window and watched as a new shipment of inmates climbed from the prison van, grouped close, shackles beating a chant on the asphalt. Most were young blacks or Latinos, already

sizing each other up. Slave to master. Who gets cut or
scored first. The few whites looked as though they might
drop and die from sheer panic before they even got to their
cells. Some of these young men were probably the sons of
men Patrolman John Fiske had arrested ten years ago.
They would have been just kids then, maybe dreaming of
something other than the public dole, no daddy at home,
mother struggling through a horror of a life with no end
in sight. Then again, maybe not. Reality had a way of
punishing one's subconscious. Dreams weren't a reprieve,
merely a continuation of the real-life nightmare.

As a cop, the dialogue he had had with many arrestees
tended to repeat itself.

"Kill you, man. Kill your whole damn family," some
would scream at him, drug-faced, as he put the cuffs on.

"Uh-huh. You have the right to remain silent. Think
about using it."

"Come on, man, ain't my fault. My buddy done it.
Screwed me."

"Where would that buddy be? And the blood on your
hands? The gun in your pants? The coke still in your
nostrils? Buddy do all that? Some buddy."

Then they might eye the dead body and lose it, blub-
bering. "Holy shit! Sweet Jesus! My momma, where's my
momma? You call her. Do that for me, oh shit, do that,
will you? Momma! Oh shit!"

"You have the right to an attorney," he would calmly
tell them.

And that now was John Fiske.

After a couple more court appearances downtown, Fiske
left the glass and brick John Marshall Courts Building,
named after the third chief justice of the United States
Supreme Court. Marshall's ancestral home was still right
next door, now a museum dedicated to preserving the
memory of the great Virginian and American. The man
would have turned over in his grave if he had known of the

vile acts being debated and defended in the building that
bore his name.

Fiske headed down Ninth Street toward the James
River. Hot and humid the last few days, the weather
patterns had angled cooler with the coming rain, and he
pulled his trench coat tighter around him. As the rain
started, he began to jog along the pavement, his shoes
cleaving through puddles of filthy water collected in dips
of asphalt and concrete.

By the time he reached his office in Shockoe Slip, his
hair and coat were soaked, the water running in miniature
rivulets down his back. Eschewing the elevator, he took
the steps two at a time and unlocked the door to his
office. It was located in a cavernous building that had
once been a tobacco warehouse, its oak and pine guts
having been given the new ribs of multiple office drywall.
The reek of the tobacco leaves forever lingered, however.
And this wasn't the only place it could be found. Cruising
on Interstate 95 south past the Philip Morris cigarette-
manufacturing facility Bobby Graham had referred to,
one could almost get a nicotine high without even lighting up. Fiske had often been tempted to fling a lighted
match out the window as he drove by, to see if the air
would simply explode.

Fiske's office was one room with a small attached bathroom, which was important, since he slept here more often
than he did at his apartment. He hung up his coat to dry,
and wiped his face and hair down with a towel he grabbed
off the rack in the bath. He put on a pot of coffee and
watched it brew while he thought about Jerome Hicks.

If Fiske did a superb job, Jerome Hicks would spend the
rest of his life behind bars instead of receiving the prick of
lethal injection at the Virginia death house. Killing an
eighteen-year-old black kid would not win Graham the
attorney general's job he coveted. A black-on-black, loser-

THE SIMPLE TRUTH 35

on-loser murder wouldn't even warrant a back-page story
in the newspaper.

As a Richmond cop, Fiske had survived, barely, the
violence of combat. It swept through neighborhood and
town, swelling large, like an aneurysm, the size of a
county, leaving behind the shattered ghettos, and the soaring, dollar-consumed spires of downtown, flowing over,
around and through the ill-conceived barricades of subur-
bia. And it wasn't just the commonwealth. Glaciers of
criminal activity flowed from all the states. When they
eventually met, then where would we go? Fiske wondered.

He abruptly sat down. The burn had started slowly at
first; it usually did. He sensed its march from his belly up
to his chest, then spreading. Finally, like lava in a trench,
the sensation of impossible heat started down his arms and
poured into his fingers. Fiske staggered up, locked his
office door and stripped off his shirt and tie. He had a T-
shirt on underneath; always wore the damn T-shirt.
Through the cotton, his fingers touched the starting point
of the thickened scar, after all these years still rough-
edged. It began just below his navel and followed the
meandering path of the surgeon's saw in an unbroken line,
until it ended at the base of his neck.

Fiske dropped to the floor and did fifty push-ups without ceasing, the heat in his chest and extremities surging
and then diminishing with each repetition. A drop of
sweat fell from his brow and hit the wooden floor. He
thought he could see his reflection in it. At least it wasn't
blood. He followed the push-ups with an equal number of
stomach crunches. The scar rippled and flexed with each
bend of his body, like a serpent unwillingly grafted to his
torso. He attached a quick-release bar to the doorway leading to the bathroom and struggled through a dozen pull-
ups. He used to be able to do twice that many, but his
strength was slowly ebbing. What lurked beneath the
fused skin would eventually overtake him, kill him, but,

for now, the heat faded; the physical exertion seemed to
frighten it off, letting the trespasser know that somebody
was still home.

He cleaned up in the bathroom and put his shirt back
on. As he sipped his coffee he looked out the window.
From this vantage point he could barely make out the line
of the James River. The water would grow rough as the
rain picked up. He and his brother had often boated down
the river, or leisurely floated down it in truck-tire inner
tubes on hot summer days. That had been years ago. This
was as close as Fiske got to the water these days. Leisure
time was over. He had no space left for it in his shortened
frame of life. He enjoyed what he did, though, at least
most of the time. It wasn't the life of a Supreme Court
superlawyer like his brother, but he took a certain pride in
his job and how he did it. He would have no money or
grand reputation when he died, but he believed he would
die reasonably satisfied, reasonably fulfilled. He turned
back to his work.

CHAPTER FIVE

Like a brooding hawk, Fort Jackson perched on the desolate topography of southwest Virginia, fairly equidistant from the Tennessee, Kentucky and West Virginia borders and in the middle of a remote scrap of coal country. There were few if any stand-alone military prisons in the United States; they were typically attached to a military facility, due both to tradition and to the constraints of defense dollars. Fort Jackson did have a military base component; however, the dominant feature of the place would always be the prison, where the most dangerous offenders in the United States Army silently counted down their lives.

There had never been an escape from Fort Jackson, and even if an inmate could manage to achieve his freedom without benefit of a court ruling, such liberty would be empty and short-lived. The surrounding countryside represented a prison of even greater menace, with jagged-faced, strip-mined mountains, treacherous roads with widowmaker drops, dense, unyielding forest laced with

copperheads and rattlers. And along the polluted water-
ways awaited their more aggressive cousin, the water
moccasin, anxious for panicked feet crashing its border.
And the self-reliant local folk in the forgotten "toe" of
Virginia—the human equivalent of razor wire—were well
schooled with the gun and the knife, and unafraid to use
either. And yet in the slope of the land, the breadth of
forest, shrub and flower, the scent of unhurried wildlife
and the quiet of ocean depths, there was much beauty here.

Attorney Samuel Rider passed through the fort's main
gate, received his visitor's badge and parked his car in the
visitors' lot. He nervously walked up to the flat, stone-
walled entrance of the prison, his briefcase lightly tapping
against his blue-clothed leg. It took him twenty minutes
to go through the screening procedure, which included
producing personal identification, verifying that he was on
the visitors' list, a pat-down of his person, walking
through a metal detector and ending with a search of his
briefcase. The guards suspiciously eyed the small transis-
tor radio, but allowed him to keep it after confirming that
it contained no contraband. He was read the standard rules
of visitation and to each he gave an affirmative, audible
reply that he understood. Rider knew that were he to run
afoul of any of these rules, the guard's polite facade would
quickly disappear.

He looked around, unable to shake the oppression of
fear, of extreme nervousness, as though the prison's architect had managed to craft these elements into the bones of
the place. Rider's bowels clenched, and his palms were
sweaty, like he was about to climb on a twenty-seat turbo-
prop in the face of a hurricane. As a member of the military during Vietnam, Rider had never left the country,
never come close to combat, to mortal danger. Damn
ironic if he were to drop dead from a coronary while standing in a military prison on United States soil. He took a
deep breath, mentally signaled his heart to calm down,

and wondered again why he had come. Rufus Harms was in no position to make him, or anyone else, do anything. But here he was. Rider took another deep breath, clipped on his visitor's badge and gripped the comforting handle of his briefcase, his leather amulet, as a guard escorted him to the visitors' room.

Alone for a few minutes, Rider eyed the dull brown of the walls that seemed designed to depress further those who probably already lived in the throes of near-suicidal intent. He wondered how many men called this place home, entombed by their fellow man and with excellent reason. And yet they all had mothers, even the vilest among them; some, Rider assumed, even had fathers, beyond the stain of semen on egg. And still, they ended up here. Born evil? Maybe so. Probably have a genetic test soon that'll tell you if your preschooler is the second coming of Ted Bundy, Rider thought. But when they drop the bad news on you, then what the hell do you do?

Rider stopped his musings as Rufus Harms, towering over the two guards trailing him, entered the visitors' room. The quick image was that of the lord to his serfs, reality the reverse of that. Harms was the largest man Rider had ever personally encountered, a giant possessed of truly abnormal strength. Even now he seemed to fill up the room with his bulk. His chest was two slabs of rebarred concrete hung side by side, arms thicker than some trees. Harms wore shackles on both his hands and feet that forced him to do the "prison shuffle." He was accomplished at it, though; the shortened strides were graceful.

He must be close to fifty, Rider thought, but actually looked a good ten years older; he noted the facial scars, the awkward twist of bone beneath Harms's right eye. The young man Rider had represented was the owner of fine, even handsome features. Rider wondered how often Rufus had been beaten in here, what other telling evidence of abuse he carried under his clothing.

Harms sat down across from Rider at a wooden table heavily scored by thousands of nervous, desperate fingernails. He didn't look at Rider just yet, but instead eyed the guard, who remained in the room.

Rider caught Harms's silent meaning and said to the guard, "Private, I'm his lawyer, so you're going to have to give us some space here."

The reply was automatic. "This is a maximum-security prison facility and every prisoner here is classified as violent and dangerous. I'm here for your safety."

The men here *were* dangerous, both prisoners *and* guards, and that was just the way things were, Rider knew.

"I understand that," replied the lawyer. "I'm not asking you to abandon me, but I'd be obliged if you could stand farther away. Attorney–client privilege—you understand, don't you?"

The guard didn't answer, but he did move to the far end of the room, ostensibly out of earshot. Finally, Rufus Harms looked over at Rider. "You bring the radio?"

"A strange request, but one that I honored."

"Take it out and turn it on, would you?"

Rider did so. The room was immediately filled with the mournful tunes of country-western music, the lyrics contrived, shallow in the face of the genuine misery sensed at this place, Rider thought uncomfortably.

When the lawyer looked at him questioningly, Harms glanced around the room. "Lotta ears around this place, some you can't see, right?"

"Bugging the conversations of an attorney and his client is against the law."

Harms moved his hands slightly, chains rattling. "Lot of things against the law, but people still do 'em. Both in and out of this place. Right?"

Rider found himself nodding. Harms was no longer a

young, scared kid. He was a man. A man in control despite being unable to control one single element of his existence. Rider also observed that each of Harms's physical movements was measured, calculated; like he was engaging in chess, reaching out slowly to touch a piece, and then drawing back with equal caution. Here, swift motion could be deadly.

The inmate leaned forward and started speaking in a tone so low that Rider had to strain to hear him above the music. "I thank you for coming. I'm surprised you did."

"Surprised the hell out of me to hear from you. But I guess it got my curiosity up too."

"You look good. The years have been kind to you."

Rider had to laugh. "I lost all my hair and put on fifty pounds, but thank you anyway."

"I won't waste your time. I got something I want you to file in court for me."

Rider's astonishment was clear. "What court?"

Harms spoke in even lower tones, despite the cover of the music. "Biggest one there is. Supreme Court."

Rider's jaw went slack. "You got to be kidding." The look in Harms's eyes would not brook such a conclusion. "Okay, what exactly do you want me to file?"

With smooth increments of motion, despite the restraints of the manacles, Harms slid an envelope out of his shirt and held it up. In an instant, the guard stepped across and snatched it from his hand.

Rider protested immediately. "Private, that is a confidential attorney–client communication."

"Let him read it, Samuel, I got nothing to hide," Harms said evenly, eyes staring off.

The guard opened the envelope and scanned the contents of the letter. Satisfied, he returned it to Harms and resumed his post across the room.

Harms handed the envelope and letter across to Rider, who looked down at the material. When he looked back up, Harms was leaning even closer to him, and he spoke for at least ten minutes. Several times Rider's eyes widened as Harms's words spilled over him. Finished, the prisoner sat back and looked at him.

"You going to help me, ain't you?"

Rider could not answer, apparently still digesting all that he had heard. If the waist chain had not prevented such a movement, Harms would have reached out and put his hand over Rider's, not in a threatening manner, but as a tangible plea for help from a man who had experienced none for almost thirty years. "Ain't you, Samuel?"

Finally, Rider nodded. "I'll help you, Rufus."

Harms rose and headed for the door.

Rider put the paper back in the envelope and tucked it and the radio away in his briefcase. The lawyer had no way of knowing that on the other side of a large mirror that hung on the wall of the visitors' room, someone had watched the entire exchange between prisoner and attorney. This person now rubbed his chin, lost in deep, troubled thought.

CHAPTER SIX

At ten A.M., the marshal of the Supreme Court, Richard Perkins, dressed in charcoal-gray tails, the traditional Supreme Court dress of lawyers from the Solicitor General's Office as well, stood up at one end of the massive bench, behind which sat nine high-backed leather chairs of various styles and sizes, and pounded his gavel. The packed courtroom grew silent. "The Honorable, the Chief Justice, and the Associate Justices of the United States," Perkins announced.

The long burgundy-colored curtain behind the bench parted at nine different places, and there appeared a like number of justices looking stiff and uncomfortable in their black robes, as though startled awake and discovering a crowd next to their beds. As they took their seats, Perkins continued. "Oyez, oyez, oyez. All persons having business before the Honorable, the Supreme Court of the United States, are admonished to draw near and give their attention, for the Court is now sitting. God save the United States and this honorable Court."

Perkins sat down and looked out over a courtroom with the square footage of a mansion. Its forty-four-foot ceiling made the eye look for drifting clouds. After some preliminary business and the ceremonial swearing in of new Supreme Court Bar members, the first of the day's two morning cases would be called. On this day, a Wednesday, only two cases during the morning would be heard, afternoon sessions being held only on Monday and Tuesday. No oral arguments were held on Thursday and Friday. On it would go, three days a week every two weeks, until the end of April, approximately one hundred and fifty oral argument sessions later, the justices assuming the modern-day role of Solomon for the people of the United States.

There were impressive friezes on either side of the courtroom. On the right were figures of lawgivers of the pre-Christian era. On the left, their counterparts of the Christian period. Two armies ready to have go at each other. Perhaps to determine who had gotten it right. Moses versus Napoleon, Hammurabi against Muhammad. The law, the handing down of justice, could be damn painful—bloody, even. Right above the bench were two figures carved in marble, one depicting the majesty of the law, the other the power of government. Between the two panels was a tableau of the Ten Commandments. Swirling around the vast chamber like flocks of doves were carvings—Safeguard of the Rights of People, Genii of Wisdom and Statecraft, Defense of Human Rights—representing the role of the Court. If there ever was a stage of perfect proportion for the hearing of matters paramount, it seemed that this landscape represented it. However, topography could be deceiving.

Ramsey sat in the middle of the bench, Elizabeth Knight at the extreme right. A boom microphone was suspended from the middle of the ceiling. The moms and

pops in the audience had noticeably tensed up when the
justices appeared. Even their gangly, bored kids sat a little
straighter. It was understandable enough even for those
barely familiar with the reputation of this place. There was
a discernible feeling of raw power, of important confronta-
tions to come.

These nine black-robed justices told women when they
could legally abort their fetuses; dictated to schoolchildren
where they would do their learning; proclaimed what
speech was obscene or not; pronounced that police could
not unreasonably search and seize, or beat confessions out
of people. No one elected them to their positions. They
held their positions for life against virtually all challenge.
And the justices operated in such levels of secrecy, in such
a black hole, that it made the public personae of other
venerable federal institutions seem vainglorious by
comparison. They routinely confronted issues that had
activist groups all over the country banging heads, bomb-
ing abortion clinics, demonstrating outside prison death
houses. They judged the complex issues that would
bedevil human civilization until its extinction. And they
looked so calm.

The first case was called. It dealt with affirmative action
in public universities—or, rather, what was left of the
concept. Frank Campbell, the counsel arguing on behalf of
affirmative action, barely got through his first sentence
before Ramsey pounced.

The chief justice pointed out that the Fourteenth
Amendment unequivocally stated that no one shall be
discriminated against. Didn't that mean affirmative action
of any sort was impermissible under the Constitution?

"But there are broad wrongs that are trying to be—"

"Why does diversity equate with equality?" Ramsey
abruptly asked Campbell.

"It ensures that a broad and diverse body of students
will be available to express different ideas, represent differ-

ent cultures, which in turn will serve to break down the ignorance of stereotypes."

"Aren't you premising your entire argument on the fact that blacks and whites think differently? That a black raised by parents who are college professors in a well-to-do household in, say, San Francisco will bring a different set of values and ideas to a university than a white person who was raised in the exact same affluent environment in San Francisco?" Ramsey's tone was filled with skepticism.

"I think that everyone has differences," Campbell responded.

"Instead of basing it on skin color, doesn't it seem that the most impoverished among us have a greater right to a helping hand?" Justice Knight asked. Ramsey looked over at her curiously as she said this. "And yet your argument draws no distinction on wealth or lack thereof, does it?" Knight added.

"No," Campbell conceded.

Michael Fiske and Sara Evans sat in a special section of seats perpendicular to the bench. Michael glanced over at Sara as he listened to this line of questioning. She didn't look at him.

"You can't get around the letter of the law, can you? You would have us turn the Constitution on its head," Ramsey persisted after finally taking his eyes off Knight.

"How about the spirit behind those words?" Campbell rejoined.

"Spirits are such amorphous things, I much prefer to deal in concrete." Ramsey's words brought scattered laughter from the audience. The chief justice renewed his verbal attack, and with deadly precision he skewered Campbell's precedents and line of reasoning. Knight said nothing more, staring straight ahead, her thoughts obviously far from the courtroom. As the red light on the counsel lectern came on indicating Campbell's time was up, he almost ran to his seat. As the counsel opposing affirmative action took his place at the lectern and began his argument, it didn't seem like the justices were even listening anymore.

"Boy, Ramsey is efficient," Sara remarked. She and Michael were in the Court's cafeteria, the justices having retired to their dining room for their traditional post-oral argument luncheon. "He sliced up the university's lawyer in about five seconds."

Michael swallowed a bite of sandwich. "He's been on the lookout for a case for the last three years to really blow affirmative action out of the water. Well, he found it. They should have settled the case before it got here."

"You really think Ramsey will go that far?"

"Are you kidding? Wait until you see the opinion. He'll probably write it himself, just so he can gloat. It's dead."

"I can partly see his logic," Sara said.

"Of course you can. It's evident. A conservative group brought the case, handpicked the plaintiff. White, bright, blue-collar, hardworking, never given a handout. And, even better, a woman."

"The Constitution does say no one shall discriminate."

"Sara, you know that the Fourteenth Amendment was passed right after the Civil War to ensure that blacks wouldn't be discriminated against. Now it's been forged into a bat to crush the people it was supposed to help. Well, the crushers just guaranteed their own Armageddon."

"What do you mean?"

"I mean that poor with hope starts to push back. Poor without hope lashes back. Not pretty."

"Oh." She looked at Michael, his manner so intense, so mercurial. Serious beyond his years. He climbed on the soapbox with regularity, sometimes to an embarrassing degree. It was one of the elements about him that she both admired and feared.

"My brother could tell you some stories about that," Michael added.

"I'm sure he could. I hope to meet him someday."

Michael glanced at her and then looked away. "Ramsey sees the world differently than it actually is. He made it in the world by himself, why can't everybody else? I admire the guy, though. He sticks it equally to the poor and the rich, the state and the individual. He doesn't play favorites. I'll give him that."

"You overcame a lot too."

"Yeah. I'm not blowing my own horn, but I've got an IQ over one-sixty. Not everybody has that."

"I know," Sara said wistfully. "My legal brain says what happened today was correct. My heart says it's a tragedy."

"Hey, this is the Supreme Court. It's not supposed to be easy. And by the way, what was Knight trying to do in there today?" Michael was perpetually in the loop on everything that happened at the Court, all the inner secrets, the gossip, the strategies employed by the justices and their clerks to further philosophies and points of view on cases before them. He felt behind on whatever Knight had alluded to in court this morning, though, and it bothered him.

"Michael, it was only a couple sentences."

"So what? Two sentences with a ton of potential. Rights for the poor? You saw the way Ramsey picked up on it. Is Knight posturing for something down the road? A case she was trying to set up in there?"

"I can't believe you're asking me that. It's confidential."

"We're all on the same team here, Sara."

"Right! How often do Knight and Murphy vote together? Not very. And this place has nine very separate compartments, you know that."

"Right, nine little kingdoms. But if Knight has something up her sleeve, I'd like to know about it."

"You don't have to know everything that goes on at this

place. Christ, you already know more than all the clerks combined, and most of the justices. I mean, how many other clerks go down to the mail room at the crack of dawn to get a jump on the appeals coming in?"

"I don't like to do anything halfway."

She looked at him, was about to say something, but then stopped herself. Why complicate things? She had already given him her answer. In reality, although a driven person herself, she could not imagine being married to someone with standards as high as Michael Fiske's. She could never reach them, sustain them. It would be unhealthy even to try.

"Well, I'm not betraying any confidences. You know as well as I do that this place is like a military campaign. Loose lips sink ships. And you have to watch your backside."

"I'm not disagreeing with you in the grand scheme of things, but I am in this case. You know Murphy, he's a throwback—a lovable throwback, but he's a pure liberal. Anything to help the poor he'd go for. He and Knight would be aligned on this, no doubt about it. He's always on the lookout to throw a wrench in Ramsey's machine. Tom Murphy led the Court before Ramsey got the upper hand. It's no fun always being on the dissenting end in your twilight years."

Sara shook her head. "I really can't go into it."

He sighed and picked at his meal. "We're just pulling away from each other at all points, aren't we?"

"That's not true. You're just trying to make it seem that way. I know I hurt you when I said no, and I'm sorry."

He suddenly grinned. "Maybe it's for the best. We're both so headstrong, we'd probably end up killing each other."

"Good old Virginia boy and a gal from Carolina," she drawled. "You're probably right."

He fiddled with his drink and eyed her. "If you think I'm stubborn, you really should meet my brother."

Sara didn't meet his gaze. "I'm sure. He was terrific during that trial we watched."

"I'm very proud of him."

Now she looked at him. "So why did we have to sneak in and out of the courtroom so he wouldn't know we were there?"

"You'd have to ask him that."

"I'm asking you."

Michael shrugged. "He's got a problem with me. He sort of banished me from his life."

"Why?"

"I actually don't know all the reasons. Maybe he doesn't either. I do know it hasn't made him very happy."

"From the little I saw, he didn't strike me as that sort of person. Depressed or anything."

"Really? How did he strike you?"

"Funny, smart, identifies well with people."

"I see he identified with you."

"He didn't even know I was there."

"You would have liked him to, though, wouldn't you?"

"What's that supposed to mean?"

"Only that I'm not blind. And I've walked in his shadow all my life."

"You're the boy genius with a limitless future."

"And he's a heroic ex-cop who now defends the very people he used to arrest. He also has a martyr quality about him that I never have been able to get around. He's a good guy who pushes himself unbelievably hard." Michael shook his head. All the time his brother had spent in the hospital. None of them knowing if he was going to make it day to day, minute to minute. He had never known such fear, the thought of losing his brother. But he had lost him anyway, it seemed, and not because of death. Not because of those bullets.

"Maybe he feels like he's living in your shadow."

"I doubt that."

"Did you ever ask him?"

"Like I said, we don't talk anymore." He paused and then added quietly, "Is he the reason you turned me down?" He had watched her as she observed his brother. She had been enraptured with John Fiske from the moment she saw him. It had seemed like a fun idea at the time, the two of them going to watch his brother. Now Michael cursed himself for doing it.

She flushed. "I don't even know him. How could I possibly have any feelings for him?"

"Are you asking me that, or yourself?"

"I'm not going to answer that." Her voice trembled. "What about you? Do you love him?"

He abruptly sat up straight and looked at her. "I will always love my brother, Sara. Always."

CHAPTER SEVEN

Rider wordlessly passed his secretary, fled to his office, opened his briefcase and slipped out the envelope. He withdrew the letter from inside, but barely glanced at it before tossing it in the wastebasket. In the letter Rufus Harms had written his last will and testament, but that was just a dodge, something innocuous for the guard to read. Rider looked at the envelope closely while he punched his intercom.

"Sheila, can you bring in the hot plate and the tea-kettle? Fill it with water."

"Mr. Rider, I can make tea for you."

"I don't want tea, Sheila, just bring the damned kettle and the hot plate."

Sheila didn't question this odd request or her boss's temper. She brought in the kettle and hot plate, then quietly withdrew.

Rider plugged in the hot plate and within a few minutes steam poured out of the kettle. Gingerly grasping the envelope by its edges, Rider held it over the steam and watched as the envelope began to come apart, just as Rufus Harms had told him it would. Rider fussed with the edges, and he soon had it completely laid out. Instead of an envelope, he now held two pieces of paper: one hand-written; the other a copy of the letter Harms had received from the Army.

As he turned off the hot plate, Rider marveled at how Rufus had managed to construct this device—an envelope that was actually a letter—and how he had copied and then concealed the letter from the Army in it as well. Then he recalled that Harms's father had worked at a printing press company. It would have been better for Rufus if he had followed his daddy into the printing business instead of joining the Army, Rider muttered to himself.

He let the pieces of paper dry out for a minute and then sat behind his desk while he read what Rufus had written. It didn't take long, the remarks were fairly brief, though many words were oddly formed and misspelled. Rider couldn't have known it, but Harms had scrawled it out in near darkness, stopping every time he heard the steps of the guards draw close. There wasn't a trace of saliva left in Rider's throat when he had finished reading. Then he forced himself to read the official notice from the Army. Another body blow.

"Good God!" He sank back in his chair, rubbed a trembling hand over his bald spot, and then lurched to his feet, rushed over and locked his office door. The fear spread like a mutating virus. He could barely breathe. He staggered back to his desk and hit his intercom button again. "Sheila, bring me in some water and some aspirin, please."

A minute later Sheila knocked on the door. "Mr. Rider," she said through the door, "it's locked."

He quickly unlocked the door, took the glass and aspirin from her and was about to shut the door again when Sheila said, "Are you okay?"

"Fine, fine," he replied, hustling her out the door.

He looked down at the paper Rufus wanted him to file with the United States Supreme Court. Rider happened to be a member of the largely ceremonial Supreme Court Bar, solely by virtue of the sponsorship of a former colleague in the military who had gone on to the Justice Department. If he did exactly as Rufus asked, he would be the attorney of record in Harms's appeal. Rider could envision only personal catastrophe resulting from such an arrangement. And yet he had promised Rufus.

Rider lay down on the leather sofa in one corner of his office, closed his eyes and commenced a silent deliberation. So many things hadn't added up the night Ruth Ann Mosley had been killed. Rufus didn't have a history of violence, only a constant failure to follow orders that had enraged many a superior, and, at first, had bewildered Rider as well. Harms's inability to process even the simplest of commands had been finally explained during Rider's representation of him. But his escaping from the stockade never had. Confronted with no defense, factually, Rider had made noises about an insanity plea, which had given him just enough leverage to save his client from possible execution. And that had been the end of it. Justice had been served. At least as much as one could expect in this world.

Rider looked once more at the notice from the Army, the stark lie of the past now firmly revealed. This information should have been in Harms's military file at the time of the murder, but it wasn't. It would have constituted a completely plausible defense. Harms's military file had been tampered with, and Rider now understood why.

Harms wanted his freedom and his name cleared and he wanted it to come from the highest court in the land. And he refused to entrust the prospect of freedom to the Army. That's what Harms had said to him while the country-western music had covered his words. And could he blame him?

All things good were in Rufus's corner. He should be heard and he should be free. But despite that, Rider remained immobile on his couch of worn leather and burnished nails. It was nothing complex. It was fear—a far stronger emotion, it seemed, than any of the others bestowed upon humankind. He planned to retire in a few years to the condo he and his wife had already picked out on the Gulf Coast. Their kids were grown. Rider was weary of the frigid winters that settled into the low pockets of the area and he was tired of always chasing new pieces of business, of diligently recording his professional life in quarter-hour increments. However, as enticing as that retirement was, it wasn't quite enough to prevent Rider from helping his old client. Some things were right and some things were wrong.

Rider rose from the couch and settled behind his desk. At first he had thought the simplest way to help Rufus was to mail what he had to one of the newspapers and let the power of the press take over. But for all he knew, the paper would either toss it as a letter from some crazy, or otherwise bungle it such that Rufus might be put in danger. What had really made up Rider's mind as to his course of action was simple. Rufus was his client and he had asked his lawyer to file his appeal with the United States Supreme Court. And that's what Rider was going to do. He had failed Rufus once before; he wasn't going to do it again. The man was in dire need of a little justice, and what better place for that than the highest court in the land? If you couldn't get justice there, where the hell could you get it? Rider wondered.

As he took out a sheet of paper from his desk drawer, sunlight from the window glanced off his square gold cuff links, sending bright dots around the room helter-skelter. He pulled over his ancient typewriter, kept out of nostalgia. Rider was unfamiliar with the Supreme Court's technical filing requirements, but he assumed he would be running afoul of most of them. That didn't bother him. He just wanted to get the story out—away from him.

When he had finished typing, he started to place what he had typed, together with Harms's letter and the letter from the Army, into a mailing envelope. Then he stopped. Paranoia, spilling over from thirty years of practice, made him hustle out to the small workroom at the rear of his office suite and make copies of both Harms's handwritten letter and Rider's own typewritten one. This same uneasiness made him decide to keep, for now, the letter from the Army. When the story broke he could always produce it, again anonymously. He hid the copies in one of his desk drawers and locked it. He returned the originals to the envelope, looked up the address of the Supreme Court in his legal directory, and next typed up a label. He did not provide a return address on the envelope. That done, he put on his hat and coat and walked down to the post office at the corner.

Before he had time to change his mind, he filled out the form to send the envelope by certified mail so he would get a return receipt, handed it to the postal clerk, completed the simple transaction and returned to his office. It was only then that it struck him. The return receipt could be a way for the Court to identify who had sent the package. He sighed. Rufus had been waiting half his life for this. And, in a way, Rider had abandoned him back then. For the rest of the day Rider lay on the couch in his office, in the dark, silently praying that he had done the right thing, and knowing, in his heart, that he had.

CHAPTER EIGHT

"Ramsey's clerks have been pestering me about the comment you made the other day, Justice Knight, about the poor being entitled to certain preferences." Sara looked over at the woman, sitting so calmly behind her desk.

A smile flickered across Knight's face as she scanned some documents. "I'm sure they have."

They both knew that Ramsey's clerks were like a well-trained commando unit. They had feelers out everywhere, looking for anything of interest to the chief justice and his agendas. Almost nothing escaped their notice. Every word, exclamation, meeting or casual corridor conversation was duly noted, analyzed and catalogued away for future use.

"So you intended for that reaction to happen?"

"Sara, as much as I may not like it, there is a certain process at this place that one must struggle through. Some call it a game, I don't choose to do so. But I can't ignore its presence. I'm not so much concerned with the chief. The positions I'm thinking about taking on a number of cases Ramsey would never support. I know that and he knows that."

"So you were floating a trial balloon to the other justices."

"In part, yes. Oral argument is also an open, public forum."

"So, to the public." Sara thought quickly. "And the media?"

Knight put down the papers and clasped her hands together as she stared at the younger woman. "This Court is swayed more by public opinion than many would dare to confess. Some here would like to see the status quo always preserved. But the Court has to move forward."

"And this ties into the cases you've been having me research about equalizing educational rights of the poor?"

"I have a compelling interest in that." Elizabeth Knight had grown up in East Texas, the middle of nowhere, but her father had had money. Thus, her education had been first-rate, and she had often wondered how her life would have been if her father had been poor like so many of the people she had grown up with. All justices carried psychological baggage to the Court and Elizabeth Knight was no exception. "And that's all I'm really going to say right now."

"And *Blankley*?" Sara said, referring to the affirmative action case Ramsey had so thoroughly decimated.

"We haven't voted on it yet, of course, Sara, so I can't say one way or the other how it will turn out." The voting conferences took place in complete secrecy, without even a stenographer or secretary in residence. However, for those who followed the Court with any consistency, and for the clerks who lived in the place every day, it wasn't too difficult to predict how votes were lining up, although the justices had surprised people in the past. Justice Knight's depressed look made it clear, however, which way the votes were aligned on the *Blankley* case.

And Sara could read the tea leaves as well as anyone. Michael Fiske was right. The only question was how sweeping the opinion would be.

"Too bad I won't be around to see the results of my research come to fruition," Sara said.

"You never know. You came back for a second term. Michael Fiske signed up with Tommy for a third. I'd love to have you back again."

"Funny you should mention him. Michael was also asking about your remarks at oral argument. He thought Murphy might welcome anything you were trying to put together concerning preferences for the poor."

Knight smiled. "Michael would know. He and Tommy are as close as clerk and justice can be."

"Michael knows more about the Court than just about anyone. Actually, sometimes he can be a little scary."

Knight eyed her keenly. "I thought you and Michael were close."

"We are. I mean, we're good friends." Sara blushed as Knight continued to watch her.

"We won't be getting any announcements from the two of you, will we?" Knight smiled warmly.

"What? No, no. We're just friends."

"I see. I'm sorry, Sara, it's certainly none of my business."

"It's okay. We do spend a fair amount of time together. I'm sure some people assume that there's more there than just friendship. I mean, Michael's a very attractive man, obviously very smart. Great future."

"Sara, don't take this the wrong way, but you sound like you're trying to convince yourself of something."

Sara looked down. "I guess I do, don't I?"

"Take it from someone who has two grown daughters. Don't rush it. Let it take its natural course. You have plenty of time. End of motherly advice."

Sara smiled. "Thanks."

Eizabeth Knight had become almost a second mother to Sara Evans, replacing the one she had lost as a young child.

As Sara walked out the door, Knight sat back in her chair. Where she was now was the culmination of a lifetime of work and sacrifice, luck and skill. She was married to a well-respected United States senator, a man she loved and who loved her. She was one of only three women who had ever donned the robes of a Supreme Court justice. She felt humble and empowered at the same time. The president who had nominated her was still in office. He had seen her as a reliable middle-of-the-road jurist. She had not been that active politically, so he could not exactly expect her to toe his party's line, but he probably expected her to be judicially passive, letting the solution to the really important questions fall to the people's elected representatives.

She had no deep-set philosophies like Ramsey or Murphy. They decided cases not so much on the facts of each one, but on the broad positions each case represented. Murphy would never vote to uphold or reverse any case in favor of capital punishment. Ramsey would wither and die before he would side with a defendant in a criminal rights case. Knight could not choose her sides in that manner. She took each case, each party, as they came. She agonized over the facts. While she thought about the broader impact of the court's decisions, she also worried about the fairness to the actual parties. It often meant she was the swing vote on a lot of cases, and she didn't really mind that. She was no wallflower, and she had come here to make a difference.

Only now was she seeing what a very great impact she could have. And the responsibility that came with such power was what humbled her. And frightened her. Made her stare at the ceiling wide awake as her husband slept soundly beside her. Still, she thought with a smile, there was no other place she would rather be; no other way she would rather be spending her life.

CHAPTER NINE

John Fiske walked into the building located in the West End of Richmond. The place was officially called a rest home, but, plain and simple, it was a place for the elderly to come to die. Fiske tried to ignore the moans and cries as he strode down the corridor. He saw the feeble bodies, heads dipping low, limbs useless, encased in the wheelchairs, stacked like shopping carts against the wall, waiting for a dance partner who was never going to show up.

It had taken all the resolve he and his father had in order to move John's mother into this place. Michael Fiske had never faced up to the fact that their mother's mind was gone, eaten away by Alzheimer's. The good times were easy to enjoy. The real worth of a person came from how he acted during the bad times. As far as John Fiske was concerned, his brother Mike had failed that test miserably.

He checked in at the desk. "How is she today?" he asked the assistant administrator. As a frequent visitor here, he knew all the staff.

"She's had better ones, John, but your being here will perk her up," the woman answered.

"Right," Fiske muttered as he walked to the visitors' room.

His mother awaited him there, dressed, as always, in her housecoat and slippers. Her eyes wandered aimlessly, her mouth moving, but no words coming out. When Fiske appeared at the doorway, she looked at him, a smile breaking across her face. He walked over and sat down across from her.

"How's my Mikey?" Gladys Fiske asked, tenderly rubbing his face. "How's Momma's baby?"

Fiske took a deep breath. It was the same damn thing, for the last two years. In Gladys Fiske's devastated mind he was Mike, he would always be his brother until the very end of his mother's life. John Fiske had somehow completely vanished from her memory, as if he had never been born.

He gently touched her hands, doing his best to quiet the absolute frustration inside him. "I'm fine. Doing good. Pop's good too." He then added quietly, "Johnny's doing good too, he asked about you. Always does."

Her stare was blank. "Johnny?"

Fiske attempted this every time, and every time the response was the same. Why did she forget him and not his brother? There had to have been some deep-rooted facet in her that had allowed the Alzheimer's to erase his identity from her life. Was his existence never that strong, never that important to her? And yet he had been the son who had always been there for his parents. He had helped them as a boy, and continued to be there for them as a man. Everything from giving them a large part of his income to getting up on the roof on a suffo-cating August day, in the middle of a hellish trial, to help his old man shingle their house, because he didn't have the cash to pay someone to do it. And Mike, always the favorite, always the one to go his own way, his own selfish way, Fiske thought . . . Mike was always hailed as the great one, the one who would do the family proud. In reality, his parents had never been that extreme in their views of their sons; Fiske knew that. But his anger had skewed that truth, empowering the bad and subverting the good.

"Mikey?" she said anxiously. "How are the children?"

"They're fine, they're good, growing like weeds. They look just like you." Having to pretend that he was his brother and had fathered children made Fiske want to collapse to the floor bawling.

She smiled and touched her hair.

He picked up on that. "Looks good. Pop says you're prettier than ever." Gladys Fiske had been an attractive woman for most of her life, and her appearance had been very important to her. The effects of the Alzheimer's had, in her case, accelerated the aging process. She would have been terribly upset with how she looked now, Fiske knew. He hoped his mother still saw herself as twenty years old and the prettiest she would ever be.

He held out a package he had brought. She seized it with the glee of a child and tore off the wrapping. She touched the brush delicately and then ran it through her hair very carefully.

"It's the most beautiful thing I've ever seen."

She said that about everything he brought her. Tissues, lipstick, a picture book. The most beautiful thing she had ever seen. Mike. Every time he came here, his brother scored brownie points. Fiske forced these thoughts away and spent a very pleasant hour with his mother. He loved her so much. He would rip from her the disease that had destroyed her brain if he could. Since he couldn't, he would do anything to spend time with her. Even under another's name.

Fiske left the rest home and drove to his father's house. As he turned onto the familiar street, he looked around the disintegrating boundaries of his first eighteen years of life: dilapidated homes with peeling paint and crumbling porches, sagging wire fences, and dirt front yards running down to narrow, cracked streets where twin streams of ancient, battered Fords and Chevys docked. Fifty years ago, the neighborhood had been a typical starter community for the post-World War II masses filled with the unshakable confidence that life would only get better. For those who hadn't crossed that bridge of prosperity, the most visible change in their worn-out lives was a wooden wheelchair ramp grafted over the front stoop. As he looked at one of the ramps, Fiske knew he would choose a wheelchair over the rot of his mother's brain.

He pulled into the driveway of his father's well-kept home. The more the neighborhood fell apart around him, the harder his old man worked to keep it at bay. Perhaps to keep the past alive a little longer. Maybe hoping his wife would come home twenty years old again with a fresh, healthy mind. The old Buick was in the driveway, its body rusted a little, but the engine in mint condition thanks to its owner's skills as a master mechanic. Fiske saw his father in the garage, dressed in his usual outfit of white T-shirt and blue work pants, hunkered over some piece of equipment. Retired now, Ed Fiske was at his happiest with his fingers full of grease, the guts of some complex machinery strewn out helter-skelter in front of him.

"Cold beer's in the fridge," Ed said without looking up.

Fiske opened the old refrigerator his father kept in the garage and pulled out a Miller. He sat down on a rickety old kitchen chair and watched his father work, just as he had done as a young boy. He had always been fascinated with the skill of his father's hands, the way the man confidently knew where every piece went.

"Saw Mom today."

With a practiced roll of his tongue, Ed pushed the cigarette he was puffing on to the right side of his mouth. His
muscular forearms flexed and then relaxed as he ratcheted
a bolt tight.

"I'm going tomorrow. Thought I'd get all dressed up,
bring some flowers, a little boxed dinner Ida is going to
make up. Make it real special. Just me and her."

Ida German was the next-door neighbor. She had lived
in the neighborhood longer than anyone else. She had
been good company to his father ever since his wife had
gone away.

"She'll love that." Fiske sipped on his beer and smiled at
the picture the two would make together.

Ed finished up what he was doing and took a minute to
clean up, using gasoline and a rag to get the grease off his
hands. He grabbed a beer and sat down on an old toolbox
across from his son.

"Talked to Mike yesterday," he said.

"Is that right?" Fiske said with no interest.

"He's doing good up there at the Court. You know they
asked him back for another year. He must be good."

"I'm sure he's the best they've ever had." Fiske stood up
and went over to the open doorway. He took a deep
breath, letting his lungs fill with the scent of freshly cut
grass. Every Saturday growing up, he and his brother
would mow the lawn, do the chores and then the family
would pile into the mammoth station wagon for the
weekly trip to the A&P grocery store. If they had been
really good, done all their chores correctly, not clipped the
grass too short, they'd get a soda from the machine next
to the paper box outside the A&P. To the boys it was
liquid gold. Fiske and his brother would think all week
about getting that cold soda. They had been so close
growing up. Carried the morning *Times Dispatch* together,
played sports together, though John was three years older

than his brother. Mike was so gifted physically that he had played varsity sports as a freshman. The Fiske brothers. Everybody knew them, respected them. Those were happy times. Those times were over. He turned back and looked at his father.

Ed shook his head. "Did you know Mike turned down a teaching job at one of them big law schools, Harvard or something, to stay at the Court? He got a slew of offers from big law firms. He showed me 'em. Lord, they were talking money I can't even believe." The pride in his voice was obvious.

"More power to him," Fiske said dryly.

Ed suddenly slapped his thigh. "What's wrong with you, Johnny? What the hell do you have against your brother?"

"I've got nothing against him."

"Then why the hell don't you two get along like you used to? I've talked to Mike. It's not on account of him."

"Look, Pop, he's got his life and I've got mine. I don't remember you being all touchy-feely with Uncle Ben."

"My brother was a bum and a drunk. Your brother ain't either of those."

"Being a drunk and a bum aren't the only vices in the world."

"Damn, I just don't understand you, son."

"Join the crowd."

Ed put out his cigarette on the concrete floor, stood and leaned against one of the garage's exposed wall studs. "Jealousy ain't right between brothers. You should feel good about what he's done with his life."

"Oh, so you think I'm jealous?"

"Are you?"

Fiske took another sip of beer and looked over at the belly-button-high wire fence surrounding his father's small backyard. It was currently painted dark green. Over the years it had seen many different colors. John and Mike had painted it each summer, the color being whatever the trucking firm Ed worked for had left over from its annual office repainting. Fiske looked over at the apple tree that spread over one corner of the yard. He motioned with his beer. "You've got caterpillars. Get me a flare."

"I'll get to it."

"Pop, you don't even like standing on a chair."

Fiske took off his jacket, grabbed a ladder from the garage and took the flare his father handed him. He ignited it, positioned the ladder under the bulging nest and climbed up. It took a few minutes, but the nest slowly dissolved under the heat of the flare. Fiske climbed back down and stamped out the flare while his father raked up the remains of the nest.

"And you just saw my problem with Mike."

"What?" Ed looked confused.

"When was the last time Mike was down here to help? Hell, just to see you or Mom?"

Ed scratched at his beard stubble and fumbled in his pants pocket for another cigarette. "He's busy. He gets down when he can."

"Sure he does."

"He's got important work to do for the government. Up there helping all them judges. It's the damn highest court in the land, you know that."

"Well, guess what, Pop, I keep pretty busy too."

"I know that, son. But—"

"But, I know, it's different." Fiske threw his jacket over his shoulder, wiped the sweat from his eyes. The mosquitoes would be out soon. That made him think of water. His father kept a trailer at a campground down by the Mattaponi River. "You been down to the trailer lately?"

Ed shook his head, relieved at the change in subject. "Naw, planning to go soon, though. Take the boat out before it gets too cold."

Fiske rubbed another bead of sweat off his forehead. "Let me know, I might run down with you."

Ed scrutinized his eldest son. "How you doing?"

"Professionally? Lost two, won two this week. I take that as an acceptable batting average these days."

"You be careful, son. I know you believe in what you're doing and all, but that's a damn rough bunch you're lawyering for. Some of them might remember you from your cop days. I lie awake at night thinking about that."

Fiske smiled. He loved his father as much as he did his mother, and, in some subtle ways of men, even more. The thought of his father still losing sleep over him was very reassuring. He slapped his father on the back.

"Don't worry, Pop, I never let my guard down."

"How about the other thing?"

Fiske unconsciously touched his chest. "Doing just fine. Hell, probably live to be a hundred."

"I hope you do, son," his father said with great conviction as he watched his boy leave.

Ed shook his head as he thought of how far his sons had drifted apart and his being unable to do anything about it. "Damn," was all he could think of to say before sitting down on the toolbox to finish his beer.

CHAPTER TEN

It was early in the morning as Michael Fiske quietly hummed his way through the broad, high-ceilinged hallway toward the clerks' mail room. As he entered the room, a clerk looked up. "You picked a good time, Michael. We just got in a shipment."

"Any con mail?" Michael asked, referring to the ever-growing number of petitions from prisoners. Most of them were filed *in forma pauperis,* meaning, literally, in the form of a pauper. There was a separate docket kept for these petitions, and it was so large that one clerk was specially designated to manage the filings. The IFPs, as they were termed by Court personnel, were usually a place to discover either humor over some ridiculous claim or occasionally a case worthy of the Court's attention. Michael knew that some of the most important Court decisions ever had resulted from IFP cases—thus his early morning ritual of panning for appellate gold in the paper piles.

"From the hand scribblings I've tried to decipher so far, I'd say that was a good bet," the clerk responded.

Michael dragged a box over to one corner. Within its confines was an array of complaints, penned miseries, a procession of claimed injustice of varying content and description. But none of them could be simply shrugged off. Many were from death row inmates; for them, the Supreme Court represented the last hope before legal extermination.

For the next two hours Michael dug through the box. He was very accomplished at this now. It was like expertly shucking corn, his mind scanning the lengthy documents with ease, effortlessly probing through the legalese to the important points, comparing them to pending cases as well as precedents from fifty years ago pulled from his encyclopedic memory; then filing them away and moving on. However, at the end of two hours he had not found much of great interest.

He was thinking of heading up to his office when his hand closed around the plain manila envelope. The address label was typewritten, but the envelope had no return address. That was strange, Michael thought. People seeking to plead their case before the Court normally wanted the justices to know where to find them in the rare event that their plea was answered. There was, however, the left side of a postal return receipt card affixed to it. He slid open the envelope and removed the two sheets of paper. One of the functions of the clerks' mail room was to ensure that all filings met the strict standards of the Court. For parties claiming indigent status, if their petitions were granted, the Court would waive certain filing requirements and fees, and even engage and pick up some of the expenses of counsel, although the attorney would not bill for his or her time. It was an honor simply to stand before the Court as an advocate. Two of the forms required to achieve indigent status were a motion for leave to file as a pauper, and an affidavit signed by the prisoner, basically swearing to the person's impoverished status. Neither was in the envelope, Michael quickly noted. The appeal would have to be kicked back.

When Michael started reading what *was* in the envelope, all thoughts of any filing deficiencies vanished. After he finished, he could see the sweat from his palms leach onto the paper. At first Michael wanted to put the pages back in the envelope and forget he had ever seen them. But, as though he had now witnessed a crime himself, he felt he had to do something.

"Hey, Michael, Murphy's chambers just called down for you," the clerk said. When Michael didn't answer, the clerk said again, "Michael? Justice Murphy is looking for you."

Michael nodded, finally managing to focus on something other than the papers in his hand. When the clerk turned back to his work, Michael put the pages back in the manila envelope. He hesitated an instant. His entire legal career, his entire life, could be decided in the next second or so. Finally, as though his hands were acting independently from his thoughts, he slipped the envelope into his briefcase. By doing so before the petition had been officially processed with the Court, he had just committed, among other crimes, theft of federal property, a felony.

As he raced out of the mail room, he almost collided head-on with Sara Evans.

She smiled at first, but the look changed quickly when she saw his face. "Michael, what's wrong?"

"Nothing. I'm fine."

She gripped his arm. "You're not fine. You're shaking and your face is white as a sheet."

"I think I'm coming down with something."

"Well, then you should go home."

"I'll grab some aspirin from the nurse. I'll be okay."

"Are you sure?"

"Sara, I really have to go." He pulled away, leaving her staring worriedly after him.

The rest of the day moved at a glacial pace for Michael and he repeatedly found himself staring at his briefcase, thinking of the contents. Late that night, his day's work at the Court finally completed, he furiously rode his bike back to his apartment on Capitol Hill. He locked the door behind him and took out the envelope once more. He grabbed a yellow legal pad from his briefcase and carried everything over to the small dinette table.

An hour later he sat back and stared at the numerous notes he had made. He opened his laptop and rewrote these notes onto his hard drive, changing, tinkering, rethinking as he did so, a longtime habit of his. He had decided to attack this problem as he would any other. He would check out the information in the petition as carefully as he could. Most important, he would have to confirm that the names listed on the petition were actually the people he thought they were. If it seemed legitimate, he would return the appeal to the clerks' mail room. If it was clearly frivolous, the work of an unbalanced mind or a prisoner blindly lashing out, he had made up his mind to destroy it.

Michael looked out the window and across the street at the cluttered line of row houses that had been converted into apartments just like his. Young disciples of government were honeycombed in this neighborhood. Half were still at work, the rest in bed, nightmaring through a list of uncompleted tasks of national importance, at least until the five A.M. awakening. The darkness Michael stared into was interrupted only by the wash of a corner streetlight. The wind had gained strength, and the temperature had dropped, in readiness for an advancing storm. The boiler in the old building was not yet engaged, and a sudden chill hit Michael through the window. He pulled a sweatshirt from his closet, threw it on, and returned to stare out to the street.

He had never heard of Rufus Harms. According to the dates in the letter, the man had been incarcerated when Michael was only five years old. The spelling in the letter was abysmal, the formation of the letters and words clumsy, resembling a child's humorous first attempts at penmanship. The typewritten letter explained some of the background of the case and was obviously composed by a far better educated person. A lawyer, perhaps, Michael thought. The language had a legal air to it, although it was as though the person typing it had intended his professional—together with his personal—identity, to remain unknown. The notice from the Army, according to the typewritten letter, had requested certain information from Rufus Harms. However, Rufus Harms denied ever being in the program the Army's records apparently indicated he was in. It had been a cover, Harms was alleging, for a crime that had resulted in a horrific miscarriage of justice—a legal fiasco that had caused a quarter century of his life to disappear.

Suddenly warm, Michael pressed his face into the coolness of the window and took a deep breath, the air frosting the glass. What he was doing amounted to blatant interference with a party's right to seek his day in court. All of his life Michael had believed in a person's inalienable franchise to have access to the law, no matter how rich or poor. It was not scrip that could be revoked or declared worthless. He comforted himself somewhat with the knowledge that the appeal would have been defeated via a host of technical deficiencies.

But this case was different. Even if false, it could still do terrible damage to the reputations of some very important people. If it was true? He closed his eyes. Please, God, do not let it be, he prayed.

He turned his head and eyed the phone. He suddenly

wondered if he should call and seek his brother's advice. John was savvy in ways his younger brother was not. He might know how to handle the situation better. Michael hesitated for a moment longer, reluctant to admit that he needed any help, especially from that troubling, estranged source. But it also might be a way back into his brother's life. The fault was not entirely on one side; Michael had matured enough to comprehend the elusiveness of blame.

He picked up the phone and dialed. He got the answering machine, a result that pleased a certain part of him. He left a message asking for his brother's help but revealing nothing. He hung up, and returned to the window once more. It was probably better that John had not been there to take the call. His brother tended to see things only in rigid lines of black and white, a telling facet of the way he lived his life.

Toward the early hours of the morning, Michael drifted off to sleep, growing ever more confident that he could handle this potential nightmare, however it turned out.

CHAPTER ELEVEN

Three days after Michael Fiske had taken the file from the clerks' mail room, Rufus Harms placed another call to Sam Rider's office, but was told the attorney was out of town on business. As he was escorted back to his cell, Rufus passed a man in the corridor.

"Lot of phone calls lately, Harms. What, you have a mail-order business going or something?" The guards laughed loudly at the man's words. Vic Tremaine was a little under six feet, had white-blond, close-cropped hair, weathered features and was molded like a gun turret. He was the second-in-command of Fort Jackson, and he had made it his personal mission to compress as much misery into Harms's life as he could. Harms said nothing, but stood there patiently as Tremaine looked him up and down.

"What'd your lawyer want? He coming up with another defense for you slaughtering that little girl? Is that it?" Tremaine drew closer to the prisoner. "You still see her in your sleep? I hope you do. I listen to you crying in your cell, you know." Tremaine's tone was openly taunting, the muscles in his arms and shoulders tensing with each word, neck veins pulling taut, as though he were hoping Harms would crack, try something, and that would be the end of the prisoner's life tenure here. "Crying like a damn baby. I bet that little girl's momma and daddy cried too. I bet they wanted to wrap their fingers around your throat. Like you did to their baby. You ever think about that?"

Harms did not flinch. His lips remained in a straight line, his eyes looking past Tremaine. Harms had been through isolation, solitary, taunts, physical and mental abuse; everything one man could do to another out of cruelty, fear and hatred, he had endured. Tremaine's words, no matter their content or how they were delivered, could not break through the wall that encased him, kept him alive.

Sensing this, Tremaine took a step back. "Get him out of my sight." As the group headed off, Tremaine called after them, "Go back to reading your Bible, Harms. That's as close as you're ever getting to heaven."

John Fiske hustled after the woman walking down the hallway of the court building.

"Hey, Janet, got a minute?"

Janet Ryan was a very experienced prosecutor currently doing her best to send one of Fiske's clients away for a long time. She was also attractive and divorced. She smiled when she turned to him. "For you, two minutes."

"About Rodney—"

"Wait, refresh my memory. I've got lots of Rodneys."

"Burglary, electronics store, north side."

"Firearm involved, police chase, priors—now I remember."

"Right. Anyway, neither one of us wants to take this sucker to trial."

"Translation, John: Your case stinks and mine is overwhelming."

Fiske shook his head. "You might have a chain-of-custody problem with some of the evidence."

"*Might* is such a funny word, don't you think?"

"And that confession has holes."

"They always do. But the fact is your guy is a career crim. And I'll get a jury who'll put him away for a long time."

"So why waste the taxpayers' money, then?"

"What's your deal?"

"Plead to the burglary, possession of stolen property. Drop the nasty little firearm count. We end up with five years with credit for time served."

Janet started walking. "See you in court."

"Okay, okay, eight, but I need to talk with my guy."

She turned around and ticked off the points on her fingers. "He pleads to all of it, including the 'nasty little firearm' count, he gets ten years, forget the time served, and he punches the whole ticket. Probation for another five after that. If he pees funny, he goes back for another ten, no questions asked. If he goes to trial you're looking at a slam-dunk of twenty. And I want an answer right now."

"Damn, Janet, where's the compassion?"

"Saving it for somebody who deserves it. As you can probably guess, my list is very short. Besides, it's a sweetheart deal. Yes or no?"

Fiske tapped his fingers against his briefcase.

"Going once, going twice," Ryan said.

"Okay, okay, deal."

"Good doing business with you, John. By the way, why don't you call me sometime. You know, off hours?"

"Don't you think there might be a conflict lurking there somewhere?"

"Not at all. I'm always hardest on my friends."

She walked off humming while Fiske leaned up against the wall and shook his head.

An hour later, he returned to his office and tossed down his briefcase. He picked up the phone and checked his messages at home, listening to the recorded voices at the same time he wrote down notes for an upcoming hearing. When he heard his brother's voice, he didn't even stop writing. One finger flicked out and erased the message. It was rare but not unheard-of for Mike to call. Fiske had never called him back. Now he thought his brother was doing it just to antagonize him. As soon as he completed this thought, he knew it was not true. He rose and went over to a bookcase jammed with trial notebooks and legal tomes. He slid out the framed photograph. It was an old picture. He was in his policeman's uniform, Mike stood next to him. Proud little brother just entering manhood and stern-faced big brother, who had already seen a lot of evil in life and expected to see a lot more before he was done. In reality he had experienced firsthand the ugly side of humanity, and was still, but now he did so without the uniform. Just a briefcase, a cheap suit and a fast mouth. Bullets exchanged for words. Till the end of his days. He put the photo back and sat down. However, he looked over at the photo, suddenly unable to concentrate.

A few days later, Sara Evans knocked and then opened the door to Michael Fiske's office. It was empty. Michael had borrowed a book and she needed it back. She looked around the room but didn't see it lying anywhere. Then she spotted his briefcase underneath the kneehole of his desk. She picked it up. From the weight, she knew there was something inside. The briefcase was locked, but she knew the combination from having borrowed his briefcase a couple of times before. She opened it and immediately saw two books and the papers inside. Neither book was the one she was looking for though. She was going to close it back up but then stopped. She pulled the papers out and then looked at the envelope they had come in. Addressed to the clerks' office. She had just glanced at the handwritten page and then the typewritten letter when she heard footsteps. She put the papers back, closed the briefcase and slid it back under the desk. A moment later Michael walked in.

"Sara, what are you doing here?"

Sara did her best to look normal. "I just came looking for that book I had lent you last week."

"I've got it at home."

"Well, maybe I can come over for dinner and get it."

"I'm kind of busy."

"We're all busy, Michael. But you've really been keeping to yourself lately. Are you sure you're okay? Not cracking under the strain?" She smiled to show she was kidding. But Michael did look like he was cracking.

"I'm fine, really. I'll bring the book tomorrow."

"It's not that big a deal."

"I'll bring it tomorrow," he said a little angrily, his face flushing, but he calmed down quickly. "I've really got a lot of work to do." He looked at the door.

Sara went over and put her hand on the knob, then looked back. "Michael, if you need to talk about anything, I'm here for you."

"Yeah, okay, thanks." He ushered her out and closed and locked the door. He went over to his desk and pulled out the briefcase. He looked at the contents and then over at the door.

Later that night, Sara pulled her car down the gravel drive and stopped in front of the small cottage located off the George Washington Parkway, a truly beautiful stretch of road. The cottage was the first thing she had ever owned and she had put a lot of work into fixing up the place. A stairway led down to the Potomac, where her small sailboat was docked. She and Michael had spent their rare free time sailing across the river to the Maryland side and then north under Memorial Bridge and then on to Georgetown. It was a haven of calm for them both, surrounded as they were by a sea of crisis at work. Michael had turned down her last offer to go sailing. In fact, he had turned down all of her get-together ideas the past week. At first she thought it was due to her rejecting his marriage offer, but after the encounter at his office, she knew that was not it. She struggled to remember precisely what she had seen in the briefcase. It was a filing, she was sure of that. And she had seen a name on the typewritten letter. It was Harms. She hadn't remembered the first name. From the little she had been able to read before Michael walked in, apparently Harms was filing some sort of appeal with the Court. She didn't know what about. There had been no signature at the bottom of the typewritten letter.

She had gone directly to the clerks' office to see if any case with the name Harms had been logged in. It hadn't. She couldn't believe she was thinking this, but had Michael taken an appeal before it had been processed and put into the system? If he had, that was a very serious crime. He could be fired from the Court—sent to jail, even.

She went inside, changed into jeans and a T-shirt and walked back outside. It was already dark. Supreme Court clerks rarely made it home while it was still light, unless it was daybreak and they were coming home to shower and change clothes before going back to work. She walked down the stairs to the dock and sat on her boat. If only Michael would confide in her, she could help. Despite his words to the contrary, Michael had pulled back from her. He had not taken rejection well. Who would? she told herself.

She abruptly jumped up and raced to the house, picked up the phone and started to dial his number, but then stopped. Michael Fiske was a stubborn man. If she confronted him on what she had seen, that could very well make matters worse. She put the phone back down. She would have to let him come to her. She went back outside and looked at the water. A jet flew by and she automatically waved to it, a ritual of hers. Indeed, the planes were so low at this point that, had it been light, a passenger on the plane could have seen her waving. When her hand dropped back down, she felt more depressed than she had since her father had passed away, leaving her all alone.

After that loss, she had started life anew. Gone to the West Coast for law school, where she had excelled, clerked at the Ninth Circuit Court of Appeals and then taken a job with the Supreme Court. That's when she had sold the farm in North Carolina and bought this place. She wasn't running from her old life, or from the sadness that gripped her whenever she dwelled on her parents not being around either to see her accomplishments, or to simply hold her. At least she didn't think she was. When the day came for her to leave the Court, she had no idea what she wanted to do. In the legal arena, she could go anywhere. The trouble was, she didn't even know if she wanted the law to be part of her life. Three years of law school, a year at the court of appeals, starting on her second year up here, she was creeping close to burnout.

She thought of her father, a farmer and also the town's justice of the peace. He had no fancy courtroom. He often dispensed sound and fair justice while perched on his tractor in the field or while washing up for dinner. To Sara, that was what the law was, what it meant to most people, or at least what it should mean. A search for the truth, and then the handing down of justice after that truth was found. No hidden agendas, no word games, simply common sense applied to the facts. She sighed. But it was never that simple. She knew that better than most.

She went back inside, stood on a chair and snared a pack

of cigarettes off the top of the cabinet in the kitchen. She sat on the glider on the back porch overlooking the water. She looked up at the clear sky and located the Big Dipper. He dad had been an avid, if amateur, astronomer, and had taught her many of the constellations. Sara often used the stars to sail by, a practice she had picked up while at Stanford. On a clear night, you could never lose the stars, and with them you could never be truly lost. That was comforting. As she smoked her cigarette, she hoped Michael knew what he was doing.

Her next thoughts turned to another Fiske: John. Michael's comment about his brother had been close to the mark despite her protests. At the very first instant she had seen John Fiske, something had clicked in all the important conduits of her heart, brain and soul that she simply had no way to explain. She did not believe that significant emotions could be aroused to such an intensity that quickly. It just didn't happen. But that was why she was so confused, because, in a way, that's exactly what had occurred to her. Every movement John Fiske made, every word he spoke, every time he made eye contact with someone, or simply laughed, smiled or frowned, she felt as though she could watch him forever and never grow tired of it. She almost laughed at the absurdity. But then again, how crazy could it be when it was how she felt?

And that wasn't her only observation of the man. Unknown to Michael, she had checked with a friend at the courthouse in Richmond and found out Fiske's trial schedule for a two-week period. She had been amazed at how often the man was in court. She had gone down once more during the summer when things were slower at the Supreme Court, and watched John Fiske argue at a sentencing hearing. She had worn a scarf and glasses, just in case she was ever introduced to him later on, or in case he had seen her the first time she had come to watch him with Michael.

She had listened to him argue forcefully for his client. As soon as he had finished, the judge had put the man away for life. His client led away to begin his prison term, Fiske packed his briefcase and left the courtroom. Outside, Sara had watched as Fiske had attempted to comfort the man's family. The wife was thin and sickly, her face covered with bruises and welts.

Fiske spoke a few words to the wife, hugged her and then turned to the oldest son, a young man of fourteen who already looked to be a committed slave of the street.

"You're the man of the house now, Lucas. You have to look after your family," said Fiske.

Sara studied the teenager. The anger in his face was painful to see. How could someone so young have all that hostility inside him?

"Uh-huh," Lucas said, staring at the wall. He was dressed for gang work, a bandanna covered his head. He wore clothes one could not afford flipping burgers at McDonald's.

Fiske knelt down and looked at the other son. Enis was six years old, cute as the devil and usually bubbly.

"Hey, Enis, how you doing?" Fiske asked, holding out his hand.

Enis warily shook Fiske's hand. "Where's my daddy?"

"He had to go away for a while."

"Why's that?"

"Cause he kill—" Lucas started to say before Fiske cut him off with the sharpest of looks. Lucas muttered an expletive, threw off his mother's shaky hand and stalked away.

Fiske looked back at Enis. "Your daddy did something he's not too proud of. Now he's going away to make up for it."

"Jail?" Enis asked. Fiske nodded.

As Sara observed this exchange it occurred to her that today Fiske, and adults in general, probably felt foolish and inadequate in these situations, like sitcom characters from the 1950s trying to deal with a second millennium child. Even at six years old Enis probably knew a great deal about the criminal justice system. In fact, the little boy probably knew far more about the evil parts of life than many adults ever would.

"When's he getting out?" Enis asked.

Fiske looked up at the wife and then back at the little boy. "Not for a real long time, Enis. But your mom's going to be here."

"Okay, then," Enis said with little emotion. He took his mom's hand and they left.

Sara watched as Fiske looked after the pair for a moment. Again, she could almost feel what he was thinking. One son perhaps lost forever, the other casually leaving his father behind, like a stray dog on the street.

Finally, Fiske had loosened his tie and walked off.

Sara wasn't exactly sure why, but she decided to follow him. Fiske kept a slow pace, and she easily was able to keep him in sight. The bar he entered was a little slit in the wall, its windows dark. Sara hesitated and then went in.

Fiske was at the bar. He had obviously already ordered because the bartender was sliding a beer across to him. She quickly went to a back booth and sat down. Despite its dingy appearance, the bar was fairly full and it was barely five o'clock. There was an interesting mixture of working class and downtown office dwellers in here. Fiske sat between two construction workers, their yellow hard hats on the bar in front of them. Fiske slipped his jacket off and sat on it. His shoulders were as broad as the burly men's next to him. Sara noted that his shirt was untucked and fell over the back of his pants. The way his dark hair covered the back of his neck and touched the white of his shirt held her gaze for some time.

He was talking to the men on either side of him. The

workers laughed heartily at something Fiske had said, and
Sara felt herself smile even though she hadn't heard it. A
waitress finally came over and Sara ordered a ginger ale.
She continued to watch Fiske sitting at the bar. He was
not joking around anymore. He stared at the wall so
intently Sara caught herself looking at it too. All she saw
were bottles of beer and liquor, neatly arranged; Fiske
obviously observed far more. He had already ordered a
second beer, and when it arrived he held the bottle to his
lips until it was empty. She noticed that his hands were
large, the fingers thick and strong-looking. They didn't
look like the hands of someone who spent all his time
punching a pencil or sitting in front of a computer screen.

Fiske slapped some money down, grabbed his jacket
and turned around. For an instant Sara thought she felt
his eyes upon her. He hesitated a moment and then
pulled his jacket on. The corner she was in was dark. She
didn't believe he had seen her, but why had he hesitated?
A little nervous now, she waited an extra minute or so
before she rose and left, leaving a couple of singles
behind for her drink.

She didn't see him as she came back out into the
sunlight. Just like that, as though in a dream, he was gone.
On an impulse she went back into the bar and asked the
bartender if he knew John. He shook his head. She wanted
to ask some more questions, but the bartender's expression
signaled that he would not be communicative if she did.

The construction workers eyed her with a great deal of
interest. She decided to leave before things turned uncomfortable for her. Sara walked back to her car and climbed
in. Half of her had wanted to run into Fiske somehow, the
other part of her was glad that she hadn't. What would she
say anyway? Hello, I work with your brother and I'm sort
of stalking you?

She had driven back to northern Virginia that night,
had two beers herself, and fallen asleep in the glider on

her rear deck. The same one she was sitting in right now as she smoked her cigarette and watched the sky. That had been the last time she had seen John Fiske, almost four months ago.

She couldn't be in love with him, since she didn't even know the man; infatuation was far more likely. Maybe if she ever did meet Fiske it would destroy her impression of him.

She wasn't a believer in destiny, though. If anything was going to happen between them, it would probably be up to her to make the first move. She was just totally confused as to what that first move should be.

Sara put out her cigarette and stared at the sky. She felt like going for a sail. She wanted to feel the wind in her hair, the tickle of water spray against her skin, the sting of rope against her palm. But right now, she didn't want to experience any of those things alone. She wanted to do them with someone, someone in particular. But with what little Michael had told her about John Fiske, and what she had seen of the man herself, she doubted that would ever happen.

A hundred miles south, John Fiske too gazed up at the sky for a moment as he got out of his car. The Buick wasn't in the driveway, but Fiske had not come to see his father anyway. The neighborhood was quiet other than a couple of teenagers two doors down working on a Chevy with an engine so big it looked like it had ruptured through the car's hood.

Fiske had just spent all day in a trial. He had presented his case, warts and all, as best he could. The ACA had vigorously represented the commonwealth. Eight hours of intense sparring, and Fiske had barely had time to go to the john to take a leak before the jury came back with a guilty verdict. It was his guy's third strike. He was gone for good. The ironic thing was Fiske really believed him innocent of this particular charge—not something he could say with most of his clients. But his guy had beat so many other raps, maybe the jury was just unconsciously evening the score. To top it off, he'd die of old age waiting for the rest of his legal fee to come. Prisoners for life seldom bothered about settling their debts, particularly debts to their loser attorneys.

Fiske went into the backyard, opened the side door to the garage, went in and pulled a beer from the fridge. The humidity still lay over them like a damp blanket, and he held the cold bottle against his temple, letting the chill sink deep. At the very rear of the yard was a small stand of bent trees and a long-dead grapevine still tightly wrapped around rusty poles and wire. Fiske went back there and leaned up against one of the elms. He looked down at a recessed spot in the grass. Here was buried Bo, the Belgian shepherd the Fiske brothers had grown up with. Their father had brought the dog home one day when Bo was no bigger than his fist. Within a year or so he had grown into a big-chested, sixty-pound, black and white beauty that both boys adored, Mike especially. Bo would follow them on their morning paper routes, taking turns with the two boys. They had had almost nine years of intense pleasure together before Bo had toppled over from a stroke while Mike was playing with him. John had never seen anyone cry that hard in his whole life. Neither his mother nor his father could console Mike. He had sat in the backyard bawling, holding the dog's bushy coat, trying to make him stand up again, to go play with him in the sunshine. John had held his brother tightly that day, cried with him, stroked the still head of their beloved shepherd.

When Mike had gone to school the next day, John had stayed behind with his father to bury the dog here. When Mike had come home they all had attended a little service in the backyard for Bo. Mike had read with great conviction from the Bible and the brothers had placed a little headstone, actually a chunk of cinder block, with Bo's name scrawled on it in pen, at the head of the simple grave. The piece of cinder block was still there, though the ink had long since vanished.

Fiske knelt down and ran his hand along the grass, so smooth and fine in this shaded spot. Damn, they had loved that dog so much. Why did the past have to recede so quickly? Why did one always recall the good times as being so brief? He shook his head, and then the voice startled him.

"I remember that old dog like it was yesterday."

He looked up at Ida German, who stood on the other side of the fence staring at him. He rose, looking a little embarrassed. "It was a long time ago, Ms. German."

The woman smelled perpetually of beef and onions, as did her house, Fiske knew. A widow for nearly thirty years now, she moved slowly, her body shrunken, squat and thick. Her long housecoat covered veiny, splotched legs and bloated ankles. But at nearly ninety years old, her mind was still clear, her words crisp.

"Everything's a long time ago with me. Not with you. Not just yet. How's your momma?"

"Holding her own."

"I've been meaning to get over there to see her soon, but this old body just doesn't have the get up and go it used to."

"I'm sure she'd love seeing you."

"Your daddy went out a while ago. American Legion or VFW, I think."

"Good, I'm glad to see he's getting out. And I appreciate you keeping him company."

"Isn't any fun being alone. I've outlived three of my own children. Hardest thing in the world for a parent to do is bury their babies. Ain't natural. How's Mike? Don't see him much."

"He keeps pretty busy."

"Who would've thought that chubby-cheeked little towhead would've gone on to do what he's done? Mind-boggling, if you ask me."

"He's earned it." Fiske stopped for a moment. That had just slipped out. But his brother *had* earned it.

"You both have."

"I think Mike hit it a little higher than I did."

"Huh. Don't you go believing that. Your daddy brags about you a mile a minute. I mean, he talks about Mike too, but you're the king of the hill with him."

"Well, he and Mom brought us up right. Sacrificed everything for us. You don't forget that." Maybe Mike had, but he never would, Fiske told himself.

"Well, Mike had three fine examples to follow." Fiske looked at her curiously. "That boy worshiped the ground you walked on."

"People change."

"You think so, do you?"

A few drops of rain started to fall. "You better get back inside, Ms. German, it looks like it might pour."

"You know you can call me Ida if you want."

Fiske smiled. "Some things don't change, Ms. German."

He watched her until she made it inside. The neighborhood wasn't nearly as safe as it had once been. He and his father had installed deadbolts on her doors, sash locks on her windows and a peephole in her front door. The elderly carried a bull's-eye on them when it came to crime.

Fiske looked down once more at Bo's grave, the vision of his brother crying his eyes out over a dead dog cemented in his mind.

CHAPTER TWELVE

"How are you, Mom?" Michael Fiske touched his mother's face. It was early in the morning and Gladys was not in a good mood. Her face darkened and she pulled back from his touch. He looked at her a moment, deep sadness in his eyes as he saw the open hostility in hers.

"I brought you something." He opened the bag he carried and pulled out a gift-wrapped box. When she made no move to open it, he did so for her. He showed her the blouse, her favorite shade of lavender. He held it out to her, but she wouldn't take it. It was like this every time he came to visit. She would rarely talk to him, her mood always foul. And his gifts were never accepted. He repeatedly tried to draw her out in conversation, but she refused.

He sat back and sighed. He had told his father about this, that his mother absolutely refused to have anything to do with him. But his old man was powerless to change things. No one could control who Gladys was nice to. Michael's visits had grown less and less frequent because of it. He had tried to talk to his brother about it, but John had refused to discuss it with him. His mother would never treat John that way, Michael knew. To her, he was the golden child. Michael Fiske could be elected the president of the United States or win the Nobel Prize, and in her eyes he would still always be second to his older brother. He left the blouse on the table, gave his mother a quick kiss and left.

Outside, the rain had started to come down. Michael pulled up the collar on his trench coat and got back in his car. He had a very long drive ahead of him. The visit to his mother was not the only reason he had driven south. He was now headed to southwest Virginia. To Fort Jackson. To see Rufus Harms. For a moment, he debated whether to stop and see his brother. John had not returned his phone call, which was no surprise. But the journey he was about to undertake had some personal risk to it, and Michael wouldn't have minded having his brother's advice and perhaps presence. But then he shook his head. John Fiske was a very busy attorney and he didn't have time to run around the state chasing wild theories of his younger brother's. He would just have to deal with it alone.

As she often did, Elizabeth Knight rose early, did some stretching exercises on the floor and then ran on the treadmill in the spare bedroom of her and her husband Senator Jordan Knight's Watergate apartment. She showered, dressed, fixed some coffee and toast and looked over some bench memos in preparation for oral argument next week. Since it was Friday, the justices would spend part of the day in conference, where they would vote on cases they had already heard. Ramsey ran the conferences on a tight schedule. To her disappointment, there was little debate at these meetings. Ramsey would summarize the salient points of each case, cast his vote orally, and wait while the other justices did the same. If Ramsey was in

the majority, which he usually was, he assigned the opinion. If he wasn't, the most senior associate justice in the
majority, usually Murphy—ideological opposites, he and
Ramsey rarely if ever voted the same way—would assign
the opinion.

As Knight finished her coffee, she thought back over her
first three years on the Court. It had been a whirlwind,
really. Because of her gender, she was automatically seen as
not only a champion of women's rights but also of causes
that many women traditionally supported. People never
considered this stereotyping, although it was a blatant
form of it, Knight knew. She was a judge, not a politician.
She had to look at each case separately, just as she had done
as a trial court judge. And yet, even she had to own up to
the fact that the Supreme Court was different. The impact
of its decisions was so far-reaching that the justices were
forced to go beyond the four corners of each case and look
at the effect of the decision on everyone else. That had
been one of the hardest things for her to do.

She looked around the luxurious apartment. She and
her husband had a good life together. They were
routinely touted as the capital's number one power
couple. And in a way they were. She carried that mantle
as well as she could, even as she combated the isolation
that each justice had to endure. When you went on the
Court, friends stopped calling, people treated you differently, were careful, guarded in what they said around
you. Knight had always been gregarious, outgoing. Now
she felt much less so. She clung to her husband's professional life as a way to lessen the impact of this abrupt
change. Sometimes she felt like a nun with eight monks
as her lifelong companions.

As if in answer to her thoughts, Jordan Knight, still
dressed in his pajamas, came up behind her and gave her
a hug.

"You know, there's no rule that says you have to start

every day at the crack of dawn. Snuggling in bed is good for the soul," he said.

She kissed his hand and turned to give him a hug back. "I don't recall you being a late sleeper either, Senator."

"We should both make a concerted effort to do it, I think. Who knows what it could lead to? I've heard sex is the best defense against aging."

Jordan Knight was tall and heavily built, with thinning gray hair and a tanned face scored with lines. In the inequitable way of the world regarding the physical appearances of men and women, he would be considered handsome even with the wrinkles and the extra pounds. He cut quite a figure on the pages of the *Post* and local magazines, and on national TV shows where even the most experienced political pundits were often overwhelmed by his wit, experience and intelligence.

"You certainly have some interesting opinions."

He poured himself a cup of coffee while she looked over her papers.

"Ramsey still grooming you to become a good member of his camp?"

"Oh, he's pushing all the right buttons, saying all the right things. However, I'm afraid some of my recent actions aren't sitting all that well with him."

"You go your own way, Beth, just like always. You're smarter than all of them. Hell, you should be chief justice."

She put an arm around his thick shoulders. "Like maybe you should be president?"

He shrugged. "I think the U.S. Senate is challenge enough for me. Who knows, this might be the last roundup for yours truly."

She pulled her arm away. "We really haven't talked about it."

"I know. We're both busy. Too many demands on our

time. When things settle down, we'll talk. I think we have to."

"You sound serious."

"Can't keep on the treadmill forever, Beth."

She let out a troubled laugh. "I'm afraid I signed on for life."

"Good thing about politics. You can always decide not to run again. Or you can lose your seat."

"I thought there was a lot more you wanted to accomplish."

"It's not going to happen. Too many obstacles. Too many games. To tell you the truth, I'm getting kind of tired."

Beth Knight started to say something and then stopped. She had jumped firmly into the "game" of the Supreme Court.

Jordan Knight picked up his coffee and kissed her on the cheek. "Go get 'em, Ms. Justice."

As the senator walked off, she rubbed her face where he had kissed it. She tried to study her papers once more, but found she couldn't. She simply sat there, her mind suddenly whirling in many different directions.

John Fiske held the photo of himself and his brother. He had sat there for almost twenty minutes with it, not even looking at it for much of that time. Finally he stood it up on his bookcase, went over to the phone and dialed his brother's number. There was no answer and Fiske didn't bother leaving a message. He then called the Supreme Court, but was told Michael was not yet in. He called thirty minutes later and was told by another person that Michael would not be in at all that day. Figures, he thought. He couldn't get hold of his brother when he had at last gotten up the nerve to call him. Was that what it was—nerve? He sat down at his desk and tried to work, but his eyes kept stealing over to that photo.

Finally, he packed his briefcase, grateful that he had to go to court, grateful to get away from some nagging feelings.

In the course of the morning, he had two hearings back to back. One he won convincingly; with the other he was torn apart by the judge, who seemingly took every opportunity to ridicule his legal arguments, while the assistant commonwealth attorney stood by politely, holding back the smiles; you had to maintain the professional facade, because it could be your butt being put through the wringer the next time. Everyone here understood that. Or at least those who stuck with it did.

He next went to the Richmond city jail and then the county jail in Henrico to speak with clients. With one, he discussed strategy for the man's upcoming trial. His inmate client offered to go on the witness stand and lie. Sorry, you won't be doing that, Fiske told him. With another client the talk was about the ubiquitous plea bargain. Months, years, decades. How much time? Will I have a shot at parole? Suspended sentence? Help me out, man. I got a woman and kids. I got bizness to take care of. Okay, right. What's a little murder and mayhem compared to that?

With the last client, things took a very different turn. "We're not in good shape here, Leon. I think we should plead," Fiske advised.

"Nope. We go to trial."

"They've got two eyewitnesses."

"Is that right?"

Leon had been charged with the shooting of a child. It had been a dispute between two gangs of skinheads, and the little girl had gotten in the way—a fairly common tragedy these days. "Well, they're not going to hurt me if they don't testify, are they?"

"Why won't they testify?" Fiske said evenly. He had been down this road before. How many times as a cop had cases disappeared before his eyes because the witnesses suddenly forgot what they had so clearly seen and remembered before?

Leon shrugged. "You know, things come up. People don't keep their appointments."

"The police took their statements."

Leon gave him a sharp glance. "Right, but I get to face people testifying against me, right? So's you can trip 'em up on the witness stand, right?"

"You certainly know your Constitution," Fiske said dryly. He took a deep breath. He was so tired of the game of witness intimidation. "Come on, Leon, tell me—I'm your attorney, it's all privileged. Why won't they testify against you?"

Leon cracked a smile. "You don't need to know."

"Yes, I do. I don't need any surprises. You never know what a prosecutor is going to try. Believe me, I've seen it happen before. If something goes down and I'm not prepared for it, your ass could go up the river."

Now Leon looked a little worried. He obviously hadn't thought of that. He rubbed at the swastika on his forearm. "Privileged, right? That's what you said."

"That's right." Fiske leaned forward. "Between you, me and God."

Leon laughed. "God? Shit, that's a good one." He hunched forward and spoke in a low voice. "Got me a couple of friends. They gonna pay a little visit to these witnesses. Make sure they forget their way to the courthouse. It's all set up."

Fiske slumped back. "Aw hell, now you've done it."

"Done what?"

"Told me the one damn thing I have to go to the judge with."

"What the hell you talking about?"

"Legally, and ethically, I can't divulge any information given to me by a client."

"So, what's the problem? I'm your client and I just gave you the damn information."

"Right, but you see, there's an important exception to that rule. You just told me about a crime you've planned for the future. That's the one thing I have to tell the court. I can't let you commit the crime. I have to advise you not to do it. Consider yourself so advised. If you'd already done it, we'd be okay. What the hell were you thinking about, telling me that?" Fiske looked disgusted.

"I didn't know that was the law. Shit, I ain't no damn lawyer."

"Come on, Leon, you know the law better than most lawyers. Now you've gone and screwed up your own case. Now we have to plead."

"What the hell do you mean?"

"If we go to trial and the witnesses don't show, I have to tell the court what you told me. If the witnesses show, your ass is cooked."

"Well, then don't you go telling nobody nothing."

"That's not an option, Leon. If I don't and it comes out somehow, I lose my license to practice. And while I like you a lot, no client is worth that. Without my license I don't eat. And you screwed up, man, not me."

"I don't believe this shit. I thought you could tell your damn attorney anything."

"I'll see what I can do on the plea. You're going to spend some time in jail, Leon, no way around that." Fiske stood and patted the prisoner on the back. "Don't worry, I'll cut you the best deal I can."

As Fiske walked out of the visitors' room he smiled for the first time all day.

CHAPTER THIRTEEN

Michael Fiske looked up ahead nervously as he drove. His wipers struggled to maintain visibility in the face of the pouring rain. Headed west, he had passed places with names like Pulaski, Bland and even something called Hungry Mothers State Park, which had conjured up in his mind a discomforting vision of huddled masses of women and children begging for food along the park's trails. For a while winds swirling off nearby Big A Mountain buffeted the car. Even though he had been born and raised in Virginia, Fiske had never been west of Roanoke, and he had only ventured there to take the bar exam. Up to this point he had made good time, because the trip had been all highway. Once he had exited Interstate 81 and headed in a northwesterly direction, that had abruptly changed. Now the terrain was rugged and unforgiving, the roads narrow and serpentine.

He glanced over at the briefcase next to him on the front

seat, drawing a long breath as he did so. He had learned a lot since reading Rufus Harms's plea for help.

Harms had murdered a young girl, who was visiting the military base where Harms had been stationed at the end of the Vietnam War. He had been in the stockade at the time but had somehow broken out. There was no motive; it just seemed a random act of violence by a madman. Those facts were uncontroverted. As a Supreme Court clerk, Michael had many information resources to turn to, and he had used all of them in compiling the background facts. However, the military wouldn't acknowledge that such a program as described in Harms's petition even existed. Michael slapped the steering wheel. If only Harms or his attorney had included the letter from the Army in his filing.

Michael had finally decided that he needed to hear the account from its source: Rufus Harms. He had tried to do it through channels other than direct confrontation. He had tracked down Samuel Rider through the postal trail, but had received no reply to his calls. Was he the author of the typewritten paper? Michael believed it was a strong possibility. He had called the prison to try to talk with Harms on the phone, but his request had been denied. That had only increased his suspicions. If an innocent man was in prison, it was Michael's job—his *duty*, he corrected himself—to see that that man became free.

And there was a final reason for this trip. Some of the names listed in the petition, the people allegedly involved in the little girl's death, were names well known to Michael. If it turned out Rufus Harms was telling the truth . . . he shuddered as one nightmarish scenario after another rolled through his thoughts.

On the seat next to him was a road atlas and a sheet of written directions he had made up for himself showing precisely the way to the prison. Over the next hour or so, he traveled through miles of back roads and over corroded wooden bridges, blackened by weather and car exhaust, through towns that weren't big enough to justify the title, and past battered house trailers tucked into narrow crevices of rock along the foothills of the Appalachians. He was passed by muddy pickup trucks with miniature Confederate flags flapping from radio antennae, and shotguns and deer rifles slung across racks in the rear window. As he drew closer to the prison, the tight, weathered faces of the few people he saw grew more and more taciturn, their eyes filled with a constant, irreversible suspicion.

As Michael rounded a curve, the prison facility loomed before him. The stone walls were thick, towering and vast, like a medieval castle transported to this miserably poor stretch of rocky soil. He wondered for a moment if the stone had been quarried by the prisoners into the assemblage of their own tombs.

He received his visitor's card, passed through the main gate and was then directed to the prison's visitors' parking. He explained his purpose to the guard at the entrance.

"You're not on the visitors' list," the young guard said. He eyed Michael's dark blue suit and intelligent features with contempt. *A rich, smartass, pretty boy from the city,* Michael could read in the man's eyes.

"I called several times, but I never got through to anyone who could tell me the procedure for being put on the list."

"Up to the prisoner. Generally speaking, if he wants you to visit, you do. If he don't, you don't. Only control these boys got." The guard cracked a grin.

"If you tell him that an attorney is here to see him, I'm sure he'll put me on his visitors' list."

"You're his lawyer?"

"I'm involved with an appeal of his right now," Michael said evasively.

The guard looked down at his ledger. "Rufus Harms," he said, evidently confused. "He's been here since before I was even born. Exactly what sort of appeal could some-body like him have going after all this time?"

"I'm not at liberty to discuss that," Michael said. "My work is covered by attorney–client privilege and is absolutely confidential."

"I know that. What, you think I'm stupid?"

"Not at all."

"If I let you in and it turns out I wasn't supposed to, then my keester's in a lot of trouble."

"Well, I was just thinking that you might want to check with your superior. That way, it's not your call and you can't get in trouble."

The guard picked up his phone. "I was already going to do that," he said in a very unfriendly tone.

He spoke into the phone for a couple minutes and then hung up.

"Somebody's coming on down." Michael nodded. "Where you from?" the guard asked.

"Washington, D.C."

"How much does somebody like you get paid?" It was clear that whatever sum Michael stated would be too much.

He took a deep breath as he observed the approach of the uniformed officer. "Actually, not nearly enough."

The young guard quickly stood and saluted his superior officer. The officer turned to Michael. "Please come with me, Mr. Fiske." The man was in his fifties, with the lean build, calm but serious manner and closely cut gray hair that helped mark him as career military.

Michael followed the man's precise strides down the hallway to a small office. For five minutes Michael patiently explained what he was doing there without really revealing any information of substance. He could do the lawyer-speak with the best of them.

"If you tell Mr. Harms that I'm here, he'll see me."

The man twirled a pen between his fingers, his eyes

dead center on the young lawyer. "This is rather puzzling. Rufus Harms just received a visit from his lawyer not too long ago. And that person wasn't you."

"Is that right? Was his name Samuel Rider?" The man didn't answer, but the momentary surprise on his features made Michael inwardly smile. His hunch had proven correct. Harms's former military counsel had enclosed the typewritten sheet of paper. "A person can have more than one lawyer, sir."

"Not someone like Rufus Harms. He hasn't had anyone for the last twenty-five years. Oh, his brother visits pretty regularly, but all this interest in the man has us puzzled. I'm sure you can appreciate that."

Michael smiled pleasantly, but his next words were spoken in a firm manner. "I hope you can appreciate the fact that a prisoner is entitled to speak with an attorney."

The officer stared at him for a few moments and then picked up the phone and spoke into it. He hung up and looked back at Michael without speaking. Five minutes passed before the phone rang again. When the man put it back down, he nodded at Michael and said curtly, "He'll see you."

CHAPTER FOURTEEN

When Rufus Harms appeared in the doorway of the visitors' room, he looked confused as his gaze settled on the young man. He shuffled forward. Michael rose to greet him and was met with a bark by the guard behind Rufus.

"Sit down."

Michael did so immediately.

The guard watched closely until Rufus took a seat across from Michael, and turned to the lawyer. "You were previously instructed as to the rules of conduct during visitation. In case you forgot any of them, they're posted clearly right over there." He pointed to a large sign on the wall. "No physical contact is permitted at any time. And you are to remain seated at all times. Do you understand?"

"Yes. Do you have to stay in the room? There is such a thing as attorney–client confidentiality. Also, does he have to be chained like that?" Michael asked.

"You wouldn't ask that if you'd seen what he did to a bunch of guys inside this place. Even all chained up he

could snap your skinny little neck in half in two seconds."
The guard moved closer to Michael. "Maybe at other prisons you get some more privacy, but this isn't like other
prisons. We only got the biggest and the baddest here, and
we have our own set of rules to operate by. This is an
unscheduled visit, so you got twenty minutes before the
big bad wolf here has to go to work cleaning toilets. And
we got some real messy ones today."

"Then I'd appreciate your letting us get started," said
Michael.

The guard said nothing else and moved over to his post
against the door.

When Michael looked at Rufus he found the big man's
gaze squarely on him.

"Good afternoon, Mr. Harms. My name is Michael
Fiske."

"That name don't mean nothing to me."

"I know, but I'm here to ask you some questions."

"They said you were my lawyer. You're not my lawyer."

"I didn't say I was. They just assumed that. I'm not
associated with Mr. Rider."

Rufus's eyes narrowed. "How do you know about
Samuel?"

"That's really not relevant. I'm here to ask you questions, because I received your writ for certiorari."

"You did what?"

"Your appeal." Michael lowered his voice. "I work at the
United States Supreme Court."

Rufus's mouth fell open. "Then what the hell are you
doing here?"

Michael nervously cleared his throat. "I know this isn't
actually orthodox. But I read your appeal, and I wanted to
ask you some questions about it. It makes a number of
very damaging allegations against some very prominent
people." As he looked into Rufus's astonished eyes,
Michael suddenly regretted ever coming here. "I looked

into the background of your case and some things don't make sense to me. I wanted to ask you some questions and then, if things check out, we can get your appeal going."

"Why isn't it going already? It got to the damned Court, didn't it?"

"Yes, but it also had a number of technical deficiencies that would have caused it to be denied processing. I can try to help you with those. But what I want to avoid is a scandal. You have to understand, Mr. Harms, that the Court receives bags of appeals from prisoners every year that have no merit."

Rufus's eyes narrowed. "Are you saying I'm lying? Is that what you're saying? Why don't you spend twenty-five years in this place for something that wasn't your fault and then come here and tell me that?"

"I'm not saying you're lying. I actually think there's something to all of this or, believe me, I wouldn't have come here." He looked around the grim room. He had never been near a place like this, sitting across from a man like Rufus. He suddenly felt like a first-grader getting off the bus and realizing he was somehow in high school. "Believe me," he said again. "I just need to talk to you."

"You got some ID shows you are who you say you are? I ain't been in a real trusting mood for the last thirty years."

Supreme Court clerks were not issued ID badges. The security personnel at the Court were required to learn to recognize them by sight. However, the Court did publish an official directory with the clerks' names and photos. That was one way to help the guards get to know their faces. Michael pulled this from his pocket and showed it to Rufus. Rufus studied it intently, looked over at the guard, then turned back to Michael. "You got a radio in your briefcase?"

"A radio?" Michael shook his head.

Rufus lowered his voice even more. "Then start humming."

"What?" Michael said, bewildered. "I can't really . . . I mean, I'm not really musical."

Rufus shook his head impatiently. "Then you got a pen?"

Michael nodded dumbly.

"Then pull it out and start tapping on the table. They've probably heard all they need to hear by now anyway, but we'll leave 'em a few surprises."

When Michael started to say something, Rufus interrupted. "No words, just tap. And listen."

Michael began to tap the table with his pen. The guard glanced over but said nothing.

Rufus spoke so softly that Michael had to strain to hear him. "You shouldn't have come here at all. You don't know the chance I took to get that piece of paper out of this place. If you read it, you know why. Killing some old black con who strangled a little white girl, people wouldn't give a damn. Don't think they would."

Michael stopped tapping. "That was all a long time ago. Things have changed."

Rufus let out a grunt. "Is that right? Why don't you go knock on Medgar Evers's or Martin Luther King's coffin and tell 'em that? Things have changed, yes sir, everything be all right now. Praise the Lord."

"That's not what I meant."

"If the people I talked about in that letter were black, and I was white—and I didn't call this place home— would you be here right now 'checking up' on my story?"

Michael looked down. When he looked back up, his expression was pained. "Maybe not."

"Sure as hell not! Start tapping, and don't stop."

Michael did so. "Believe it or not, I want to help you. If the things you described in your letter did happen, then I want to see justice served."

"Why the hell you care about somebody like me?"

"Because I care about the truth," Michael said simply.

"If you're telling the truth, then I will do everything in my power to get you out of this place."

"That's sure easy enough to say, ain't it?"

"Mr. Harms, I like to use my brains, my skills, to help people less fortunate than I am. I feel it's my duty."

"Well, that's real nice of you, son, but don't go patting me on the head. I might bite your hand off."

Michael blinked in confusion, and then it registered. "I'm sorry, I didn't mean to be condescending. Look, if you've been wrongly imprisoned, then I want to help you get your freedom. That's all."

Rufus didn't say anything for a minute, as though attempting to gauge the sincerity of the young man's words. When he finally leaned forward again, his features were softer, but his manner remained guarded.

"It ain't safe to talk about this stuff here."

"Where else can we talk?"

"No place that I know of. They don't let people like me out for vacation. But everything I said is true."

"You made reference to a let—"

"Shut up!" Rufus said. He looked around again, his eyes locking for a moment on the large mirror. "Wasn't it with what was filed?"

"No."

"All right, you know my attorney. You said his name before."

Michael nodded. "Samuel Rider. I tried to call him, but he didn't call me back."

"Tap louder." Michael picked up the beat. Rufus glanced around and then began speaking. "I'll tell him to talk to you. Whatever you need to know, he'll tell you."

"Mr. Harms, why did you file your appeal with the Supreme Court?"

"Ain't no higher one, is there?"

"No."

"Didn't think so. We get newspapers in here. Some TV,

radio. I've been watching them people over the years. In here you think a lot about courts and such. Faces change, but them judges can do anything. Anything they want to. I seen it. Whole country's seen it."

"But from a purely legal technical point of view there are other avenues you really have to pursue in the lower courts before your appeal can be heard there. You don't even have a lower court ruling from which you're appealing, for instance. In sum, your appeal has numerous flaws."

Rufus shook his head wearily. "I been in this place half my life. I ain't got all that much time left. I ain't never been married, I ain't never gonna have no kids. The last thing I'm gonna do is spend years messing around with lawyers and courts and such. I want out of here, and I want out of here just as fast as I can. I want to be free. Them big judges, they can get me outta here, if they believe in doing the right thing. That's the right thing, you go back and tell 'em that. They call 'em justices, well, that's justice."

Michael looked at him curiously. "Are you sure there's not another reason you filed it with the Supreme Court?"

Rufus looked blankly at him. "Like what?"

Michael let out a breath he hadn't realized he was holding. It was certainly possible that Rufus wouldn't know the positions now held by some of the men named in his appeal. "Never mind."

Rufus sat back and stared at Michael. "So what do them judges think about all this? They sent you down here, didn't they?"

Michael stopped tapping and said nervously, "Actually, they don't know I'm here."

"What?"

"I haven't actually shown anyone your appeal, Mr. Harms. I . . . I wanted to be sure, you know, that it was all aboveboard."

"You're the only one that's seen it?"

"For now, but like I said—"

Rufus looked at Michael's briefcase. "You didn't bring my letter with you, did you?"

Michael followed his gaze to the briefcase. "Well, I wanted to ask you some questions about it. You see—"

"Lord help us," Rufus said so violently that the guard braced himself to pounce.

"Did they take your briefcase when you come in? Because two of the men I wrote about are at this prison. One of them is in charge of the whole damn place."

"They're here?" Michael went pale. He had confirmed that the men named in the appeal were in the Army back in the seventies. He knew the current whereabouts of two of them, but he hadn't bothered to locate the others. He froze, suddenly realizing that he had just made a potentially fatal mistake.

"Did they take your damn briefcase?"

Michael stammered, "Just—just for a couple of minutes. But I put the documents in a sealed envelope, and it's still sealed."

"You done killed us both," Rufus screamed. Like a hot geyser, he exploded upward, flipping the heavy table over as though it were made of balsa wood. Michael leaped out of the way and slid across the floor. The guard blew his whistle and grabbed Rufus from behind in a choke hold. Michael watched as the giant prisoner, shackled as he was, flipped the two-hundred-pound guard off like a bothersome gnat. A half dozen other guards poured into the room and went at the man, swinging their batons. Rufus kept tossing them off like a moose against a pack of wolves, for a good five minutes, until he finally went down. They dragged him from the room, first screaming and then gagging as a baton was wedged against his throat. Right before Rufus disappeared, he stared at Michael, horror and betrayal in his eyes.

After an exhausting struggle that had continued all the way down the hallway, the guards managed to strap Rufus to a gurney.

"Get him to the infirmary," somebody screamed. "I think he's going into convulsions."

Even with the shackles and thick leather restraints on, Rufus wildly gyrated, the gurney rocking back and forth. He kept screaming until someone stuffed a cloth into his mouth.

"Hurry up, dammit," the same man said.

The group burst through the double doors and into the infirmary.

"Good God!" The physician on duty pointed to a clear space. "Over here, men."

They swung the gurney around and slid it into the empty spot. As the doctor approached, one of Rufus's thrashing feet almost clipped him in the gut.

"Take that out of his mouth," the doctor said, pointing at the handkerchief balled up in Rufus's mouth. The prisoner's face was turning a deep purple.

One of the guards looked at him warily. "You better take care, Doc, he's gone nuts. If he can reach you, he'll hurt you. He already took out three of my men. Crazy SOB." The guard looked menacingly at Rufus. As soon as the cloth was pulled from his mouth, Rufus's screams filled the room.

"Get a monitor on him," the doctor said to one of the attending nurses. Seconds after they managed to attach the sensors to Rufus, the doctor was closely watching the erratic rise and fall of Rufus's blood pressure and pulse. He looked at one of the nurses. "Get an IV over here." To another nurse he said, "An amp of lidocaine, stat, before he goes into cardiac arrest or has a stroke."

Both guards and medical personnel crowded around the gurney.

"Can't your men get out of here?" the doctor yelled into the ear of one of the guards.

The man shook his head. "He's strong enough to maybe break those restraints, and if he does and we're not here, then he could kill everybody in this room within a minute. Believe me, he could."

The doctor eyed the portable IV stand as it was placed next to the gurney. The other nurse raced up with the amp of lidocaine. The doctor nodded at the guards. "We're going to need your help to hold him down. We need a good vein to get the IV started, and from the looks of things we're only going to get one shot at it."

The men gathered around Rufus, holding him down. Even with their combined weight, it was barely enough.

Rufus looked back at them, so enraged, so terrified, he could barely keep his senses. Just like the night when Ruth Ann Mosley had perished. They ripped his shirt-sleeve up, exposing his sinewy forearm, the veins strong and pronounced. He shut his eyes and then opened them again as he saw the shiny needle coming his way. He shut his eyes one more time. When he opened them he was no longer in the infirmary at Fort Jackson. He was in the stockade in South Carolina a quarter of a century ago. The door burst open and a group of men walked in like they owned the place, like they owned him. There was only one he didn't know by sight. He had expected to see the batons come out, to feel the sharp thrusts into his ribs, against his buttocks and forearms. It had become a morning and evening ritual. As he absorbed the blows in silence, his mind would recite a Bible prayer, his spiritual side carrying him past the physical torture.

Instead, a gun was placed against his head. He was told to kneel down on the floor and to close his eyes. That's when it happened. He remembered the surprise, the shock he had felt as he stared up at the grinning, triumphant group. The smiles vanished when, a few minutes later,

Harms rose, threw off the men as though they were weightless, burst through his cell door, bowled over the guard on duty and was out of the stockade, running wild.

Rufus blinked again and he was back in the infirmary, looking at the faces, the bodies bearing down on him. He saw the needle coming closer to his forearm. He was looking up, the only person doing that. That's when he saw the second needle puncture the IV bag, the fluid from the hypodermic flowing into the lidocaine solution.

Vic Tremaine had carried out his task calmly and efficiently, as though he were watering flowers instead of committing murder. He didn't even look at his victim. Rufus jerked his head back around and eyed the IV needle held by the doctor. It was just about to puncture his skin, discharging into his body whatever poison Tremaine had chosen to kill him with. They had taken half his life already. He was not about to let them take the rest, not yet.

Rufus timed it as best as he could.

"Shit!" the doctor yelled, as Rufus ripped free from the restraint, grabbed his hand and whipped it across his body. The IV stand came tumbling down; the IV bag hit the floor and burst. A furious Tremaine took the opportunity to quickly leave the infirmary. Rufus's chest suddenly tightened, and his breathing became constricted. When the doctor managed to stagger up, he looked at Rufus. So still was the prisoner that the doctor had to check the monitor to make sure he was still alive. As he stared at vital signs that had dropped to dangerously low levels, he said, "Nobody can take this many extremes. He could be going into shock." He turned to a nurse. "Get a medevac helicopter up here." He looked at the head guard. "We're not equipped to handle this kind of situation. We'll stabilize him and then fly him to the hospital in Roanoke. But we need to move fast. I assume you're sending a guard with him."

The guard rubbed his bruised jaw and looked at the docile Rufus. "I'd send a whole platoon if they could fit in the damn chopper."

CHAPTER FIFTEEN

Escorted by an armed guard, Michael Fiske walked unsteadily down the hallway. Waiting at the end of the corridor was the uniformed officer who had questioned him earlier. Michael could see that he was holding two pieces of paper.

"Mr. Fiske, I didn't identify myself when we first met. My name is Colonel Frank Rayfield. I'm the commanding officer here."

Michael licked his lips. Frank Rayfield was one of the men Rufus had named in his appeal. The name had meant nothing to Michael at the time. Inside this prison, it meant that he was going to die. Who could have imagined that two of the men Rufus had accused of, essentially, murder in his appeal would be here of all places? But now that he thought about it, this would be a perfect place for them to keep close watch on Rufus Harms.

Focusing on Rayfield once more, Michael wondered where they would dump his body. As he had done as a

child, he suddenly found himself wishing that his big
brother would appear to help him. He looked on dully as
Rayfield handed him the papers and motioned the guard
to leave. As Michael clutched the papers, Rayfield looked
apologetic.

"I'm afraid my men were a little overzealous," said
Rayfield. "We don't usually photocopy documents in a
sealed envelope." Actually, Rayfield had opened the envelope and photocopied its contents himself. None of his
men had seen the documents.

Michael looked down at the papers. "I don't understand.
The envelope was still sealed."

"The envelope is a very common one. They just put it
back in a new one and sealed it."

Michael inwardly cursed himself for missing something
that obvious.

Rayfield broke into a chuckle.

"What's so funny?" Michael demanded.

"This is the fifth time Rufus Harms has named me in
some cockamamie lawsuit, Mr. Fiske. What else am I
supposed to do but laugh?"

"Excuse me?"

"He's never gone as high as the United States Supreme
Court before—that's who you're with, isn't it?"

"I don't have to answer that."

"Okay. But if you are, then your presence here is a
little unusual."

"That's my business."

"And my business is running this prison in a precise,
military way," Rayfield snapped back. But then his voice
softened. "I don't blame you, though. Harms is slick.
Looks like he conned his old military lawyer to help him
this time, and Sam Rider should know better."

"You're saying Rufus Harms makes a practice of filing
frivolous lawsuits?"

"You think that's unusual for prisoners? Too much

time on their hands. Anyway, last year he accused the president of the United States, the Secretary of Defense and yours truly of conspiring to frame him for a murder he committed, and which was witnessed by at least a half dozen people."

"Really?" Michael looked skeptical.

"Yes, really. It was finally dismissed, but it cost a few thousand bucks in government attorney time to get it done. I know the courts are open to everybody, Mr. Fiske. But a nuisance suit is a nuisance suit and, quite frankly, I'm getting tired of them."

"But he said in his petition—"

"Right, I read it. Two years ago, he claimed it was Agent Orange suffered in combat that caused him to do it. And you know what? Rufus Harms was never exposed to Agent Orange, because he was never in combat. He spent most of his two-year Army career in the stockade for insubordination, among other things. It's no secret—look it up yourself if you want. That is, if you haven't already done so." He gazed at Michael, who was looking down. "Now take your little papers, go back to Washington and let it work its way through the system. It'll get dismissed like all the others. Some innocent people are going to get embarrassed as hell, but that's the American way. I guess it's why I fought for this country: to sustain all those freedoms. Even when they're abused."

"You're just going to let me go?"

"You're not a prisoner here. I've got a lot of real inmates to worry about, including one that just beat the crap out of three of my guards. You're going to have to answer some questions that one of my men will be here shortly to ask you. It will relate to what happened in the visitors' room. We need it for our incident report."

"But that means it will go into the official record. My being here, everything."

"That's right, it will. It was your choice to come here, not mine. You have to live with the consequences."

"I know. But I wasn't counting on any of this."

"Well, life is full of little surprises."

"Look, do you really have to file anything?"

"Your presence here is a matter of official record anyway, Mr. Fiske, regardless of what happened in that visitors' room. You are in the visitation book with an assigned badge number."

"I guess I hadn't thought that all the way through."

"I guess not. I take it you're not really experienced in military matters?" While Michael stood there looking miserable, Rayfield thought for a moment. "Look, we need to fill out the report, but other things being equal, I may not officially file it. Maybe your presence here at the prison gets expunged too."

Michael breathed a sigh of relief. "Could you do that?"

"Maybe. You're a lawyer. What about a *quid pro quo*?"

"What do you mean?"

"I throw away the report and you throw away that appeal." He paused as he stared at the young man. "It would save the government another lawyer bill. I mean, God bless anybody's rights to seek their day in court, but this is getting a little old."

Michael looked away. "I'll have to think about that. It has some technical deficiencies anyway. Maybe you're right."

"I am right. I'm not looking to mess up your career. We'll just forget this ever happened. And hopefully I won't be reading about this case in the papers. If I do, then maybe your being down here has to come out too. Now, if you'll excuse me." Rayfield turned on his heel and walked off, leaving behind a visibly distressed Michael Fiske.

Rayfield went directly to his office. Rufus's suspicions had been well founded; a listening device designed to blend in with the wood grain had been planted on the underside of the table in the visitors' room. Rayfield listened once more to the conversation between Michael and Rufus. Some of it had been disrupted by Michael tapping his pen. The radio had obliterated all of Rufus's earlier conversation with Rider. Rufus was no idiot. But Rayfield had heard and read enough to know that potentially they had a big problem. And his conversation with Michael had not solved the dilemma, at least not permanently. He picked up the phone and placed a call. In concise sentences Rayfield recounted the events to the party at the other end.

"Holy shit, I can't believe this."

"I know."

"All of this happened today?"

"Well, I told you about Rider coming in earlier, but yes, all of these events happened just now."

"Why the hell did you let him in to see Harms?"

"If I didn't, don't you think he would've gotten more suspicious? After reading what Harms had written in his damn letter to the Court, what choice did I have?"

"You should have taken care of the sonofabitch before this. You've had twenty-five years to do it, Frank."

"That was the plan twenty-five years ago, to kill him," Rayfield fired back. "And look what happened. Tremaine and I have spent half our lives watching over his ass."

"You two aren't exactly doing it for free. What's your little nest egg up to so far? A million? Retirement's going to be awfully nice. But it won't be, for any of us, if this gets out."

"It's not like I haven't tried to kill the guy. Hell, Tremaine tried to do him today in the infirmary, but damn, it's like the guy's got a sixth sense. Rufus Harms is as mean as a snake when his back's against the wall. The guards will only go so far and we've got people looking over our shoulder, surprise inspections, the damn ACLU.

The bastard just won't die. Why don't you come down here and try?"

"All right, all right, there's no use us arguing about it. You're sure we were all named in the letter? How is that possible? He didn't even know who I was."

Rayfield didn't hesitate. The person he was speaking with had *not* been named in Rufus's letter, but Rayfield wasn't going to tell him that. Everybody was on the hook for this one. "How should I know? He's had twenty-five years to think about it."

"So how did he get the letter out?"

"That blows my mind. The guard saw the damn thing. It was his last will and testament, that was it."

"But he got it out somehow."

"Sam Rider is involved. That's for sure. He brought a radio with him and the noise messed up the bug we installed, so I couldn't hear what they said to each other. That should've told me something was up."

"I never trusted that guy. Except for Rider's insanity BS, Harms would've been dead a long time ago, courtesy of the Army."

"The second letter we found in Fiske's briefcase had been done on a typewriter. There were no initials at the bottom, you know, like when it's typed by a personal secretary, so Rider probably did it himself. They were both original documents, by the way."

"Dammit, why now? After all this time?"

"Harms received a letter from the Army. He referenced it in the paper he filed. Maybe that jogged his memory. I can tell you that up to now he either didn't remember what happened, or he's been keeping it inside for the last twenty-five years."

"Why would he do that? And why in the hell would the Army be sending him anything after all this time?"

"I don't know," Rayfield said nervously. He actually did know. The reason had been referenced in Rufus's court petition. But Rayfield was going to keep that card hidden for now.

"And of course you don't have this mysterious letter from the Army, do you?"

"No. I mean, not yet."

"It must be in his cell, although I can't imagine how it slipped through." The voice was again accusatory.

"Sometimes I think the guy's a magician," said Rayfield.

"Has he had any other visitors?"

"Just his brother, Josh Harms. He comes about once a month."

"And what about Rufus?"

"Looks like he's just about bought it. Stroke or heart attack. Even if he makes it, he probably won't be the same."

"Where is he?"

"En route to the hospital in Roanoke."

"Why the hell did you let him out?"

"The doc ordered it. He has an obligation to save the man's life, prisoner or not. If I overruled him, don't you think it would raise suspicion?"

"Well, keep on top of it, and pray his heart blows up. And if it doesn't, make it."

"Come on, who'd believe him?"

"You might be surprised. This Michael Fiske? He's the only other one who knows, besides Rider?"

"That's right. At least I think so. He came here to check out Harms's story. Didn't tell anybody—at least that's what he told Harms. We caught a big break there," Rayfield said. "I gave him the song and dance about Harms being a chronic jailhouse lawyer. I think he bought it. We got leverage because he could get in big trouble for being here. I don't think he's going to let the appeal go through."

The voice on the other end went up a few decibels. "Are you nuts? Fiske isn't going to have a choice in the matter."

"He's a Supreme Court clerk, for chrissakes. I heard him tell Harms."

"I know that. I damn well know that. But let me tell you exactly what you're going to do. You're going to take care of Fiske and Rider. And you're going to do it pronto."

Rayfield paled. "You want me to kill a Supreme Court clerk and a local lawyer? Come on, they don't have any proof of this. They can't hurt us."

"You don't know that. You don't know what was in the letter from the Army. You don't know what new information Fiske or Rider might have found out in the interim. And Rider's been practicing law for thirty years. He wouldn't have filed something he thought was frivolous, not with the damn Supreme Court. And maybe you're not aware of this, but Supreme Court clerks aren't exactly dummies. Fiske didn't drive all the way down there because he thought Harms was a lunatic. From what you told me, the contents of the letters were very specific on what happened in that stockade."

"They were," Rayfield conceded.

"So there you are. But that's not the biggest hole in all this. Remember, Harms *isn't* a jailhouse lawyer. He's never filed anything else in court. If Fiske checks out your claim, he'll find out you lied. And when Fiske does that—and I have to believe he will—then everything blows up."

"It's not like I had a lot of time to think up a plan," Rayfield said hotly.

"I'm not saying otherwise. But by lying to him, you just made him a big liability. And we have yet another problem."

"What's that?"

"Everything Harms said in his appeal happens to be true. Did you forget that? The truth is funny. You start looking here and there and all of a sudden the wall of lies starts to topple over. Guess where it's going to land? Do you really want to take that chance? Because when that wall comes down, the only place you're going to be retiring to is Fort Jackson. And this time on the other side of the prison cell door. That sound good to you, Frank?"

Rayfield took a weary breath and checked his watch.

"Shit, I'd take Nam over this any day."

"I guess we all got a little too comfortable. Well, it's time to earn your money, Frank. You and Tremaine just get it done. And while you're taking care of business, remember this: We all either survive this together, or we all go down together."

Thirty minutes later, after his debriefing by Rayfield's assistant, Michael left the prison building and walked in the light rain to his car. What a sucker he'd been. He felt like tearing up the appeal papers, but he wouldn't. Maybe he'd put them back into the process. Still, he felt sorry for Rufus Harms. All those years in prison had taken their toll. As Michael pulled out of the parking lot, he had no way of knowing that most of his radiator fluid had been collected in a bucket and poured into the nearby woods.

Five minutes later he looked on in dismay as the steam poured out from the hood of his car. He got out, gingerly raised the hood and then jumped back as a cloud of steam momentarily engulfed him. Swearing angrily, he looked around: not a car or human in sight. He thought for a moment. He could walk back to the prison, use the phone and call a towing service. As if on cue, the rain picked up in intensity.

As he looked up ahead of him, his spirits brightened. A van was approaching from the direction of the prison. He waved his arms to flag it down. As he did so he looked back at the car, steam still pouring out. Funny—he had just had it serviced in preparation for the trip. As he looked back at the van, his heart started to beat rapidly. He looked around, and then turned and sprinted away from the van. It sped up and quickly overtook him, blocking his way. He was about to race into the woods when the window came down and a gun was pointed at him.

"Get in," Victor Tremaine ordered.

CHAPTER SIXTEEN

It was Saturday afternoon when Sara Evans drove to Michael's apartment and looked at the cars parked on the street. His Honda wasn't there. He had called in sick on Friday, something she had never known him to do before. She had called his apartment, but he hadn't answered the phone. She parked, went in the building and knocked on his door. There was no answer. She didn't have a key. She went around to the rear of the building and climbed up the fire escape. She looked in the window of his small kitchen. Nothing. She tried the door, but it was locked. She drove back to the Court, her worries increased tenfold. Michael was not sick, she knew that. All this had something to do with the papers she had seen in his briefcase, she was sure of it. She silently prayed that he was not in over his head. That he was safe, and would be back to work on Monday.

She went back to work for the rest of the day and then had a late dinner with some of the other clerks at a restaurant near Union Station. They all wanted to talk shop, except for Sara. Usually a devoted fan of this ritual, she simply could not get into the conversations. At one point she wanted to run screaming from the room, sick of the endless strategizing, predictions, case selections, the subtlest nuances analyzed to death; mushroom clouds from mere mushrooms.

Later that night she lingered on the rear deck of her home. Then she made up her mind and took her boat out for a late-night sail on the river. She counted the stars, made funny pictures from them in her mind. She thought of Michael's offer of marriage and the reasons she had refused it. Her colleagues would be amazed that she had. It would be a brilliant match, they would say. They would have a wonderful, dynamic life together, with the almost absolute certainty that their children would be highly intelligent, ambitious and athletically gifted. Sara herself had been a scholarship lacrosse player in college, although Michael was the better athlete of the two.

She wondered whom he would ultimately marry. Or if he even would. Her rejection might cause him to remain a bachelor the rest of his life. As she sailed along, she had to smile. She was giving herself far too much credit. In a year's time, Michael would be off doing something incredibly fantastic. She would be lucky if he even remembered who she was five years from now.

As she docked her boat and wrapped the sails, she stopped for a moment to catch one last breeze off the water before she headed back to the house. Barely a twenty-minute non-rush-hour trip due north would deliver her to the most powerful city on earth, to her place with the most awe-inspiring legal minds of her time. And yet all she really wanted to do right now was snuggle under her blanket with the lights off and pretend she never had to go back there. Reasonably ambitious all her life, she suddenly had no drive to accomplish anything else of note in her professional life. It was like she had used up all her energy in getting to this point. Marriage and being a mom? Was that what she wanted? She had no siblings and had been pretty spoiled growing up. She wasn't used to being around kids all that much, but something pulled at her in this direction. Something very strong. But even so, she wasn't sure. And shouldn't she be by now?

As she went inside, undressed and climbed into bed, she realized that having a family required one thing to start: finding someone to love. She had just turned down one opportunity to do so with a truly exceptional man. Would another chance come along? Did she want a man in her life right now? Still, sometimes one shot was all you got. One shot. That was her last thought before falling asleep.

CHAPTER SEVENTEEN

It was Monday and John Fiske sat at his desk, digesting yet another arrest report on one of his clients. By now he was extremely adept at this process. He was only halfway through the report and he could already tell the sort of deal the guy could expect to get. Well, it was nice being good at something.

The knock on his office door startled him. His right hand slid open the top drawer of his desk. Inside was a 9mm, a leftover from his cop days. His clientele were not the most trustworthy. So while he would represent them zealously, he was not naive enough to turn his back on them either. Some of his clients had shown up at his door drugged or drunk, with a grudge against him for some perceived wrong. Thus, his spirits were lifted considerably by the feel of hard steel against his palm.

"Come on in, door's unlocked."

The uniformed police officer who stepped through the

doorway brought a smile to Fiske's lips, and he closed his desk drawer. "Hey, Billy, how you doing?"

"I've been better, John," Officer Billy Hawkins said.

As Hawkins came forward and sat down, Fiske saw the multicolored bruises on his friend's face. "What the hell happened to you?"

Hawkins touched one of the bruises. "Guy went nuts at a bar the other night, popped me a couple of good ones." He added quickly, "That's not why I'm here, John."

Fiske knew Hawkins to be a good-natured sort who didn't let the constant pressures of his job overwhelm him. He was always as reliable and serious about his job as he was casual and friendly off duty.

Hawkins glanced nervously at Fiske.

"It's not anything with Bonnie or the kids, is it?" Fiske asked.

"It's not about *my* family, John."

"Is that right?" As he looked into Hawkins's troubled eyes, Fiske's gut clenched.

"Damn, John, you know how much we hated going around to the next of kin, and we didn't even know them."

Fiske slowly stood up, his mouth instantly dry. "Next of kin? Oh my God, not my mom? My dad?"

"No, John, it's not them."

"Just tell me what the hell you need to tell me, Billy."

Hawkins licked his lips and then started speaking quickly. "We got a call from the police up in D.C."

Fiske looked confused for an instant. "D.C.?" As soon as he said it, his body froze. "Mike?"

Hawkins nodded.

"Was it a car accident?"

"No accident." Hawkins paused for a moment and cleared his throat. "It was a homicide, John. Looks like a robbery gone bad. They found his car in an alley. Bad part of town, I understand."

Fiske let this horrific news sink in for a long minute. As

a cop and now a lawyer, he had seen the results of many murders on other people, other families. This was new territory. "You haven't told my dad, have you?" he said quietly.

Hawkins shook his head. "Figured you'd want to do that. And what with your momma the way she is."

"I'll take care of it," Fiske said.

His thoughts were interrupted by Hawkins's next words.

"The detective in charge has requested an ID from next of kin, John."

As a police officer, how many times had Fiske told a grieving parent that same thing?

"I'll go on up."

"I'm so sorry, John."

"I know, Billy, I know."

After Hawkins had left, Fiske walked over to the photo of him and his brother and picked it up. His hands were shaking. It was not possible, what Hawkins had just told him. He had survived two gunshot wounds and spent nearly a month in the hospital, his mother and his little brother next to him for much of that time. If John Fiske could survive that, if he could be alive right now, how could his brother be dead? He put the photo back down. He tried to move to get his coat, but his legs were frozen. He just stood there.

CHAPTER EIGHTEEN

Rufus Harms slowly opened his eyes. The room was dim, shadowy. However, he was accustomed to seeing without benefit of light, becoming, over the years, an expert of sorts. The years in prison had also boosted the acuity of his hearing such that he could almost hear someone thinking. You did both a lot in prison: listening and thinking.

He shifted slowly on his hospital bed. His arms and legs were still in restraints. He knew there was a guard right outside the door to his room. Rufus had seen him several times now, as people had come and gone from his room. The guard was not a cop; he was in fatigues, and he was armed. Regular Army or maybe reserves, Harms couldn't be sure. He took a shallow breath. Over the course of the last two days, Harms had listened to the doctors checking him. He had not suffered a heart attack, although apparently he had come close. He couldn't remember what the doctors had called it, but his heartbeat had been irregular enough for him to stay in intensive care awhile.

He thought back to his last hour at Fort Jackson. He wondered if Michael Fiske had even made it out of the prison before they killed him. Ironically, Rufus's near heart attack had saved his life. At least he was out of Fort Jackson. For now. But when his condition improved, they would send him back. And then he would die. Unless they killed him in here first.

He had scrutinized each of the doctors and nurses attending him. Anyone administering drugs to him was given special attention. He was confident that, if he thought himself in danger, he could rip the sides of the hospital bed off. For now, all he could do was get his strength back, wait, watch, and hope. If he could not gain his freedom through the court system, then he would obtain it another way. He was not going back to Fort Jackson. Not while he was still breathing.

For the next two hours he watched people come and go. Every time the door to his room opened, he would look at the guard outside. A young kid, looking very self-important in his uniform and wearing his gun. Two guards had flown with him on the helicopter, but neither was the one posted outside now. Perhaps they were doing a rotation. When the door opened, the guard would nod and smile at the person entering or leaving, especially if the person happened to be young and female. When the guard had occasionally looked into the room, Rufus had seen two emotions in his eyes: hatred and fear. That was good. That meant he had a chance. Both could lead to the one thing Rufus desperately needed the guard to commit: a mistake.

Leaving a single guard, they must think him pretty well incapacitated, Rufus figured; only he wasn't. The monitors with their numbers and jumpy lines meant nothing to him. They were metal-cased buzzards waiting for him to fade before moving in. But he could feel his strength returning; that was something tangible. He curled and uncurled his hands in anticipation of being able eventually to fully move his arms.

Two hours later he heard the door swing inward, and then the light came on. The nurse carried a metal clip-board and smiled at him as she checked his monitor. She was in her mid-forties, he guessed. Pretty, with a full figure. Looking at her wide hips, he figured she had been through several childbirths.

"You're doing better today," she said when she noticed him watching her.

"I'm sorry to hear that."

She stared at him openmouthed. "You better believe a lot of people in this place would love to have that kind of prognosis."

"Where exactly am I?"

"Roanoke, Virginia."

"Never been to Roanoke."

"It's a pretty town."

"Not as pretty as you," said Rufus with an embarrassed smile, the words having slipped through his lips. He had not been this close to a woman in almost three decades. The last woman he had ever seen in person was his mother, weeping at his side as they carried him off to serve his life sentence. She had died within the week. Something exploded in her brain, his brother had told him. But he knew his mother had died from a broken heart.

His nose wrinkled up as the scent touched it. It seemed out of place in a hospital. At first, Harms did not realize that he was simply smelling the nurse's scent, a mixture of slight perfume, moisturizing lotion and woman. Damn. What else had he forgotten about living a real life? A tear started to tremble at the corner of his right eye as he thought this.

She looked down at him, her eyebrows raised, a hand on one hip. "They told me to be careful around you."

He looked at her. "I'd never hurt you, ma'am." His tone

was solemn, sincere. She saw the tear barely clinging to his eye. She didn't really know what to say next.

"Can't you put on that chart that I'm dying or something?"

"Are you crazy? I can't do that. Don't you want to get better?"

"Soon as I do, I go right back to Fort Jackson."

"Not a nice place, I take it."

"I been in the same cell there for over twenty years. Kind of nice seeing something else for a change. Not much to do there except count your heartbeats and stare at the concrete."

She looked surprised. "Twenty years? How old are you?"

Rufus thought for a moment. "I don't know exactly, to tell you the truth. Not over fifty."

"Come on, you don't know how old you are?"

He eyed her steadily. "The only cons who keep a calendar are the ones getting out someday. I'm serving a life sentence, ma'am. Ain't never getting out. What's it matter how old I am?" He said this so matter-of-factly that the nurse felt her cheeks flush.

"Oh." Her voice quavered. "I guess I see your point."

He shifted his body slightly. The shackles pinged against the metal sides of the bed. She drew back.

"Can you call somebody for me, ma'am?"

"Who? Your wife?"

"I don't got no wife. My brother. He don't know where I am. Wanted to let him know."

"I think I have to check with the guard first."

Rufus looked past her. "That little boy out there? What's he got to do with my brother? He don't look like he can go pee-pee by hisself."

She laughed. "Well, they sent him to guard big old you, now, didn't they?"

"My brother's name is Joshua. Joshua Harms. He goes by Josh. I can tell you his phone number if you got yourself a pencil. Just call him and tell him where I am. Gets kind of lonely in here. He don't live all that far away. Who knows, he might come on over and see me."

"It does get lonely here," she said a little wistfully. She looked down at him, at his tall, strong body, all covered with tubes and patches. And the shackles—they held her attention.

Rufus noted her staring. Chains on a man usually had that effect on people, he had found.

"What'd you do anyway? To be in prison for."

"What's your name?"

"Why?"

"Just like to know. My name's Rufus. Rufus Harms."

"I knew that. It's on your chart."

"Well, I ain't got no chart to look up your name."

She hesitated for a moment, looked around at the door and then back at him. "My name's Cassandra," she said.

"Real pretty name." His eyes passed over her figure. "It fits you."

"Thank you. So you're not going to tell me what you did?"

"Why you want to know?"

"Just curious."

"I killed somebody. A long time ago."

"Why'd you do it? Were they trying to hurt you?"

"Didn't do nothing to me."

"So why'd you do it?"

"Didn't know what I was doing. Was out of my mind."

"Is that right?" She drew back a little farther as he said this. "Isn't that what they all say?"

"Just happens to be the truth with me. You gonna call my brother?"

"I don't know. Maybe."

"Tell you what, I'll give you the number. If you don't, you don't. If you do, then I thank you very much."

She looked at him curiously. "You don't act like a murderer."

"You ought to be careful about that. It's the sweet-talking ones end up hurting you. I seen enough of that kind."

"So I shouldn't trust you, then?"

His eyes seized on hers. "You got to make up your own mind on that."

She considered this for a moment. "So what's your brother's number?"

She took down the telephone number, slipped it in her pocket and turned to leave.

"Hey, Ms. Cassandra?" She turned back around. "You're right. I ain't no killer. You come back and talk to me some more . . . if you want to, that is." He managed a weak smile and rattled the shackles. "I ain't going nowhere."

She eyed him from across the room and he thought he saw a smile flicker across her mouth. Then she turned and went out the door. Rufus craned his neck to see if she spoke to the guard, but she walked right past him. Rufus lay back and stared at the ceiling. He inhaled deeply, letting the remnants of her scent soak into him. A few moments later a smile spread across his face. As did, finally, the tears.

CHAPTER NINETEEN

It was an unusual gathering of all of the clerks and the justices. Marshal of the Court Richard Perkins and Supreme Court Police Chief Leo Dellasandro were there too, looking stonily around the table in the large room. Elizabeth Knight's eyes were moist and she dabbed continually at them with a handkerchief.

As Sara Evans looked at the grim-faced justices, her eyes stopped on Thomas Murphy. Murphy was short and flabby, with white hair and tufted eyebrows. His face held cheekbones the shape of almonds. He still favored three-piece suits and wore large, showy cuff links. His dress, however, did not attract Sara's attention; rather it was his expression of complete mourning. She quickly finished checking the occupants of the room: Michael Fiske was not there. She felt the blood rush to her head. When Harold Ramsey rose from the head of the table, his deep voice was oddly subdued; she could not really hear him that well, but she knew exactly what he was saying, as though reading his lips.

"This is terrible, terrible news. In fact, I can't remember anything like it." Ramsey surveyed the room, his hands making fists in his anxiety, his tall frame shaking.

He took a heavy breath. "Michael Fiske is dead."

The justices obviously already knew. All the clerks, however, collectively missed a breath.

Ramsey started to say something else but then stopped. He motioned to Leo Dellasandro, who nodded and stepped forward while the chief justice collapsed into his chair.

Dellasandro was about five-ten, face wide, with flat cheeks and a pug nose, and a layer of fat over a muscular physique. He had an olive complexion, with wiry black and gray hair. Arising from his pores was the smell of cigar. He wore his uniform with a proud air, his thick fingers tucked inside the gun belt. The other man in uniform standing immediately behind him was Ron Klaus, his second-in-command. Klaus was trim and professional in appearance, the darting activity of his blue eyes suggesting a nimble mind. He and Dellasandro were the watchdogs of this place. They seemed to move about in tandem. Most people who worked at the Court could not think of one man without the other.

"The details are sketchy right now, but apparently Michael was the victim of a robbery. He was found in his car in an alley in Southeast near the Anacostia River. His family has been notified, and one of them is coming up to officially identify the body. However, there's no question that it's Michael." He looked down for a moment. "When they learned he was employed here, the police brought over a photograph."

One nervous-looking clerk raised his hand. "Are they sure it was a robbery? It didn't have to do with his working here?"

Sara looked over at him angrily. Not the question you

really wanted to hear five seconds after learning someone you worked with, cared about, was dead. But then she supposed violent death did that to people: made them instinctively fear for their own lives.

Dellasandro put up his big calming hands. "We have heard nothing that would make us believe that his death had anything whatsoever to do with the Court. However, out of an abundance of caution, we are increasing security around here, and should anyone notice anything suspicious or out of the ordinary, please contact either myself or Mr. Klaus. We'll make available to you any future details about this situation at the appropriate time." He looked over at Ramsey, who had his head bowed in his hands and was making no move to get up. Dellasandro stood there awkwardly until Elizabeth Knight rose.

"I know this has been a terrible shock to all of us. Michael was one of the most popular people ever to work here. His loss touches us all, especially those who had become close to him." She paused and looked at Sara for a moment. "If any of you wishes to talk about anything, please feel free to do so with your justice. Or you can stop by and see me. I'm not sure how we can continue to function, but the work of the Court must go on, despite this horrible, horrible . . ." Knight stopped again and gripped the table to stop herself from collapsing to the floor. Dellasandro quickly took her arm, but she motioned him away.

Knight rallied herself enough to call an end to the meeting and the room quickly cleared. Except for Sara Evans. She sat there, numb, staring at the spot where Knight had stood. The tears freely streamed down her face. Michael was dead. He had taken an appeal, acted very strangely for over a week, and now he was dead. Murdered. A robbery, they said. She didn't believe the answer was that simple. But right now it didn't matter. All that mattered was she had lost someone very close to her. Someone who, under different circumstances perhaps, she might have gladly spent her life with. She put her head down on the table as the sobs burst from her.

From the doorway, Elizabeth Knight watched her.

CHAPTER TWENTY

A little over three hours after Billy Hawkins had announced his brother's death, John Fiske was walking through the hallways of the D.C. morgue, a white-coated intake specialist leading the way. Fiske had had to show identification and prove to the man that he was really Michael Fiske's brother. He had been prepared for that and had brought pictures of the two together. He had tried to reach his father before leaving town, but there had been no answer. Fiske had driven by the house, but no one had been home. He left a note for his dad, including no details. He had to be sure it was his brother, and the only way to be certain was where he was headed.

Fiske was surprised when they entered an office, and even more puzzled when the morgue attendant pulled a Polaroid from a file and held it out to him.

"I'm not identifying a photo. I want to see the body."

"That's not the procedure we have here, sir. We're in the process of installing a video system so that IDs can be

made via remote television, but it's not functional yet.
Until then, it's done with a Polaroid."

"Not this time."

The man tapped the photo against his palm as though
trying to arouse Fiske's curiosity in it. "Most people would
much prefer to do it with a photograph. This is very
unusual."

"I'm not 'most people,' and having a brother murdered
is unusual. At least it is for me."

The attendant picked up the phone and conveyed
instructions to prepare the body for viewing. Then he
opened the door to his office, motioning Fiske to follow
him. After a short walk, they entered a small room that
carried a medicinal smell several times stronger than that
in a hospital. In the center of the room stood a gurney.
From under the white sheet rose a number of edges representing the head, nose, shoulders, knees and feet of the
body. As Fiske headed toward the gurney, he clutched at
the same irrational hope that everyone in his position
would leap for: that the person under the sheet was not his
brother, that his family was still reasonably intact.

As the attendant gripped the edge of the sheet, Fiske
slid one hand around the metal side of the gurney and
squeezed tightly. As the sheet rose upward, exposing the
head and upper torso of the deceased, Fiske closed his eyes,
looked upward and mouthed a silent prayer. He took a
deep breath, held it, opened his eyes and then looked
down. Before he knew it, he was nodding.

He tried to look away but couldn't. Even a stranger
could have looked at the slope of the forehead, the arrangement of the eyes and mouth, the flow of the chin, and
concluded that the two men held some close familial bond.
"That's my brother."

The sheet was replaced and the attendant gave Fiske
the ID card to sign. "Other than the items the police
have retained, we'll release his personal effects to you."

The attendant glanced at the gurney. "We've had a busy week, and we're backed up with bodies, but we should have autopsy results fairly soon. This one looks pretty simple anyway."

Anger flared on Fiske's face but then quickly faded. The man was not paid to be tactful. "Did they find the bullet that killed him?"

"Only the autopsy can determine cause of death."

"Don't bullshit me." The attendant looked startled. "I saw the exit wound on the left side of his head. Did they find it?"

"No. At least not yet."

"I heard it was a robbery," said Fiske. The attendant nodded. "He was found in his car?"

"Right, wallet gone. We had to trace his identity through his license plate."

"So if a robbery, why didn't they take the car? Carjacking's the hot thing right now. Beat the victim's ATM password out of him or her, kill them, take the car and hit a few banks, load up on money, ditch the car and go on to the next one. Why not with this one?"

"I don't know anything about that."

"Who's handling the case?"

"It happened in D.C. Must be D.C. Homicide Division."

"My brother was a federal employee. United States Supreme Court. Maybe the FBI will be involved too."

"Again, I don't know anything about that."

"I'd like the name of the detective at D.C. Homicide."

The attendant didn't answer, but jotted some notes down in the file, perhaps hoping that if he remained quiet Fiske would just go away.

"I'd really like that name, please," Fiske said, edging a step closer.

The attendant finally sighed, pulled a business card out of the file and handed it to Fiske. "Buford Chandler. He'll probably want to talk to you anyway. He's a good guy. Probably'll catch the person who did this."

Fiske looked briefly at the card before putting it in his coat pocket. He settled a clear-eyed gaze on the attendant. "Oh, we're going to get whoever did this." The odd tone in his voice made the attendant look up from his file. "Now I'd like some time alone with my brother."

The attendant glanced over at the gurney. "Sure, I'll be outside. Just let me know when you're done."

After the man left, Fiske pulled a chair next to the gurney and sat down. He had not shed a tear since learning of his brother's death. He told himself it was because positive ID had not been made yet, but now it had and still no tears. On the drive up, he had caught himself counting out-of-state license plates, a game the brothers had played growing up. A game Mike Fiske had usually won.

He lifted the side of the sheet and took one of his brother's hands. It was cold, but the fingers were supple. He squeezed them gently. Fiske looked down at the concrete floor and closed his eyes. When he reopened them a few minutes later only two tears had collected on the concrete. He quickly looked up and a gush of air came out of his lungs. It felt forced, all of it, and he suddenly felt unworthy to be here.

As a cop, he had sat with the parents of too many drunken kids who had wrapped themselves around a tree or telephone pole. He had consoled them, expressed empathy, even held them. He had truly believed that he had approached, even touched the depths of their despair. He often wondered what it would feel like when it happened to him. He plainly knew this was not it.

He forced himself to think about his parents. How exactly would he tell his father that his golden child was dead? And his mother? At least there was an easy answer to that question: He couldn't and shouldn't tell her.

Raised Catholic, but not a religious man, Fiske chose to speak with his brother instead of God. He pressed his brother's hand against his chest and talked to him of things he was sorry for, of how much he loved him, how much he wanted him not to be dead, in case his brother's spirit was lingering behind, waiting for this communication, this quiet rupture of guilt and remorse from his older brother. Then Fiske fell silent, his eyes closed again. He could hear each solid drum of his heart, a sound that was somehow dwarfed by the stillness of the body next to his.

The attendant poked his head in. "Mr. Fiske, we need to take your brother on down. It's been half an hour."

Fiske rose and passed the attendant without a word. His brother's body was going to a terrifying place, where strangers would forage through his remains for clues as to who had killed him. As they wheeled the gurney away, Fiske walked back out into the sunlight and left his little brother behind.

CHAPTER TWENTY-ONE

"You're sure you covered your tracks?"

Rayfield nodded into the phone. "Every record of his being here has been expunged. I've already transferred all the personnel who saw Fiske to other facilities. Even if someone figures out somehow that he came here, there won't be anyone left to tell them anything."

"And no one saw you dump the body?"

"Vic drove his car back. I followed him. We picked a good place. The police will think it was a robbery. Nobody saw us. And even if they did, it's not the sort of place where people are real cooperative with the law."

"Nothing left in the car?"

"We took his wallet to further the robbery angle. His briefcase too. A map. There wasn't anything else. Of course we filled the radiator back up with fluid."

"And Harms?"

"He's still in the hospital. Looks like he's going to make it."

"Damn. Just our luck."

"Don't sweat it. When he comes back here, we'll deal with him. Weak heart and all, you never know what might happen to you."

"Don't wait too long. You can't hit him in the hospital?"

"Too dangerous. Too many people around."

"And you've got him well guarded?"

"He's chained to the bed with a guard posted twenty-four hours a day outside his door. He's being released tomorrow morning. By tomorrow night he'll be dead. Vic's already working on the details."

"And there's nobody out there who can help him? You're sure?"

Rayfield laughed. "Hell, no one even knows he's there. He's got nobody. Never has, never will."

"No mistakes, Frank."

"I'll call you when he's dead."

Fiske sat in the car and cranked up the air-conditioning, which, in his fourteen-year-old Ford, merely caused the slow movement of muggy air from left to right. Sweat trickling down his face and staining his shirt collar, Fiske finally eased down the window as he stared at the building. Average-looking on the outside, it was not on the inside. There, the people spent all of their time searching for those who killed other people. And Fiske was trying to decide whether to join them in their pursuit or drive back home. He had identified his brother's remains, his official duty as next of kin completed. He could go home, tell his father, make the funeral arrangements, see to his brother's final affairs, bury him and then get on with his life. That's what everyone else did.

Instead, Fiske pulled himself out of the car and into the muggy air, and entered the building at 300 Indiana Avenue, home to the D.C. Police Homicide Division. After passing through security and being directed by a uniformed police officer, he stopped at a desk. He had tried his father once again from the morgue, but still no answer. Frustrated, he was now also worried that his father had somehow found out and was on his way up here.

He looked down at the card the attendant at the morgue had given him. "Detective Buford Chandler, please," he said, looking down at the young woman behind the desk.

"And you are?" The sharp angle of her neck, and her superior tone, immediately made Fiske want to stuff her in one of her own desk drawers.

"John Fiske. Detective Chandler is investigating my brother's . . . my brother's murder. His name was Michael Fiske." She stared at him, no recognition on her features. "He was a clerk at the Supreme Court," he added.

She glanced at some papers on her desk. "And somebody killed him?"

"This is the Homicide Division, isn't it?" She settled her gaze back on him, her look of annoyance pronounced. He continued: "Yes, somebody killed him"—he glanced down at the nameplate on her desk—"Ms. Baxter."

"Well, what exactly can I do for you?"

"I'd like to see Detective Chandler."

"Is he expecting you?"

Fiske leaned forward and spoke in a low voice. "Not exactly, but—"

"Then I'm afraid he's not in," she said, cutting him off.

"I think if you put a call into—" Fiske stopped and watched as she turned away from him and started typing on her computer. "Look, I really need to see Detective Chandler."

She typed as she spoke. "Let me educate you on the situation here, okay? We have lots of cases and not too many detectives. We don't have time for every drop-in off the street. We have to have priorities. I'm sure you can understand that." Her voice drifted off as she looked at the computer screen.

Fiske leaned forward until his face was only a couple of inches from the woman. When she looked around, they were eye to eye. "Let me make you understand something. I came up from Richmond to identify the remains of my brother at *Detective Chandler's* request. I did that. My brother is dead. And right about now the medical examiner is cutting a Y incision in his chest so that he can lift out his insides, organ by organ. Then he's going to take a saw and cut an intermastoid incision like a wedge of pie through his skull, right about here." Fiske made an imaginary cut along Ms. Baxter's head with his finger, overcoming a very strong impulse to snatch up a handful of the woman's permed blond hair. "That's so he can lift out his brain and trace the path of the bullet that killed him and perhaps get some shell fragments. Now, I thought I'd come and have a chat with Detective Chandler and see if he and I can come up with some leads on who might have killed him."

She said coldly, "Well, that's not your job, is it? We have enough problems without family members getting involved in police investigations. I'm sure Detective Chandler will be in touch if he needs you." She again turned away from him.

Fiske gripped the edge of her desk and took a deep breath, trying his best not to lose it. "Look, I can understand the caseload problem you must have here, and the fact that you don't know me from Adam—".

"I'm really busy right now, sir. So if you have a problem, I suggest you put it in writing."

"All I want to do is talk to the man!"

"Am I going to have to call a guard, or what?"

Fiske slammed his hand down on the desk. "My brother is dead! And I would really appreciate if you would take that piss-poor attitude you're wearing and replace it with just an ounce of compassion. And if you can't force yourself to mean it, lady, then just pretend."

"I'm Buford Chandler."

Both Fiske and Baxter turned. Chandler was black, in his early fifties, with curly white hair, a matching mustache and a tall, thickened frame that managed to retain a certain athleticism from his youth. He wore an empty shoulder holster, a smudge of pistol oil on his shirt where the grip had lain against it. He looked Fiske up and down from behind a pair of trifocals.

"I'm John Fiske."

"I heard. In fact I've been standing over here listening to the whole thing."

"Then you know what he said to me, Detective Chandler?" Baxter said.

"Every word."

"And don't you have something to say?"

"Yes, I do."

Baxter looked over at Fiske with a look of satisfaction on her face. "Well?"

"I think this young man gave you some pretty good advice." Chandler hooked a finger at Fiske. "Let's talk."

Chandler and Fiske made their way through busy hallways to a small, cluttered office. "Have a seat." Chandler pointed to the only chair in the room other than the one behind his desk. There were files stacked on the chair. "Just put those on the floor." Chandler held up a warning finger. "Be careful you don't taint any evidence. These days if I belch while I'm looking at tissue samples, all I'm going to hear is, 'Inadmissible! Free my mass-murdering sonofabitch of a client.'"

Fiske very carefully moved the files while Chandler settled behind his desk.

"Now, I don't want you feeling sorry for what you said to Judy Baxter."

"I wasn't planning on it."

Chandler suppressed a smile. "Okay, first things first. I'm sorry about your brother."

"Thank you," Fiske said in a subdued manner.

"Probably the first time you heard that since arriving up here, isn't it?"

"Actually, it is."

"So you were in law enforcement?" Chandler casually remarked, then smiled at Fiske's surprise. "The average citizen doesn't usually know about Y incisions and inter-mastoid cuts. With the way you got in Ms. Baxter's face, the manner in which you carry yourself, and your build, I'd say you were a patrolman."

"Past tense?"

"If you were still on the force the folks in Richmond would've told me when we contacted them. And besides, I know very few police officers who wear suits off duty."

"Right on all counts. I'm glad you were assigned to this case, Detective Chandler."

"You and forty-two other active cases." Fiske shook his head, and Chandler continued: "Budgetary cuts and all. I don't even have a partner anymore."

"So in other words, don't expect any miracles?"

"I will do my best to catch whoever killed your brother. But I can give no guarantees."

"Then how about a little unofficial help?"

"How do you mean?"

"I worked a lot of homicides with the detectives down in Richmond. Learned a lot, remember a lot. Maybe I can be your new partner."

"Officially, that's absolutely impossible."

"Officially, I absolutely understand."

"What do you do now?"

"I'm a criminal defense attorney," said Fiske. Chandler rolled his eyes. "And I take pride in my work too, Detective Chandler."

Chandler nodded over Fiske's shoulder toward the door. "Shut that, will you?" He remained silent until Fiske did so and returned to his seat.

"Now, despite my better judgment, I will take your offer of assistance under advisement."

Fiske shook his head. "I'm here now. Considering that after forty-eight hours the success rate on homicides heads to China, that's not going to cut it." Fiske thought this might set the man off, but Chandler remained calm.

"You got a business card where you can be reached?" Chandler asked.

Fiske passed across his card after writing his home number on the back.

In return, Chandler handed him a card with a series of phone numbers on it. "Office, home, beeper, fax, cell phone—when I remember to carry it, which I never do."

Chandler opened a file on his desk and studied it. Reading upside down, Fiske saw his brother's name on the label.

"I was told he was killed during a robbery."

"That's what the prelim indicated anyway."

Fiske caught the odd tone in Chandler's voice. "And has that opinion changed?"

"It was only a prelim to begin with." He closed the file and looked at Fiske. "The facts of this case, at least what we know so far, are pretty simple. Your brother was found in the front seat of his car in an alleyway near the Anacostia River with a gunshot contact wound to the right side of his head and an exit wound on the left. Looked to be fairly heavy caliber. We have not found the slug, but that search continues. The killer could have found it and taken it with him so that we couldn't do a ballistics test, if we ever get a gun to do a match."

"It would take a cool hand to root around in an alley looking for a slug while a dead body is sitting a few feet away."

"I agree. But again, the bullet may still be found."

"I understand his wallet was missing."

"Let's put it another way. No wallet was found on him. Was he in the habit of not carrying one?"

Fiske looked away for an instant. "We haven't seen each other much the last few years, but I think you can assume he was carrying a wallet. So you didn't find it in his apartment?"

"Give me a little slack, John. Your brother's body was only found yesterday." Chandler opened his notebook and picked up a pen. "The alley where he was found is a high-use drug area, among other things. To your knowledge was he a drug user? Casual or otherwise?"

"No. He was not a drug user."

"But you can't be sure, can you? You just said you hadn't seen much of each other. Right?"

"My brother set the highest goals for himself with everything he did, and then he surpassed those goals. Drugs did not enter into that equation."

"Any idea why he would've been in that area?"

"No, but he could have been kidnapped somewhere else and driven there."

"Any reason why someone would want him dead?"

"I can't think of a one."

"No enemies? Jealous boyfriends? Money problems?"

"No. But again I'm probably not the best source for that. Do you have a prelim on the time of death?"

"Pretty vague. I'm waiting on the official word. Why?"

"I just came from the morgue. I felt my brother's hand. It was soft, supple. Rigor had long since passed. What was the condition of the body when it was found last night?"

"Let's just say he had been there awhile."

"That's surprising. From what you said, it's not an isolated area."

"True, but in that area dead bodies in alleys aren't all that uncommon. Then again, about ninety-nine percent of the homicides in that area involve black victims for the very simple fact that whites just don't frequent the place."

"So my brother should have stood out, you're saying. Any ATM withdrawals? Credit card purchases?"

"We're checking all that. When did you last speak with your brother?"

"He called me over a week ago."

"What'd he say?"

"I wasn't in. He left a message. Said he needed my advice on something."

"Did you call him back?"

"Not until recently."

"Why'd you wait?"

"It wasn't high on my priority list."

"Is that right?" Chandler twirled his pen between his fingers. "Tell me something. Did you even like your brother?"

Fiske looked at him squarely. "Somebody killed my brother. I want to catch whoever did it. And that's really all I'm going to say about it."

The look in Fiske's eyes made Chandler decide to move on. "Maybe he wanted to talk about something to do with work? See, what makes this case intriguing is your brother's occupation."

"Meaning, is his murder related to something at the Supreme Court?"

"It's a long shot, absolutely, but what you just told me about your brother's phone call might just make it slightly less of a long shot than it seemed a minute ago."

"I doubt if he wanted my two cents on the latest abortion case."

"Then what? How to pick up women?"

"You must not have seen a picture of him. He never needed help with that one."

"I have seen a picture of him, but the dead don't photograph all that well. But he said he wanted some advice. Maybe it *was* legal."

"Well, you can always make a trip to the Court to see if there are any conspiracies going on up there."

"We have to tread lightly, you know."

"*We?*"

"I'm sure your brother has personal effects there, and it would not be unusual for next of kin to visit his place of work. I'm assuming you've been there before?"

"Once, when Mike first started. My dad and I."

"And your mother?"

"Alzheimer's."

"Sorry to hear that."

"Any other developments?"

In answer, Chandler rose, took down his jacket from a hanger on the back of the door and slipped it on. "I'd like to take you down to your brother's car."

"And after that?"

Chandler checked his watch before looking up and smiling. "Then we'll have just enough time to go to Court, Counselor."

CHAPTER TWENTY-TWO

Rufus watched the door as it slowly opened. He braced himself for the sight of a mass of men in green fatigues moving in on him, but then his apprehension slid away when he saw who it was.

"Time to check me again?"

Cassandra came and stood next to the bed. "Now, isn't that a woman's plight in life, always checking up on men?" Her words were funny, her tone was not. She looked at the monitors and made some notations in his chart, glancing at him as she did so.

"It feels good. I ain't used to that." He took care not to rattle his restraints as he sat up a little.

"I called your brother."

Rufus's expression grew serious. "Is that right? What'd he say?"

"He said he'd be coming to see you."

"He say when?"

"Sooner than later. Today, in fact."

"What all did you tell him?"

"I told him you were sick, but getting better fast."

"He tell you anything else?"

"I found him to be a man of few words," Cassandra remarked.

"That's Josh."

"Is he as big as you?"

"Nah. He's a little guy. Six-three or so, not much over two hundred pounds." Cassandra shook her head and turned to leave. "You got time to sit and talk?" Rufus asked.

"I'm supposed to be on my break. I just came to tell you about your brother. I've got to go." She seemed a little unfriendly.

"You okay?"

"Even if I'm not, there isn't anything you can do about it." Her tone was now edgy, rough.

Rufus studied her for a moment. "Is there a Bible around here?"

She turned back, surprised. "Why?"

"I read the Bible every day. Have for as long as I can remember."

She looked over at the table next to the bed, went across and pulled out a Gideon's Bible. "I can't give it to you. Can't get that close. The people from the prison were real, real clear on that point."

"You don't have to give it to me. If you would, I'd appreciate if you could read a passage to me."

"Read to you?"

"You don't have to," he said quickly. "You may not even be interested, you know, in the Bible and churchgoing."

She looked down at him, one hand on her hip, the other closed around the green Bible. "I sing in the choir. My husband, God rest his soul, was a lay minister."

"That's real good, Cassandra. And your kids?"

"How do you know I have kids? Because I'm not skinny?"

"Uh-uh."

"What, then?"

"You look like you're used to loving little things."

His words startled her, a smile quickly breaking through the cloud over her features. "I *am* going to have to watch you." She noted that he looked at the Bible like he was thirsty and needed a drink, and she was holding the freshest, coldest glass of water in the history of the world.

"What do you want me to read?"

"Hundred and third Psalm."

Cassandra debated for a moment and then pulled up a chair and sat down.

Rufus lay back on the bed. "Thank you, Cassandra."

As she read, she glanced at him. His eyes were closed. She read a few more words, looked up and saw his lips moving and then stopping. She looked at the next sentence, quickly memorized it, and read it, while watching him. Rufus was silently mouthing each of the words at the same time she was saying them. She stopped, but he continued to the end of the sentence. When she did not start up again, he opened his eyes. "You know the Psalm by heart?" she asked.

"Know most of the Bible by heart. All the Psalms and Proverbs."

"That's pretty impressive."

"I've had a long time to work on it."

"Why did you want me to read it to you, then, if you already knew it?"

"Looked like you were a little troubled. I thought visiting the scriptures might help you some."

"Help me?" Cassandra looked down at the page and read to herself. "He forgives all my sins. He heals me. He ransoms me from Hell. He surrounds me with loving kindness and tender mercies." Work was depressing. Her

teenage children were more and more beyond her control
every day. She was on the north side of forty, fifty pounds
overweight, and there wasn't an eligible man in sight.
With all that, as she watched this prisoner, this chained-
up killer who was going to die in prison, she felt like
bursting into tears in the face of his kindness, his
unsolicited consideration for her plight.

The Hundred and Third Psalm also held special appeal
for Rufus, one line in particular. He mouthed it to himself:
"He gives justice to all who are treated unfairly."

"Recognize it?" Chandler asked as they approached the
1987 silver Honda sedan parked in the police lot.

Fiske nodded. "We got it for him when he graduated
from college. We all chipped in, my parents and me."

"I've got five brothers. They never did that for me."

Chandler unlocked the driver's-side door and stepped
back for Fiske to look inside.

"Where did you find the car keys?"

"On the front seat."

"Any other personal items?" Chandler shook his head.
Fiske examined the front seat, dash, windshield and side
windows, his puzzlement clear. "Has it been cleaned?"

"No. Just like we found it, except for the occupant."

Fisk straightened back up and looked at the detective.

"If you put a heavy-caliber pistol flush against somebody's temple and pull the trigger in a confined space like
this you'll have blood splatters on the seat, steering wheel,
windshield. You'd also have bone and tissue throw-off. All
I see are a few stains here and there, probably where his
head was touching the seat."

Chandler looked amused. "Is that right?"

Fiske clenched his jaw. "I'm not telling you anything you
didn't already know. I take it this was another little test of
yours?"

Chandler nodded slowly. "Could be. Could be another reason. Remember I said I had five brothers?"

"Yeah."

"Well, I started out with six. One of my brothers was murdered thirty-five years ago. Working at a gas station and some punk came in and popped him for the twelve bucks in the register. I was only sixteen at the time, but I remember every detail like it was maybe five minutes ago. Anyway, most families who come in to identify their loved ones don't head over to my office and offer their services. They grieve and console each other, which is entirely proper. Oh, they rant and rave for a while about wanting to catch the SOB who did it, but they don't really want to get involved in the process. I mean, who would? And they don't usually have a law enforcement background. Add it all up, and I spotted you as somebody who might be able to really contribute. And you just proved it.

"I can understand the rage you must be feeling, John, whether you liked your brother or not. Somebody took something from you, something important—ripped it from you, in fact. It's been thirty-five years and I still feel that rage."

Fiske looked around at all the civilian cars in the police lot. He assumed each hunk of metal was waiting its turn to spill the secrets of another tragedy. He turned back to Chandler. "I guess rage will do." He added quietly, looking down, "Until something else comes along." His tone did not hold out much hope.

"Fair enough." Chandler continued his analysis. "The absence of all the physical evidence you just mentioned does have me puzzled."

"It doesn't look like he was killed in the car."

"That's right. It looks like he was killed somewhere else and his body was then put in the front seat. Now, that single conclusion takes us into a whole new realm of possibilities."

"Then we're talking about something more deliberate than a random kidnapping and murder."

"Possibly, although some punks could have kidnapped him, taken him out of the car to maybe hit an ATM. He refuses, they pop him. Get scared and then dump him back in his car."

"Then there would have been some physical evidence at the ATM. Any sign of that?"

"No, but there are a lot of ATMs."

"And a lot of people use them. If it's been at least a day, you'd think someone would have noticed."

"You'd think, but you can't be sure. We're trying to isolate your brother's movements and whereabouts for the last forty-eight hours. He was last seen at his apartment on Thursday night. After that, nada."

"If somebody carjacked him, what about prints? Most perps looking for ATM cards aren't sophisticated enough to wear gloves."

"We're still processing that."

"Would you like another observation?"

"Fire away."

Fiske held open the car door and pointed at the inside part of the doorjamb, the section that you don't see when the door is closed. Chandler fumbled for his glasses, put them on and saw what Fiske was pointing at. Chandler slapped on a pair of latex gloves he pulled from his coat pocket, gently lifted the small piece of sticky plastic off and held it in his palm, observing it carefully.

"Your brother just had his car serviced at Wal-Mart."

"It recommends that the next oil service takes place in three months or three thousand miles, whichever comes first. They put the future date and future mileage reading on that sticker as a reminder for when you're supposed to come back in. According to the date on that sticker, and subtracting out three months, my brother went in for service three days before his body was found.

Now look at the mileage for when the next service is recommended and subtract three thousand miles from it. That'll give you approximately what the odometer should read right now."

Chandler swiftly did the math. "Eighty-six thousand, five hundred and forty-three."

"Now look at the Honda's current odometer reading."

Chandler leaned back in the car and checked. Then he looked back at Fiske, his eyes slightly wide. "Somebody put about eight hundred miles on this car in the last three days."

"That's right," Fiske said.

"Where the hell did he go?"

"The sticker doesn't have which Wal-Mart he used, but probably it was one close to his home. You should call around, they might be able to tell us something useful."

"Right. Can't believe we missed this," said Chandler. He slipped the plastic sticker in a clear zippered bag he pulled from his coat pocket and wrote some information on the outside of it. "Oh, and John?"

"Yeah?"

He held up the zippered bag. "No more tests, okay?"

CHAPTER TWENTY-THREE

A half hour later, Chandler and Fiske walked through the front entrance of the United States Supreme Court.

Inside, the place was large and intimidating. What really engaged Fiske's attention, though, was the quiet, so extreme as to be unsettling. It seemed to border on the hallucinatory—trying to imagine a functioning world right outside the doors. Fiske thought of the last very silent place he had been today: the morgue.

He said, "Who are we supposed to be meeting?"

Chandler pointed to a group of men walking purpose-fully down the hallway toward them. "Them." As they drew nearer, their collective footsteps became the boom of cannon in this acoustical tunnel. One of the men wore a suit; the other two were in uniforms and carried sidearms.

"Detective Chandler?" The man in the suit extended his hand. "I'm Richard Perkins, marshal of the United States Supreme Court." Perkins was about five-nine, skinny, with the stuck-out ears of a boy, and white hair combed straight over his forehead like a frozen waterfall. He introduced his companions. "Chief of Police Leo Dellasandro; his second-in-command, Ron Klaus."

"Good to meet you," Chandler said, and he watched Perkins look expectantly over at Fiske. He added, "John Fiske. Michael Fiske's brother."

All of them rushed to provide their condolences.

"A tragedy. A mindless tragedy," Perkins said. "Michael was so highly thought of. He'll be sorely missed."

Fiske managed an appreciative demeanor in the face of all this instant sympathy.

"You've locked up Michael Fiske's office, as I requested?" Chandler asked.

Dellasandro nodded. "It was difficult, because he shared it with another clerk. Two to an office is the norm."

"Let's hope we won't need to keep it off limits long."

"We can meet in my office if you'd like and go over your agenda, Detective Chandler," Perkins offered. "It's right down the hallway."

"Let's do it."

As Fiske started off with them, Perkins stopped and looked at Chandler.

"I'm sorry. I was assuming that Mr. Fiske was here for another reason unrelated to your investigation."

"He's helping me out with some background information on his brother," Chandler said.

Perkins looked at Fiske with what Fiske gauged as unfriendly eyes.

"I didn't even know Michael had a brother," said Perkins. "He never mentioned you."

"That's okay, he never mentioned you either," Fiske replied.

Perkins's office was right off the hallway leading to the courtroom. It was furnished in an old-fashioned colonial style, the architecture and craftsmanship from an era of government unburdened with trillion-dollar national debts and budgets awash in red.

At a side table of Perkins's office sat a man in his late forties. His blond hair was cut very short, and his long narrow face carried an unshakable air of authority. His self-assured manner suggested that he enjoyed the exercise of that authority. When he rose, Fiske noted that he was well over six feet tall and looked as though he spent regular time in the gym.

"Detective Chandler?" The man extended one hand and with the other flashed his identification card. "FBI Special Agent Warren McKenna."

Chandler looked at Perkins. "I wasn't aware that the Bureau had been brought in on this."

Perkins started to say something, but McKenna said briskly, "As I'm sure you know, the attorney general and the FBI have the legal right to fully investigate the murder of any person employed by the United States government. However, the Bureau is not looking to take over the investigation or step on your toes."

"That's good, because even the tiniest bit of unwanted pressure and I just go nuts." Chandler smiled.

McKenna's expression remained unchanged. "I'll try to keep that in mind."

Fiske held out his hand. "John Fiske, Agent McKenna. Michael Fiske was my brother."

"I'm sorry, Mr. Fiske. I know it must be damn tough for you," McKenna said, shaking his hand. The FBI agent focused again on Chandler. "If conditions dictate a more active role for the Bureau, then we would expect your full cooperation. Remember that the victim was a federal employee." He looked around the room. "Employed by one of the most revered institutions in the world. And perhaps one of the most feared."

"Fear out of ignorance," Perkins pointed out.

"But feared nonetheless. After Waco, the World Trade

Center and Oklahoma City, we've learned to be extra careful," McKenna said.

"Too bad you people weren't faster learners," Chandler said dryly. "But turf battles are big wastes of time. I do believe in share and share alike, though, okay?"

"Of course," McKenna said.

Chandler asked a half hour's worth of questions, trying basically to establish if any case Michael Fiske had been working on at the Court could have led to his murder. The same answer kept coming back to him from each of the Court representatives: "Impossible."

McKenna asked very few questions but listened intently to the ones asked by Chandler.

"The precise details of cases pending before the Court are so well insulated from the public that there would be no way anyone could know what a specific clerk is or isn't working on." Perkins smacked the tabletop with his palm to emphasize the point.

"Unless that clerk told someone."

Perkins shook his head. "I personally run them through the drill on security and confidentiality as part of their orientation. The ethical rules which apply to them are very stringent. They're even provided with a handbook on the subject. No leaks are permitted."

Chandler looked unconvinced. "What's the average age of the clerks here? Twenty-five? Twenty-six?"

"Something like that."

"They're kids, working at the highest court in the land. You telling me that it's impossible that they might let something slip? Not even to impress a date?"

"I've been around long enough to know better than to use the word *impossible* to ever describe anything."

"I'm a homicide detective, Mr. Perkins, and believe you me, I got the same damn problem."

"Could we back up to square one here?" Dellasandro said. "From what I know about the case, it seemed that robbery was the motive." He spread his hands and looked expectantly at Chandler. "How does that involve the Court? Have you searched his apartment yet?"

"Not yet. I'm sending a team over tomorrow."

"How do we know it's not something connected to his personal life?" Dellasandro asked.

Everyone looked at Chandler for an answer. The detective glanced down at his notes without really focusing on them. "I'm just covering all the bases. Going to a homicide victim's place of work and asking questions is not even remotely unusual, gentlemen."

"Certainly," Perkins said. "You can count on our full cooperation."

"Now why don't we have a look at Mr. Fiske's office," Chandler said.

CHAPTER TWENTY-FOUR

The man glided cat-smooth down the corridor. He was
six-foot-three, lean but strongly built, with wide shoulders fanning out from a thick neck. He had a long and
narrow face; the skin chestnut brown and smooth, except
for deep tracings of lines at the eyes and mouth, like the
whorls of a fingerprint. He wore a crumpled Virginia Tech
baseball cap. A short-haired black and gray beard outlined
his jaw. He was dressed in worn jeans and a faded, sweat-
stained denim shirt with the sleeves rolled up, showing off
a pair of thick, veiny forearms. A pack of Pall Malls poked
out of the shirt's front pocket. He approached the end of
the hallway and rounded the corner. As soon as he did so,
the soldier sitting next to the doorway of the last room on
the hall rose and held up a hand.

"Sorry, sir, this area is off limits to everyone except
necessary medical personnel."

"My brother's in there," Joshua Harms said. "And I'm
going to see him."

"I'm afraid that's impossible."

Harms eyed the soldier's name tag. "I'm afraid it ain't, Private Brown. I visit him at the prison all the time. Now you let me in there, you hear me?"

"I don't think so."

"Well, then I'm gonna go round up the head of this hospital and the local police and the damn commandant over at Fort Jackson and tell 'em you refused to allow a family member to visit a dying relative. Then they'll all take turns kicking your butt on down the road, soldier boy. Did I mention I spent three years in Vietnam and got me enough medals to cover your whole damn body? Now you gonna let me in or we gonna have to go down that other street? I want your answer and I want it right this damned minute."

An unnerved Brown looked around for a minute, unsure of what to do. "I need to call somebody."

"No, you don't. You can search me, but I'm going on in there. Won't be long. But it's gonna be right now."

"What's your name?"

"Josh Harms." He pulled out his wallet. "Here's my driver's license. I been over the prison a lot over the years, but I don't recall ever seeing you."

"I don't work at the prison," he said. "I'm on temporary assignment here. I'm in the reserves."

"The reserves? Pulling guard duty on a prisoner?"

"The correctional facility specialists who flew in with your brother went back yesterday. They're bringing in some replacements tomorrow morning."

"Hallelujah for them. Now, we ready to get this done?"

Private Brown stared at him for another few seconds. "Turn around," he said finally.

Josh did so. Brown started to pat him down. Right before he reached his front pants pocket, Josh said, "Don't get excited, but there's a pocketknife in there. Just pull it out and hold it for me. You hold it good and tight, son, I'm right partial to that knife."

Private Brown finished the pat-down and straightened. "You got ten minutes, and that's it. And I'm going in with you."

"You go in with me, then you're deserting your post. You desert your post in the Army or the reserves and you gonna end up where my brother is." He looked at the man's youthful features. A wannabe weekend warrior, he concluded. Probably pushed a pencil Monday through Friday before slipping on his fatigues and gun looking for adventure. "And let me tell you, prison ain't where somebody looks like you wants to be."

Private Brown swallowed nervously. "Ten minutes."

The two men locked eyes. "Thank you kindly," Josh Harms said, not meaning one word of it.

He entered the room and closed the door behind him.

"Rufus," he said quietly.

"Didn't think you were gonna get here so quick, brother."

Josh went over to the side of the bed and stared down at him. "What in the hell happened to you?"

"Ain't sure you want to know."

"It's all about that damn letter you got, ain't it?" Josh pulled a chair over next to the bed.

"How long the guard give you?"

"Ten minutes, but I ain't worried about him."

"Ten minutes ain't going to be long enough to tell you much. But I'll tell this. I go back to Fort Jackson and they're gonna kill me soon as I step inside."

"Who's 'they'?"

Rufus shook his head. "I tell you, then they gonna just come after you."

"I'm in here with you, ain't I? That baby soldier out there is stupid, but he ain't that stupid. He's gonna put me down on the visitors' roster. You know that."

Rufus swallowed with difficulty. "I know, probably never should've got you to come on down here."

"I'm here now. So start talking."

Rufus thought about it for a minute. "Look, Josh, that letter from the Army, when I got it, I remembered everything that happened that night. I mean everything. It was like somebody shot it right into my head."

"You talking about the girl?"

Rufus was already nodding. "Everything. I know why I did it. And the fact is, it wasn't my fault."

His brother looked at him skeptically. "Come on, now, Rufus, you did kill that little girl. No way around that."

"Killing and meaning to kill's two different things. Anyway, I got my lawyer from back then—"

"You mean your piss-poor excuse for a lawyer."

"You read the letter?"

"Sure I did. Came to my house, didn't it? Guess that was the last civilian address the Army had for you. Big, dumb carcass, didn't know it had you smack in one of its own damn prisons."

"Well, I got Rider to file something for me. In court."

"What'd he file?"

"A letter I wrote."

"Letter? How'd you get it out?"

"Same way you got the letter from the Army in."

Both men smiled.

Rufus said, "They got a printing operation inside the prison. The machinery's hot and dirty, so the guards give you a little space. Let me work my magic."

"So you think the Court's gonna look at your case? I wouldn't bet my life on it, little brother."

"Don't look like the Court's gonna do nothing."

"Well, gee, that's a big-ass surprise."

Rufus looked past his brother at the door. "When the guards coming back from the prison?"

"Boy said tomorrow morning."

"Well, that means I got to get out of here tonight."

"Woman who called me said you had some kind of heart problem. Look at you, all strapped to this crap. How far you think you can run?"

"How far you think I can run dead?"

"You really think they gonna try and kill you?"

"They don't want this to come out. You said you read the letter from the Army."

"Yep."

"Well, I was never in the program they said I was."

Josh eyed him hard. "How you mean?"

"Just what I said. Somebody put me in the records. They wanted me to look like I was in it, to cover up what they did to me. Why I killed that little girl. In case somebody checked, I reckon they had to do it. They thought I was going to be dead."

Josh took this in slowly until the truth hit him. "Jesus Lord Almighty. Why would they do that shit to you?"

"You asking me that? They hated me. Thought I was the biggest screw-up in the world. Wanted me dead."

"If I had known all that was happening, I sure as hell would've come back and kicked some butt."

"You were busy trying to keep the VC from tearing you up. But I go back to prison now, they gonna make sure they get me this time."

Josh looked at the door and then down at his brother's restraints.

"I need your help to do this, Josh."

"You're damn right you do, Rufus."

"You ain't gotta help me. You can turn and walk straight out of here. I still love you. You stood by me all these years. What I'm asking ain't fair, I know that. You worked hard, you got yourself a good life. I'd understand."

"Then you don't know your brother."

Rufus slowly reached out and took his brother's hand.

They gripped each other tightly, as though trying to give strength and resolve to one another for what lay ahead.

"Anybody see you come in?"

"Nobody except the guard. I didn't exactly come in the front door."

"Then I can pretend to knock you out, get out of here on my own. They know I'm a crazy SOB. Kill my own brother and never think twice about it."

"Bullshit. That dog just won't hunt, Rufus. You wouldn't even know where the hell to go. They'd catch your butt in ten minutes. I worked on repairs at this hospital for almost two years, know it like the back of my hand. Way I came in is supposed to be locked, only the nurses taped over the lock. They sneak their smokes out there."

"How you wanta work it, then?"

"We just go back out the way I came in. It's right down the hall on the left. Don't pass no nurses' station or nothing. My truck's right outside the door. I got a buddy thirty minutes from here. He owes me a favor. I'll leave my truck in one of his old barns and borrow his rig for a while. He won't ask no questions and he won't answer any if the police come along. We hit the road and don't look back."

"You sure you want to do this? How about your kids?"

"They all gone. Don't see 'em much."

"What about Louise?"

Josh looked down for a moment. "Louise walked out the door five years ago and I ain't seen her since."

"You never told me that!"

"What you gonna do about it if I had?"

"I'm sorry."

"I'm damn sorry about a lot of things. I ain't the easiest person to live with. Can't say I blame any of them." Josh shrugged his shoulders. "So it's just the two of us again. Make Momma happy if she was alive."

"You sure?"

"Don't ask me that again, Rufus."

Rufus raised his manacled hands. "What about these?"

His brother was already sliding something out of his boot. When he straightened back up he was holding a slender piece of metal with a slight hook at one end.

"Don't tell me that boy didn't search you?"

"Shit, like he knew where to look. Once he took my pocketknife, he figured he had all my *dangerous* weapons. Didn't even bother to do my boots." Josh grinned and then inserted the metal in the lock on the restraints.

"You think you can pick it?"

Josh stopped and looked at his brother with contempt. "If I can escape from the damn Viet Cong, I can sure as hell pick an Army-issued pair of handcuffs."

Out in the hallway, Private Brown looked at his watch. The ten minutes were up. He cracked open the door to the room. "All right, Harms, time's up." He pushed the door open farther. "Mr. Harms? Did you hear me? Time's up."

Brown heard a small groan. He drew his pistol and pushed the door all the way open. "What's going on in here?"

The groaning became louder. Brown looked around for the light switch. That's when he stumbled over something. He knelt down and touched the man's face as his vision focused.

"Mr. Harms? Mr. Harms, you okay?"

Josh opened his eyes. "I'm fine. How 'bout you?"

Then a big hand clamped down on Brown's gun and stripped it clean away. The other hand went around his mouth and he was lifted completely off the floor, one massive fist colliding with his jaw and knocking him out.

Rufus put Brown in the bed, covering him with the sheet. Josh put the restraints around the unconscious soldier's arms and legs and locked them up tight. Then he used adhesive tape and gauze he found in one of the cabinets to tape his mouth shut. The last thing he did was search the soldier and retrieve his pocketknife.

As Josh turned toward him, Rufus wrapped his arms around his brother and squeezed tight. Josh returned the hug, the first time the men had been able to do this in twenty-five years. His eyes moist, Rufus shook a little as Josh finally pulled away.

"Now, don't get too mushy on me. We ain't got no time for that."

Rufus smiled. "Still feels good to hold you, Josh."

Josh put a hand on his brother's shoulder. "Never thought we'd get a chance to ever do that. Never gonna take that for granted again."

"So what now?"

"You can't see where the boy was sitting from the hallway. But they got private security here." Josh checked his watch. "When I was working here they made rounds every hour on the hour. It's quarter past now. Those boys are on the six-singles-an-hour plan and don't give much of a shit about guarding bedpans, but they'll probably notice he's gone at some point. You ready?"

Rufus had already pulled on his prison pants and shoes. He had left off the shirt, opting for just his T-shirt instead. He had one thing clutched in his hand: the Gideon Bible. He didn't feel free yet, but he was only seconds from it. "Twenty-five years' worth of ready."

CHAPTER TWENTY-FIVE

Chandler looked around Michael Fiske's office. Located on the second floor of the building, it was large, with high ceilings, and half-foot-wide moldings. There were two massive wooden desks, each with a computer workstation, shelves filled with volumes of law books and case reporters, and a portable book caddy. There were wooden cabinets and stacks of files placed on the desks. The place was organized in a disorderly fashion, he concluded.

Perkins looked at Chandler. "There has to be someone from the Court present while you search. There are many confidential documents in here. Drafts of opinions, memos from justices and other clerks, that sort of thing, pertaining to undecided cases."

"All right. We won't remove anything that may relate to pending cases."

"But how can you know if it does or not?"

"I'll ask you."

"I don't know. I'm not even a lawyer."

Chandler said, "Well, then get somebody down here who is, because I'm going through this office."

"It may not be possible today. Can it wait until tomorrow? I believe all the clerks have gone home. Chief Justice Ramsey didn't think they should work late considering what happened."

"Some of the justices are still here, Richard," Klaus said.

Perkins cast an unfriendly glance at Klaus, who looked over at Dellasandro. "I didn't want to bring the justices into this until it was absolutely necessary. But let me see what I can do," he said. "I'm afraid I'll have to lock this door until I get back."

Chandler took a step closer to Perkins. "Look, Richard, I'm the police. Now, maybe I'm wrong and you don't mean what I thought you did by that very stupid remark."

Perkins's face flushed, but he left the door unlocked, motioned to Klaus to accompany him, and they walked off. Dellasandro stayed behind, talking to McKenna.

Chandler went over to Fiske. "I get the feeling this has all been scripted out long before we got here."

"McKenna knew your name before you were introduced."

"They've obviously already done some digging."

"Well, I guess you can't blame them."

"I'm gonna go over and talk to McKenna," said Chandler. "Never know when we might need a favor from the Feds."

Fiske leaned back against the wall and checked his watch. He still hadn't reached his father.

The door a short way down the hall from his brother's office opened and a young man came out.

Fiske nodded his head. "Busy place."

"Are you with the police?"

Fiske shook his head and extended his hand. "Just an observer. I'm John Fiske. Mike was my brother."

The young man went pale. "Oh God, it's awful. Awful. I'm so sorry." He shook Fiske's hand. "I'm Steven Wright."

"Did you know Mike well?"

"Not really. I just started this session. I clerk for Justice Knight. I know everyone thought the world of him."

Fiske looked at the door Wright had come out of. "Is that your office?" Wright nodded. "I guess there's been a lot of activity at my brother's office."

"You bet. People have been in and out all day."

"Like Mr. Perkins, Chief Dellasandro?"

"And that gentleman over there."

Fiske looked to where he was pointing. "That's Agent McKenna from the FBI," Fiske said.

Wright shook his head sadly. "I've never known anyone who's been . . ." He stopped and looked embarrassed.

"It's okay. I know what you mean." Suddenly all of Fiske's attention was trained on a pair of people walking toward him. His focus, actually, was on only one. Despite her obvious physical attractiveness, the woman looked, Fiske concluded, like the tomboy next door. Someone you could play touch football or chess with. And end up losing.

Sara Evans eyed Fiske. She had seen him come into the building earlier and guessed what he was here for. She had stayed close by in case they needed one of the clerks to talk to. That's why Perkins had "found" her so quickly. She stopped directly in front of Fiske, causing Perkins to abruptly do the same.

"Oh," he said, "John Fiske, this is Sara Evans."

"You're Michael's brother?"

"Let me guess, he never mentioned me," said Fiske.

"As a matter of fact, he did."

They shared a firm handshake. The whites of her eyes were smudged with red, as was the tip of her nose. Her voice sounded tired. Fiske noted that she clutched a handkerchief in her other hand. He had the feeling they had met before.

"I'm very, very sorry about Michael," she said.

"Thank you. It came as a tremendous shock." Fiske blinked. Was there something in her eyes when he said that? Something that said it wasn't all that shocking to her?

Perkins looked at Wright. "I didn't know you were in your office."

"You might have tried knocking," Fiske suggested.

Perkins cast him an unfriendly glance and walked over to Chandler and McKenna.

"Hi, Sara," Wright said, a smile breaking across his face.

From the way Wright was looking at her, it was obvious to Fiske that he was infatuated with the woman.

"Hello, Steven. How are you holding up?"

"I don't think anyone's gotten much work done today. I'm thinking about leaving soon."

Sara looked at Fiske. "Everyone thought the world of your brother. It's rocked all of us, from the chief justice on down. But it doesn't come close to equaling your loss, I know."

She said this so strangely that Fiske did a double-take. Before he could say anything, Perkins rejoined them.

"All right, Detective Chandler from D.C. Homicide is waiting along with a gentleman from the FBI," Perkins said to Sara.

"Why do they want to search Michael's office?"

Perkins's tone was blunt. "That's none of our business."

"It's part of the investigation, Ms. Evans," Fiske explained, "in case there's a connection with his murder."

"I thought it was a robbery."

"It was a robbery, and the sooner we can convince Detective Chandler that it has nothing whatsoever to do with the Court, the better," Perkins said huffily.

"*If* that happens to be the case," Fiske said.

"Of course, but it *is* the case." Perkins turned to Sara. "As I explained on the way down, your task is to ensure that no confidential documents are seen or taken."

"Confidential meaning exactly what?" she asked.

"You know, anything having to do with pending court cases, opinions, memos, that sort of thing."

"Shouldn't I be involved in that decision, Richard," came a new voice, "or is that outside my jurisdiction?"

Fiske easily recognized the man approaching them. Harold Ramsey strode toward them like a vintage ocean liner grandly pulling into harbor.

"Chief, I didn't see you there," Perkins said nervously.

"Obviously not." Ramsey looked at Fiske. "I don't believe we've met."

"Michael's brother, John Fiske," offered Sara.

Ramsey held out his hand; his long, bony fingers seemed to wrap twice around Fiske's. "I cannot tell you how sorry I am. Michael was a very special young man. I know that you and your family must feel his loss terribly. If there's anything we can do, please let us know."

Fiske acknowledged Ramsey's sentiments, feeling like a stranger at a wake, awkwardly receiving condolences for a deceased he could not name.

"I will," he said solemnly.

Ramsey looked at Perkins and inclined his head toward Chandler and McKenna. "Who are those men and what do they want?"

Perkins explained the situation in a fairly efficient manner, although it was clear that Ramsey had already thought five steps ahead by the time Perkins finished his account.

"Would you ask Detective Chandler and Agent McKenna to step over here, please, Richard?"

When introductions had been made, Ramsey turned to Chandler. "It seems to me that the better way of approaching the problem is to sit down with Justice Murphy and his clerks and take an oral inventory of the cases on which Michael was engaged. Understand that I'm trying to balance your right to investigate this crime with the Court's responsibility to keep confidential its opinions, until such time as they become publicly known."

"Okay." And I don't want anyone trying to pin any leak on me, Chandler thought to himself.

Ramsey continued. "I see no reason why you can't examine Michael's personal effects, if he kept any here. I only ask that any documents pertaining to the Court's work be set aside until you have had your discussion with Justice Murphy. Then, should there appear to be a connection between a case Michael was working on and his death, arrangements can be made for you to investigate any link thoroughly."

"All right, Mr. Chief Justice," Chandler said. "I've actually already spoken briefly with Justice Murphy."

McKenna quickly agreed with this approach.

Ramsey turned to Perkins. "Richard, please advise Justice Murphy and his clerks that Detective Chandler will want to meet with them as soon as possible. I'm assuming tomorrow after oral argument would do?"

"That'll be fine," Chandler replied.

"I'll also make available the Court's legal counsel to assist you in coordinating matters and addressing any concerns of confidentiality that may arise. Sara, you'll be available tomorrow, won't you? You were close with Michael."

Fiske eyed her. How close? he wondered.

Ramsey once again extended his hand to Fiske. "I would also appreciate being advised of funeral arrangements."

Ramsey then turned to Perkins. "Richard, after you speak with Justice Murphy, please come to my office." The meaning in his tone was clear.

After Ramsey and Perkins had left, Chandler watched as McKenna looked into Michael Fiske's office again. "Chief

Dellasandro," Chandler said, "to be as least disruptive as possible, I'll bring a team in tomorrow to search the office, so we only have to do it once."

"We appreciate that," Dellasandro replied.

"However, I want this door locked until I come back," Chandler continued. "Nobody goes in, and that means you, or Mr. Perkins, or"—he looked pointedly at Agent McKenna—"anybody else."

McKenna glared at Chandler as Dellasandro nodded his agreement.

Fiske looked around and caught Wright staring at Chandler. Wright abruptly closed his office door, and Fiske heard the lock turn. Smart man, he thought.

As Fiske and Chandler were leaving the building, a voice made them stop.

"Do you mind if I see you out?" Sara said.

"Okay with me," Chandler said. "John?"

Fiske shrugged noncommittally.

Chandler smiled as they walked along. "Why do I have the feeling we were just in the presence of the Almighty?"

Sara smiled. "The chief has that effect on people."

"So you clerk for Justice Knight?" Fiske asked.

"Going on my second year."

As they rounded a corner, they almost collided with Elizabeth and Jordan Knight.

"Oh, Justice Knight, we were just talking about you," Sara said. She made introductions all around.

"Senator," Chandler said, "we appreciate what you're doing for the District. Without the special funding you just pushed through for the police department, I'd be conducting homicide investigations via bicycle."

"We've got a lot more to do, as you know. The problems were built up over a long time, and they're going to take just as long to correct," Knight said in a political stumping tone. He looked at Fiske and his voice softened. "I am sorry about your brother, John. I didn't personally know him. I don't make it up to the Court much. If I have lunch with my wife too often the media thinks I'm trying to influence her decision making. I guess they forget we share the same house and bed. But please accept my heartfelt condolences to you and your family."

Fiske thanked him and then added, "For what it's worth, I voted for you."

"Every vote counts." He looked over at his wife and smiled warmly. "Just like it does up here, right, Mrs. Justice? How did Brennan put it? You need five votes to do anything? God, if I only had five votes to worry about I'd be thirty pounds lighter and my hair would still be black."

Elizabeth Knight didn't smile. Her eyes were as red as Sara's, her skin paler than usual. "Sara," she said, "I'd like to meet with you after the afternoon session tomorrow." She cleared her throat. "And I'd like you to speak with Steven about the bench memo on *Chance*. I have to have it by tomorrow at the latest. If he has to work through the night, I have to have it." Her voice was almost shrill.

Sara looked shaken. "I'll tell him right away, Justice Knight."

Knight gripped one of Sara's hands. "Thank you." She swallowed with difficulty. "Please also remember that the dinner for Judge Wilkinson is tomorrow night at seven o'clock at my home."

"It's on my calendar," Sara said a little reluctantly.

Elizabeth Knight finally looked at Fiske. "Your brother was a very gifted lawyer, Mr. Fiske. I know it may sound callous discussing these details, but the business of the Court stops for no one." She added a little wearily, "I learned that lesson a long time ago. Again, I'm very sorry." She checked her watch. "Jordan, you're going to be late for your meeting on the Hill. And I have some work to finish." She looked at Fiske. "If you'll excuse us."

Fiske shrugged. "Like you said, the machine stops for no one."

After the Knights had departed, Sara commented, "Justice Knight is tough, but fair." She glanced quickly at Fiske. "I'm sure she didn't mean it to sound that way."

"Sure she did," Fiske said.

Chandler stepped in. "Well, she probably had to work three times as hard as a man to get where she is. You don't ever forget that sort of experience."

"That's a very liberated mind-set," Sara said.

"If you knew my wife, you'd understand."

Sara smiled. "Ramsey and Knight are from different walks of life, although they tend to work together on many issues. He seems overly accommodating to her. Maybe he doesn't like confrontation with women. He's from a different generation."

"I don't think gender has anything to do with it," Fiske remarked bluntly.

"She's a brilliant jurist," Sara said defensively.

They all heard the beeping sound. Chandler reached down to his belt, held up the pager and looked at the number on its screen. "Can I use a phone?" he asked Sara.

She led the way.

Chandler rejoined them a minute later and shook his head wearily. "Couple of new customers for me to interview. Shotgun wounds to the heads. Lucky, lucky me."

"Can you take me back to the station so I can pick up my car?" Fiske asked.

"Actually, I was heading the other way."

"I can drive you," Sara said quickly. Both men looked at her. "I'm finished for the day. Not that I got much accomplished." She looked down and smiled a little wistfully. "The ironic thing is, I know Michael wouldn't approve. I've never seen anyone so dedicated, so hardworking." She looked at Fiske keenly, as though giving added strength to her words.

"Grab some dinner or something," Chandler suggested. "You two might find a lot to talk about."

Fiske glanced around, clearly uncomfortable with this suggestion, but he finally nodded. "You ready?"

"Give me a minute." She shook her head wearily. "I have to tell Steven he has to work all night," she said, and headed off.

Chandler said, "John, find out what you can. She was close to your brother." He added, "Unlike you."

"I'm not real good at spying," Fiske said, feeling guilty about plotting like this behind Sara's back. He had to catch himself, though; he didn't even know the woman.

As if he were privy to Fiske's thoughts, Chandler said, "John, I know she's smart and pretty, and she worked with your brother and she's shook up about his death. But remember one thing."

"What's that?"

"Those are *not* reasons to trust her." With that parting comment, Chandler walked off.

CHAPTER TWENTY-SIX

Jordan Knight stood in the doorway of his wife's office and watched her. Elizabeth Knight's head was bowed as she sat at her desk. Several books were open in front of her, but she was obviously not reading any of them.

"Why don't you call it a day, honey?"

She looked up, startled. "Jordan, I thought you had left for your meeting."

He came over and stood next to her, massaging the back of her neck with one hand. "I canceled it. And now it's time to go home."

"But I have some more work to go. We're all behind. It's so hard—"

He put a hand under her arm and helped her up. "Beth, no matter how important it is, it's not that important. Let's go home," he said firmly.

A few minutes later they were being driven in a government car to their apartment. After a relaxing shower, something to eat and a glass of wine, Elizabeth Knight finally started to feel halfway normal again as she lay on her bed. Her husband came in and sat down next to her, putting her feet on his lap and rubbing them.

"Sometimes I think we're too hard on our clerks. Work them too hard. Expect too much from them," she said after a while.

"Is that right?" Jordan Knight cupped her chin in one hand. "What, are you somehow trying to blame yourself for Michael Fiske's death? He wasn't working late the night he was probably killed. You told me he called in sick. His being in an alleyway in a bad part of town has nothing to do with you or the Court. Somebody, some piece of street trash, killed him. Maybe it was a robbery, or maybe he was just in the wrong place at the wrong time, but you had nothing to do with it."

"The police think it was a robbery."

"I'm sure it's early on in the investigation, but it'll be given the highest priority."

"One of the clerks today asked if Michael's death might be connected to the Court somehow."

Jordan Knight considered this for a moment. "Look, I suppose it's possible, but I can't see how." He suddenly looked worried. "If it is, though, I'm going to make sure you have added protection. I'll make a call tomorrow and you'll have your own Secret Service or FBI agent, round the clock."

"Jordan, you don't have to do that."

"What, make sure that some nut doesn't take you away from me? I think about that a lot, Beth. Some of the Court's decisions are very unpopular. You all get death threats from time to time. You can't ignore that."

"I don't. I just try not to think about it."

"Fine, but don't get upset if I do."

She smiled, touched his face. "You take much too good care of me, you know."

He smiled. "When you have something precious, that's the only way to go."

They tenderly kissed and then Jordan pulled the covers up over her, turned out the light and left to finish up some work in his study. Elizabeth Knight didn't go to sleep right away. She stared into the darkness, a series of emotions hitting her. Right when they all threatened to overwhelm her, she thankfully drifted off.

"I can't imagine what you're going through, John. I know how badly I'm feeling, and I'd only known Michael for a relatively short time."

They were in Sara's car and had just crossed over the Potomac River and into Virginia. Fiske wondered if she was trying to impress upon him that she had little information to provide.

"So how long did you two work together?"

"A year. Michael talked me into coming back for a second year."

"Ramsey said you and Michael were close. How close?"

She looked sharply at him. "What are you implying?"

"I just want to gather facts about my brother. I want to know who his friends were. If he was seeing anyone." He glanced over at her to gauge her reaction. If she had one, she wasn't showing it.

"You only lived two hours away and you know nothing about his life?"

"Is that your opinion or someone else's?"

"I can actually make observations all by myself."

"Well, that's a two-way street."

"The observations, or the two-hour drive?"

"Both."

They pulled into the parking lot of a restaurant in northern Virginia. They went inside, got a table and ordered their drinks and food. A minute later, Fiske took a swallow of his Corona; Sara sipped on a margarita.

Fiske wiped his mouth. "So, do you come from a family of lawyers? We tend to run in packs."

She smiled and shook her head. "I'm from a farm in North Carolina. Single-stoplight town. But my father had a connection to law."

Fiske looked mildly interested. "What was that?"

"He was the justice of the peace for the area. Officially, his courtroom was a little space in the back of the jail. More often he'd hear cases while sitting on his John Deere tractor in the middle of the field."

"Is that what got you interested in law?"

She nodded. "My dad looked more like a judge sitting on dusty farm equipment than some others I've seen in the fanciest courts."

"Including the one you're in now?"

Sara blinked and suddenly looked away. Fiske felt guilty for having made the comment. "I bet your dad was a good JP. Common sense, fair in his decisions. Man of the soil."

She glanced at him to see if he was being sarcastic, but Fiske's look was genuine. "That's exactly what he was. He mostly dealt with poachers and traffic tickets, but I don't think anyone walked away feeling they had been treated unfairly."

"You see him often?"

"He died six years ago."

"I'm sorry. Is your mom still around?"

"She died before Dad. Rural life can be rough."

"Sisters or brothers?"

She shook her head and seemed relieved to see their food arrive.

"It just occurred to me that I haven't eaten today," Fiske said as he took a large bite of his tortilla.

"I do that a lot. I think I had an apple this morning."

"Not good." His gaze swept over her. "You don't have a lot of excess on you."

She looked him over. Despite his broad shoulders and

full cheeks, he almost looked gaunt, his shirt collar loose against his neck, his waist a little too small for his size. "Neither do you."

Twenty minutes later Fiske pushed away his empty plate and sat back. "I know you're busy, so I won't waste your time. My brother and I didn't see a lot of each other. There's an information void I need to fill if I'm going to find out who did this."

"I thought that was Detective Chandler's job."

"Unofficially, it's mine."

"Your cop background?" Sara asked. Fiske arched his eyebrows. "Michael told me a lot about you."

"Is that right?"

"Yes, that's right. He was very proud of you. From cop to criminal defense attorney. Michael and I had some interesting discussions about that."

"Look, it bothers me that someone I don't know has been having discussions about my life."

"There's no reason to get upset. We just thought it was an interesting career change."

Fiske shrugged. "When I was a cop I spent all my time getting criminals off the streets. Now I make my living defending them. To tell you the truth, I was starting to feel sorry for them."

"I don't think I've ever heard a cop admit that."

"Really? How many cops have you dealt with?"

"I have a heavy foot. I get lots of traffic tickets." She smiled teasingly. "Seriously, why did you make the switch?"

He absently played with his knife for a moment. "I busted a guy who was carrying a brick of coke. He was a mule for some drug runners, a real minor role; just transport the stuff from point A to point B. I had other probable cause to do a stop and search. I turn up the brick and then the guy, with the vocabulary of a first-grader, tells me he thought it was a hunk of cheese." Fiske looked directly as her. "Can you believe that? He would've been better off claiming he didn't know how it got in there. Then his attorney could've at least had a shot at raising reasonable doubt on the possession charge. Trying to sell a jury on the fact that somebody who looks, acts and talks like a slime-ball really thought ten thousand bucks worth of misery for their kids was a chunk of Swiss, well, you got problems." He shook his head. "You put ten of these guys in jail, there's a hundred more just waiting to take their place. They've got nowhere else to go. If they had, they would. The thing is, you don't give people hope, they don't care what they do to themselves or each other."

Sara smiled. "What's so funny?" he asked.

"You sound a lot like your brother."

Fiske paused and rubbed his hand across a water ring on the table. "You spent a lot of time with Mike?"

"Yes, quite a lot."

"Socially too?"

"We had drinks, dinner, outings." She took a sip of her drink and smiled. "I've never been deposed before."

"Depositions can actually be quite painful."

"Really?"

"Yes, like this for instance: Something tells me Mike's death didn't seem to surprise you all that much. Is that true?"

Sara instantly dropped her casual manner. "No. I was horrified."

"Horrified, yes. But surprised?"

The waitress stopped by and asked if they would like some dessert or coffee. Fiske asked for the bill.

Then they were back in the car and heading toward the District. A light rain had begun to fall. October was a quirky month, weatherwise, for the area. It could be hot, cold or mild during any given stretch. Right now it was very hot and humid outside, and Sara had the AC on high.

Fiske looked at her expectantly. She caught his gaze, took a troubled breath and started speaking slowly.

"Recently, Michael did seem nervous, distracted."

"Was that unusual?"

"For the last six weeks we've been cranking out bench memos. Everybody's short-fused, but Michael thrived under those conditions."

"You think it was related to something at the Court?"

"Michael didn't have much of a life outside the Court."

"Other than you?"

She glanced at him sharply but said nothing.

"Any big controversial cases pending?" he asked.

"Every case is big and controversial."

"But he never mentioned specifics to you?"

Sara stared ahead but again chose not to answer.

"Whatever you can tell me will help, Sara."

She slowed the car slightly. "Your brother was funny. Do you know that he would go down to the clerks' mail room at the crack of dawn to get an early jump on any interesting cases?"

"I'm not surprised. He never did things halfway. How are the appeals normally processed?"

"The clerks' mail room is where the filings are opened and processed. Each filing goes to a case analyst to make sure that it complies with the requirements of the rules of the Court, and so forth. If it's handwritten, like a lot of the *in forma pauperis* appeals are, they even make sure the handwriting is legible. Then the information goes into a database under the last name of the party filing the appeal. Lastly, the filing is copied and sent to all the justices' chambers."

"Mike once told me how many appeals the Court gets. The justices can't possibly read all of them."

"They don't. The petitions are divided up among the justices' chambers, and the clerks are assigned to do certorari pool memos on them. For example, we might get in a hundred or so appeals in a week's time. There are nine justices, so each chamber gets roughly a dozen appeals. Of the dozen appeals sent to Justice Knight's chambers, I might write a memo on three. That memo is circulated to all the chambers. Then the other justices' clerks look over my memo and make a recommendation to their justice on whether the Court should grant cert or not."

"You clerks have a lot of power."

"In some areas, but not really with the opinions. A clerk's draft of an opinion is mostly a recap of the facts of the case and then stringing together cites. The justices just use the clerks to get the grunt work done, the paper pulp. We have the greatest impact in the screening of the appeals."

Fiske looked thoughtful. "So a justice may not even see the actual documents filed with the Court before deciding whether to hear the case or not? He'd just read the pool memo and the clerk's recommendation."

"Maybe not even the memo, perhaps just the clerk's recommendation. The justices hold discussion conferences usually twice a week. That's when all the petitions screened by the clerks are discussed and voted upon to see if there are at least four votes, the minimum you need, to hear the case."

"So the first person to actually see an appeal filed with the Court would be someone in the clerks' mail room?"

"That's normally the case."

"What do you mean, 'normally'?"

"I mean there's no guarantee that things will always be done by the rules."

Fiske thought about this for a moment. "Are you suggesting that my brother might have taken an appeal before the clerks' mail room could process it?"

Sara let out a muffled groan but quickly composed herself. "I can only tell you this in confidence, John."

He shook his head. "I'm not going to promise you something I can't deliver."

Sara sighed and in concise sentences told Fiske about finding the papers in his brother's briefcase. "I didn't really mean to snoop. But he had been acting strangely, and I was worried about him. I ran into him one morning coming from the clerks' mail room. He looked really distraught. I think he had just taken the appeal I found in his briefcase."

"The filing you saw, was it the original or a copy?"

"Original. One of the pages was handwritten, the other typewritten."

"Are originals normally circulated?"

"No. Only copies. And the copied files certainly don't have the original envelope the filing came in."

"I remember Mike telling me that clerks sometimes take home files, even originals sometimes."

"That's true."

"So maybe that was the case here."

She shook her head. "It wasn't set up like a normal case file. There was no return address on the envelope, and the typewritten page had no signature at the bottom. The handwritten page made me think it was an *in forma pauperis* petition, but there was no motion or affidavit of indigency that I could see."

"Did you see any name on the papers, anything that could identify who was involved?"

"I did. That's why I knew Michael had taken a filing."

"How?"

"I managed to glance at the first sentence of the typewritten page. The person identified as the party filing the appeal was named there. As soon as I left Michael's office I checked the Court's filing database. There was no one by that name listed."

"What was the name?"

"The last name was Harms."

"First name?"

"I didn't see it."

"Do you remember anything else?"

"No."

Fiske eased back in his seat. "The thing is, if Mike took the appeal, he had to be sure that no one would call up about the disappearance of the file. Like the attorney who filed it, if an attorney did."

"Well, the envelope had a return receipt requested label. The sending party would've gotten notice that it was delivered to the Court."

"Okay. And why one handwritten page and one type-written page?"

"Two different people. Maybe the person didn't want to be recognized, but still wanted to help Harms."

"From all the appeals the Court gets, Mike takes this one. Why?"

She glanced at him nervously. "Oh God, if it turns out that this had anything to do with Michael's death. I never thought . . ." She suddenly looked as though she would burst into tears.

"I'm not going to tell anyone about this. For now. You took a risk for Mike. I appreciate that." There was a lengthy silence until Fiske said, "It's getting late."

As they drove along, Fiske finally said, "We've been able to ascertain that Mike put eight hundred or so miles on his car in the last couple of days. Any idea where he might have gone?"

"No. I don't think he liked driving. He rode his bike to work."

"How was he perceived by the other clerks?"

"Highly respected. He was incredibly motivated. I guess all Supreme Court clerks are, but Michael seemed incapable of turning it off. I consider myself a hard worker too, but I think a balance in life is good."

"Mike was always that way," Fiske said a little wearily. "He started at perfection and moved up from there."

"Must run in the family. Michael told me that, growing up, you worked two and three jobs almost all the time."

"I like to have spending money."

The money had not remained long in Fiske's pocket. It had gone to his father, who had never earned more than fifteen lousy grand a year in over forty years of working his ass off. Now it went to his mother and her massive health bills.

"You also went to college while working as a cop."

Fiske impatiently tapped his fingers against the car window. "Good old Virginia Commonwealth University, the Stanford of the next century."

"And you read for the law." Fiske looked at her angrily. "Please don't get upset, John. I'm just curious."

Fiske sighed. "I apprenticed to a Richmond criminal defense attorney. Learned a lot. Got my certificate and passed the bar." He added dryly, "It's the only way to become a lawyer if you're too dumb to score high enough on the LSATs."

"You're not dumb."

"Thanks, but how would you know?"

"We watched you do a trial."

He turned to look at her. "Excuse me?"

"Over the summer, Michael and I came down to Richmond and watched you do a trial in circuit court." She was not going to mention her second trip to watch him in court.

"Why didn't you let me know you were there?"

Sara shrugged. "Michael thought you'd be upset."

"Why would I be upset at seeing my brother?"

"Why are you asking me? He was your brother." When Fiske said nothing, Sara continued, "I was really impressed. I think you might have motivated me to become a criminal defense lawyer someday. At least for a while, try it out, see what it's really like."

"Oh, you think you'd like to do that?"

"Why not? The law can still be a noble calling. Defending the rights of others. The poor. I'd love to hear about some of your cases."

"Would you really?"

"Absolutely," she said enthusiastically.

He settled down, pretended to think hard. "Let's see, there was Ronald James. That was his real name, but he preferred to be called Backdoor Daddy. That referred to his sexual position of choice with the six women he brutally raped. I plea-bargained that one, even though all six women identified him from a police lineup. I had some leverage, though. Four of the women couldn't face Backdoor in court. That's what terror will do for you. Or *to* you. The fifth victim had a few nasties in her past that maybe we could've used to attack her credibility. The last woman wanted nothing less than to crucify him. But one good witness isn't the same as a half dozen. Bottom line: The prosecutor got cold feet and Backdoor got twenty years with a shot at parole.

"Then there was Jenny, a nice kid who put a cleaver into her grandmother's skull because, as she tearfully explained to me, the old, dumb bitch wouldn't let her go to the mall with her friends. Jenny's mother, the daughter of the woman little Jenny butchered, is paying my legal bill in installments of two bucks a month."

"I think I get the point," Sara said tersely.

"Now, I don't want to disillusion you. The guy I just got off for burglary paid my bill in full, probably with the cash he got from fencing the property he stole. I've learned not to ask. So my rent's paid for the month, and I haven't had to pull a gun on one of my clients in a long time. And tomorrow's always a new day." Fiske leaned back. "Go get 'em, Ms. Evans."

"You really enjoy shocking people, don't you?"

"You asked."

"So why the hell do you do it, then?"

"Someone has to."

"That wasn't exactly the answer I was expecting, but let's just drop it," she said harshly. "Thanks for bursting my balloon, though, I really appreciate it."

"If I burst your little balloon, you should thank me," he said angrily. Then he added more calmly, "Look, Sara, I'm no white knight. Most of my clients are guilty. I know that, they know that, everybody knows that. Ninety percent of my cases are plea-bargained for that very reason. If somebody actually came to me proclaiming their innocence, I'd probably die of a heart attack. I'm not a defender of anybody, I'm a negotiator of sentencing. My job is to make sure that the prison time is fair relative to what everybody else gets. On the rare occasion I do go to trial, the trick there is to blow enough smoke around that a jury just loses the energy to figure it all out and gives up. Like they really want to sit around debating the fate of somebody they don't even know, and could give a shit about."

"Gee, whatever happened to the truth?"

"Sometimes the truth is a lawyer's biggest enemy. You can't spin it. Nine times out of ten, with the truth I lose. Now, I'm not paid to lose, but I try to be fair. So we all do our little shuffle during the day, the tuna nets go out at night and catch a batch of fresh meat, and we all come back and do the dance again. And on and on it goes."

"Your version of real life?" she asked.

"Don't worry, you're never going to see it. You'll be teaching at Harvard, or working at some gold-plated New York law firm. If I'm ever up there, I'll be sure to wave to you from the Dumpster."

"Can you please stop?" Sara exclaimed.

They drove on in silence until something occurred to Fiske.

"If you had already seen me at the trial, why did you make a show of not knowing who I was back at the Court when Perkins introduced us?"

Sara took a short breath. "I don't know. I guess because in front of Perkins, I couldn't think of a clever way to tell you how I had already seen you."

"Why did it have to be clever?"

"You know what they say about first impressions." She shook her head at the thought now. *Christ!*

As Fiske watched her, the last of his hostility faded. "Don't let my cynical ass dampen your enthusiasm, Sara." He added quietly, "Nobody has that right. I'm sorry."

Sara looked over at him. "I think you care more than you let on." She hesitated for a moment, debating whether to tell him or not. "You know a little boy named Enis, don't you?" Fiske stared over at her. "I saw you talking to him."

It finally hit Fiske. "The bar. I knew I had seen you before. What were you doing, following me?"

"Yes."

Her frankness caught Fiske off guard. "Why?" he asked quietly.

She spoke slowly. "That's a little difficult to explain. I don't think I'm up to it right now. I wasn't spying on you. I could see how difficult it was for you, talking to Enis and his family."

"Best thing that ever happened to them. Next time the old man might have killed them."

"Still, to lose your father like that . . ."

"He wasn't Enis's father."

"I'm sorry, I thought he was."

"Oh, Enis is his son. But that doesn't make somebody your father. Fathers don't do what that guy did to his family."

"What'll happen to them?"

Fiske shrugged. "I give Lucas two more years before

they find him in some alley with a dozen holes in him. The really sad thing is, he knows it too."

"Maybe he'll surprise you."

"Yeah. Maybe."

"And Enis?"

"I don't know about Enis. And I don't want to talk about it anymore."

They remained silent until they pulled up in front of the Homicide building.

"I'm parked right in front."

Sara looked at him in surprise. "Pretty lucky. In the two years I've lived in this city, I don't think I've ever found an empty parking space on the street."

Fiske stared at one spot. "I could've sworn I parked right here."

Sara looked out the window. "You mean right next to that tow-away zone sign?"

Fiske jumped out of the car just as the rain picked up, and looked at the sign and then at the space where his car used to be. He climbed back in her car, leaned back against the seat and closed his eyes. Water droplets clung to his face and hair. "I really can't believe this day."

"They have a number you can call to get your car back." Sara picked up the cell phone and punched in the numbers as she read them off the street sign. The phone rang ten times, but no one answered. She hung up. "It doesn't look like you're going to get your car back tonight."

"I can't go to sleep until my dad knows."

"Oh." She thought for a moment. "Well, I'll drive you."

Fiske looked outside at the pouring rain. "You sure?"

She put the car in gear. "Let's go find your dad."

"Can we make one stop first?"

"Sure, just tell me where."

"My brother's apartment."

"John, I'm not sure that's a good idea."

"I think it's a great idea."

"We can't get in."

"I've got a key," said Fiske. She looked puzzled. "I helped move him in when he started working at the Court."

"Won't the police have it taped off or anything?"

"Chandler said he was going to go over it tomorrow." He looked at her. "Don't worry, you're staying in the car. If anything happens, just take off."

"And if maybe the person who killed Michael is there?"

"You got a tire iron in the trunk?"

"Yes."

"Then it's my lucky day."

Sara took a shallow breath. "I hope you know what you're doing."

Me too, Fiske thought.

CHAPTER TWENTY-SEVEN

When they reached Michael Fiske's apartment, Sara pulled into a parking space around the corner. "Pop the trunk," Fiske said, before getting out.

She could hear him rummaging through the compartment for a moment. She was startled for an instant when he appeared at her window. She quickly rolled it down.

"Keep the car doors locked, the engine running and your eyes open, okay?" he said.

She nodded, noting the tire iron in one hand and a flashlight in his other.

"If you get nervous or anything, just leave. I'm a big boy. I'll get to Richmond okay."

She shook her head stubbornly. "I'll be right here."

As she watched him head around the corner, a thought occurred to her. She waited a minute or so to allow him time to get into the building, then she pulled around the corner, back onto Michael's street and parked across from the row house. She picked up her cell phone and held it ready. If she spotted anything remotely suspicious, she was going to call the apartment and warn Fiske. A good emergency plan, but one she hoped she wouldn't have to use.

Fiske closed the door behind him, clicked on the flashlight and looked around. He saw no obvious signs that anyone had searched the place.

He entered the small kitchen, which was separated from the living room by a waist-high bar. He looked for and found a couple of plastic baggies in one of the kitchen drawers and covered his hands with them, so as not to leave any prints. There was a small door leading to the pantry, but Fiske didn't bother with it. His brother wasn't the type to have neatly arranged rows of canned corn and peas. It was no doubt empty.

He went through the living room, checked the small coat closet, but there was nothing in any of the coat pockets. Next he headed to the single bedroom at the rear of the apartment. The floors were worn tongue-in-groove and the creaks followed him with each step. He pushed open the door and looked in. Bed was unmade, clothes here and there. He checked the pockets—nothing. There was a small desk in the corner. He searched it carefully but came up empty. Hidden behind the desk he saw a power cord plugged into the wall and frowned as he held up the other end. He looked next to the desk but didn't see what he had expected to see there: the laptop computer the cord should have been attached to. And his brother's briefcase; Fiske had actually bought it for Mike upon his graduation from law school. He made a mental note to ask Sara about both the briefcase and the laptop.

Finished with the bedroom, he moved back down the hallway and toward the kitchen. He stopped for a moment, listening intently. As he did so, he tightly gripped the tire iron. With a sudden lunge he jerked open the pantry door, the tire iron raised, the light shining directly into the small space.

The man burst out and hit Fiske right in the stomach with his shoulder. Fiske grunted, the flashlight flew away, but he held his ground and managed to clip the man across the neck with the tire iron. He heard a pained cry; but the man recovered more quickly than Fiske had anticipated, lifted him off the floor and threw him over the bar. Fiske landed hard and felt his shoulder go numb. Even so, he managed to twist sideways and kick the legs out from under the guy as he hurtled past, going for the door. He swung with the tire iron again, but in the darkness missed and it hit the floor instead. A fist connected with his jaw. Fiske swung out and hit solid flesh as well.

The guy was on his feet and through the door in a few seconds. Fiske finally lurched up and raced to the door, holding his shoulder. He heard feet clattering down the steps. He hustled after the man and heard the front door to the building crash open. Ten seconds later Fiske was out on the street. He looked right and left. A horn blew.

Sara rolled down her window and pointed to the right. Fiske sprinted hard through the rain in that direction and turned the corner. Sara put the car in gear, but had to wait for two cars to pass, and then she spun rubber after him. She turned the corner, raced down the next block but didn't see anyone. She backed the car up and turned down another side street, and then another, growing more and more frantic. She let out a shriek of relief when she saw Fiske in the middle of the street, sucking in air.

She jumped out of the car and ran over to him.

"John, thank God you're okay."

Fiske was furious that the man had gotten away. He stomped around in tight circles. "Dammit! Shit!"

"What the hell was that all about?"

Fiske calmed down. "Bad guys one, good guys zip."

Sara put an arm around his waist and walked him

over to the car. She eased him into it. Then she climbed in the driver's side and they started off. "You need to see a doctor."

"No! It's just a stinger. Did you see the guy?"

Sara shook her head. "Not really. He came out so fast, I thought it was you."

"My size? Distinguishing clothing? White, black?"

Sara thought hard for a moment, trying to visualize what she had seen. "I don't know about his age. He was close to your size. He had on dark clothing and a mask, I think." She sighed. "It happened so fast. Where was he?"

"In the pantry. I didn't hear him on my first pass through, but I heard the floor squeak on my way back out." He rubbed his shoulder. "And now comes the hard part." He picked up her cell phone and pulled a business card from his wallet. "Telling Chandler what just happened."

Fiske paged Chandler and the detective called back a few minutes later. When Fiske told him what he had done, he had to hold the phone away from his ear.

"Slightly upset?" Sara asked.

"Yeah, like Mount Saint Helens *slightly* erupted." Fiske brought the receiver back to his ear. "Look, Buford—"

"What the hell were you thinking, doing something that stupid?" yelled Chandler. "You were a cop."

"That's how I was thinking. Like I was still a cop."

"Well, you're not a damn cop anymore."

"Do you want the description of the guy or not?"

"I'm not finished with you yet."

"I know, but there's plenty of me to go around."

"Give me the damn description," Chandler said.

After Fiske finished, Chandler said, "I'll get a squad car over there right now to secure it, and I'll request a tech team ASAP to go over the place."

"My brother's briefcase wasn't at his apartment. Was it in his car?"

"No, I told you we found no personal items."

Fiske looked at Sara. "Is the briefcase in his office? I don't remember seeing it. Or his laptop computer."

She shook her head. "I don't remember seeing the brief-case. And he usually didn't bring his laptop to work, since we all have desktops."

Fiske spoke back into the phone. "Looks like his brief-case is missing. And so is his computer; I found the power cord to it."

"Did the guy maybe have either of the items on him?"

"He was empty-handed. I know. He clocked me good with one of those empty hands."

"Okay, so we got a missing briefcase, missing laptop and a dumb-as-shit ex-police officer who I've got half a mind to arrest right this instant."

"Come on, you guys already towed my car."

"Put Ms. Evans on the line."

"Why?"

"Just do it."

Fiske handed the phone over to a perplexed Sara.

"Yes, Detective Chandler?" she said, nervously twirling a strand of her hair.

"Ms. Evans," he began politely, "I thought you were simply going to drive Mr. Fiske to his car and maybe get a little dinner, not engage in filming a James Bond movie."

"But you see, his car was towed and—"

Chandler's tone quickly changed. "I don't appreciate you two making my job even more difficult. Where are you?"

"About a mile from Michael's apartment."

"And where are you headed?"

"To Richmond. To tell John's father about Michael."

"Okay, then you drive him to Richmond, Ms. Evans. Don't let him out of your sight. If he wants to play Sherlock Holmes again, you call me, and I will come directly over and shoot him myself. Do I make myself clear?"

"Yes, Detective Chandler. Absolutely."

"And I expect to see both of you back in D.C. tomorrow. Is that also understood?"

"Yes, we'll be back."

"Good, Tonto, now put the Lone Ranger back on."

Fiske took back the phone. "Look, I know it was stupid, but I was only trying to help."

"Do me a favor, don't try to help anymore unless I'm with you. Okay?"

"Okay."

"John, any number of things could've happened tonight, most of them bad. Not only to you, but to Ms. Evans."

Fiske rubbed his shoulder and glanced over at the woman. "I know," he said quietly.

"Give my condolences to your father."

Fiske put down the phone.

"Can we go to Richmond now?" Sara asked.

"Yes, we can go to Richmond now."

CHAPTER TWENTY-EIGHT

In his friend's pickup truck, Josh Harms drove along the deserted country road. The dense forest bracketing the narrow lanes gave him a certain comfort. Isolation, a buffer between himself and those who would hassle him, had been Josh's one constant goal in life. As a carpenter of considerable skill, he worked alone. When he was not working, he was either hunting or fishing, again alone. He did not desire the conversation of others, and he very rarely offered any of his own. All of that had changed now. The responsibility he had just acquired had not yet fully sunk in, but he knew it was considerable. And he also knew his decision had been the right one.

The truck had a camper and his brother was back there supposedly resting, although Josh had doubts as to whether the man could really be sleeping. The back of the camper was also filled with a month's worth of food and bottled water, two deer rifles and a semiautomatic pistol in addition to the one he had tucked in his belt. That arsenal was insignificant compared to what would soon be coming after them, but he had faced long odds before and survived.

He lit a cigarette and blew the smoke cleanly out the window. They were already two hundred miles from Roanoke and he was putting as much distance between it and them as he could. The escape would have been discovered by now, he knew. The roadblocks would be set up, but not out this far, he figured. They had gotten a head start, but that gap would quickly close. The boys in green had a big advantage in manpower and equipment. But Josh had fished and hunted around the area for the last twenty years. He knew all the abandoned cabins, all the hidden valleys, the smallest opening in otherwise solid forest. His survival skills had been honed as much from scraping for an existence in America as from dodging death halfway around the world in Vietnam.

Even with his outright distrust of all authority, he didn't break the law lightly. He had never figured his little brother for some crazed killer. Rufus never should have joined the Army, wasn't cut out for it. Ironically, Josh had been the decorated war hero, and he had been drafted. His brother had volunteered and had spent his career in the stockade. Josh hadn't been too thrilled about taking up a rifle for a country that had largely failed him and anyone his color. But once in the service he had fought with great distinction. He had done it for himself and the men in his company, and for no other reason. He had no other motivation to fight and kill men with whom he had no personal quarrel.

Josh slowed the truck and turned down a dirt road that led deeper into the woods. Rufus had filled him in on some of the details of what had happened twenty-five years ago, what those men had done to him. Josh felt his face grow hot as he now recalled an incident he had kept buried. It was principally what drove the anger, the hatred in him. What their little town in Alabama had done to the Harms family after the news of Rufus's crime. He had tried to protect his mother then, but had failed. Let me meet up with the men who did this to my brother. *You hear that one, God? You listening?*

His plan was to hide out for a while and then hit the road again when the pressure died down. Maybe try to get to Mexico and disappear. Josh wasn't leaving all that much behind. A disintegrated family, a carpentry business that was always on the wrong side of profitability despite his skill. He guessed Rufus was all the family he had left. And he was certainly all Rufus ever would have. They had been cut off from each other for a quarter century. Now, in middle age, they had a chance to be closer than brothers normally were at this time in their lives. If Josh and Rufus could survive. He tossed out the cigarette and kept on driving.

In the back of the camper, Rufus was, indeed, not asleep. He lay on his back, a black tarp partially over him—Josh's doing, the tarp designed to blend in with the dark truck bed liner under him. Stacked around him were boxes of food, secured by bungie cords—also Josh's doing, a wall to prevent anyone from seeing in. He tried to stretch out a little, relax. The motion of the truck was unsettling. He had not been in a civilian automobile since Richard Nixon had been president. Could that really be? How many presidents ago was that? The Army had always transported him between prisons via helicopters, apparently unwilling to let him get this close to the road, to freedom. When you escape from a chopper, there wasn't much place to go except down.

Rufus tried to peek between cardboard, out at the passing night. Too dark now. Freedom. He often wondered what it would feel like. He still did not know. He was too scared. People, lots of them, looking for him. Wanting to kill him. And now his brother. His fingers gripped the

unfamiliar texture of the hospital Bible. The one his
mother had given him was back in the cell. He had kept
it beside him all these years, turned again and again to the
scriptures as sustenance against all that was his existence.
He felt empty of brain and heart without it. Too late now.
He felt his heart start to accelerate. He figured that was
bad—too much strain on it. From memory he recited
comforting words from the Bible's bounty. How many
nights had he mumbled the Proverbs, all thirty-one chap-
ters, the one hundred and fifty Psalms, each one telling
and forceful, each one with particular meaning, insight
into elements of his existence.

When he finished his "readings," he half rose and slid
open the window of the camper. From this angle he
could see his brother's face in the reflection of the
rearview mirror.

"I thought you were sleeping," Josh said.

"Can't."

"How's your heart feel?"

"My heart ain't troubling me none. If I die, it ain't
gonna be because of my heart."

"Not unless it's a bullet ripping through it."

"Where we headed?"

"A little place in the middle of nowhere. I figure we stay
there a bit, let things die down, and then we head out
again when it's dark. They probably think we're shooting
south, going for the Mexican border, so we're going north
to Pennsylvania, at least for now."

"Sounds good."

"Hey, you said Rayfield and that other sonofabitch—"

"Tremaine. Old Vic."

"Yeah, you said they've been watching over you all this
time. After all those years went by, how come they were
still hanging in there? Didn't they figure if you remembered what happened you would've said something before
now? Like maybe at your trial?"

"Been thinking about that. They maybe thought I couldn't remember nothing then, but maybe I might one day. Not that I could prove nothing, but just me saying stuff might get them in trouble or at least get people looking around. Easiest thing was to kill me. Believe me, they tried that, but it didn't work. Maybe they thought I was messing with 'em, playing dumb and hoping they'd give up the guard, and then I start talking. With them at the prison, they pretty much had me under their thumb. Read my mail, checked out people coming to see me. Anything look funny, then they just take me out. Probably felt better about doing it like that. After so many years, though, they got a little lazy, I guess. Let Samuel and that fellow from the Court come see me."

"I figured that. But I still got that letter from the Army in to you. I didn't know all this shit was going on, but I didn't want them having a look-see at it either."

The two stayed quiet for a while. Josh was naturally reserved and Rufus wasn't used to having anyone to talk to. The silence was both liberating and oppressive to him. He had a lot he wanted to say. During Josh's thirty-minute visits at the prison each month, he would talk and his brother would mostly listen, as though he sensed the accumulation of words, of thoughts in Rufus's head.

"I don't think I ever asked you: You been back home?"

Josh shifted in his seat. "Home? What home?"

Rufus started slightly. "Where we was born, Josh!"

"Why the hell would I want to go back to that place?"

"Momma's grave is there, ain't it?" Rufus said quietly.

Josh considered this for a moment and then nodded. "Yeah, it's there, all right. She owned the dirt, she had the burial insurance. They couldn't *not* bury her there, although they sure as hell tried."

"Is it a nice grave? Who's keeping it up?"

"Look, Rufus, Momma's dead, okay? Long time now. Ain't no way in hell she's knowing nothing about how her grave looks. And I ain't going all the way down to damn Alabama to brush some leaves off the damn ground, not after what happened down there. Not after what that town done to the Harms family. I hope they all burn in hell for it, every last damn one of 'em. If there is a God, and I got me some big-ass doubts on that, then that's what the Big Man should do. If you want to worry about the dead, you go right ahead. I'm gonna stick to what counts: keeping you and me alive."

Rufus continued to watch his brother. There is a God, he wanted to tell him. That same God had kept Rufus going all these years when he had wanted to just curl up and sink into oblivion. And one should respect the dead and their final resting place. If he lived through this, Rufus would go see to his mother's grave. They would meet up again. For all eternity.

"I talk to God every day."

Josh grunted. "That's real good. I'm glad He's keeping company with somebody."

They fell silent until Josh said, "Hey, what was the name of that fella come visit you?"

"Samuel Rider?"

"No, no, the young fella."

Harms thought for a moment. "Michael somebody."

"From the Supreme Court, you said?" Rufus nodded. "Well, they killed him. Michael *Fiske.* Anyway, I guess they killed him. Saw it on the TV right before I came to get you."

Rufus looked down. "Damn. I figured that would happen."

"Stupid thing he did, coming to the prison like that."

"He was just trying to help me. Damn," Rufus said again, and then fell silent as the truck rolled on.

CHAPTER TWENTY-NINE

With Fiske directing her, Sara drove to his father's neighborhood on the outskirts of Richmond and pulled into the gravel driveway. The grass was brown in spots after another heat- and humidity-filled Richmond summer, but fronting the house there were carefully tended flower beds that had benefited from consistent watering.

"You grew up in this house?"

"Only house my parents have ever owned." Fiske looked around, shaking his head. "I don't see his car."

"Maybe it's in the garage."

"There's no room. He was a mechanic for forty years, and accumulated a lot of junk. He parks in the driveway." He looked at his watch. "Where the hell is he?" He got out of the car. Sara did as well.

He looked at her over the roof of the car. "You can stay here if you want."

"I'll come in with you," she said quickly.

Fiske unlocked the front door and they went in. He turned on a light, and they moved through the small living room and into the adjacent dining room, where Sara stared at a collection of photos on the dining room table. There was one of Fiske in his football uniform; a little blood on the face, grass stains on the knees, sweaty. Very sexy. She caught herself and looked away, suddenly feeling guilty.

She looked at some of the other pictures. "You two played a lot of sports."

"Mike was the natural athlete of the family. Every record I set, he broke. Easily."

"Quite the jock family."

"He was also valedictorian of his class, a GPA on the north side of four-point-oh, and a near-perfect score on the SATs and LSATs."

"You sound like the proud big brother."

"A lot of people were proud of him," Fiske said.

"And you?"

He looked at her steadily. "I was proud of him for some things, and not proud of him for others. Okay?"

Sara picked up a photo. "Your parents?"

Fiske stood beside her. "Their thirtieth anniversary. Before Mom got sick."

"They look happy."

"They were happy," he said quickly. He was growing very uncomfortable with her seeing these items from his past. "Wait here." Fiske went to the back room, which had once been the brothers' shared bedroom and now had been turned into a small den. He checked the answering machine. His father had not listened to his messages. He was about to leave the room when he saw the baseball glove on the shelf. He picked it up. It was his brother's, the pocket ribbing torn, but the leather well oiled—by his father, obviously. Mike was a lefty, but the family had no money to buy a special glove for him, so Mike had learned to field the ball, pull off his glove and throw. He had gotten so good that he could do it all faster than a righty could. Fiske recalled that blur of efficiency, no obstacle his brother couldn't overcome. He put the glove down and rejoined Sara.

"He hasn't listened to my phone messages."

"Any idea where he could've gone?"

Fiske thought a moment and then snapped his fingers. "Pop usually tells Ms. German."

While he was gone, Sara looked around the room some more. She eyed a small framed letter, set on a wooden pedestal. Wrapped around it was a medal. She picked up the frame and read the letter. The medal was for valor, awarded to Patrolman John Fiske, and the letter commemorated the event. She looked at the date it had been given. Quickly calculating, she concluded that the award would have been given at about the time Fiske had left the force. She still didn't know why he had, and Michael never would say. When she heard the back door open, she quickly put the letter and medal down.

Fiske entered the room. "He's at the trailer."

"What trailer?"

"Down by the river. He goes there to fish. Go boating."

"Can you call the trailer?"

Fiske shook his head. "No phone."

"Okay, so we drive. Where is it?"

"You've gone way beyond the call of duty already."

"I don't mind, John."

"It's about another hour and a half from here."

"The night's sort of shot anyway."

"You mind if I drive? It's off the beaten path."

She tossed him the keys. "I thought you'd never ask."

CHAPTER THIRTY

"Let me get this right: On top of everything else that's happened, you let him escape."

"First of all, I didn't *let* him do anything. I thought the guy had just had a friggin' heart attack. He was chained to the damn bed. He had an armed guard outside his door, and nobody was supposed to know he was even there," Rayfield snapped back into the telephone. "I still don't know how his brother found out."

"And his brother's some kind of war hero, I understand. Superbly trained in all forms of eluding capture. That's just great."

"It is for our purposes."

"Why don't you explain that one to me, Frank?"

"I've ordered my men to shoot to kill. They'll put a bullet into both of them as soon as they get a chance."

"What if he tells somebody first?"

"Tells them what? That he got a letter from the Army that says something he has no way to prove? Now we've got a dead Supreme Court clerk on our hands. That just makes our job a lot tougher."

"Well, we were supposed to have a dead country lawyer too, but, funny, I haven't read his obituary anywhere."

"Rider went out of town."

"Oh, good, we'll just wait until he gets back from vacation and hope he's not in discussions with the FBI."

"I don't know where he is," Rayfield said angrily.

"The Army has an intelligence component, Frank. What do you say you try to use some of it? Take care of Rider and then concentrate on finding Harms and his brother. And when you do, you put them six feet under. I hope that's clear enough for you." The phone went dead.

Rayfield slammed the receiver down and stared up at Vic Tremaine.

"This is going to hell in a handbasket."

Tremaine shrugged his shoulders. "We take Rider out and then those two black SOBs, we're home free," he said in a gravelly voice that seemed perfectly calibrated to command men to fight.

"I don't like it. We're not in a war here."

"We are at war, Frank."

"The killing never did bother you, did it, Vic?"

"All I care about is the success of my mission."

"Do you mean to tell me that right before you pulled the trigger on Fiske you didn't feel anything?"

"Mission accomplished." Tremaine put his palms down on Rayfield's desk and leaned forward. "Frank, we've been through a lot together, combat and otherwise. But let me tell you something. I've spent thirty years in the Army, the last twenty-five in various military prisons just like this one when I could've gotten a civilian job that paid a lot more. We all made a pact that was supposed to protect us from a stupid thing we did a long time ago. I've kept my end of the bargain. I've baby-sat Rufus Harms while the others went on with their lives.

"Now, in addition to my military pension, I've got over one million bucks sitting in an offshore account. In case you've forgotten, you've got the same little nest egg. That's our comp for all these years of doing this crap. And after all the shit I've been through, no one and nothing is going to keep me from enjoying that money. The best thing Rufus Harms ever did for me is escape. Because now I've got a bulletproof reason to blow his sorry ass away and nobody'll ask any questions. And as soon as that sonof-abitch has breathed his last, this uniform I'm wearing goes into mothballs. For good."

Tremaine straightened up. "And, Frank, I will destroy anyone who even remotely tries to mess that up." His eyes became black dots as he said the next word. "Anyone."

CHAPTER THIRTY-ONE

On the drive to the trailer, Fiske stopped at an all-night convenience store. Sara waited in the car. A rusty Esso sign clanked back and forth from the force of a semi sailing past and made her jump. When Fiske got back in the car, Sara stared at the two six-packs of Budweiser. "You intend to drink your sorrows away?"

He ignored the question. "Once we get down there, there's really no way for you to get back by yourself. It's really in the middle of nowhere; sometimes *I* get lost."

"I'm prepared to sleep in the car."

About thirty minutes later, Fiske slowed the car, turned into a narrow gravel drive and drove up to a small, darkened cottage. "You're supposed to check in here and pay the guest fee before going into the grounds," he explained. "I'll do it before we leave tomorrow."

He pulled the car past the cottage and into the middle of the campground. Sara looked at the trailers, which were laid out in a street grid style. Most of them were bril-

liantly outlined with Christmas lights and had flagpoles
either attached to the trailer or porch, or sunk into
concrete. With the strings of lights and the moonlight,
the area was surprisingly well illuminated. They passed
late-blooming flower beds of impatiens, and red and pink
mums. Clumpy vines of clematis gripped the sides of some
homes. Everywhere Sara looked were outdoor sculptures of
metal, marble and resin. There were a number of cinder-
block grills and a large smoke pit; the commingled smells
of cooked meat and charcoal lingered tantalizingly in the
hot, humid air.

"This place is like a little gingerbread town built by
gnomes," Sara said. She eyed the numerous flagpoles and
added, "Patriotic gnomes."

"A lot of the people are from the American Legion and
VFW crowd. My dad has one of the tallest flagpoles. He
was in the Navy in World War II. The all-year Christmas
lights became sort of a tradition a long while back."

"Did you and Michael spend much time here?"

"My dad only got a week's vacation, but Mom would
bring us down for a couple weeks at a time during the
summer. Some of the old guys taught us to sail, swim and
fish. Things Pop never had time to do. He's made up for it
since he retired."

He stopped the car in front of one trailer. It had bright
Christmas lights and was painted a soothing, muted blue.
His father's Buick, with a SUPPORT YOUR LOCAL POLICE
bumper sticker, was parked next to the trailer. Fronting
the trailer was a bed of bulky plantation hostas. Next to
the Buick was a golf cart. The flagpole in front of the
trailer went a good thirty feet into the air.

Fiske eyed the Buick. "At least he's here." Well, this is
it, John, no more reprieves, he thought.

"Is there a golf course nearby?"

Fiske glanced at her. "No, why?"

"So what's with the golf cart?"

"The owners of the trailer park buy them secondhand from golf courses. The roads are pretty narrow here and, while you can drive your car to your trailer, you can't drive it around the grounds. And the people down here are elderly, for the most part. They use the golf carts to get around."

Fiske got out of the car with the two six-packs. Sara didn't move to join him. He looked at her questioningly.

"I thought you might want to talk to your dad alone."

"After everything we've been through tonight, I think you've earned the right to see it through. I'll understand if you don't want to." He looked over at the trailer and felt his nerves slowly disintegrate. He turned back to her. "I could sort of use the company."

She nodded. "Okay, give me a minute."

She flipped down the visor mirror and checked her face and hair. She grimaced and reached for her purse, doing the best she could with lipstick and a small hairbrush. She was sweaty and sticky too, her dress clingy, her hair beyond salvation thanks to the rain and humidity. As trivial as worrying about her appearance seemed under the circumstances, she felt like such a fifth wheel that it was the only thing she could think to address.

With a sigh, she flipped the visor back up, opened the door and got out. As they headed up the wooden porch, she smoothed down her dress and fiddled some more with her hair.

Fiske noted this and said, "He's not going to care how you look. Not after I tell him."

She sighed. "I know. I guess I just didn't want to look like too much of a disaster."

Fiske took a deep breath and knocked on the door. He waited and knocked again. "Pop." He waited a moment and knocked again, louder this time. "Pop," he called out, and kept knocking.

They finally heard movement in the trailer and then a

light came on. The door opened and Fiske's father, Ed, peered out. Sara looked at him closely. He was as tall as his son, and very lean, although he had vestiges of the powerful musculature shared by both his boys. His forearms were enormous, like thick pieces of sun-baked wood. Sara was able to observe this because he had on a tank-top shirt. He was deeply tanned, his face lined and starting to sag, but she could see he had been handsome as a younger man. His hair was thinning and curly and almost totally gray except for small flecks of black at the temples. She fixed for a moment on his long sideburns, a holdover from the seventies, she guessed. He had on a pair of pants halfway zipped up, the clasp unbuttoned so that his striped boxers were clearly in sight. He was barefoot.

"Johnny? What the hell you doing here?" A broad smile cracked his face. When he registered Sara, he looked startled and quickly turned so his back was to them. They watched him fumble with his pants until they were right. Then he turned back to face them.

"Pop, I need to talk to you."

Ed Fiske glanced over at Sara again.

"I'm sorry—Sara Evans, Ed Fiske," John said.

"Hello, Mr. Fiske," she said, trying to sound both pleasant and neutral at the same time. She awkwardly held out her hand.

He shook it. "Call me Ed, Sara, pleased to meet you." He looked back at his son curiously. "So what's up? You two getting married or something?"

Fiske glanced at Sara. "No! She worked with Mike at the Supreme Court."

"Oh, well, hell, where are my manners, come on in. I got the air going, sticky as the damn devil out there."

They went inside. Ed pointed to a worn sofa and Fiske and Sara sat down there. Ed pulled a metal chair from the small dinette and sat down opposite them.

"Sorry I took so long. Just nodded off to sleep."

Sara looked around the small space. It was paneled with thin plywood stained dark. Several stuffed fish were mounted on plaques and hung on the wall. Slung across a rack on another wall was a shotgun. In the corner she saw a long, round container with one end of a rod and reel poking out. A folded newspaper was lying on the dinette table. Next to that was a small kitchen area with a sink and a little refrigerator. There was a worn-out recliner in one corner, a small TV across from it. There was one window. Mounted on the ceiling was an air conditioner that was making the room deliciously cool. She actually shivered as she adjusted to the temperature. The floor was cheap, uneven linoleum with a thin rug covering a portion of it.

Sara sniffed and then coughed. She could almost see the cigarette smoke lingering in the air. As if in response to her thoughts, Ed pulled a pack of Marlboros from a knicked-up side table and deftly popped a cigarette in his mouth, taking a moment to light up, then blew the smoke to the nicotine-coated ceiling. He grabbed a small ashtray off the same table and tapped his cigarette in it. He put his hands on his knees and leaned forward. She noted that his fingers were abnormally thick, the nails cracked, and blackened in spots from what looked like grease. He had been a mechanic, she recalled.

"So what brings you two down here so late?"

Fiske handed his father a six-pack. "Not good news."

The elder Fiske tensed, and he squinted at them through the smoke. "It's not your mom. I just saw her, she's okay." As soon as he said this, he shot a glance at Sara. The look on his face was clear: She "worked" with Mike.

He looked back at John. "Why don't you tell me whatever the hell it is you need to tell me, son."

"Mike's dead, Pop." As he finished saying it, it was as though he were hearing the news for the first time. He could feel his face grow hot as though he had leaned too

close to a fire. Perhaps he had waited to see his father, to
join his grief with his. He could believe that, couldn't he?

Fiske could sense Sara looking at him, but he kept his
gaze on his father. As he watched the devastation wash
over the man, Fiske suddenly found he could barely
breathe.

Ed took the cigarette out of his mouth and dropped the
ashtray, his fingers shaking. "How?"

"Robbery. At least they think so." Fiske paused and then
added the obvious, since he knew his father was going to
ask anyway. "Somebody shot him."

Ed tore off one of the Buds from the plastic holder and
popped the tab. He drank it down almost in one swallow,
his Adam's apple moving up and down.

Ed crushed the beer can against his leg and threw it
against the wall. He stood up and went over to the small
window and looked out, the cigarette dangling from his
mouth, his big hands closing and opening, the veins in his
forearms swelling and then diminishing.

"Have you seen him?" he asked without turning around.

"I went up to identify the body this afternoon."

His father whirled around, furious. "This afternoon?
Why the hell did you wait so long to come tell me, boy?"

Fiske stood up. "I've been trying to track you down all
day. I left messages on your answering machine. I only
knew you were here because I asked Ms. German."

"That should've been the first damn place you
started," his father countered. "Ida always knows where
I am. You know that." He took a step toward them, one
fist balled up.

Sara, who had risen along with Fiske, shrank back. She
glanced over at the shotgun and suddenly wondered if it
was loaded.

Fiske moved closer to his father. "Pop, as soon as I found
out, I called you. Then I went by your house. After that I
had to go up to the morgue. It wasn't any fun identifying

Mike's body, but I did it. And the rest of the day has been pretty much downhill from there." He swallowed hard, suddenly feeling guilty that his father's angry reaction was more painful to him than his brother's death. "Let's not argue about the timing, okay? That's not going to bring Mike back."

All the anger seemed to go out of Ed as he listened to those words. Calm, rational words that did nothing to explain or reduce the anguish he was feeling. They hadn't invented the words that could do that, or the person to deliver them. Ed sat back down, his head swinging loosely from side to side. When he looked back up, there were tears in his eyes. "I always said you never had to chase bad news, it always got to you faster than anything good. A helluva lot faster." There was a catch in his throat when he spoke. He absently crushed his cigarette out on the carpet.

"I know, Pop. I know."

"Do they got whoever did this?"

"Not yet. They're working on it. The detective in charge is first-rate. I'm sort of helping him."

"D.C.?"

"Yes."

"I never liked Mike being up there."

He glared at Sara, who completely froze in the face of that accusing look.

He pointed a thick finger at her. "People kill you for nothing up there. Crazy bastards."

"Pop, they'll do that anywhere these days."

Sara managed to find her voice. "I liked and deeply respected your son. Everyone at the Court thought he was wonderful. I'm so, so very sorry about this."

"He was wonderful," Ed said. "He damn sure was. Never figured out how we turned out such a one as Mike."

Fiske looked down at the floor. Sara picked up on the pained expression on his face.

Ed looked around the trailer's interior, memories of

good times with his family nudging him from all corners. "Got his mother's brains." His lower lip trembled for an instant. "Least the one she used to have." A low sob escaped from his mouth and he slumped to the floor.

Fiske knelt down next to his father and wrapped his arms around him, their shoulders shaking together.

Sara looked on, unsure of what to do. She was embarrassed at witnessing such a private moment, and wondered if she should just get up and flee to her car. Finally she simply looked down and closed her eyes, silently releasing her own tears onto the cheap carpet.

Thirty minutes later, Sara sat on the porch and sipped on a warm can of beer. She was barefoot, her shoes next to her. She absently rubbed her toes and stared out into a darkness that was occasionally broken by the wink of a lightning bug. She swatted at a mosquito and then swiped off a trickle of sweat that meandered down her leg. Holding the beer can to her forehead, she contemplated getting into her car, cranking up the AC and trying to fall asleep.

The door opened and Fiske appeared. He had changed into faded jeans and an untucked short-sleeved shirt. He was barefoot as well. He held a plastic package strip with two beers dangling from it. He sat down beside her.

"How is he?"

Fiske shrugged. "Sleeping, or at least trying to."

"Does he want to come back with us?"

Fiske shook his head. "He's going to come over to my place tomorrow night." He glanced at his watch and realized that dawn was not very far away. "I mean tonight. I need to stop by my apartment on the way back so I can pick up some clean clothes."

Sara looked down at her dress. "Tell me about it. Where'd you get those?"

"I left them down here from the last fishing trip."

She wiped her forehead. "God, it's so humid."

Fiske looked toward the woods. "Well, there's a cooler breeze down by the water." He led her over to the golf cart. As they drove along the quiet dirt roads, Fiske handed her a beer. "This one is cold."

She popped it open. It felt good going down, and managed to lift her spirits a little. She held the can next to her cheek.

The narrow road took them through a mass of scrub pine, holly, oak and river birch with its bark unraveling like pencil shavings. Then the land opened up and Sara could see a wooden dock with several boats tied to it. She watched as the wooden structure moved up and down with the lap of the water.

"It's a floating dock; rests on fifty-gallon drums," Fiske explained.

"I gathered. Is that a boat ramp?" she asked, pointing to a place where the road angled sharply into the water.

Fiske nodded. "The people bring their cars up another road to get here. Pop has a little motorboat. That one over there." He pointed to a white boat with red stripes that bobbed in the water. "They usually pull them out at night. He must have forgotten. He got it cheap; we spent a year fixing it up. It's no yacht, but it'll get you where you want to go."

"What river is this?"

"Do you remember on the drive down 95 seeing signs for the Matta, the Po and the Ni Rivers?" Sara nodded. "Well, up near Fort A. P. Hill, southeast of Fredericksburg, they converge and it's called the Mattaponi River." He looked out at the water. There were few things more relaxing than skimming along the water, and he could think out there. "There's a full moon, the boat has running lights and a guide beacon and I know this part of the river real well. And it's a lot cooler on the water." He looked at her questioningly.

Sara didn't hesitate. "Sounds good."

They walked out to the boat and Fiske helped her in.

"Do you know how to cast off?" he asked.

"I actually did some competitive racing when I was an undergrad at Stanford."

Fiske watched her expertly undo the knots and cast off the line. "The old Mattaponi must seem pretty dull, then."

"It's all in who you're doing it with."

She sat next to Fiske, who stuck his hand into a storage compartment next to the captain's chair and pulled out a set of keys. He started the engine and they slowly pulled away from the dock. They got out into the middle of the river and he eased the throttle forward until they were moving at a fairly decent clip. The temperature was about twenty degrees cooler on the water. Fiske kept one hand on the wheel, his beer in the other. Sara folded her legs up under her and then raised herself up so that her upper torso was above the low-slung windshield. She held her arms out from her sides and let the wind grip her.

"God, this feels wonderful."

.Fiske looked out over the water. "Mike and I would race each other across the river. It gets pretty wide at some points. Couple of times I thought one or the other of us was surely going to drown. But one thing kept us going."

"What was that?"

"We couldn't bear the thought of the other winning."

Sara sat back down and swung her chair around until she was facing him, smoothing out her hair as she did so.

"Do you mind a really personal question?"

Fiske stiffened slightly. "Probably."

"You won't take this the wrong way?"

"I will now."

"Why weren't you and Michael closer?"

"There's no law that says siblings have to be close."

"But you and Michael seemed to have so much in common. He spoke so highly of you, and you obviously were proud of him. I sense you had some differences. I'm just confused as to what went wrong."

Fiske shut the engine down and allowed the boat to drift. He cut off the beacon and the moon became their only source of light. The river was very calm, and they were at one of the widest points. Fiske pulled his pants legs up, went to the side of the boat, sat on the edge and swung his feet into the water.

Sara sat down next to him, hiked her skirt up a little and lowered her feet in.

Fiske gazed out over the river, sipping his beer.

"John, I'm really not trying to pry."

"I'm not really in the mood to talk about it, okay?"

"But—"

Fiske sliced the air with his hand. "Sara, it's not the place to do it, and it's damn sure not the time, okay?"

"Okay, I'm sorry. I just care. About all of you."

They sat there as the boat drifted along, the noise of the cicadas barely reaching them from shore.

Fiske finally stirred. "You know, Virginia's such a beautiful place. You've got water, mountains, forest, beaches, history, culture, high-tech centers and old battlefields. People move a little slower, enjoy life a little more here. I can't imagine living anywhere else. Hell, I've never been anywhere else."

"And they have really nice trailer parks," Sara said.

Fiske smiled. "That too."

"So does your segue into the travelogue mean the topic of you and your brother is officially closed?" Sara bit her tongue when she finished. Stupid mouth, she berated herself.

"Guess so." Fiske abruptly stood up. The boat rocked and Sara almost ended up in the river. Fiske's hand shot out and gripped her arm. He squeezed tightly and looked down at her. She looked up at him, her eyes as big as the moon over them, her legs splayed out and gently drifting in the water, her dress wet where the river had touched it.

"How about a swim?" she said. "To cool off?"

"I don't have any swimsuits," he said.

"My clothes are wet enough."

He pulled her up into the boat and then went over and started the engine, destroying the peace. "Okay."

"Why not swim here?"

"Current's a little too strong."

He swung the boat around and headed toward the dock. Three-quarters of the way there, he cut across and headed to the shoreline. Here the bank sloped gradually down to the water, and as they drew closer Sara could make out fifty-gallon drums floating about twenty feet apart. As they kept heading in, she could see that they were tied together by mesh rope forming a huge rectangular-shaped pool.

Fiske cut the engine near one of the drums and let the boat's momentum propel them along until he could reach out and touch the big container. Then he tied a line to a hook mounted on the drum and dropped a small anchor, actually a gallon paint bucket filled with concrete, over the side for added security.

"It's about eight feet at its deepest point inside the ropes. There's a fence of wire mesh that circles the whole area and goes all the way to the bottom. That way if the current catches you, you won't end up in the Atlantic."

When Sara started to slip out of her dress, Fiske quickly turned around.

She smiled. "John, don't be a prude. My bikini shows more than this." In her panties and bra, she dove over the side, coming up a moment later treading water.

She called out, "I'll turn *my* back, if you're too embarrassed."

"I think I'll sit this one out."

"Oh, come on, I won't bite."

"I'm a little old for skinny-dipping, Sara."

"Water's really great."

"It looks it." He still made no move to join her.

A disappointed look on her face, she finally turned and swam away from him, her arms cutting powerful strokes through the smooth surface.

As Fiske watched her, he absently ran his finger the length of the wound, touching the two circular humps of burned flesh where the bullets had entered him. He abruptly removed his hand and sat down.

The name "Harms" kept reverberating in his head. An *in forma pauperis* petition probably would have come from a prisoner, if that's what the handwritten document amounted to. He shifted in his seat and once more looked in Sara's direction. Under the moonlight he could barely make her out, in the shallow end, drifting. Whether she was looking at him or not, he couldn't tell.

He looked out over the river, his mind taking him back. There was splashing in the water, the two young men swimming for all they were worth, one pulling ahead a bit and then the other. Sometimes Mike would win, other times John. Then they would race back. Day after day, growing more tan, leaner and stronger. So much fun. No real worries, no heartaches. Swim, explore the woods, devour bologna-and-mayo sandwiches for lunch; for dinner, skewered hot dogs on straightened hangers and cooked over the coals until the meat split open. So much damn fun. Fiske looked away from the water and forced himself to concentrate.

If Harms was a prisoner, finding him would be easy. As a former police officer, Fiske knew that there were no categories of humanity better monitored than America's inmate population of nearly two million. The country might not know where all its children or homeless were, but it religiously kept track of the cons. And most of the information was on computer database now. He looked back over and saw Sara swimming toward the boat. He didn't notice the glow of a burning cigarette as someone sat on the shore and watched them.

A couple minutes later Fiske was helping Sara into the boat. She sat on the deck, breathing deeply. "I haven't swum that much in a long time."

Fiske held out a towel he had pulled from the small cabin, averting his eyes as he did so. She quickly toweled down and then slipped her dress on. When she handed him back the towel, their arms brushed. That made him look at her. She was still breathing deeply from her swim, the rise and fall of her eyelids hypnotic.

He studied her face in silence for a moment, then looked past her at something in the sky. She turned her head to look too. Pink swirls were lapping against the dark edges of the sky as dawn began to break. Everywhere they looked, the soft glow of the coming light was apparent. The trees, the leaves, the water were cast as a shimmering facade, as the boat gently rocked them.

"It's beautiful," she said in a hushed tone.

"Yes, it is," he said.

As she turned back to him, she reached up her hand, slowly at first, her eyes searching his for some reaction to what she was doing. Her fingers touched his chin, cupping it, his beard stubble rough against her skin. Her hand moved higher, tracing his cheeks, his eyes and then pressing against his hair, each touch gentle, unhurried. As she gripped the back of his neck and pulled his head toward her, she felt him flinch. Her lips trembled when she saw his glistening eyes. Sara removed her hand and stepped back.

Fiske suddenly looked out over the water, as though still seeing two young boys swimming their hearts out. He turned back to her. "My brother's dead, Sara," he said simply, his voice shaking slightly. "I'm just really messed up right now." He tried to say something else, but the words would not come.

Sara slowly walked over and sat in one of the seats. She wiped at her eyes and then self-consciously gripped the hemline of her skirt, trying to smooth it, to wring out some of the wetness. The breeze had picked up and the river bounced them. She glanced up at Fiske.

"I really did like your brother. And I'm so damned sorry that he's gone." She looked down, as though searching at her feet for the right words. "And I'm sorry for what I just did."

He looked away. "I could have said something to you before now." He glanced up at her, bewilderment on his features. "I'm not sure why I didn't."

She stood up, wrapped her arms around her shoulders. "I'm a little cold. We should go back now, shouldn't we?"

Fiske hauled up the anchor while Sara cast off, and then he fired up the motor and they headed back to the dock, each unable to look at the other, for fear of what might happen, of what their bodies might do, despite the words they had just spoken.

On the shore, the owner of the glowing cigarette had departed just as Sara had drawn close to Fiske.

CHAPTER THIRTY-TWO

Fiske and Sara docked the boat, walked in silence to the golf cart and climbed in. The footsteps made Fiske look around. "Pop? What are you doing here?"

His father didn't answer but kept coming toward them. Fiske walked to him, his arms outstretched. "Pop, you okay?"

A puzzled Sara watched from the golf cart.

The men were about a foot apart when the elder Fiske lunged forward and punched his son in the jaw.

"You bastard," Ed shouted.

Fiske fell back from the blow, as Ed pounced on his son and hammered away with both fists.

Fiske pushed himself away from his father and staggered backward, blood coming from his mouth and nose. "What the hell is wrong with you?" he screamed.

Sara was halfway out of the cart, but she froze when Ed pointed at her.

"Get that slut and your ass out of here! Get the hell out of here, you hear me?"

"Pop, what are you talking about?"

Enraged, Ed rushed his son again. This time Fiske sidestepped the charge, wrapping his arms around his father and holding tight as the older man spun wildly, trying with all his might to hit him again.

"I saw you, damn you both. Half naked, kissing, while your brother lies dead on some slab. Your brother!" He screamed the words so loudly his voice broke.

Fiske's voice cracked as he realized what his father had seen. Or thought he had seen. "Pop, nothing happened."

"You bastard." He tried to pull his son's hair, clothing, anything to get at him again. "You heartless sonofabitch," he kept screaming, his face brick red, his breathing becoming more and more labored, his movements sluggish.

"Stop it, Pop, stop it. You're gonna have a coronary."

The two men struggled fiercely as they slipped, pitched and swung around in the loose dirt and gravel.

"My own son doing that. I don't have a son. Both my sons are dead. Both my sons are dead." Ed spat out these words in a crescendo of fury.

Fiske let his father go, and the old man spun around and dropped to the ground in exhaustion. He tried to rise, but then slumped back down, his T-shirt stained with the sweat of his efforts, the merged smells of alcohol and tobacco enveloping him. Fiske stood over him, chest heaving, his blood mixed with salty tears.

A horrified Sara stepped out of the cart, knelt down next to Ed and put a hand gently on his shoulder. She didn't know what to say.

Ed swung his arms around blindly and struck Sara on the thigh.

She gasped in pain.

"Get the hell out of here. Both of you. *Now!*" Ed screamed.

Fiske gripped Sara's arm and pulled her up. "Let's go, Sara." He looked at his father. "Dad, take the cart back." As they entered the forest, Fiske and Sara could still hear the screams of the old man.

Her leg aching, her tears half blinding her, Sara said, "Oh, my God, John, this is all my fault."

Fiske didn't answer. His insides were on fire. The pain had never been this bad, and he was scared. The dispassionate warnings of scores of doctors engulfed him. He kept walking faster and faster, until Sara had to half trot to keep up.

"John, John, please say something."

She reached over to wipe some blood from his chin, but he quickly pushed her hand away. Then, without warning, he started to run.

"John!" Sara started to run too, but she had never seen anyone accelerate as Fiske had. "John," she screamed, "please come back. Stop! Please!"

In the next moment, he had rounded a bend in the forest path and disappeared completely from her sight.

She slowed down, her own chest burning now. Then she stepped on a loose clod of dirt and fell heavily to the ground amid the scattered pine needles. She sat there sobbing, her thigh already bruised and aching from where Ed had hit her.

A minute later she started as a hand touched her shoulder. Terrified, she looked up, certain that Ed had come to beat her too, for blackening the memory of his dead son.

Fiske was breathing hard, his T-shirt soaked in sweat, the blood already hardened on his face. "Are you okay?"

She nodded and stood up, gritting her teeth as the pain in her leg increased. If Ed's blind swipe at her leg had caused so much hurt, she could hardly imagine what John was feeling, after taking a direct blow to the face. She balanced against him while he bent down, edged her skirt up and examined her thigh.

Fiske shook his head. "It's bruised pretty good. He didn't know what he was doing. I'm sorry."

"I deserved it."

With Fiske's help she was able to walk pretty normally. "I'm sorry, John," she said. "This . . . this is a nightmare."

As they neared the trailer, she heard him say something. At first she thought he was talking to her, but he wasn't.

He said it again, in a low voice, his eyes straight ahead, his head slowly turning in disbelief. "I'm sorry."

The apology was not directed toward her, she instinctively knew. Perhaps to the screaming man back at the dock. And maybe to the dead brother?

When they reached the trailer, Sara sat down on the steps while Fiske went inside. He came back out a minute later with some ice and a roll of paper towels. While she held the ice wrapped in a paper towel against her bruised thigh, she used one of the ice cubes and another paper towel to wipe the blood from his face and clean the cut on his lip. After she had finished, he stood, went down the steps and headed down the dirt road.

"Where are you going?" she asked.

"To get my father," he said without turning around.

She watched until he disappeared into the forest. While he was gone, Sara limped into the trailer and cleaned herself up in the small bathroom. She spotted Fiske's suit and shoes and carried them out to her car. She ran her hand along the smooth metal surface of the flagpole and wondered if Ed would manage to raise the Stars and Stripes today. Maybe he would, at half-mast, in memory of his son. Perhaps mourning *both* sons?

She began trembling with that thought, moved away from the flagpole and leaned up against her car. She

scanned the woods nervously as though anticipating the
abrupt charge of all sorts of terror from its underbelly.

An elderly woman came out of the trailer next door and
stopped when she saw Sara.

Sara smiled in an embarrassed fashion. "I'm, uh, a friend
of John Fiske's."

The woman nodded. "Well, good morning."

"Good morning to you too."

The woman disappeared down the road toward the
cottage.

Sara looked anxiously back toward the woods, clutching
her hands together. "Come on, John. Please, come on."

Fifteen minutes later the golf cart came into view. Fiske
was driving. His father was slumped in the rear, apparently asleep.

Fiske pulled up to the trailer, got out, carefully lifted his
father and put him over his shoulder. He marched up the
steps and disappeared inside. He came out a few minutes
later carrying the shotgun.

"He's asleep," Fiske said.

"What's that for?" Sara pointed at the weapon.

"I'm not leaving it here with him."

"You don't think he'd shoot anybody."

"No, but I don't want him sticking it in his mouth and
pulling the trigger either. Guns, alcohol and bad news
don't mix real well." He put the shotgun in the back seat
of the car. "You'd better let me drive."

"Your clothes are in the trunk."

They climbed in the car and a minute later were back at
the owner's cottage. Fiske went in and slapped four singles
down for the guest fee. He bought some pastries and a
couple cartons of orange juice.

The woman who had greeted Sara was also there. "I saw
your lady friend, John. Real cute girl."

"Uh-huh."

"You leaving already?"

"Yep."

"I'll bet your daddy wishes you were staying longer."

Fiske paid for the food and didn't wait for a bag. "I'll take that bet," he told the puzzled woman, before heading back out to the car.

CHAPTER THIRTY-THREE

Samuel Rider arrived at his office early after being away a few days for business. Sheila hadn't come in yet. It was just as well, since Rider wanted to be alone. He picked up his phone and called Fort Jackson, identified himself as Harms's attorney and asked to speak with him.

"He's no longer here."

"Excuse me? He's serving a life sentence. Where exactly could he have gone?"

"I'm sorry, but I'm not allowed to give out that information over the phone. If you would like to come down in person or make an official inquiry in writing—"

Rider slammed down the phone and collapsed in his chair. Was Rufus dead? Had they somehow discovered what he was up to? Once Rider had filed the appeal with the Supreme Court, Rufus should have had instant security.

Rider clamped his fingers around the edge of his desk. *If* it had reached the Court. He tore open his desk drawer and pulled out the white receipt with the tracking number on it. The green receipt should have come back to his office. Sheila! He jumped up and raced to Sheila's work area. Normally, any return receipts would be included in the appropriate case file. However, there was no case file for Rufus Harms. What could she have done with the damn receipt?

As if in answer to his thoughts, the woman herself walked in the door. She was surprised to see him.

"Why, you're in awful early, Mr. Rider."

Rider assumed a casual tone. "Trying to catch up on a few things." He edged away from her desk; however, she had picked up on his intentions.

"Are you looking for something?"

"Well, now that you mention it, I was, actually. I had sent a letter out and, you know, I had sent it return receipt requested, and then it occurred to me that I hadn't told you anything about it. Stupid of me."

Her next words brought an inward sigh of relief.

"So that's what that was. At first I thought I had forgotten to open a case file. I was meaning to ask you about it when you got back."

"So you got it back, then," Rider said, trying to veil his eagerness.

Sheila opened a drawer of her desk and pulled out a green receipt. "The United States Supreme Court," she said with awe, passing it over to him. "I remember thinking, are we going to be doing something with them or what?"

Rider put on his best lawyer's face. "Naw, Sheila, just something to do with a bar function. We don't need to look to Washington for our daily bread."

"Oh, here are your phone messages that came in while you were out of town. I tried to prioritize them for you."

He gave her hand a nice squeeze. "You're the essence of efficiency," he said gallantly.

She smiled and started to fuss at her desk.

Rider went back to his office, closed the door and looked down at the receipt. The filing had been delivered. The signature was right there. But then where was Rufus?

Rider planned to spend much of the morning in meetings discussing the possible development of a shopping mall on a vast tract of land that had been used since the forties as an auto wrecking yard. One of the men he was meeting with had flown a prop plane into Blacksburg, Virginia, from Washington early that morning and was driving over to Rider's office. With everything on his mind it was all Rider could do to act normal when the man arrived at his office a while later. The man had brought with him a copy of the morning's *Washington Post.* While the man accepted a cup of coffee from Sheila, Rider idly ran his eye over the *Post*'s headlines. One in particular caught his attention. The man noticed what Rider was doing.

"Damn shame," he said, nodding at the story Rider was focused on. "One of the best and brightest," he said as Rider silently mouthed the headline again: SUPREME COURT CLERK SLAIN.

"Did you know him?" Rider asked. It couldn't be connected. There was no way in hell.

"No. But if he was clerking up there, you know he had to be top of the top. Murdered too. Shows you how dangerous times have become. Nobody's safe anymore."

Rider stared at him for a moment, and then looked down at the paper and the accompanying photo. Michael Fiske, age thirty. He had earned a Ph.D. from Columbia University and then gone on to the University of Virginia Law School, where he had been editor-in-chief of the *Law Review.* He was the senior law clerk for Justice Thomas Murphy. No suspects, no clues, other than a missing wallet. *Nobody's safe anymore.* He tightly gripped the paper as he stared at the grainy, depressing photo of the dead man. It couldn't be. However, there was one way to find out.

He excused himself and slipped into his office, where he called the Supreme Court clerks' office.

"We have no case with the name Harms, sir, either on the regular or IFP docket."

"But I've got a return receipt that shows it was delivered to you people." The voice on the other end again delivered the perfunctory message.

"Don't you have some way of keeping track of your mail up there?" The polite answer Rider received did not sit well with him. He yelled into the phone. "Rufus Harms is rotting in the damn stockade and you people can't keep track of your mail." He threw down the phone.

Somewhere between its arrival and the point where a case was actually placed in the official system, Rufus Harms's filing had apparently disappeared. And so had Rufus Harms. Rider suddenly felt chilled.

Rider looked down once more at the newspaper. And a Supreme Court clerk had been murdered. It all seemed so far-fetched, but then so had the story Rufus told him. Then another thought hit him even harder: If they had killed Rufus and the clerk, they surely wouldn't stop there. If they had what Rider had filed with the Court, then they would know that Rider had played a role in all of it. That meant he could be next on their hit list.

But come on, he told himself, you're just being paranoid. And that's when it finally dawned on him. The sheaf of phone messages that Sheila had collected while he had been away. He had idly skimmed through them, returning the ones he felt were most important. The name, the damn name.

He clawed through his desk until he found the pink pieces of paper. His hands flew through them, scanning, scanning, finally ripping the pile apart in his rising anxiety, until he found it. He looked down at the name, the blood slowly draining from his face. Michael Fiske had called him. Twice.

Oh, my God. In an avalanche of thought, visions of his wife, the condo in Florida, his grown children, all the years of billable hours, flew through his mind. Well, damn if he was waiting around for them to come get him. He punched his intercom and told Sheila he wasn't feeling well, to convey that to his visitor and the other gentlemen who would shortly arrive, and accommodate them any way she could.

"I won't be back today," he told her as he hurried through the reception area. I hope I will someday. And not in a coffin, he added silently.

"All right, Mr. Rider, you take care."

He almost laughed at her remark. He had phoned his house before leaving the office, but his wife wasn't in. As he drove along, he had already made up his mind what he was going to do. The two had kicked around the idea of taking a late fall vacation, maybe down to the islands, one last dose of sun and water before the ice set in. Only they might stay awhile. He'd prefer to pour his savings into staying alive than into securing the view of a Florida sunset he might never get a chance to see.

They could drive to Roanoke, hop a commuter flight and take it into Washington or Richmond. From there they could go anywhere. He would explain it to his wife by saying he was just being spontaneous, something she had said he never was and never could be. Good old steady, reliable Sam Rider. Did nothing more with his life than work hard, pay his bills, raise his kids, love his wife and try to catch a few strands of happiness along the way. Lord, I'm already writing my obituary, he realized.

He wouldn't be in a position to help Rufus, but he figured the man was probably dead anyway. I'm sorry, Rufus, he thought. But you're in a much better place, far better than the one those bastards saddled you with on this earth.

A sudden thought made him almost turn the car around. He had left the copies of the filing he had made for Rufus back at the office. Should he go back? He finally decided that his life was worth more than a few pieces of paper. What could he do with them now anyway?

He concentrated on the road. There wasn't much between his office and his home except windy roads, birds and the occasional deer or black bear. The isolation had never bothered Rider until now. At this moment, it terrified him. He had a shotgun at home that he used for quail hunting. He wished he had it with him.

He rounded an elbow-shaped bend in the road, a rusted guardrail the only thing standing between him and a five-hundred-foot drop. As he tapped his brakes to slow down, his breath caught in his throat. His brakes. Oh, my God, I've lost my brakes! He started to scream. But then the brakes held. Don't let your senses run away from you, Sam, he cautioned himself. A few minutes later he turned the last corner and saw his mailbox. A minute after that he pulled the car into his garage. His wife's car was next to his.

As he passed by her car, he glanced at the front seat. His feet seemed to sink right into the concrete floor. His wife was lying facedown in the front seat. Even from where he was standing, Rider could see the blood pouring from the head wound. That was the next to last memory Rider would have. The hand came around and clamped across his face a large cloth that had a sickening medicinal odor. Another hand slipped something into Rider's hand. As the lawyer looked down with eyes that were already beginning to close, he saw and felt the still-warm pistol as his fingers were wrapped around it by a pair of latex-gloved hands. It was Rider's pistol, one he used for target shooting. The one he now also knew had been used to kill his wife. From the heat left in the metal, they must have done it as soon as he turned into the driveway. They must have been watching for him. He arched his head and stared into the cold, clear eyes of Victor Tremaine as his face was thrust deeper and deeper into the clutches of unconsciousness. This man had killed her, but Rider would be blamed for it. Not that it would matter much to him. He was dead too. As he finished this thought, Samuel Rider's eyes closed for the last time.

CHAPTER THIRTY-FOUR

Driving down the George Washington Parkway south of Old Town Alexandria, Fiske glimpsed a bike rider as he flitted, phantomlike, among the line of trees that ran along the asphalt bike path paralleling the river. Fiske nudged Sara awake and she told him where to turn off the parkway. She glanced quickly at him. The encounter with his father had not been mentioned on the drive back. It was as though they had silently agreed not to discuss it.

With Sara directing, Fiske pulled down another blacktop road, and then turned right onto a gravel lane that ran steeply down toward the water. He stopped the car in front of the small, wood-framed cottage, which stood there prim and dour among the untidy backdrop of tree, bramble and wildflower, like the preacher's wife at a church picnic turned rowdy. The clapboard was layered with fifty years' worth of white paint; the structure also had black shutters, and a wide brick chimney the color of terra-cotta. Fiske watched as a squirrel sprinted across the phone line, leaped to the roof and corkscrewed up the chimney.

Anchoring one corner of the property was a crape myrtle in full bloom, its bark the texture and color of deerskin. Wedged against the other side of the cottage was a twenty-foot holly, red berries peeping out, ornamentlike, from among the dark green leaves. In between was a hedge of burning bush, the ground underneath it sprinkled with cardinal-red leaves. Behind the house Fiske noted the stairway angling down to the water. From there he thought he saw the bob of a sail mast. From the back seat, he grabbed the clean clothes he had gotten from his apartment. They got out of the car.

"Nice place," he commented.

Sara stretched and yawned deeply. "When I got the clerkship at the Court, I flew in to look at housing. I thought I'd just rent at first, but found this place and fell in love with it. So I went down to North Carolina, sold the farm, and bought this."

"Must have been hard selling the homestead."

Sara shook her head. "The two reasons it was important to me were dead. All that was left was a bunch of dirt that I couldn't do anything with."

Still stretching, she headed to the house. "I'll get the coffee going." She looked at her watch and moaned. "I'm going to be late for oral argument. I should call in, but I'm afraid to."

"I'm sure they'll understand, given the circumstances."

"You'd think so, wouldn't you," she said doubtfully.

Fiske hesitated. "Do you have a map around here?"

"What kind?"

"Eastern half of the United States."

She thought a moment. "Check the glove compartment."

He did so and pulled out the map. As they went into the house she asked, "What are you looking for?"

"I've been thinking about the eight hundred miles that were on Mike's car."

"You want to see what's eight hundred miles from here?"

"No, four hundred." Sara looked puzzled. "Four hundred miles out, but he, or someone else, had to drive back to D.C."

"Although it could be a number of smaller trips, a hundred miles here and there."

Fiske shook his head. "Human remains inside a trunk on a hot day aren't real pleasant to be around. I've found a couple that way," he added grimly.

While she fixed coffee in the kitchen, Fiske looked out the window that faced the river. From this vantage point he could now see the pressure-treated lumber dock and the sailboat tied up to it.

"You get to sail much?"

"Black or cream?"

"Black."

She got out two cups. "Not as much as I used to. Where I lived in North Carolina was pretty landlocked. Some fishing with my dad, swimming at a pond a few miles down the road. But out at Stanford, I really got into it. You never know how big something can be until you see the Pacific Ocean. It dwarfs everything else I've ever experienced."

"Never been there."

"Let me know if you ever decide to. I could show you around." She wiped the hair out of her eyes, poured his coffee and handed him his cup.

"I'll put that on my list," he said dryly.

"I've only got one bathroom, so we'll have to take turns showering."

"You go first. I want to check out this map."

"If I'm not down in twenty minutes, pound on the door; I'll probably have fallen asleep in the shower."

Fiske was looking at the map, sipping his coffee, and didn't comment. Sara paused on the stairs.

"John?" He looked up. "I hope you can forgive me for last night." She stopped, as though mulling over what she had just said. "The problem is, I don't think I deserve to be forgiven."

Fiske put his cup down and stared at her. The sunlight poured through the window at a graceful angle, falling full upon her face, accentuating the sparkle of her eyes, the sensual margins of her lips. Her hair was limp from the river water, sweat and sleeping on it. The little makeup she wore had long since lost its life, staining her eyelids and cheeks, her entire body pushed to the point of exhaustion. This woman had been the source of a major, perhaps cataclysmic rift between him and his father, a man he worshiped. And yet Fiske had to fight the impulse to slip off her clothes and lie down next to her right there on the floor.

"Everybody deserves to be forgiven," he finally said, and then looked back at the map.

While Sara was showering, Fiske went into a room off the kitchen. She obviously used it as a home office of sorts, since it had a desk, computer, bookshelf full of law books and a printer. He spread the map out on the desk. He found the scale at the bottom, converting inches into miles, and rummaged around in the desk drawer until he found a ruler. Using Washington as the epicenter, he drew lines outward in north, west and southerly directions and then drew a line attaching the end points. He ignored the east, since four hundred miles out would put him well into the Atlantic. He made a list of the various states within this rough circumference, picked up the phone and called directory assistance. Within a minute he was on the phone with someone from the Federal Bureau of Prisons. He gave the name Harms to the person on the other end, along with the geographic radius he might be within. It had occurred to Fiske that his brother may have gone to visit Harms in prison. The call his brother had made to him seeking some advice would then make sense. John Fiske knew a lot more about prisons than his younger brother did.

When the bureau representative came back on the line with the results, Fiske's face sagged. "You sure there's no prisoner with that last name in any federal prison in the geographic area I gave you?"

"I even went out an extra couple hundred miles."

"Well, how about state prisons, then?"

"I can give you the phone numbers for each state. You'll have to contact them separately. Do you know which ones are in that area?"

Fiske looked at the map and rattled them off. There were over a dozen. Fiske wrote down the telephone numbers he was given and hung up.

He thought for a moment and then decided to check messages at his home and office. One was from an insurance agent. Fiske returned the call to the agent, who was located in the D.C. metropolitan area.

"I was very sorry to read about your brother's death, Mr. Fiske," the woman said.

"I didn't know my brother had any life insurance."

"Sometimes the beneficiaries aren't aware. In fact, it's not the insurance company's obligation to notify the beneficiaries even if we're aware of the insured's death. Bluntly speaking, insurers don't go out of their way to pay out claims."

"So why did you call me?"

"Because I was horrified by Michael's death."

"When did he take the policy out?"

"About six months ago."

"He had no wife or kids. Why did he need insurance?"

"Well, it's why I called you. He said he wanted you to have the money in case anything happened to him."

Fiske felt a catch in his throat and he held the phone away for a moment. "Our parents could use the money a lot more than me," he finally managed to say.

"He told me you'd probably give the money to them, but he wanted you to use some of it for yourself. And he thought you'd know better than your parents how to deal with it."

"I see. Well, how much money are we talking about?"

"A half million dollars." She read his address to him to confirm that it was still accurate. "For what it's worth, I write a lot of policies for people, for a lot of different reasons, not all of them good, but in case you didn't realize it, your brother loved you very much. I wished I was as close to my brother."

As Fiske hung up the phone, he realized that he was not on the verge of tears. He was on the verge of putting his fist through a wall.

He got up, put the list in his pocket and went outside, down the stairway, past the vertical rise of cattail on one side, the sprawl of fern on the other, his feet taking him to the small dock. The sky was deep blue, with dabs of cloud, the breeze encouraging, the humidity vanished for now. He looked to the north, to the four-story reach of the million-dollar town houses on the outer ring of the Old Town Alexandria area, and then at the long, serpentine shape of the Woodrow Wilson Bridge. Across the water he made out the Maryland shore, a tree-lined mirror image of the Virginia side. A jet powered by, its landing gear down as it headed into National Airport a few miles distant. The fuselage was so close to the earth that Fiske almost could have hit it with a rock.

As the plane passed by and the silence returned, he stepped onto the bow of the sailboat. The craft gently swayed under him; the sunlight stroked his face. He sat down and put his head against the mast, sniffed the canvas of the unfurled sail and closed his eyes. He was so damn tired.

"You look awfully comfortable."

Startled awake, Fiske looked around before turning and seeing Sara standing there. She wore a black two-piece business suit; a white silk blouse peeked out at the neckline. Her neck was encircled with a small strand of pearls, her hair tied in a simple bun, a touch of makeup and pale red lipstick tinting her face.

She smiled. "I'm sorry I had to wake you. You were sleeping so peacefully."

"Have you been watching me long?" Fiske asked, and then wondered why he had.

"Long enough. You can take your shower now."

He stood up and stepped back from the dock. "Nice boat."

"I'm lucky, the riverbank drops off steeply here. I don't have to keep it at one of the marinas. I'll take you out if you want. We have time left before it has to be winterized."

"Maybe."

He walked past her toward the cottage.

"John?" He turned back. She put one hand on the stair rail and looked over at her sailboat, as though hoping to carve a wedge of calm from its tranquil frame.

"If it's the last thing I ever do, I will make it right with your father," she said.

"It's my problem. You don't have to do that."

"Yes, John, I do," she said firmly.

Thirty minutes later, Fiske drove the car out onto the private road leading to the parkway. The two black sedans flashing in front of their car made Fiske slam on the brakes. Sara screamed. Fiske jumped out of the car. He stopped as soon as he saw the guns pointed at him.

"Hands in the air," one of the men barked.

Fiske immediately put his hands up.

Sara climbed out of the car in time to see Perkins emerge from one vehicle and Agent McKenna from the other.

Perkins spotted Sara. "Holster your weapons," he said to the two men in suits.

McKenna's voice boomed out. "Those men are under my command, not yours. They will holster their weapons upon my order only." McKenna stopped directly in front of Fiske.

"Are you all right, Sara?" Perkins asked.

"Of course I'm all right. What the hell is going on?"

"I left an urgent message with you."

"I didn't check my messages. What's wrong?"

McKenna's eye caught the shotgun lying in the back seat. Now he pulled his own weapon and pointed it directly at Fiske. He studied Fiske's injured face. "Is this man holding you against your will?" McKenna asked Sara.

"Will you stop with the dramatic crap?" said Fiske. He lowered his hands and caught a sucker punch in the gut from McKenna. Fiske dropped to his knees, gasping. Sara raced to him, helping him lean back against the car tire.

"Keep your hands up until the lady answers the question." McKenna reached down and jerked Fiske's hands up in the air. "Keep your damn hands up."

Sara screamed, "No, for God's sake, he's not holding me. Stop it. Leave him alone!" She pushed McKenna's hand away.

Perkins stepped forward. "Agent McKenna—" he began, but McKenna cut him off with a cold stare.

"He's got a shotgun in the car," McKenna said. "You want to take a chance with your men, fine. I don't operate that way."

Another sedan pulled up and Chandler and two un'formed Virginia police officers climbed out, guns drawn.

"Everybody freeze!" Chandler boomed out.

McKenna looked around. "Tell your men to put away their weapons, Chandler. I've got the situation under control."

Chandler walked right up to McKenna. "Tell your men to holster their weapons right now, McKenna. Right now or I'll have these officers arrest you on the spot for assault and battery." McKenna didn't move. Chandler leaned directly in his face. "Right now, Special Agent Warren McKenna, or you'll be calling the Bureau's legal counsel from a Virginia lockup. You really want that in your record?"

Finally, the man flinched. "Holster your weapons," McKenna ordered his men.

"Now move the hell away from him," Chandler ordered.

McKenna very slowly edged away from the fallen Fiske, his eyes burning into Chandler's with every backward step.

Chandler knelt down and gripped Fiske's shoulder. "John, you okay?"

Fiske nodded painfully, his eyes on McKenna.

"Will someone please tell us what is going on?" Sara cried out.

"Steven Wright was found murdered," Chandler said.

CHAPTER THIRTY-FIVE

The shack rested in the center of a heavy forest in a remote part of southwestern Pennsylvania, where it notched into West Virginia. A muddy, tire-gouged strip of dirt was the only way in or out. Josh came in the front door, his 9mm poking out of his waistband, red clay and pine needles sticking to his boots. The truck was parked under a leafy shield of a soaring walnut tree, but Josh had taken the added precaution of covering the vehicle with camouflage netting. His biggest worry was being spotted from overhead. Luckily, the nights were still warm. He couldn't risk building a fire; you couldn't control where smoke went.

Rufus sat on the floor, his broad back resting against the wall, his Bible in his lap. He was drinking a soda, the remains of his lunch beside him. He had changed into some clothes that his brother had brought him.

"Everything okay?"

"Just us and the squirrels. How you feeling?"

"Happy as hell and scared as the devil." Rufus shook his head and smiled. "Feels good to be free, sitting here drinking a Coke, not having to worry about somebody trying to get the jump on me every second of my life."

"The guards or the other cons?"

"What do you think?"

"I think both. I was on the inside for a while too, you know. We could probably write us a book."

"How long we gonna stay here?"

"A couple of days. Let things die down a little. Then we'll head on, make our way down to Mexico. Live good on a tenth of what it takes up here. Went a few times after the war. Got some old Army buddies who live there. They'll help us get in and then set us up. Find us a boat, do some fishing, live on the beach. That sound good to you?"

"Living in the sewer would sound good to me." Rufus stood up. "Got a question for you."

His brother leaned against the wall and started carving up an apple with his pocketknife. "I'm listening."

"Your truck was full of groceries, two rifles and that pistol you're carrying. And the clothes I'm wearing."

"So?"

"So you just happen to be carrying all that stuff when you come visit me?"

Josh swallowed a slice of apple. "I got to eat. That means I got to go to the store, now, don't it?"

"Yeah, but you didn't buy nothing that'd go bad, no milk or eggs, stuff like that. All cans and boxes."

"I ate out of a can in the Army. I guess I just fell in love with meals ready to eat."

"And you always carry all them guns with you?"

"Maybe I'm still screwed up from Nam, got some syndrome or other."

Rufus tugged at his shirt, which was the size of a blanket. "My size don't exactly come off the rack. You came ready to bust me out, didn't you, Josh?"

Josh finished working on his apple and then threw the core out the open window. He wiped the apple juice from his hands onto his jeans before facing his brother.

"Look, Rufus, I never knew why you killed that little girl. But I knew you weren't right in the head when you done it. When I got that letter from the Army it crossed my mind there was something there. Now, I didn't know it was some cover for what they done to you. But the fact is, nowadays, people go crazy and do bad shit, they stick 'em in the nuthouse, and when they're better, they just let 'em go. You been in prison for twenty-five years for something I know for a fact you didn't even mean to do. Let's just say I took it on myself to say that was long enough. You served your time, you know, 'paid your debt to society' crap. It was time for you to get out, and I was gonna bring the key. If you hadn't wanted to come, I was going to make you change your way of thinking. Call me right or wrong, I don't give a damn. It's what I made up my mind to do."

The two brothers looked at each other for at least a minute without speaking.

"You a good brother, Josh."

"You damn right I am."

Rufus sat on the floor again and picked up the Bible, his hands gently turning the pages until he found the part he wanted. Josh eyed him.

"You still reading that stuff after all this time?"

Rufus looked up at him. "Gonna read it all my life."

Josh snorted. "You do what you want with your time, but wasting it ain't such a good idea if you ask me."

Rufus eyed him stonily. "The word of the Lord kept me alive all these years. That ain't no waste of time."

Josh shook his head, looked out the window and then back at Rufus. He touched the grip of his pistol. "This is

God. Or a knife, or a stick of dynamite, or a don't-piss-on-me attitude. Not some holy book full of people killing each other, men taking other men's women, just about every sin you can think of—"

"Sins of man, not God."

"God ain't the one busted you out. I did."

"God sent you to me, Josh. His will is everywhere."

"So you're saying God made me come get you?"

"Why did you come?"

"I told you. Get you out."

" 'Cause you love me?"

Josh appeared a little startled. "Yes," he said.

"That's the will of God, Josh. You love me, you help me. That's God's way of working."

Josh shook his head and looked away. Rufus went back to his reading.

A squawking sound came from Josh's portable police scanner, which he had set on the floor along with his radio. Josh had managed to tune in a radio station from southwest Virginia for any local news on Rufus's escape.

"Heard your name on the police band anymore?" Josh asked.

Rufus Harms had been mentioned in the news the day before. All the military authorities would say was that Harms was a convicted murderer who had a history of violence inside prison. He had escaped with the help of his brother, a dangerous man in his own right. The standard lingo was used, namely that both men were believed to be armed and dangerous. Translation: No one should be surprised or ask any questions when the authorities dragged their corpses in.

"A little," Rufus replied. "They're looking south, like you thought."

Just then the afternoon news came on the radio. The first two news stories meant nothing to either brother. The third news story was a late-breaking one and it made both brothers stare at the radio. Josh hustled over and turned up the sound. The story only lasted about a minute and when it was over Josh turned the radio off. "Rider and his wife," he said.

"Made it look like he killed her and then turned the gun on himself," Rufus added, his head shaking slowly in disbelief. "Two men come to see me and now they're both dead."

Josh stared over at his brother. He knew exactly what he was thinking. "Rufus, you can't bring him back, you can't bring none of them back."

"It's my fault they're dead. For trying to help me. And Rider's wife, she didn't know nothing about any of this."

"You didn't ask that Fiske boy to come down to the prison."

"But I asked Samuel. He'd be alive except for me."

"He owed you, Rufus. Why you think he came on down in the first place? He felt guilty. He knew he didn't fight hard for you back then. He was trying to make up for that."

"He's still dead, ain't he? Because of me."

"Supposing that's true, you can't do nothing about it."

Rufus looked over at him. "I can make sure they didn't die for nothing. Them folks took most of my life away. And now they took these other peoples' lives. You say we'll be okay in Mexico, but they ain't never gonna stop looking for us. Vic Tremaine is crazy as hell. Just have to look in the man's eyes to see that. Old Vic been trying to get me all these years. Probably think he's got his chance now. Fill us both up with lead."

"The Army catches up with us before the police do, they'll damn sure keep firing till their mags are empty," Josh agreed. He pulled out his Pall Malls and lit up, blowing smoke across the room. "Well, I can shoot straight too. They'll know they been in a damn fight if they don't know nothing else."

Rufus shook his head stubbornly. "Nobody should be able to get away with what they done."

Josh flicked cigarette ash to the floor and stared at him. "Well, exactly what are you gonna do? March in to the police and say, 'Listen up, boys, I got some story to tell. Now y'all come on help a brother put these big-important white folk away'?" Josh took the cigarette out of his mouth and spit on the dirt floor. "Shit, Rufus."

"I need to get me that letter from the Army."

"Where'd you leave it?"

"I hid it back in my cell."

"Well, we ain't going back to the prison. You try to do that, I'll shoot you myself."

"I ain't going back to Fort Jackson."

"What, then?"

"Samuel was a lawyer. Lawyers make copies of things."

Josh arched his eyebrows. "You wanta go to Rider's office?"

"We got to, Josh."

Josh smoked his Pall Mall down to the filter before answering. "*I* ain't got to do nothing, Rufus. The whole damn United States Army is out looking for your ass. And mine too. You can't exactly melt into the crowd. Hell, you'd make George Foreman look like a damn sissy."

"We still got to do it, Josh. Least I got to do it. If I can get that letter, then maybe I can get it to somebody who can help. Maybe write another letter to the Court."

"Yeah, look at all the good it done you last time. Them big-ass judges just come running to help you, didn't they?"

"It don't matter if you don't want to come, Josh. But I got to do it."

"What about Mexico? Damn, Rufus, you free. For now. We try poking around this thing, they gonna take you back to prison or most likely shoot you down first. We got to go while we got the chance, man."

"I want to be free. But I can't leave it like this. I go to Mexico now and I'll die of guilt, if the Lord don't strike me down before then."

"Guilt? You done twenty-five years for nothing. When you die you going to heaven and you gonna be sitting in God's lap. You a lock for that."

"No good, Josh. You ain't changing my mind."

Josh spit again and looked out the dirty, cracked window. "You sonofabitchin' crazy. Prison's screwed you for good. Damn!"

"Maybe I am crazy."

Josh glared at him. "Where the hell is Rider's office?"

"About thirty minutes outside Blacksburg. That's all I know. Shouldn't be hard to find out where it is exactly."

"Probably crawling with cops."

"Maybe not, if they think Samuel done it all."

"Shit." Josh violently kicked the wall and then turned to his brother. "Okay, we'll wait until nightfall and then head on out."

"Thanks, Josh."

"Don't thank me for helping us both get killed. That kind of thanks I surely don't want."

CHAPTER THIRTY-SIX

The flag at the United States Supreme Court was flying at half-mast. Newspaper, TV and radio reports nationwide were filled with accounts of the two murdered clerks. The phones in the Court's Public Information Office refused to stop ringing. The adjoining press room was standing room only. Major TV and radio networks were broadcasting live from booths on the ground floor of the Court. Supreme Court police, reinforced by fifty D.C. police officers, National Guardsmen and FBI agents, ringed the Court's perimeter.

The private hallways outside the justices' chambers were filled with clusters of people nervously talking. Most of the justices were secluded inside their chambers, having barely made it through the oral argument sessions, their minds far from the advocates and issues before them. The young faces of the law clerks too bore the terror inspired by the killings.

The small first-floor room normally used for the

justices' conferences was filled. The walls were dark-paneled and lined with bookshelves containing the bound volumes of two hundred years of the Court's decisions. Another wall held a fireplace, unlit on this very warm day. A grand chandelier hung overhead. Ramsey sat at the head of the table. Justices Knight and Murphy sat in their regular chairs.

While Knight's gaze darted around the table, Murphy, fiddling with an old pocket watch strung on a chain across his puffy middle, kept his eyes downcast. Also present were Chandler, Fiske, Perkins, Ron Klaus, and McKenna. Fiske and McKenna occasionally made eye contact, but Fiske had kept his temper under control.

Wright had been found in a park a half dozen blocks from his Capitol Hills apartment, with a single gunshot wound to the head. His wallet, like Michael Fiske's, was missing. Robbery was the superficial motive, although no one in the room believed the answer could be that simple. Preliminary indications were that Wright had been killed between midnight and two in the morning.

On the ride over to the Court, Chandler had filled Fiske in on recent developments. He had had Michael Fiske's autopsy expedited, although he was still awaiting the official report and the exact time of death. The cause of Michael Fiske's death, however, had definitely been a single gunshot to the head. Chandler had tracked down the northern Virginia Wal-Mart where Fiske had had his car serviced, but no one there could give them any useful information.

Fiske had had one thought that prompted him and Chandler to make a short detour on the way to the Court: They had returned to the car impoundment lot to have another look at Michael's Honda. Fiske had looked in the back pockets of the front seat.

"He kept a map in here, always did. He had this weird fear of getting lost. Had to plot out his whole trip before he set foot on the road. There's no map here, but there is this." He held up a couple of yellow Post-its that he had found wadded up at the bottom of the seat pocket. There was writing on them, names of interstates and roads—directions, given the faded condition of the ink, from some trip taken long ago.

Chandler looked at the pieces of yellow paper. "So why take the map book?"

"He would've had the directions to wherever he was going in there."

"So the miles had something to do with his death."

Fiske hesitated for a moment, debating whether to tell Chandler about the Harms filing. Revealing that information would open a can of worms that he didn't want to deal with right now. "Maybe," he finally said.

After that, he and Chandler had driven to the Court.

Now they were all in the conference room staring at each other. Without disclosing how he had come by the information, Chandler had just reported that there had been an intruder at Michael Fiske's apartment the night before.

"We're in your hands, Detective Chandler," Ramsey said. "Although now I think it much more likely that we have some madman at work with a grudge against the Court, rather than it pertaining to some matter Michael was working on."

McKenna said, "I want you to know that the Bureau has assigned a hundred agents to this matter. We've also arranged around-the-clock protection for the justices."

"What about the clerks?" Fiske said. "They're the ones getting killed."

Chandler stepped in. "I've compiled the home addresses of all the clerks. I've beefed up patrols in those areas. Most of them live on Capitol Hill close to the Court. We've offered to house any clerk who so chooses at a local hotel where full-time security is available. I've also instructed one of our experts to talk to the clerks about ways to keep safe, be on the lookout for suspicious persons, avoid going out alone or at night, that sort of thing." He looked around for a moment. "By the way, where is Dellasandro?"

"He's trying to coordinate all the new security measures," Klaus reported. "I've never seen him this worried. I think he's taking it personally."

"I've been on the Court for almost thirty-three years, and I never thought I would ever see the likes of this," Justice Murphy said sadly.

"None of us did, Tommy," Knight said forcefully. She looked pointedly at Chandler. "You have no leads at all?"

"I wouldn't go that far. We have several things to go on. I'm talking about Michael Fiske's death. With Wright's murder it's still too early to say."

"But you believe them to be connected?" Ramsey said.

"I really don't have a belief on that one way or the other."

"What do you recommend that we do?"

"That you go about your business as usual. If this is the work of some nut out to disrupt the Court, then you'd be playing into his hands by canceling your docket."

"Or we could risk infuriating whoever's doing this, with the result that he will strike again," Knight said.

"That's always a possibility, Justice Knight," Chandler conceded. "But I'm not convinced that what the Court does or doesn't do will have any effect on that. If the cases are connected." He looked at Ramsey. "I do think it's worth going over the cases both clerks were involved in, just to cover that base. I know it's a long shot, but I could end up kicking myself later on if I don't address it now."

"I understand."

Chandler turned to Justice Murphy. "Will you and your other clerks still be available today to go over cases Michael Fiske was handling?"

"Yes," Murphy replied quickly.

"And I would appreciate if all of you would confer with the other justices and try to determine if any one case you've heard over the last few years may have prompted some action like this," said Chandler.

Knight looked at him and shook her head. "Detective Chandler, many of the cases we deal with stir incredible emotions in people. It would be impossible to know where to start."

"I see your point. I guess you've all been lucky that no one's tried to do something like this before."

"Well, if you want us to go about our normal routines, then I suppose that the dinner honoring Judge Wilkinson will go forward tonight," Knight said.

Murphy sat straight up in protest. "Beth, if nothing else, I think the murders of two Court personnel would dictate that the dinner be put off."

"That's easy enough to say, Tommy, but you didn't happen to plan the event. I did. Kenneth Wilkinson is eighty-five years old and he has pancreatic cancer. I won't risk putting it off, unfortunate as the timing may be. This is very important to him."

"And to you as well, correct, Beth?" Ramsey said. "And your husband?"

"That's right. Are we going to have another debate on legal ethics, Harold? In front of all these people?"

"No," he said. "You know my feelings on the subject."

"Yes, I do, and the dinner will proceed."

Fiske was fascinated by the exchange. He thought he saw a hint of a smile pass across Ramsey's face as the man said, "All right, Beth. Far be it from me to attempt to change your mind on any matter of importance, much less those bordering on the trivial."

CHAPTER THIRTY-SEVEN

Tremaine set the Army helicopter down in the grassy field. As the circling of the copter blades slowed, he and Rayfield looked over at the sedan parked near the edge of the tree line. They lifted off their seat harnesses, climbed out and, torsos bent forward as they passed beneath the blades, headed toward the car. When they reached it, Rayfield sat in the front seat while Tremaine slipped into the back.

"Glad you could make it," said the man in the driver's seat, turning to face Rayfield.

The colonel's jaw fell. "What happened to you?"

The bruises were purplish in the center, leaching out to yellow around the edges. One clung to the side of his right eye, the two others spread out from his collar.

"Fiske," he answered.

"Fiske? He's dead."

"His brother, John," the man said impatiently. "He caught me at his brother's apartment."

"Did he recognize you?"

"I was wearing a mask."

"What was he doing at his brother's apartment?"

"Same thing I was, looking for anything that the cops could use to find out the truth."

"Did he find anything?"

"Nothing to find. We'd already gotten Fiske's laptop." He looked at Tremaine. "And you got his briefcase from his car before you killed him, right?" Tremaine nodded. "Where is it?" the man asked.

"A pile of ash."

"Good."

"Is this brother a problem?" Rayfield wanted to know.

"Maybe. He's an ex-cop. He and one of the other clerks are snooping around. He's helping the detective investigate the clerks' murders."

Rayfield started. "Murders? More than one?"

"Steven Wright."

"What the hell's going on?" Rayfield demanded.

"Wright saw someone come out of Michael Fiske's office. He also heard something he shouldn't have. We couldn't trust him to be quiet, so I had to bluff him out of the building and kill him. We're okay on that one."

"Are you nuts? This thing is totally out of control," Rayfield said angrily.

The man looked at Tremaine. "Hey, Vic, tell your superior to stay cool. I think Nam took away some of your nerve, Frank. You've never been the same since."

"Four murders, and you say stay cool? And Harms and his brother are still out there."

"So we've got two more bodies to go. The two most important. You understand that, don't you, Vic?"

"I do," Tremaine answered.

The man looked over at Rayfield with a pair of very cold eyes.

Rayfield swallowed nervously. "I guess there's no going back now."

"You're right there."

"John Fiske and this clerk: What are you doing about them? If Fiske is on some mission to find his brother's killer, he may be a problem."

"He already is a problem. They're on a real short leash. And they'll stay there until we decide what to do with them."

"Meaning?" Rayfield asked.

"Meaning we might have four more bodies to go instead of two."

Sara sat in her new office. Chandler had declared the space she shared with Wright off limits, but he had allowed Court personnel to move Sara's computer and work files to this overflow space. She had taken the list of state prison agencies Fiske had given her and started calling. At the end of a half an hour she hung up the phone, depressed. There was no one with the last name Harms in any prison in any of those states. She tried to remember any other helpful word or phrase from the documents she had seen, but she finally gave that up.

Suddenly she had a mental flash: the letter R sticking in her mind. Harms's first name started with an R; she had seen that in the filing. It was maddening that she couldn't remember anything else.

She stood, and that's when it caught her eye. She had just grabbed a stack of files with her abrupt move and hadn't noticed it until now. It was the *Chance* bench memo. The one she had told Wright he had to work on last night until he finished. A handwritten note was attached asking Sara to review it.

She sat down and her head sank to the desktop. What if there really was some psychopath targeting clerks? Was it just chance that Wright had been killed instead of her? For

a minute she sat there, frozen. Come on, Sara, you can beat
this. You have to beat this, she urged herself. Using every
bit of resolve she could marshal, she stood and walked out
the door.

A minute later, she entered the clerks' office, and went
over to a clerk who was manning one of the Court's
computer database terminals. The question she was about
to ask was one she had asked earlier, but she wanted to be
absolutely certain.

"Could you check and see if there's any case at the Court
with the name Harms as one of the parties?"

The clerk nodded and started tapping buttons. After
about a minute he shook his head.

"I'm not finding anything. When was it filed?"

"Recently. Within the last couple of weeks or so."

"I've gone back six months—there's nothing coming up.
Didn't you ask me about this a while ago?"

Before Sara could answer, another voice spoke.

"Did you say Harms?"

Sara stared at the other clerk. "Yes. Harms was the last
name."

"That's strange."

Sara's skin started to tingle. "What?"

"I got a call early this morning from a man asking about
an appeal and he used that name. I told him we didn't have
any case filing with that name."

"Harms? You're sure?" The clerk nodded. "How about a
first name?" Sara asked, trying to suppress her excitement.

The clerk thought a moment.

"Maybe starting with an *R*?" Sara prompted.

The clerk snapped his fingers. "That's right. Rufus,
Rufus Harms. Sounds like a hick."

"Did the caller identify himself?"

"No. He got pretty upset."

"Anything else you can remember?"

The man thought a bit longer. "He said something about the guy rotting in a stockade, whatever that meant."

Sara's eyes opened wide and she started to race out.

"What's this all about, Sara? Does this have anything to do with the murders?" the clerk asked. Sara kept going without answering. The clerk hesitated for a moment and then looked around to see if anyone was watching. Then he picked up his phone and dialed a number. When it was answered, he spoke quietly into the receiver.

Sara almost sprinted up the stairs. The reference to the *stockade* had shown her that there was a big hole in Fiske's list. She reached her office, grabbed a card from her Rolodex and dialed the number. She was calling Military Police Operations. Fiske had covered both the federal and state prison populations, but he had not thought of the military. Sara's favorite uncle had retired from the Army as a brigadier general. She knew very well what a stockade was: Rufus Harms was a prisoner of the United States Army.

She got through to Master Sergeant Dillard, the corrections specialist on duty. "I don't have his prison ID number, but I believe he's incarcerated at a military facility within four hundred miles or so of Washington," she said.

"I can't give you that information. The official procedure is to send a written request to the deputy chief of staff for operations and plans. Then that department, in turn, will send your request to the Freedom of Information Act people. They may or may not answer your request depending on the circumstances."

"The thing is, I really need the information now."

"Are you from the media?"

"No, I'm calling from the United States Supreme Court."

"Right. How do I know that?"

Sara thought for a moment. "Call directory assistance for

the general number for the Supreme Court. Then call the number they give you and ask for me. My name is Sara Evans."

Dillard sounded skeptical. "This is highly unusual."

"Please, Sergeant Dillard, it's really important."

There was silence on the other end of the line for a few seconds. "Give me a few minutes."

Five very long minutes later the call was put through to Sara's phone. "You know, Sergeant Dillard, I've gotten information from your office before about military prisoners without going through the FOIA process."

"Well, sometimes the people here are a little generous with the information."

"I just want to know where Rufus Harms is, that's all."

"Actually, it wouldn't really be a problem with any other prisoner."

"I don't understand. Why is Rufus Harms so special?"

"Haven't you been reading your newspaper?"

"Not today, no, why?"

"Maybe it's not real big news, but the public ought to know, for its own safety if nothing else."

"The public ought to know what?"

"That Rufus Harms escaped." In concise sentences, Dillard filled her in on the details.

"Where was he incarcerated?"

"Fort Jackson."

"Where is that?"

Dillard told her and Sara wrote down the location.

"Now I got a question for you, Ms. Evans. Why is the Supreme Court interested in Rufus Harms?"

"He filed an appeal with the Court."

"What sort of appeal?"

"I'm sorry, Sergeant Dillard, but that's all I can tell you. I have rules to go by too."

"All right, but I tell you what. If I were you, I'd hold off working on his appeal. The courts aren't open to dead people, are they?"

"Actually, they can be. What exactly did the man do?"

"You'll have to check his military file."

"How do I do that?"

"You're a lawyer, aren't you?"

"Yes, but I don't do a lot of work with the military."

She could hear him muttering a bit over the phone.

"Since he's a prisoner of the military, Rufus Harms is no longer technically in the United States Army. Along with his conviction he would have been given either a dishonorable or a bad-conduct discharge. His military records would have been sent to the St. Louis Military Personnel Records office. Hard copies are kept there. It's not on a computer database or anything. Harms was convicted about twenty-five years ago, so his records should have been transferred to microfilm, although the personnel office is a little behind on that process. If you or anyone other than Harms wants his records, you have to use a subpoena."

Sara wrote all of this down. "Thank you again, Sergeant Dillard, you've been a huge help."

She had map software on her computer. Sara brought the screen up and, using her mouse, drew a distance line from Washington, D.C., to the approximate location of Fort Jackson.

"Almost four hundred miles exactly," she said to herself. She hurried upstairs to the Court's third-floor library and went on-line via one of the computer terminals there. None of the law clerks' office terminals were connected to phone modems for obvious reasons of security and confidentiality. But the library terminals had on-line access. Using an Internet explorer service she typed in Rufus Harms's name. She looked around at the hand-carved oak paneling as she waited for the computer to sprinkle its technological pixie dust.

A few minutes later she was reading all the latest news accounts on Rufus Harms, his background and that of his brother. She printed out all of these. One of the stories had a quote from the newspaper editor in Harms's hometown. Using an Internet telephone directory, she looked up the man's number. He still lived in the same small town near Mobile, Alabama, where both brothers had grown up.

The phone was answered after three rings. Sara introduced herself to the man, George Barker, still editor-in-chief of the local paper.

"I already talked to the papers about that," he said flatly.

His deep southern drawl made Sara think of braying coon dogs and clear jugs of 'shine. "I'd appreciate if you could answer a few questions for me, that's all."

"Who are you with again?"

"An independent news service. I'm a freelancer."

"Well, what exactly do you want to know?"

"I've read that Rufus Harms was convicted of killing a young girl on the military base where he was stationed." She glanced at the news accounts she had printed out. "Fort Plessy."

"Killed a little *white* girl. He's a Negro, you know."

"Yes, I know," Sara said curtly. "Do you know the name of the attorney who represented him at the trial?"

"Wasn't really a trial. He did a plea arrangement. I covered the story some, because Rufus was local, sort of the reverse of the local boy makes good."

"So you know the name of his attorney?"

"Well, I'd have to look it up. Give me your number and I can call you back."

Evans gave him her home number. "If I'm not there, just leave it on the answering machine. What else can you tell me about Rufus and his brother?"

"Well, the most noticeable thing about Rufus was his size. He must have already been six-foot-three by the time he was fourteen. And he wasn't skinny or lanky or anything. He already had a man's body."

"Good student? bad? In trouble with the police?"

"From what I recall, he wasn't a good student. He never graduated high school, although he was real good with his hands. He worked at a little printing press with his daddy growing up. His brother did too. Why, I remember one time the press at my newspaper broke down. They sent Rufus over to fix it. He couldn't have been much more'n sixteen. I gave him the manual for the machinery, but he wouldn't take it. 'Words just mess me up, Mr. Barker,' he said, or something to that effect. He went in there and within one hour he had the whole damn thing up and running, good as new."

"That's pretty impressive."

"And he was never in trouble with the police. His momma wouldn't have let him. You got to understand, this is one small town, no more than a thousand souls have ever lived here, even fewer today. I'm pushing eighty, still run the newspaper. Nobody's been here longer than me. Now, the Harmses lived in the colored section of town, of course, but we still knew 'em. Now, I don't have colored folk over to my house, but they seemed like good people. She worked at the meat processing factory here just like most everybody else. Cleaning crew, not one of the good-paying jobs. But she took care of her boys."

"What happened to their father?"

"He was a good man, not prone to drink or wild living like so many of their kind. He worked hard, too hard, because one day he just didn't wake up. Heart attack."

"You have a good memory."

"I wrote out his obituary."

"What about his brother?"

"Now, Josh was a different story. Around here, he's what we call a bad black. Hotheaded, arrogant, trying to be better than he was. Now, I'm not prejudiced or anything and I don't tolerate the use of the *n* word in my presence, but if I did use that particular word I'd use it to describe Josh Harms. He rubbed a lot of people the wrong way."

"I read that he fought in Vietnam and was actually a war hero."

"Sure, that's right," Barker conceded quickly. "He was the most decorated war hero to ever come out of this town, by a long shot. People were damn surprised about that, let me tell you. But he could fight, I'll give the man that."

"What else?"

"Well, Josh actually graduated high school." Barker's voice changed. "But where he really showed up everybody was in sports. I'm a one-man shop here and I cover all the news. Josh Harms was the greatest pure athlete I have ever had the privilege to see. White, black, green or purple, that boy could run faster, jump higher, stronger, quicker than anybody else. Now, I know the coloreds can do all that really well anyway, but Josh was truly special. He lettered in just about every sport there was. Do you know he still holds about a half dozen state athletic records?" He added proudly, "And you know Alabama's got more than its share of great athletes."

Sara sighed. "Did he play at the collegiate level?"

"Well, he got a slew of scholarship offers for football and basketball. Bear Bryant even wanted him at 'Bama, that's how good he was. Probably would've been a star in the NBA or the NFL. But he got sidetracked."

"How so?"

"Well, you know how so. His government asked him to defend his country in the war against communism."

"In other words, he got drafted and was shipped to Vietnam."

"That's right."

"Did he come back home afterward?"

"Oh, sure. His momma was still alive, but not for long. See, right about that time was when Rufus got in all that trouble. I actually think Rufus volunteered for the Army because of Josh. Maybe he wanted to be like his older brother, you know, a hero. Really I think he just wanted something to go right with his life for a change. After his daddy died there wasn't anything for him in this town. Of course, it ended up going about as wrong as it could. Anyway, Josh came to see me, to see if there was anything I could do. You know, the power of the press, but there wasn't anything I could do."

"Did Rufus killing the girl surprise you? I mean, had he ever been violent, that you knew?"

"He never hurt anyone that I know of. A real gentle giant. When I heard about the little girl I couldn't believe it. Now, if it had been Josh, I wouldn't have blinked twice, but not Rufus. But with all that, the evidence was clear as could be."

"Did Josh keep living there?"

"Well, now you take me to a particularly troubling part of this town's history."

"What's that?"

"I'd rather not say."

Sara thought quickly. What was the journalistic phrase? "It can be off the record."

"Is that right?" Barker sounded wary.

"Absolutely. It's off the record."

"I want you to know that I just recorded what you said. So if I read in some newspaper what I'm about to tell you, I'll sue you and your paper for every last cent you got," he said sternly. "I'm a journalist, I know how these things work."

"Mr. Barker, I promise that whatever you're about to tell me will not be used in any way for a story."

"All right. Actually, I guess so much time has passed that it doesn't matter anymore—legally, anyway. But you can never be too careful in this old world." He cleared his throat. "Well, the story of what Rufus had done got around town, no way it wouldn't. A bunch of boys started drinking, got together and decided to do something. Now, they couldn't do anything to Rufus, he was in the custody of the United States Army. But they could do something about the other Harms living here."

"What did they do?"

"Well, what they did was they burned Mrs. Harms's house to the ground."

"Good God! Was she in it?"

"She was until Josh pulled her out. And let me tell you what, Josh went after those boys. They went at it right up and down the town's streets. I watched it from my office. You know, it must've been ten against one, but Josh put half of them boys in the hospital, until the rest beat him up bad, real bad. Never seen anything like it, hope I never do again."

"It sounds almost like a riot. Didn't the police come?"

Barker coughed in an embarrassed fashion. "Well, just so happens that it was rumored that a couple of the boys that were in on it, you know, who had burned the house down—"

"Were the police," Sara finished the sentence for him. Barker didn't say anything. "I hope Josh Harms sued for all the money the town had," she said.

"Well, actually, they sued *him*. I mean, the boys he put in the hospital did. Josh couldn't prove anything about the fire. I mean, I had my speculations, but that was all. And the police sort of put together this story about him resisting arrest and all. It was ten people's word against one, and a colored's word at that. Well, the long and the short of it was he spent some time in jail and they took everything he and his momma had, little enough that it was. She died soon thereafter. What happened to both her boys, I guess, was too much for her."

It was all Sara could do not to start screaming at the man. "Mr. Barker, that is the most disgusting story I have ever heard," she said. "I don't know much about your town, but I do know I would never want anyone I cared about to live there."

"It has its good points."

"Really—like welcoming home a war hero like that?"

"I know. I thought about that too. You fight for your country, get shot up and then come home to something like that, probably makes you wonder what the hell you were fighting for."

"You sound like you knew the truth. Didn't you use the power of the press that time?"

Barker sighed deeply. "This has always been my home, Ms. Evans, and you can only offend the powers that be so many times, even if they deserve it. Now, I can't say that I'm any great friend of the blacks, because I'm not. And I wouldn't lie to you and say I championed Josh Harms's cause, because frankly I didn't."

"Well, I guess that's partly what the courts are for: to keep people like those in your town from screwing people like Josh Harms. Please call me back with the name of Harms's lawyer."

She hung up the phone. Her whole body was tingling with rage from what she had just heard. But then, how many blacks had she known growing up in Carolina? The generations of squatters down the road? Or during harvest time when her father would bring in the part-timers to help? She had watched these men from the porch, sweat soaking the thin fabric of their shirts, their skin growing ever darker under the bite of the sun. She and her mother would bring them lemonade, food. They would mumble their thanks, never making eye contact, eat their meal and toil on into the darkness. Sara's school had been all white, despite the string of Supreme Court cases demanding otherwise. These cases were the twentieth century battlefields of racial equality, replacing the Antietams, Gettysburgs and Chickamaugas of the last century. And some would argue with equal futility. And here at the Court there was one black justice, who occupied the so-called Thurgood Marshall seat, and currently one black clerk, out of thirty-six. Many of the justices had never had a minority person clerk for them. What sort of message did that send? At the highest court of justice in the land?

As she hurried down the hallway in search of Fiske, Sara wondered if they would ever really find out the truth. If the Army caught up to the Harms brothers before anyone else, the truth might very well die with them.

CHAPTER THIRTY-EIGHT

Fiske was standing outside his brother's office while Chandler was overseeing the progress of his evidence-collection team under close supervision of the Court's staff counsel. However, with now two dead clerks, concerns over confidentiality had taken a back seat to finding the killer or killers. When they finished with Michael Fiske's office, they would go down the hallway and start on Steven Wright's.

Fiske looked over at his brother's office door and then back at Wright's. He did so a couple more times as an idea began to percolate through his head. He went over to Chandler.

"Exactly where was Wright's body found?"

Chandler flipped open his notebook and started looking through his notes. "By the way, I got your car out of impound. It's at my office in a nice, legal parking space."

"Thanks for doing that for me."

"Don't thank me. With the tow and fine and all, it's gonna cost you about two hundred bucks."

"Two hundred bucks? I don't have that kind of money for a lousy parking ticket."

"Is that right? Well, maybe I can pull a few strings, you know, do you a favor. But you'll have to work it off. I got some painting that needs to be done at my house." Chandler cracked a smile and then stopped leafing through his notes. "Okay, here we are. Wright lived about a block from the Eastern Market metro station. His body was found in Garfield Park. That's at F and Second Streets. It's about a half dozen blocks from the Court."

"How did Wright usually get to and from work?"

"According to several people here, he either walked, took a cab or occasionally the metro."

"Was this Garfield Park on his way home?"

Chandler tilted his head as he studied his notes. "Not really. Normally he would've hung a left from Second onto E to go home. He wouldn't have continued on down to the park."

"Did he have a dog or anything? Maybe he went home and then took it for a walk in the park."

"He did have a dog, but he hadn't been home. At least we don't think he had. And if he was going to walk his dog, Marion Park is a lot closer to his home."

"That is strange."

Chandler's eyes narrowed as he thought of something.

"But Marion Park has something that Garfield doesn't."

"What's that?"

"A police substation right across the street."

"Whoever killed him might have known that."

"The substation's not exactly a big secret. We want our presence known there as a deterrent to crime."

"Does it look like he was killed at the park, or maybe somewhere else and dumped there?"

"The grass had blood on it. No shell casings—that we

found yet, anyway. Shooter probably would've used a silencer, unless it was some random robbery. A silencer on a revolver is too tricky. If he used a semiautomatic, then we should find a shell casing unless it was picked up."

"Bullet still in the body?"

Chandler nodded. "Hope we lay our hands on a gun to match it against."

"Considering what happened at Mike's apartment, you should probably have someone posted at Wright's."

"Gee, now, why didn't I think of that."

"Sorry. Any idea when Wright left the Court last night?"

"We're still checking on that. After regular hours there's only one door open for entering and exiting. That door is constantly guarded and it closes up at 2 A.M. After that you need a guard to let you out. You can leave via the garage too, but it's also secured. However, Wright didn't drive, so the garage is irrelevant."

"Then someone must have seen him leave."

"My people are checking with the guards on duty last night."

"Doesn't this place have surveillance cameras?"

"You mean in the courtroom?" Chandler asked with a smile. "The answer is yes, but not everywhere and unfortunately not along this part of the hallway. But we're checking the tapes right now to see if there's anything relevant on them." Chandler scanned his notes once more. "At that time of night, really the only activity on this floor would have been a clerk working late."

"Anything in Wright's background helpful?"

Chandler shook his head. "No skeletons that we found so far. Motive is going to be tough on this one."

"But his wallet was missing."

"Yeah, I thought about that. A little too convenient."

"Like somebody wants to make us think both murders are connected?"

"You know, it actually could be some nut with a grudge against the Court."

"I believe the murders are connected but not for the reasons everyone probably thinks," Fiske said.

"How do you mean?"

"If Mike was killed for a reason someone doesn't want us to find out about, then killing another clerk and making it look related would be a great way to divert our attention."

Chandler looked intrigued. "So what's the *real* reason someone killed your brother and is trying to cover it up?"

Fiske hesitated again. Keeping the stolen appeal a secret was beginning to become very awkward. "I don't know, but I might have an idea why Wright was killed."

"Other than as a red herring?"

"Let's say his death might have served a dual purpose."

At that moment Sara joined them, trying very hard to conceal her excitement.

"John, can we talk for a minute?"

"Ms. Evans," Chandler said with a broad smile, "I hope your drive to Richmond was pleasant and uneventful."

"Let's just say it was different," she said quickly. "John, I really need to talk to you."

"Can I catch up with you later, Buford?"

"And you can tell me your theory."

As they walked off together, Chandler's smile faded. He was wondering if he had just lost his "unofficial" partner to Sara Evans.

Minutes after Sara had left her office, Justice Knight had stopped by to see her. She started to leave a written message when she saw the *Chance* bench memo with Wright's attached note. She sat down in Sara's chair and read the note. After she finished, it suddenly dawned on Knight what she had done. She had instructed Wright to work late, all night if necessary. He had done so, left the building late and someone had killed him. Her precious bench memo. She had never really focused on this chain of events before. A gush of air came out of her lungs so hard it almost choked her. She put the memo down and rushed from the room.

A minute later she raced past her astonished staff and locked the door to her office. She looked around the spacious, beautiful room, with even its own fireplace. Here she had sat and contemplated her little strategies, her philosophies of life. And it had cost a young man his life. She threw off her pumps, collapsed in a corner, covered her face and wept.

CHAPTER THIRTY-NINE

Back at her office, Sara spent the next thirty minutes filling Fiske in on everything she had found out. "When Barker calls back with the attorney's name, we can talk to him and maybe really start getting somewhere."

"That would be nice."

"Do you believe Michael went to see Harms in prison?"

"It really complicates matters that the guy's escaped."

Sara had a sudden terrifying thought. "You don't think Michael was somehow mixed up in that, do you?"

"My brother would not be part of anything illegal."

"I didn't mean intentionally."

"According to the newspaper reports, Harms escaped from a hospital in Roanoke *after* Mike's body was found. But I'm not saying that the timing is just coincidental."

"Do you have any brilliant deductions?"

"I think I know why Wright was killed."

"Why? Because he knew about Harms? About what Michael had done?"

"No, he was killed because he saw something. Something he shouldn't have."

Sara drew her chair closer to his. "What do you mean?"

"Wright's office—*your* former office—is right down the hallway from Mike's. Wright was going to be working all night."

Sara slumped in her chair. "Right. Because I told him he had to."

"No, because Knight told you to tell him he had to. Well, his body was found in a park that wasn't on his way home. Chandler told me that he was killed between midnight and two last night. If he was working all night here, what was he doing in that park?"

"You believe someone took him there and killed him?"

"More to the point, someone took him from inside the Court to the park and killed him."

Sara gaped. "Meaning the killer was here?"

Fiske nodded. "I don't know if the person works here, but I believe he was physically present here last night."

"What could Steven have seen that cost him his life?"

"I think he saw someone go into Mike's office. Yesterday, Wright heard Chandler tell everyone that the office was off limits to *everyone*. Whoever went into Mike's office might not have known that Wright was in *his* office. I assume you don't broadcast when you're working late."

"Like last night, often we don't even know until the last minute."

"Right. So somebody goes into the office looking for something—"

"Like what?"

"Who knows? Copies of the appeal that Mike took. Telephone messages, something on his computer."

"But that's an awfully big risk. There's security here twenty-four hours a day."

"Well, if the person knew the police were going to

search the office thoroughly the next morning, he'd only have a limited amount of time to do it."

"That makes sense."

"So Wright hears something, or he's finished his memo, he comes out, and runs right into whoever."

"If your theory is correct, do you think Steven knew the person who killed him?"

Fiske took a deep breath and sat back. "I think he had to. Otherwise he would've raised the alarm right away. And I saw Dellasandro lock the door to Mike's office. There's no sign of forced entry. The person had a key."

"But someone must have seen something, then."

"Not necessarily. If the killer is familiar with the layout of the Court, then he'd know ways to avoid being seen with Wright until they got out of the building."

"So it might be somebody he trusted."

Fiske looked at her. "Like one of the justices?"

Sara stared back, horrified. "I'll accept a lot, but I can't accept that." She had a sudden thought. "Maybe it was McKenna? Steven would have trusted him, FBI and all."

"How could McKenna be involved in this?"

"I don't know. He's the first one who occurred to me."

"Because he's not with the Court and he slugged me?"

Sara sighed. "Probably." Then she remembered something and tore through the papers on her desk until she found it. "I can tell you about what time Steven left." She picked up the memo Wright had left for her. Across the top of the memo was a date and time stamp. She flipped the papers around so Fiske could see it.

"The word-processing system automatically puts the date and time stamp on documents because we go through so many drafts. That way we can quickly tell what's current or not."

Fiske looked at the time stamp. "This was printed out at one-fifteen this morning."

"That's right. Steven finished the memo, printed it out, put it on my desk and then presumably left."

"And saw whatever he saw."

Sara suddenly looked puzzled. "Wait a minute. Something doesn't make sense here. When a clerk works late, ordinarily what happens is one of the Court police officers will give the clerk a ride home, if you live nearby." She looked at Fiske. "The police here are really good to us."

"And at one-fifteen the metro's not running, is it?"

"No. Besides that, Steven lived barely a five-minute car ride from here. He's gotten rides home before."

"So the chances are very good that Wright got a ride home from somebody at the Court?"

"Leaving here at one-fifteen in the morning, I'd say it was a really safe bet."

"How about a cab, though? Maybe at that hour there weren't enough guards to spare to take him home."

Sara looked doubtful. "I guess it's possible."

"If a police officer did take him home, that should be easy enough to check. I'll tell Chandler."

"So where does that leave us?"

Fiske shrugged. "We need to see Harms's military file. I've got an old friend with the Army JAG. I'm going to call and see if he can help expedite the process. Until we know who's involved in all this, I want as few people as possible to know we're looking around."

Sara shuddered and wrapped her arms around herself.

"You know what?" she said. "I'm starting to become terrified of what the truth might be."

CHAPTER FORTY

While Sara went back to work, Fiske telephoned his lawyer friend at the JAG office, Phil Jansen, and relayed his request. Among other things, he asked Jansen to obtain a list of the personnel stationed at Fort Plessy during the time Rufus Harms was there.

When Fiske rejoined Chandler, he related his theory of why Wright had been killed. Chandler was impressed. "We'll check the cab companies too. We can only hope somebody saw or heard something."

Chandler stared intently at the young man. "So, did you find out anything interesting with Ms. Evans during your time together last night?"

"I think she's a good person. A little impulsive, but a good person. Very smart."

"Anything else? At our initial meeting, Ramsey said that she and your brother were close. She have any reason why he might have been killed?"

"You might want to ask her that."

"Well, I'm asking you, John. I thought we were a team."
He moved closer to Fiske. "I've got way too much I don't
understand on the front end of this case without having to
watch my backside. You were a police officer; you should
understand about covering somebody's backside."

Fiske said angrily, "I never let a partner down."

"Good to hear. So tell me about last night."

Fiske looked away, thinking how best to handle this.
Withholding information was not the best course. So how
could he do the right thing with Chandler and avoid
destroying Sara's life and his brother's reputation?

"Can we get some coffee around here?"

"In the cafeteria. I'll even buy."

A few minutes later they were in the ground-floor cafeteria. The Court's afternoon session was in progress and
thus the cafeteria was fairly empty.

Fiske sipped on his coffee while Chandler watched him.

"John, it can't be that bad, unless you tell me you're the
one running around popping people."

"Buford, if I tell you something, then you have very
specific rules as to what you do with that information and
who else learns that information."

"That's true. And those rules are what's stopping you
from coming clean?"

"What do you think?"

"I think let's talk hypotheticals, okay? Now, my job is
to collect the facts and to use those facts to ultimately
arrest somebody for a crime. If we're not talking facts, but
just theories—like your theory of why Wright was
murdered—then I can follow up that theory but I don't
have an obligation to report it to anyone until it's proven
correct by the discovery of facts to corroborate it."

"So we can talk theoretically and it'll just stay between
you and me?"

Chandler shook his head. "Can't promise it will *stay*
between you and me. Not if it becomes a fact."

Fiske looked down at his coffee cup. Sensing he was losing him, Chandler tapped his spoon against Fiske's cup.

"John, the bottom line here is finding out who murdered your brother and Wright. I thought that's what you wanted."

"It is. That's all I want."

Really? Chandler suddenly doubted that. "Then what's the problem?"

"The problem is you can hurt people at the same time you're trying to help them."

"Just your brother? Or somebody else?"

Fiske knew he had already said too much. He decided to go on the offensive.

"Okay, Buford, let's discuss theories for a minute. Let's suppose that somebody at the Court took an appeal before it was put into the Court's system."

"Why and how?"

"Apparently the *how* is easy. The *why* isn't."

"Okay, go on."

"Now let's suppose that somebody else at the Court saw this appeal, discovered that it wasn't on the system, but didn't say anything about it."

"I take it the *why* on that is also complicated?"

"Maybe not. Let's further assume that the person who took the appeal did so for a good reason. And that this person went somewhere, to visit the person who had filed the appeal."

"The eight hundred miles on your brother's car?"

Fiske stonily eyed the detective. "That's a fact, Buford, I'm not discussing facts."

Chandler took a drink of coffee. "Go on."

"And let's suppose that the person filing the appeal was a prisoner."

"Is that a fact or just speculation?"

"I'm not prepared to say."

"Well, I'm prepared to ask. Where is this prisoner?"

"I don't know."

"What do you mean, you 'don't know'? If he's a prisoner, he has to be in some prison somewhere, doesn't he?"

"Not necessarily."

"What the hell does that—" Chandler abruptly closed his mouth and stared across the table. "Are you saying this person escaped from prison?" Fiske didn't answer. "Please don't tell me that your brother got all suckered by some con's BS plea for help, went to the prison, helped bust him out and then the guy killed him. Dammit, please do not tell me that." Chandler's voice rose in his agitation.

"I'm not telling you that. That's not what happened."

"Okay. This appeal . . . do you know what it says?"

They had gone well beyond theories now, Fiske knew. He shook his head. "I've never even seen it."

"So how do you know it exists?"

"Buford, I'm not going to answer that question."

"John, I can make you answer that question."

"Then you're going to have to."

"You know you're taking a risk here."

"I do." Fiske finished his coffee and stood up. "I'll grab a cab back to pick up my car."

"I'll drive you. I do have other cases I'm working, even if this is the only one the world cares about right now."

"I think it would be better for both of us if you didn't drive me."

Chandler pursed his lips. "Suit yourself. Your car's in the back lot. Keys are on the front seat."

"Thanks."

Chandler watched Fiske leave the cafeteria. "I hope she's worth it, John," the detective said quietly.

Chandler had put some inquiries of his own into play, and when he returned to his office he found a stack of paper on his desk. One standard line of investigation had been to obtain the phone records of Michael Fiske's office and home phones over the last month. The results were catalogued in the ream of paper. The phone call to his brother was on there. There were others to family. A dozen of them to a phone number that had been identified as Sara Evans's. That was interesting, he thought. Had both Fiske brothers fallen for the same woman? When Chandler got near the end of the list, his pulse quickened. After all the years on the job, that rarely happened anymore. Michael Fiske had called Fort Jackson in southwest Virginia several times, the last only three days before his body had been discovered. Fort Jackson, Chandler knew, housed a military prison. And that wasn't all. Chandler scattered the piles on his desk until he found what he was looking for. The telex had been sent nationwide asking for assistance on apprehending the man. When he had seen it earlier, Chandler hadn't thought much about it.

Now he intently studied the photo of Rufus Harms. He picked up his phone and made a quick call. Chandler needed one piece of information and he got it within a minute. Fort Jackson was approximately four hundred miles from Washington, D.C. Had Harms been the one to file the appeal John Fiske had mentioned? And if he had, why, according to Fiske's "theory," had his brother taken it?

Chandler looked back at the list of phone calls. His eyes flitted over one number without registering, perhaps because it was to some law office and there were several law-related calls on the list. But the name Sam Rider would have meant nothing to the detective even if he had focused on it for some reason. Chandler put down the phone list and contemplated bringing in Fiske and Sara Evans, and making them tell him what was going on. But then the instincts built up over thirty years kicked in with one precept clearly emerging: You can't trust anyone.

"Come on, John," Sara pleaded. They were in her office near the end of the workday.

"Sara, I don't even know Judge Wilkinson."

"But don't you see? If someone at the Court *is* involved, this would be a perfect opportunity to find out some information because practically everybody from the Court will be there."

Fiske was about to protest again but then stopped. He rubbed his chin. "What time does it start?"

"Seven-thirty. By the way, have you heard from your JAG friend?"

"Yeah. There are actually two files that are applicable. Harms's service record, which contains not only his record of service, but also evaluations, personal info, enlistment contract, pay and medical histories. The second file, the record of his court-martial proceedings, would be with him at Fort Jackson. His lawyer's work product would be maintained at the JAG office that handled Harms's defense. That is, if they've kept it all these years. Jansen's checking. He'll send what he can."

As Sara started gathering her things to leave, Fiske remained sitting. "So what can you tell me about the Knights? Their pasts and all that?"

"Why?"

"Well, we're going to a party that they're hosting. She's a big part of the Court and he's a VIP in his own right. That qualifies them to be part of our investigation, don't you think?"

"You probably know more about Jordan Knight's past than I do. He's from your hometown."

Fiske shrugged. "True. Jordan Knight is big business in Richmond. At least he was until he entered politics. He made a lot of money."

"And a lot of enemies?"

"No, I don't think so. He's given a lot back to Virginia. Besides, he's a low-key, nice guy."

"Then he's an odd match for Elizabeth Knight."

"I could see how she'd bruise a few egos on the way up."

"More than a few. It came with the territory. Tough federal prosecutor turned tougher trial judge. Everybody knew she was being groomed for a seat on the Court. She's the swing vote on most of the major cases, which drives Ramsey crazy. I'm sure that's why he treats her the way he does. Kid gloves most of the time, but every once in a while he can't resist jabbing her."

Fiske thought back to the confrontation between the two justices at the conference. So that's what it was.

"How well do you know the other justices? You seem to know them well enough to believe they couldn't commit murder."

"Like in any other large organization, I know them mostly superficially."

"What's Ramsey's background?"

"He's the chief justice of the country's highest court and you don't know?"

"Humor me."

"He was an associate justice before being elevated to the top spot about ten years ago."

"Anything unusual in his background?"

"He was in the military. Army or Marines, maybe." She caught Fiske's look. "Don't even think it, John. Ramsey is not going around killing people. Other than that, just what's in his official bio."

Fiske looked puzzled. "I would have thought you'd know everything about the other justices by talking to the clerks."

"The clerks for one justice tend to stick together to a certain degree, although every Thursday afternoon there's a happy hour when we all get together. And periodically the clerks of one justice take another justice out to lunch just as a get-to-know-you sort of thing.

Otherwise, each chamber is pretty self-contained"—she paused—"except for the famed clerk opinion network."

"Mike mentioned something like that to me after he first came to the Court."

Sara smiled. "I'm sure he did. The clerks are the mouth-pieces for their justices. We send up trial balloons all the time, feeling each other out on a justice's position. For example, Michael used to ask me what Knight needed in a majority opinion to join Murphy."

"But if Murphy is already writing the majority opinion, why does he need to court other votes?"

"You really are in the dark about how we work."

"Just a simple country lawyer."

"Okay, Mr. Simple Country Lawyer, the fact is if I had ten bucks for every time a majority opinion turned into a dissent because enough support wasn't garnered for it, I'd be wealthy. The trick is you have to craft an opinion that'll get five votes. And of course the opposition doesn't just sit idly by. One or more dissenting opinions might be circulated simultaneously. The use of dissenting opinions, or even the threat of them, is a fine art."

Fiske looked at her curiously. "I thought the dissenters were on the losing side. What kind of leverage could they have?"

"Let's say a justice doesn't like how a majority opinion is shaping up, so the justice either circulates a draft of a scathing dissent that may make the whole court look bad if it's published or that even undercuts the majority's opin-ion. Or better yet, and easier, the justice will let it be known that he intends to write such a dissent, unless the majority opinion is scaled back. They all do it. Ramsey, Knight, Murphy. They go at it tooth and nail."

Fiske shook his head. "Like one long political campaign, always scrounging for votes. The legal version of porkbel-lies. Give me this and you got my vote."

"And knowing when to pick your battles. Let's say one

or more justices doesn't like how a case was decided five years ago. Now, the Court doesn't lightly overturn its own precedent, so you have to think strategically. Those justices might use a case in the present to start laying the building blocks for overturning the precedent they didn't like years from now. That also goes for case selection. The justices are always on the outlook for just the right case to use as a vehicle to change a precedent they don't like. It's like a chess game."

"Let's hope one thing doesn't get lost in all the game playing."

"What's that?"

"Justice. Maybe that's what Rufus Harms wants. Why he filed his appeal. You think he can get justice here?"

Sara looked down. "I don't know. The fact is the individual parties involved in the cases at this level really aren't all that important. The precedents established through their cases, that's what counts. It all depends on what he's asking for. How it will impact others."

"Well, that really sucks." Fiske shook his head and gave her a penetrating look. "A damn interesting place, this Supreme Court."

"So you'll come to the party?"

"Wouldn't miss it."

CHAPTER FORTY-ONE

Josh Harms assumed the police would now be covering the back roads, so he had taken the unusual tactic of driving on the interstate. It was dusk, though, and with the windows rolled up, they were okay; a police cruiser would have a tough time seeing inside. But despite all his precautions, he knew they were steering toward disaster.

Funny, he thought, after all the hell his brother had been put through, that he would even think about wanting to do the right thing at the risk of dying, of losing the freedom that never should have been taken away from him in the first place. He felt like both cursing and praising Rufus in the same breath. Josh's outlook on life wasn't complicated: It was him against everybody else. He didn't go looking for trouble, but he had a hair trigger when confronted with anybody looking to piss on him. It was a wonder he'd lived this long, he knew.

Still, you had to admire a person like Rufus, who could fight through all that, through people who didn't want to see the world change one iota since they were riding on top of it. Maybe the truth *will* set you free, Rufus, he thought. Suddenly out of the corner of his eye he saw something in the truck's sideview mirror that made him ease his hand over and grip his gun.

"Rufus," he called back through the open window connecting to the camper, "we got a problem here."

Rufus's face appeared at the window. "What is it?"

"Stay low! Stay low!" Josh cautioned. He again eyed the police cruiser, which was a fixture in the truck's side mirror. "Trooper's passed us twice and then dropped back."

"You speeding?"

"Five clicks under."

"Something wrong with the truck, taillight out?"

"I ain't that dumb. Truck's fine."

"So what, then?"

"Look, Rufus, just because you've been in prison all these years doesn't mean the world's changed any. I'm a black man in a real nice-looking vehicle on the highway at night. Cops think I either stole it or I'm running drugs. Shit, going to the store for milk can be a real adventure." He looked in the side mirror again. "Looks like he's just about to hit his light."

"What we gonna do? I can't hide back here."

Josh didn't take his eyes off the mirror even as he slipped his gun under the seat. "Yep, any second now he's gonna hit that light, and we are done. Get down on the floor and pull that tarp on top of you, Rufus. Do it now." Josh pushed his baseball cap down low so that only the white hair of his temples showed. He stuck out his chin and pushed his bottom lip out, giving the impression that he had no teeth. He leaned over, flipped open the glove box and took out a tin of chew and put a big plug of it in his mouth, which made his cheek bulge. He let his strong frame collapse. Then he rolled down the window and stuck his arm out, motioning in long, slow waves for the police cruiser to pull over to the highway shoulder. Josh eased the truck off the road and stopped. The cruiser quickly pulled in behind the truck, its roof lights throwing off a startling, ominous blue into the darkness.

Josh waited in the truck. You let the boys in blue come to you, no hurried movement. He winced as the cruiser's searchlight beam reflected off the side mirror. A cop tactic to disorient you, he knew well. Josh heard the boots crunching on the bite of gravel. He could envision the trooper approaching, hand on his gun, eyes trained on the door.

Three times in the past, cops had pulled him over and then Josh would hear the tinkling of glass as the baton just happened to collide with a taillight, with the result that he had been cited for an equipment infraction. It was done just to piss him off, see if he'd do something that would warrant some jail time. It had never worked.

Yes sir, no sir, mister policeman, sir, even as he wanted to beat the man unconscious.

At least they had never planted drugs in his car and then tried to pin that on him. He had several buddies idling in prison right now after being hit with that shit.

"Fight it," his ex-wife Louise had always said.

"Fight what?" he had retorted. "Might as well be fighting God for all the good it'll do me."

As the footsteps stopped, Josh looked out the window.

The state trooper stared back at him. Josh noted that he was Hispanic.

"What's the matter, sir?" the trooper asked.

The chew bulging against his cheek with each syllable, Josh said, "Wanta git me on Luzzana." He pointed down the road. "Dis a'ight?"

The puzzled trooper crossed his arms. "Now where do you want to go again?"

"Luzzana. Bat' Rouge."

"Baton Rouge, Louisiana?" The trooper laughed. "You're a long way from there."

Josh scratched his neck and looked around. "Got me chil'ren on down dare ain't seen they's daddy in a while."

The trooper's expression turned serious. "Okay."

"Man say I gone git dare from dis here road."

"Well, the man didn't tell you exactly right."

"Huh, you know's how's I git dare, den?"

"Yeah, you can follow me, but I can't drive the whole way."

Josh just stared at the man. "My chil'ren, dey bin good. Dey wanta see Daddy. You hep me?"

"Okay, I tell you what, we're close to the exit you need to take to head on down that way. You follow me there, and then you're on your own. You stop and ask somebody else. How's that sound?"

"A'ight." Josh touched the bill of his cap.

The trooper was about to return to his cruiser when he glanced at the camper. He hit his light through the side window and saw the stacked boxes. "Sir, you mind my taking a look in the camper?"

Josh didn't flinch, although his hand edged toward the front of the seat, where his gun was. "Hell, no." The trooper went to the rear of the camper and opened the upper glass door. The wall of boxes stared back at him. Behind the stacks, Rufus huddled under the tarp in the darkness of the camper.

"What you got in here, sir?" the trooper called out.

"Food," Josh called back, leaning out the window.

The trooper opened one box, shook a soup can, opened the box of crackers and then replaced it, closed the box and then the camper window. He walked back to the driver's-side window.

"Lot of food. The trip isn't that long."

"Axed my chil'ren what dey want. Dey say food."

The trooper blinked. "Oh. Well, that's good of you. Real good of you."

"You got chil'ren?"

"Two."

"A'ight, den."

"Have a safe trip." The cop walked back to his cruiser. Josh pulled back onto the road after the cruiser did.

Rufus appeared at the camper window. "I was sweating a damn river back there."

Josh smiled. "You got to take it cool. You play badass, they cuff you. You act too polite, they figure you scamming their ass and they cuff you. Now, you be old and dumb, they don't give a shit."

"Still a close call, Josh."

"We caught us a break with the Mexie. They're real big on family, kids. Talk that shit and they're cool with you. If he'd been white, we might have had us a big problem. Once he made up his mind to look, Whitie would've pulled everything out of that camper until he found your ass. Now, a bro' might've cut me some slack, but you never know. Sometimes, they got that uniform on, they start to act white."

Rufus stared at his brother with a look of displeasure.

"Now, the Asians, they the worst," Josh continued. "You can't say shit to them. They just stand there and look at you, not listening to a damn word, and then go off and do what they're gonna do. Might as well just shoot them mothers before they kung fu your ass. Yeah, it's real good we met up with Officer Pedro." Josh spit the chew out the window.

"You got everybody figured out?" Rufus said angrily.

Josh glanced at him. "You got a problem with that?"

"Maybe."

"Well, you live your life the way you want, I live mine the way I want. We see who makes it farther. I know you had it hard inside, but it ain't no picnic on the outside. I got me my own little prison right out here. And nobody's convicted me of a damn thing."

"God made all of us, Josh. We all his children. Ain't no good trying to divide us all up. I seen plenty of white folk beaten up in prison. Evil comes in all forms, all colors. Bible says so. I ain't judging nobody except on themselves. Only way to do it."

Josh snorted. "Look at you, saying that. After all Tremaine and them done to you. You telling me you don't hate them, want to kill 'em?"

"No. If I felt that way, that'd mean Vic took the love from my heart. Took my Lord away from me. He does that, that means he's controlling me. Ain't nobody on this earth strong enough to take God from me. Not old Vic, you or anybody else. I'm not dumb, Josh. I know life ain't fair. I know black folk ain't riding on top of the world. But I ain't adding to the problem by hating people."

"Shit. You got the gold card from God to hate every white person ever born."

"You're wrong. I hate them, it's like hating myself. I went down that road when I first went to prison. Hated everybody. The Devil had me, but the Lord took me back. Can't do it. Won't do it."

"Well, that's your problem. Sooner you get over that the better."

"That was a big oversight on your part, Frank. You take out Rider and his wife, but you didn't search his office?"

Rayfield's grip tightened around the phone. "Well, tell me exactly when I was supposed to do that. If I had done it before we killed him, he would've gotten suspicious and maybe gotten away. If we had gotten caught going through it now, there would've been questions I don't have answers for."

"But you just told me they ruled it a murder-suicide. The cops aren't going to investigate that anymore."

"Probably true."

"So you can hit his office. Like tonight."

"If the coast is clear, we'll do it."

"Have you found the letter Harms got from the Army?"

"Not yet—" He broke off as Tremaine burst into his office, waving a piece of paper. "Hold on."

Tremaine slid the paper in front of Rayfield, who went pale as he read it. He looked up at a grim Tremaine.

"Where'd you find it?"

"That SOB hollowed out one of the bed supports. Pretty slick," Tremaine grudgingly conceded.

Rayfield spoke into the receiver. In terse sentences he conveyed the contents of the letter.

"Was this your doing, Frank?"

"Look, if the guy had died in the stockade the way we planned, they would've done an autopsy, right? Well, this was the only way to cover that hole. We all agreed."

"But, Christ, Harms didn't die. Why didn't you have it expunged from the system later?"

"I did! Don't you think if I hadn't, it would've come out during the investigation? Rider wasn't stupid, he would've pounced on that as a defense."

"So if you took it out of the record back then, why did the Army send him that letter all these years later?"

"Who knows? Some dipshit clerk could have come across a piece of paper and put it back in, or these days entered it into a database. Once in the Army's official record, you never know if something's going to resurface, no matter how hard you tried to bury it. It's the biggest damn bureaucracy in the world. You can't account for everything."

"But it was your job to stay on top of it."

"Don't tell me what my job is. I tried to stay on top of it, but it's not like I could check on it every stinking day for the last quarter century."

The voice sighed. "So now we know what triggered Harms's memory."

"Any strategy comes with risks."

"Well, maybe Rider had a copy of this letter."

"I don't see how Rufus Harms could've had access to a copier, and the letter wasn't part of what he filed with the Court, we know that for a fact."

"But we can't be sure that he didn't. That's all the more reason for you to go over Rider's office tonight."

Rayfield looked up at Tremaine and then said into the phone, "All right, we'll hit it tonight. Fast and hard."

CHAPTER FORTY-TWO

Senator Knight warmly greeted Fiske and Sara as they entered the foyer. Behind him, they could see the place was filled with the business and political elite of the nation's capital.

"Glad you could come, John," Jordan Knight said, shaking his hand. "Sara, you look radiant as always." He gave her a hug and they exchanged pecks on the cheek.

Fiske looked over at Sara. She had changed out of her business attire and into a light summer dress of soft pastel colors that accented nicely her suntanned skin. The bun was gone and her hair swept appealingly around her face.

She caught Fiske staring at her and he quickly looked away, embarrassed, before accepting a drink from one of the waiters. Sara and Jordan Knight did the same.

Jordan looked around, seemingly a little embarrassed himself. "I know the timing on this damn thing is atrocious." He eyed Sara closely when he said this. "I know Beth feels the same way, although she won't admit it."

Sure she does, thought Fiske.

Jordan pointed his drink toward an elderly man in a wheelchair and spoke softly. "Kenneth Wilkinson unfortunately isn't long for this world. He's a scrapper, though, and he might fool us all. But he's lived a long, inspiring life. My mentor and my friend. I'm a better man for having known him."

"Didn't he introduce you and your wife?" Sara asked.

"That's another reason I owe him so much."

Fiske watched Elizabeth Knight methodically work the room, as polished and poised as any experienced politico. Fiske scanned the room again but didn't see any sign of Ramsey or Murphy. He wondered if they had boycotted the event. He did note several of the other justices looking nervous and uncomfortable. The fear that a madman wanted to mount your head in his trophy case could do that to you.

His eyes passed over Richard Perkins hovering in the background. There were armed guards everywhere and Fiske knew the hot topic of the evening was the two murdered clerks. Fiske's eyes narrowed as he spied Warren McKenna knifing through the crowd like a shark looking for flesh to devour.

"You two make a great team," Sara said.

Jordan Knight touched his glass to hers. "I think so too."

"Your wife ever think about running for political office?" Fiske asked.

"John, she's a Supreme Court justice. It's a lifetime appointment," Sara exclaimed.

Fiske kept his eyes on Jordan. "Wouldn't be the first time someone left the Court in pursuit of another job, would it?"

Jordan looked at him keenly. "No, it wouldn't, John. As a matter of fact, over the years Beth and I have talked about that. I'm not going to be in the Senate forever. I've got a seven-thousand-acre ranch out in New Mexico. I can easily see myself running that until the end of my days."

"And maybe your wife becomes the Virginia senator in the household?"

"I never presume to know what Beth will do. It actually adds a level of excitement to our marriage that I think is incredibly healthy." He smiled at his remark and Fiske felt himself smile in return.

Sara was raising her glass as a thought hit her. "Senator, can I use a phone?"

"Use the one in my study, Sara. It's more private."

She glanced at Fiske but said nothing. After she had gone, Jordan said, "She's quite a young woman."

"I wouldn't disagree with that," Fiske said.

"Since she's been clerking for Beth, I've come to know her quite well. I've been almost like a father figure, I guess you could say. She has a brilliant future ahead of her."

"Well, she's got a great role model in your wife." Fiske almost choked on his drink as he said this.

"The absolute best. Beth does nothing halfway."

Fiske thought about this remark for a moment. "I know your wife is a real go-getter, but she might want to cut back on her schedule until the case is solved. You don't want to give some maniac a free shot."

Jordan studied Fiske over the rim of his glass for a moment. "Do you really think the justices might be in danger?"

Fiske didn't really think so, but he wasn't about to say that to Jordan. If he and Sara were wrong in their conclusions, he didn't want anyone letting down his guard.

"Let's put it this way, Senator, if anything happens to your wife, no one will care what I think."

Jordan's face slowly went pale. "I see your point."

Fiske noticed a line forming to talk to the man. "I won't take up any more of your time. Keep up the good work."

"Thank you, John, I intend to."

Senator Knight started to receive the other guests. He needn't have bothered to work the room, Fiske thought. His wife had probably already hit all the important players.

In Jordan Knight's study, Sara dialed home for messages. She had forgotten to check earlier, and she was desperately hoping to hear back from George Barker, the newspaper editor from Rufus Harms's hometown. Her hopes were rewarded when she heard the old man's deep voice on her answering machine: He sounded a little contrite, she thought.

She snatched a piece of paper from the notebook on the desk and wrote the name down: Samuel Rider. George Barker had left only the man's name; apparently, after twenty-five years, that was all the information his files had contained. She had to find out Rider's office address and telephone number right away. As she looked up, she saw the way to do it. The bookshelves on the far wall of the study held a set of current Martindale-Hubbells, the official directory of the legal profession, which purported to have the name, office address and phone number of virtually every attorney licensed to practice in the United States. It was divided by states and territories, and she decided to opt for the local jurisdictions first. As she looked through the index for the commonwealth of Virginia, her search was rewarded as she spotted the name Samuel Rider. Flipping to the page indicated, she found a brief bio of Rider. He had been in the JAG in the early seventies. That had to be the man.

She dialed the phone number to his office, but received no answer. She dialed Information for his home phone number, but it was unlisted. She hung up, thoroughly frustrated. She had to talk to the man. She thought a moment. The timing would be very tight, so there was only one way to do it. A phone directory was on the desk and she used it to look up a number. It took only a few minutes to arrange things. She and Fiske had a couple of hours before they could leave. With any luck they would be back by early tomorrow morning.

As Sara opened the door to the study, Elizabeth Knight was standing there.

"Jordan told me you might be back here."

"I had to make a phone call."

"I see."

"I guess I'll get back to the party."

"Sara, I need to talk to you in private for a moment."

Elizabeth Knight motioned her back into the study and then closed the door behind them. The justice had on a simple white dress, minimal makeup and a tasteful sapphire necklace. The white dress made her skin seem even more pallid. However, she wore her hair down and the dark strands were striking against the white background. When she made the effort, Sara thought, Elizabeth Knight could be a very attractive woman. She apparently picked those moments with great care. At this moment, Elizabeth Knight looked very uncomfortable.

"Is there something wrong?" Sara asked.

"I dislike delving into the personal lives of my clerks, Sara, I really do, but when it reflects on the image of the Court, then I feel that it is my duty to say something."

"I'm not sure I understand."

Knight collected her thoughts for a moment. Ever since the realization that she had, however unwittingly, condemned Steven Wright to death, her nerves had been in tatters. She felt like lashing out at someone, even if unfairly. It was not her habit to do such a thing, but the fact was she *was* upset with Sara Evans. And she did care about her. Thus, the young woman was going to feel the justice's wrath. "You're a very smart woman. A very attractive and smart young woman."

"I'm afraid I still don't—"

Knight's tone changed. "I'm talking about you and John Fiske. Richard Perkins reported that he saw you and Fiske leaving your home together this morning."

"Justice Knight, with all due respect, that is my personal business."

"It is certainly more than your personal business, Sara, if it reflects negatively on the Court."

"I don't see how that could possibly be the case."

"Let me see if I can make it clearer for you. Do you think it would sully the Court's reputation if it became known that one of its clerks was sleeping with the brother of her slain colleague on the day after his murder was discovered?"

"I am not sleeping with him," Sara said forcefully.

"That is quite beside the point. Public opinion is driven by perception rather than by fact, particularly in this town. If a newspaper reporter had seen you and Fiske leave your home this morning, what do you think the headline would've read? Even if it just recounted the actual facts of the reporter's observations, what do you think would be the likely perception of the reading public?" When Sara didn't answer, Knight continued. "Right now we don't need any additional adverse complications, Sara. We have quite enough of them to deal with."

"I guess I never thought that part through."

"That is exactly what you must do if you want to have anything other than a mediocre legal career."

"I'm sorry. I won't repeat the mistake."

Knight stared hard at her, then she opened the door. "Please see that you don't."

As Sara passed her, Knight added, "Oh, Sara, until the identity of the murderer is definitively ascertained, I wouldn't put your complete faith or trust in anyone. Whether you're aware of it or not, a large percentage of murders are committed by *family members.*"

Astonished, Sara turned to face her. "You're not imply-ing—"

"I imply nothing," Knight said sharply. "I'm only conveying a fact. You do with it what you will."

Bored, Fiske meandered through the apartment when he felt someone at his shoulder.

"There's a question I've been meaning to ask you."

Fiske looked around. Agent McKenna was staring at him.

"McKenna, I'm seriously considering a lawsuit against you, so get the hell away from me."

"Just doing my job. And right now I want to know where you were at the time your brother was murdered."

Fiske finished his glass of wine and then looked out the broad bank of windows. "Haven't you forgotten some-thing?"

"What's that?"

"They haven't ascertained the time of death yet."

"You're a little behind in the investigation."

"Is that right?" Fiske said, a little taken aback.

"Between three and four A.M. Saturday. Where were you during that time?"

"Am I a suspect in this case?"

"If and when you become a suspect, I'll let you know."

"I was working at my office in Richmond until about four in the morning on Saturday. Now you're going to ask me if anyone can corroborate that, right?"

"Can anyone?"

"No. But I went to the Laundromat around ten that morning."

"Richmond's only a two-hour drive from Washington. You'd have plenty of time."

"So your theory is I drove up to Washington, killed my brother in cold blood, dumped his body in the middle of a heavily black area, with such skill that no one noticed me do it, drove back to Richmond and washed my underwear. And the motive is?" As soon as Fiske said the last sentence, his next breath caught in his throat. He had the perfect motive: five hundred thousand dollars in life insurance. *Shit!*

"Motives can always come later. You have no alibi, which means you had the opportunity to commit the murder."

"So you think I murdered Wright too? Remember, you told the justices that you think the two murders are related. I do have an alibi for that one."

"Just because I said something doesn't mean it's true."

"Fascinating. Do you take that same philosophy with you to the witness stand?"

"During the course of an investigation I've found it's not always good to show your hand. The killings could be completely unrelated, which means any alibi you have for Wright's murder means nothing."

As Fiske watched McKenna walk off, a very unsettling sensation went down his spine. Even McKenna wouldn't be so stupid as to try to pin the murder of his brother on him, would he? And why hadn't Fiske known about the autopsy results ascertaining the time of his brother's death? Fiske immediately answered that question: The information flow from Chandler had dried up.

"John?"

Fiske turned around and looked at Richard Perkins.

"Got a minute?" the man asked nervously. The two men went over to a corner. Perkins looked out the window for a moment as though preparing what he was about to say. "I've only been the marshal at the Supreme Court for two years. It's a great job, prestigious, not too much stress, pays quite well. I oversee almost two hundred employees, everybody from barbers to police officers. I worked at the Senate before that, thought I'd probably retire there, but then this opportunity came up."

"Good for you," Fiske said, but he wondered why Perkins was telling him this.

"Even though your brother's death didn't take place at the Court I felt a real responsibility for his safety, for everyone who works at the Court. Now with Wright's death, I'm just reeling. I'm not used to handling things like this. I'm a lot better at payroll issues and overseeing the orderly functioning of bureaucracies than I am being in the middle of a homicide investigation."

"Well, Chandler is really good at his job. And of course you've got the FBI on the case too." Fiske almost bit his tongue when he said this. Perkins picked up on it.

"Agent McKenna seems to hold some kind of grudge against you. Have you ever met the man before?"

"No."

Perkins looked down at his hands. "Do you really think there's some crazy out there with a vendetta?"

"It's not out of the realm of possibility."

"But why now of all times? And why target clerks? Why not the justices?"

"Or other court personnel."

"What do you mean?"

"You might be in danger too, Richard."

Perkins looked astonished. "Me?"

"You're the head of security. If this person wants to show that he can pick people off at will, then he's flouting the security of the Court. He's flouting you."

Perkins seemed to consider this. "So you think the deaths are definitely connected?"

"If they're not, it's one helluva coincidence. Frankly, I don't believe in coincidences that big."

"And Chandler too?"

"Maybe. I'm sure he'll keep you informed."

As Perkins walked off, Elizabeth Knight powered by. It was as though the crowd automatically parted for her.

A hand pressed against his shoulder. "Meet me outside

the building in ten minutes." It was Sara's voice, but by the time Fiske turned around he could only see her disappearing into the crowd.

Visibly frustrated, he looked around and picked up on Elizabeth Knight's movements again. She probably forgot Kenneth Wilkinson was even here, he thought. At his own party too. He was thus very surprised when Elizabeth went over to Wilkinson and spoke with him briefly. He watched as she wheeled him out onto the lighted and empty terrace, where he could see her kneeling beside the wheelchair, holding one of Wilkinson's hands and talking to him.

Fiske mingled a bit more and then couldn't keep himself from heading out to the terrace. Elizabeth Knight looked up and then quickly rose from her kneeling position.

"I'm sorry for interrupting, but I have to leave and I wanted to say hello to Judge Wilkinson."

Knight stepped back and Fiske went forward and introduced himself. He shook Kenneth Wilkinson's hand and passed along his congratulations for the elderly man's long career in public service. As he started back into the room, Knight stopped him.

"I assume you're leaving with Sara."

"Is that a problem?"

"I guess that's up to you."

"What's that supposed to mean?"

"Sara has a wonderful future ahead of her. But little things can sometimes disrupt careers with great potential."

"You know, Justice Knight, I think you have a real problem with me, and I'm not sure why."

"I don't know you, Mr. Fiske. If you're anything like your brother, then maybe I don't have a big problem."

"I'm not like anybody else. I try not to compare people or make nice, neat assumptions. They seldom prove true."

Knight appeared taken aback by this but said, "I actually agree with you."

"I'm glad we could agree on something."

"However, I do know Sara, and I care about her very much. If certain actions you take reflect negatively on her and thus on the Court, then you're right, I do have a problem with that."

"Look, all I'm concerned about is finding out who killed my brother."

She looked at him keenly. "Are you sure that's all?"

"If I weren't sure, well, you know what, it's a free country." Fiske thought he saw an amused expression pass across her face.

She crossed her arms. "You don't seem the least bit intimidated by a Supreme Court Justice, Mr. Fiske."

"If you knew something about me, you'd understand why."

"Perhaps I should make a point of finding out about you. Perhaps I already have."

"I guess that can be a two-way street."

Knight's expression turned dark. "Confidence is one thing, Mr. Fiske, disrespect is quite another."

"I've found that also to be a two-way street."

"I hope you appreciate my concerns for Sara. They are genuine."

"I'm sure they are."

She started to turn away and then looked back at him. "Your brother was a very special person. Highly intelligent, the consummate legal analyst."

"He was one of a kind."

"With that said, I'm not sure he was the most able lawyer in his family."

Knight walked away, leaving a surprised Fiske behind. He stood there for a minute trying to analyze her words. Then he left the terrace and made his way down in the elevator to the lobby. He looked around but didn't see

Sara. A horn beeped and he saw her car ease up to the front door. He climbed in and looked over at her. "Where are we going?"

"To the airport."

"What are you talking about?"

"We're going to see Samuel Rider, Esquire."

"And who is Samuel Rider, Esquire?"

"Rufus Harms's attorney. George Barker called back with the name. I looked Rider up. He practices outside of Blacksburg, only a couple hours east of the prison. I tried his office, but there was no answer. His home phone's unlisted."

"So why are we flying out there then?"

"We have his office address. It'll be late by the time we get there, so it's a long shot he'll be in his office. But it's also not a big town: We should be able to find somebody there who can give us his home address or at least his phone number. And if we're right about his involvement, he could be in danger. If something happens to him, we may never find out the truth."

"So you really think he's the one who called the Court? The one who filed the appeal?"

"I wouldn't bet against it."

CHAPTER FORTY-THREE

Twenty-five minutes later Fiske and Sara arrived at National Airport, and Sara pulled into one of the parking garages. After that they made their way to the general aviation terminal. "Are you sure we can get a flight out?" Fiske asked.

"I chartered a private plane to take us there."

"You did what? Do you know how much that costs?"

"Do *you* know how much it costs?"

Fiske looked sheepish. "No, I mean it's not like I ever chartered a friggin' plane before. But it can't be cheap."

"It's about twenty-two hundred dollars for a round-trip flight to Blacksburg. I maxed out my credit card."

"Then I'll pay you back somehow."

"You don't have to do that."

"I don't like owing people."

"Fine, I'm sure I can figure out lots of ways for you to pay it off." She smiled.

A few minutes later they approached a small twin-engine jet sitting on the tarmac. Fiske watched as a boxy 737 lumbered down the main runway and then lifted gracefully into the air. Everywhere was the nauseating smell of jet fuel and the irritating whine of engines.

Sara and Fiske headed up the steps of the sleek jet, where they were met by a man in his fifties with short white hair and a wiry build. He introduced himself as the pilot, Chuck Herman.

Herman looked up at the skies. "I got the flight plan filed okay, but we're a little behind in the takeoff schedule. They had some delays earlier because of a software glitch in the control tower and everybody's paying for it."

"We're on a short time fuse, Chuck," Sara said. The later they arrived at Rider's office, the less likely it was that they'd find someone to help them. In addition, she couldn't be late for work again.

Herman looked proudly at his aircraft. "Not to worry. We're only talking a seventy-minute trip, and I can step on the gas if need be."

They all moved into the cabin and Herman indicated chairs for them to sit in.

"I'm sorry, but I couldn't get a cabin steward in here on such short notice. Do you two want anything?"

"A glass of white wine," Sara said.

"How about you, John? Can I get you anything?" Fiske declined. "The fridge is fully stocked with food. Please help yourself."

Ten minutes after takeoff, the flight became very smooth, like gliding on a calm pond in a canoe. Sara unstrapped her belt and looked over at Fiske. He stared out the window at the sinking sun.

"How about I fix up something to eat? And I've got some interesting things to tell you."

"Same here." Fiske unstrapped himself, followed her back and sat down at the table, where he watched Sara make up some sandwiches.

"Coffee?"

Fiske nodded. "Something tells me it's going to be a long night."

Sara finished making the food and poured out two cups of coffee. She sat down across from Fiske and looked at her watch. "The flight is so short we don't have all that much time. There aren't any rental car places at the airport in Blacksburg. We can take a cab to a rental place in town and get a car there, though."

Fiske took a bite of sandwich and swallowed it down with some coffee. "You mentioned some things that happened at the party."

"I had a run-in with Justice Knight." She recounted the story to Fiske. He then shared his own experience with Knight.

"A hard woman to figure out," Fiske remarked.

"Anything else?"

"McKenna asked me if I had an alibi for the time my brother was murdered."

"Are you serious?"

"I don't have an alibi, Sara."

"John, it's not like anyone believes that you could have murdered your own brother. And how would that tie in to Steven's death?"

"If the two are connected."

"So did McKenna have a theory as to what your motive might be?"

Fiske put his coffee down. It might be good to get somebody else's view, he thought. "No, but the fact is, I have a perfect motive."

Surprised, she put down her coffee. "What?"

"I found out today that Mike had taken out a half-million-dollar life insurance policy on himself and named me as the beneficiary. That qualifies as a top-rank motive, don't you think?"

"But you said you just found out today."

"Do you seriously think McKenna will believe that?"

"That's strange."

Fiske cocked his head at her. "What is?"

"Justice Knight said something along the lines that most homicides are committed by family members, and that I shouldn't trust anybody—meaning, I'm sure, you."

"Was she ever in the Army that you know?"

Sara almost laughed. "No, why?"

"I was just wondering if she could have anything to do with Rufus Harms."

Sara smiled. "But now that we're on the subject, how about Senator Knight? He might have been in the Army."

"He wasn't. I remember reading in the Richmond papers during his first Senate campaign that he was physically unable to be in the Armed Forces. His political opponent at the time was a war hero and he tried to make a big deal out of Knight not serving his country. But he did, in an intelligence capacity, good record and all, and the whole thing went away." Fiske shook his head in frustration. "This is silly. We're trying to pound square pegs in round holes." He took a long breath. "I hope Rider can help us."

Dressed in overalls, the man pushed the bulky cleaning cart down the hallway and then stopped outside one office, noting the stenciled lettering on the frosted glass door: SAMUEL RIDER, ATTORNEY-AT-LAW. The man cocked his head and looked around, listening intently. The office building was small and Rider's law office was one of only a half dozen places of business on the second floor. At this hour, the town and the building were pretty much deserted.

Josh Harms tapped against the door and waited for a response. He tapped again, this time a little louder. Josh had left Rufus in the truck parked in the alley while he reconnoitered the area. He had found the cleaning supply closet and hatched his plan in case someone showed up. He tapped on Rider's office door once more, waited another couple of minutes, pursed his lips and gave a low whistle. Within twenty seconds, Rufus, who had been trailing him in the darkness of the hallway, joined him. Rufus wasn't wearing a cleaning uniform; there hadn't been one in the storage closet that came close to fitting him.

Josh pulled his lock-pick equipment and within a few seconds they were on the other side of the office door in the receptionist's area.

"We got to move fast. Somebody might show up," Josh said. Tucked inside his belt was his pistol, fully loaded, a round chambered.

"I'll look here and you go into Samuel's office and start looking around."

Rufus was already going through a file cabinet using the flashlight he had brought with him from the truck. Josh went into Rider's office. The first thing he did, after checking the street for activity, was close the drapes. He pulled out a flashlight of his own and started searching. He came to the locked desk drawer and jimmied it. He gave a low whistle as his hand closed around the packet that had been taped to the underside of the desk drawer. He went to the doorway. "Rufus, I got it."

His brother rushed in and took the papers. He scanned them under the flashlight's arc.

"You still ain't told me how having these pieces of paper is gonna help your butt any which way."

"I ain't thought that all the way through, but I'd rather have them than not have them."

"Well, let's get out of here before somebody has *us.*"

They had barely made it to the receptionist area when they both heard the footsteps, two sets of them. They glanced quickly at each other. Josh pulled the pistol and punched off the safety. "Cops. They know we're here."

Rufus looked at him and shook his head. "It ain't the cops. And it ain't the Army. Building's deserted. If it was them they'd come in here sirens going and the next sound we'd be hearing is glass breaking when the tear gas canisters come through the damn window. Come on." Rufus led the way back into Rider's interior office and softly closed the door. All they could do now was wait.

CHAPTER FORTY-FOUR

Chandler walked around Michael Fiske's apartment. He knelt down and examined the gouge mark in the floor caused by John Fiske's swing with a tire iron. If the blow had found its mark, this mystery might have been solved. Chandler rose and shook his head. It was never that easy. His men were putting the finishing touches on the apartment. Black carbon dusting powder lay everywhere in piles like magic sprinkles, which in a way they were. They had taken Michael Fiske's prints for purposes of elimination. They would have to get his brother's as well. Since John Fiske was a lawyer licensed in Virginia, his fingerprints would be on file with the Virginia State Police. He should get Sara Evans's prints as well, he figured. She had undoubtedly been here too. He looked down the hallway. In the bedroom, perhaps? However, his inquiries had revealed only that the two had been good friends.

He had met with Murphy and his clerks. They had gone over all the cases Michael had been working on. Nothing really stuck out. That line of investigation would simply take too long. And people were dying.

John Fiske's unwillingness to confide in Chandler had cost him. As Fiske had earlier deduced, Chandler had cut off the flow of information to him. Chandler had played fair with the Feds, though, and passed along what he had to McKenna, including his newfound information on Rufus Harms's escape from prison and Michael Fiske's earlier calls to the prison. He had also informed McKenna of the missing appeal Fiske had told him about. McKenna had thanked him but had been unable to add any new information of his own. As if on cue, he heard a sound at the front door and the FBI agent walked into the room— after showing his ID card to the uniform outside and being added to the crime scene list, Chandler assumed. Crime scene. Well, it was one of sorts, Chandler said to himself.

"You're working late tonight, Agent McKenna."

"So are you." The FBI agent's gaze swept the area, starting at the center and marching outward grid by grid.

"So, is the director of the FBI just a little bit on your butt, or a lot, to get this thing solved?"

"Same as your boss. In the Bureau you get double kudos if you solve the crime in time for the evening news." McKenna flashed a rare smile, although it was as though his mouth didn't know quite how to manage it, because the effect came off as lopsided.

Chandler wondered if the man did it on purpose to throw people off. Because he'd had a weird feeling about the guy, Chandler had discreetly checked out Warren McKenna. His career at the Bureau was first-rate in all respects. He had been assigned to the Washington Metropolitan Field Office at Buzzard Point for eight years after transferring from the Richmond Field Office. Before his career at the FBI, he had done a brief stint in the military, then completed college. Since that time McKenna had done nothing except make positive impressions on his superiors. One curious thing Chandler had found out: McKenna had refused several promotions that would have taken him out of the field.

"You're lucky John Fiske hasn't slapped you with a lawsuit yet. He still might."

"Maybe he should," was McKenna's surprising reply. "I probably would if I were him."

"I'll be sure and tell him that," Chandler said slowly.

McKenna's gaze darted all over the place for a couple of minutes, seemingly absorbing every detail like a sheet of Polaroid, before he glanced back at Chandler. "What are you, anyway, his mentor?"

"Didn't know the man until a couple days ago."

"You make friends a lot faster than I do, then." McKenna inclined his head at Chandler. "Mind if I look around?"

"Go ahead. Try not to touch anything that doesn't look like it's got a pound of print dust on it."

McKenna nodded and stepped carefully around the living room. He noted the mark on the floor.

"Fiske going after his purported attacker?"

"That's right. Only I didn't know he was purported."

"He is until we have a corroborating account. At least that's how I work."

Chandler unwrapped a piece of gum and popped it in his mouth, slowly chewing over both the agent's words and the gum.

"Sara Evans reported to me that she also saw a man flee from the building and that Fiske was chasing him. Is that good enough for you?"

"That's convenient corroboration. Fiske is one lucky guy. He should run out right now and play the lottery while he's so hot."

"I wouldn't call losing your brother being lucky."

McKenna stopped walking and looked at the pantry

door, which was ajar and covered with print dust. "I guess it depends on how you look at it, doesn't it?"

"What the hell do you have against him? You don't even know the guy."

McKenna's eyes flashed at him. "That's right, Detective Chandler, and you know what? Neither do you."

Chandler wanted to say something back but couldn't think of anything. In a way the man was right. This thought was interrupted by one of his men.

"Detective Chandler, we found something I think you might want to see."

Chandler took the sheaf of papers from the tech and looked down at it. McKenna joined him.

"Looks like an insurance policy," McKenna said.

"We found it on one of the shelves in the pantry. No food in there. Guy used it for storage. Tax returns, bills and stuff like that are in there too."

"Half a million bucks worth of life insurance," Chandler muttered. He flipped rapidly through the pages, passing by the legalese until he got to the end, where more specific information was set forth.

"Michael Fiske was the insured."

McKenna's finger suddenly stabbed at the bottom of the page. Chandler paled a little as he read the line the man had so energetically indicated. "And John is the primary beneficiary."

The two men looked at each other. "Would you like to take a walk and hear a theory of mine?" McKenna asked.

Chandler wasn't sure exactly what to do.

"It won't take long," McKenna added. "In fact, some of it you're probably thinking right now, I would imagine."

Chandler finally shrugged. "You got five minutes."

The two men walked out onto the sidewalk in front of the row house. McKenna took a moment to light up a cigarette and then offered one to Chandler. The detective held out his pack of gum. "I can be overweight or I can smoke. I like to eat, so there we are."

They strolled along the dark street as McKenna began talking. "I found out that Fiske doesn't have an alibi for the probable time his brother was murdered."

"Might be something in his favor. If he killed his brother, he would've worked hard to establish one."

"I disagree for a couple of reasons. First, he probably never thought he would become a suspect."

"With a half-million-dollar life insurance policy?"

"He might have thought we wouldn't find out. We go down a different trail and that's it. He waits awhile and then collects his money."

"I don't know about that. What's your second point?"

"If he had some perfect alibi—which there is no such thing if you're guilty—then a hole would come up in it somewhere, sometime, somehow. So why bother? He was a cop and now a lawyer. He knows all about alibis. He says he doesn't have one and then he doesn't have to worry about it blowing up in his face. And then he counts on everybody reaching the conclusion you just did, namely, that if he's guilty he would've concocted a good one."

McKenna took a long drag on his cigarette and looked up at the few stars visible in the sky. "So he's got motive and, by his own admission, opportunity. I checked him out. He's got a dip-shit law practice in Richmond, defending the scum of the earth. Guy never even went to law school. He's third-rate at best. Unmarried, no kids, lives in a shithole. A real loner. Oh, and he left the Richmond police force under a somewhat dark cloud."

"How do you mean?" Chandler asked sharply.

"Let's just say that there was a shooting incident that was never fully explained other than the fact a civilian and another police officer were dead as a result."

Chandler looked shaken, but recovered. "So why does he come up and offer his assistance in the investigation?"

"Again, a cover. Fiske's position would be, 'How could I have pulled the trigger? I'm up here working my butt off to find the person who murdered my brother.'"

"How does that explain Wright's death?"

"Who says it has to? Like you said, the two murders could be unrelated. If they are, then if I were Fiske I'd jump on it and argue that they are connected. See, he's got an alibi for Wright's murder."

Evans again, Chandler thought.

McKenna continued, "So if we believe they're connected, he's home free."

"And Sara Evans? Remember? She said she saw the guy running out of Michael Fiske's apartment building. You say she's lying too?"

McKenna stopped walking and so did Chandler. McKenna took a last puff of his cigarette and then crushed it out on the sidewalk with several twists of his foot. "Sara Evans too," McKenna repeated Chandler's words, eyeing the detective closely.

Chandler shook his head. "Come on, McKenna."

"I'm not saying she's in on the whole thing. I'm saying maybe she has a thing for Fiske and she's doing what he tells her to."

"They just met."

"Is that right? You know that for sure?"

"Actually, no."

"Okay, he convinces her he's done nothing wrong, but some people might try to frame him."

"Why do you have such a thing against Fiske?"

Now McKenna erupted. "He's got a smart mouth. He comes off as holier than thou, the defender of his brother's memory, only they seemed to have no contact recently. He and Evans spent the night at her house doing who knows what the day after his brother's body is found. He's got a shotgun for some reason. He's nosed his way into the investigation, which means he knows just about everything we do. He's got no alibi for the night of the murder and five minutes ago we found out he's a half million bucks richer because his brother is dead. What the hell am I supposed to think? Are you saying your cop radar's not even tingling over this?"

"Okay, you've made your point. Maybe I have been too lax with him. Rule number one: Don't trust anybody."

"Good rule to live by." McKenna paused and then added, "Or die by." He walked off leaving a very shaken Chandler staring after him.

CHAPTER FORTY-FIVE

Fiske knocked on Rider's office door. He squinted through the glass. "Dark inside."

"He's probably at home. We need to find out where that is."

"Well, the guy also might be eating dinner out, or out of town on business. He might even be on vacation. Or—"

"Or something could have happened to him," Sara said.

"Don't get overly dramatic." Fiske clasped the doorknob and it turned easily. He and Sara exchanged a significant glance. Fiske looked up and down the hallway. That's when he saw the cleaning cart and relaxed slightly. "Cleaning crew?"

"And they're cleaning in the pitch-dark because . . . ?" Sara responded.

"That's just what I was thinking." He pulled Sara away from the door and over to the cart. He rummaged around, before pulling out a pair of Vise-Grips from a toolbox.

Whispering, he said, "Go down near the exit stairs. If you hear anything, run to the car and call the cops."

She grabbed his arm and whispered back, "I have a much better idea. Let's go call the police together right now and report a burglary."

"We don't know that it is a burglary."

"We don't know that it isn't either."

"If we leave, they could get away."

"And if you go in there and get killed, what exactly is that going to accomplish? You don't even have a gun— you have that thing, whatever the hell that is."

"Vise-Grips."

"Great, they could have guns and you have a tool."

"Maybe you're right."

"Lady is for sure right. Too bad you didn't listen."

Fiske and Sara whirled around.

Josh Harms stood there, his pistol aimed at them.

"Wall's mighty thin. Figured when we heard the door start to open, and then all that whispering, you two were going to go for the cops. Can't let you do that."

Fiske studied him. He was big but not bulky. Unless they had run into a routine burglary, this man had to be Josh Harms. He eyed the gun and then scrutinized Josh's features, trying to size up quickly whether he had it in him to pull the trigger. He had killed in Vietnam; Fiske knew that from reading the news reports. But killing them would have to be in cold blood, and Fiske just did not see that in Josh Harms's eyes. But that could always change. Mouth, do your magic, he told himself.

"Hello, Josh, my name's John Fiske. This is Sara Evans with the United States Supreme Court. Where's your brother?"

Behind him, from the open doorway leading into Rider's office, appeared a man of such huge proportions that both Sara and Fiske knew he could only be Rufus Harms. He had obviously heard Fiske's words.

"How you know all that?" Rufus said while his brother kept his pistol tightly on the pair.

"I'd be glad to tell you. But why don't we talk inside the office? You have that APB out on you and everything."

He motioned to Sara. "After you, Sara." Out of the Harms brothers' line of sight, he gave her a reassuring wink. He only wished he could feel as confident on the inside. They were confronted with a convicted murderer who had been in a hellhole for twenty-five years, which had probably not made him any nicer, and a wily Vietnam vet whose trigger finger was looking itchier with every passing second.

Sara walked into the office, with Fiske behind her.

Josh and Rufus eyed each other quizzically. Then they followed the pair inside and shut the door behind them.

The Jeep sailed through the back roads on the way to Samuel Rider's office. Tremaine was driving; Rayfield sat beside him. The two-seater Jeep was Tremaine's private vehicle. They were both off duty now and had decided against checking out a military vehicle from the motor pool. In case anyone came upon them while they were searching Rider's office, they had settled upon a cover story: Sam Rider, Rufus Harms's old military attorney, practiced in the area and had recently visited Harms in prison for an unknown reason. Rider and his wife had been killed. Harms and his brother could have committed the murders; perhaps Rider had mentioned to Harms that he kept cash or other valuables at his home or office.

Tremaine glanced over at Rayfield.

"Something wrong?" Tremaine asked.

Rayfield stared straight ahead. "This is a big mistake. We're taking all the risks here."

"You think I don't know that?"

"If we get the letter that Harms filed, along with Rider's letter, maybe we can forget about Harms."

Tremaine looked sharply over at him. "What the hell are you talking about?"

"Harms wrote that letter because he wanted out of prison. He killed the little girl, but he really didn't *murder* her, right? Well, he's out of prison. He and his brother are probably in Mexico right now waiting on a plane to South America. That's exactly what I'd be doing."

Tremaine shook his head. "We can't be sure of that."

"What else is he going to do, Vic? Write another letter to the Court and say, what? 'Your Honor, I wrote you before with this crazy story I can't prove, but something happened to my appeal, and my lawyer and the clerk who got it are now dead. So I escaped from prison, I'm on the run and I want my day in court.' That's bullshit, Vic. He's not going to do that. He's going to run like hell. He *is* running like hell."

Tremaine considered this. "Maybe. But on the off chance that he isn't as smart as you think he is, I'm going to do everything I can to blow him away. And his brother. I don't like Rufus Harms. I've never liked the guy. I'm getting my ass shot up in Nam and he's back in the States safe and sound, three squares a day. We should've just let him rot in the stockade, but we didn't," Tremaine added bitterly.

"Too late for that now."

"Well, I'm going to do him a big favor. When I find him, his next cell is going to be seven feet long, four feet wide and made of pine. And he ain't getting a damn flag on it." Tremaine punched the gas even more.

Rayfield shook his head and settled back down in his seat. He checked his watch and then looked down the road. They were almost at Rider's office.

Sara and Fiske sat on the leather couch while the Harms brothers stood in front of them.

"Why don't we just tie them up and get the hell out of here?" Josh said to his brother.

Fiske jumped in. "I think you're going to find we're on the same side."

Josh scowled at him. "Now, don't go taking this the wrong way, but you're full of shit."

"He's right," Sara said. "We're here to help you." Josh snorted but didn't bother to respond.

"John Fiske?" Rufus said. He studied Fiske's features, remembering where he'd seen similar ones. "That clerk they killed was family, wasn't he? Brother?"

Fiske nodded. "Yes. Who killed him?"

Josh broke in: "Don't tell them nothing, Rufus. We don't know who they are or what they want."

"We came here to talk to Sam Rider," Sara said.

Josh looked over at her. "Well, unless you're gonna put on a séance or something you're gonna have a real hard time doing that."

Fiske and Sara looked at each other and then back at the brothers.

"He's dead?" Sara asked.

Rufus nodded. "He and his wife. Made it look like suicide."

Fiske noted the file clutched in his hand. "Is that what you sent to the Court?"

"You mind if I ask the questions?" Rufus said.

"I'm telling you, Rufus, we're your friends."

"Sorry, but I don't make friends nowhere near that easy. What'd you want to talk to Samuel about?"

"He filed that for you at the Court, didn't he?"

"I ain't answering no questions."

"Okay, I'll just tell you what we know and then you can take it from there. How's that sound?"

"I'm listening."

"Rider filed it. My brother got it and took it out of the Court's system. He came to the prison to see you. Then he ended up dead in an alley in Washington. They made it look like a robbery. Now you tell us Rider is dead. Another clerk was killed too. I think it's connected to my brother's death, but I'm not sure why." Fiske stopped talking and studied the two men. "That's all we know. Now, I think you know a lot more. Like why all this is happening."

"You know so much. You with the cops?" Josh demanded.

"I'm helping the detective in charge."

"See, Rufus, I told you. We got to get out of here. Cops probably on their way right now."

"No, they're not," Sara said. "I saw your name in the papers Michael had, Mr. Harms, but that's all I saw. I don't know why you filed it or what was in it."

"Why does a prisoner file something with a court?" Rufus asked.

"Because you want out," Fiske said. Rufus nodded. "But you have to have grounds to do that."

"I got me the best grounds of all: the simple truth," Rufus said forcefully.

"Tell me what it is," said Fiske.

Josh edged toward the door. "Rufus, I got a bad feeling about all this. We stand here talking to them and the cops are closing in. You've already said too much."

"They killed his brother, Josh."

"You don't know if he really is his brother."

Fiske pulled out his wallet with his driver's license.

"This'll at least prove we have the same last name."

Rufus waved it off. "I don't need to see that. You got the same way about you too."

"Even if they ain't in on it, what the hell can they do to help?" Josh asked.

Rufus looked over at Fiske and Sara. "You both talk real good and quick. You got an answer to that one?"

"I work at the Supreme Court, Mr. Harms," Sara said. "I

know all the justices. If you have evidence that shows you're innocent, then I promise you it will be heard. If not by the Supreme Court, then by another court, believe me."

Fiske added, "The detective on the case knows something is fishy. If you tell us what's going on, we can go to him and get him to explore that angle."

"I know the truth," Rufus said again.

"That's great, Rufus, but the fact is, in a court of law it's not the truth unless you can prove it," Fiske said.

Sara said, "What was in your appeal, then?"

"Rufus, don't you answer that, dammit!" Josh yelled.

Rufus ignored him. "Something the Army sent me."

"Did you kill the little girl, Rufus?" Fiske asked.

"I did," he said, looking down. "At least my hands did. The rest of me didn't know what the hell was going on. Not after what they done to me."

"What do you mean by that? Who did what to you?"

"Rufus, he's looking to trick you," Josh warned.

"Messed with my head, that's what," Rufus said.

Fiske eyed him sharply. "Are you pleading some sort of insanity? Because if you are, you don't have a chance in hell." He watched Rufus intently. "But it's more than that, isn't it?"

"Why you say that?" Rufus said.

"Because my brother took whatever was in that appeal very seriously. Seriously enough that he broke the law by taking it, and lost his life trying to help you. He wouldn't have done that for some twenty-five-year-old insanity plea. Tell me what it was that cost my brother his life."

Josh put one big hand on Fiske's chest and pushed him hard against the back of the couch. "Look here, Mr. Smart-ass, Rufus here didn't ask your brother to do jack-shit for him. Your brother was the one that blew this whole thing up sky-high. He had to come check Rufus out cuz he's some old colored man sitting in some old prison for some old crime. So don't sit there singing that song 'bout your 'righteous brother.' "

Fiske ripped the hand away. "Why don't you go to hell, you sonofabitch!"

Josh moved the pistol closer to Fiske's face and said menacingly, "Why don't I send you there first? I catch up with you later. How's that sound, whitebread?"

"Please don't," Sara implored. "Please, he's just trying to help."

"I don't need no damn help from the likes of you."

"We're only trying to get your brother justice in a court of law."

Josh shook his head. "I can get me justice in a court all by myself. We done overwhelmed your white asses. Prisons full of us and you just too cheap to build more. So I can get me mor'n justice in a court. Problem is I can't get me none on the outside, and damn if that ain't where I spend most of my time."

"This ain't the way to handle things," Rufus said.

"Oh, so now you know the way to handle everything all of a sudden?" said Josh.

Fiske was growing more nervous. Josh Harms sounded like he was at the point where maybe even his brother would have no control over him. Should he make a jump for the gun? Josh was probably fifteen years older than he, but the man looked as strong as an oak tree. If Fiske made a grab and got tossed on his head, he would probably be eating several rounds from the 9mm.

The screeching of rubber against asphalt made them all look toward the window. Rufus hustled across and cautiously looked out. When he turned back from the window they all could see the fear in his eyes.

"It's Vic Tremaine and Rayfield."

"Shit!" Josh exclaimed. "What they carrying?"

Rufus took one long breath. "Vic's got a machine gun."

"Shit!" Josh said again as they all listened to the heavy

boots clattering into the building. In another couple of minutes, maybe less, they would be here. He suddenly glared at Fiske and Sara. "I told you. They set us up. We been sitting here jawing with them while the Army surrounds this place."

"In case you didn't notice, we're not in uniform," Fiske said. "Maybe they followed you."

"We didn't come from the direction of the prison. When they see the two of us, they're gonna shoot, and that's it."

"Not if you give yourselves up, they won't."

"That ain't an option," Josh said loudly.

"It ain't an option," Rufus repeated. "They ain't gonna let me live, knowing what I know."

Fiske looked at Rufus Harms. The man's eyes darted left and right. He had admitted to killing the girl. Shouldn't that be an end to it? Why not let the Army put him back in his cage? But Mike had wanted to help him.

Fiske jumped up.

Josh covered him with his pistol. "Don't make this no harder than it is."

Fiske didn't even look at him; his eyes were squarely on Rufus. "Rufus? Rufus!"

Rufus finally seemed to break out of his inertia and looked at him.

"Maybe I can get you out of this, but you have to do exactly what I say."

Josh said, "We can damn well get ourselves out of this."

"In about thirty seconds those two guys are going to come through that door and it'll be over. You can't match their firepower."

"How 'bout I put one of my bullets in you right now?" Josh said.

"Rufus, will you trust me? My brother came to help you. Let me finish what he started. Come on, Rufus. Give me a chance." A bead of sweat trickled down Fiske's forehead.

Sara couldn't even speak. All she could hear were those boots, all she could see was that machine gun, coming closer and closer.

Finally, almost imperceptibly, Rufus nodded.

Fiske launched into action. "Get in the bathroom, both of you," he said.

Josh started to protest until Rufus cut him off and pushed him toward the private bath adjoining the office.

"Sara, you go with them."

She looked at him, stunned. "What?"

"Just do what I say. If you hear me call your name, flush the toilet and then come out. You two"—he nodded at the brothers—"stay behind that door. If you don't hear me say your name, Sara, stay put."

"And you don't think them Army boys might just want to come take a peek at the toilet, especially if the door's closed?" Josh asked sarcastically.

"Let me worry about that."

"Okay," Josh said slowly. "But let me give you another thing to worry about, smart boy. You sell us out and the first bullet I fire is gonna hit you right about here." Josh placed his pistol against the base of Fiske's skull. "But you won't even hear my pistol fire. You'll be dead before your damn ears tells your damn brain."

Fiske nodded at Josh as though accepting his challenge, which, in effect, he was. He looked at Sara; her face was pale. She leaned into him, shaking hard, trying, without success, to catch her breath, as the pounding feet drew closer.

"John, I can't do this."

He gripped her shoulders hard. "Sara, you *can* do this. You are going to do this. Now go. Go." He squeezed her hand and then she and the Harms brothers went into the bathroom and Sara shut the door behind them. Fiske looked around the office, fighting hard to get his composure. He spied a briefcase against one wall, grabbed it and unsnapped the lid. It was empty. He stuffed files from the top of Rider's desk into the briefcase. As the boots boomed down the hallway, he raced to the small conference table set up in one corner. As he sat down, he heard the outer door open. As he pulled a file from the briefcase and opened it, he heard the inner door start to open. He leaned back in the chair and pretended to study some of the papers as the door opened. He stared up into the faces of the men.

"What the hell—" he started to say until he saw the machine gun pointed at him and fell silent.

"Who are you?" Rayfield demanded.

"I was about to ask you that question. I'm here for a meeting with Sam Rider. I've been waiting ten minutes already and he hasn't bothered to show up."

Rayfield edged closer. "You're a client of his?"

Fiske nodded. "Flew in from Washington this evening on a chartered plane. The meeting's been planned for several weeks now."

"Little late for a meeting, isn't it?" Tremaine's eyes bored into Fiske.

"I have a very busy schedule. This was the only time I could meet." He looked at both men sternly. "And why is the Army bursting in here with machine guns in the first place?"

Tremaine's face flushed angrily, but Rayfield assumed a more diplomatic tone. "It's not our business, Mr—"

Fiske started to say his real last name, but then decided not to. Rufus had known these men by name. That meant these men were somehow involved with whatever had happened to Rufus. If that was true, they might have killed Mike.

"Michaels, John Michaels. I run a real estate development company and Rider is my land-use attorney."

"Well, you're going to have to get another lawyer," Rayfield said.

"I'm happy with Sam's work."

"That's not the point. The point is Rider's dead. He committed suicide. Killed his wife and then himself."

Fiske stood up, trying to make his expression as horrified as possible. It wasn't too hard, given the fact that he was trying to scam two armed men, with two more armed men in the adjoining room. If he failed, he would be the first casualty, if Josh Harms had anything to say about it.

"What the hell are you talking about? I spoke with him recently. He seemed fine."

"That's all well and good, but the fact is he's dead," Rayfield said.

Fiske sat down abruptly, looking numbly at the files in front of him. "I can't believe it," he said, slowly shaking his head. "I feel like an idiot. Sitting in the man's office waiting to hold a meeting. But I didn't know. No one told me. The door to his office was unlocked. Christ!" He pushed the files away, then looked up sharply. "So what are you two doing here? Why is the Army involved?"

Tremaine and Rayfield exchanged glances. "There's been an escape from the military prison nearby."

"Good Lord, you think whoever escaped is around here?"

"Don't know. Fact is, Rider was the escapee's lawyer. We thought he might hit this place for some cash or something. Who knows, the prisoner might have murdered Rider, for all we know."

"But you said it was a suicide."

"That's what the police think. That's why we're here. To look around, catch the guy if he's here."

Fiske watched with a sinking heart as Tremaine headed to the bathroom door.

"Susan, can you please come out here?" Fiske called in a loud voice.

Tremaine stared hard at Fiske as they all heard the toilet flush. And then the door opened partially and Sara came out, trying her best to look astonished. She did a pretty good job, Fiske thought, probably because she too was scared shitless.

"John, what's going on?"

"I told these gentlemen about our meeting with Sam Rider. You're not going to believe this, but he's dead."

"Oh, my God."

"Susan is my assistant." She nodded at both men.

"I didn't get your names," Fiske said.

"That's right," Tremaine shot back.

Fiske hurriedly continued: "These men are from the Army. They're looking for an escaped prisoner. They think the person might have had something to do with Sam's death."

"Oh, my God. John, let's just get back on the plane and get out of here."

"That's not a bad idea," Tremaine said. "We can search the place a lot faster with you two out of the way." He once again looked over at the bathroom door. Holding his gun with one hand, he reached out to push the door all the way open.

"Well, I can tell you there's no one hiding in there," she said with as straight a face as she could.

"If you don't mind, ma'am, I like to see these things for myself," Tremaine said curtly.

Fiske watched Sara. He was sure she was going to start screaming. Come on, Sara, hold on. Don't lose it.

Behind the door of the darkened bathroom, Josh Harms had his pistol pointed directly at Tremaine's head through the slight gap between the door and doorjamb.

Josh had already sized up the tactical advantages he had, slight though they were. Vic Tremaine first, and then Rayfield, unless Rayfield got him first, which was a real possibility given Josh's very limited field of vision. Well, there was no way he could miss the little Sherman tank of a target Vic Tremaine represented. His hand tightened on the trigger as his brother loomed over his shoulder, pressing his bulk up as far as he could against the wall. But there was barely an inch of space between him and the door. As soon as Tremaine touched the wood, it would be over.

At that moment Fiske started to stuff the files in his briefcase. "I can't believe it. First two black guys almost run us over and now this."

Tremaine and Rayfield jerked around and stared at him. "What two black guys?" they said in unison.

Fiske stopped what he was doing and looked at them. "We were coming in the building and they ran by us, almost knocked Susan down."

"What'd they look like?" Rayfield asked, his voice strained as he edged closer to Fiske. Tremaine quickly moved away from the bathroom door.

"Well, they were black, like I said. Now, one of them looked like he was ex-NFL or something. You remember how big he was, Susan?" She nodded and then started breathing again. "I mean, he was huge. And the guy with him was pretty big too, six-two, six-three at least, but a lot leaner. They were running like the devil and they weren't young either. Forty-five, fifty if they were a day."

"Did you see which way they went?" Tremaine asked.

"They jumped in some old car and took off on the main road heading north. I'm not good with cars, I don't know the make or anything, but it was an old model. Green, I think." He suddenly looked frightened. "You don't think it was the escaped prisoner, do you?"

Tremaine and Rayfield didn't answer because they were rushing out the door. As soon as they heard the outer door open and the boots running down the hallway, Fiske and Sara looked at each other and then they both, as though tied together with string, collapsed onto the sofa. They reached for each other and huddled together.

"Glad I didn't have to shoot you. You think fast on your feet."

They looked up at the grinning face of Josh Harms as he jammed his pistol into his pants. "We're both lawyers," Fiske said hoarsely, still clutching Sara tightly.

"Well, nobody's perfect," Josh said.

Rufus appeared behind his brother. "Thanks," he said quietly.

"I hope you believe us now," Fiske said.

"Yeah, but I ain't gonna take your help."

"Rufus—"

"Everybody's tried to help me up till now, they're dead. Except Josh, and we all almost bought it tonight. I ain't having that on my conscience. You two get back on that plane of yours and stay the hell out of this."

"I can't do that. He was my brother."

"Suit yourself, but you're gonna do it without me." He went to the window and watched as the Jeep sped off, heading north. He motioned to Josh. "Let's get going. No telling when they might get the itch to come back."

As the two men started to turn away, Fiske reached in his pocket and took out something, which he held out to Rufus. "This is my business card. It's got my office and home numbers on it. Rufus, think about what you're doing. By yourself, you're not going to get anywhere. When you finally realize that, call me."

Fiske looked surprised as Sara lifted the card from him and wrote something on the back. She held it out to Rufus. "That's my home and car phone numbers on the back. Call either one of us, day or night."

Slowly, the huge hand reached out, took the card. Rufus slipped it in his shirt pocket. In another minute Sara and Fiske were all alone. They again stared at each other, completely drained. A full minute passed before Fiske broke the silence.

"Well, I have to admit, that was pretty close."

"John, I never, ever want to do that again." Sara walked unsteadily to the bathroom.

"Where are you going?"

She didn't bother to look back at him. "To the bathroom. Unless you want me to throw up out here."

CHAPTER FORTY-SIX

An hour after his conversation with Warren McKenna, Chandler climbed out of his car and walked slowly to his house. It was a comfortable brick and siding split-level set in a neighborhood of like structures. A nice, safe place to raise kids—at least it had been twenty years ago. It wasn't as safe or as nice today, but then what was? he thought.

Many years ago, when he wanted to unwind after work, he would shoot a few hoops in the driveway with his kids using the basketball net he had hung over the garage doors. That net had long since rotted away and the hoop and backboard had been removed. Now he went into the small backyard, where he sat down on a weathered gray cedar bench, situated near a spreading magnolia and in front of a small in-ground fountain. His wife had pestered him into putting in the fountain and he had bitched and complained the whole time. It was only after he had finished the project that he had understood her insistence. Building the thing had been cathartic for him: the planning, the measurements, the selection of materials. It was a lot like detective work, meaning a jigsaw puzzle where, if you were equal parts competent and lucky, all the pieces fit.

After ten minutes of quiet he finally lurched to his feet, his coat thrown over his shoulder, and ambled into the house. He looked around the quiet, dark kitchen. It was well decorated, the whole house was, due entirely to the efforts of his wife, Juanita. Kids raised, doctor visits made, bills paid, flowers tended to, grass clipped, beds made, clothes washed and ironed, meals cooked, dishes cleaned—she did all those things while he worked horrendous hours on his way up. That had been their partnership. After the kids were gone, she had gone back to school, become a nurse and worked at a local hospital on the pediatric wing. Married thirty-three years now and still going strong.

Chandler had no idea how much longer he could continue being a detective. It was all getting to him. The stench of the work, the feel of his hands in rubber gloves, the taking of tiny, measured steps for fear of trampling a bit of evidence that might cost somebody his life or let a butcher go free. The paperwork, the slick defense attorneys asking the same questions, plotting the same verbal traps, the bored judges reading off the sentencing guidelines like they were parceling out test results. The robotic looks of the defendants who said nothing, showed no emotion, went to prison with all their buddies, their institution of higher learning, coming out much more accomplished criminals.

The ringing phone cut short these depressing thoughts. "Hello?" He listened for a couple of minutes, gave a series of instructions and hung up. A slug had been found in the alleyway where Michael Fiske's body had been discovered. It apparently had ricocheted off one wall and gotten wedged in some trash that had fallen behind a Dumpster. From what Chandler had been told, the slug was in very good shape with little projectile deformity. The lab would have to confirm that it was actually the bullet that had killed the young clerk. That would be fairly easy to determine for a sickening reason: The slug would have blood, bone and brain tissue residue on it that could be linked pretty much conclusively to the head of Michael Fiske. With the bullet in hand, they could now search hard for the murder weapon. Ballistics could match the slug to the gun that had fired it with the reliability of matching fingerprints to a human hand.

Chandler rose and went into the living room, purposely leaving his own gun behind. He sat down in a recliner that matched his bulky proportions. The room was dark and he did not move to turn on a light. He had too many lights around him at work. Lights in his office beating down on him every day. Harsher lights in the autopsy room, that made every piece of flesh enormous, ominously raw, memorable to the point of Chandler's excusing himself every once in a great while to go to the men's room, where his stomach showed its appreciation for the polished skill of official dismemberment. The popping lights of the photographers at a crime scene or a courthouse. Too many damn lights. Darkness was quiet, darkness was soothing. Darkness was how he wanted his retirement to be. Cool and dark. Like his fountain in the backyard.

Warren McKenna's words had disturbed Chandler, though he had tried hard not to show it. He couldn't bring himself to accept that John Fiske could murder his own brother. But, truth be known, wouldn't that be exactly what Fiske wanted Chandler to believe? But then he had something else to think about. Michael Fiske's phone calls to Fort Jackson. And now Rufus Harms's escape. Were they connected? Fiske was covering for Sara Evans, that was clear. Chandler shook his head. He would have to sleep on it, because his old brain was running on empty.

He started to get up and then stopped abruptly. The

arms suddenly encircled his neck, startling him. His hands gripped the person's forearms as his eyes popped huge. His gun—where the hell was his gun?

"Working hard or hardly working?"

He immediately relaxed and looked up into Juanita's face. The edges of her mouth were crinkled into the beginnings of a smile. Her face always held that same look, as though she were about to tell a joke or laugh at one. That look never failed to cheer him up no matter how lousy his day had been, no matter how many bodies he had poked and probed.

He put a hand on his heaving chest. "Damn, woman, you sneak up on me like that again, the only thing I'm going to be working is my angel wings."

She sat down on his lap. She was wearing a long white robe, bare feet showing. "Come on, now, a big, strong fella like yourself? And aren't you being a bit presumptuous about those angel wings?"

He slid an arm around her waist, which, after three children, wasn't as small as on their wedding night, but then neither was his. They had *grown* together, he often liked to say. Balance was essential in life. One fatty and one skinny was just heading for disaster.

There was no one alive who knew him better than Juanita. Maybe that was really the one important product of a successful marriage: the knowledge that there was one other soul out there who had your number, all the way down to the last possible decimal place, out there with pi, maybe more; if that was possible, Juanita had his.

He smiled back at her. "Sure, I'm one big, strong guy, but sensitive, baby. Us sensitive types, you just never know what might knock us over. And after a life spent fighting crime, I thought the Lord would be up there right now sewing together a nice fancy pair of angel wings for me, size extra-large, of course. He's all-knowing, so He'll be aware of the fact that I've spread some in my old

age." He gave her a kiss on the cheek and they held hands.
She swept her fingers through his disappearing hair. She
could sense that his humor was forced.

"Buford, why don't you tell me what's bothering you so
we can talk about it and then you can come to bed? It's
getting pretty late. Tomorrow's always another day."

Chandler smiled at her remark. "Hey, what happened to
my poker face? As I look a culprit in the eye and wear him
down without ever revealing what I'm really thinking."

"You stink at poker. So talk to me, baby."

She rubbed at his kinked-up neck and he reciprocated
by massaging her long feet.

"You remember that young man I was telling you
about? John Fiske? His brother was a clerk at the Supreme
Court?"

"I remember. And now another clerk dead too."

"Right. Well, I was over at his brother's apartment
tonight, going through it for evidence collection.
McKenna, that agent from the FBI, showed up."

"The one you said was wound up like a grenade ready to
blow? Couldn't figure him out?"

"He's the one."

"Mmm-hmm."

"Well, we found a life insurance policy that pays John
Fiske half a million dollars upon his brother's death."

"So, they were family, weren't they? You have life insurance, don't you? I get rich if you die, right?" She lightly
smacked the top of his head. "You better have, anyway.
Promising me all this nice stuff my whole life and never
delivering. I better be rich when your sorry butt kicks off."

They both laughed and exchanged lingering hugs.

"Fiske never told me about the insurance policy. I mean,
come on, that's a classic motive for murder."

"Well, maybe he doesn't know about the policy."

"Maybe," Chandler conceded. "Anyway, McKenna laid
out this whole theory that has Fiske killing his brother for

the money, getting another clerk at the Court to help him because she's got a thing for him and then throwing all this misdirection at us, offering to help with the investigation and whatnot. Even lying about an intruder at his brother's apartment. I have to admit, he put together a pretty convincing argument, at least on the surface."

"So John Fiske was at his brother's apartment?"

"Yep. Claims some guy hit him there and took off. Maybe stole some stuff from the apartment, something that tied in to the murder."

"Well, if John Fiske was at his brother's apartment and made up the story about this intruder person, and he knew about the life insurance policy, why didn't he search his brother's apartment for the policy? Why leave it for you to find and get suspicious?"

Chandler stared at her, wide-eyed.

"Buford, are you okay?"

"Damn, sweetie, I thought I was the detective in the family. Now, how the hell did I miss that one?"

"Because you're overworked and underappreciated, that's why." She got up and extended her hand to his. "But if you come upstairs right now, I will show you some extra-special appreciation. Leave your sensitive side down here, though, baby, and just bring your other parts upstairs." She looked at him with heavy-lidded eyes that he knew did not indicate sleepiness.

Chandler quickly rose, took her hand and together they walked up the stairs.

CHAPTER FORTY-SEVEN

As the Jeep raced down the road, Tremaine scrutinized the passengers of each car they passed.

"The damn luck," Rayfield moaned. "We couldn't have missed them by more than a few minutes."

Tremaine ignored him, focusing instead on the car in front of them. The dome light of the car came on as they passed, revealing the driver and passenger. The passenger was unfolding a map.

As Tremaine stared at the car's interior he hit the brakes, ripped the Jeep to the left and went across the median. The vehicle bumped and jostled in the grassy ditch before the tires found asphalt again and they were heading back toward Rider's office.

Rayfield grabbed Tremaine's shoulder. "What the hell are you doing?"

"They suckered us. The guy and the gal. Their story was bullshit."

"How do you know that?"

"The light in the bathroom."

"The light? What about it?"

"It wasn't on. The bitch was in there in the dark. It hit me when I saw the dome light go on in the car back there. There was no light coming from under the bathroom door when she was in there. When she opened the door she didn't hit the light switch because the bathroom was already dark. She wasn't using the can. She was standing in the bathroom in the pitch-dark. And guess why?"

Rayfield's face went pale. "Because Harms and his brother were in there too." While he looked at the road ahead he had another thought. "The guy said his name was John Michaels. Could it have been John Fiske?"

"And the girl was Sara Evans. That's what I'm thinking. You better call and let the others know."

Rayfield picked up the cell phone. "We'll never catch up to Harms now."

"Yes, we will."

"How the hell can we?"

Tremaine drew on thirty years of Army training, studying what the other side would do in a particular scenario. "Fiske said he saw them get in a car. Opposite of a car is a truck. He said it was an old car. Opposite of that is a *new* truck. He said they were going north, so we go south. It's only been five minutes. We'll catch them."

"I hope to God you're right. If they were at Rider's office—" He broke off and looked anxiously out the window.

Tremaine looked over at him. "Then that means the Harms brothers ain't running. That means they were looking for something Rider had. And that sure as hell is not good news for us." He nodded at the phone. "Make that call. We'll take care of Harms and his brother. They'll have to deal with Fiske and the woman."

Because of the high-profile nature of the case, the FBI had offered the use of its laboratory to perform the analysis on the slug found in the alley. After comparing tissue samples taken from Michael Fiske's remains, the slug was deemed to have been fired through his brain. The slug was a 9mm of a type typically carried by law enforcement personnel.

With that information, Agent McKenna sat down in front of a computer terminal at the Hoover Building and typed in a high-priority request to the Virginia State Police. Within a few minutes he had his answer. John Fiske had a 9mm SIG-Sauer registered to his name, a carryover from his cop days. Within minutes McKenna was in his car. Two hours later he turned off Interstate 95 and headed through the darkened streets of downtown Richmond. His car rumbled over the aged and uneven streets of Shockoe Slip. He parked in a secluded area near the old train station.

Ten minutes later he was standing in John Fiske's office, having picked the locks of the building and the lawyer's office with remarkable ease. He looked around the darkened space using a small light. He had decided to search Fiske's office first rather than his apartment. It only took a couple of minutes until he found it. The 9mm pistol was relatively light and compact. Wearing gloves, McKenna palmed it for a moment and then put it in his pocket.

He shone his light around the rest of the office. The beam caught on something and he went over to the bookcase. He picked up the framed picture. The flashlight kicked up too much glare on the glass covering the photo, so McKenna took it over to the window and looked at it under the moonlight.

The Fiske brothers looked like any others, standing side by side. Michael Fiske was taller and better-looking than his older brother, but the fire in John Fiske's eyes burned with a greater intensity. John had on his police uniform, so this had been taken a while back, McKenna knew. The older brother had seen much of life wearing that uniform, just as McKenna had in his career at the FBI. Sometimes those experiences gave you that fire, or else harshly took it away.

He put the photo back and left the office. In another five minutes the FBI agent's car was heading north once again. Two hours later, back at his home in a well-to-do northern Virginia suburb, McKenna sat in his small study and alternated sipping on a beer and pursing his lips around a cigarette. He held the pistol he had taken from Fiske's office. It was nicely maintained, a solid piece of work. Fiske had made a good choice in ordnance. As a cop he would have relied on this weapon to survive. Years ago policemen rarely had to pull their sidearm. That had changed.

Fiske had killed a man with this gun, McKenna knew. Fired the shot that had taken another's life. McKenna understood the complexities of that journey—a journey that was typically compressed within the span of a few seconds. The heat of the metal, the nauseating smell of exploded powder. Unlike in the movies, a bullet didn't blow a man backward several feet. A man fell where you shot him; made him crap and pee in his pants, plunged him to the dirt without a word. McKenna had killed a man too. It was quick, reflexive; he had seen the eyes bulge out, the body twist. Then McKenna had gone back to the spot where he had fired from and noted the two bullet holes on the wall on either side of where he had stood. The dead man had gotten off his own shots. They had miraculously passed on either side of the FBI agent. McKenna would later learn that the dead man had an eye disability that threw off his depth perception. McKenna had gone on, lived to see his wife and kids because the dead man had a wobbly pupil. On the drive home, McKenna had soiled his pants.

He put the pistol down and cast his thoughts forward

now. His snitch in the clerks' office had paid off. Tomorrow, both Fiske and Evans would face some tough questioning. He would get hold of Chandler first thing, lay the facts before him, and let the pugnacious homicide detective do his duty. McKenna got up and walked around the room. On the walls were framed photos of him with a number of important people. Carefully arranged on a side table were the numerous awards and commendations Warren McKenna had earned with his wits and his courage as an FBI agent. He had led a long, productive career on the side of law enforcement, but that had not made up for one event that had caused him great shame ever since. It had happened so many years ago, and yet was still one of the clearest memories he possessed. What he had done back then was, today, compelling him to frame John Fiske for a crime.

He put out the cigarette and moved silently through the house. His wife had long since gone to bed. His two children were grown and on their own. He had done all right financially, although FBI agents never earned the big dollars, unless they gave up the badge. But his wife, a partner in a major D.C. law firm, had. Thus, the house was large, expensively furnished, and basically empty. He looked back in the direction of the den. His distinguished career, neatly tallied on that table, lastingly captured in those photos. He took a long breath as the darkness clung to him. Penance was a lifelong responsibility.

The plane touched down and taxied to a stop. Commercial jets and some private planes could not land at National after ten o'clock at night because of noise-level restrictions, but the small aircraft Fiske and Sara were flying in could take off and land pretty much wherever it wanted. A few minutes later Fiske and Sara were headed toward the parking garage at National Airport.

"We flew all the way out there, nearly got slaughtered

and we came back empty-handed," Sara muttered. "Brilliant idea on my part."

"That's where you're wrong," Fiske said.

They reached the car and climbed in. "So what exactly did we learn?" she asked.

"Quite a few things. One, we saw Rufus Harms face-to-face. I think he's telling the truth, whatever the truth happens to be."

"You can't be sure of that."

"He came to Rider's office, Sara, when he should be doing his best to get out of the country. He came to get the appeal he had written. Why would he do that unless he believed it to be true?"

"I don't know," Sara admitted. "If it was his appeal, why not just write it again?"

"Rider had filed his own document with it. You saw that in my brother's briefcase. Now that Rider's dead, that was something Harms couldn't duplicate. He also mentioned something he got from the Army. A letter. Maybe he thought that would help, so he came to get both."

"That makes more sense."

"The Army guys were on a blood hunt. They didn't come there to look for Rufus Harms. They came there to search Rider's office."

"How do you know that?"

"They didn't even ask us if we'd seen anyone suspicious, anyone who looked like Rufus. I had to volunteer the information. And they weren't doing it in their official capacity. The middle of the night, machine guns. They weren't MPs or anything. They were of fairly high rank, judging from their age and attitude. Barging into civilian offices with machine guns at midnight, that's not how the Army does things."

"Maybe you're right."

"So I'm thinking whatever was in that appeal had something to do with those guys personally."

"But we don't even know who they are."

"Yes, we do. Rufus said their names at Rider's office. Tremaine, Vic Tremaine—and the other guy's name is Rayfield. They're in the Army, which means they must be connected with Fort Jackson somehow. Rufus said they did something to him. I'm sure he meant back in the stockade."

"John, even if they somehow encouraged him to kill that little girl, or even ordered him to do it for some hellish reason, the most they'd get pinned on is some sort of accessory. And after all these years? If that's all Harms has, he has nothing, you damn well know that."

"The problem is we don't know enough about the actual events back then. If some people visited Harms in the stockade on the night the little girl was killed, there should be a record of that."

Sara looked skeptical. "After twenty-five years?"

"And then there's the letter from the Army that Harms mentioned. What sort of letter would the Army be sending a court-martialed con?"

"Do you think the letter somehow triggered this?"

"It could have had some information that Harms didn't know about before. I don't know what it could be or why he wouldn't have known it before, though."

"Wait a minute. If Tremaine and Rayfield are from Fort Jackson, why would they let that kind of a letter reach Harms? Isn't a prisoner's mail censored?"

Fiske thought for a moment. "Maybe it just slipped through."

"Or maybe it didn't come to the prison at all. Josh Harms seems to know all about it; maybe he got the letter, put two and two together and told Rufus about it."

"And then Rufus maybe fakes a heart attack somehow,

gets taken to the nearest hospital and that's where Josh breaks him out?"

"That works."

"I just wish we knew what happened at Fort Jackson that day. It's pretty clear from what Josh and Rufus said that my brother visited him at the prison."

"Why not call or go to the prison? Then we can find out if Michael was there."

Fiske shook his head. "If those two guys are at the prison, they'll have covered that up, maybe transferred anyone who saw Mike out of the place. And we can't go to Chandler with it, because what would we say? Two Army guys are looking for a prisoner who escaped from their custody. So what?"

"Well, if Rayfield and Tremaine work at the prison, then Michael walked right into the lion's den. Even though you two weren't close, I'm really surprised Michael didn't try to call you for help. He might still be alive if he had."

Fiske froze at her words and then closed his eyes. He said nothing more as they drove along.

When they reached Sara's cottage, Fiske went directly to the refrigerator and grabbed a beer.

"Do you have any cigarettes?"

She raised her eyebrows. "I didn't think you smoked."

"I haven't for years. But I really need one right now."

"Well, you're in luck." She pulled a chair over and set it next to the kitchen counter. She slipped off her pumps and stepped onto the chair's seat. "I've found that if I make it as difficult as possible to get to my little stash, I crave them less. I guess I have a real lazy streak."

Fiske watched as she stood on tiptoe and reached up over the highest cabinet, her fingers barely scraping the top edge.

"Sara, come on, let me do that. You're going to kill yourself."

"I've got it, John. Just about there." She stretched her body as far as she could and Fiske found himself staring at the tops of her exposed thighs as her dress had risen. She started to sway a bit, so he placed a hand on her waist to steady her. On the back of her right thigh was a small birthmark, almost perfectly triangular in shape and a dull red in color. It seemed to pulse with each of her exertions. He glanced down at her feet as he continued to hold on to her, the bottom of his hand resting lightly on the softness of her hip. Her toes were long and uncramped, as though she went barefoot often. He looked away.

"Got 'em." She held up the pack. "Camels okay?"

"As long as you can light one end, I don't really care." He helped her down, took out a cigarette, and then looked at her. "You in? You did all the work." She nodded and he nudged one out for her. They took a moment lighting up and Sara joined Fiske with a beer. They went out onto the small rear deck that looked out over the river and sat down in a faded wooden glider.

"You made a good choice in housing," he commented.

"The first time I saw it, I could see myself living here forever." She drew her legs up under her, tapped her cigarette against the deck rail, and watched as the breeze carried the ash away. She arched her long neck and took a long sip of beer.

"Impulsive of you."

She put the beer down and studied his face. "Haven't you ever felt that way about something?"

He thought about it for a moment. "Not really. So what's next? Husband, kids? Solely the career path?" He took a puff and waited for her to answer.

She took another swallow of beer and watched the car lights pass over the Woodrow Wilson Bridge in the distance. Then she stood up. "Want to go sailing?"

He looked up at her in surprise. "A little late for that, isn't it?"

"No later than our last boat trip. I've got the permit and the boat lights. We'll just do a lazy circle and come back in." Before he could answer, she disappeared into the cottage. Within a couple minutes she came back out wearing jean cutoffs, a tank top and deck shoes, her hair pulled back in a bun.

Fiske glanced down at his dress shirt, slacks and loafers. "I didn't bring my sailor suit."

"That's okay. You're not the sailor, I am." She had two fresh beers. They walked down to the dock. It was miserably humid, and Fiske quickly broke a sweat helping Sara ready the sails. While standing on the bow to rig the jig sail, Fiske slipped and almost tumbled into the water. "If you had fallen into the Potomac, we wouldn't need the moon to sail by, you'd be glowing all by yourself," Sara said, laughing.

The water was flat, no shore wind evident, so Sara fired up the auxiliary engine and they motored out into the middle of the river, where the sails finally caught a breeze and swelled with the warm air. For the next hour they moved in slow ovals across the river. The boat had a light, and the moon was at three-quarters and there were no other craft on the river.

Fiske took a turn at the helm, with Sara coaching him at the tiller until he felt comfortable. Each time they tacked into the wind, the mainsail would shudder and drop, Fiske would duck and Sara would swing the boom around and watch as the canvas filled again and propelled them along.

She looked over at him and smiled. "It feels magical to catch something invisible and yet so powerful, and compel it to do your bidding, doesn't it?" The way she said it, so girlish, with so much frank wonder, he had to smile. They drank beer and both smoked another cigarette after several

humorous attempts at lighting up in the face of a stiff
wind. They talked about things unrelated to present
events, and both felt relieved to be able to do so even for a
short time.

"You have a nice smile," Sara remarked. "You should use
it more often."

By the time they headed back in, Fiske had a blister on
the inside of his thumb from clutching the boom line.

They docked the boat and tied down the sails. Sara went
up to the cottage and came back with more beer and a bag
of chips and salsa. "Don't let it be said that I don't feed my
guests."

They sat on the boat and drank, and whittled down at
the chips. The wind started to pick up and the temperature dipped suddenly as a late night storm rolled in. They
watched as the clouds turned black-edged and pops of
lightning appeared on the horizon. In her tank top shirt,
Sara shivered a little and Fiske put his arm around her. She
leaned into him. Then a few drops of rain hit and Sara
jumped up. With Fiske's help she pulled out the vinyl
covers and snapped them into place across the open
compartments of the boat.

"We better head in," she said.

They walked up to the cottage, running the last few feet
as it started to pour.

"Long day tomorrow," Sara said, looking at the kitchen
clock while patting her wet hair with a paper towel.

"Especially after no sleep last night," Fiske added,
yawning. They turned the lights off and headed upstairs.

Sara said goodnight and went to her room. Fiske
watched through the doorway as she opened the window,
letting the breeze in along with some of the rain. A shaft
of lightning flared across the sky and connected with the
earth somewhere. The boom was deafening. So much
power, Fiske thought. He went down the hallway to the
other bedroom and undressed. He sat on the bed in his

undershorts and T-shirt, listening to the rain. His room was stuffy, but he made no move to open a window. The house was too old to have central air, but it didn't have window-mounted air conditioners either. Apparently Sara preferred the river breeze to cool her. A clock hanging on the wall ticked the seconds at him. He caught himself measuring his pulse against it. His heart was pumping fast, gallons of blood gushing through him.

He pulled on his trousers, rose and went down the hall-way. Her room was dark now, but the door was still open. The curtains kicked up and down with the bursts of wind. He stood in the doorway and watched her as she lay in bed, only a sheet over her.

She was watching him watching her. Was she waiting for him? Letting him come to her this time? He moved into the room, hesitantly, as though this was the first time he had entered a woman's bedroom. She didn't move or speak, neither encouraging nor discouraging.

He lay down next to her and she immediately moved next to him, as though refusing to give him the opportunity to rethink his decision, to flee from her. She wore no clothes. Her body was warm, her skin smooth; the breasts spongy and heat-filled; the scent of the outside air thick over them. Sara's hair was tangled and falling in her face. Her lips clenched and then opened; her fingers stroked him gently, everywhere. Together, they worked his pants off and let them fall to the floor.

They kissed, lightly at first, and then with greater depth. She moved to raise his T-shirt, to rub his chest, his belly against hers. He moved her hand away and pulled his shirt back down. As the rain hit the roof and glanced off the windows, Fiske slid off his undershorts, lifted his body up, and eased himself down on top of her.

Sara awoke early, the first shafts of sunlight just drop-ping over the windowsill. Behind the storm had come waves of deliciously chilly air, and a sky that would transform fully from pink and gray to a deep blue in another hour. She put out her arm to touch him and felt the empty space next to her. She quickly sat up and looked around. Wrapping the sheet around her, she rushed down the hallway and checked the guest room. Empty. So was the bathroom. In a panic she reached the top of the stairs and stopped, a smile edging across her face.

She watched Fiske as he poured a cup of coffee and then returned to cracking eggs in a bowl, to which he then added grated cheddar cheese. Sara stood there, the smell of simmering onion reaching her nostrils. Fiske was fully dressed, his hair damp from the shower. As he turned to pull open the refrigerator door, he saw her.

Sara clutched the sheet a little tighter around her.

"I thought you might have left."

"Thought I'd let you sleep in. It was a late night."

A wonderful night, she wanted to say, but didn't. "You okay?" she asked as casually as she could, unable as yet to fully read the subtle messages behind his words, his movements and expressions. Especially about something as recent as their lovemaking. Was the choice of eggs over lying next to her until they both awoke a bad sign?

"I'm fine, Sara." He smiled, as if to show her that this was actually so.

She smiled back. "Whatever you're making smells wonderful."

"Nothing fancy. Western omelet."

"I usually have dry toast and kitchen sink coffee. It's a nice change. Do I have time to shower?"

"Make it fast."

"Not like last night." She smiled, flicked her eyebrows and turned away. The sheet was fully open in the back.

Fiske watched her go, aroused again at the sight of her naked body, the delicate, sensual tensing of her back, legs and buttocks. He sat down at the kitchen table and looked around the cozy space. He had stood on the rear deck for a while and watched the sun slowly rise over him. Dawn always seemed so much purer over water, as though these two essential elements of life, heat and water, produced a near-spiritual performance. He glanced back at the stairs as the sound of the shower started. He had watched Sara after she had fallen asleep. In the darkness of the night, their mingled scents a second skin, it had seemed as though he belonged next to her, and she to him. But then the blunt clarity of morning had come. Fiske lifted the coffee cup to his lips, but then quickly put it back down. If he had called his brother back right away, Mike would be alive right now. Fiske could never dodge that truth. He would, in fact, have to live with it forever.

CHAPTER FORTY-EIGHT

Elizabeth Knight also awoke at the crack of dawn, showering and dressing quickly. Jordan Knight still slept soundly and she made no move to wake him. She brewed the coffee, poured a cup, took her notebook and sat out on the terrace and watched the sun come up. She looked over every page of her materials for oral argument today, which included the last bench memo Steven Wright would ever author. His blood seemed to replace the ink on the page. As she thought this, she had to fight back the tears again. She swore to herself that he wouldn't die in vain. Ramsey would not carry this day, this case. Knight already had great incentive to make sure that Barbara Chance and women like her could sue the Army for damages for, in essence, condoning the cruel, sadistic and illegal behavior of its male personnel. The organization had not been invented that deserved immunity from such action. But now her motivation, her will to win, to beat Ramsey, had grown a thousandfold. She finished her coffee, packed her briefcase and took a cab to the Supreme Court.

*   *   *

Fiske rubbed his reddened eyes and tried to put the memory of the night before and its bewildering complexities out of his mind. He sat in a special section reserved for members of the Supreme Court bar. He looked over at Sara, who sat with the other clerks in a section of seats perpendicular to the bench. She looked over at him and smiled.

When the justices appeared from behind the curtain and took their seats, Perkins finished his little speech and everyone came to rigid attention. Fiske looked over at Knight. Her subtle movements, an elbow resting lightly here, a finger sifting through paper there, were those of nearly uncontrollable raw energy. She looked, he thought, like a rocket straining at its tethers, desperately wanting to explode. He looked over at Ramsey. The man was smiling, looking calm, in control. If Fiske were a betting man, though, his chips would be at the extreme right of the bench, directly in front of Justice Elizabeth Knight.

The case of *Chance v. United States* was called.

Chance's attorney, a hired gun from Harvard Law School, who made a practice of appearing before the Supreme Court with much success, launched into his argument with vigor. Until Ramsey cut in.

"You're aware of the *Feres* Doctrine, Mr. Barr?" Ramsey asked, referring to the 1950 Supreme Court opinion first granting immunity from lawsuits to the military.

Barr smiled. "Unfortunately, yes."

"Aren't you asking us to overturn fifty years of Court precedent?" Ramsey looked up and down the bench as he said this. "How can we decide this case in favor of your client without turning the military and this Court on their heads?"

Knight did not let Barr answer. "The Court did not
allow that argument to dissuade it from overturning the
segregated school system in this country. If the cause is
right, the means are justified, and precedent cannot stand
in the way of that."

"Please answer my question, Mr. Barr," Ramsey
persisted.

"I think this case is distinguishable."

"Really? There is no question that Barbara Chance and
her male superiors were in uniform, on government property and performing their official duties when the sexual
episodes occurred?"

"I would hardly call coerced sex, 'official duties.' But
nonetheless, the fact that her superior used his rank to
coerce her into what amounted to a rape, and—"

"And," Knight cut in, seemingly unable to remain
quiet, "the superior officers at the base in question and the
regional command were aware these events had taken
place—had been advised in writing of them, even—and
had taken no action to even investigate the matter other
than in a cursory fashion. It was Barbara Chance who
called in the local police. They undertook an investigation
which resulted in the truth coming to light. That truth
clearly establishes a cause of action that would result in
damages with respect to any other organization in this
country."

Fiske stared from Ramsey to Knight. It was suddenly as
though, instead of nine justices, there were only two. In
Fiske's mind, the courtroom had been transformed into a
boxing ring, with Ramsey the champ and Knight the
talented contender, but still an underdog.

"We're talking about the military here, Mr. Barr,"
Ramsey said, but he looked at Knight. "This Court has
ruled that the military is *sui generis.* That is the precedent
you face. Your case deals with chain-of-command issues.
An inferior personnel to her superior. That is just the issue

that this Court has—several times in the past—addressed and unequivocally decided that it would not intrude upon the military's presumptive immunity. That was the law yesterday, and it is the law today. Which gets me back to my original statement. For us to hold for your client, this court must reverse its position on a long and deeply followed line of precedents. That is what you are asking us to do."

"And as I mentioned earlier, *stare decisis* is clearly not infallible," Knight said, referring to the Court's practice of adhering to and upholding its previous decisions.

Back and forth Knight and Ramsey went at it. For every salvo fired by one, there was an answer fired by the other.

The other justices, and Mr. Barr, Fiske thought, were reduced to interested spectators.

When the lawyer for the United States, James Anderson, stepped forward to deliver his argument, Knight did not even let him begin a sentence.

"Why does allowing a damage suit against the Army for condoning a hostile environment for women interfere with the chain of command?" she asked him.

"It clearly impacts negatively on the integrity of the relationship between superior and subordinate personnel," Anderson promptly replied.

"So let me see if I understand your reasoning. By allowing the military over the years to poison, gas, maim, kill and rape its soldiers with impunity, and stripping the victims of any legal recourse, that will somehow improve the relationship, the integrity, of the military and its personnel? I'm sorry, but I'm not quite getting the connection."

Fiske had to stop himself from laughing out loud. His respect for Knight as a lawyer and judge increased tenfold as she finished her statement. In two sentences, she had reduced the Army's entire case to the level of absurdity. He looked over at Sara. Her gaze was trained on Knight, with, Fiske thought, a great deal of pride.

Anderson reddened slightly. "The military, as the chief justice has pointed out, is a unique, special entity. Allowing lawsuits to fly at will can only inhibit and destroy that special bond between personnel, the need for discipline that is at the very core of military preparation and readiness."

"So the military is special?"

"Right."

"Because it serves to defend and protect us?"

"Exactly."

"So we have the four branches of the Armed Forces which are already covered by that immunity. Why don't we extend this immunity to other special organizations? Like the fire department? The police department? They protect us. The Secret Service? They protect the president, arguably the most important person in the country. How about hospitals? They save our lives. Why not let hospitals be immune from suit in the event male doctors rape female personnel?"

"We are getting far outside the boundaries of this case," Ramsey said sternly.

"I think those boundaries are precisely what we're trying to determine," Knight fired back.

"I believe that *U.S. v. Stanley*—" Anderson began.

"I'm glad you mentioned it. Let me briefly recount the facts of that case," Knight said. She wanted this heard. By her fellow justices, several of whom were on the Court when the case had been decided, as well as by the public. To Knight, the *Stanley* case was one of the worst miscarriages of justice in history and represented everything that was wrong with the Court. That had also been Steven Wright's conclusion in his bench memo. And she intended to make those conclusions heard both today and when it came time to win a majority vote on this case.

When Knight spoke, her voice was strong and resonating.

"Master Sergeant James Stanley was in the Army in the fifties and volunteered for a program which he was told had to do with testing protective clothing against gas warfare. The testing was conducted in Maryland, at the Aberdeen Proving Grounds. Stanley signed up for it, but he was never asked to wear any special clothing or do testing with gas masks or anything. He only talked to some psychologists for great lengths of time about a variety of personal subjects, was given some water to drink during these sessions and that was it. In 1975, Stanley, whose life had gone downhill—inexplicable behavior, discharge from the Army, divorce—received a letter from the Army asking him to participate in a follow-up exam by members of the Army who had been given LSD in 1959, because the Army wanted to study the long-term effects of the drug. Under the pretense of testing clothing against gas warfare, the Army had slipped him and other soldiers LSD without his knowledge."

A collective gasp went up from the general public's seats as they heard this, and the spectators started talking to each other. Perkins actually had to bang his gavel, an almost unheard-of event.

As Fiske sat there and listened, it occurred to him how important this case was. Rufus Harms had filed an appeal with this Court. Was he also seeking to sue the Army? Something terrible had happened to him while in the military. Certain men had done something to him that had ruined his life and resulted in the death of a little girl. Rufus wanted his freedom, wanted justice. He had the truth on his side, Rufus had proclaimed. And yet even with the truth, under the current law, it didn't matter. Just like Sergeant Stanley, Private Rufus Harms would lose.

Knight continued, secretly well pleased with the audience's reaction. "The psychologist was employed by the CIA. The CIA and the Army had undertaken a joint effort on the study of the drug's effects, because the CIA had received reports that the Soviet Union had stockpiled the drug and the Army wanted to know how it might be used against its soldiers in wartime. That sort of thing. Stanley, who rightly blamed the Army for destroying his life, sued. His case finally made it to the Supreme Court." She paused. "And he lost."

Another gasp came from the public.

Fiske looked around at Sara. Her eyes were still fixed on Knight. Fiske peered over at Ramsey. He was livid.

"In effect, what you're asking is for this court to deny to Barbara Chance and similar plaintiffs one of the most cherished constitutional rights we possess as a people: the right to our day in court. Isn't that what you're asking? Letting the guilty go unpunished?"

"Mr. Anderson," Ramsey broke in. "What has happened to the men who perpetrated these sexual assaults?"

"At least one has been court-martialed, found guilty and imprisoned," Anderson again promptly replied.

Ramsey smiled triumphantly. "So hardly unpunished."

"Mr. Anderson, the record below clearly establishes that the actions for which the man was imprisoned have been going on for a very long time and were known to higher-ups in the Army, who declined to take any action. In point of fact only when Barbara Chance went to the local police did an investigation ensue. So tell me, have the guilty been punished?"

"I would say it depends on your definition of guilt."

"Who's policing the military, Mr. Anderson? To make sure what happened to Sergeant Stanley doesn't happen again?"

"The military is policing itself. And doing a good job."

"*Stanley* was decided in 1986. Since that time we've had Tailhook, the still-unexplained incidents in the Persian

Gulf War, and now the rape of female Army personnel. Do you call that doing a good job?"

"Well, every large organization will have small pockets of trouble."

Knight bristled. "I rather doubt if the victims of these crimes would describe them as small pockets of trouble."

"Of course, I didn't mean—"

"When I alluded to extending immunity to police, firemen, hospitals, you didn't agree with that, did you?"

"No. Too many exceptions to the rule disproves the rule."

"You recall the *Challenger* explosion, of course?" Anderson nodded. "The survivors of the civilians on board the shuttle were entitled to sue the government, and the contractor that built the shuttle, for damages. However, the families of the military personnel on board were denied that right because of the immunity granted to the military by this court. Do you consider that fair?"

Anderson fell back upon the old reliable. "If we allow lawsuits against the military it will unnecessarily complicate the national security of this country."

"And that's really the whole ball of wax," Ramsey said, pleased that Anderson had raised the point. "It's a balancing act, and this court has already determined where that balance lies."

"Precisely, Mr. Chief Justice," Anderson said. "It's bedrock law."

Knight almost smiled. "Really? I thought bedrock law was the constitutional right of citizens of this country to seek redress of their grievances before the courts. No immunity from suit was granted to the military by any law of this country. Congress did not see fit to do it. In fact, it was this court in 1950 which invented, out of broadcloth, such specialized treatment, and they apparently did so, in part, because they were afraid that allowing such suits would bankrupt the U.S. Treasury. I would hardly call that bedrock."

"However, it is the controlling precedent now," Ramsey pointed out.

"Precedents change," Knight replied, "particularly if they're wrong." Ramsey's words truly irked her, since the chief justice had no problem overturning precedents of long standing when it suited him.

Anderson said, "With all due respect, I think the military is better suited to handle this matter internally, Justice Knight."

"Mr. Anderson, do you dispute this court's jurisdiction or authority to hear and decide this case?"

"Of course not."

"This court has to determine whether serving your country in the military ironically carries the price of stripping away virtually all protections one has as a citizen."

"I wouldn't phrase it quite that way."

"However, I would, Mr. Anderson. It's really a question of justice." She locked eyes with Ramsey. "And if we can't deliver justice here, then I truly despair to think of where one could find it."

As Fiske listened to these impassioned words, he looked again at Sara. As though she somehow knew he was looking, she glanced at him.

Fiske had the strong sense that she was thinking the same thing he was: Even if they somehow solved this whole mystery and the truth finally came out, would Rufus Harms ever really find justice?

CHAPTER FORTY-NINE

J osh Harms finished his sandwich and then idly smoked a cigarette as he watched his brother doze in the front seat of the truck. They were parked on an old logging road in a dense forest. Driving through the night, they had finally stopped because Josh could barely keep his eyes open, and he didn't trust his brother to drive, since Rufus hadn't been behind the wheel of a vehicle for almost thirty years. Besides, when they were on the road, Rufus, for obvious reasons, had to be in the back of the truck. Rufus had kept watch while his brother had dozed and now Josh had taken up the sentinel.

They had talked during the drive about what they were going to do. Much to his own surprise, Josh found himself arguing that they shouldn't go to Mexico.

"What the hell's going on with you? I didn't think you'd want any part of that. You said you didn't," Rufus had said in wonderment.

"I didn't. But once we made up our mind—hell, once I

made up *my* mind—then all I'm saying is we should stick to it. I don't like being no wimp on shit like that. If you're going to do something, then you should do it."

"Look, Josh, if Fiske hadn't thought real fast, we'd both be dead right now. I don't want you on my conscience."

"See, that's where you ain't thinking. Hell, it ain't going to get any worse than it is. Why don't we see what we can do to help it get better? You were right: They deserve what's coming to 'em. Seeing those two boys at Rider's office, I almost shot 'em down in cold blood, and I ain't never done nothing like that in my whole life. Fiske and that woman, they stood up for us. Maybe they're shooting straight."

Rufus had stared at him. "And you don't have a problem with them?"

"What the hell, you think I'm racist?" Josh had pulled out a cigarette as he said this, a grin lighting his face.

"I can't figure you out, Josh."

"You ain't got to figure me out. I ain't figured me out, and I've had a long time to do it. All you got to do is decide if you want to go to Mexico or you want to stick it out. And don't worry about me. If there's anybody that can take care of himself, then you're looking at him."

That had done it, and as soon as his brother woke up, they were going to head back toward Virginia, hook up with Fiske and see what they could do. If it was proof that was needed, then they could get proof, somehow, some way, Josh believed. They had the truth on their side, and if that still didn't count for something, then they might as well go ahead and get themselves shot up.

Josh eyed the surrounding woods. The leaves had already started to turn here, and the way the sunlight cut and dipped through the foliage presented a pleasing combination of colors and textures. He often sat in the woods when hunting; he'd find an old log and rest his bones, taking in the simple beauty of the country, a marvel that didn't cost you a dime. After coming back from Southeast Asia, he had avoided the woods for several years. In Vietnam, the trees, the dirt, everything around you meant death by some of the most ingenious methods the Vietnamese could devise. He checked his watch. Another ten minutes and they would have to be on their way.

He looked back out the window and squinted as the sunlight reflected off something and hurt his eyes. He sucked in his next breath instead of letting it go, spit his cigarette out the window, started the engine and put the truck in gear.

"What the hell," Rufus said as he was jolted awake.

"Get your gun and keep your damn head down," Josh hollered at him. "It's Tremaine."

Rufus gripped his pistol and ducked down.

Tremaine charged from the woods and opened fire. The first shots from the machine gun hit the tailgate of the truck, blowing out one of the lights and riddling the frame with holes. A cone of dirt kicked up in the truck's wake and momentarily blinded Tremaine, who stopped shooting and ran forward, trying desperately to get a clear field of fire on the truck.

Sensing what Tremaine was trying to do, Josh cut the wheel to the left and the truck went off-road and onto what appeared to be the dry remains of a shallow creek bed. It was a good move for another reason, as Rayfield came flying down the road in the Jeep from the other direction, trying to box the truck in.

Rayfield stopped to let Tremaine climb in and they went after the truck.

"How in the hell did they catch up to us?" Rufus wondered aloud.

"Ain't no sense wasting time thinking about that. They're here," Josh shot back. He glanced in the rearview mirror and his eyes narrowed. The Jeep was more nimble and better built to maneuver through the woods than the bulky truck.

"They're going to shoot out the tires and then they got us like sitting ducks," Rufus said.

"Yeah, well, Vic should've shot those tires out first thing. That was his second mistake."

"What was his first?"

"Letting the sunlight hit his binoculars. I saw that long before I spotted that little bastard."

"Let's hope they keep making mistakes."

"We count on ourselves, and hope that's enough."

Back in the Jeep, Tremaine hung out the side and fired his weapon. The machine gun wasn't really worth a spit long-range, although in close quarters it could take out an entire platoon of men in a few seconds; he wanted just two. He slipped the machine gun strap off his shoulder and pulled out his sidearm.

"Get as close as you can," he barked to a very nervous-looking Rayfield. "If I can take out one of their tires, they'll plow right into a tree and our problems are over."

Rufus looked back through the window in the camper and saw what Tremaine was attempting to do. He slid open the glass separating the cab from the interior of the camper and drew a bead on the Jeep. He had not touched a gun in almost thirty years, basic training with a rifle his last experience with a firearm. When he fired, the explosion pierced his ears, the truck's cabin immediately full of the sickening fumes of burned metal, flashed powder. The bullet shattered the rear glass door of the camper shell and then flew at the Jeep like an angry, metal-jacketed hornet. Tremaine ducked back into his vehicle and the Jeep swerved a little.

"Hit anything?" Josh asked.

"Bought us a little time." Rufus's hand was shaking, and he rubbed at his ears. "I forgot how loud these things are."

"Try firing an M-16 for three years. They're real loud, especially when they explode in your face. Hold on."

Josh cut the wheel to the right and then to the left to avoid several trees that had toppled across the creek bed. Beyond was a mass of scrub pines, oaks and brambles. With the Jeep closing in, Tremaine was again taking up his shooting position. Josh cut the truck to the right and through a narrow cleft in the trees and brush, leaves and slender branches slapping and tearing at the truck. But the maneuver had its intended effect because Tremaine had to duck back inside the Jeep to avoid having his head torn off by a tree limb.

The Jeep slowed down. The narrow lane ahead opened up a little, and Josh decided to take advantage, hoping Rayfield was losing a little of his nerve.

"Hold the wheel," he shouted to his brother.

Rufus gripped the steering wheel hard, alternating between looking at his brother and eyeing where the truck was heading.

Josh pulled his pistol and scanned the trees ahead. They were on a fairly level bit of ground now, so the truck didn't rock as much. He gripped the pistol with both hands, doing his best to figure distance and speed, and then selected what he wanted: a thick oak branch high up on a forty-footer. The branch was at least twenty feet long and four inches thick, with other, smaller branches growing from it, and it hung directly over the narrow lane. What had drawn Josh's attention was the fact that the branch was so long and heavy it had started to crack where it was attached to the trunk.

Josh slid his arm out the window, kept it parallel to the truck, took aim and started firing. The first bullet hit the tree trunk directly above where the branch joined it. Having now gauged the trajectory, Josh continued to fire, and each bullet after that hit squarely at the juncture of branch and trunk as the truck hurtled closer. For him it wasn't that extraordinary a display of marksmanship. As a game, he had been shooting at tree branches since he was old enough to carry a .22 rifle. Scaring coons and squirrels, having fun. Still, he had never attempted it in a moving vehicle with two men shooting at him.

Rufus had to keep his eyes open to steer, but he scrunched up his face with each shot. His ears were ringing so loudly you could have shouted in his face and he would not have been able to hear you. The heavy branch dropped a couple of inches as its support weakened. Josh kept firing, as sprays of wood chips shot off the oak like steam from an old train engine.

Tremaine saw what he was doing. "Gun it, gun it."

Rayfield hit the gas.

Josh never took his eyes off the branch as he kept firing. It gave some more, and finally gravity took over and it cracked and swung down. A layer of bark clung to the tree, then the branch slapped hard against the trunk, broke free completely and started coming down. Josh slammed on the accelerator and took the steering wheel back, passing by the tree as he did so.

"Go, go," Tremaine screamed at Rayfield.

However, Rayfield slammed on the brakes as about a thousand pounds of tree branch smashed into the middle of the narrow lane directly in front of them. Tremaine was almost thrown from the vehicle.

"Dammit, why in the hell did you stop?" Tremaine looked ready to turn his pistol on the man.

Rayfield was breathing very hard. "If I hadn't, that damn thing would've crushed us. This Jeep doesn't have a hard top, Vic."

Josh looked up ahead and then to the right where the path opened up some. He braked hard, swerved to the left, swung the truck around and then headed right and gunned the motor. The truck broke free from the brush, lifted a little off the ground as it went over a shallow gully,

and landed in a clearing. Rufus's head hit the top of the
cab's interior as the truck came back to earth.

"Damn, what're you doing?"

"Just hold tight."

Josh slammed on the gas again and Rufus looked up in
time to see the small shack ahead of them that his brother
had spotted seconds before.

Josh looked back and saw what he expected to see.
Nothing. But it wouldn't take Tremaine and Rayfield long
to work the Jeep around the obstacle.

Josh looked past the shack at an angle and could see the
road that lay beyond it. He had been right. Where there
was a shack in the woods, there usually was a road. He
pulled the truck around onto the other side of the old
structure. Both brothers' hearts sank. There was a road
there, all right. But it had a large steel barricade blocking
any passage. And on either side of the barricade were
impenetrable woods. Josh looked back. They were
trapped. Maybe he could hoof it, but Rufus wasn't built
for speed, and Josh wasn't leaving his brother behind.

Josh's eyes narrowed again as he looked at the shack.
The Jeep would be on them in another minute or so. Even
now he could hear the machine gun efficiently tearing the
tree limb apart so the Jeep could shove it aside.

A minute later the Jeep scaled the gully and made its
way to the clearing. Rayfield slowed down as they scanned
ahead and immediately saw the shack.

"Where'd they go?" he asked.

Tremaine checked the area with his binoculars and spotted the road as it snaked off through the woods. "That
way," he shouted, pointing ahead.

Rayfield hit the gas and the Jeep shot around the corner
of the shack. Instantly both men saw that the road was
blocked off and Rayfield slammed the Jeep to a stop. With
a roar, the truck, which had been hidden on the far side of
the shack, exploded forward and hit the vehicle broadside,

knocking it over on its side and flinging Rayfield and
Tremaine out.

Rayfield landed on top of a pile of rotted stumps, his
head at a vicious angle. He lay still.

Tremaine took cover behind the overturned Jeep and
opened fire, forcing Josh to back the truck up, his head
below the dashboard. Finally the truck engine died, steam
pouring out from the hood, the front tires flattened by the
machine-gun fire.

Josh came out the driver's side while Rufus covered him.
Josh lunged, dropped to his knees and rolled until he
made it to the rear of the truck, and then he peered out.
Tremaine hadn't moved from his position. Josh could see
the tip of the machine gun. Tremaine was probably
putting in another clip just as Josh was doing, and taking
a moment to study the tactical situation.

Josh's heart was pounding, and he rubbed at his eyes to
clear the dirt and sweat away. He had been in many battles
on both foreign and American soil, but the last one had
been almost thirty years ago. Besides, it didn't matter:
Every time, you were terrified that you were going to die.
When somebody was shooting at you, it didn't exactly
make you think more clearly. You reacted more than
anything else.

Josh had an edge, though. There were two of them and
only one of Tremaine. Josh peered out once more and then
sprinted from behind the truck and made it to the edge of
the shack.

"Rufus," he hollered. "On the count of three."

"Start counting," Rufus shouted back, tremors of fear in
his voice.

Three seconds later Josh opened fire on Tremaine, the
bullets pinging off the Jeep's frame. Rufus hustled to the
back of the truck. He was stopped there, however, when
Tremaine managed to fire a burst between the truck and

the shack. The air smelled of gunfire, and of the sweat of frightened men.

Josh and Rufus looked at each other, and then Josh cracked a smile, sensing the rising panic in his brother.

"Hey, Vic," Josh yelled out, "how 'bout you throw down that damn widowmaker and come on out with your hands up?"

Tremaine responded by blowing a chunk of wood off the shack a little above Josh's head.

"Okay, okay, Vic, I hear you. Now, you be cool, you hear me, little buddy? Don't you worry, we'll bury you and Rayfield. Ain't gonna leave you for the bears and shit to chew on. That's bad shit. Animals eating dead bodies. You saw that in Nam, didn't you, Vic? Or maybe you was running too fast the other way to see that." While he was talking, Josh was motioning for Rufus to stay put and then pointing around the shack to show his brother what he was going to do.

Rufus nodded to show he understood. Josh was going to try to flush the man into his brother's field of vision and let Rufus cut him down. Rufus gripped his gun and slipped in a new clip, grateful that his brother had taken the time to show him how. He was having trouble breathing; his arms felt heavy holding the gun. He was afraid that he would not have the nerve, the killer instinct, much less the skill to shoot the man down, even if Tremaine came at him, firing with that damn machine gun. Rufus had fought many men in prison in order to survive—with his hands only, even though his opponents had always been armed with a shiv or piece of pipe. But a gun was different. A gun could kill from a distance. But if he didn't shoot, his brother would die. And for once he could not pray to God to help him. He could not speak to his Lord for assistance in killing another.

In a half crouch, Josh made his way across the front of the shack, stopping at intervals to listen intently. Once he

dared to raise his head up to one of the windows, in order
to perhaps see through it and out the rear window to
where the Jeep was, but the angle was wrong and his view
was blocked. Josh was totally focused now. The fear was
still there, it was very much there, but he had done his
best to transform it into adrenaline, to heighten every
sense he possessed. He pointed his pistol directly in front
of him, knowing full well that if Tremaine had figured
what his plan was, his best course of action would be to
slip out from behind the Jeep and come around the shack
the other way, with the result that he would meet Josh
head-on somewhere in the middle. Machine gun against
pistol, a hundred rounds to one, meaning Josh would die,
and then so would Rufus.

He moved forward another foot. Then he heard the
machine gun open fire again and listened as the bullets
tore into the pickup truck. He raced forward and rounded
the corner. While Tremaine was busy firing at Rufus, Josh
could outflank him and silence the sonofabitch once and
for all.

This plan vanished when he went around the corner, for
Tremaine was standing there, his pistol pointed at Josh's
head. An astonished Josh stopped so abruptly that his feet
slid in the gravel and his legs went out from under him.
This was fortunate, since the bullet slammed into his
shoulder instead of his brain. His momentum carried him
forward and his legs clipped Tremaine's, and they went
down hard, both their pistols sailing out of reach.

Tremaine came up first; Josh, holding his bloody shoulder, was slower to rise. Tremaine pulled a knife from his
belt. In the background the machine gun stopped firing.
Josh yelled out as Tremaine lunged into him and both men
hit the wall of the shack, shaking the primitive structure
right down to its wooden joints. Josh managed to block
Tremaine's arm with his forearm. His whole side hurt like
hell. Whatever piece of ordnance was in him had gone

beyond his shoulder to explore other parts of his body. He managed to kick at Tremaine and caught him once in the belly, but the man was up and was on Josh again in an instant. Josh felt the knife cut through his shirt and into his side, and he started to lose consciousness. The pain from this fresh wound was barely felt, so overwhelmed was it by the first. He could hardly make out the image of Tremaine pulling the knife free from his body and rearing his arm back for a final thrust. Probably at his throat, Josh dimly thought, as his brain started to shut down. The throat was quick and always fatal. That's what he would do, he thought, as the darkness started to close around him.

The knife never made its downward plunge. It stopped at its highest point and moved no closer to Josh Harms. Tremaine kicked and jerked as he was torn off the wounded man. Rufus was directly behind him. One hand gripped the wrist holding the knife. He smashed it against the shack until Tremaine's finger lock was finally broken and the knife dropped to the ground. Tremaine was solid muscle and superbly trained in hand-to-hand combat. But he was half Rufus's size. One on one, there were few men who could match Rufus. The big man was like a grizzly bear once he got hold of somebody. And he had a good hold of Vic Tremaine, the man who had made his life a nightmare he'd thought would never end.

As Tremaine tried to wedge a forearm against Rufus's windpipe, Rufus changed his tactic and lifted Tremaine completely off the ground, slamming his face again and again into the wall until Tremaine was groggy from the impacts, his face bloody. Finally Rufus put Tremaine's head right through the window, the jagged glass cutting deeply into the man's face. Then Josh screamed in pain from his wounds, and Rufus looked at him, his grip loosening a bit. Tremaine, sensing this, kicked out Rufus's knee and whipsawed an elbow into his kidney, dropping the big man to the ground. Tremaine rolled free, gripped his knife and lunged toward the defenseless man. The bullet hit him smack in the back of the head and dropped him on the spot.

Rufus heaved upward and looked at his brother, wisps of smoke still seeping from the barrel of the 9mm Josh held. Then he put the pistol down and lay back in the dirt. Rufus raced over and knelt next to him. "Josh! Josh?"

Josh opened his eyes and looked over at Tremaine's twisted body, both relieved and sickened by what he had done. Even the worst enemy in the world didn't look so terrifying dead. He looked back at Rufus. "You done good, little brother. Shit, better'n me."

"I'd be dead if you hadn't killed him."

"Ain't gonna let him get you. Ain't gonna let him . . ."

Rufus ripped open his brother's shirt and looked at the wounds. The knife had only cut a slice in his side. Probably hadn't hit anything vital, Rufus concluded, but it was bleeding like a bitch. The bullet, though, was something else. He saw the blood dripping from his brother's mouth, the rising glaze to his eyes. Rufus could stop the bleeding on the outside, but he could do nothing about what was going on inside. And that's what could kill him. Rufus took off his shirt and put it over his brother, who was now shivering despite the heat.

"Hold on, Josh." Rufus ran over to the Jeep and quickly looked through it. He found the first-aid kit and hustled back over to his brother. Josh's eyes were now closed and he didn't seem to be breathing.

Rufus shook him gently. "Josh, Josh, don't do it, keep your damn eyes open. Don't be going to sleep on me. Josh!"

Finally Josh opened his eyes and appeared lucid. "You got to get outta here, Rufus. All the shooting, people might be coming. You got to go. Now."

"*We* got to get out of here—that's right."

Rufus lifted Josh up a little and checked his back. The bullet hadn't gone through; it was still in him somewhere. Rufus started cleaning both wounds.

At one point Josh gripped his arm. "Rufus, get the hell out of here," he said again.

"You don't go, I don't go, so that's what we got."

"You still crazy."

"Yeah, I'm crazy as hell, let's leave it at that." He finished cleaning and then dressing the wounds and tightly bandaged them. He gently lifted his brother, but the movement sent Josh into a coughing spasm, blood from his mouth pooling down his shirt. Rufus carried him over to the truck and laid him down next to it.

"Shit, Rufus, this thing ain't going nowhere," Josh said desperately, looking at the battered truck.

"I know that." Rufus pulled a bottle of water from the camper, twisted it open and put it to Josh's lips. "Can you hold it? You need to get some liquid in you."

Josh answered by gripping the bottle with his good hand and drinking a little.

Rufus rose and went to the overturned Jeep. He pulled the machine gun free from where Tremaine had wedged it between the seat and the metal side of the Jeep. The man had used wire, a piece of metal and a string to rig the trigger for full automatic fire while he set up his ambush of Josh. Rufus eyed the situation for a moment and then tried to push against the hood to right the vehicle, but he couldn't get any leverage that way, and his feet slipped in the loose gravel. He studied the situation some more. There was really only one way that he could see.

He put his back against the edge of the driver's-side seat and then squatted down. He dug his fingers into the dirt and gravel until they got underneath the Jeep's side, and then he clenched the metal tightly. He gave one good pull to gauge what he was up against. The Jeep was heavy, damn heavy. Thirty years ago, this wouldn't have been that much trouble for him. As a young man he had lifted the front end of a full-sized Buick, engine and all, clean off the ground by a good three feet. But he wasn't twenty anymore. He pulled again and he could feel the Jeep rise a little before settling back down. He pulled once more, straining and grunting, the muscles in his neck tensing hard beneath his skin.

Josh put the bottle down and even managed to lift himself partially off the ground by leaning against the shredded truck tire, as he watched what his brother was trying to do.

Rufus was tired already. His arms and legs weren't used to this anymore, not for a long time. He had always been strong, stronger than anyone else. Now, when he really needed it, when his brother would surely die if he couldn't turn this damn Jeep upright, would he not be strong enough?

He hunkered down again, closed his eyes and then opened them. He looked skyward where a big, black crow lazily circled. Not a care in the world, just long, unhurried brush strokes against the canvas of blue.

As sweat poured off Rufus's face he clenched his eyes again and did what he always did when he was troubled, when he thought he wouldn't make it. He prayed. He prayed for Josh. He asked the Lord to please grant him the strength he needed to save his brother's life.

He gripped the sides of the Jeep once more, tensed his massive shoulders and legs. His long arms began to pull, his bent legs began to straighten. For a moment, Jeep and man were suspended in a precarious equilibrium, moving neither up nor down—the Jeep unwilling to yield and Rufus just as stubborn. But then Rufus slowly started to fall back a little as the weight was just too much for him. Rufus sensed he would not have another chance. Even as the Jeep began to win the battle, he opened his mouth and let out a terrible scream that forced tears from his eyes. As

Josh looked on at the impossible thing his brother was trying to do for him, tears started to fall down his exhausted face.

Rufus's eyes opened again as he felt the Jeep rise, inch by agonizing inch. His joints and tendons afire with what he was accomplishing, Rufus grunted and pulled and heaved and ignored the pain as it snapped perilous signals through his trembling body. The Jeep fought him every punishing inch. It creaked and groaned, cursing him. But then he was standing upright, and he gave the hunk of metal one last heave. Like a wave about to pitch onto a beach, the Jeep cleared the point of no return and fell hard to earth, rocking upon impact and then coming to rest on all four wheels.

Rufus sat down in the Jeep, his whole body shaking from his immense exertions.

Josh looked on in silent wonderment. "Damn," was all he could finally say about what he had just witnessed.

Rufus's heart was racing so hard now, he worried his success might prove to be an empty one. He clutched at his chest, breathed deeply. "Please," he quietly said, "please don't." A minute later Rufus slowly rose, shuffled over to his brother and carefully lifted him into the Jeep. He rearranged the cloth top, which had become dislodged when Tremaine and Rayfield had been thrown clear. He gathered up as many supplies as he could from the truck, including his Bible, and put them into the back of the Jeep along with the weaponry. He climbed in the driver's seat and then stopped and looked over at Tremaine and Rayfield. Then he stared up once again at the circling crow, which had now been joined by several brethren, large enough to be buzzards. In less than a day the two dead men would be picked to the bone if left out in the open.

Rufus climbed out of the Jeep and went over to Rayfield. He didn't have to check the man's pulse. The eyes didn't lie. That and the stench of released bowels. He slid first Rayfield's and then Tremaine's bodies into the shack. He said a few simple words over both men before rising and closing the door. One day he would forgive them for all they had done, but not today. Rufus climbed back in the Jeep, gave Josh a reassuring look and started the Jeep. The engine didn't catch the first time, but it did the second. Gears grinding as Rufus got a quick lesson in driving a stick shift, the Jeep jolted forward, and the brothers left this impromptu battlefield behind.

CHAPTER FIFTY

The justices traditionally had a private lunch in the Court's second-floor dining room after oral argument. Fiske had left Sara in her office to catch up on some work. He had decided to use the opportunity to make some inquiries on his own. If his flow of information had been cut off from D.C. Homicide, Fiske decided he'd better make it up somehow. One possible source was Police Chief Leo Dellasandro.

As he walked along the hallway, he thought about the oral argument he just listened to. Even as a lawyer, he had never really understood how much power was wielded from this building. The Supreme Court over its history had taken some very unpopular positions on a myriad of significant issues. Many had been brave and, at least in Fiske's opinion, correct. But it was unnerving to realize that if a vote or two had gone the other way on some or all of those prior decisions, the country might be very differ-

ent today. By any definition that seemed to be a precarious, if not perilous, state of events.

Fiske also thought about his brother, and how much
good he had undoubtedly brought to this place, even in
the role of a clerk. Mike Fiske had always been fair and just
in his opinions and actions. And when he made up his
mind, a person could not ask for a more loyal friend. Mike
Fiske was good for this place. The Court had indeed
suffered a great loss when someone had taken his life. But
not as great as the Fiske family's loss.

Fiske made his way to Dellasandro's ground-floor office,
knocked on the door, waited. He knocked again, and then
opened the door and peered inside. He was looking at the
anteroom to Dellasandro's office, where his secretary
worked. That space was empty. Probably at lunch, Fiske
assumed. He stepped into the office. "Chief Dellasandro?"
He wanted to know if anything had turned up on the
surveillance videos. He also wanted to know if one of the
officers had driven Wright home.

He approached the inner office door. "Chief
Dellasandro, it's John Fiske. I was wondering if we could
talk." Still no answer. Fiske decided to leave the man a
note. But he didn't want to leave it at the secretary's desk.

He slipped into Dellasandro's office and over to his desk.
He picked up a piece of paper and, using a pen from the
holder on the desk, scrawled out a brief note. As he
finished and positioned the note prominently on the desk,
he looked around the office for a moment. There were
many ceremonial tokens on shelves and walls, attesting to
a distinguished career. On one wall was a photo of a much
younger Dellasandro in his uniform.

Fiske turned to leave. Hanging on the back of the door
was a jacket. It had to belong to Dellasandro, obviously
part of his Court uniform. As Fiske passed by it, he noticed
several smudges on the collar. He rubbed it with his finger
and examined the residue: makeup. He went out into the

anteroom and looked at the photos on the desk there. He
had seen Dellasandro's secretary once before. A young, tall
brunette with quite memorable features. On her desk,
there was a photo of her and Chief Dellasandro. His arm
was around her shoulder; they were both smiling into the
camera. Probably many secretaries had a photograph with
their bosses. There was something in the eyes, how close
they were standing together, however, that might suggest
something more than a platonic working relationship. He
wondered if the Court had specific rules on fraternization.
And there was another reason why Dellasandro would be
well advised to keep his pants on and his hands off his
secretary: Fiske glanced back into Dellasandro's office at
the photo on his credenza—of his wife and kids. A very
happy-looking family. Only on the surface, obviously. As
he left the office, he concluded that it pretty much
summed up how this place and the world in general operated: Surface appearances could be very deceiving; one had
to dig deeper to get to the real truth.

Rufus stopped the Jeep. "I'm going to flag down the
first cop I see. Get you some help," Rufus said.

With an effort, Josh sat up. "The hell you are. Cops get
hold of you, they find Tremaine and Rayfield, they'll bury
you."

"You need a doctor, Josh."

"I don't need shit." With a lunge, he gripped his pistol.
"We started this, we gonna finish it." He wedged the
barrel of the pistol against his gut. "You stop for anybody,
I'm gonna put a hole right here."

"You're crazy. What the hell you want me to do?"

Josh coughed up blood. "You find Fiske and that girl. I
can't help you no more, maybe they can." Rufus looked at
the gun. "Don't go thinking it—bullet's pretty damn
fast."

Rufus put the Jeep in gear and pulled back on the road.

Josh watched him, his eyes coming in and out of focus. "Stop that shit."

"What?"

"I see you doing that mumbling shit. Don't be praying for me."

"Ain't nobody telling me when I can talk to the Lord."

"Just keep me out of it."

"I'm praying for Him to watch over you. Keep you alive."

"Does it look like it's troubling me any? You just wasting your breath."

"God gave me the strength to lift this Jeep."

"*You* lifted this damn hunk of metal. Ain't no angels come down from no heaven and help you do shit."

"Josh—"

"Just drive." The intensity of his pain forced Josh to suddenly hunch forward. "I'm tired of talking."

While she was in her office, Sara received an urgent summons from Elizabeth Knight. She was surprised by this, because on Wednesday afternoons the justices were usually in conference, going over the cases heard on Monday. Each justice had two secretaries and a personal assistant. As she entered Knight's chambers, Sara greeted Knight's longtime secretary, Harriet, who had been with the justice through several careers. Normally cheerful and friendly, Harriet spoke in a cold tone. "Go right in, Ms. Evans."

Sara passed by Harriet's desk and paused at the door to Knight's office. She turned around and caught Harriet staring at her. Harriet quickly turned back to her work. Sara took a deep breath and opened the door.

Within the office, either standing or perched upon chairs, were Ramsey, Detective Chandler, Perkins and Agent McKenna. Seated behind her antique desk,

Elizabeth Knight was nervously fiddling with a letter opener when she saw Sara.

"Please come in and sit down." Her tone was barely cordial, Sara thought.

She sat in an upholstered wing chair that had been, she thought, carefully positioned because it allowed everyone in the room to directly face her. Or confront her, perhaps?

She looked at Knight. "You wanted to see me?"

Ramsey stepped forward. "We all wanted to see you, and, more to the point, hear you, Ms. Evans. However, I will let Detective Chandler do the honors." Ramsey was as stern as Sara had ever seen him. He leaned back against the fireplace mantel and continued to stare at her, his large hands clasping and unclasping nervously.

Chandler sat down across from her, his knees almost touching hers. "I've got some questions I need to ask you, and I want the truth in return," he said quietly.

Sara looked around the room. Only half joking, she said, "Do I need a lawyer?"

"Not unless you've done something wrong, Sara," Knight quickly pointed out. "However, I think you should make the determination whether to have legal counsel present or not."

Sara swallowed with difficulty and then looked back at Chandler. "What do you want to know?"

"Have you ever heard the name Rufus Harms?"

Sara closed her eyes for a moment. *Oh, shit.* "Let me explain—"

"Yes or no, please, Ms. Evans," Chandler said. "Explanations can come later."

She nodded, then said, "Yes."

"Exactly how are you familiar with that name?"

She fidgeted in her chair. "I know that he's a military prisoner who escaped. I read that in the papers."

"Was that the first you'd heard of him?" When she didn't answer, Chandler continued, "You've been asking questions at the clerks' office about an appeal presumably filed by Rufus Harms. In fact, you did that before he escaped from prison, didn't you? What were you looking for?"

"I thought . . . I mean—"

"Did John Fiske put you up to it?" Knight asked sharply. She looked searchingly at Sara, the disappointment on her features making Sara feel even more guilty.

"No. I did it on my own."

"Why?" Chandler asked. From his vague conversation with Fiske in the Court's cafeteria, he already had a notion as to what the truth was. But he needed to hear it from her.

Sara let out a deep breath and looked once more at the army aligned against her. She wished that Fiske would suddenly appear to help her, but that was not going to happen. "One day I happened to see what looked like an appeal with Rufus Harms's name on it. I checked at the clerks' office, because I didn't recall seeing it on the docket. The clerks' office had no record of it."

"Where did you see this appeal?" Ramsey interjected, before Chandler could get the same question out.

"Just somewhere," Sara said, looking miserable.

"Sara," Knight said harshly, "it's no use covering up for somebody. Just tell us the truth. Don't throw your career away for this."

"I don't remember where I saw it, I just saw it. For maybe two seconds. And I only saw Rufus Harms's name, not what was in the filing," Sara said stubbornly.

"But if you suspected it was an appeal that was not logged into the system," Perkins said, "then why didn't you take it down to the clerks' office and have it logged in?"

How was she supposed to answer that? "It really wasn't convenient at the moment, and I didn't get another chance."

"Wasn't convenient?" Ramsey looked ready to erupt.

"It's my understanding that you just recently inquired at the clerks' office about this 'missing' appeal. Was it still not convenient for you to have it logged in then?"

"At that point I didn't know where it was."

McKenna spoke up forcefully. "Listen, Ms. Evans, either you tell us or we find out from another source."

Sara stood up. "I resent your tone and I don't appreciate being treated this way."

"I think it's in your interests to cooperate," McKenna said, "and stop trying to protect the Fiske brothers."

"What are you talking about?"

"We have reason to suspect that Michael Fiske took that appeal for his own purposes, and that somehow you're involved in all of that," Chandler informed her.

"If he did and you knew about it but remained silent, that is a very serious ethical offense, Ms. Evans," said Ramsey.

"You're doing all of this running around, asking questions, because John Fiske put you up to it, didn't he?"

"This may come as quite a shock to you, but I can think and act all by myself, Agent McKenna," she said hotly.

"You know that Michael Fiske had a half-million-dollar insurance policy naming his brother as beneficiary?"

"Yes, John told me."

"And do you also know that Fiske has no alibi for the time of his brother's death?"

Sara shook her head and smiled tightly. "You're wasting valuable time trying to pin Michael's murder on his brother. He had nothing to do with it, and he's trying as hard as he can to find out who did murder Michael."

McKenna put his hands in his pockets and studied her for a moment, changing his tactic. "Would you say the Fiske brothers were close?"

"What do you mean by 'close'?"

McKenna rolled his eyes. "Just the ordinary meaning of the word, that's all."

"No, I don't think they were particularly close. So?"

"We found the life insurance policy at Michael Fiske's apartment. Tell me why he insured his life for all that money and made his not-so-close older brother the beneficiary. Why not his parents? From what I've found out, they can certainly use the money."

"I don't know what Michael was thinking when he did that. I guess we'll never know."

"Maybe it wasn't Michael Fiske who did it at all."

Sara was momentarily stunned. "What do you mean?"

"Do you know how easy it is to take out a life insurance policy on somebody else? There's no photo identification necessary. A nurse comes to your house, takes some measurements and fluid samples. You forge a few signatures, pay the premiums through a dummy account."

Sara's eyes widened. "Are you suggesting that John impersonated his brother in order to take out the life insurance policy on him?"

"Why not? It would make it a lot clearer why two estranged brothers would have such a big financial pact."

"You obviously do not know John Fiske."

McKenna gazed at her in a way that she found unnerving. "The point is, Ms. Evans, neither do you."

McKenna's next words almost put her on the floor.

"Did you also know that Michael Fiske was killed by a slug fired from a nine-millimeter?" He paused for effect. "And that John Fiske has a nine-millimeter registered to his name? And this appeal, I'm sure he's telling you it's connected to his brother's murder, isn't he?"

Sara looked at Chandler. "I can't believe this."

"Well, none of it's been proven yet," Chandler said.

Perkins nodded thoughtfully, his arms crossed. "We received a phone call from the Office of Special Military Operations, Ms. Evans. A Master Sergeant Dillard. He said you had called about Rufus Harms, that you said an appeal had been filed by Rufus Harms with the Court and you were checking into his background."

"There's no law that says I can't make a phone call to clarify something, is there?"

"So you admit having called him," Perkins said triumphantly, looking first at Ramsey and then at Knight. "That means you admit to having used Court facilities and Court time on some personal investigation into some escaped convict. And you happened to have lied to the military, since no such appeal is on file here, as you pointed out."

"Your offenses are quickly adding up," added McKenna.

"I admit to no such thing. As far as I'm concerned, it was Court business and I had a perfect right to do it."

"Ms. Evans, are you going to tell us who exactly had that appeal?" Ramsey was staring at her just as he had peered down at the lawyers during oral argument that morning. "If someone at this Court stole an appeal before it was filed—the very idea is unthinkable—and if you know who it was, you have a duty to this institution to tell us who it was."

They all knew the answer to that question, Sara realized, or at least they thought they did. However, she wasn't providing any clarification. Summoning a reserve of strength she was unaware she possessed, she rose slowly. "I think I've answered enough questions, Mr. Chief Justice."

Ramsey looked over at Perkins and then at Elizabeth Knight. Sara thought she could see a slight nod pass among all of them.

"Then, Sara, I have to ask you to voluntarily resign your clerkship, effective immediately," Knight said, her voice breaking as she made this announcement.

Sara looked at her with very little surprise. "I understand, Justice Knight. I'm sorry it's come to this."

"Not nearly as sorry as I am. Mr. Perkins will escort you

out. You may gather your personal belongings from your office." Knight abruptly looked away.

As Sara turned to go, Ramsey's voice boomed out again. "Ms. Evans, be advised that if your actions cause this institution any harm whatsoever, all appropriate action will be taken against you and any other responsible parties. However, if I am reading the situation correctly, I think the harm has already come to pass, and may well be irreversible." His voice rose dramatically. "If so, then may your conscience haunt you with that damnable fact for the rest of your natural life!"

Ramsey's face was red with indignation; his gaunt body seemed ready to burst through his suit. Sara could read it all in his smoldering eyes: A scandal on his watch. At the one institution that had been above scandal in a town constantly and infamously mired in it. His place in history, his long-earned career of jurisprudence, to be blemished by the blunders of an insignificant clerk; the history of his professional life reduced to a series of explanatory footnotes. If she had struck down his entire family right in front of him, Sara Evans could not have devastated the man any more. She fled the room before she burst into tears.

CHAPTER FIFTY-ONE

Fiske was waiting for Sara in her office. When she appeared in the doorway, he rose and started to speak, but then Perkins appeared behind her. Sara went over to her desk and started cleaning it out, while Perkins watched from the doorway.

"Sara, what happened?"

"This is none of your concern, Mr. Fiske," Perkins said. "However, I will let Detective Chandler and Agent McKenna know you're here. They have something to ask you."

"Well, why don't you run off and tattle on me so I can talk to Sara in private."

"I am going to escort Ms. Evans from the building."

Sara continued to pack her things into a large shopping bag and then picked up her purse and laid it on top in the bag. As she passed Fiske, she whispered, "I'll meet you in the garage."

As she went by Perkins, he said, "I'll also need all of your keys to this building."

Sara put her bag down, fished through her purse, pulled the keys off her key ring and tossed them to Perkins.

"It's not like I'm enjoying any of this," Perkins said indignantly. "The Court's in shambles, we're surrounded by a media army, people being murdered, the police swarming everywhere. It's not like I wanted you to lose your job."

Sara wordlessly pushed past him.

On the way down the main hallway, the group slowed as Chandler and McKenna approached from the other way.

"I need to talk to you, John," Chandler said.

Fiske looked at Sara. "I'll catch up with you, Sara."

She and Perkins walked off.

"You want to ask me something?" Fiske said.

"That's right."

"Would this be about my brother's life insurance policy?"

"Yes it would," Chandler said grimly. "McKenna thinks you might have taken it out yourself in your brother's name without his knowledge and then killed him."

"You found the policy in my brother's apartment?" Chandler nodded. "Well, then he obviously knew about it."

Chandler looked over at McKenna with an inquiring look. However, McKenna remained silent.

"Look, I didn't know my brother had taken out the policy. The insurance agent talked with me. I'll give you her name. She actually met with my brother, if you're really thinking I set this whole thing up myself." He looked at McKenna and saw the man's face darken. "Sorry to pop your balloon, McKenna. The money's going to our parents—Mike knew that's what I'd do with it. Talk to the insurance agent, she can confirm it. Unless you think I'm also in cahoots with her. Why stop there? I've probably got all nine justices in the back of my pocket too. Right?"

"So you talked your brother into taking out a life insurance policy to help your parents. But you and only you are the beneficiary. That's still terrific motivation to kill him," McKenna said. He turned to Chandler. "You want to ask him or do you want me to?"

Chandler looked at Fiske. "Your brother was killed by a nine-millimeter slug."

"Really?"

"You own a nine-millimeter pistol, don't you?"

Fiske looked at both men. "Been talking to the Virginia State Police?"

"Just answer the question," McKenna said.

"Why answer it, if you already know the answer?"

"John—" Chandler began.

"All right, yes. I own a nine-millimeter. SIG-Sauer P226, to be specific, with a fifteen-round mag."

"Where is it?"

"In my office, back in Richmond."

"We'd like to have it."

"For ballistics?"

"Among other things."

"Buford, this is a waste of time—"

"Do we have your permission to go to your office and get the gun?"

"No."

McKenna said, "Well, we'll have a search warrant issued in about one hour."

"You don't need a warrant. I'll give you the gun."

McKenna looked stunned. "But I thought you just said—"

"I don't want them breaking into my office to get it. I know how cops can be sometimes. They're not the most gentle souls, and it'd take me forever to get reimbursed on the cost of fixing my door." Fiske looked at Chandler. "I assume I'm not part of the unofficial team anymore, but a couple of things: Did you talk to the guards on duty the night Wright was murdered, and have the video cameras been checked?"

"I would advise you to say nothing to him, Chandler," McKenna said.

"Advice duly noted." Chandler looked at Fiske. "For old times' sake. We talked to the guards. Unless one of them's lying, none of them gave Wright a lift home. One of them offered, but Wright declined."

"What time was that?"

"About one-thirty A.M. or so. The film from the video cameras was checked and showed nothing out of the ordinary."

"Did Wright give a reason for not wanting a ride home?"

"The guard said he just walked out the door and he didn't see him after that."

"Okay, let's get back to the gun," McKenna said. "I'm going with you to your office."

"I'm not driving anywhere with you."

"I meant I'll follow you down."

"Do whatever you want, but I want a uniformed Richmond police officer there, and I want him to take the gun into custody and then have it transferred to D.C. Homicide. I will not let you be anywhere near the chain of custody."

"I really don't like what you're implying."

"Fine, but that's the way it's going to be, or you can go get your warrant. It's up to you."

Chandler spoke up, "Okay, anybody in particular?"

"Officer William Hawkins. I trust him and so can you."

"Done. I want you to leave right now, John. I'll arrange things with Richmond."

Fiske looked down the hallway. "Give me a half hour. I need to talk to somebody."

Chandler put a hand on Fiske's shoulder. "Okay, John, but if the Richmond police don't have your gun in about three hours or so, then you got a big problem with yours truly, understood?"

Fiske hustled off to the garage in search of Sara.

A couple minutes later, Dellasandro joined Chandler and McKenna.

"I'd like to know what the hell is going on around here," Dellasandro said angrily. "Two clerks murdered and now another fired over some missing appeal."

McKenna shrugged. "Pretty complicated."

"That's real encouraging," Dellasandro said.

"I'm not paid to be encouraging," McKenna shot back.

"No, you're paid to find out who's doing this. And you too, Detective Chandler," Dellasandro replied.

"And that's what we're doing," Chandler snapped.

"Okay, okay," Dellasandro said wearily. "Perkins filled me in earlier. You really think John Fiske killed his brother? I mean, okay, he had the motive, but, damn. Five hundred thousand sounds like a lot, but it's really not these days."

McKenna answered. "When you've got zip in your bank account, anything seems like a lot. He's got the motive, he's got no alibi, and in a few hours we'll see if he has the murder weapon."

Dellasandro looked unconvinced. "And what about Wright's death? How does that tie in?"

McKenna spread his hands. "Look at it this way. Sara Evans may have somehow been duped into helping Fiske. Evans and Wright shared an office. It's not out of the realm of possibility that Wright overheard something or saw something that made him suspicious about those two."

"But I thought Fiske has an alibi for the time of Wright's death," Dellasandro said.

"Yeah, Sara Evans," McKenna said.

"And all this stuff with this escaped convict Harms and the questions Evans was asking?"

Chandler shrugged. "I can't claim we have it all figured out, but that could be just another red herring."

McKenna said, "I don't think, I know. If there was anything to it, they would've told somebody. Evans couldn't even tell us what was in the appeal. Maybe Michael Fiske took some appeal, so what? John Fiske pops him for the money and he uses this missing appeal as a bunch of mumbo-jumbo to dupe Evans and everybody else."

"Well, I'm not letting my guard down until we know for sure," Dellasandro said. "The people in this building are my responsibility and we've already lost two of them." He looked over at McKenna. "I hope you know what you're doing with Fiske."

"I know exactly what I'm doing with him."

Fiske caught up with Sara in the parking garage. It didn't take her long to explain what had happened.

"Sara, I hoped I would never have to tell you this, but Chandler boxed me into a corner the other day. I'm sure I'm the reason you just lost your job."

Sara put the shopping bag in the trunk of her car. "I'm a big girl. I'm responsible for my own actions."

Fiske leaned up against the car. "Maybe I can go and talk to Ramsey and Knight, try and explain things to them?"

"Explain it how? What they're alleging I did, I did." Sara closed the trunk and joined him. "I assume they told you about your gun?"

Fiske nodded. "McKenna's giving me an armed escort to my office so I can hand it over." He looked at her closely. "So what are you going to do now?"

"I don't know. But I've suddenly got a lot of free time on my hands. I'll try to find out about Tremaine and Rayfield."

"You sure you still want to help?"

"At least I won't have ruined my career for nothing. What about you?"

"I don't have any choice in the matter."

He looked at his watch. "How about I come by your place around seven tonight?"

"I think I can manage dinner. Buy some food, a nice bottle of wine. I might even get real ambitious and dust. We can celebrate my last day at the Court. Maybe go for another sail." She paused and touched his arm. "And finish it off the same way?"

"I can bag Richmond and stay with you. I know how you must be feeling."

"But what about Chandler and McKenna?"

"I don't have to do what they say."

"If you don't go, McKenna will probably push for the electric chair. Besides, to tell you the truth, I feel really good."

"Are you sure?"

"I'm sure, John, but thanks." She stroked his face. "Tonight you can be with me."

After Fiske left, Sara was about to get in her car when she realized she had left her purse, with her car keys, in the bag in the trunk. She popped the trunk and reached in the bag to get her purse. As she lifted it out, the photo on top caught her eye. She had taken it from Michael Fiske's office before the police had searched it. It suddenly occurred to her that she did have something very important to take care of. She got in her car and pulled out of the garage.

She had just been fired as a Supreme Court clerk. Oddly, she didn't feel like bursting into tears, or slipping her head in an oven. She felt like going for a drive. Down to Richmond. She needed to see somebody. And today was as good a day as any.

When she drove past the columned facade of her old

place of work, a great wave of relief swept over her. It was so sudden that it left her breathless. Then, bit by bit, she was okay. She accelerated down Independence Avenue and didn't look back.

CHAPTER FIFTY-TWO

Fiske hurried down to Knight's chambers and, surprisingly, was allowed in. Knight sat behind her desk. Ramsey was still there, slumped in a chair. He quickly rose when Fiske entered.

Fiske plunged in. "I want you to know that anything Sara did or didn't do was to protect my brother. All she's trying to do now is help me find who killed him."

"And you're sure that question wouldn't be answered by your simply looking in a mirror?" Ramsey said forcefully.

Fiske paled. "You're way off the mark, sir."

"Am I? The authorities don't seem to think so. If you are a murderer, then I hope you spend the rest of your life in prison. As for your brother's actions, they reside not far down the ladder from taking someone's life, at least in my book."

"My brother did what he thought was right."

"I find that statement positively laughable."

"Harold—" Knight began, but he cut her off with a sweep of his hand.

"And I want you"—he pointed at Fiske—"to get out of this office and out of this building before I have you arrested for trespassing."

Fiske looked at the two of them. The anger he was feeling right now was the culmination of the last three days of sheer hell. It was as though everything bad that had ever happened to him had been caused by Harold Ramsey. "I've seen the nice little sign over the front door of this place: 'Equal Justice Under Law'? I find that laughable."

Ramsey looked ready to attack Fiske. "How dare you!"

"I've got a client on death row right now. If I ever have the 'honor' of appearing before you, can you tell me you'll actually care whether my guy lives or dies? Or will you just be using him and me to overturn a precedent that pissed you off ten years ago?"

"You insufferable—"

"Can you tell me that?" Fiske shouted. "Because if you can't, then I don't know what you are, but you're sure as hell not a judge."

Ramsey was livid. "What do you know about anything? The system—"

Fiske smacked his chest. "I'm the system. Me and the people I represent. Not you. Not this place."

"Do you realize the magnitude of the issues we deal with here?"

"When's the last time you sat and 'judged' a battered wife? Or a molested child? Have you ever watched a man die in the electric chair? Have you? You sit up here and you never even see a real person. You don't hear from any live witnesses, you never hear from any of the people you'll destroy or help by your actions. All you get is a bunch of high-powered lawyers throwing a bunch of paper at you. You have no idea of the faces, the people, the heartbreak and pain behind any of it. To you it's some intellectual game. A game! Nothing more." Fiske stared at the man. His voice shook as he said, "You think the big issues are so hard? Try dealing with the little ones."

"I think you should leave," Knight said, almost pleadingly. "Right now."

Fiske stared at Ramsey for a few seconds longer and then, calming down, he looked at the woman. "You know, that's good advice, Counselor, I think I'll take it." Fiske turned to the door.

"Mr. Fiske," Ramsey boomed out. Fiske slowly turned back. "I have several good friends at the Virginia state bar. I think they should be apprised of the situation. I would think that appropriate action should be taken against you, perhaps resulting in suspension and subsequent disbarment."

"Guilty until proved innocent? That's your idea of how the criminal justice system should work?"

"It's my strong opinion that it's only a matter of time until you're found guilty."

Fiske started to say something else, but Knight, one hand on the phone, said, "John, I would much prefer if you left without the assistance of the guards."

After Fiske was gone, Ramsey shook his head. "Beyond all doubt, the man's a psychopath."

He turned and looked at Knight. She sat there, staring straight ahead. "Beth, I just want to let you know that you're welcome to use one of my clerks until you find a replacement for Sara."

She looked over at him. The offer of a clerk seemed very nice. On the surface. A spy in her camp underneath that surface?

"I'll be fine. We'll just have to work harder."

"You put up a good fight at oral argument today, though I do wish you wouldn't take it personally. It's a little unseemly when we bicker back and forth like that in public."

"How can I not take the cases personally, Harold? Tell me how." Her eyes were swollen, her voice suddenly hoarse.

"You have to. I never lose sleep over a case. Even a death penalty one. We don't decide guilt or innocence. We interpret words. You have to think of it in those terms. Otherwise you'll burn out."

"Maybe burning out early is a preferable alternative to having a long, distinguished career that only challenges my *intellect*." Ramsey glanced sharply at her. "I want to hurt, I want to feel the pain. Everyone else does. Why are we an exception? Dammit, we should be agonizing over these cases."

Ramsey shook his head sadly. "Then I'm afraid you'll never endure. And you have to if you want to make a real difference up here."

"We'll see. I may surprise you. Starting today."

"You don't have a chance of overturning *Stanley*. But I admire your tenacity, even though it was wasted today."

"The votes haven't been counted yet that I recall."

Ramsey smiled. "Of course, of course. A formality only." He put his hands in his pockets and stood in front of her. "And just so you know, I also am aware of your plans to reexamine the issue of the rights of the poor—"

"Harold, we've just lost our third clerk. A third human being. One whom I care greatly about. The place is in shambles. I don't feel like talking about Court business right now. I may never feel like it again, in fact."

"Beth, we must move on. True, it's been one crisis after another, but we will persevere."

"Harold, please!"

Ramsey would not back down. "The court goes on. We—"

Knight stood up. "Get out."

"I beg your pardon?"

"Get out of my office."

"Beth—"

"Get out! Get out!"

Without another word, Ramsey left. Knight stood there for another minute or so. Then she quickly left her office.

After his confrontation with Ramsey, Fiske entered the Court's underground garage and went straight to his car. He felt numb. He had gotten Sara fired, was being set up for murdering his brother and had just told off the chief justice of the United States. All in less than an hour. In any realm other than total lunacy, that would be called a bad day. He sat in his car. He had no desire to drive to Richmond and watch McKenna try to put the finishing touches on the destruction of his life.

He pushed his fists against his eye sockets. A groan escaped from him and then he jerked forward as he heard the sound. His eyes widened as he saw Elizabeth Knight tapping on the car window. He rolled it down.

"I would like to talk to you."

He composed himself as best he could. "What about?"

"Can we go for a short drive? I don't think I'd risk bringing you back in the building. I'm not sure I've ever seen Harold quite that upset."

Fiske thought he saw a trace of a smile on the woman's face as she said this. "You want to go for a drive in my car?" he asked.

"I don't have a car here. Is there a problem with yours?"

Fiske looked at her expensive dress. "Well, my car's interior is basically rust covered with a veneer of grime."

Knight smiled. "I grew up on a ranch in East Texas. When my family drove to the little shacks that consti- tuted the town we lived near, we did so on a backhoe with me and my six siblings hanging on for dear life and enjoy- ing every minute of it. And I *would* like to talk to you."

Fiske finally nodded and Knight slipped in the front seat.

"Where to?" Fiske asked as they left the garage.

"Take a left at the light. I hope you don't have anything pressing. It was rude of me not to ask."

Fiske thought of McKenna waiting for him. "Nothing important."

After he made the turn, Knight started speaking. "You shouldn't have come back and said those things, you know."

"I hope you didn't come here just to tell me that," Fiske said sharply.

"I came to tell you that I feel terribly about Sara."

"Join the crowd. She tried to help my brother and then me. I'm sure she just loves the day she ran into the Fiske brothers."

"Well, at least one of you anyway."

"What does that mean?"

"Sara liked and respected your brother. But she didn't love him, although, quite frankly, I think he was in love with her. But her heart lies elsewhere."

"Is that right? And she told you this?"

"John, I really don't like to admit to any gender bias, but I also refuse to ignore some basic realities: I doubt if my eight male colleagues have any clue whatsoever, but it's clear to me that Sara Evans is very much in love with you."

"Your womanly intuition?"

"Something like that. I also have two girls of my own." She noted his curious look. "My first husband died. My daughters are grown and on their own." Knight put her hands in her lap and looked out the window. "However, that's not really why I wanted to talk to you," she said. "Turn right, up here," she said.

As Fiske did so, he asked, "So what is on your agenda? You people seem to always have one."

"And you find that somehow wrong?"

"You tell me. Seeing the games you people play doesn't give me warm fuzzies."

"I can respect that point of view."

"I'm in no position to really judge what you do. But, to me, you're not judges, you're policymakers. And what that policy will be depends on who lobbies hard enough to get five votes. What does that have to do with the rights of one plaintiff and one defendant?" As soon as Fiske had finished speaking he had a sudden, depressing thought: He had no room to complain about the Court and how it operated. He spent all his time dodging the truth on behalf of his clients. In a way, that was worse than anything the Court did or didn't do in the name of justice.

They drove in silence for a minute until Knight broke it. "I started out as a prosecutor. And then became a trial judge." She paused. "I can't tell you that your feelings are wrong." Fiske looked mildly surprised. "John, we could debate this until we're both sick of it, but the fact is there is a system in place and one must work within that system. If that means playing by its rules and, on occasion, bending them, so be it. Perhaps that's an oversimplified philosophy for a complex situation, but sometimes you have to go with your gut." She looked at him. "Do you know what I mean?"

He nodded. "My instincts are pretty good."

"And what do your instincts tell you about Michael and Steven's deaths? Is there anything to this story of the missing appeal? If there is, I would really like to know about it."

"Why ask me?"

"Because you seem to know more than anyone else. That's why I wanted to talk to you in private."

"Are you really hoping that I killed my brother and I'm using this appeal as a red herring? That way the Court doesn't get a black eye."

"I didn't say that."

"You said as much to Sara at your party."

Knight sighed and sat back. "I'm not sure why I did. Perhaps to scare her away from you."

"I didn't kill my brother."

"I believe you. So this missing appeal may be important?"

Fiske nodded. "My brother was killed because he knew what that appeal said. I think Wright was killed because he was working late, came out of his office and saw someone at the Court going through my brother's office."

She turned pale. "You believe someone at the Court murdered Steven?" Fiske nodded. "Can you prove that?"

"I hope so."

"That can't be, John. Why?"

"There's a guy who's spent half his life in prison who'd like to know the answer to that."

"Does Detective Chandler know all this?"

"Some of it. But Agent McKenna has pretty much convinced him I'm the bad guy."

"I'm not sure Detective Chandler believes that."

"We'll see."

As Fiske dropped Knight back at the Court, she said, "If everything you suspect is true and someone at the Court is involved in this . . ." She stopped, unable to continue for a moment. "Do you realize what this could do to the Court's reputation?"

"I'm not sure of a lot in life, but I'm certain of one thing." He paused and then said, "The Court's reputation isn't worth an innocent man dying in prison."

CHAPTER FIFTY-THREE

Rufus looked anxiously over at his brother, who had just finished an exhausting coughing fit. Josh tried to sit up a little, thinking that would help his breathing. His insides, he knew, were all but destroyed. Something important to keeping him alive might burst at any moment. He still held the pistol against his side. But it didn't look like a bullet would be needed to end his life. At least, not another one.

It was fortunate for them that Tremaine and Rayfield hadn't come in an Army vehicle. But the Jeep did have one crushed side from being broadsided by the truck and this would draw unwanted attention to them. At least it had a cloth top, which prevented anyone from getting a good glimpse of what was inside.

Rufus didn't know where he was going, and Josh moved in and out of lucidity too much to really help him. Rufus flipped open the glove box and pulled out a map. He studied it quickly and traced the route to Richmond with his

finger. He had to get to the highway. If he had to he would
stop and ask directions. He pulled the little card out of his
shirt pocket and glanced at the names and telephone
numbers. Now he just had to find a phone.

*   *   *

When Fiske and McKenna arrived at Fiske's office, the
FBI agent said, "Let's get to it."

"We wait for the police," Fiske said firmly.

Just as he said that, a police cruiser pulled up and
Officer Hawkins climbed out.

"What the heck's going on here, John?" Hawkins asked,
perplexed.

Fiske pointed at McKenna. "Agent McKenna thinks I
killed Mike. He's here to get my gun so he can do a ballistics test."

Hawkins looked at McKenna with hostile eyes. "If that's
not the biggest bunch of bullshit I ever heard . . ."

"Right, thanks for your official assessment—Officer
Hawkins, is it?" McKenna said, coming forward.

"That's right," Hawkins said grimly.

"Well, Officer Hawkins, you have the consent of Mr.
Fiske to search his office for a nine-millimeter pistol registered to his name." He looked at Fiske. "I'm assuming you
are still giving that consent." When Fiske didn't respond,
McKenna looked back at Hawkins. "Now, if you have a
problem with that, then let's go talk to your boss and you
can start planning another career outside of law enforcement."

Before Hawkins could do something foolish, Fiske
grabbed his sleeve and said, "Let's just go get this over
with, Billy."

As they walked into the building, Fiske commented,
"Your face looks a lot better."

Hawkins smiled, embarrassed. "Yeah, thanks."

"What happened?" McKenna asked.

Hawkins looked at him sullenly. "Guy decided to take a ride on drugs. He was a little difficult to arrest."

There was a stack of mail and packages in front of Fiske's office door. He picked them up and unlocked the door. They went inside and Fiske walked over to his desk and dropped the stack of mail on it. He slid open the top drawer and looked inside. He stuck his hand in and fumbled through the contents before looking up at both men. "It was right in this drawer. I actually saw it the day you came to tell me about Mike, Billy."

McKenna crossed his arms and eyed Fiske sternly. "Okay, has anybody else had access to your office? Cleaning crew, secretary, delivery people, window washers?"

"No, nobody. Nobody else has a key, except for the land-lord."

Hawkins said, "You've been gone, what, two days or so?"

"That's right."

McKenna was looking at the door. "But there's no signs of forced entry."

Hawkins said, "That doesn't mean anything. Person who knew what they were doing could pick that lock and you'd never even know it."

"Who knew you kept the gun here?" McKenna asked.

"Nobody."

"Maybe one of your clients took it so he'd have a piece of ordnance to knock over a bank with," McKenna said.

"I don't interview clients in my office, McKenna. They're usually in prison by the time I get the call."

"Well, it looks like we have a little problem here. Your brother was killed by a nine-millimeter slug. You have a nine-millimeter Sig registered to you. You admit it was actually in your possession as of a few days ago. Now that pistol is missing. You have no alibi for the time of your brother's death and you're a half million bucks richer because of his death."

Hawkins glanced over at Fiske.

"A life insurance policy Mike took out," Fiske explained. "It was for Mom and Dad."

"At least that's your story, right?" McKenna added.

Fiske edged closer to McKenna. "If you think you have enough to charge me, then do it. If not, get the hell out of my office."

McKenna wasn't fazed. "I believe Officer Hawkins has your consent to search your entire office for the gun, not just the drawer you said it was in. Now, friend or not, I would expect him to carry out his sworn duty."

Fiske backed off and looked over at. Hawkins. "Go ahead, Billy. I'm going down to the corner café for something to drink. You want anything?" Hawkins shook his head.

"I could use a cup of coffee," McKenna said, following Fiske out. "It'll give us a chance to have a little talk."

Sara pulled her car into the driveway. She took a deep breath. The Buick was there. As she got out of the car, the smell of cut grass hit her. It was comforting, taking her back to high school football games, lazy summers in the peace of the Carolinas. When she knocked on the door, it was jerked open so quickly she almost fell off the stoop. Ed Fiske must have watched her drive up. Before he could slam the door in her face, she held the photo out to him.

There were four people in the photo: Ed and Gladys Fiske and their two sons. They all wore broad smiles.

Ed looked questioningly at Sara.

"Michael had it in his office. I wanted you to have it."

"And why's that?" His tone was still cold, but at least he wasn't screaming obscenities at her.

"Because it seemed like the right thing to do."

Ed took the photo from her. "I got nothing to say to you."

"But I have a lot to say to you. I promised someone something, and I like to keep my promises."

"Who? Johnny? Well, you can tell him that it's no good sending you over to try to mend things."

"He doesn't know I'm here. He told me not to come."

He looked surprised. "So why are you here?"

"That promise. What you saw the other night wasn't John's fault. It was mine."

"It takes two to tango and you ain't telling me no different."

"May I come in?"

"I don't see why."

"I'd really like to talk to you about your sons. I think you need to know some things. Some information that might make things a little clearer. It won't take all that long and I promise you, after I'm done, I won't ever bother you again. Please?"

After a long moment, Ed finally moved aside and let her pass. He closed the door noisily behind them.

The living room was much the way it had been the first time she had seen it. The man liked things tidy. She imagined his garage full of tools kept in the same manner. Ed motioned to the sofa and Sara sat down. He went into the dining room and carefully placed the photo among the others there. "You want something to drink?" he asked grudgingly.

"Only if you're having something."

Ed sat down in a chair across from her. "I'm not."

She looked at him closely. Now she could more clearly see the rough outlines of both sons in his face, his build. The mother was there too, though more in Michael than in John. Ed started to light up a cigarette and then stopped.

"You can smoke if you want. It's your house."

Ed replaced the pack of smokes in his pocket and slid the lighter back in his pants pocket. "Gladys wouldn't let me smoke in the house, just outside. Old habits are hard to break." He crossed his arms, waiting for her to start talking.

"Michael and I were very close friends."

"I'm not sure how close you could've been after what I saw the other night." Ed's face started to flush.

"The fact is, Mr. Fiske—"

"Look, just call me Ed," he said gruffly.

"All right, Ed, the fact is we were close friends. That's how I saw it, but Michael wanted more than that."

"What do you mean?"

Sara swallowed hard, her own face reddening. "Michael asked me to marry him."

Ed looked shocked. "He never said anything to me."

"I'm sure he didn't. You see"—she hesitated for a moment, very nervous about what his reaction would be to these next words—"you see, I told him no." She shrank back a little, but Fiske just sat there, trying to digest this.

"Is that right? I take it you didn't love him."

"I didn't—not like that, anyway. I'm not sure why I didn't. He seemed perfect. Maybe that's what scared me, sharing my life with someone like that, trying to keep my standards up that high for a lifetime. And he was so caught up in his work. Even if I had loved him, I'm not sure there would have been room for me."

Ed looked down. "It was hard raising those two boys. Johnny was good at most everything, but Mike . . . Mike was flat-out great at anything he wanted to do. I was working all the damn time and didn't really see it that good when they were growing up. I see it a whole lot better now. I bragged a lot on Mike. Too much. Mike told me Johnny wouldn't have nothing to do with him, and wouldn't really say why. Johnny really keeps to himself. Hard to get him to talk."

Sara looked past him, out the window, where a cardinal flitted by and settled on the branch of a weeping willow.

She said, "I know. I've spent a lot of time with him the last few days. You know, I always thought I'd be able to tell, almost instantly: This is the person I want to spend my life with. I guess that notion seems silly. And unfair. Doesn't it?"

A tiny smile creased the man's face. "The first time I saw Gladys, she was waitressing at this little diner across from where I worked. I walked in the door with a bunch of my buddies one day and from the moment I saw her I didn't hear a word they said. It was like it was just me and her in the whole damn world. Went back to work and made a mess of a Cummins diesel engine. Couldn't get her out of my head."

Sara smiled. "I'm well acquainted with the stubbornness of John and Michael Fiske. So I doubt if you just left it at that."

Ed smiled too. "I went back over to that diner for break-fast, lunch and dinner for the next six months. We started going out. Then I got up the courage to ask her to marry me. I swear to God I would've done it that first day, but I thought she'd think I was crazy or something." He paused for a moment and then said with finality, "We've had a damn good life together too." He studied her face. "Is that what happened to you when you saw Johnny?" Sara nodded. "Did Mike know?"

"I think he figured it out. When I finally met John I asked him if he had any idea why the two of them didn't seem to be close. I thought that might have been part of it, but they seemed to have drifted apart before then." Sara tensed. "So that night in the boat, what you saw was me pushing myself on your son. He had been through the most hellish day imaginable and all I could think about was myself." She looked directly at him. "He turned me down flat." She thought of last night, the tenderness she and John Fiske had exchanged, both in and out of her bed. And then the morning after. She thought she had figured it all out. That had been a good feeling. Now she was close to overwhelmed by the sense that she knew nothing about the man or his feelings. She let out a troubled laugh. "It was a very humbling experience." She pulled a tissue from her pocketbook and dabbed at her eyes. "That's all I came to tell you. If you want to hate anyone, hate me, not your son."

Ed studied the carpet for a minute and then stood. "Just finished cutting the grass. I'd like an iced tea, how about you?" With a surprised look, Sara nodded.

A few minutes later Ed came back with glasses of ice and a pitcher of tea. As he filled the glasses he said, "I've thought a lot about that night. I don't remember all of it. Had a damn bad hangover the next day. As mad as I was, I never should've hit Johnny. Not in the damn gut."

"He's pretty tough."

"That's not what I meant." Ed took a swallow of tea and sat back, chewing on his lip. "Did Johnny ever tell you why he left the police force?"

"He said he had arrested some young kid for a drug offense. That the kid was so pathetic and everything, that he decided to start helping people like that."

Ed nodded. "Well, he didn't actually arrest him. That boy died at the scene. And so did the officer that backed Johnny up on that call."

Sara almost spilled her tea. "What?"

Ed looked a little uncomfortable now that he had opened this subject, but he continued. "Johnny never really talked about it, but I got the story from the officers who arrived after it all happened. Johnny stopped the car for some reason. It was stolen, I think. Anyway, he called in for backup. He got the two boys out of the car. Found the drugs. That's when his backup came. Right before they were going to search them, one of the boys dropped like he was having a seizure. Johnny tried to help him. His backup should've kept his gun on the other, but he didn't, and the other fellow pulled a gun and killed him. Johnny managed to fire, but the boy put two rounds into him.

"They both went down, facing each other. The other boy had just been faking it. He jumped up and took off in the car. They caught him a little while later. The other fellow and Johnny were about a foot apart, both bleeding like crazy."

"Omigod!"

"Johnny stuffed a finger in one of the holes. It stopped the bleeding a little. Well—and I heard some of this from him while he was in the hospital half out of his head—the boy said some things to Johnny. I'm not exactly sure what, Johnny never would say, but they found the boy dead and Johnny next to him, his arm around him. Must've dragged himself over there or something. Some of the cops didn't exactly like that, what with one of their own lying dead because of the kid. But they checked everything out and Johnny was cleared. It was the other cop's fault. Anyway, Johnny almost died on the way to the hospital. As it was, he was in there for about a month. Whatever load the boy was carrying in that pistol ripped Johnny's insides to shreds."

Sara suddenly thought back to Fiske's pulling his shirt back down before they made love. "Does he have a scar?"

Ed looked at her funny. "Why do you ask?"

"Something he said."

He nodded slowly. "From his gut to his neck."

"Too old for skinny-dipping," Sara said to herself.

"Guess they could've done some plastic surgery, but Johnny had had enough of hospitals. Besides, I think he figured if they couldn't fix him on the inside, what the hell did it matter what he looked like on the outside?"

Sara's face took on a stricken look. "What do you mean? He fully recovered, didn't he?"

Ed shook his head sadly. "Those bullets ripped him bad, bounced around inside him like a damn pinball. They patched him up, but just about every one of his organs was damaged for good. Maybe they could make it all right if Johnny wanted to spend a bunch of years in the hospital, have transplants and stuff like that. But that ain't my son. Docs say eventually things inside him are just going to stop working. They said it was like diabetes—you know, how a person's organs get worn out and all?" Sara nodded as her own stomach started to churn. "Well, the docs said those two bullets will eventually cost Johnny about twenty years of his life, maybe more. And there wasn't really nothing they could do about it. Back then we didn't care. Hell, he was alive, that was enough. But I know he thinks about it. He pumped iron, ran like a damn demon, got himself in good shape, at least on the outside. Quit the police force. Wouldn't even take damn disability, although he was sure as hell entitled. Became a lawyer, works like a dog for what amounts to chickenshit, and gives me and his momma most of it. I got no pension and Gladys's medical bills added up to more than I made in my whole life. Hell, we had to mortgage this place again after spending thirty years paying it off. But you do what you got to do."

As Ed paused, Sara glanced over at the table where John Fiske's medal for valor sat. A little piece of metal for all that pain.

"I tell you all this so you'll see Johnny doesn't really have the same goals as you and me might. Never got married, never talks about having no kids of his own. Everything is sped up for him. He figures if he makes it to fifty, he's the luckiest man on earth. He told me that himself." Ed Fiske looked down, his voice catching. "Never figured I'd outlive Mike. I hope to God I don't outlive my other boy."

Sara finally found her voice. "I appreciate your telling

me this. I realize it was hard for you. You don't really know me."

"Depending on the situation, sometimes you can know a person better in ten minutes than someone you've crossed paths with all your life."

Sara rose to leave. "Thank you for your time. And John really needs to hear from you."

He nodded solemnly. "I'll do that."

As her hand touched the doorknob, Ed spoke one last time. "You still love my son?"

Sara walked out without answering.

At the small café down from his office building, Fiske bought his coffee and sat down at an outside table. McKenna did the same. At first Fiske chose to completely ignore the hovering FBI agent and idly watched the passersby while he drank his coffee. He slipped on his sunglasses as the sun cleared the top of the building across the street and drew both men's shadows across the bricks. McKenna silently munched on some crackers he had bought and fingered his Styrofoam cup of coffee.

"How's the gut? Sorry I had to punch you like that."

"The only thing you're sorry about is that you didn't hit me harder."

"No, really. I saw the shotgun and got concerned."

Fiske looked up at him. "I guess you thought I might be able to somehow open the car door, pull the shotgun out, swing it around and get off a shot before you could blow me away from a distance of, what, six inches?"

McKenna shrugged. "FYI, I read up on your police record. You were a good cop. Right up until the end, anyway."

"What the hell is that supposed to mean?"

McKenna sat down at the table. "Nothing, other than there being some questions about that last event in your record. Care to fill me in on it?"

Fiske took off his glasses and stared at the man. "Why don't you put a bullet in my head instead? I think that would be more fun for me."

McKenna leaned his chair back against the side of the building and lit up a cigarette. "You know, if you're so anxious to prove your innocence, then you might want to start being a little more cooperative."

"McKenna, you're convinced I killed my brother, so why should I bother?"

"I've worked a lot of cases over the years. Half the time my original theory didn't turn out to be right. My philosophy is: Never say never."

"Boy, you really sound sincere."

McKenna assumed a friendlier tone. "Look, John, I've been doing this stuff a long time, okay? Nice, neat little cases aren't the norm. There are twists on this one and I'm not ignoring them." He stopped and then added as casually as he could, "So why was your brother interested in Rufus Harms, and what exactly was in the appeal?"

Fiske put his sunglasses back on. "That doesn't fit into your theory of me killing my brother."

"That's only one of my theories. I'm down here following that up by looking for your suddenly vanished nine-millimeter. While I'm waiting on that, I'm looking at it from another angle: Rufus Harms. Your brother took the appeal, it looks like he visited the prison."

"Chandler told you that?"

"I have a lot of information sources. You and Evans have both been snooping around into Harms's background. He escaped from a prison in southwest Virginia. And you two took a chartered plane to that area last night. Why don't you tell me about that? Where'd you go and why?"

Fiske sat back, stunned. McKenna had put them under surveillance. That wasn't unusual, yet somehow Fiske hadn't even thought about the possibility. "You seem to know so much—why ask me?"

"You might have some information I could use to solve this case."

"Ahead of Chandler?"

"When people are getting killed, what does it matter who stops it first?"

That statement made a lot of sense, Fiske knew. On the surface, at least. But of course it mattered a great deal who stopped it. People in law enforcement kept score, just like people in other lines of work. Fiske stood up. "Let's check in with Billy. By now he's probably found those two bodies I stuffed in my file cabinet last week."

Hawkins was just finishing up when they returned.

"Nothing," he said in response to McKenna's look. "You can search it yourself if you want," he added defiantly.

"That's okay, I trust you," McKenna said amicably.

Fiske was staring at Hawkins. "What's that, Billy?" Fiske pointed at his neck and collar.

"What's what?"

Fiske touched Hawkins's collar with his finger and then held it up for the man to see.

Hawkins blushed a little. "Oh. Damn, that was Bonnie's idea to cover the bruises. That's why my face doesn't look so beat up. I've never been hit that hard in my life. I mean, the guy was big, but so am I."

McKenna said, "I would've emptied my clip in the bastard."

Fiske stared openmouthed at McKenna as he said this.

Hawkins nodded. "I was tempted. But anyway, the guys would give me hell if they knew, but it's so hot outside and you start sweating, and the stuff just comes off on your clothes. I don't know how women do it."

"Then you're saying it's—"

"Yeah, it's makeup," he said sheepishly.

Despite the revelation that had just occurred to him, Fiske tried his best to appear calm. He unconsciously rubbed his still-tender shoulder.

McKenna was staring at him.

Just then the phone rang. Fiske picked it up. It was the nursing home where his mother lived.

"I read about Michael in the paper. I'm so sorry, John." The woman had worked at the home for years and Fiske knew her very well.

"Thanks, Anne. Look, right now is a real bad time—"

"I mean, Michael was just here and now he's gone. I can't believe it."

Fiske tensed. "'Here,' as in at the nursing home?"

"Yes. Just last week. Thursday—no, Friday."

The day he disappeared.

"I remember because he usually comes on Saturday."

Fiske shook his head clear. "What are you talking about? Mike didn't visit Mom."

"Sure he did. I mean, not nearly as often as you did."

"You never told me that."

"Didn't I? Well, I guess if you have to know, Michael didn't want you to know."

"Why in the hell didn't he want me to know? I'm sick and tired of people not telling me things about my brother."

"I'm sorry, John," the woman said, "but he asked me not to say anything and I honored his request. That's all. But now that he's gone, I . . . I didn't think it would hurt for you to know."

"He saw Mom on Friday? Did he talk to you?"

"No, not really. He seemed a little nervous, actually. I mean, sort of anxious. He came really early and only stayed about a half hour."

"So they talked?"

"They met. I don't know how much they actually talked. Gladys can be difficult sometimes. When do you think you might stop by to see her? I mean, she couldn't possibly know about Michael, but still she seems very depressed for some reason."

It was clear to Fiske that the woman believed a mother's
link to her children could trump even the grip of
Alzheimer's. "I'm really busy right——" Fiske broke off
what he was saying. It would be a miracle if his mother
could remember anything of any conversation she might
have had with Mike that could possibly help them. But if
she did?

"I'll be right over."

Fiske hung up the phone, picked up his briefcase and
stuffed the stack of mail in there.

"Your brother visited your mom on the day he disappeared?" McKenna asked. Fiske nodded. "Then she might
be able to tell us something."

"McKenna, my mom has Alzheimer's. She thinks John
Kennedy is still president."

"Okay, what about somebody who works there?"

Fiske wrote down an address and phone number on the
back of one of his cards. "But leave my mom out of it."

"You're going to see her, aren't you? How come?"

"She's my mother." Fiske disappeared out the door.

Hawkins looked over at McKenna. "You ready to leave?
Because I want to lock up. Don't want anybody else
coming in here and stealing any more stuff."

The way Hawkins said it made McKenna blink. The
guy couldn't know that he had taken the gun, could he?
Still, he felt guilty about it. But he had bigger things to
feel guilty about. Far bigger.

CHAPTER FIFTY-FOUR

Sara was stopped at a red light on her way to Fiske's office when she saw him drive through the intersection heading west. She didn't have time even to blow her horn. She thought about flagging him down, but a glimpse of his tense face stopped her. She turned right and followed him.

Thirty minutes later she slowed as Fiske's car turned into the parking lot of a long-term care facility located in the West End of Richmond. Sara had been here once before, with Michael, to visit his mother. She kept her car hidden behind a broad-leaved evergreen next to the entrance and watched as Fiske stepped out of his car and hurried inside.

Fiske met up with Anne, the woman who had just called him, who apologized again and led him to the visitors' lounge, where Gladys sat docilely in her pajamas and slippers. When Fiske appeared, she looked up and silently clapped her hands together.

Fiske sat down across from her, and Gladys put out her

hands and tenderly touched his face. Her smile broadened, her eyes wide and catching absolutely nothing of reality.

"How's my Mike? How's Momma's baby?"

He gently touched her hands. "I'm fine. Doing good. Pop's good too," he lied. "We had a nice visit the other day, didn't we?"

"Visits are *so* nice." She looked behind him and smiled. She often did that. It was hard keeping her attention. She was an infant now, the cycle complete.

She touched his cheek again. "Your daddy was here."

"When was that?"

She shook her head, "Last year sometime. He got leave. His ship went down. Japs done it."

"Really? He's okay, isn't he?"

She laughed long and loud. "Oh yes, that man is A-okay." She leaned forward and whispered conspiratorially, "Mike, honey, can you keep a secret?"

"Sure, Mom," Fiske said hesitantly.

She looked around, blushing. "I'm pregnant again."

Fiske took a deep breath. This was a new one. "Really? When did you find out?"

"Now, don't you worry, sweetie, Momma's got enough love to go around for all of you." She pinched his cheek and kissed his forehead.

He squeezed her hand and managed a smile. "We had a good talk the other day, didn't we?" She nodded absently. This was crazy, he thought, but he was here and he might as well try. "I had a good trip. You remember where I went?"

"You went to school, Mike, just like every day. Your daddy took you on his ship." She frowned. "You be careful out there. Lot of fighting going on. Your daddy's out fighting right now." She punched a fist in the air. "Get 'em, Eddie."

Fiske sat back and stared at her. "I'll be careful." Looking at her was like watching a portrait that was fading daily under unforgiving sunlight. Eventually, he would come to visit and all the paint would be gone, the only image left would come from his memory. And so life goes. "I have to get going. I'm, uh, I'm late for school."

"So pretty." She looked past him and waved. "Hello, there." Fiske turned around and froze as he saw Sara standing there.

"I'm pregnant, honey," Gladys told her.

"Congratulations," was all Sara could think to say.

Fiske stormed down the hallway to the exit, Sara trailing him. He threw open the door so hard it smacked against the wall.

"John, will you stop and talk to me?" she pleaded.

He whirled around. "How dare you come and spy on me."

"I wasn't spying."

"It's none of your damn business." He pulled out his keys and got into his car. She jumped in.

"Get the hell out of my car."

"I'm not budging until we talk about this."

"Bullshit!"

"If you want me out, throw me out."

"Damn you!" Fiske shouted, before climbing out of the car.

Sara followed him. "Damn *you*, John Fiske. Will you please stop running away and talk to me?"

"We've got nothing to talk about."

"We have *everything* to talk about."

He pointed an unsteady finger at her. "Why the hell are you doing this to me, Sara?"

"Because I care about you."

"I don't need your help."

"I think you do. I know you do."

They stood there staring at each other.

"Can't we go somewhere and talk about this? Please."

She slowly walked around the car and stood next to him. Touching his arm, she said, "If last night meant half as much to you as it did to me, we should at least be able to talk." She stood there, convinced that his response would be to climb in his car and drive out of her life.

Fiske looked at her for a moment, dropped his head and wearily leaned against his car. Sara's hand slipped down to his and tightened around it. Fiske looked beyond her to a car parked on the road and the two men inside. "We'll have the Feds along for a ride." His manner and tone were now resigned. At least it wasn't McKenna back there.

"Good, I'll feel very safe," she said, her gaze refusing to leave his, until finally she saw she hadn't lost him, at least for now.

They climbed in their cars and Sara followed Fiske to a small shopping mall about a mile away, where they sat at an outdoor table and sipped lemonade in the heat of the late afternoon.

"I can understand how you could hold that against your brother, although it's not his fault," Sara said.

"Nothing was ever Mike's fault," Fiske said bitterly.

"It's not like your mother can help herself. It could just as easily be that she called Michael by your name."

"Yeah, right. She chose not to remember me."

"Maybe she calls you that because you visited her a lot more than Michael did and that's her way of reacting to it."

"I'm not buying that."

Sara looked angry. "Well, if you want to be jealous of your brother even now that he's dead, then I guess that's your right."

Fiske settled a very cold gaze on her. She expected him to erupt. Instead, he said, "I am, was, whatever, jealous of my brother. Who wouldn't be?"

"But that doesn't make it right."

"Maybe it doesn't," Fiske said, his voice tired. He

looked away. "The first time I visited Mom and she called me Mike, I thought it was a temporary thing, you know, she was having a real bad day. After two months of it . . ." He paused. "Well, that's when I cut Mike off. For good. Everything that had ever ticked me off about him, no matter how stupid, I just blew up into a huge picture of this evil sonofabitch with no heart, nothing good. He had taken my mother away from me."

"John, the day we came to see you at trial, I went with Michael to see your mother."

He tensed. "What?"

"Your mother wouldn't even talk to him. He brought her a gift, she wouldn't take it. He told me she was always like that. He assumed that it was because she loved you so much, that she didn't care about him."

"You're lying," Fiske said in a hushed tone.

"No, I'm not. It's the truth."

"You're lying!" he said again, more forcefully.

"Ask some of the people who work there. They know."

A few minutes of silence passed. Fiske's head was bowed. When he looked back up, he said, "I never really thought about him losing his mother too."

"Are you sure about that?" Sara asked quietly.

Fiske stared at her, his hands clenched. "What do you mean?" he said, his voice shaking.

"What stopped you from talking to your brother? Michael told me you had shut him out, and you just admitted that. Even so, I can't believe you never knew how she treated him."

For a full minute Fiske said nothing. He stared at Sara, perhaps through her; his eyes revealed nothing of what he was thinking. Finally, he closed his eyes and said in a barely audible tone, "I knew."

He looked at her. The terrible pain on his features made her tremble.

"I just didn't want to care," Fiske said. Sara gripped his

shoulder tightly. "I guess I used it as an excuse not to have anything to do with my own brother." He took another deep breath. "There's something else. Mike did call me, before he went to the prison. I didn't call him back. Not until it was too late. . . . I killed him."

"You can't blame yourself for that." Sara's words had no effect, she could see that, so she changed tactics. "If you want to blame yourself, then do it for the right reason. You unfairly cut your brother out of your life. You were wrong to do that. Very wrong. Now he's gone. That's something you'll have to live with forever, John."

Now he looked at her. His face grew calmer. "I guess I've been living with it already."

Since he had confided in her, Sara decided it was only fair to reciprocate. "I saw your father today." Before Fiske could say anything, she hurried on. "I promised you I would. I told him what really happened."

"And he believed you," Fiske said skeptically.

"I was telling the truth. He's going to call you."

"Thanks, but I wish you had kept out of it."

"He filled in some gaps for me."

"Like what?" Fiske said sharply.

"Like what happened to make you stop being a cop."

"Dammit, Sara, you had no need to know that."

"Yes, I did. A great reason."

"What is it?"

"You know what!"

Neither of them spoke for several minutes. Fiske looked down at the table too, and fiddled with his straw. Finally, he sat back and crossed his arms. "So my dad told you everything?"

Sara glanced up at him. "About the shooting, yes." Her tone was cautious.

"So you know I'm probably not going to be alive and kicking when I'm sixty or maybe even fifty."

"I think you can beat any odds someone throws at you."

"And if I don't?"

"If you don't, that doesn't matter to me."

He leaned forward. "But it matters to me, Sara."

"So you give up the life you do have?"

"I think I'm leading my life exactly how I want to."

"Maybe you are," she quietly conceded.

"It would never work, you know."

"So you've thought about it?"

"I've thought about it. Have you? How do you know this isn't another impulse decision? Like buying your house?"

"It's what I feel."

"Feelings change."

"And it's so much easier to admit defeat rather than work at something."

"When I want something, I work very hard at it." Fiske had no idea why he said that, but he saw the devastated look on Sara's face.

"I see. And I guess I have no choice in the matter?"

"You really don't want to have to make that kind of a choice." She said nothing and Fiske remained quiet for a moment. "You know, my dad didn't tell you everything, because he doesn't know everything."

"He told me how you almost died, how the other officer did die. And the man who shot you. I can understand how that could change your life. How it could make you do what you do. I think it's very noble, if that's the right word."

"That's not even close. Do you really want to know why I do what I do?"

Sara could sense the sudden change of mood. "Tell me."

"Because I'm scared." He nodded at her. "Fear drives me. The longer I was a cop, the more it became 'us against them.' Young, angry, attitude, with a pistol to back it all up." Fiske stopped speaking and watched through the glass partition as people inside bought refreshments. They appeared carefree, happy, pursuing some tangible goal in their lives; they were everything he wasn't, couldn't be.

He looked back at Sara. "I kept arresting the same guys over and over and it seemed like before I filed the paperwork they were back on the streets. And they'd blow you away like stepping on a cockroach. See, they lived the game of 'us against them' too. You lump people together. Young and black, catch 'em if you can. Blues coming at you? Kill 'em if you can. It's quick and you don't have to make choices about individuals. It's like a drug addiction."

"Not everybody does that. The whole world isn't made up of people like that."

"I know that. I know that most people, black, white or whatever, are good people, lead relatively normal lives. I really want to believe that. It's just that as a cop I never saw any of that. Normal ships didn't sail by my dock."

"So did the shooting make you rethink things?"

Fiske didn't answer right away. When he did, he spoke slowly. "I remember dropping to my knees to check the guy, who it turned out was faking a seizure. I heard the gun go off, my partner scream. I pulled my pistol at the same time I was turning. I don't know how I got a round off, but I did. It hit him right in the chest. We both went down. He lost his gun, but I kept mine. Pointed it right at him. He wasn't more than a foot from me. Every breath he took, blood kicked out of the bullet hole like a red geyser. It made this swishing sound I still hear in my sleep. His eyes had started to freeze up, but you never knew. All I knew was that he had just shot my backup, and he had just shot me. My insides felt like they were dissolving." Fiske let out a long breath. "I was going to just wait for him to die, Sara." Fiske stopped talking as he recalled how close he had come to being another blue in a box, buried and mostly forgotten.

"Your father said you were found with your arm around him," Sara gently prompted.

"I thought he was trying to grab my gun. I had one finger on the trigger and one finger stuck in the hole in my gut. But he didn't even put his hand out. Then I heard him talking. I could barely make out what he was saying at first, but he kept saying it until I did."

"What did he say?" Sara asked gently.

Fiske let out a breath, half expecting to see blood kick out of his old wounds, his tired, betrayed organs calling it quits on him forty years early. "He was asking me to kill him." As if in answer to her unspoken question, Fiske said, "I couldn't. I didn't. It didn't matter, though, he stopped talking a few seconds later."

Sara slowly sat back, unable to say anything.

"I actually think he was terrified he *wasn't* going to die." Fiske shook his head slowly, the words becoming more difficult to put together. "He was only nineteen. I'm an old man already, next to him. His name was Darnell—Darnell Jackson. His mother was a crack addict, and when he was eight or nine she would whore him out for drug money."

He looked at her. "Does that sound horrible to you?"

"Of course it does. Yes!"

"To me, it was the same old shit. I saw it all the time. I'd become immune to it, or at least I thought I had." He licked his dry lips. "I didn't think I had any compassion left. But after Darnell, I got some back." He flashed a troubled smile. "I call it my steel-jacketed epiphany. Two slugs in my body, a kid dying in front of me, wanting me to finish him off. It's hard to imagine one event having enough force to make you question everything you've ever believed. But it happened to me that night." He nodded thoughtfully. "Now I think of the whole future of the world solely in the context of Darnell Jackson. He's my version of nuclear holocaust, only it won't be over in a few seconds." He looked at her. "That's the terror that drives me."

"I think you really do care. You do a lot of good."

Fiske shook his head, his eyes glimmering. "I'm not some rich, brilliant white attorney running around nobly saving the little Enis's of the world. And it took a lost kid blowing up my insides with a cannon to make me even give a damn. How many people do you think really care?"

"You can't be that cynical, can you?"

Fiske stared at her a moment before answering. "Actually, I'm the most hopeful cynic you'll ever meet."

CHAPTER FIFTY-FIVE

"You did the right thing, Beth. As much as it hurts. I still can't believe it about Sara, though." Jordan Knight shook his head. They were in the back seat of his government limousine, which was threading its way through bumper-to-bumper traffic toward their Watergate apartment. "Maybe she just cracked. The pressures are enormous."

"I know," Elizabeth Knight said quietly.

"It all seems so bizarre. A clerk steals an appeal. Sara knows about it but keeps quiet. The clerk is then murdered. Then the clerk's brother comes under suspicion. John Fiske just doesn't strike me as the murderous type."

"He doesn't strike me that way either." Her discussion with John Fiske had only deepened her fears.

Jordan Knight patted his wife's hand. "I've checked on Chandler and McKenna. Both are rock-solid. McKenna has an excellent reputation at the Bureau. If anybody can solve this thing, I think those two can."

"I find Warren McKenna rude and obnoxious."

"Well, in his line of work I suppose he sometimes has to be," he pointed out.

"That's not all. There's just something about him. He's so intense, but he almost seems to be"—she paused, searching for the right word—"playacting."

"In the middle of a murder investigation?"

"I know it sounds crazy, but it's just how I feel."

The senator shrugged and stroked his chin thoughtfully. "I've always said a woman's intuition is worth more than a man's best judgment. I guess in this town we're all on a stage. Sometimes one does grow tired of it."

She eyed him closely. "The New Mexico ranch beckons?"

"I've got a dozen years on you, Beth. Every day becomes a little more precious."

"It's not like we're not together."

"Time together in D.C. is not really the same. We're both so busy here."

"My appointment to the Court is a lifetime one, Jordan."

"I just don't want you to have any regrets. And I'm trying my best not to have any."

They both fell silent and looked out the window as the car traveled along Virginia Avenue.

"I heard you and Ramsey went at it tooth and claw today. Do you think you have a chance?"

"Jordan, you know I don't feel comfortable talking to you about these things."

Jordan reddened. "That's one thing I hate about this town, and our jobs. Government should not interfere in the covenant of marriage."

"Funny talk, coming from a politician."

Jordan laughed deeply. "Well, as a politician, I have to get up on the damn soapbox every now and then, don't I?" He stopped and took her hand. "I appreciate your going forward with the dinner for Kenneth. You took some heat for it, I know."

Elizabeth shrugged. "Harold takes any opportunity, no matter how trivial, to tweak me, Jordan. I've built up a very strong resistance." She gave him a kiss on the cheek, while he lovingly stroked her hair.

"We really have prevailed, despite all the odds, haven't we? We have a nice life, don't we?"

"We have a wonderful life, Jordan." She kissed him again and he put a protective arm around her.

"I say tonight we cancel all of our appointments and just stay home. Have some dinner, watch a movie. And talk. We don't get to do that much anymore."

"I'm afraid I won't be good company."

Jordan squeezed her tightly. "You're always good company, Beth. Always."

When the Knights arrived at their apartment, Mary, their housekeeper, handed a phone message to Elizabeth. A curious expression crossed her face as she looked at the name on the paper.

Jordan appeared in the hallway rubbing his hands together. He looked at Mary. "I hope you have something nice planned for dinner."

"Your favorite. Beef tenderloin."

Jordan smiled. "I think we're going to have a late dinner. Tonight the missus and I are going to relax completely. No interruptions." He looked at his wife. "Anything wrong?" He noted the paper in her hand.

"No. Court business. It never ends."

"You don't have to tell me that," he said dryly. "Well, I'm for a hot shower." He went down the hallway. "You're welcome to join me," he called over his shoulder.

Mary went off to the kitchen, a smile on her lips at the senator's remark.

Elizabeth took the opportunity to slip into the study and dialed the number on the message.

"I'm returning your call," she said into the phone.

"We need to talk, Justice Knight. How's right now?"

"What is this about?"

"What I'm about to tell you will come as quite a shock. Are you prepared for that?"

For some reason, Elizabeth Knight sensed that the man was enjoying this. "I really don't have time for the cloak-and-dagger rhetoric that obviously amuses you."

"Well, I'm going to give you a crash course in it."

"What are you talking about?"

"Just listen."

And she did. Twenty minutes later she threw the phone down, raced out of the room and almost knocked down Mary, who was coming down the hallway. Elizabeth raced into the powder room, where she splashed water on her face. She gripped the edges of the sink, composed herself, opened the door and moved slowly down the hallway.

She could still hear Jordan in the shower. She looked at her watch. She went out into the lobby and down the elevator to the reception area of the building and waited over by the main entrance. Time seemed to pass slowly. Actually only ten minutes had gone by since her phone call. Finally, a man she didn't recognize, but who clearly knew her by sight, appeared and handed her something. She looked down at it. When she looked back up, he had already disappeared. She put what he had given her into her pocket and hurried back up to her apartment.

"Where's Jordan?" she asked Mary.

"I believe he's in the bedroom getting dressed. Are you all right, Ms. Knight?"

"Yes, I . . . my stomach was just a little upset, but I'm fine now. I decided to stretch my legs and do some window shopping downstairs, get some fresh air. Would you mix up some cocktails and put them out on the terrace?"

"It's starting to rain."

"But the awning's up. And I feel very claustrophobic all

of a sudden. I need the air. It's been so hot and humid lately, and the rain has made things so cool. So very cool," she said wistfully. "Make Jordan's favorite, will you?"

"Beefeater Martini with a twist, yes, ma'am."

"And the dinner, Mary . . . please make sure it's absolutely wonderful. Just perfect."

"I will, ma'am." Mary headed to the bar with a puzzled look on her face.

Elizabeth Knight squeezed her hands together to fight the waves of panic. She just had to stop thinking about it. If she was going to make it through this, she had to merely act, not think. Please, God, help me, she prayed.

CHAPTER FIFTY-SIX

Fiske stared moodily out the car window at the dark clouds. He and Sara were halfway to Washington, and neither one had said much on the drive up.

Sara turned on the wipers as the rain started to fall. She looked over at him and frowned. "John, we've got a lot of information to work with. We might want to use the next hour making some sense of it all."

Fiske glanced at her. "I guess you're right. Do you have pen and paper anywhere?"

"Don't you have that in your briefcase?"

He undid his seat belt, pulled his briefcase from the back seat and popped it open. He pushed through the stack of mail until his hands closed around a bulky package. "Christ, that was fast."

"What?"

"I think this is Harms's service record." Fiske tore it open and started reading. Ten minutes later, he looked at her. "It's in two different parts. His service record, portions

of the record of court-martial, and the personnel list from
Fort Plessy during the time Harms was stationed there."
Fiske pulled out a section marked MEDICAL RECORDS. He
studied the pages and then stopped. "Would you like to
guess why Rufus Harms was so insubordinate, wouldn't
take orders, was always in trouble?"

"He was dyslexic," Sara answered promptly.

"How the hell did you know that?"

"A couple of things. Even the little I saw of it, the handwriting and spelling on the appeal was so bad. That's a
sign of dyslexia, although it's not conclusive. But when I
talked to George Barker, remember he told me that story
about Rufus fixing his printing press?" Fiske nodded.
"Well, he recalled Rufus saying that he didn't want to look
at the manual for the printing press, that the words would
just mess him up. I went to school with a girl who had
dyslexia. She once told me more or less the same thing. It's
like you can't communicate with the world. Although,
from our encounter last night, it looks like Rufus has
conquered his disability."

"If he can survive in prison all those years with people
trying to kill him, he can do anything he sets his mind to."
Fiske looked back at the records. "Looks like he was diag-
nosed with it after the murder. Probably during the court-
martial proceedings. Maybe Rider discovered it. Preparing
a defense requires some client cooperation."

"Dyslexia is not a defense to murder."

"No, but I know what is."

"What?" Sara asked excitedly. "What?"

"First, a question: Leo Dellasandro—is he having an
affair with his secretary?"

"Why are you asking that?"

"He had makeup on his coat collar."

"Maybe it was from his wife."

"Maybe, but I don't think so."

"I really doubt he was having an affair, because his secretary just got married."

"I didn't think they were."

"So why did you ask me?"

"Just covering all the bases. I don't think Dellasandro got it from his wife either. I think he was wearing it."

"Why would a man—a chief of police, no less—be wearing makeup?"

"To cover the bruises he got when I hit him in my brother's apartment." Sara's breath caught as Fiske continued. "I haven't seen Dellasandro since that night. He wasn't at the meeting at the Court after Wright was murdered. I've been with Chandler a lot and the man never came by to check up on the investigation. At least while I was there. I think he was avoiding me. Maybe afraid I'd recognize him somehow."

"Why in the world would Leo Dellasandro have been at your brother's apartment?"

In response, Fiske held up a sheaf of papers. "The list of personnel stationed at Fort Plessy. Luckily, it's alphabetized." He turned toward the end of the roster. "Sergeant Victor Tremaine." He turned another page. "Captain Frank Rayfield." He flipped back through some pages and stopped. "Private Rufus Harms." Then he went back near the beginning, circled a name with his pen, and said triumphantly, "And Corporal Leo Dellasandro."

"Good God. Then Rayfield, Tremaine and Dellasandro were the men in the stockade that night?"

"I think so."

"How did you know Dellasandro was in the military?"

"I saw a photo of Dellasandro in his office. He was much younger, in uniform. His *Army* uniform. I think the three of them went there to teach Rufus Harms a lesson. I think we'll find they all fought in Vietnam, and Rufus didn't. He wouldn't follow orders, was always in trouble."

"But what the hell did they *do* to Rufus Harms?"

"I think they—"

The car phone rang. Sara glanced at Fiske and then picked it up. Her face went pale as she listened. "Yes, I'll accept the call. Hello? What? Okay, calm down. He's right here." She handed the phone to Fiske. "Rufus Harms. And he doesn't sound good."

Fiske gripped the phone. "Rufus, where are you?"

Rufus was inside the Jeep parked next to a pay phone. He had one hand on the phone, the other on Josh, who was now slipping into longer periods of unconsciousness, but still had the pistol wedged against his side. "Richmond," he answered. "I'm two minutes from the address on the card you gave me. Josh is hurt bad. I need a damn doctor and I need him quick."

"Okay, okay, tell me what happened."

"Rayfield and Tremaine caught up to us."

"Where are they now?"

"They're dead, dammit, and my brother's about ready to join 'em. You said you'd help me. Well, I need help."

Fiske glanced in the rearview mirror. The black sedan was still back there. He thought quickly. "Okay, I'll meet you at my office in four hours tops."

"Josh ain't got four hours. He's shot the hell up."

"We're going to take care of Josh right now, Rufus. I'm meeting you, not Josh."

"What the hell you talking about?"

"I'm going to call a buddy of mine who's a cop. He'll get an ambulance. They'll take care of him. MCV Hospital is only a few minutes from my office."

"No police!"

Fiske yelled into the phone, "Do you want Josh to die? Do you?" Fiske took the silence as Rufus's surrender to whatever help Fiske could give him. "Describe the car to me and give me the intersection where you are right now." Rufus did so. "My friend will have help there in a few minutes. Leave Josh in the car. As soon as you hang up, walk to my office building. It's open. Go in the front door and go down the flight of stairs on your left. You go through another door. There's a door on your right marked 'Supplies.' It's unlocked. Get in there and sit tight. I'll be down quick as I can. I also want you to take your brother's wallet because I don't want him to have any ID. If they know it's Josh, they're going to start looking for you nearby. That includes my office. The police cordoning off the area would throw a real wrench in my plan."

"What if somebody sees me? Maybe recognizes me?"

"We don't have much choice now, Rufus."

"I'm trusting you. Please help my brother. Please don't let me down."

"Rufus, I'm trusting you too. Don't let me down."

When Rufus hung up, he looked at Josh. He slipped a gun under his shirt and reached out to touch his brother. He thought Josh was completely unconscious now, but when Rufus brushed his shoulder gently with his finger, Josh opened his eyes.

"Josh—"

"I heard." The voice was weak; everything about him was now.

"He wants me to take your wallet, so they won't know who you are just yet."

"In my back pocket." Rufus slid it out. "Now get going."

Rufus considered this for a moment. "I can stay with you. We go together."

"No good." Josh spit up some more blood. "Docs'll sew me up. I been hurt a lot worse than this." Josh moved a shaky hand out, touched his brother's face, brushed away the wetness from his eyes.

"I'm gonna stay with you, Josh."

"You stay, all this is for nothing."

"I can't leave you alone. Not like this. Not after all these years away."

With a painful grimace, Josh sat up. "You ain't leaving me alone. Give it to me."

"Give you what?"

Josh said, "The Bible."

Without taking his eyes off his brother, Rufus slowly reached behind the seat and handed him the book. In return, Josh held out the pistol that had been wedged against his ribs for all these hours. Rufus looked at him questioningly. "Fair swap," Josh said hoarsely.

Rufus thought he saw a smile flicker across his brother's lips before Josh closed his eyes, his breathing shallow but steady. One large hand gripped the Bible so tightly the spine of the book twisted.

As Rufus climbed out of the Jeep, he looked back once more, and then left his brother behind.

Fiske finally reached Hawkins at home. "Don't ask me why or how, Billy. I can't tell you who it is. For now he's a John Doe. Stall the paperwork and drive the Jeep to the hospital." Fiske hung up.

"John, how are we going to meet Rufus with the FBI right behind us?" Sara said.

"I'm meeting Rufus, you're not."

"Wait a minute—"

"Sara—"

"I want to see this through."

"Believe me, you will. You have to make a phone call for me, to my friend at the JAG."

"What about? And you still haven't told me what you think happened in that stockade twenty-five years ago."

He put one hand on top of hers. "*U.S. v. Stanley.* An innocent soldier and LSD," Fiske said, watching her eyes go wide. "Only worse," he added.

After making a quick stop at Sara's home, they drove to National Airport and parked. Fiske tugged the trench coat around him and pulled his hat down tightly over his head as the rain began to fall harder. He opened a big umbrella and covered Sara with it. They went to the general aviation terminal, and then out the other side to the boarding area, where they climbed in a sedan with tinted windows. A couple minutes later the car pulled away from the curb.

Behind them were two FBI agents, one of whom was already communicating this development to his superiors. Then he went over to the service counter to determine the destination of the flight Fiske and Sara were about to get on. The other agent went out and watched as the sedan pulled up to the private jet.

Inside the sedan, Fiske and the driver, Chuck Herman's copilot, were busy switching places. The driver put on the trench coat and hat. From a distance he would look like Fiske. Their plan was to have Sara stay on the plane for an hour, during which time she would attempt to contact Fiske's JAG friend, Phil Jansen. Then she would leave. They knew the FBI would question her about Fiske's disappearance, but they would have no grounds to detain her.

The FBI agent watched as a thin, white-haired man came down the steps from the plane and greeted Sara and the man whom he assumed was Fiske as they climbed out of the car. The group went up the steps and into the plane. The sedan pulled away. The FBI agent kept his eyes on the plane as the sedan passed by him and continued on to the main road leading out of the terminal.

Driving the sedan, Fiske let out a deep breath as he pulled onto the George Washington Parkway. Within ten minutes he was headed south on Interstate 95 toward Richmond. Traffic was heavy; it was almost three hours before he pulled the car up to his office building. He had already checked in with Billy Hawkins. Josh Harms was in surgery at MCV. It didn't look good, Hawkins had told

DAVID BALDACCI

him. Fiske parked the car and went around to the office's rear entrance, just in case.

He made his way to the lower level and approached the supply room. Please be there, he urged Rufus. He tapped on the door. "Rufus?" he said quietly. "It's John Fiske."

Rufus cautiously opened the door.

"Let's get out of here."

Rufus gripped his arm. "How's Josh?"

"He's in surgery. All you can do is pray."

"That's all I been doing."

They went out the rear entrance, walked quickly to Fiske's car and climbed in.

"Where we going?" Rufus said.

"You want to tell me about the letter from the Army?"

"What about it?"

"They wanted to follow up on the phencyclidine testing, right?"

Harms stiffened. "Phen-what?"

"You know, PCP."

"How did you know about that?"

"Same thing happened to another guy in the Army named Stanley, who was in a bogus program. They used LSD on him."

"I wasn't in no damn PCP program, even if they said I was." He pulled out the letter and gave it to Fiske.

Fiske took a moment to read it and then looked at him. "Tell me about it, Rufus."

Harms sat back as much as he could. He was so large that his knees touched the dash and his head brushed the car's ceiling. "They'd been out to get me for a while. Tremaine and Rayfield."

"And Dellasandro? Corporal Leo Dellasandro?"

"Yeah, him too. I guess they didn't take too kindly to me sitting nice and snug in the States, even if it was in the stockade."

"They didn't know about your dyslexia?"

"You seem to know a damn lot."

"Go on."

"I'd had plenty of run-ins with that group before. Tremaine got thrown in the stockade with me one night for drinking. He told me real directly what he thought about me. I guess they planned this thing out. They came in the stockade one night. Leo had a gun. They made me close my eyes, get on the floor. The next thing I knew, they stuck something in me. I opened my eyes and saw the needle coming out of my arm. They all stood there laughing, waiting for me to die. I could tell from what they said, that was their plan. OD me on the stuff."

"How the hell did you go from getting shot up with PCP to escaping from the stockade?"

"My whole body seemed to swell up like somebody was pumping air in me. I remember getting up and it felt like the room wasn't big enough to hold me. I tossed 'em all aside like they were made of straw. They had left the door unlocked. The guard on duty came running up, but I hit him like a truck and then I was running free." His breathing had accelerated, his huge hands clasping and unclasping, as though reliving what he had done with them so long ago.

"And you ran into Ruth Ann Mosley?"

"She was there visiting her brother." Rufus slammed his fist down onto the dash. "If only God had struck me down before I got to that little girl. Why'd it have to be a child? Why?" Tears streamed down the man's face.

"It wasn't your fault, Rufus. PCP can make you do anything, anything. It wasn't your fault."

In answer Rufus held up his hands and bellowed, "These did it. No matter what shit they put in me, ain't nothing gonna change the fact that I killed that beautiful little girl. Ain't nothing on this earth gonna make that go away. Is it? Is it?" Rufus's eyes blazed at Fiske, but then he closed them and slumped back, as though lifeless.

Fiske tried to keep calm. "And you remembered nothing, until you got the letter?"

Finally Rufus came around. "Hell, all those years the only thing I remembered from that night was sitting in the stockade reading the Bible my momma give me. The next thing I knew I'm next to this dead little girl. That's all." He wiped the tears away with his sleeve.

"PCP can do that too. Screw with your memory. Probably the shock of it all too."

Rufus took a heavy breath. "Sometimes I think that crap's still in me."

"But you pleaded guilty to the murder anyway?"

"There was a bunch of witnesses. Samuel Rider said if I didn't take the deal, they'd convict me and then they'd execute me. What the hell else was I supposed to do?"

Fiske thought about that for a moment and then said quietly, "I guess I would've done the same thing."

"But when I got that letter, it was like somebody turned this big light on inside my head, and some part of my brain that had been all dark got real bright and everything came back to me. Every damn little bit."

"And so you wrote the letter to the Court and asked Rider to file it for you?"

Rufus nodded. "And then your brother came to see me. Said he believed in justice, wanted to help me if I was telling the truth. He was a good man."

"Yes, he was," Fiske said hoarsely.

"The thing was, he had brought my letter with him. Rayfield and old Vic weren't going to let him go. No way. I went crazy when I found out. They took me to the infirmary, tried to kill me there. I got to the hospital and Josh busted me out."

"You said Tremaine and Rayfield are dead."

Rufus nodded. He took another deep breath, watched the rain falling over the darkened Richmond skyline and then looked over at Fiske. "Now you know everything I know. So what are we going to do?"

"I'm not sure," was all Fiske could manage to say.

CHAPTER FIFTY-SEVEN

An hour after Fiske had driven off, Chuck Herman smiled as he passed Sara in the plane aisle. "This is the only time I've ever been paid *not* to fly."

"This is Washington, Chuck. They pay farmers not to grow crops too," Sara said dryly.

She picked up the cell phone for the tenth time and dialed Phil Jansen's home number. His office had already told Sara that Jansen had left for the day. Luckily, Fiske had given her Jansen's home number too. She was relieved when Jansen finally answered. She quickly introduced herself and explained her connection to Fiske.

"I don't have much time, Mr. Jansen, so I might as well get to the point. In the past has the Army been involved in PCP testing programs?"

Jansen's voice tensed. "Why exactly are you asking that, Ms. Evans?"

"John thinks that Rufus Harms was involuntarily given PCP when he was in an Army stockade at Fort Plessy twenty-five years ago. He thinks the exposure to PCP caused Harms to go berserk and kill a little girl. He's been in prison for the crime ever since."

Sara recounted all that she and Fiske had deduced, along with what they had learned from Rufus at Rider's office. Sara continued, "Rufus Harms recently received a letter from the Army asking him to participate in a follow-up test to determine the long-term effects of PCP. That's what happened to Sergeant James Stanley, right? The Army sent him a letter. That was the only reason he knew the Army had given him LSD. Well, we think a group of Army personnel forcefully administered PCP to Harms in the stockade, but not as part of any program. We think they intended to use the drug to kill him. Instead he broke free and committed the murder."

Jansen said, "Wait a minute. Why did the Army send him a letter saying Harms was in the program, if he wasn't?"

"We think whoever gave Harms the PCP enrolled him in the program."

"And why would they do that?"

"If they killed him with the PCP and there was an autopsy, presumably the substance would have been found in his bloodstream."

"Yes, it would," Jansen said slowly. "So they enrolled him in the program to cover that up. The coroner would chalk it up to an unfortunate reaction to the drug. I can't believe this."

"Right. So such a program existed?"

"Yes," Jansen conceded. "It's public information now. All declassified. It was run jointly by the Army and CIA in the seventies. They wanted to determine if PCP could be used to 'build' super soldiers. If Harms was listed in the program's records, he would have recently received a follow-up letter." Jansen paused for a moment. "What are you and John going to do now?"

"I wish we knew." Sara thanked Jansen and hung up.

She waited awhile longer and then left the plane and walked across the tarmac to the terminal. She was immediately stopped by the two FBI agents.

"Where's Fiske?" one of them demanded.

"John Fiske?" she asked innocently.

"Come on, Ms. Evans."

"He left a while back."

The agents looked startled. "Left. How?"

"I assume he drove. Now, if you'll excuse me."

She smiled as the stunned men took off at a dead run toward the plane. They had no grounds to detain her. She took the opportunity to hop on the shuttle bus to the garage and got her car. She drove out of the airport and headed south. A sudden thought hit her and she pulled off the road and into a gas station. Keeping the motor running, she opened Fiske's briefcase and took out the packet of documents they had received from St. Louis. She wasn't sure how closely Fiske had examined them, but it had occurred to her that it was possible the Army might have put a copy of the letter they had sent to Rufus Harms in his official file— although technically it had been closed upon the occasion of his court-martial. It was worth a look.

A half hour later she sat back, disappointed. She started returning the papers to the briefcase when her hand closed around the personnel list from Fort Plessy. She leafed through the pages, noting the names of Victor Tremaine and Frank Rayfield. Then her eye sadly passed over the name of Rufus Harms. So many years of his life gone.

As she was thinking this, she was continuing to turn pages, running her eye down the personnel list; as soon as she saw the name, she froze. When she finally broke out of her trance, she did so with such force that she bumped her head against the window. She threw the file down and slammed the car into gear, burning rubber on the slick pavement as she sped out of the gas station. She glanced down at the floorboard where the personnel list had landed, where the name Warren McKenna seemed to stare back at her, taunting her. She never looked back, so she didn't notice the car that had followed her from the airport.

CHAPTER FIFTY-EIGHT

Harold Ramsey leaned back in his chair, a grave look on his face. "I never imagined that anything like this could have happened here."

McKenna and Chandler sat in Ramsey's chambers. McKenna watched the chief justice closely. They seemed to make eye contact for a moment, and then McKenna looked away and glanced over at Chandler.

"Well, we don't have any solid proof one way or another about whether Michael Fiske actually stole an appeal, or if there even was an appeal," Chandler said.

Ramsey shook his head in disagreement. "After the discussion with Sara Evans, can there be any doubt?"

Discussion? Inquisition was more like it, Chandler thought. "It's still speculation. And I would advise against going public with this information."

"I agree," McKenna said. "It could complicate the investigation."

"I thought you were convinced that John Fiske was

behind it all," Ramsey said. "If you're changing your position now, I don't see how we're any farther ahead than we were two days ago."

"Murders don't just solve themselves. And this one is a little more complex than usual. And I never said I had changed my position," McKenna said. "Fiske's gun was missing from his office. No big surprise there. Don't worry, things are falling into place."

Ramsey looked unconvinced.

"I really don't see why waiting a bit will hurt," Chandler said. "And if things turn out the way we hope, maybe the public never has to know."

"I don't see how that is possible," Ramsey said angrily. "But I suppose it won't make this disaster any more horrible by taking your advice. For now. What about Fiske and Evans? Where are they?"

"We have them under surveillance," McKenna answered.

"So you know where they are right now?" Ramsey asked.

McKenna maintained his stone face. He wasn't about to admit that in fact both Sara and Fiske had managed to elude his FBI surveillance team. McKenna had just gotten that message a minute before he had stepped into this meeting.

"Yes," McKenna answered.

"Where are they?" Ramsey asked.

"I'm afraid I can't give out that information, Mr. Chief Justice." He added quickly, "As much as I'd like to accommodate you. We really need to keep that confidential."

Ramsey looked sternly at him. "Agent McKenna, you promised to keep the Court informed about the progress of this case."

"I did. That's why I'm here right now."

"The Court has its own police force. Chief Dellasandro and Ron Klaus are out right this very minute trying to solve this thing. We have our own investigation ongoing and it's in the best interests of everybody that we have full disclosure. Now please answer my question. Where are they?"

"What you say makes a lot of sense, but I'm afraid I still can't divulge that information," he said. "FBI policy, you understand."

Ramsey arched his eyebrows. "I think I should speak to someone else at the Bureau, then," he said. "I don't like going over people's heads, Agent McKenna, but this is a unique situation."

"I'd be glad to give you some names to call at the Bureau, starting with the director himself," McKenna offered pleasantly.

"Do you have anything of actual importance to report," Ramsey said dryly, "or is that it?"

McKenna stood up. "We're trying as hard as we can to get to the bottom of this. And I'm convinced that, with a little luck, we will."

Ramsey stood up too, towering over them. "A word of advice, Agent McKenna. Never leave anything to chance. Anyone who does that usually lives to regret it."

Sara unlocked the door to her cottage and hurried inside. From her car she had tried phoning Fiske's home and office; then had tried Ed Fiske too, but he had heard nothing from his son. She threw her purse down on the kitchen table, went upstairs and changed out of her wet clothes and into jeans and a T-shirt. She was nearing panic and she wasn't sure what to do. If Dellasandro was in on this, that was bad enough. He was privy to what was happening with the investigation. The fact that FBI Agent Warren McKenna was also involved was poten-tially catastrophic. He was practically running the damn investigation. She could now see the subtle manipulations of the FBI agent at every juncture in the case. Fiske implicated, herself forced to quit the Court; all of it building motive for John's killing his brother. It was all untrue, and yet, for someone just looking at the bare facts, it would make sense.

She tried Chandler's office. She wanted to know definitively if Agent McKenna had been stationed at Fort Plessy, or if it had been simply someone else with the same name. She couldn't believe two McKennas would be involved here, but she needed to be sure. Unfortunately, Chandler wasn't in. Who else could she call who would have that information? Jansen might be able to find out, but it would probably take him a while. She tried his number anyway, but there was no answer. Who else? It suddenly hit her. She dialed the number. After three rings a woman answered. It was the housekeeper.

"Is he in? It's Sara Evans."

A minute later Jordan Knight's voice came on the line. "Sara?"

"I know this is terrible timing, Senator."

"I heard what happened today." His tone was cold.

"I know what you must think, and I'm sure nothing I could say would change your mind."

"You're probably right about that. However, for what it's worth Beth feels terrible about what happened. She was one of your strongest supporters."

"I appreciate that." Sara held the phone away from her ear as she struggled to hold her nerves in check. Every second counted now. "I need a favor."

"A favor?" Jordan sounded perplexed.

"Some information on someone."

"Sara, I hardly think this is appropriate."

"Senator, I will never, ever call you again, but I really need to know the answer to my question, and with all your information resources, and your personal clout, you're the only person I can think of to ask. Please? For old times' sake."

Jordan pondered this for a moment. "Well, I'm not at my office right now. I was just settling down to a late dinner with Beth, in fact."

"But you could call your office, or maybe the FBI."

"The FBI?" he said loudly.

She hurried on. "A phone call would be all that it would take. I'm at home. You can even have the person call me back directly. You and I won't even have to speak again."

Finally, Jordan relented. "All right, what's your question?"

"It's about Agent McKenna."

"What about him?"

"I need to know if he ever served in the Army. Specifically at Fort Plessy during the seventies."

"Why in the world do you need to know that?"

"Senator, it would take me far too long to explain."

He sighed. "All right. I'll see what I can do. I'll have someone from my office check and then call you. You'll be at home?"

"Yes."

"Sara, I hope you know what you're doing."

"If you can believe it, Senator, I really do."

"If you say so," he replied, not sounding convinced.

When he went back into the dining room about fifteen minutes later, Elizabeth looked up at him. "What in the world did Sara want?"

"The strangest thing. You know that FBI agent fellow? The one you were complaining about?"

She tensed. "Warren McKenna? What about him?"

"She wanted to know if he had ever served in the Army."

Elizabeth Knight dropped her fork. "Why would she want to know that?"

"I don't know. She wouldn't tell me." Jordan looked over at her curiously, noting her tension. "Are you all right?"

"I'm fine. This has just been the day from hell."

"I know, honey, I know," he said soothingly. He looked down at his cold meal. "I guess our relaxing evening just went out the window."

"What did you tell her?"

"Tell her? I told her I'd check. And that I'd have somebody get back to her. That's what I was doing, calling my office. I guess they can check on the computer or something."

"Where is Sara?"

"At home, waiting for the answer to her question."

Elizabeth got up, her face pale.

"Beth, are you all right?"

"A headache just hit me. I need some aspirin."

"I can get it for you."

"No, that's all right. Finish your dinner. Then maybe we can finally relax."

A worried-looking Jordan Knight watched his wife go down the hallway. Elizabeth Knight did indeed get some aspirin, since she did have a very real headache. Then she slipped down the hallway to her bedroom, picked up the phone and dialed a number.

"Hello," the voice said,

"Sara Evans just called. She asked Jordan a question."

"What was the question?"

"She wanted to know if you had ever been in the Army."

Warren McKenna loosened his tie and took a sip of water from the glass on his desk. He had just returned from the meeting at the Court. "And what did he tell her?"

"That he'd check and get back to her." Elizabeth did her best to fight back the tears.

McKenna nodded to himself. "Where is she?"

"She told Jordan she was at home."

"And John Fiske?"

"I don't know. Apparently she didn't say."

McKenna grabbed his coat. "Thanks for the information, Justice Knight. It might prove to be even more valuable than one of your opinions."

Elizabeth Knight slowly hung up the receiver and then picked it up again. She couldn't leave it like this. She dialed Information and got the number. The call was answered. "Detective Chandler, please. Tell him it's Elizabeth Knight and it's urgent."

Chandler came on the line. "What can I do for you, Justice Knight?"

"Detective Chandler, please don't ask me how I know, but you have to get to Sara Evans's house. I think she's in grave danger. Please hurry."

Chandler didn't waste time asking questions. He raced out of his office without even hanging up the phone.

Elizabeth Knight slowly put down the receiver. She had thought her work at the Court was pressure-filled, but this . . . She knew that no matter how this turned out, her life was going to be devastated. For her, there was no way out. How ironic, she thought, that justice would end up destroying her.

*   *   *

The figure was outfitted in dark clothing, a ski mask pulled over his face. He had followed Sara down to Richmond and then trailed her and Fiske and the FBI agents back to Washington. He was very grateful that she had lost the FBI agents; it would make his job much easier. Crouching down, he made his way over to the car and opened the driver's-side door. The dome light came on when he did so, and he quickly twisted the control to dim it. He looked at the windows of the house. He saw Sara pass by once, but she didn't look outside. He pulled a small flashlight from his pocket and swept the beam around the car's interior. He saw the papers on the floorboard, glanced at them and noted the encircled name. He gathered up the files and put them in a knapsack he was carrying. He pulled a pistol from his holster and attached a silencer to the muzzle. Looking up at the house again, he saw no sign of Sara this time. But she was in there. Alone. He put out the light and headed toward the house.

Sara had been nervously pacing the kitchen, constantly checking her watch and waiting for a phone call from Jordan Knight's office. She stepped out onto the rear deck and watched as a jet slid past under the canopy of dark clouds. Then she looked down at her sailboat as it nudged against the rubber tires that were affixed to the dock to act as buffers between the smooth fiberglass and the rough wood. She had to smile as she thought back to the events of last night. The smile disappeared as she recalled what she and Fiske had discussed after their encounter at the nursing home. She pressed her bare toes against the damp wood, and took a moment to breathe in the soothing smells of the wet, rustic surroundings.

She went inside and up the stairs, stopping at the doorway of her bedroom and looking inside. The bed was still unmade. She sat down on the mattress and picked up one edge of the sheet as she recalled their lovemaking. She thought of how Fiske had pulled his T-shirt back down. The scar went from navel to neck, Ed had told her. As if it could ever actually make a difference to her. And yet Fiske obviously believed it could.

She listened as another jet passed overhead and then the complete silence returned in its wake, as though all sound had disappeared into a Pratt & Whitney-made vacuum. The silence so profound she could clearly hear the side door of the cottage open. She jumped up and raced to the stairs. "John?" There was no answer, and when the downstairs light went out, a shiver of fear hit her spine. She ran into her bedroom, shut and locked the door. Her chest heaving, her own pulse bursting in her eardrums, she looked around desperately for a weapon, because there was no way to escape. The window was small and even if she could manage to wriggle through, the grade of the land was such that the room was two stories off the ground, with a concrete sidewalk down below—and breaking both her legs didn't seem like a good idea.

Her sense of desperation turned to panic when the sounds of the footsteps reached her. She now cursed herself for not having a phone in the bedroom. She held her breath as she saw the doorknob slowly turn until the lock halted the movement, but both the lock and the door were very old. As something hit the door with a solid blow, she instinctively jumped back, a small scream escaping her lips. She scanned the room before her gaze settled on the four-poster bed. She raced over and grabbed one of the pineapple-shaped finials off one of the bedposts. Thank God she had never gotten around to having the bed actually canopied. The finial was solid wood and weighed at least a pound.

She held it in one upraised hand and stepped quickly over to the door. It shook as another blow landed, the lock bending under the force of it; the doorframe started to splinter. After that impact she reached over, quietly unlocked the door and then stood back. With the door unbolted, the next blow sent it and the man flying into the room. Sara's arm came down swiftly and the finial hit flesh. She raced through the doorway and down the hall-way. The man she had struck lay on the floor holding his shoulder and moaning.

Sara knew that Rayfield and Tremaine were dead. Then the man she had just hit was either Dellasandro or—she shuddered at the thought of the man being in her home—Warren McKenna. She navigated the stairs in two jumps, grabbed her car keys off the table and threw open the door on her way to the car. She let out a shriek of terror.

The second man stared back at her, calmly, coolly. As he stepped forward, Leo Dellasandro pointed a pistol directly at her. The man in black came racing down the stairs holding his shoulder, his gun trained on her as well. Dellasandro closed the door. Sara looked at the man behind her. It must be McKenna. But then her expression changed. This man wasn't nearly big enough to be the FBI agent.

The ski mask came off and Richard Perkins glared at her. Then he smiled at her obvious astonishment and pulled some papers from his knapsack. "You must have overlooked my name on the Fort Plessy service roster, Sara. How sloppy of you."

She stared at him angrily. "The marshal of the Supreme Court and the chief of its police, parties to a despicable crime."

"Harms killed that girl, not me," Dellasandro said.

"Have you made yourself believe that, Leo? You killed her, not Rufus, just as sure as if your hands were around her neck."

Dellasandro's face turned ugly. "That sonofabitch. If I had my way I would've pumped him full of lead instead of some damn drug. He was a disgrace to the uniform."

"He was dyslexic," Sara screamed at him. "He didn't follow orders because he couldn't understand them, you idiot. You destroyed his life and that girl's for nothing."

A smirk appeared on Dellasandro's face. "I don't see it that way. Not at all. He got what he deserved."

"How's the face, Leo? John really popped you. He knows everything, of course."

"We'll just have to visit him too."

"You, Vic Tremaine and Frank Rayfield?"

"You're damn right," Dellasandro said with a sneer.

"Your buddies are dead." Sara's smile emerged as Dellasandro's faded. "They ambushed Rufus and his brother, but just like last time they couldn't finish the job," she added tauntingly.

"Then I hope I get the chance to do it for them."

Sara stared him up and down and finally shook her head in disgust. "Tell me something, Leo. How did vermin like you ever get to be a police chief of anything?"

He slapped her across the face, and would have hit her again if Perkins hadn't stopped him. "We don't have time for this crap, Leo." He gripped Sara by the shoulder. That's when the phone rang.

Perkins looked at Dellasandro. "Fiske?" He looked again at Sara. "Fiske is with Harms, isn't he? That's why you had to split up, isn't it?" Sara looked away as the phone rang again. Perkins stuck his pistol under her chin and his finger tightened on the trigger. "I'll ask you one more time. Is Fiske with Rufus Harms?" He pushed the gun harder against her skin. "In two seconds your head will disappear, I swear to God. Answer me!"

"Yes! Yes, he's with him," she said in a strangled voice as the metal pushed against her windpipe.

He shoved her to the phone. "Answer it. If it's Fiske, pick a place to meet. Make it somewhere around here, but private. Tell him you've found some more information. You say anything to warn him, you're dead." She hesitated. "Do it! Or die!" Sara could see now that the mild-mannered Perkins was actually the more dangerous of her two captors. She slowly picked up the phone. Perkins stood next to her listening, his gun pressed against her temple. She took a quick breath to try to calm herself.

"Hello?"

"Sara?" It was Fiske.

"I've been trying to reach you everywhere."

"I'm with Rufus."

Perkins pushed the gun against her head as he listened. "Where are you?" she asked.

"We're halfway to D.C. At a rest stop."

"What's your plan?"

"I think it's time we went to Chandler. Rufus and I have talked it over."

Perkins shook his head and pointed at the phone.

"I don't think that's such a good idea, John."

"Why not?"

"I've . . . I've found out some things that you need to know first. Before you go to Chandler."

"Like what?"

"I can't tell you over the phone. It could be bugged."

"Come on, I kind of doubt that, Sara."

"Look, I tell you what, give me the number where you're at and I'll call you from the car." She looked over at Perkins. "We can arrange to meet someplace. Then we can go to Chandler. The FBI has the tag number of the car you're in. You have to get rid of it anyway."

He gave her the number and she wrote it down on a pad by the phone and ripped off the top sheet.

"Are you sure you can't tell me over the phone?"

"I talked to your friend at the JAG," Sara said, whispering a silent prayer for what she was about to say next. If Fiske reacted the wrong way, she was dead. She had to trust him. "Darnell Jackson told me all about the PCP testing."

Fiske stiffened and looked over at Rufus, who sat in the car at the darkened rest stop. *Darnell Jackson.* He answered quickly. "Darnell's never let me down before."

Sara let out an inaudible breath. "I'll call you back in five minutes." She hung up and looked at the two men.

Perkins grinned malevolently. "Good job, Sara. Now let's go see your friends."

CHAPTER FIFTY-NINE

After Sara called him back with the meeting place, Fiske made one more phone call. The news was not good. Not good at all. Then he got in the car and looked at Harms. "He's got Sara."

"Who's got her?" Harms asked.

"Your old buddy. Dellasandro. He's the only one left."

"What you talking about, the only one left?"

"Rayfield and Tremaine are dead. That leaves Dellasandro. Sara tipped me off without him catching on—" Fiske stopped and stared at Rufus, who was staring back at him quizzically. Fiske spoke haltingly. "Rufus, how many men were in the stockade that night?"

"Five."

Fiske slumped back. "I only know about the three I just mentioned. Who are the other two?"

"Perkins. Dick Perkins."

Fiske thought he might be sick. "Richard Perkins is the marshal of the Supreme Court."

"I ain't seen him since that night and damn glad of it. Except for Tremaine, he was the worst of the bunch. He'd come in and beat me with his damn baton. He's the one who shot me up with the PCP."

"And the fifth man?"

"Didn't know him. Never seen him before."

"That's okay. I think I know who it is." Sara had not told him about finding the man's name on Fort Plessy's personnel roster, but Fiske had finally figured it out himself. Warren McKenna's image appeared starkly in his thoughts. That's why the FBI agent was trying to frame him. It all made sense. Fiske started up the car.

"Where we going?"

"Sara just called back. She . . . they want us to meet them at a place off the GW Parkway in Virginia. I tried to get hold of Chandler, but he wasn't in. I left a message telling him where we'll be. I just hope he gets it in time."

"And we're going to go?"

"If we don't, they'll kill Sara. If you want to stay behind, you can."

In response, Rufus slid a pistol out of his pocket and handed it to Fiske. "You know how to use one of these things?"

Fiske took the pistol, pulled back the slide and made sure a round was chambered. "I think I can manage," he said.

It was well after midnight now and the parkway was deserted. At various points there were pull-offs with picnic areas and small parks where, during the day, families would gather for barbecues and quality time. But now, as Fiske pulled the car down the road, the area was dark, isolated and, he knew, deadly. He eyed the exit signs until he found the one he wanted. At the same time that he saw the sign, he spotted Sara's car parked in the otherwise empty parking lot. Large trees served as a backdrop to the grassy picnic area. Beyond them Fiske could make out the deeper darkness that was the Potomac River.

Rufus was crouched in the back seat, his eyes level with the bottom edge of the window. His gaze swept the darkened landscape. "Somebody's in the car. Can't tell if it's a man or woman, though," he said.

Fiske squinted and then nodded in confirmation. They had devised a plan of sorts on the way up. Now that the lay of the land had been established, they could implement that plan. He pulled ahead a little until they passed a bend in the road that took them beyond the line of sight from Sara's car. Fiske pulled to a stop. The back door of the car opened, and Rufus quickly disappeared into the surrounding trees and headed through the woods toward the parking lot.

Fiske drove into the parking lot and pulled up a couple of spaces from Sara's car. He looked over and was relieved to see her in the driver's seat. He pulled his gun and slowly got out. He looked over the top of his car. "Sara?"

She looked at him, nodded and smiled tightly. The smile disappeared when the man next to her rose up and pointed a gun against her head. They both got out the driver's side. Dellasandro locked one arm around her neck, his free hand holding the gun tightly against her temple.

"Over here, Fiske," Dellasandro said. Fiske did his best to look shocked. "Where's Harms?" Dellasandro said.

Fiske made a show of rubbing his cheek. "He had a change of heart. Didn't want to go to the cops. Hit me and took off."

"And left you the car? I don't think so. Give me the answer I want or your girlfriend gets a chunk of lead in her brain."

"I'm telling you the truth. You know he's been in prison all these years. He didn't take the car because he can't even drive."

Dellasandro considered this for a moment. "Come over here. I want your hands way, way up in the air."

Fiske slipped the pistol in the back of his waistband and put his hands up in the air. He stepped slowly around the car and walked toward them. When he got close enough, he saw the ugly bruise on Sara's cheek. "Are you all right, Sara?"

She nodded. "I'm sorry, John."

"Right, right—look, just shut up," Dellasandro said. "Exactly where did Harms get away from you?"

"When we got off the interstate. We came up Route One."

"That was pretty stupid of him to go off like that. He'll never get far."

"Well, like they say, you can lead a horse to water . . ."

"Why don't I believe a word you're saying?"

"Maybe because you've been a lying sack of shit all your life and you figure everybody is the same way."

Dellasandro pointed his gun at Fiske's head. "It's gonna be so much fun blowing you away."

"Kind of hard disposing of a couple bodies."

Dellasandro glanced toward the river. "Not when you've got the best of Mother Nature to help you."

"And you don't think Chandler will suspect anything?"

"What's to suspect? The cops think you killed your brother for the insurance money. The chick here got fired today because of you and your dumb brother. Her whole career ruined. You two meet up, things get violent. Maybe you kill her and then pop yourself. Maybe it's the other way around. Who cares? They'll find her car, and a few days or weeks later, they'll find your bodies floating some-where—what's left of them, anyway. Case closed."

"Actually, that's a good plan. And since I know there's no way you could have thought of it, where are your partners?"

"What are you talking about?"

"The other two guys in the stockade that night."

"Perkins is one," Sara blurted out. "He's here too."

"Shut up!" Dellasandro yelled.

"I actually knew that one. I think I can guess who the other one is."

"Run your theories by the fish. Let's go."

They all started to move toward the riverbank. Fiske glanced back at Dellasandro. "Don't even think about it, Fiske. I could blow you away from fifty yards, much less two feet. And if your plan is to have that stupid lummox jump me from the trees, well, then just bring him on."

Since that was their plan, Fiske's heart sank. Then a bullet hit the dirt next to Dellasandro's leg. He shouted and moved the pistol away from Sara's head.

Fiske hit him hard in the belly, doubling him over, and then clocked him in the head with his fist. Before Dellasandro could recover, Rufus exploded from behind a tree and hit him with the force of a runaway tank. The man sailed down the bank and into the water from the impact. Fiske pulled his gun. Rufus was about to go after Dellasandro when more shots zipped past them and everybody hit the ground.

Fiske had one protective arm over Sara. "You see anything, Rufus?"

"Yeah, but you ain't going to like it. I think those shots came from two different places."

"Great, both his backups are here. Shit!" He clenched his pistol. "Look, Rufus, here's the plan. We'll fire two shots each and draw their fire in return so we can see where the muzzle flashes are coming from. Then I'll cover you and you take Sara and get the hell out of here. Make it to her car and go." Before Sara could say anything, he added, "Somebody's got to go get Chandler."

Rufus said, "I can stay behind. I owe these suckers a lot more than you."

"I think you've carried the ball long enough." Fiske

aimed his gun. "You fire left and check left, one-two-three, now!" Sara covered her ears as the shots rang out. A few seconds later their fire was returned.

Fiske and Rufus quickly analyzed the muzzle flashes. Fiske said, "One of them's aiming wild. Maybe we hit him. Okay, I'm going to fire in both directions. Keep your gun ready, but don't shoot. I'm going to move to my right about ten yards. I'll draw the fire my way. Give me to the count of twenty and then when you hear the first round go, hit it."

Fiske started to move away, but Sara clutched at his hand, unwilling to let him go.

Fiske wanted to say something confident, cocky even, to her, to show he wasn't scared. But he was. "I know what I'm doing, Sara. And I guess fifty years of living is better than nothing."

She stared at him as he crawled off, convinced it would be the last time she would see him alive.

A minute later the shots began. Rufus half carried Sara as they raced for the car. They made it and Rufus threw open the door and pushed Sara inside before climbing in.

Fiske moved slowly through the underbrush, the smell of hot metal and flamed gunpowder clinging to him. His spirits had faded to nothing. He had counted his shots carefully, but, unknown to him, his clip had not been full to begin with; he had no more ammo. As he heard the car crank up, he smiled grimly. With his thoughts distracted for a moment, his ears still ringing from the shots he had fired, he didn't hear the sound behind him until it was too late.

Dellasandro, dripping filthy river water, pointed the gun at him. Fiske couldn't speak, his mouth too dry. He also couldn't breathe, as though his lungs had sized up the situation and decided to stop working a few seconds before the slug would force them to. Two bullet holes in him, the third would do the trick. Darnell Jackson had been facing

Fiske's gun, had been off balance after killing Fiske's partner; Dellasandro would have no such problems. Fiske
looked in the direction of the river. A week in that water
and not even his father would be able to identify him. He
looked back at Leo Dellasandro: his last image before
death.

When the shot came, Fiske watched in stunned silence
as Leo Dellasandro pitched forward and lay still.

Fiske looked up. What he saw made him wish
Dellasandro had been able to get off his own round.
McKenna looked down at him. Fiske could only shake his
head. Why couldn't it have been Chandler? Why couldn't
he catch a damn break just this once? And then he saw
Dellasandro's pistol where it had landed very near to him.

"Don't try it, Fiske," McKenna said sharply.

"You sonofabitch!"

"Actually, I thought you'd want to thank me."

"Why? For killing your accomplice before you kill me?"

In response, McKenna pulled another pistol from his
pocket. "Here's your pistol. I just happened to find it."

"Right. Some way, someday you're going to get what's
coming to you."

McKenna glanced at Dellasandro. "Actually, in a way, I
just did."

The man's next actions absolutely astonished Fiske.

McKenna flipped the gun around and handed it to him,
grip first. "Now don't go and shoot me." He put a hand
out and helped Fiske up. "Chandler's on his way. I
managed to catch him at Evans's house. I got there just as
Perkins and Dellasandro were leaving with Sara. I figured
they were trying to use her to set you up. I followed along
as your unofficial backup. A little better than the last one
you had. I *never* let my guard down."

Fiske just stared at him, unable to speak.

"Perkins took off. He was the other guy firing. I tried to

hit him, but he was too far off. I also fired the shot to distract Leo. I figured Rufus was around here somewhere."

"I thought you were one of the guys in the stockade that night," said Fiske.

"I was."

"Then what are you doing? Clearing your conscience? If you are, you're the only one of the five to do it."

"I wasn't one of the five."

"But you just said you were in the stockade that night."

"There were *six* men there that night other than Rufus."

Fiske looked bewildered. "I don't understand."

"I was the guard on duty that night, John. It took me twenty-five years to figure out what happened, but I couldn't have done it without you and Sara. I think the PCP angle hit me right after it did you at your office. I never even knew about the drug testing at Fort Plessy, although I guess it wasn't something they broadcast."

"Whether anybody else knew or not, I don't think anyone back then cared about what happened to Rufus Harms."

"Actually, I cared." McKenna looked down. "I just didn't have the balls to do anything about it until it was too late. I could have stopped this whole thing." His body seemed to sag for a second as his mind went back to the past. "But I didn't."

Fiske studied the man for a moment, still reeling from this last development. "Well, you're doing something about it now."

"Twenty-five years too late."

"Rufus is going to be free, isn't he? That's all he cares about."

McKenna looked up. "Rufus is free now, John. No one will ever put him back in prison. If they try to, they have to go through me first. And believe me, they won't be able to."

Fiske looked toward the road. "What about Perkins?"

McKenna smiled. "I know exactly where Perkins is going. We can call Sara in the car and let her know. As soon as Chandler gets here, we'll go."

"Go? Go where?"

"Perkins is going to see the fifth person who was in the stockade that night."

"Who? Who was it?"

"You'll find out. Soon you'll know everything."

CHAPTER SIXTY

When the woman opened the door, Richard Perkins burst in past her. "Where is he?"

"In his study."

Perkins raced down the hallway and threw open the door. The tall man looked back at him, a calm look in his eyes.

Perkins shut the door. "Everything's gone to hell and I'm getting out of here."

Jordan Knight sat back and shook his head. "If you run, they'll know you're guilty."

"They know I'm guilty now. I kidnapped Sara Evans. Leo is probably dead by now."

"You followed her ever since she left the Court today. I hoped, when I contacted you, it would all have been taken care of. But it's still only her word against yours."

"Why would she make up something like that?"

Jordan rubbed his chin. "Think about it. She was fired today. You escorted her out the door. She makes wild accusations against you; perhaps you can invent some others to bolster your position."

"Rufus Harms is still out there. I saw him."

Jordan's face darkened. "Ah, the celebrated Mr. Harms."

"He killed Frank and Vic."

"Two fewer people to worry about, then."

"That's damn cold-blooded of you. You were the one who told them to kill Michael Fiske. You got all this started."

Jordan looked thoughtful. "I still don't know how Rufus Harms was able to identify me in that appeal. He knew all of you. I wasn't even in the Army."

"He didn't ID you."

Knight looked shocked at first; then there was a glint of hope in his eyes.

Perkins explained, "I talked to Tremaine. Rayfield lied to you. You weren't named in the appeal. Just the four of us."

"So I'm the only unknown." Jordan stood up and looked at Perkins. God, that meant he still had a way out. Only one more thing, one more person to deal with, and this nightmare was over. He almost trembled at the thought of it.

"Who knows for how long. God, all this for what? We shoot the bastard up with PCP and it comes down to this."

"You actually shot him up, Richard."

"Don't act high and mighty now. It was your idea to use the PCP, Mr. CIA."

"Well, naturally—I was there conducting the testing. And listening to all of you complain about Harms. Just trying to do you a favor." He eyed Perkins with an unnerving calmness. "I'm very anti-drug now, of course."

"Stumping to the end? How about anti-murder? How do you feel about that, Senator?"

"I never killed anybody."

"How about that little girl, Jordan? How about her?"

"Rufus Harms pled guilty to that crime. As far as I'm concerned, that plea hasn't changed."

"Well, it will soon enough if we don't do something."

"Are you certain you want to run?"

"I'm not hanging around for the ax to fall."

"I suppose you'll need money?"

Perkins nodded. "I don't have a nice little retirement package like we put together for Vic and Frank. I have the bad habit of always living beyond my means."

Jordan took a key from his pocket and unlocked his desk drawer. "I have some cash here. The rest will have to be by check. I can give you fifty thousand, to start."

"That sounds good. To start."

Jordan turned and pointed a pistol at Perkins.

"What the hell are you doing, Jordan?"

"You burst in here, clearly out of your mind, telling of these outrageous crimes you've committed, including kidnapping Sara Evans, for what purpose I don't know. You threaten me. I manage to get out my gun and kill you."

"You're crazy. No one will believe that."

"Oh, they will, Richard." Jordan pulled the trigger and Perkins dropped to the floor. He heard a scream from the hallway. Jordan moved to the body, quickly searched Perkins, found his gun, placed it in the dead man's hand and fired a shot into the wall. "It's all right," he called out, rising from the floor and putting the pistol down. "I'm all right." He opened the door and froze as Rufus Harms stared back at him. Behind Rufus were Chandler, McKenna, Fiske and Sara.

Jordan finally pulled his gaze from Rufus and looked at Chandler. "Richard Perkins burst in here making wild threats. He had a gun. Fortunately I was a better shot."

McKenna stepped forward. "Senator, you don't remember me, do you? I mean, outside the FBI?" Jordan stared at him without recognition. McKenna edged closer to the man. "Perkins and Dellasandro didn't remember me either. It's been a long time and we've all changed a lot. Besides, everybody was pretty drunk that night. Everybody except you."

"I have no idea what you're talking about."

"I was the guard on duty the night you and your friends came calling on Rufus at Fort Plessy. It was my first and last time pulling guard duty at the stockade. Probably why nobody remembered me."

Jordan Knight flinched. "Am I supposed to know what you're talking about?"

"I let you in to see Rufus because I was a greenhorn scared private and I had a captain ordering me to. And then Rufus came busting out of his cell, knocked me down and changed everybody's life forever. For twenty-five damn years I've wondered what really happened in there. I kept quiet about all of you because I was scared. Rayfield was the most senior. He probably would've remembered me. Guess no one mentioned my name to him. Lucky. Rayfield fixed it up so I wouldn't get in trouble, but he made it clear I had better keep my mouth shut about all of you being in there. And I never knew what had happened anyway. And by the time I got the courage to say something, it was all over, and Rufus was in prison. I've lived with that guilt all these years. But I got off easy." McKenna looked over at Rufus. "I'm sorry, Rufus. I was weak, a coward. It probably doesn't make any difference to you, but there hasn't been a day gone by that I didn't hate myself for it."

Jordan cleared his throat. "Very touching, Agent McKenna. However, if you think you saw me in the stockade that night, you're mistaken."

"CIA records will show that you were at Fort Plessy conducting PCP tests on soldiers stationed there," McKenna pointed out.

"If you can get those records, get them. Even if I was

there, so what? I was in the intelligence service back then. That's no secret. The public is aware of that."

"I wonder if your constituents would be bothered by the fact that you were administering PCP to soldiers," Chandler said heatedly.

"Even if I did—and I'm not admitting anything—the program was perfectly aboveboard and legal, as my wife could certainly tell you."

"*U.S. v. Stanley?*" Sara said bitterly.

Jordan's gaze did not leave McKenna. "Quite a coincidence that you claim to have been in the stockade and now you're involved in this matter," he said.

"It was no coincidence, it was intentional," was McKenna's surprising reply. "After I left the Army I finished college, and then went to the FBI academy. But I kept tabs on you and the others. Guilt is very strong motivation. Rayfield and Tremaine moved around with Rufus. That I found suspicious, but not conclusive. Perkins and Dellasandro moved around with you. They had positions in your various businesses. I got myself transferred to the Richmond Field Office so I could be close to you. When you jumped into politics they again went with you. When you went to D.C., you got Dellasandro and Perkins jobs at the Senate. So I got transferred to D.C. When you were given a seat on the Senate Judiciary Committee a few years ago, you got them their positions at the Court. Real nice of you. It must be part of the payback, the agreement all of you made. Rayfield and Tremaine baby-sat Rufus. You took care of Perkins and Leo. I bet if we checked their accounts, we'd find some nice little retirement funds somewhere.

"When I got wind of Michael Fiske's murder, I jumped on it only because it was at the Court. When I discovered Rufus was connected somehow, I prayed all those years of following you were going to pay off. Now the truth has finally come out."

"Absurd speculation, you mean," Jordan Knight countered. "From your own words, it's obvious you have some deranged vendetta against me. I find it outrageous that you've come into my home making all these accusations, particularly after I've had a man try to murder me, forcing me to kill him. And other than Detective Chandler, who has to investigate this act of obvious self-defense, I want the rest of you to get the hell out of my home."

McKenna pulled a cell phone from his pocket, spoke into it and listened to the response. "I'm placing you under arrest, Senator Jordan. I'm sure Detective Chandler will do the same."

"Get the hell out of here. Now!"

"I'm going to read you your rights now."

"I'll have you in the FBI equivalent of Siberia by dawn. You have no proof of anything."

"Actually, I'm basing my arrest on your own words." While everyone watched, McKenna knelt under the desk kneehole, probed for a moment and pulled out a listening device. "Your statements came through loud and clear in the surveillance van parked outside." He looked at Fiske. "Knight was the one who told Rayfield to kill your brother."

Jordan was furious. "That is completely illegal. There's not a judge in this city who would have given you a warrant for that. I'm not going to prison, you are."

"We didn't need a warrant. We had consent."

"Bullshit!" Jordan roared. He looked like he was about to attack the agent. "I demand you give me those tapes immediately. You're an imbecile if you think anyone will believe that I gave such consent."

"You didn't, Jordan. I did."

The blood drained from Jordan's face as his wife stepped into the room. She didn't even look at Perkins's body. Her gaze remained fixed on her husband.

"You?"

"I live here too, Jordan. I gave that consent."

"In God's name, why?"

Elizabeth held his gaze for a moment, then touched the sleeve of Rufus Harms. "This man is why, Jordan. This man is the only reason strong enough to make me do what I did."

"For him? He's a child killer."

"It's no good, Jordan. I know the truth. And damn you for what you've done."

"What I've done? All I've ever done is serve my country." He stabbed a finger at Rufus. "This man never did shit for anything or anybody. The bastard deserved to die."

Moving faster than his bulk would seem to have allowed, Rufus reached Jordan, his big hands encircling the senator's neck as he slammed him up against the wall.

"Damn you!" Rufus screamed. His grip tightened and Jordan started turning red.

McKenna and Chandler trained their guns, but couldn't bring themselves to shoot. They looked helpless. They grabbed Rufus, but it was like pulling on a mountain.

"Jordan," Elizabeth screamed.

"Rufus, stop," Sara yelled.

Jordan was nearly unconscious.

Fiske stepped forward. "Rufus, Rufus?" Fiske took a quick breath and then just said it. "Josh didn't make it." Rufus instantly loosened his grip on Jordan's throat and stared at Fiske. "He's dead, Rufus. We both lost our brothers." Fiske was visibly trembling and Sara put a hand on his shoulder. "If you kill him, you'll go back to prison and Josh will have died for nothing." Rufus relaxed his grip even more as tears wound down his face. "You can't do it, Rufus." Fiske took another unsteady step forward. "You just can't."

As the two bereaved men looked at one another, Rufus simply let go, and a gasping Jordan Knight slumped to the carpet.

Jordan did not look at his wife as he was led away in handcuffs by McKenna. An hour later the forensics team had completed its work and Perkins's body was removed. Chandler, Rufus, Sara and Fiske remained behind. Elizabeth Knight was in her bedroom.

"So how much did you know about the truth, Buford?" Fiske asked.

"Some of it. McKenna and I had talks. At first I think he really believed you were involved, or at least he genuinely didn't like you." Chandler smiled. "But after he learned Rufus was somehow connected, his opinion changed. I didn't like the idea of him setting you up for the fall, though. And he pushed the buttons on Sara getting fired."

"Why?" Sara asked.

"You two were getting close to the truth. That meant you both were in danger. McKenna knew the people involved were capable of a lot. But he didn't have any proof. He had to make them think you two were the primary suspects. And every time we were around Perkins and Dellasandro, McKenna made it clear he thought Rufus's appeal was bogus and John was the killer. He took your gun and made sure Perkins and Dellasandro knew it was missing. He hoped that meant they would feel safe and might slip up. Also it was meant to keep you two safe."

"I don't think it accomplished the last part," Sara said with a shiver.

"Well, he didn't count on you losing his surveillance team either. Once McKenna got Justice Knight to agree to the bug, he just had to spring the trap. McKenna had already told Justice Knight that he knew her husband from Fort Plessy, so when the senator told her he had to call to get that information, she knew he was lying."

"So Justice Knight's quick thinking probably saved my life," Sara commented.

Chandler nodded in agreement. "When everything

went down, McKenna knew Perkins would make a run for it and would need Jordan's help. It worked out okay. Jordan killing Perkins was not in the game plan. But I'm not going to lose any sleep over that." Chandler looked at Rufus Harms. "I need to take you into custody, but it won't be for long."

"I want to see my brother."

Chandler nodded. "I can arrange that."

"I'll go with you, Rufus," Fiske said.

As they walked to the door, Elizabeth Knight met them in the hallway.

"Justice Knight, you did a very brave thing tonight. I know how painful it was for you," Chandler said.

Elizabeth reached out her hand to Rufus Harms. "It can't possibly be worth anything to you after all you have suffered, Mr. Harms, but I am so sorry for everything. So very, very sorry."

He took her hand gently. "It's worth a lot, ma'am. To me and my brother."

As they headed out the door, Elizabeth Knight looked at them all and said with finality, "Good-bye."

The group headed to the elevator. When the three men stepped on the elevator car, Sara hesitated. "I'll catch up with you later," she said. As the elevator doors closed, she raced back to the apartment. Mary opened the door.

"Where's Justice Knight?"

"She went into the bedroom. Why—"

Sara flew past her and burst into the bedroom. Sitting on the bed, Elizabeth Knight looked up at her former clerk. The justice's hand was clenched in a fist; a prescription bottle lay empty next to her.

Sara walked slowly over to her, sat down and took her hand. She opened it and the pills spilled out. "Elizabeth, that's not the way to deal with this."

"Deal with it?" Elizabeth said hysterically. "My life just walked out that door in handcuffs."

"Jordan Knight just walked out that door. Justice Elizabeth Knight is sitting right here next to me. The same Justice Knight who will be leading the Supreme Court into the next century."

"Sara . . ." The tears spilled down her face.

"It's a lifetime appointment. And you have a lot of life left." Sara squeezed her hand. "I'd like to help you with your work, your very important work. If you'll have me back."

Sara put her arms around the woman's trembling shoulders.

"I don't know if I can do this . . . survive this."

"I'm certain that you can. And you won't be doing it alone. I promise."

Elizabeth clutched at the young woman's shoulder. "Will you stay with me tonight, Sara?"

"I'll stay as long as you want."

CHAPTER SIXTY-ONE

On the strength of his being the possessor of the Silver Star, Purple Heart and Distinguished Service Medal, Josh Harms was entitled to burial with modified honors—the highest an enlisted man could attain—at Arlington National Cemetery. However, the Army representative who had come to speak to Rufus about the arrangement seemed bent on talking him out of it.

"He got shot up, saved a bunch of the men in his company, won himself a box full of medals," Rufus said, eyeing the man's uniform, the single row of colored metal on it. "A lot mor'n you got."

The man twisted his lips. "His record was not the cleanest in the world either. He had a real problem with authority. From what I could gather, he didn't like or respect one thing about the institution he was representing."

"So you think burying him up there with all them generals and such would be disrespectful?"

"The cemetery is running out of space. I think it would

be a nice gesture to reserve those spaces for soldiers who actually were proud to wear the uniform, that's all I'm saying."

"Even though he earned it?" Rufus said.

"I'm not disputing that. But I can't believe your brother would *want* to be buried there either."

"I guess he'd spend all of eternity telling those dead brass exactly what he thinks of them."

"Something like that," the man said dryly. "So then we're in agreement? You'll arrange burial for him elsewhere?"

Rufus eyed the man. "I made up my mind."

Thus, on a cool, clear day in October, former Sergeant Joshua Harms, USA, was laid to rest at Arlington National Cemetery. From an angle, the ground was so covered with white crosses that it looked like an early snow had fallen. As the honor guard fired off its salute and the bugler launched into taps, the simple coffin was lowered into the ground. Rufus and one of Josh's sons received the flag, folded tricornered, from a somber and respectful Army officer, while Fiske, Sara, McKenna and Chandler looked on.

Later, as Rufus prayed over his brother's grave, he thought about all of the bodies buried here, most in the name of war. There were both men and women who had this as their final resting place, although, historically, it was the men who were the instigators and chief wagers of armed conflict. For those who traced their history though the Book of Genesis and beyond, as did Rufus, the bodies buried here could blame the existence of wars on the man called Cain and the mortal blow he struck his brother Abel.

As Rufus finished his prayer, his talk with his Lord and his brother, he rose and put an arm around the nephew he had never seen until today. His heart was sad, but his spirits were lifted. He knew that his brother had passed on to a better place. And for as long as Rufus lived, Josh Harms would never be forgotten. And when Rufus went to join his Lord he would also, once again, embrace his brother.

CHAPTER SIXTY-TWO

Two days later, Michael Fiske was buried at a private cemetery on the outskirts of Richmond. The well-attended funeral service included each justice of the United States Supreme Court. Ed Fiske, dressed in an old suit, his hair neatly combed, awkwardly stood next to his surviving son and received condolences from each of the jurists, together with many of Virginia's political and social elite.

Harold Ramsey spent an extra minute giving comfort to the father and then turned to the son.

"I appreciate all that you did, John. And the sacrifice that your brother made."

"The ultimate one," Fiske said in an unfriendly tone.

Ramsey nodded. "I also respect your views. I hope that you can respect my views as well."

Fiske shook the man's hand. "I guess that's what makes the world go round."

Looking at Ramsey made Fiske think of what lay ahead for Rufus. Fiske had encouraged him to sue everybody he could think of, including the Army and Jordan Knight. There was no statute of limitations on murder, and the ensuing cover-up orchestrated by Jordan and the others had broken numerous other laws.

Rufus had refused Fiske's advice, however. "All of 'em except for Knight are in a far worse place than any judge on this earth could send 'em to," he had said. "That's their true punishment. And Knight's got to live with what he done. That's enough for me. I got no reason to get mixed up with courts and judges no more. I just want to live as a free man, spend a lot of time with Josh's children. Go see my momma's grave. That's all."

Fiske had tried to get him to change his mind, until he realized that the man was right. Besides, Fiske thought, according to the precedents established by the Supreme Court, Rufus couldn't sue the Army anyway. Not unless Elizabeth Knight could use the Barbara Chance case to give military personnel the same basic rights as the rest of the country's citizens. To do that, she had to get past Ramsey. As he thought about it, though, Fiske concluded that if anyone could do it, Elizabeth Knight could. He'd like to be a fly on the wall of the Supreme Court in the coming years.

But there were two things Fiske—with the assistance of JAG attorney Phil Jansen—was going to accomplish for Rufus: an honorable discharge, and a full military pension and benefits. Rufus Harms wasn't going to scrape for an existence, not after all he had been through.

As Fiske finished this thought, Sara walked up with Elizabeth Knight. Sara had returned to the Court as Knight's clerk. The place was slowly returning to normal. Or as normal as it was going to get with Knight and Ramsey in the same building.

"I feel deeply responsible for all of this," Knight said.

She and the senator, Fiske knew, were divorcing. The government, the Army in particular, wanted to keep all of this quiet. Important strings in Washington were being pulled. That meant that Jordan Knight might not go to prison for all that he had done. Even with Elizabeth Knight's consent, the legality of the electronic surveillance of the man had already been drawn into serious question by the senator's very skillful lawyers. In a private meeting with McKenna, the FBI agent had told Fiske that the wiretap had been a risky strategy, since they did not have the consent of one of the parties being taped, but it was the only way McKenna could think of to implicate Jordan Knight. But without the recording, Chandler and McKenna really had nothing to take to court. The thought that Jordan would go unpunished made Fiske want to visit the man late at night with his 9mm. But the man had suffered, and would continue to do so. The wiretap had carried some leverage. Jordan had resigned his senate seat and, more devastatingly, lost the woman he cherished. He still had his New Mexico ranch, though. Let it be your seven-thousand-acre prison, Fiske thought.

"If there's anything I can ever do for you . . ." Elizabeth Knight said.

"You have the same offer from me," Fiske said.

Thirty minutes after the last mourners were gone, Fiske, his father and Sara watched as the chairs and green carpet were removed. The coffin was lowered, and the slab was laid over the vault. Then the dirt was shoveled on top. Fiske spoke with his father and Sara for a few minutes and told them he would meet them back at his father's house. He watched them drive off. When he looked back over at the fresh hump of earth, he was startled. The cemetery workers were gone now, but on his knees next to the new grave, eyes closed, Bible clutched in one hand, was Rufus Harms.

Fiske walked over and put a hand on the man's shoulder. "Rufus, you okay? I didn't even know you were still here."

Rufus didn't open his eyes, and he didn't say anything.

Fiske watched as his lips moved slightly. Finally, Rufus opened his eyes and looked up at him.

"What were you doing?"

"Praying."

"Oh."

"How about you?"

"How about me, what?"

"Have you prayed over your brother yet?"

"Rufus, I haven't been to Mass since high school."

Rufus gripped Fiske's sleeve and pulled him down next to him. "Then it's time you started up again."

His face suddenly pale, Fiske looked at the grave site. "Come on, Rufus, this isn't funny."

"Nothing funny about saying good-bye. Talk to your brother, and then talk to your Lord."

"I don't remember any prayers."

"Then don't pray. Just talk, plain words."

"What exactly am I supposed to say?"

Rufus had already closed his eyes and didn't answer.

Fiske looked around to see if anyone was watching. Then he turned back, looked over at Rufus, awkwardly put his hands together and, embarrassed, finally let them dangle at his sides. At first he didn't even close his eyes, but then they just seemed to do so on their own. He felt the moisture from the ground soak through his pants legs, but he didn't move. He felt the comforting presence of Rufus next to him. He didn't know if he could have remained here without it.

He focused on all that had happened. He thought of his mother and his father. The insurance money had given Gladys Fiske her first trip to the beauty parlor in years, and some new clothes to admire herself in. To her he was still Mike, but at least she remembered one of them. Ed Fiske would soon be driving a new Ford pickup, the loan on the house paid off. He and his father were planning a fishing trip for the next year, down in the Ozarks. A lot to be thankful for.

With a smile Fiske thought of Sara, gratefully, even with all the complexities that came with the woman. Fifty, sixty, maybe seventy years old? Why not give himself the benefit of the doubt? He had a life to live. Potentially a very satisfying one. Particularly when it included Sara. Then he tilted his head up and smelled the wet air, caught the scent of leaves burning somewhere. The air also carried to him an infant's cry, followed by the silence of the dead around him. Growing more comfortable, he squatted back on his haunches, easing himself more firmly into the embrace of the ground, the cool touch of the dirt now welcome somehow.

Finally, with difficulty, he thought of his brother. He was so tired of grudges held. He now focused on reality. On the truth. On his baby brother, a person he would have done anything for. He recalled the pride he shared with his mother and father for the exceptional human being they had jointly raised. For the good man Mike Fiske had grown into, graceful faults and all, just like the rest of them. A brother who had shown, through his actions, that he respected John Fiske, cared about him. Loved him. Through the half dozen feet of dirt, past the bound flowers on top, inside the bronze coffin, he could clearly see his brother's face, the dark suit he had been buried in, the hair parted on the side, the hands folded across the chest, the eyes closed. At rest. At peace. The limbs stilled much too early. The exceptional mind shut down far from its potential.

It did not take long for the tremors to start. The two-year void that John Fiske had artificially forced upon the pair was nothing compared to the one he was suddenly stricken with now. It was as though Billy Hawkins had just walked through the door and told him that Mike, the other half of his life growing up, was dead. Only he

wouldn't have to identify the body. He wouldn't have to
search for and falsely share grief with his father. He
wouldn't have to watch as his mother called him by
another's name. He would not have to risk his life to find
his brother's killers. But he would have to do something
else. The one task left was the hardest of all.

He felt the burn in his chest, but it was not the underbelly of his scar come calling. This pain was not capable of
killing him, but it was worse by legions than that inflicted
on him by the two bullets. The things he had found out
about his brother lately only highlighted how unfair Fiske
had been in shutting him out. But if he had tried, Fiske
would have realized all those things while Mike was still
alive. Now his brother was dead. John Fiske was kneeling
in front of his grave. Mike was not coming back. He had
lost him. He had to say good-bye and he didn't want to.
He desperately wanted his brother back. He had so much
he wanted to do with him, suddenly so much love he
wanted to convey. He felt his heart would burst if he didn't
get it out.

"Oh God," he said with an outward breath. He couldn't
do this. He felt his body start to give on him. The tears
suddenly poured with such force he thought his nose was
bleeding. He started to go down, but a strong hand
grasped him, easily held him up; Fiske's body felt light,
fragile, as though he had left part of it somewhere else.
Through the blur of tears he looked at Rufus. The man
had one hand under Fiske's arm, thrusting him up. Yet his
eyes were still closed, his head looking to the sky; the lips
still rising and falling in the narrowest of ranges as he
continued his prayers.

Right then John Fiske envied Rufus Harms, a man who
had lost his own brother, a man who really had nothing.
And yet in the most important way, Rufus Harms was the
richest man on earth. How could anyone believe in

anything that much? Without doubt, without debate, without an agenda, with all his substantial heart?

As Fiske looked at the calm face of his friend next to him, he thought how very fine it must be to know for certain that your loved one is in a better place, embraced and held for all time by the phenomenon of unassailable good. So comforting a notion at the precise time you needed to feel it. How often did such timing occur in life? Death as joyous. Death as the beginning. Meaning life was both more and less precious because of it.

Fiske looked away from Rufus and stared down at the grave, the image of a pale hand under a white sheet coming back to him, and then leaving, like a bird in search of food. He dug his knees into the earth, closed his eyes, bowed his head, placed his hands firmly together and started making his peace. With his brother below. And with whatever lay above.